Katie had grown up without a father.
She was determined that her child
would never know the loneliness she had known.
So she lived a lie
in order to stay with her husband—
and almost lost her son.

A WORLD FULL OF STRANGERS
a novel by Cynthia Freeman

Bantam Books by Cynthia Freeman
Ask your bookseller for the titles you have missed

THE DAYS OF WINTER
FAIRYTALES
PORTRAITS
A WORLD FULL OF STRANGERS

A WORLD FULL OF STRANGERS

by Cynthia Freeman

This low-priced Bantam Book has been completely reset in a type face designed for easy reading, and was printed from new plates. It contains the complete text of the original hard-cover edition. NOT ONE WORD HAS BEEN OMITTED.

A WORLD FULL OF STRANGERS
A Bantam Book

PRINTING HISTORY
Arbor House edition published August 1975
2nd printing .... October 1975

Bantam edition / August 1976

2nd printing	*........ August 1976*	*10th printing*	*.... January 1977*
3rd printing	*........ August 1976*	*11th printing*	*.... January 1977*
4th printing	*........ August 1976*	*12th printing*	*.......... May 1977*
5th printing	*.. September 1976*	*13th printing*	*.... October 1977*
6th printing	*.. September 1976*	*14th printing*	*. November 1977*
7th printing	*.. September 1976*	*15th printing*	*............ July 1978*
8th printing	*...... October 1976*	*16th printing*	*. September 1979*
9th printing	*...... October 1976*	*17th printing*	*.. February 1980*

18th printing .... June 1980

ISBN 0-553-14062-0

Published simultaneously in the United States and Canada

Bantam Books are published by Bantam Books, Inc. Its trademark, consisting of the words "Bantam Books" and the portrayal of a bantam, is Registered in U.S. Patent and Trademark Office and in other countries. Marca Registrada. Bantam Books, Inc., 666 Fifth Avenue, New York, New York 10103.

PRINTED IN THE UNITED STATES OF AMERICA

27 26 25 24 23 22 21 20

To my dearest husband, whose love, understanding and encouragement sustained me through the dark days of self doubt.

The characters depicted herein are wholly fictional and any resemblance to any person is purely coincidental . . . However, I would not have hesitated to bring this story to light were it the other way around, for people seldom recognize themselves as they really are.

I wish to thank the deity that watches over our stars, and directed my destiny, via Allan Barnard and Linda Price, into the hands of Don Fine, my publisher, mentor and friend. For the long arduous hours so lovingly belabored, there are only two words, inadequate though they may be—thank you.

Words would gct in the way were I to try to articulate what I feel for Elizabeth Pomada and Michael Larsen who have become more, much more than my agents.

CHAPTER ONE

Winter, 1932

Soon there would be a simple marker placed here with the inscription that would read

HANNAH KOVITZ
1898–1932
Beloved Mother of Katie

the words that bore witness that once Hannah had walked upon the earth. Standing in the dense gray London fog that enveloped her slowly, Katie lifted her eyes toward the heavens. She listened, but there was no sound in the silence—no celestial chorus of angels singing, not even the song of the mournful dove. In time the grass would grow tall hiding the marker with no onc to protcct this sacred plot for posterity: the last time she would stand here was now. Who would know or care that beneath the freshly turned sod that had become home for Hannah was all that remained of a life born in poverty, lived in loneliness, ended in agony, whose passing went unnoticed as though she had never been?

Oh God, Katie whispered, is this all to mark the coming and the going of the genteel woman who had borne her life with dignity, who had buried two young sons and a beloved husband? Hannah, Katie remembered gratefully, had said it was she, the last surviving child, who had sustained her most of all. Hannah had prayed that she might live to see this child grow to womanhood, but even that was not fulfilled, for Katie was not quite a woman yet; tomorrow she would be seventeen. She called out softly, "Why, dear God, why? Please let there be meaning in my mother's death, more than there was in her life, I beg you, dear God." She picked up a handful of dirt, held the small, cold piece of earth close to her for a long moment, then threw it into the abyss. Giving in to blinding tears, she turned and walked away.

That evening she packed her belongings. The next day she took a train from Waterloo station, and at Southampton boarded a freighter that would take her to New York.

The crossing seemed like an eternity. For days on end the ship pitched violently, leaving Katie ill and confined to the cabin, windowless and foreboding. She would lie in her bunk with only the bleak, uncertain future to contemplate and suddenly living seemed more frightening than dying. Although during those last inevitable months, with Katie sitting at her bedside, Hannah had tried to prepare her for the eventuality that soon she would have to find a new life, hopefully better and happier than the one that she now had, Katie found little solace. But for Hannah, comforted with the thought that somehow out of all travail God did provide, there were compensations. In her absence there would be Malka Greenberg, her dearest and oldest friend, to whom she could vouchsafe her child and with whom Katie would find a haven.

However, when the time came Katie was not prepared. What would it be like, going to live as a stranger with Malka Greenberg and her family? She reached into her handbag and took out the faded photograph taken of Malka and Hannah so many years ago when they were small children in Poland, trying to read the face of her new benefactress. But nothing was revealed to indicate that she would really be wanted.

Malka Greenberg and Hannah Kovitz had developed a friendship that went back to a small village in Poland where both had been born. Their young lives were inseparable until Malka, at the age of fifteen, met and married Jacob Greenberg. Shortly after their marriage, Jacob decided to leave Poland, where life was unbearably hard, and go to America. Amidst promises of returning some day and a pledge of everlasting friendship, the two clung together, tears streaming down their cheeks, saying their goodbyes, each knowing secretly that they would never see each other again, as the Greenbergs departed, by cattle boat, for New York.

Ensuing years kept them in touch. They waited impatiently for a letter, a photograph. When Malka read that Hannah was dying, she wrote immediately that she was to put her mind at rest so far as Katie was concerned, that when the time came the child was to come to her as soon as possible. In spite of all her mother had told her about Malka, Katie realized that the two had not seen each other for many years, and that the years had a way of changing people. Katie thought perhaps Jacob Greenberg would object to her, even if Malka were willing. Maybe the two Greenberg children would not accept her. Maybe Birdie Greenberg, who was only a year older, would dislike having her around, and maybe Sammy, who was eleven years old, might resent having a stranger living in his house. Maybe she would be in the way. But the most important thing was that maybe Malka had merely made the promise as a gesture to a dying woman. And maybe she should have stayed in London; maybe she could have gotten a job and taken care of herself. . . .

The ship reached New York harbor one day earlier than was scheduled and there was no one to meet her. Katie was desolate: she had no way of contacting Malka Greenberg because they had no phone. She had only their address, and Malka was expecting her the next day. After she had undergone customs, she sat on the shabby suitcase completely exhausted from the whole ordeal, unable to cry, and for a very long time watched the crowd disperse.

Finally, she realized what she must do. She picked up the suitcase, went out into the street, and experienced New York for the first time. And after she couldn't say how many inquiries and struggles through the impersonal crowds, she found herself standing in front of Malka Greenberg's door. Breathless by the time she reached the top of the five flights of stairs in the old tenement building, she leaned against the wall, felt the labored beating of her heart and waited for it to subside. All that she had anticipated was now here: the end of the journey had brought her to this moment.

She stood staring at the door and then timidly knocked, half hoping it would not be heard. When there was no answer she knocked again, this time with more vigor; still no answer. She took the letter out of her purse and looked again at the address; it had to be right, she had followed all the instructions for how to get here. This time, frantic, she pounded on the door. Suddenly it opened and there, framed in the doorway, was Malka, the front of her dress soaking from the washing she had just done. Awkwardly Katie said, "You're Mrs. Greenberg?"

Malka stood looking at the girl. What happened that she was standing here? She was to have met her tomorrow. She could not find her voice. The resemblance between Hannah and Katie was so unmistakable it was as though she were looking at Hannah, and for one moment she was abruptly taken back to her own childhood. Slowly she held out her large arms, drew the young girl to her and kissed her with such tenderness that Katie easily placed her head on Malka's bosom and the two held onto one another as though they would never let go. Katie knew that she had come home at last.

London seemed very far away now. Soon Katie became adjusted to the sights and the sounds of this strange land, and at times she had difficulty remembering she was the same confused and terrified girl who stood before Malka's door only a few short months before. How wonderful it is, she thought, that one can shut out all the unhappy memories when there is love. At night she would lie awake and think of what might have become of her were it not for the Greenbergs and the love they had given her. It was they who had held her hand and led her beyond the dark of her bereavement. They had given her back her life, and now there was again reality in living, and contentment she'd never thought possible. The Greenberg family shared all they had with her, even the three-room flat where five of them now lived, without even making her feel she had intruded.

Birdie had gotten her a job in the same dress factory where she worked and each day brought with it new experience. And new enthusiasm, especially when she brought home the paycheck, which each week she gave to Malka, and each week Malka went through the ritual of refusing. She would say, "So tell me, Katie darling, how much do you eat? So Birdie's got a bed, so how much room do you take up?"

"But Malka, dearest, let me share whatever I have with you, please." Katie realized the Greenbergs were not really poor, they just didn't have any money. She felt overwhelming gratitude for having a home to which she belonged, thinking what a beautiful word was *belong*. She now had a family, a job; she had reached the millennium.

Katie's bliss was not felt completely by Malka. A girl going on eighteen should begin to think seriously of love and marriage, and quite frankly she was concerned about the absence of romance in Katie's life. Wisely she reasoned that with Katie's great need to feel safe and secure she might find things too comfortable in their family embrace. This and Katie's shyness made Malka think that she might become an old maid. To Malka Greenberg this was unthinkable.

How wrong it was for Katie to be sitting around the kitchen table with Jacob and herself on a Saturday night, keeping Sammy amused while Birdie was at the movies with Solly Obromowitz seeing a Buddy Rogers picture. What was to become of Katie, wasting her entire girlhood, losing it in such a way? Youth disappeared fast enough. Something had to be done.

It was only ten o'clock when Birdie returned home. Malka looked up from her darning. "You're home early. The movie wasn't good?"

"It was good, I guess."

"You guess?" Malka said. "So how come you didn't stay?"

"Oh that lousy Solly," Birdie said. "We had a fight."

"This is how you talk about a nice boy like Solly? So what was the fight about?"

Birdie looked at her mother and smiled. How shocked her sweet mother would be if she told her that not only was it getting tougher all the time to keep Solly from going up to the roof, but to get him to keep his grubby paws off her was a whole battle. But damn it, she was going to fight him, and she didn't know how long she was going to be able to hold out if she continued to see Solly, which she secretly hoped she would.

"Listen to me, Birdie," Malka continued.

"So I'm listening."

"Not only have I got a problem with Katie but I've got a problem with you."

"So what's the problem you got with me, mama?"

"I want you should be nice with Solly, that's all." She thought, oy vay, all she needed was two old maids in the house, one wasn't enough.

"What's nice?"

"I mean you shouldn't always make out like you're so stuck up. You see, Birdala, your problem is you go out with a boy a few times and right away you don't like him."

"So stop worrying, it's not so serious. I'm going to see Solly tomorrow. Where's Katie?"

"She went to bed early. You want a cup of tea?"

"You sit still, I'll fix it."

As Birdie put the kettle on the stove, she said to her father, "You want a cup, papa?" He mumbled something under his breath which meant no and kept on reading his paper.

"Take a piece of sponge cake, Birdie."

Malka held the cup with both hands to her lips and peered over the rim, thinking how best to bring up the subject of Katie. "Birdie, why is it you never take Katie with you when you go out?"

"Because she doesn't want to go."

"Did you ever ask her?"

"Yes, mama, I did and I do. Tell me, what brought this up?"

"What brought it up is, I'm worried."

"For you that's nothing new. I don't understand you, mama. What is she, an old maid?"

Malka was startled by the phrase. It was almost as if Birdie had read her thoughts. With pretended annoyance she said quietly, "Don't get fresh, Birdie. Maybe in America they talk like that to a mother, but not to me."

"O.K., mama, I'm not being fresh, but what's to worry about?"

"I shouldn't worry about a beautiful young girl who sits in a house every night and Sammy is her big companion?"

"Well what's wrong if I am her companion?" Sammy asked. They'd forgotten him sitting round-eyed, listening to everything.

Birdie looked at him. "Big shot, you go to bed. This is not your business."

"It's as much my business as yours."

"Don't get fresh, Sammy."

"That's enough, children. Sammala, darling, go to bed," Malka said. He objected but obeyed. On the way out he kissed first his mother, his father and then his sister, said good night, and went to bed in the hall between the kitchen and Birdie's room, pulling closed the floral, cretonne drapery which separated them.

"Now listen to me, mama. I know how much you love Katie and all you want is what's good for her, but you've got to realize she's different from the boys on Hester Street. She doesn't take to them and they don't take to her. But she'll meet hers, believe me."

"Not unless you introduce her to someone," Malka said adamantly. "I don't want her whole young life to be wasted only working. She's got to go out and have a little fun like other girls."

Jacob, a man of few words, folded his glasses, put them in his shirt pocket, laid the paper down on the table, got up, and in a voice louder than usual, said, "That's enough already with the boys and the marriage and the marriage and the boys. When she's thirty you'll worry already. Come to bed, Malka." He walked to the back bedroom off the kitchen and Malka followed.

Walking up and down in front of the Bijou Theater where he had been waiting for Birdie for the last thirty minutes, Solly wondered why he even bothered. Cold, never gave an inch. Who the hell did she think she was anyway? True, he was no Adonis, but he'd already stopped counting the girls he'd screwed since he was twelve, so anybody with a track record like that couldn't be so bad. He should be furious with her for slapping his face—and hard—the night before, as they sat in the back row upstairs. In a gesture of pure love he'd thrust his right hand down inside her low-cut blouse, cupping her warm and round full breast in his sweating palm while, with his other hand under her dress, his fingers crept slowly up her thigh. But as he kissed her and tried forcing his tongue into her mouth, Birdie became so angry that she stood up and kicked him knowingly with her knee, slapped his face so hard he thought she'd broken his jaw, and through clenched teeth said, "You son-of-a-bitch Solly Obromowitz, don't you ever do that to me again!"

Birdie had run out of the theater and into the street for several blocks with Solly calling out after her, "Wait a minute, wait a minute!" Tired, angry, and perspiring, she sat down on a door stoop when she heard Solly saying, "O.K., O.K., what the hell did I do that was so terrible? Tell me, what?"

Instead of answering, she sat clutching her purse and staring ahead of her. Solly simply could not stand the coldness, the being shut out. "Damn it, fight with me. Scream, holler, but don't stop talking," he said.

She finally looked at him, bit back the tears, but still there were tiny crystals of glistening moisture in the corners of her eyes. She said, "O.K., Solly, you want me to tell you why I'm so mad? So O.K., I'll tell you. I'm no Hester Street tramp, the kind you can take to the movies for fifty cents and screw. I think I'm a little better than that. When I do get laid, it won't be in the back of the Bijou Theater. Oh no, it's going to be beautiful—you hear what I say—and with someone who loves me. So O.K., now you know."

Solly was surprised at feeling unexpected guilt instead of his usual hostility and pain at her tirade of rejection. "You mean to tell me that you never necked?"

"That's right, not the kind of necking you're talking about. The trouble with you, Solly, is you think the same as every other Hester Street bum, that everybody's alike, looking for a cheap, quick screw, button up your pants and go home. But you're wrong. Life's tough enough; it's even tougher if you want to live it like a decent human being and for that you've got to work a lot harder in this place." She started to cry.

Solly looked at her, then cautiously he put his arms around her, brushed away the tears with the back of his hand and kissed her softly on the mouth. He whispered in her ear. "I love you, Birdie. I'm sorry."

They walked home in silence. When they reached Birdie's house Solly said, "Can I take you to the Bijou tomorrow?" Birdie nodded yes and went up the stairs while Solly waited below until she disappeared, then he turned and walked home through the hot summer night.

Now, when he saw Birdie coming toward him as she crossed the street, he pretended he wasn't hurt about the things that had happened the night before. "How come you're late?" he said agreeably.

"I'm sorry, I had to help Mama. Solly, do you mind if we don't go to the movies tonight, it's so hot?" She added quickly, "It has nothing to do with last night, really. I just don't feel like going, if you don't mind."

He grimaced slightly, thinking he really wanted to see the movie, but here he was saying, "O.K., we'll do what you want."

"Let's go and have a soda, then we'll see, O.K., Solly?"

They sat at a small round ice-cream table at Plotkin's delicatessen and ordered a celery tonic. Solly was halfway through his when he noticed that Birdie had hardly tasted hers. "You don't like it?" he asked. After all, it cost a nickel.

"It's fine. Look, Solly, I have a problem I want to talk to you about."

He felt flattered that she was seeking his advice. "Yeah, so what's the problem?"

"You know Katie?"

He nodded his head. "So what's the problem?" As she hesitated Solly popped a piece of ice in his mouth.

"Well, Solly," she started out slowly, "I want you to do me a big favor." She paused, then added quickly, "I want you to introduce Katie to David Rezinetsky."

Solly nearly choked on the ice. "Say that again."

"David Rezinetsky. I want you to introduce him to Katie."

"You must be out of your mind—you think I'm going to ask him for anything."

"Please, Solly, don't get mad, this is important."

"I will not. That guy never even talks to me. Like dirt under his feet he treats me."

"Don't be like that, Solly. You've known him all your life. You could overlook it if you wanted to do this for me."

Solly scratched the back of his head. "I don't know why it's so important that she meets him. That's number one, and number two is that that guy has lived in the same house two floors above me I forget for how many years, I went to school with him, I see him every day and never does he say hello Solly, drop dead Solly, go to hell, Solly, and you want me to go up to him and say, 'Look Dave, have I got a girl for you'? He'd knock me on my can." This was the advice she needed him for? The problem she wanted him to help her with? Like hell it was. She didn't need his advice; she needed to use him, pure and simple, so her skinny girl friend could get a boyfriend she couldn't get on her own. The hell he would humble himself, for what, why should he? What was in it for him? Not even the promise of feeling her tits in the dark movie.

Birdie's eyes were cast down as she peeled off tiny bits of the cracked, dirty oil cloth that should have been replaced years ago. They both looked up when Mr. Plotkin called from behind the counter in Yiddish, "How long you going to sit there, till next shabbes? For a dime yet. I should charge you for sitting."

Solly looked up, then around. There was no one in the store except Mr. Plotkin and themselves and the flies buzzing around the big slab of smoked salmon that lay on the counter. "You need the table for the big rush you've got coming in?" Up yours, he wanted to say to Mr. Plotkin, but he thought better of it because he knew his mother would give him one across the face even if he was going on twenty-one, because leave it to Mr. Plotkin to tell her how a son from the house of Obromowitz has profaned in his fine establishment. Aloud he said, "Come on, Birdie, let's get out of here."

They walked aimlessly for a while. There was really no place to go. Without looking at Solly, Birdie said, "Would you like to go up to the roof?" hoping that he would not misunderstand her motives, which were purely to divert his attention back to the mainstream of their conversation—her purpose. From the tone of his voice as he grumbled, "Oh what the hell," she knew she could dismiss that problem.

They sat on the empty orange crates and felt the special heat of dusk. Birdie said, "I guess I hurt your feelings, Solly. I really didn't mean to. I was just trying to do something nice for Katie."

"Why that particular louse? I don't understand, why him?"

"Because it's a little bit complicated."

"So uncomplicate it for me. I've got no place to go."

"You know Katie lived in London with her mother when she was a little girl after she left Poland? Well, she's had a really good education and the boys around here don't appeal to her."

"So that makes her some kind of a princess?"

"No, but what would she be able to talk to them about?"

"How would I know?"

Ignoring the sarcasm she went on, "I think my mother realized that she'd have a tough time getting a guy. Let's face it, Solly, we're slobs."

That did it, Solly thought. "So I'm a slob? But David Rezinetsky the louse isn't?"

"Now wait a minute, Solly. Don't get mad—"

"Who the hell is he because he graduated from high school and I didn't?"

"He's a classy guy, that's who he is."

"Some classy guy, because he read a few more books than I did, so that makes him the Prince of Walcs and me a slob?" He got up and paced back and forth, then angrily said, "Damn it, I had to go to work while he went to school because he had four older brothers. I got three younger ones. Him with his superior attitude, he runs around selling his fifty-cent insurance policies, big insurance man!" He turned to Birdie, looking her square in the eye, "Well I'm going to tell you, Birdie Greenberg, maybe you don't think I'm good enough for you but someday the big insurance man will choke from envy because I got plans too, see?" Pointing to himself with both his thumbs he said, "I'm going to own my own theater someday, see?"

Birdie stood up and shook her finger at Solly as her voice crescendoed. "Damn you, Solly, that's not what I meant and you know it. Skip it, forget it, if you couldn't do this for me then you and I are through, understand? You and your crummy pride!" She ran down the stairs to her flat and slammed the door.

Solly remained on the roof for a long time, his head in his hands, shifting and kicking under his feet the small pebbles that stuck to the tar paper. Why was he debating with himself, he thought, when all the time he knew that he was going to eat crow for that frigid broad downstairs. He knocked on the door, and Birdie opened it.

Startled to see Solly but quickly composing herself and narrowing her eyes on him, she demanded, "Yea, what do you want?"

"Come out into the hall."

She hesitated for a moment, then shut the door behind her.

He took a deep breath and said, "I don't know how but I'm going to do it for you."

She put her arms around Solly's neck and kissed him hard. Maybe, he thought, this would have been an opportunity to make a deal with her in exchange for what he was going to do for her. But just as quickly he realized that Birdie would not be tricked into any barter. "Come on," he said, resigned, "let's go and get a knishe and cream soda at Erna Schimmel's."

Solly hung around the tenements, scarcely going anywhere for two nights trying to meet David coming or going. Finally, as Solly stood leaning against David's crumbling banister, David came bouncing down the stairs two at a time. Before Solly could say a word he was away and down the street, with Solly running behind him up one street and down another until David reached the Christie Street gym, where he sat waiting his turn and watching intently the four other players as they ran and swatted the ball back and forth.

Solly quietly edged onto the seat next to David, being careful not to disturb him. Finally he spoke up. "Hi, Dave. They're pretty good, huh?"

David looked quickly at Solly, thought momentarily what the hell was he doing here, then mentally shrugged, what did he care? and nodded.

Solly said, "You play a lot?"

David didn't answer, he simply pretended not to hear. Solly tried again to engage him in conversation, and David again paid no attention.

The first four players left; it was David's turn now. Taking the handball out of his pocket, he hit it hard against the wall and began the rally. Solly waited through forty-five minutes of torture, and boredom, for David to finish. He hated sports of any kind. There were really only two things he loved or even liked in this whole universe—Birdie Greenberg and the movies. The movies he loved, he ate, he slept. He would rather have worked as a part-time usher for no money, if necessary even getting up each morning at four to work at Lipkin's Bakery so his evenings would be free to usher at the Bijou . . . he would rather do that than be, well, than be the mayor of New York.

Thank God, Solly thought, the game was over. He resented this arrogant creep. It was all too obvious David wanted nothing to do with him, but damn it he couldn't turn back now; he wasn't about to go back to Birdie and say he'd failed without even trying. He moved closer to David.

"You play great handball, Dave."

David answered without looking at him, "Thanks."

"You play often?"

Now David looked at him. This guy wants something. Maybe to make a touch, maybe he's selling something. "O.K., Solly, what's on your mind?"

Solly worried David could read his thoughts. "Nothing, I just happened by and saw you. Nothing wrong with being a little friendly, is there?"

David knew he didn't just happen by. Gyms were not exactly Solly's natural habitat. But David decided not to pursue it and got up and started to walk away, saying, "O.K., Solly, see you around."

Solly jumped up and called out, "Hey wait a minute, Dave, I want to talk to you."

Here it comes, David thought. He turned abruptly around. "What about?"

No use prolonging it. "Dave, I know we've never been friends, I mean real friends, but I'm going to ask you to do me a very, very big favor."

"What kind of favor?"

It didn't make it any easier for Solly that David impatiently volleyed the small ball between his hands as he stood there. Solly cleared his throat. He just couldn't find the right words. It wasn't easy standing in front of a guy you knew felt so damn superior to you —not at all the same as rehearsing the dialogue, taking both parts at three o'clock in the morning. The things he did for Birdie . . . so who asked him to be so crazy for her? Who forced him? "I'd like to ask you to double date with me and Birdie Greenberg and her best girl friend," he finally blurted out.

David looked at him in amazement. "Solly, what do you want, what are you really after?"

"Nothing, Dave, honest, that's it."

"Oh, come on, Solly."

"I know it sounds crazy. We were never out together before, and for me suddenly to ask you to blind date a girl sounds nuts, but please, Dave, would you do this for me? It means a lot, honest."

"You're right, it does sound crazy. But why me?"

"Well it's kind of a mixed-up thing. Birdie gets an idea, nobody can talk her out of it."

"What's this got to do with me?"

"Nothing, really. Birdie thinks you've got class, she thinks you're a regular Buddy Rogers, and she wants you to meet a girl friend she thinks you'd like."

"And I suppose she looks just like Jean Harlow." He turned and began to walk out of the building. Solly hurried after him and stood in the doorway, but David pushed by him. He hated anyone who begged. Solly's anger came out, his face grew red.

"David, can't you even listen? I just asked you to do me a favor, that's all. But no, your nose might fall off. Who the hell do you think you are, anyway? You always thought you were too good for me, for anyone around here. You were born in the same place as me. We went to school together. We're cut from the same cloth. So what makes you think you're so damn great?" Even though the anger had subsided, leaving him drained, Solly rambled on. "I'm in love with a meshuggena . . . she's crazy but I'd go to hell for her if she wanted me to . . . I didn't want to do this, I knew what you'd say . . ."

The consequences of failure came rushing at him as he thought of Birdie. Now more quietly he said, "I know she'll hate me and think I'm stupid because I couldn't get you to go. Knowing her she'll never talk to me again and if that happens I'll go kill myself somewhere. She doesn't know you the way I do." Then quietly he said, "All it would have meant to you was one lousy night. So she was pretty, or she wasn't pretty, or you liked her or you didn't like her, what the hell difference would it have made? Big deal. Only one night, Dave, that's all for you, but for me it could mean the rest of my whole life." Shoulders hunched, Solly looked very alone as he walked out to get lost in the crowd.

David watched Solly walking away, his teeth clenched, the muscles in his jaw taut. His first reaction when Solly had begun his attack on him was a desire to smash him one. That's what he had wanted to do . . . but he didn't, which was not a role that became David. He'd never taken any grief from anybody. When it came to defending himself, he was afraid of no one. He could never remember a time when he had deliberately started a fight, but if someone wanted to take him on that was O.K. with him. He was angry with himself because he let Solly get away with this, but even more angry because he didn't know why, and that was what bothered him. He didn't owe Solly anything. Besides, who had ever done anything for him, why should he do anything for Solly? Or for that matter for anybody, except his best and only friend, Abe Garfinckel, who had proved over and over again that he was a friend. Why should he? He asked for nothing from anybody, gave nothing in return. That was the way he wanted it, no obligations.

By his own design, David had been considered somewhat eccentric all his life by everyone in the community. A loner was a phenomenon in this closely knit society, and his aloofness was interpreted as conceit. David himself did nothing to dispel this impression and the effect snowballed. But conceit was the result rather than the cause of his isolation, and there were depths of intelligence and sensitivity within David that few would ever know existed.

To outward appearances David had all the physical attributes to attract people to him, but on the other hand he didn't have the desire to attract the people who surrounded him. He had never been able to accept this network of humanity into which he had been born. They lived always with the fear of tomorrow, always with the threat of hunger, of illness, of old age, of dying. It was true that all of them had fled from the threat, or near threat, of annihilation, and understandably what they found here, if not utopian, was better than what they had before. Here was something they called freedom, but David constantly asked himself how much better was it, this kind of freedom? A ghetto without fences, a Diaspora without dignity?

What plagued David above everything else was the fear of poverty there seemed to be no escape from. He was driven to study in secrecy and to bear his doubts and dreams in loneliness. He would not capitulate to life, this he promised himself. If he had to remake himself he would; he would rise above the complacency of his family and his contemporaries, even if he had to forsake relationships that might have brought some companionship and comfort. To him, though, the risk of being *like* them was greater than the pain of being separate. He could bear that . . . he would be somebody, if only in his own eyes. It took discipline and loneliness, and David found his own private island, reading everything he could get his hands on, even from time to time going to a concert or a play with Abe. He held to his dream, and these things he did were less important for themselves than as part of his overriding plan of escape.

His aloofness did make him particularly attractive to the opposite sex. The more "hard to get," the more desirable he became, and the girls pursued him. However, he didn't avoid them just to play hard to get. They never bettered themselves, they never even tried, which was what he hated most of all.

So David Rezinetsky remained a loner, and let life swarm around him without being touched by it. Poverty and the ghetto bred mutual suffering, but David refused to share in any part of their lives. Still . . . that night, he had difficulty in getting to sleep. Solly stuck in his craw like a hard morsel he couldn't spit up. He had to be honest with himself that Solly had touched a sore spot. The armor he had forged over the years had been chipped away just a little bit by some of the things Solly had said.

There was no denying, as Solly had said, that they were cut from the same piece of cloth, never mind how hard he tried to pretend otherwise, the truth was that—no matter how offensive the thought—chances were he would never escape from this sewer any more than Solly would. Face it, for every one who had, there were a hundred who couldn't. The only lines of escape were either crime or education. The first was out of the question, so was the second. He had no diploma, no profession; he had no family to help him rise out of all this the way Abe's family had done, and besides, what kind of a world waited outside for David Rezinetsky? He was a Jew living in a time when there were signs of blatant discrimination, signs that even literally read "No Jews Allowed." At least here in this dismal ghetto, discrimination was one thing they didn't have to contend with. Token compensation from a world that said "Leave this place and we'll crush the dignity out of you, we'll annihilate you." Quotas at universities so subtle they hit you between the eyes, and you wanted to lash out and smash to pieces the world that didn't want you. He asked himself where he did belong; and in a moment of honesty he had to say . . . here. Maybe he and Solly were not so different after all. They were Jews, a fact he could not be reconciled to, a fact that even in acknowledgment did not comfort him.

In his mind's eye David again saw Solly standing there trying to reach him, his face sweating, his hair in his eyes, his glasses askew—and for some reason that David couldn't sort out Solly now made him feel pity and admiration. It was as though he were looking at Solly for the first time in his life, Solly standing up to him. That had taken a hell of a lot of courage—David was also a head taller and thirty pounds heavier—fighting for a girl he loved so much he would take the chance of getting beaten up. David wondered what it would feel like to love someone with that much passion, and whether he ever would, or if in fact he were capable.

Anyway, it really wouldn't hurt him if he did this for Solly . . . And now suddenly he wondered if Solly might actually have been serious about killing himself. At first he told himself it was a show of dramatics, but Solly was awfully convincing for once . . . what if Solly really meant to do what he had threatened . . . then David would be at least partly responsible . . . he had not even been willing to give Solly a chance, show him the courtesy of listening. Like it or not, he at least owed him that much. Everybody owed somebody something—even David Rezinetsky.

CHAPTER TWO

David did not go home to supper the next night. Instead he ate at Plotkin's delicatessen right next to the Bijou Theater, sitting at a window table and keeping his eyes on the street to catch Solly before he went to work. As Solly crossed the street, David got up quickly, went out, and called to him.

When Solly saw David he became frightened. The other night had been different. He had been geared up by anger that reinforced his boldness. But standing here in front of David, in his usher's uniform, which was baggy and ill-fitting, its tarnished braid making him look like a reject from Kaiser Wilhelm's army, he didn't feel so brave. "O.K., O.K., Dave, don't hit. I'm sorry about last night. What the hell, you don't owe me anything."

"That's all right, Solly, forget it. Did you eat?"

Solly blinked. What was this, David being civil to *him?* Maybe David had a plot to poison him, he was being so nice. Sheepishly, without looking at David, he answered, "Sure, I ate at three when I came home from the bakery. Who doesn't eat at my mother's house?"

"Well, come on in anyway and have a cup of coffee before you go to work."

As he brought Solly his coffee, Mr. Plotkin said in Yiddish, "The big general is here. You want a piece of strudel, General?"

Solly wanted to say, you know where you can put your strudel, Mr. Plotkin, but he thought of his mother and nodded yes.

It was still a little new for David, giving in to Solly,

so for just a moment more he diverted the conversation by asking Solly—and not much caring—"How do you like your job?"

"Don't ask, Dave. Outside of Birdie it's my whole life, I love it. Someday I'm going to own my own theater, you wait and see, I promise you . . ."

David thought, there it was . . . the dream, the wait-and-see that nobody really believed. Still, everyone needed an island. For David it was books that took him out of the world he could not otherwise escape, for Solly it was the movies. Were they so different . . . "What time do you go to work, Solly?"

"Six-thirty. I got time."

"About last night—"

"I'm real sorry, Dave, honest I am. I don't know why I got so damned mad, honest—"

"Look, it doesn't matter what happened last night. Did you tell Birdie we had no date?"

Solly bit his lip. "No, not yet, and I'm not looking forward to it either." Hurriedly he added, "But that's got nothing to do with you, Dave. That's not your problem."

"Why would she be so mad at you if I didn't want to go?"

"You ever have a steady girl?"

David shook his head. "No."

"Well, let me tell you about Birdie. I love her, but like they say, nothing's perfect. She's got her faults and I got mine. I know what she thinks of me, that I'm a slob, I've got no class." He hesitated, bit into the strudel, chewed, swallowed, then began again. "One thing I'll say about Birdie, she's got a lot of guts. When she wants something, she never takes no and she wants to think I'm the same. I'm not." He paused, looked at David, and then slowly continued, "I guess I was trying to prove to her that maybe I had more guts than I have. No use talking, I guess what it all amounts to is, I wanted to look good in her eyes. That's really what it is, Dave."

David watched as he sipped the coffee; there was silence between them for a moment, then carefully: "Tell me about this girl."

Solly shrugged his shoulders. "What's to tell? I might as well be honest with you. You're not going to take her out anyway, so why should I give you the old baloney. She's a girl, a plain girl."

"What is she like?"

"What is she like?" Solly repeated, groping for a description. "She's a skinny girl, not like Birdie with two gorgeous grapefruits out in front. I like her because she's Birdie's friend."

"She's really so bad?"

"No, she's a very nice girl. A little bit strange, but she's really a very nice girl."

"What does she look like?"

"To say I would call her a beauty, I wouldn't. A contest she wouldn't win. And she speaks funny. I'll tell you the truth, I don't understand her half the time."

"What do you mean?"

"With an accent like I never heard. She's a greenhorn."

"Oh, she hasn't been in this country very long then?"

"Yeah, that's right."

"Where does she live?"

"With Birdie and her family. Her mother and father are dead and it's some kind of a long story who the hell wants to go into."

David had been sitting with his own thoughts, not really listening too hard as Solly spoke on. It wasn't too necessary to describe her. Hester Street was full of such girls coming from Europe; he knew the type. He didn't even have to ask her name, and as he looked at Solly he asked himself how different could this girl be from Birdie or any of the others? But he said, "Look Solly, let's forget all that. I'm going to ask you a question."

"Sure, Dave, anything." He took another bite of the strudel.

"If . . . I decided to go out with her, would that take you off the hook with Birdie? I mean just once, that's all," he added emphatically.

Solly almost choked on the strudel, and small morsels spewed from his mouth as he shook his head in disbelief. Catching his breath he said, "You mean you would?"

"Maybe, just once, Solly, just one time. Let's get that straight, no strings attached."

"Oh my God, Dave, I can't believe this!" He almost screamed, he wanted to kiss David. "Yes, yes and how!"

"O.K., then, I'll take her out, but not alone."

"You'd do this after what I told you about her? God, Dave, how can I ever thank you?"

"Forget it. What night do you want to go?"

"Sunday night I don't have to work, if that's O.K. with you?"

"That's fine with me. What do you want to do?"

"The best thing is go to the movies, but I'm going to pay," he insisted.

"Forget that. You just make all the plans and let me know."

Solly looked up at the clock on the wall and saw that it was almost six-thirty. He shook David's hand and thanked him profusely, wondering what had changed David so.

After he'd left, David sat at the small round table, feeling a little uneasy that he had allowed Solly to get under his skin.

Solly couldn't wait to tell Birdie about his victory. When his little brother came to the theater at eight o'clock to bring a hot corned beef sandwich, which his mother sent to him every night in fear that the big breadwinner might die of malnutrition between the hours of five and eleven, he said, "Hymie, go to Birdie's house on the way home and tell her to meet me here after the show."

Birdie was standing in front of the theater when the marquee was turned off. Solly came out whistling and said smugly, "O.K., baby," trying to imitate Humphrey Bogart, "what's there in it for me if I tell you I got the job done, baby?"

"Solly! You mean Katie's got a date with David Rezinetsky?"

"That's right . . . baby."

"Oh, Solly, how did you do it? Tell me quick."

"Wait a minute, not so fast, what's there in it for me?"

"Stop all this foolishness, for God's sake, and tell me what happened."

But Solly was going to savor this for a while. Let Birdie get a little excited, this was his moment. "Let's go and get ice cream and sit down and I'll tell you all about it." This moment was too sweet, like honey in the mouth, to be wasted on the street. He needed a relaxed atmosphere to confide his saga of conquest. No hurry, let her wait . . .

Solly was now deliberately licking the cone, very slowly, but Birdie couldn't wait, not another minute. "All right, Solly, *what happened?*"

He took a bite of ice cream and let it melt slowly in his mouth. Then, eyes smiling, he began to tell her how difficult it had been to get David to go out with Katie. Without telling her any of the real facts he made it seem that now David was eating out of his hand; he had sold him so completely on Katie's charms he could hardly stand waiting to meet her, wanting to do it that very same night. He sounded so convincing that even he began to believe his story, then laughed to himself as he decided the movies might be make-believe but they sure set you up to deal with the big problems of the world.

She listened to him with elbows on the table, face cupped between her hands. When he finished she said, "Solly, I love you. That's terrific, I honestly didn't think you could do it."

He felt ten feet tall. "Why not? It really wasn't that tough."

Birdie spoke to him with new respect. "Did you make any arrangements?"

"No, only that we have a date on Sunday night to go to the movies, the four of us."

"Oh, Solly, I can't believe this, I'm so thrilled! And mama will be too."

"Wait a minute, wait a minute, slow down." He put his hand up. "He didn't ask her to marry him yet, so don't get that excited."

"I know, Solly, but it's a beginning for Katie." Then her expression changed, she looked at Solly and said, "You know, we got another problem?"

"Oh, for God's sake, now what? You and your problems—"

"Don't get mad, not a real problem. I mean we have to figure out a way to get them together, because if I tell Katie we've cooked up this whole thing behind her back, it would embarrass her so much that maybe she wouldn't go. So how do we do it?"

"Well," said Solly confidently, as though he suddenly knew all the answers, "that is absolutely no problem. What we'll do is this. You tell Katie you want her to go with you to buy a new dress."

"Where would I look for a new dress, Solly?"

He looked at her as though he was getting tired of her being so dumb. "At Saks Fifth Avenue," he said, waving his hand. "Where would you go to buy a dress? To Bloom's Emporium! Pick out a dress, tell them you're bringing your girl friend in. You don't have to buy it." He stopped, looked at her and then, shaking his head, said, "What's the matter with you, can't you use your imagination, a smart girl like you? I'm surprised."

She pursed her lips together and squinted her eyes, "O.K., smart ass, don't get so fresh. I didn't know if Katie would believe me. I don't want her to catch on, that's all."

"All right, now let's continue on with the plan, O.K.?"

"O.K."

"Go to Bloom's at four o'clock and look at the dress which should take you what, five, ten minutes? Then walk down toward the Bijou. Now Dave and me by coincidence will be walking up the street at four-fifteen, got it?"

She nodded in an unaccustomed show of deference.

"When you see us, you say hello to me and Dave; then like it wasn't planned, you introduce Katie, and the four of us just walk along the street together. Then

I'll say, 'How about us all going to the movies?' How does that sound?"

Instead of jumping up and kissing him for his inventiveness, she just sat mulling it over in her mind, every detail. Did it seem too made-up, she wondered? Would Katie catch on? . . . Maybe not. She hoped not. "Do you think it'll work?"

"Sure, why not?"

"Won't she think it funny bumping into you and Dave and him joining us to go to the movies?"

"Of course not, why should she? You only think so because you know all about it."

"O.K., I'll take your word." Her eyes were warm; to Solly she looked incredibly sweet sitting across from him, even in the harsh overhead light. There was softness in her voice as she said, "Solly, darling, I love you so much. I'll just never forget what you've done."

Slowly they walked through the night holding each other's hand, and when they got to Birdie's house they went up to the roof.

Sunday had finally come and not too soon for Birdie. For four days now she had endured the suspense of not letting on to Katie; the deception and the secrecy were driving her wild. For one thing she was afraid that either she or her mother might let a word slip and give the whole thing away, so she carried the burden of romance alone. Nervously she contemplated how she could get Katie to wear her beautiful French dress.

Hannah had seen it one day in the window of a small exclusive London shop and had made up her mind that Katie was going to have that dress, no matter how; and she saved and scrimped until she finally had accumulated the money. For Hannah it represented more than just a dress, much more. She knew that perhaps this would be her only legacy to her child. Not a dress, really, but a cherished memory, a memory to recall through the years so that out of Katie's lonely, sequestered childhood she would remember that one precious moment. Everyone needed an important memory in a lifetime. It made no difference that Katie would wear it only once. Once was enough for Hannah, the day she saw her child graduate from school. She had wept tears of pride and gratitude that God had allowed her to live to see that day. . . .

Saturday night accidentally on purpose Birdie washed the only other dress that Katie could have worn out on the street on a Sunday afternoon. The dress had shrunk so that Katie would never be able to wear it again. For this Birdie was sorry, but she knew God would forgive her for being so devious. How else could she have gotten Katie to wear her best dress just to go to Bloom's? Now she would have no alternative. When Katie objected Birdie said, "So what if you do wear it? It's such a beautiful day." To make it appear that she too would make a sacrifice Birdie said, "Tell you what, as long as you're going to wear yours, I'll get dressed up too and we'll go to the Jewish Center dance. It'll be fun."

But as she dressed, Katie thought this was not the time or the place to wear her most treasured possession. This dress had been meant to wear only on the most important occasions of her life. To wear it to Bloom's was almost an affront to her mother's memory. Gently taking it from its resting place, she held it up to herself and looked at her reflection in the mirror, remembering the day her mother had given it to her, and in spite of herself she began to cry. "Oh, Mama, I miss you so." And then suddenly as she stood looking at herself, she did want to wear the dress. By some magic, for this brief moment it seemed she and her mother were terribly close, as though her mother were here now and that they were once more, miraculously, together.

When she finished dressing, Katie took one last look at herself. How she loved this dress. She felt again the excitement she had felt that first time she had taken it out of the box. Never had there been such a dress, never! She touched the exquisite white embroidered silk organza with a tiny bunch of French violets attached to the black velvet ribbon around her waist, feeling as she stood here the same as she did that other day, like a fairy princess, and one loved so very much.

After Birdie had rushed Katie through Bloom's, the two girls walked through the multitudes of screaming people—women trying to buy a bunch of carrots for a penny cheaper than they had been that morning; the push-cart peddlers haggling over a pound of potatoes; the ragged children playing in the street which was their playground, their park; old men in skull caps discussing the Testaments, each one arguing the fine points of the Talmud and each one thinking that the others were idiots. The garbage cans overflowed. But for Katie there was nothing squalid, nothing ugly, nothing sordid in all of this, feeling as she did that she belonged to all of them and they to her, all bound together by a heritage that had survived so much. She didn't feel at all out of place in her lovely dress as they now walked toward the Bijou Theater.

From a distance Birdie saw David and Solly approaching them. She had butterflies in her stomach by the time Solly said in feigned surprise, "Hi, Birdie, where are you going?"

She swallowed hard, and when the words came out she was so nervous she stuttered a little. "We're coming from Bloom's," and pointed in its direction. Then she heard herself asking, "How are you, Dave?" For a second her mind was blank; she was so rattled by the strain of deception that she forgot to introduce Katie. Then, finally, "Dave, I want you to meet my very best girl friend, Katie Kovitz, and Katie, I want . . ."

David didn't hear the rest of the introduction, he was so shocked that *this* was Birdie's friend. Where did she come from? How long had she been here? Why had he never seen her on the street or in the neighborhood? Solly's measure of beauty would be the movie queens he spent so much vicarious time with, but how, David asked himself, could Solly not have seen how exquisite this girl was? My God, couldn't Solly see for himself how she stood out from the rest? He looked at the delicate face with the porcelain-like skin; her long hair, tied back simply with a narrow velvet ribbon, gently falling like heavy strands of silk to her shoulders. He had visualized her looking like another Birdie, with an overly red mouth that made her look like a kewpie, painted nails, short hair permanent-waved to match.

But Birdie was thinking, I should have insisted she use some lipstick, she looks so plain.

Katie stood back and just listened to the rapid conversation; she heard Solly saying, "How would you like for all of us to go to the movies?" Then Birdie was saying, "Gee, that sounds swell. We'd love it." Then Solly was saying, "How about you, Dave, if we all go to the movies?" with Birdie interrupting, "Sure, why not?" and Solly echoing, "Sure, why not?" While David looked at Katie and said, "How would you like to take a boat ride, Miss Kovitz?"

Unprepared, Katie didn't know what to say and looked to Birdie, who quickly said, "That's a great idea, we'd love to go."

But David gave Solly a quick look he understood, and taking the hint he said, "No, Birdie, I want to go to the movies tonight. I don't want to go no place else."

Birdie understood and looked at Katie. "You'll have a swell time, but I'm going to go to the movies with the big shot general here, O.K.?"

Katie simply nodded. She was bewildered, all this had happened so fast.

As Birdie and Solly sat in their seats at the Bijou, Birdie thought, if that David touches Katie, I'll kill Solly, so help me, I'll kill him with my bare hands.

CHAPTER THREE

In awkward silence Katie stood at the boat rail and listened to the gentle sound of the waves as the boat seemed to glide along without effort. In the distance Manhattan looked majestic, the lights just beginning to go on.

"What are you thinking of?" David asked.

"How magnificent the different colors are between dusk and evening, and how beautiful New York looks from here."

So far as he was concerned it looked beautiful neither from here nor from anywhere. "Really? Do you like it here?"

He expected her to say no, not really. "I adore it; I've never been so happy in all my life."

"Happy?"

"Yes, very."

They strolled around the deck. There was an Italian family en masse having a Sunday excursion.

"Hey, Tony, play *Sorrento* again," the grandfather shouted. The young boy took up his concertina and the concert began.

"Oh, David, this is such fun, more than I've ever had."

The more she spoke the more intrigued he became. Solly didn't understand her, he thought she spoke with an accent? Never had he heard his name until she said it; she made it sound soft, and gentle. David, he repeated to himself slowly. Nobody called him David; his family called him by his Jewish name, Duvid, and his friends, Dave.

They found a bench and sat down.

"How do you happen to be living with the Greenbergs?"

"My mother and Mrs. Greenberg had known each other all their lives, and when my mother died I came here to live with them."

"Tell me about yourself." He was so curious about her—a rare thing for him.

"There's nothing to tell, I've really had a very uninteresting life."

"Tell me just the same."

Uncertainly she said, "I was born in Poland but I lived in London all of my life until I came here."

"How did you happen to be in London?"

"It's really all so boring, David."

"I don't mind. If it gets too boring I'll tell you all about mine, which is very exciting!" They both laughed.

"Are you sure you want to hear all this?"

"Yes."

She thought for a while; where did he want her to begin? At the beginning.

Hannah's oldest brother Max had escaped the Polish army by fleeing to England. In London there was a benevolent society that secured jobs for these men, and among them was Max. Naturally, none of them could speak English, so the problem was they had to wait until they could be employed, mostly by Jewish firms. One such firm that absorbed many of these men was the Felix Block Company, manufacturers of leather goods from fine luggage and ladies' handbags to gloves, and this is where Max Iscoff found work. He was a man of many qualities. One of the qualities that endeared him to Felix Block was his giving more than just a day's work. He worked long after the others left, he was the first one waiting for the factory to open in the morning, and Mr. Block watched with a canny eye. Large as the factory was, he knew the prowess of every one of his workers. Within a year he promoted Max to superintendent and eventually to sales manager, while all the time Mr. Block had even bigger plans for Max. His English had become so good that after two years he spoke with only a slight trace of a Polish accent, having applied the same verve and tenacity to learning English that he did to his work. So the time had come for Mr. Felix Block to invite Max to dinner. The mistress of his home was his daughter, his wife having passed away four years ago. His life revolved around her; she was the reason for his whole existence, and it was her future which mainly concerned him now that Rosalind Block had just turned thirty-one with no prospects of marriage on the horizon.

Felix looked painfully at his one and only child and secretly had to admit that she looked just like him. On a man the large features didn't seem too terribly out of place, but unfortunately she had inherited the worst of his looks as well as the worst that was in his nature, and none of her mother's charm and beauty. Had it been the other way around, Felix would not now be unhappy over the fact that perhaps there might never be an heir to carry on the firm of Block, a firm whose lineage went back five generations. Felix Block wanted grandchildren. If fate had designed it differently there would be no need to have someone like Max to dinner, a mere peasant to sit at the table of Mr. Felix Block. But *c'est la vie,* and Mr. Felix Block, being a very practical man, began to evaluate the potential of Max, figuring that in him he just might be able to have his life-long ambition come true. This was not the man he would have chosen if the gods had been kinder to Rosalind; but Max had charm, and above all, obedience. He worked hard and diligently, and with him there would be no risk of the business falling out of Felix' hands. After his demise it would still be Rosalind's, because Felix realized that where Max was extremely bright, he was also soft and pliable. Felix knew that his daughter could never be married to a strong, dominating man such as, for example, himself. They were too much alike. So with all things considered, without his knowing it, Max had been chosen.

And they were married. Felix waited impatiently for that one year but there were no children. When Rosalind told her father there would likely be none because she had been unable to conceive, Felix laughed bitterly to himself at the games life played with him. He had accepted a man he felt was beneath him to live in his house, to sleep with his daughter and eat at his table—and all for nothing.

And then seeming miracle of miracles happened: Felix Block was told that his dream was going to be fulfilled—Rosalind was going to have a child. Max immediately was moved out of Rosalind's bed chamber and given a small room down the hall. His task was completed, his function was done.

The nine months passed miserably for Rosalind. In the beginning she was terribly ill with morning sickness, which persisted for hours, adding to her irritability. Her enormous bulk toward the end became so cumbersome that she spent most of the time in bed, was unbearably moody, and promised herself that never again would she submit to anything as undignified as pregnancy.

When the moment of birth arrived she lay prostrate in her bed, hating Max for having subjected her to the tyrannies of childbirth. After forty-eight hours, Julian Iscoff was born. Almost immediately after being separated from the placenta of his mother he found himself in the arms of his doting grandfather, who looked upon the child from the moment of birth as the product of his own self-will and determination.

As Julian began to grow, so did Rosalind's disdain for Max. He was never permitted to take the child out alone; Julian was either in the care of a nanny, his mother, or grandfather. Primarily Felix Block would direct Julian's destiny.

One day out of desperation Max took the three-year-old from his nanny's arms, disregarding her wild objections, took Julian out, sat him alongside him in the car, having decided to spend the day alone with the child in spite of them all. He bought him a ball, then took him to Hyde Park and frolicked with him in the grass, threw the ball back and forth. To Max's great delight the child responded to him.

After several hours three-year-old Julian became

tired, lay down on the grass and fell asleep while Max hovered over him. When the child awoke refreshed, Max picked him up in his arms, hugged and held him, and walked back to where the car was. For one moment Max looked into the window of the toy store, thinking perhaps he should have bought Julian another toy. As he did so the ball that Julian was holding dropped from his hand and rolled into the street; the child ran after it. In all the confusion after the screech of brakes a crowd gathered and Julian lay lifeless.

Rosalind was inconsolable. She beat Max with her fists until the blood ran from his mouth, screaming that he was a monster and had killed her child.

For the rest of his life Max was enslaved, beholden to her out of his guilt. Rosalind could now do with him absolutely what she would. From then on he was never to know another moment of tranquility. Rosalind never let him forget that it was he who was responsible for Julian's death; she never let him forget that he lived on her bounty, that he was a nobody, a nothing without the Block name. Disregarding that he contributed to what she now regarded as his charity, no matter how much he produced he still received a relatively small salary despite being responsible for making thousands and thousands of pounds for the firm each year.

Max accepted all the indignities, until matters became so unbearable he felt he had to escape. But how? He could not divorce her, the laws forbade that, and so he stayed. He built an unbreachable wall between himself and her—the only way he could have gone on living with Rosalind without eventually killing her, which is what he would like to have done many times. He became deaf to her rantings and mute to her caprices. Only once did he really oppose her, when he received the letter from his sister.

Hannah had become widowed and was left penniless with a five-year-old child. There was no one left, now that Mama and Papa were gone and all the rest had scattered. So she wrote to Max. It was her dream to be near her brother, the person she loved the most from childhood. She had to get away from the ghosts of the past and the tragic memories that haunted her. She begged Max to rescue her.

Max, badly shaken by the news, sent two tickets and sufficient money to bring her to London. He would worry about Rosalind later. . . .

As he waited at Victoria station for the train to arrive he looked back to a day so long ago and remembered that rosy-cheeked young girl with the long heavy silken braids, standing at the roadside dressed in a peasant blouse his mother had made, waving good-bye to him as he left on his life's journey. Now when Hannah and her child stepped off the train he hardly recognized her; she was only in her late twenties but looked ten years older than himself.

"Hannah!" he called out as he ran to her. They went into each other's arms. He kissed her cheeks, her eyes and her forehead; he stroked her hair, which was still shining and beautiful, placed her head on his shoulder as they swayed gently back and forth. For one fleeting moment as he held her in his arms he recalled another day in an orchard, when they lay on their backs under a tree eating sweet summer pears and gazing up at a so blue sky, watching white foamy clouds float by and in childish fantasy dreamed about wondrous things they would do when they grew up. A bittersweet memory now as he held the fragile body against him.

"Hannah," he whispered, "Hannah, what have they done to you . . . Hannah, my Hannah . . ." They stood in silence now, each with their own thoughts. Finally Hannah separated herself from Max and held him at arm's length.

"Max, dearest brother, let me look at you. Am I really seeing you? Is this a dream? Will I wake up?"

"It's me, Hannala. It is real and you are here."

Katie waited patiently with the rag doll in her hand. Max looked down at her; swooping her up in his arms, he kissed and hugged her.

"Katie, this is little Katie! Hannah, this could have been you when you were five. My precious child," he said, and hugged her to him.

Max drove them through the cold London night to

Rosalind's house. Hannah looked around in awe as they entered the oak-paneled hall with its original paintings, the vibrant antique Persian rug which she was reluctant to walk on, and thought that in her wildest dreams never would she see such a house, much less her brother's.

"Max," she said, "Max, you never mentioned once in your letters you lived in such a palace. Oh, Max, I'm so proud of you, but I'm not surprised; you were always the smartest one of all. If only mama and papa could have seen this."

Max could not meet the gaze of those lovely eyes full with admiration, love, and innocence. He just nodded his thanks and changed the subject.

"My wife would like to have been here to meet you,"—he listened to himself as he continued to lie—"but she's not been too well lately and wishes to be forgiven for tonight; you'll meet in the morning." At least he had spared her the morbid details for this one evening, hoping through some divine intervention Rosalind might relent, though never really believing it for a moment. "Let me take you to your room; you must be exhausted, and the poor child is half asleep. Come to Uncle Max, my *schöen kind.*" He carried her up the stairs to the servants' quarters on the third floor. Looking over his shoulder, he said, "Leave your suitcase, I'll come down and get it later." Hannah had started to pick it up and follow him.

"Now you'll rest. I've had a little supper prepared."

They reminisced about their childhood and their youth, about papa, such a scholar, the challehs, the strudel and the mandelbrot which mama made. They laughed when they thought about her, that she was the envy of every woman in the village. They tried to speak about the good things and the happy things and then, as happens with shared memories, they could not avoid the bad things. But for Hannah this was all behind them now. It would be a better life, a new life, and above all for her, no longer the loneliness. Now she had Max.

After supper he said, "It's getting late, my dearest, get some rest; we'll talk tomorrow." He kissed her on the forehead. "Sleep well, Hannah, my little sister, sleep well."

He left, walked down the stairs, then along the hall. Opening the door to his room, he found Rosalind waiting for him, silhouetted against the fireplace. "How dare you defy me?" She raged, and rushed over to Max, standing so close to him that when she spoke he felt the fine spray of saliva on his face. *"I told you not to bring them into my house."*

Backing away from her—not out of fear but because he found her nearness repulsive—he said calmly, "I had no other choice but to bring them here. Besides, this is my house too. I believe I make my contribution toward bed and board."

"Your house indeed, I want them out of here in the morning, do you hear me, in the morning! I have no intention of supporting three peasants!"

For the first time he laid hands on her, grabbed her arm and twisted it behind her back. He wanted to kill her. He wished he had the courage to match his anger. "Now you listen to me and listen very carefully. I will not send my sister and her child out into the streets. She will go when I find a suitable place for her." He released her arm, sickened by her and by his own violence. "I don't know how long that will take. She will go to work, so take heart, she won't be in your debt. However, Katie will remain in this house until such a time as my sister can provide a decent home for herself and the child. Do you understand what I say? Or if not, the three of us will leave, and you, my dear, and Mr. Felix Block, my benefactor, and the Felix Block Company can drop dead with my best wishes." Opening the door and waiting for her to exit, he added, "Do I make myself clear?"

She stood looking at him. This was a new Max, not the mild lamb she had led to the altar. Still—she wasn't Felix Block's daughter for nothing—she quickly pulled herself together. Her father was getting older and soon he would have to go into complete retirement. In fact, he had never recovered from the loss of Julian. She needed Max to run that business. He knew it now as well as Felix did. So she said to herself that this was not too much to negotiate for an employee as valuable as Max.

"All right, she can stay, on one condition: that she keep out of my sight and that I have no responsibilities toward her." Not wanting to linger in her moment of relative defeat, she turned smartly and like a proud general momentarily unhorsed, strode from the room, slamming the door behind her.

Who better than Max understood the problems that confronted Hannah? She spoke not a word of English, only Yiddish. What was she qualified for? Nothing, really, except to be a servant, and for Max this was simply unacceptable. He wanted to support her, but she refused, grateful enough that Katie could remain. Max regretfully agreed there seemed to be no other answer. Hannah got a job as a cook for a lovely family in Kensington by the name of Goldsmith with four growing children who maintained a kosher kitchen and spoke Yiddish in a most delightful way, with traces of a cockney accent.

Katie lived from one Saturday to the other; being the sabbath, that was the only day her mother did not work. Impatiently she would wait downstairs at the side entrance. When Hannah approached, Katie would run to her, kissing and hugging her around the legs. Proud of the way she had dressed herself, she would look up and ask, "Do you like the way I look, Mama?"

"Yes, like the most beautiful Shabbas queen," and off the two of them would go to synagogue.

Hannah was a very religious woman, but she realized how impossible it would be to adhere to the old ways. If she didn't ride or spend money on the sabbath it would mean depriving Katie of the one, all too short day they spent together. She decided that the Lord would have to forgive her this one transgression.

After synagogue she would take Katie to lunch. On some Saturdays they would go to Hyde Park for a picnic, which Hannah brought with the compliments of the Goldsmiths; or to the cinema, which neither of them understood, but Katie loved the movies and she began to learn from them. When the day was over and Hannah brought her home, Katie would run up the back stairs to her room, take out the present she brought home each week—a lovely hair ribbon, a box of biscuits, a small doll, a coloring book—and then cry inconsolably.

Max spent an hour every evening with Katie, trying to teach her English. He would love to have indulged her, to have done great and wonderful things for her, but he was grateful that if this were not really a home, it was at least a roof over her head. From time to time he protested, but not too insistently, when she was not permitted to take her meals in the dining room with them, instead eating with the servants. It crushed Max, but this after all was Rosalind's house. He despised the room on the third floor in the servants' quarters where Katie slept when there were five bedrooms that were unused. The room had a large, round dormer window where the roof sloped and when the moon shone brightly it terrified Katie so that she slept with the covers over her head. In winter the rain pounded on the pane making sounds that frightened her so that she would lie shivering, holding tight to her doll.

With the purse strings held fast by Rosalind, what could Max really do for Katie? Knowing that he would not be able to endow her with anything, he decided the most he could do was provide her with a fine education. He enrolled her at Greycoats School for Girls, where eventually she learned not only impeccable English but French as well. Katie had expressed a great desire to play the piano, and Max found a teacher at whose home she could practice every day. When she played at her first recital he bought her a lovely dress appropriate for just such an occasion, a white starched organdy with a wide pink satin sash tied in the back with an enormous bow, long white cotton stockings, and black patent leather party pumps.

She sat at the piano playing a simple Chopin waltz, her black curls bouncing up and down as she arpeggioed back and forth. When Katie finished and curtsied, Hannah took Max's hand in hers and looked at him. Her quiet eyes spoke what no lips could have said; no words were needed to speak of the pride and the gratitude she felt toward Max for making all this possible.

Ironically, Katie's love of music was really due to Rosalind, without Rosalind's realizing it. She had become a patron of the arts, introducing and encouraging young musicians. To fill the void in her life since her son's death, she pursued this with as much fervor as she indulged her loathing for Max and now for Katie, who lived in her home that should have been for Julian.

On Sunday evenings she presided over soirées to which she would invite important people in the music world to listen to her newest protégé. The music and excitement would find its way to Katie's room and she would listen, enchanted.

One evening, barefooted, she tip-toed down to the second floor and peeked between the banister railing, listening for a long time, then crept down the stairs, careful not to be noticed. When she got to the bottom she saw the beautifully gowned women and distinguished gentlemen sitting in their gilt chairs facing the pianist. Impulsively Katie walked quietly into the dining room. The sight enthralled her. The table was set with the gleaming Sheffield silver service which had belonged to Rosalind's great-grandmother; there were deep red roses in a silver and crystal epergne that had belonged to her grandmother. The table was laden with small canapés, tiny petits-fours, and exquisitely frosted French pastries in different colors. She stood in wonder at the beauty of all she saw, and without thinking of the consequences, she reached for one. As she did so, one of Rosalind's finest Minton plates came crashing to the floor, breaking into a dozen pieces. Terrified, she bent down to pick up the fragments. As she got up, Rosalind was standing there, the doors closed behind her so that no one could hear.

She pulled Katie to her feet and slapped her so hard across the face that Katie staggered. Rosalind's face was fury itself, but Katie was too stunned to cry.

Rosalind's anger still not exhausted; she shook her again, this time harder. "I've told you never to come into this room, you bad, bad girl! Now go upstairs. I'll deal with you and your uncle about this in the morning."

Katie ran hysterically from the room, through the kitchen, and out into the street in her bare feet. She had to find her mother or Aunt Rosalind would do something dreadful to her in the morning—she had said so. She ran for blocks, tears streaming down her face, her nose running, her feet bleeding, not knowing where she was going. Finally she went back to Rosalind's house, crouched under the door stoop, cried until there were no more tears, and finally fell asleep.

The next morning Ellen, the cook, going out to gather up the morning paper and milk, found Katie feverish and half-conscious. Picking up the frozen girl in her arms, she carried her to her room, put her under the covers, and then went to summon Max. Frantic with grief, Max couldn't understand what had happened. He had looked in at her last night when she had gone to bed at her regular bedtime, which was eight in the evening. Bewildered he called the doctor, who after he had examined Katie, told Max, "We have a very sick little girl on our hands. I'm afraid it's pneumonia. I'll make all the arrangements to have her put in the hospital."

The next forty-eight hours were a nightmare. Unshaven, exhausted from lack of sleep, Max remained with his sister, consoling her, begging her to rest in the small room next to Katie's that he had arranged for. He ordered meals to be brought to them, which neither of them touched, and they prayed as never before. It was four o'clock in the afternoon on Tuesday when the doctor said, "We have a great deal to be grateful for; our little lady has passed the crisis."

The next two weeks were the happiest Katie had ever known. She was showered with loving attention from both her mother and uncle. Each day Uncle Max brought her a new toy, a box of chocolates, a coloring book; but best of all he brought her a bunch of pink baby roses in a pink-and-white container that looked like a precious lamb. She adored it and was sure she would keep it forever.

The Goldsmiths were very understanding when they learned about Hannah's girl being ill. They insisted that she not work for the time that Katie was in the hospital. Mrs. Goldsmith sent a large tin of Danish cookies and some toys her children no longer played with.

When Katie finally was released from the hospital, Max spent as much time as he could with her, which of course brought on an outbreak of Rosalind's hostility; but by now it mattered not at all to Max. When Hannah would have her holiday for one week away from the Goldsmiths, he would take Katie and her to Brighton.

On Katie's sixteenth birthday they went to Rules in Maiden Lane near Covent Garden. It was a restaurant frequented by theatrical people; he had taken Katie there once before to see a Noël Coward play. Now he ordered a very special dinner and a birthday cake.

As he sat across from his niece he looked at her face, radiant and young, her voice full of the excitement of youth. The contrast with his sister was shocking—the dim candlelight made Hannah appear even more sallow; her cheeks were sunken, there were dark rings around her eyes, she was thinner than he had ever seen her. "How are you feeling, Hannala?"

"I'm fine, really."

Max knew this was not so; she looked too ill. "You're working too hard?" he demanded.

"No, Max, I don't work hard at all. The Goldsmiths are such nice people, and besides, there really isn't all that much to do."

As he ate his dinner, he thought, if she were ill would she tell? Probably not, knowing Hannah. He promised himself one thing, that although he had to go abroad for a few days, when he came home he would insist that she either change her job and allow him to care for her, which up to now she had vehemently refused, or find a situation where she would not work so many days. The problem, of course, was the same; she had learned to speak very little English through all the years, even now knowing just enough to get by.

After dinner Max turned to Katie and said, "I'm going to Paris for a few days on business. If it's all right with your mother, would you like to go?"

"Oh, Uncle, could I really? I would love nothing quite so much!"

"Then it's settled. We go on Wednesday and we'll be back on Monday."

She clapped her hands in excitement and said, "I love you, Uncle, I love you."

"I'm delighted that you do, but I'm really only taking you because I need an interpreter. Why else do you think I spent all that money on those French lessons?"

They laughed.

She wasn't sure how someone felt when they'd had too much champagne, but knew it had to be very much the same kind of sensation she was feeling now, reeling with happy intoxication. Four glorious, exciting days of visiting the Louvre, of dining in some marvelous French restaurant where she ordered in French. She adored her room with the small gray marble fireplace, the entire room done in rough toile, the bedspread, draperies and the pair of petite chairs on either side of the mantel. But best of all was the diminutive balcony that looked out over the Seine. What girl had ever been so lucky? If nothing else ever happened in her life this memory would be sufficient to last her forever.

When they returned there was a message for Max from Mrs. Goldsmith to phone her immediately. He was told that his sister had become very ill on Friday evening and not knowing what to do since he was away, she had taken it upon herself to call her own doctor, who had advised that Hannah be put in a hospital as quickly as possible. She was now at St. Thomas's. Mrs. Goldsmith gave Max the doctor's name and telephone number. He called right away and Max was asked to come to the doctor's office to discuss his sister's case.

"I know this is very difficult for you, but you must know how seriously ill your sister is," the doctor told him. "The kind of cancer she has . . ." He shrugged his shoulders. "Perhaps a year, we can never be sure."

Hannah died almost a year later to the day.

After the funeral they drove home in silence, Katie and Max. She went to her room and packed her belongings in the same suitcase her mother had brought from Poland. In the evening, Max had Ellen take her a tray.

Rosalind did not come to offer one word of condolence; Katie never really expected she would. She looked at the tray but could not touch it. Max knocked on the door. Opening it, her uncle stood before her. He had aged so much in the last few weeks; his eyes were sunken and red, he looked like an empty vessel. The lapel of his coat had been cut in the traditional gesture of mourning.

They sat looking at each other for a long while and then quietly she said, "I must leave now that my mother is gone." She took his hand in hers and said, "Painful as it is to leave you I cannot remain in this house any longer. I've caused you enough grief with your wife, I feel very responsible for that—"

"No, no, Katie. You and I are all that is left of our family. Please stay and I'll try to work something out, just the two of us. Please stay."

"Dearest uncle, some things are too late. My mother wanted me to go to America to be with Malka Greenberg. Truly, I must, for your sake as well as mine. I cannot stay and sit shivah for my mother. I'd like to leave as quickly as possible." She swallowed hard, holding back tears. "I love you, uncle, and never in my life will I be able to tell you how dear you are to me. Thank you, thank you for everything."

She was right, Max thought. If anything happened to him, if he died, she would be completely alone, then there would not even be Malka. Life's commands

—when to stay, when to go . . . He had never learned, he never would. What was left for him now? Only the prospect of death. Soon, he hoped, soon.

Now, across an ocean, David and Katie remained strangely silent. She looked down at her hands folded in her lap. How many things, she thought, had happened to her. How many lives had been spent and how many events had taken place through all the years so that she could be sitting here next to a young man she did not even know existed until a few short hours ago, revealing things to him that she had not even told Birdie, things she had not wanted to remember. But once started, she found herself unable to stop, and here she had said it all to him, a stranger. When she thought about how casually they had met this afternoon she had the strange feeling of being caught up in something inevitable. Could she call it her destiny. . . ?

"David, forgive me, I hadn't meant to go on and on."

Deeply touched, he said, "I'm glad you told me."

"I've done all the talking. Now, David, what about you?"

He looked at her. "What's there to tell? I've used up twenty-three years of my life doing nothing, and the only thing I know for certain is that someday I'm going to grow old and die."

His hopelessness was like a sharp pain cutting through her. She did not press him, but silently wondered.

The benches they were seated on were back-to-back, and a small boy of about four climbed up behind Katie, examined her hair ribbon, then in one quick gesture untied it, jumped off the bench and ran away, with David chasing quickly after him. After David caught the child and retrieved the ribbon, he returned to where they were sitting and handed it to Katie.

As she pulled her hair back to retie the ribbon David said, "No, please don't, I think your hair looks so, well, so nice that way." He looked at her—her hair falling softly about her shoulders, her lovely eyes the color of blue hyacinths as she sat so near him in her white dress, she reminded him of a Goya painting he'd seen once at the Metropolitan Museum.

The ferry had come into port and now was docking. They sat and waited for the others to get off, wanting to be the last to leave.

After David had taken her home and said good night, he waited for her to disappear inside the doorway. Leaning against the lamp post, he lit a cigarette, drawing the smoke deep into his lungs. He looked up, hoping she would come to the window, before finally flipping the cigarette away and walking toward home.

It was twelve o'clock before Katie slid past Sammy's narrow bed in the hall. Quietly she opened the bedroom door, but Birdie was sitting up in bed in the dark, waiting. All evening she had been a nervous wreck anticipating the most horrendous things. She knew that she could handle men—look how she handled Solly—but Katie was something else again; she was green and David knew his way around plenty. All evening she'd been apprehensive over letting her go alone on a boat ride. After all, what did Birdie really know about David? What if she had gone to school with him, what did that mean? She didn't know him as a date, and what girl could resist that gorgeous hunk of flesh? For a minute she wondered if she would have used the same tactics with David that she had used with Solly, confessing that she doubted it very much. With her arms folded across her chest, she demanded, "All right, so tell me, where have you been since four-thirty today?"

Katie threw her arms around Birdie's neck. "Birdie, I've met the most wonderful boy!" She hesitated, drew in her breath, and said, "You won't laugh if I tell you something?"

"No, I won't laugh, I hope. So what is it?"

"I think I'm in love."

"Oh that's great, one time you go out and you're already in love. Congratulations. Now tell me, what did you do?"

"We went on the boat ride and then David took me to dinner. And after dinner we went for a long walk and just talked about everything . . ."

"What kind of everything?"

"Oh, about books, and paintings, and music."

"Well, that sounds just lovely," Birdie said sarcastically, as though she believed for one minute that anybody could talk for eight hours about books, music and paintings. She knew better than that, knowing all too well these east side Romeos. Sure she'd wanted Katie to meet David, but not this way. There should have been a chaperone along and who better than Birdie since she had been the shadchen, the matchmaker, especially with an innocent like Katie on her first date with a boy, and someone like David Rezinetsky, no less! "O.K., now be honest with me, I'll understand. What did he do? Did he get fresh, did he try to do something like . . . Oh, you know what I mean. Did he?" Birdie was so serious that Katie started to laugh when she became irritated and repeated, "Well, *did* he?"

"Oh, Birdie, you darling goose. He didn't even kiss me good night."

All her careful planning down the drain . . . hadn't even kissed her good night. She should have known that someone like David wouldn't go for Katie. Sweet and lovable as she was, she was so plain; Birdie should have insisted that she at least use some lipstick. After all, David had turned down the best-looking girls on Hester Street—her, for example. She kept her thoughts to herself and finally fell asleep, to dream of new and bolder stratagems. . . .

David stood outside his flat now. Looking at the closed door, he realized how impossible it would be for him after the evening he had just spent with this lovely girl to go to bed and lie alongside his brother Ben's sweating body, to go to sleep smelling freshly fermenting garbage in the alley below. He turned and went up the stairs to the roof, then over to the parapet and looked over. It was not quite the same sight he had seen earlier today. All he had come back to was the ghetto's imprisonment that he felt deep inside himself. For him there was no beauty here, and no love. He turned around and saw the wash drying on the clothes line, walked over and took down a towel, rolled it up into a ball to use as a pillow and lay down with his hands behind his head, looking up at the stars. Close enough to reach out and touch.

He thought about Katie. Certainly he'd never imagined meeting anyone like her, or that someone like her existed. She had been to Paris, she played the piano, she had attended a private school. How strange that she was happy here with the Greenbergs in the ghetto when she had known that other life, that she was happy in a place that he found so oppressive. How could she settle for this? Of course her life had been lonely and he could understand why she'd needed to leave; but to be happy and content here, this was something he found impossible to understand.

He could sense her now, sitting alongside him. He had wanted to run his fingers through her hair earlier, but he had resisted then. Suddenly he became warm from desire for her, wishing she could be next to him at this very moment. He'd felt this way when they said good night, yet he hadn't even kissed her. Why? He shrugged it off, telling himself he had only been fascinated by her, she was so different. . . . That's all it was, really, but . . . the question still persisted. If he found her all that fascinating and desirable, why hadn't he kissed her good night. Was it because he thought she was so naïve and untouched? No, it had nothing to do with her naïveté. And then the thought rushed at him: it was quite simple—he had fallen in love with her. Yes, unbelievably, impossibly, it apparently had happened to him the way the oldest stories said it did, and the way he had long since promised himself it never would. . . .

In love? Oh, my God, no, he couldn't be in love, he wasn't *ready*, he couldn't afford to be in love! How could he? He couldn't even support himself, much less a wife. What was he thinking of? Why had he even thought of the words *wife* or *support?* To support someone meant that you had to get married. Married? My God, he was insane! He just met this girl;

one didn't fall in love so quickly, it took time. You don't take a girl for a boat ride and right away think about getting married. He didn't even know her. Maybe it was an illusion. He wasn't going to see her ever again. Isn't that what he told Solly, just once? By tomorrow he'd forget her; by next week he wouldn't even remember she existed. He made up his mind, he was not going to be in love.

Running downstairs to his flat, he undressed in the dark, got into bed and spent the worst, most miserable night he could ever remember. Not only that night, but for three nights and three days he kept arguing, fighting, debating with himself. He was not going to see Katie, he was going to forget her, cut her out of his thoughts. Why not? He was too strong-willed to allow a girl, *a mere girl* he met once, to make him fall in love with her. Nothing was strong enough to make him change his mind. Fine, finished, period.

Except now, he found himself waiting just beyond the tenement where the Greenbergs lived, waiting for Katie and Birdie to come home from work. Maybe, he reasoned, if he saw her once more he would realize how stupid he had been to have plagued himself. He took out a cigarette. When he struck the match his hand shook. Taking a deep breath, he moistened his lips and tried to compose himself. He wanted to run away, he still had time; but when he saw Katie and Birdie approach, he knew . . . knew it was too late. Birdie was already saying, "Hi, Dave." He shrugged his shoulders. Later he couldn't even remember whether he had answered or not. All he could focus on was trying to disguise his joy at seeing Katie, a joy mingled with irritation and surprise at his own weakness—he still thought of it that way. "How are you, Katie?" He hoped it sounded casual. When she smiled in reply he felt his heart pound. When he heard her voice . . . "Fine, David, and you? How are you?" . . . just those few words, that's all . . . she was *real* all right. Just the smile. . . . And he heard himself saying, as though he had no will of his own, "Fine . . . thanks, are you busy tonight?" "No." "Would you like to go for a walk or to a movie?"

Birdie interrupted, "What about supper? Mama's got supper ready. Want to come up, Dave, and eat first?" He had forgotten Birdie was there. "No, *thanks.*"

"But you got to eat," she said, suddenly disliking him enormously. After all, she had been the matchmaker and he was treating her like some kind of intruder. Maybe Solly was right, he was a schmuck, a snob. What, her house wasn't good enough for him? She wished she had never started the whole affair. She didn't feel less offended when David passed over her again and asked Katie directly, "Would you like to eat out?"

Katie looked at Birdie, "Do you think it would be all right?"

"Why . . . what's not to be all right? Go . . . go and have fun."

Katie knew Birdie was hurt. David had been rude, but why he had been rude, she didn't know nor could she understand. She felt vaguely guilty, but she wanted so badly to be with David that her loyalties to Birdie were overruled. She kissed Birdie on the cheek and said she would be home early, then left with David as Birdie stood watching them walk down the street until they were out of sight.

The Greenbergs were seated in their usual places at the kitchen table when Katie came in. Birdie looked at the clock. It was only seven-thirty. "How come you're home so early?" Katie shrugged. "I don't know. It seemed David was tired and said he had a big day tomorrow."

"Some date. The Romeo, the big Beau Brummell of Hester Street was tired." Birdie was about to go on when Malka asked, "Did you eat, Katala?"

"No . . . I wasn't hungry."

"Come, sit down. The stuffed cabbage is still hot."

Before Katie could answer, Birdie interrupted, "What? The big spender couldn't take you somewhere for a bite. In our house, he didn't want to eat."

"Please, Birdie, that's not true, I just didn't feel hungry. We did have coffee."

"Ha—that must have set him back a whole dime."

Malka was mystified at Birdie's attitude. "That's enough already, Birdie, with the big mouth. Now, Katala, sit down and I'll fix tea."

Katie bit her lip to stop from crying, "Thank you, but may I be excused?" Before anyone could say another word, Katie walked quickly to the bedroom and shut the door behind her, stood at the window and let the tears tumble down her cheeks. She wasn't even sure why she was crying. She didn't look around as Birdie entered and for the first time Katie was angry, confused with Birdie. In fact, she was confused about a great many things. Most of all about David's reactions to her during their brief time together. He had said little. In fact, they seemed to have little to say to one another. Sitting across the table at Plotkin's, drinking coffee, there was an awkward silence between them, as though David's mind was a million miles away. To break the silence she asked, "David, do you like your work?" He looked up from the coffee and said, "You bet I love it. In fact, you know, I had the opportunity to be a banker, but I turned it down. Sure, I even turned down being gentile and picked Jewish." . . .

Her thoughts were interrupted by Birdie's, "I'm sorry, I don't know what got into me." She walked over to Katie, put her arms around her. "You're crying because of what I said. I'm sorry."

Katie wiped her tears, "No, Birdie, I'm crying because I'm so—"

"You're crying because you're in love."

"Yes, I am in love, very much. But I always thought being in love was a wonderful happy thing. Tonight was so curious . . ."

"What do you mean?"

"I mean I'm not sure how David feels about *me*."

"O.K., so tell me, what is it you see in him that makes you love him so. I grant you, he's handsome, but what the hell else is he? He's an arrogant louse, always was. He's not good enough for you."

"Oh, Birdie, you don't know David at all."

"And you do."

"Yes."

"So tell me, what's so great to understand?"

She hesitated, then looked at Birdie. "David is a very lonely man who lives inside himself. He's so afraid to allow anyone to understand him he has built up a hard shell so not to be hurt, and I believe life has hurt David deeply in a way I don't entirely understand but I know instinctively. David feels deprived somehow . . . it's as though he were wounded, and he holds back as though he were afraid of what might happen if he didn't. And yet I feel a kindness and tenderness in him . . . Do you understand what I'm saying?" Birdie thought, a little education can be a very dangerous thing. This was how David looked to Katie? Lonely, deprived? Tough luck, Dave, we're all millionaires and we come home from the factory in our Rolls-Royces. What she said was, "Did he kiss you good night?" "No, but I think he wanted to."

Oh boy, and Katie knows about men? A guy likes a girl, he grabs her in the hall and plants one right on the mouth and says I'll see you tomorrow, next day, the next 4th of July, Chanukah. Didn't even kiss her, and she thinks he likes her. "So," said Birdie, "when's your next date?"

"David didn't say."

"What the hell did he say?"

"Just that it was nice being together. And thank you."

"Oh, that's great. He didn't even *try* to kiss you?"

"No, but I know that I'll see him."

"Mazel tov!"

When David had left Katie, he felt there was no place to hide. He wanted to be anything in this world but alive in this moment. The evening had been a disaster. He was afraid of talking too much, afraid to betray himself by one word leading to another until without realizing what he was saying, blurt out, I love you. Saying good night without touching her, not kissing her . . . it had been agony.

All week, he walked around like a zombie, again unable to sleep, eat, work. He would walk past her house hoping to catch a glimpse of her. At the end of ten days, he thought he would go out of his mind. His mother, noticing how drawn he had gotten and how nervous he was, pleaded with him to eat. He couldn't. He tried calling Abe Garfinckel, but he was away for the week. There had to be someone to talk to, so he tried his brother.

Ben was something less than sensitive. "This is the second time you took her out?"

"Yes."

"You're screwy—who falls so crazy in love with a broad? And so serious yet." In between cutting the soup meat on his plate, he went on, "You know what you need, Dave, is a good lay to get your nuts off. Take it from me."

David was so angry at this sage advice he ran out of the house and down the street until he was out of breath. Then he walked for blocks, aimlessly, without seeing. He stopped and looked in a pawnshop window. The owner came to the door and called out, "There's something you want, maybe? Come in, I'll show you nice stuff."

David shook his head, walked on and turned down Mott Street. There, hung on two chains, he saw the wooden sign of Goldstein the optometrist, with the huge eye that swayed gently back and forth in the breeze. The eye seemed to follow him to the door beyond where Madame Vanetti ran a house of prostitution above Goldstein's store.

Maybe Ben was right, maybe this was exactly what he needed to get Katie off his mind, maybe that was all that was wrong with him. David rang the bell at the bottom of the stairs, and Madame Vanetti released the lever from the top as the door opened. She called out to him as he walked up the steep flight, "I'm-a-glad to see you, bambino." When he reached the top of the stairs she ushered him into a small waiting room.

"You-a wait, it ain't-a-gonna be long. You-a gonna get-a my best-a girl."

She said that to every customer, in the exaggerated American-Italian. He waited nervously. Finally he went into a room that smelled of too many sweating bodies and too much cheap perfume. He began to take off his shoes, tie and shirt. As he let his trousers drop to the floor, he looked down and saw the overblown body in bed where someone else had just been—and the lurid red hair, the exaggerated outline of the sensuous mouth, the green eyelids. He wanted to throw up. Quickly he put on his clothes, grabbed his jacket, took two dollars out of his pocket and tossed them to her.

As he went out she said, "Well, I'll be god damned," and then, picking up the money, "Well, what the hell . . . win some, lose some."

It was eleven o'clock when David knocked on Malka Greenberg's door. Jacob opened it and stood before David in his long union suit that bagged out at the seat. It bagged even more because one of the buttons was missing.

"So what do you want, bummukeh?"

"May I see Katie? It's very important, please."

"I should throw you out. At eleven o'clock, he comes. It couldn't wait until tomorrow, there would be a revolution? You should only go in hell." He went to get Katie, and as he walked back to bed he mumbled under his breath, "Malka couldn't wait for her to get a boy, nu, so now she's got one. A bum. Who comes to see a girl at eleven o'clock? Oi, yoi, yoi, America goniff."

Katie quickly slipped out of bed and into her robe as Birdie bolted up in bed. "Should I go with you?"

"No, Birdie, I'm sorry to disturb you."

"What's wrong, Katie?" Sammy said as she passed his bed.

"I don't know. Now go back to sleep, dear."

"You want me to protect you?"

"I know you could if I needed you, but no, darling." She bent down and kissed him on the cheek, then hurried to the door. There was David, looking shockingly haggard and disheveled. "David, what's the matter?"

"Nothing," he said. "Go get dressed quickly—I want

to talk to you." She started to speak but he interrupted. "Don't ask any questions. Just trust me and get dressed."

Katie hurried back. Birdie asked nervously, "What did he want at eleven o'clock? Talk about chutzpa, nerve, guts, he's got it. Doesn't call a girl all week, doesn't see her all week, and eleven o'clock he's here. Do you know something I didn't tell you? I'm sorry you ever met him."

Katie was paying no attention as she proceeded to dress.

"What do you think you're doing?" Birdie asked.

"David wants to talk to me. I know it must be important or he wouldn't have come at this hour."

"How do you know, tell me? How do you think you know so much about men? Listen, you're a big girl now and I'm going to tell you for your own good, when a guy comes to a girl's house this late it ain't because he respects her. He thinks she's easy, a pushover, you understand what I mean? In other words, he couldn't sleep because he's got hot pants."

Katie was dressed by now. "Birdie, do me a favor—go to sleep and don't worry."

She met David in the hall. Without a word he took her by the hand, led her down the stairs and out into the street. They walked silently along by the river for a long time, then found a bench and sat down. She looked closely at him under the yellow lamplight.

"David, if you have a problem I'd like to help you with it. May I?"

"Yes, I have a problem." He hesitated, then said, "You're my problem."

"What do you mean?

"I mean I'm in love with you."

". . . I can't believe what you're saying—"

"Believe it, believe it—I'm in love with you."

She turned to him. "Why didn't you try to see me all week?"

"Because I don't *want* to be in love with you."

"You don't want to—"

"That's right, I'm not ready. What can I give you,

what can I do for you? If you married me, well, this is what you'd have for the rest of your life."

She got up, walked to the edge of the sidewalk and watched the river. He followed and stood next to her.

"David, what can I say to you, except that I'm sorry I made you so unhappy?"

He took her face in his hands. "Maybe you could say that you could love me. I guess that's what I really want to hear."

"I can't say that yet."

"In other words you don't feel anything—"

"That's not what I meant. It's just that before I can answer I have to be sure."

"And you're not?"

"Yes, I'm sure of myself, but one week has gone by and, well, I imagined you hadn't even thought about me—"

"That's some joke! I haven't slept or eaten."

"Well, why *did* you stay away. Why should falling in love be so difficult for you?"

"Because the timing is all wrong, I just haven't the right—"

She took his hand and held it. "David, I believe love is a matter of the heart; it doesn't ask the time, it just happens."

"Have you thought about me at all?"

"Yes, a great deal."

"What did you think?"

"That you were kind and understanding. I walked on a cloud the whole week."

"And I was afraid to come tonight, afraid you'd think I was crazy."

"How *wrong* you were. The first time we were together I felt a bond between us, the way two people do when they feel these things. It's just something you sense . . . I waited for you to call or at least come and see me, but then as the days went by I decided I must have been mistaken."

"What did you do then?"

"I spoke to Birdie, who's so smart about these things and—"

"What did she say?"

"She told me I was wrong."

"Which only proves she's not so smart. Then what?"

"Even then I still felt I couldn't have been so mistaken. I thought you liked me, but when I didn't see you I began to think—"

"To think what?"

"I began to think about all of the things that I said."

"What things?"

"That maybe I had talked too much, that maybe a girl doesn't tell about herself to a boy she's just met."

"Did I seem bored?"

"No, but I did think that perhaps you might have been. You see, David, I've never been in love with anyone before."

"Neither have I."

"I knew that I was in love with you but being in love takes two."

"Well, I've already told you how I felt."

"I know, David, but for me it's terribly important. I just don't want to be hurt."

"I would never hurt you, Katie."

"But it took you ten days to see me again—"

"I *told* you, I have some problems."

"I know, but here you are. Are your problems solved?"

"No, not by a long shot, and when I found out how I felt about you, well, I've been going around in crazy circles ever since."

"David, let's start from the beginning, I really must know why."

"All right." He took a deep breath. "I had never met anyone like you before; in fact I never thought a girl like you existed, or if she did that she would ever come into *my* life. You were just everything I ever wanted. The props were knocked out from under me."

"Yes, but why—"

"When you love someone you want to share your life with them, don't you?"

"Yes."

"Well, what do I have to share? Share? . . . Hell, I don't have anything to share."

"And that bothers you so much?"

"Sure, and what bothers me most is I couldn't stand not being able to give you something better than this. You don't know what it's like, feeling so helpless . . ."

"Why should you think I wouldn't understand? I've been poor all my life."

"Your poverty wasn't the kind I'm talking about. This kind drags you down so far you can't get away from it; it holds onto you like a vise."

"But there are still people who fall in love. Why should it be so difficult for you?"

"Because, well, I suppose because I'm afraid of the future."

"David, don't ever be afraid of the future. Don't you know that when people fall in love they bring each other luck? They really only need each other. I know that what I need most of all in my life is to be loved and to give someone love. Let me love you, David, please let me . . ."

He took her in his arms, kissed her and held her for a very long time. Then, rushing the words, he said, "Will you marry me, Katie? I don't want to wait. Next week."

"Yes, David."

She leaned against the door in the dark kitchen. Could this be *true*, was she really going to share life's joy with David? Was she at last going to belong to someone, to be a complete woman, a complete person? She had never known that there could be so much happiness in a kiss. To be held by someone who loved you so much he wanted to share the rest of his life with you . . . Closing her eyes she said, "Thank you, God. Mama, mama, thank you."

She ran past Sammy's bed. "Is anything wrong?" he asked.

"No, no, Sammy, everything is wonderful. I'll tell you in the morning."

Katie sat on the edge of the bed and hugged and

kissed Birdie. "Birdie, Birdie, I don't know where to begin. I know you won't believe this but David has asked me to marry him."

Birdie switched on the light and screamed. "I don't understand, what happened?"

"I don't know that I do, but David and I love each other and he wants us to be married next week and—"

"Oh, my God, I don't believe it! David Rezinetsky that didn't think any girl was good enough for him. Come on, let's wake up mama and tell her."

It was six o'clock in the morning when Jacob came into the kitchen. "What's the matter, you're all up so early, Malka?"

"Early? We never went to bed. You don't know the good news about Katie. She's going to get married."

"To that bummukeh that was here last night?"

"Never mind," Birdie said. "That kind of a bummukeh every Jewish girl should only get."

All night they had discussed the wedding. Let's see, the chairs they would get from Aunt Fega, they would be married in synagogue and have the two families for supper.

"Are you sure it won't be too much?" Katie asked.

"It wouldn't be too hard," Malka said, dismissing it as though this was the only fitting and proper thing for her first daughter, which she felt by now that Katie had become. They would bake cakes and cook all week. Later today she would go and see Mrs. Rezinetsky and they would plan the wedding together, it was only right. Katie would be married in a long veil and a white dress. It would be a wedding that Lilly Platt would envy, whose mother boasted that hers was the best wedding in the neighborhood.

"Believe me," Malka said, "she would be plenty jealous." And then remembered in all the excitement that they had to hire Mendel the photographer to take wedding pictures, and Yankel Levinsky, the great violinist, who played at all the bar mitzvahs and weddings, to be sure and be free next Saturday night (she was sure he'd be available). The week was a frenzy of shopping for Birdie's rose taffeta dress, which she had to be squeezed into because the dress was a size 14 and she wore a 16. No problem, so from the big bow in the back, they took a little piece out which no one would notice and sewed it into the bust line, and of course David and Katie walked around as though the world had come to a standstill. Each day that went by brought them closer to that moment when they would be one.

Katie stood before the mirror, looking at her image as Birdie adjusted the veil. She felt as though she were gazing at a stranger, a beautiful lovely stranger who had come such a long distance to stand in this place, waiting for a life to begin with a young man who was to become her existence forever. She was caught up in the feeling that fate truly did predestine the lives of people. Oh, mama . . . dearest mama, have you intervened for me, is it you who have brought me to this day? Oh, God, I love you so, if only you were here, but you feel what I feel and know the love I have for David. Make me a good and devoted wife.

At that moment Malka walked in, dressed in the new blue rayon taffeta dress she'd bought at Bloom's. (So never mind how she would pay it out.) This was one of the most important days of her life . . . she had lived to see Hannah's child given in marriage. God works in mysterious ways. You see, Hannala, I gave a promise to you that has blessed me. Malka looked at Katie, then embraced her.

"You have been my mother, how can I thank you, what can I say that is enough?"

Malka took Katie's face in her hands. "*Mein schön kind,* God calls on us so seldom to do good that when we do it the reward is ours. You should thank me for the happiness and naches? No, *mein schöne,* Katala, you have blessed us by becoming ours." Katie was crying now. "It's enough, mein Katala, remember a kallah shouldn't go to the chuppa with red eyes, now finish dressing." Malka looked at Katie once again, "Oy—what a bride. You'll see, Lilly Platt's mother will plotz!"

The little shul on Hester Street was filled to capacity by guests who had been invited and by guests who had not been invited, and it seemed, from Malka's observation, there were more guests that had not been invited than those that were. Some chutzpa. Shnorrers! Now she was worrying if there would be enough chopped liver. She could just see Mrs. Rifkin filling up the brown paper sack, which she took with her to every wedding and bar mitvzah, filling it up to capacity with all the cookies, the strudel, the salami sandwiches to take home for her little Boris so he should have enough to eat for the next week. Not only her, but all the rest of the yentas. Oy vay! There should only be enough for the family.

But now the moment had come when she was compelled to set aside such worldly thoughts. The first star had appeared in the heaven. Shabbas was over and night had come and it was time for Jacob on one side of Katie and herself on the other to walk Katie down to the end of the aisle, where David, alongside his parents, awaited his future wife. As the tapering candles were lit and handed to each of the parents under the blue velvet chuppa, the rabbi began the sacred and solemn ceremony in Hebrew. The bride and both sets of parents circled the groom seven times in the truest of orthodoxy. Next the parents stood at their separate sides and the last blessings for everlasting peace, devotion and love were said. The goblet was handed to the bride as she lifted her veil for the first time and drank from the cup offered her by her husband. The veil was then dropped so as not to reveal her face, and the goblet was handed back to David, who nervously drank from it. They were pronounced man and wife and, amid shouts of mazel tov, the wine goblet was stomped upon by David. He then picked up the veil once again, held it so only he could see his bride's face in the candlelight, slipped it over her head and held and kissed her so long and so tenderly that everyone began to sing joyously, "Chassen kallah mazel tov."

CHAPTER FOUR

Spring, 1934

The sounds of the city gathered momentum and the night now rested elsewhere on the face of the globe while here the sun had just arisen. It found its way down the broad avenues, past the modern towers of Babel that jutted ever upward, down the decadent streets, the alleys and the hopelessly dirty tenements. Though no crocus bloomed through the concrete, spring had come to Hester Street, and the warmth of the early morning sun made Katie feel like dancing. For a moment she shut her eyes and raised her face toward the sky. How marvelous that spring could arouse this feeling of renewal, of rebirth. Smiling to herself she thought . . . and all through the land the voice of the turtle could be heard . . . and proceeded on happily to Lipkin's Bakery.

After climbing the five flights of stairs she let herself into the flat, where she had left David and the baby asleep. She leaned against the door, waiting for the sound of her heart thumping to subside, then went to the kitchen and placed the bag of sweet rolls on the table, took off her sweater and glanced at the clock on the window sill. Good Lord, it was already six o'clock. Soon she would have to wake David, but there was still time. Delighted, she thought again how lovely the day was with its new light, its hope, its promise. This day was special. David was going to New Jersey to sell someone an insurance policy. What was the man's name? She couldn't remember, perhaps because David had been so elusive in his discussion with her. Poor David, Katie thought, how lonely he must be when he withdrew and found it impossible to unburden himself, to discuss the problems that weighed so heavy with him. In their short marriage she'd observed that such private matters David could not share. There seemed never to have been anyone whose confidence he could really trust, and so he was suspicious of everyone. She felt sure that as their marriage grew stronger over the years he would come to her with any problem that disturbed him, that she would be there to listen and to comfort him when the time came. She chastised herself; if this were his only fault then her marriage was perfect. Indeed, she was fortunate to have such a husband. After all, what counted most was that he loved her.

Although the details of his mission were vague in her mind, she knew how vital it was to David, this enormous thing that was going to happen to him today. It meant more than just a commission check, it was a great challenge—a challenge he had hoped so long for: it would be the first time he would venture away from the East Side.

The baby awoke with outraged cries of hunger. Softly she called out, "Shh, Mama's coming." Picking the child up, she unbuttoned the front of her blouse and guided the soft pink distended nipple to his mouth as she sat down in the rocker. Soon the sounds of hungry fury were replaced with murmurs of contentment as he sucked greedily and happily, exploring the firm white flesh of his mother with his tiny fingers. At last with no more to be desired, he lay back his small head in the curve of her arm as the tiny fingers still remained on her breast. Gently she took the hand into hers and looked at it. Never would she get over the miracle of his being and that he was the result of their love. Who was he and whom did he really belong to? Was she not only the custodian for this gift that had been vouchsafed in her keeping? What would this hand do? Would it hold the knife of a surgeon or the brush of an artist? Never mind . . . the whole magnificent mystery would forever be a source of her gratitude.

She decided there was no woman in the world as rich as she. When she wheeled him in his buggy in the afternoons or sat with the rest of the mothers on the doorsteps below, she was overcome with pride, with the sense of being David's wife, and each time she received her husband was more wonderful than the last, lying there in the night, clinging together as though they were one. How mistaken David had been when he said he could never give her anything. He had given her everything. She was a mother, she was a wife, she was a woman loved . . . what else was there in life?

This was the time of day she loved the best, this moment when the world was still half silent, the noises of the street still muted, without the shouts of children who sounded too old to be so young. Soon the pushcart vendors would be rolling their carts on the cobblestones below, hawking their wares. In a short while the women would be up and bustling, all in full and good voice . . . trying to outshout one another as though in competition to prove the fact of their survival to begin another day.

She had become so accustomed now to the sights and noises of the East Side that this rustle of spring almost went unnoticed, including even the El train whose roar as it passed by was like giant cymbals being clashed together, and leaving in its wake the flimsy buildings actually swaying slightly; how they remained standing through all the years was indeed another of God's miracles. Almost all went unnoticed, except for the shriek of an exceptionally loud siren, which now aroused her out of her reverie. Come on, Katie my girl, why are you dreaming? This is an important day for your husband and here you sit as though you didn't have a care in the world.

Placing the infant gently in his crib in the corner of the front room, she carefully changed his diaper while he slept. Then, hurrying off to the kitchen, she supported the ironing board between the table and a chair as she glanced at the clock: six-thirty. She examined David's trousers as she ironed them; they had not taken a crease, so she ironed them again, this time with a damp towel, and again to no avail. David would be unhappy, but this was the best she could do. She walked to the bedroom off the kitchen, put them over a chair, went to the bed and looked down at her husband, his black hair tousled and curled from the night's sleeping. She hated to awaken him from such a sound sleep after he had been so restless during the night; when he had finally fallen asleep, she had no idea.

Hesitatingly she shook him and said softly, "David, David dear, it's five to seven." Somewhere in the valley of his mind he heard his name. Opening his eyes, he saw her standing over him. Pulling her down on him, he ran his hands through her hair, holding her face next to his and whispered, "Come on, you, let's make love."

She smiled but pulled away from him. "David, you didn't hear what time I said it was." He straightened his long legs and yawned, "What time?"

"About seven now."

"Oh my God!" He threw the covers back and jumped out of bed. "Why did you let me sleep so late?"

"Because you didn't sleep well last night, and if you hurry, you'll still have plenty of time. I'll start breakfast."

David put on his socks, which had been darned and tucked inside his shoes, then reached for the trousers, holding up the miserably misshapen raiment. How the hell could he see a man like Bates to try to sell him insurance looking like he'd slept in his suit all night? How the hell could he do that? Did he have a choice? No, damn it, he didn't. But if he sold Bates that policy, sure as hell he'd buy a new suit with his first commission check, no second hand-me-down. He found the white shirt Katie had placed on the same chair, so meticulously ironed and the collar carefully turned from the frayed side to the good side that it could hardly be seen. What the hell, what difference did it make. Who saw the inside of your shirt?

On edge, he left the flat, with his suspenders hanging over his trousers, his shirt and jacket over his arm, and walked down the hall to the only bathroom on the floor. If there was any solace in this morning it was that he had beaten the Ginsberg twins to the bathroom; this was apparent as he passed their flat and heard the cursing of Mrs. Ginsberg. The woman took advantage of Friday mornings, when she bathed her children one after the other in the same dirty bath water, trying to make sure they would be clean for the week to come.

With an entire twenty minutes of no one pounding on the door saying, "What the hell did you do, fall in?" he washed, shaved, combed his hair carefully and put his shirt and jacket on. He observed himself in the mirror. Maybe not so bad after all. Refreshed, he walked back to the flat and opened the door to the aroma of hot boiling coffee. He sat down at the kitchen table as Katie poured him a cup, but it was scalding and he burned his tongue.

"Damn it, that's hot!"

She ran to the sink, turned on the tap, poured some cold water into a glass and handed it to him. "David, I'm so sorry."

"Forget it, it'll be all right." He let the coffee sit in front of him.

"Do you feel better?" she asked. He shook his head.

"What do you want for breakfast?"

"Nothing, I'll just have coffee when the damn stuff cools off."

"David, that's simply not enough. You always get sick when you don't eat breakfast."

"Katie, don't sound like my mother, please."

"Darling, you have a big day ahead of you and I think you should have something. Scrambled eggs and toast, how does that sound?"

"No, I don't feel hungry."

"At least have the sweet rolls; they're so fresh and still hot."

She poured another cup of coffee for him and one

for herself, and sat across from him and watched. He seemed so tense, it was more than just the hot coffee that made him irritable and apprehensive this morning. Although he hadn't said it in so many words, she knew his misgivings about going to New Jersey today; it meant more than selling just a new policy. True, it was the first big policy he would have sold, but it went even beyond that; it was a test in his mind about whether he could even handle something new. It literally meant getting his foot in the door for the first time with a new firm; once that was accomplished he'd have the impetus he felt he badly needed.

Until now his policies were small and bought by people who could barely scrape together fifty cents a week to pay the premium. This morning was a maiden voyage, hopefully a whole new beginning. He had slept little during the night, staring into the darkness and thinking about every argument that Mr. Bates might present, what his answers would be. Could he sell, could he be convincing, could he at least seem to be experienced? This was different from selling Cohn a cemetery plot, or a policy to the butcher, or even a policy to Abe, to whom he owed so much. He never would have gotten to first base with a firm like Abe's if it weren't that they had been friends.

Small wonder he had slept so badly the night before. In the dark he had gotten out of bed and walked to the kitchen, took out a bottle of cold water from the ice box, and poured himself a drink. He lit a match and looked at the clock: it was four. He sat down at the kitchen table. As he smoked his cigarette he thought, if he didn't break out now, when would he? There had to be a place where he could begin. This, he felt, was the good omen, the opportunity he had been waiting for, and by God he was going to sell to Bates if it was the last thing he ever did. Abe had made the introduction and he would do the rest, but with all this resolve and courage why did he feel so frightened? The name Rezinetsky kept ringing in his ears. "Good morning, Mr. Bates, sir, my name is

David Rezinetsky." . . . There was a sinking feeling at the pit of his stomach. Trying to dismiss it, he asked himself if Garfinckel was any better sounding? In his heart, he knew it was more than a name that bothered him. Suddenly David recalled something Abe had said to him one night.

"Look, Dave, it's really not such a tough world if you remember that you don't have to prove anything."

"Sure, you can say that because you have a father that helped you make it."

"That's true, Dave, but my father made it because *he* felt he didn't have anything to prove. Don't you see, it's not what the world thinks you are or these ignorant bastards that don't even know what a Jew is. They have the problem. What's important is that you like yourself, that you know who you are."

"I suppose you're right. You and your father made it in spite of being Jewish."

Abe shook his head and said, "That's where you're wrong. We made it because we *are* Jewish." Then jokingly Abe asked, "Don't you know that there are only two kinds of people in the world?"

"Who are they?"

"Jews, and those who wished they were."

There was no arrogance, no superiority in anything that Abe said; he stated his opinion and his conviction matter-of-factly. Abe knew the anti-Semitism that they were all subjected to, rich or poor. The anti-Semitism wasn't important, what was important was that he never allowed it to get inside him. He accepted and handled it as a part of living, a struggle that all Jews had in one form or another. The struggle would always be there, but if you permitted it to eat away at you it would destroy you. The problem would still be there no matter what one did. In the end, though, as always before, Abe was sure his people would even out by surviving.

God, he thought, what would I have done without Abe through all the years? Abe had been the only warmth in his life until he met Katie. He listened to him—not just the sound of his voice, but to him,

David, the person. Abe had always encouraged him. Because of him, he was selling insurance instead of working with his brothers in some sweat shop making clothes for other people to wear. Through Abe he found a world that possessed beauty. He would never have heard of Carnegie Hall, much less have gone to hear Rubinstein play, which he could prove by the stubs and the program he had hidden away in a drawer should anyone have questioned him. But, oh God, how he envied Abe. If only he had that quality of forbearance Abe was blessed with.

His thoughts were interrupted as Katie said, "David, you seem so far away."

Startled. "Did I? It's nothing. I was just thinking what we'd do first with the money," and glanced at the clock on the window sill. "God, I've got to get going." He got up from the table, walked to the bedroom and put on his straw hat. Then he went to the front room and looked down at his son. He kissed the child gently while Katie waited for him at the door.

"I love you darling." It was what she had to give him. She wondered if it were enough.

He kissed her goodbye. Almost halfway down the stairs he looked up. Katie, leaning over the banister, called after him, "David, don't be late if you can help it. Remember, we're going to your father's house for Shabbas dinner. He hates us to be late. And please, eat something for lunch."

He laughed, "You still sound like my mother," and then his footsteps were lost as he walked out into the spring sun and down the street toward the B.M.T. subway and the train to New Jersey.

He turned the knob on the door that read "John Bates & Son, Importers and Exporters" and found himself in the outer office. There was a short oak railing that separated him from the secretary; to the right of her was a bookkeeper sitting on a tall stool in front of a high desk and bent over an enormous ledger. He wore a green eye shade and a short alpaca jacket with the sleeves pushed up to his elbows.

He did not look up nor did the secretary as her fingers rhythmically moved back and forth on the typewriter.

David, his straw hat in his hand, shifted nervously from one foot to the other. She finished so abruptly that when she looked up and said, "Yes, is there something I can do for you?" David's stomach turned over. Without smiling, she had asked the simple question with the kind of authority easy to someone who knows her position is very secure.

"I'm Mr. Rezinetsky. I have an appointment with Mr. Bates this morning."

"Oh, yes, Mr. Rezi. . . ." the rest of the name trailed off into non-syllables. David repeated, "Mr. Rezinetsky . . . David Rezinetsky."

"What is it you want to see Mr. Bates about?" she asked, checking the appointment book.

"I have an appointment to see Mr. Bates about some insurance."

"Oh? Well, Mr. Bates hasn't come in yet."

David quickly answered, "Then I'll wait."

Ignoring him, she went on with her typing as David walked to a wooden bench against the wall and sat down. He looked around at the office and up at the ceiling while turning the straw hat around in his hands and feeling damned uncomfortable. He crossed one leg, then the other, then just sat waiting. He began to count the black and white squares in the floor linoleum and after counting to 600 he looked up at the clock—one hour and fifteen minutes had gone by. He walked over to the secretary and stood in front of her. She did not look up. Finally, clearing his throat, he said, "Pardon me, but do you know what time Mr. Bates will be in?"

She continued on with her typing. "I have no idea, I'm sure."

"Do you think it might be before noon? I had an appointment at nine this morning—"

"I really can't say. Why don't you leave your card and I'll tell him to get in touch with you?"

"No thanks, I'll just wait. But you do think he'll be in today?"

"Look, when Mr. Bates comes in I'll tell him you're here."

He walked back to the bench, which by now had begun to feel like his natural habitat. It felt strange in this strange world—so cold, impersonal. Outside the ghetto everything seemed so, well, orderly.

He picked up his straw hat and began to extract small fragments from it. Then waited, and waited, and waited. His forehead was dripping; he reached in his back pocket for a handkerchief to wipe away the perspiration. As he did so his hat slipped to the floor and absentmindedly he placed the handkerchief on the bench. He sat, waiting for an audience with the king. Not exactly like walking into Adler's fish store. Well, this was big business. Success in it demanded a lot of things he would have to learn—and patience was obviously prime among them.

Diverted by his own thoughts he was startled when he heard the intercom phone ring. Mr. Bates had come in at the side entrance to his office and was calling his secretary.

"Good morning, Molly, any phone calls?" David could hear the voice faintly.

"Good morning," she said. "No, nothing important. Oh, incidentally, there's someone who wants to see you about some insurance, a Mr. R-e-z-i-n-e-t-s-k-y." She spelled it out with emphasis. There was a long pause in her conversation and finally she said, "I see," hung up, and attempted to call David by name but thought better of it. She couldn't pronounce those foreign-sounding things. Instead she cleared her throat to gain his attention.

"Mr. Bates won't be able to see you today. He's going to be tied up all afternoon." David tried not to show his feelings.

"I'd like to make another appointment," he said, hoping his voice would not betray his anger as he stood in front of her.

Without a pause in her typing she said, "I think it would be better if Mr. Bates got in touch with you."

How the hell could Bates get in touch with him?

Where, at his plush office with no phone, only the landlady's on the first floor? He had been sitting here since eight-thirty and now it was ten of twelve, almost four hours. Goddamn it, why hadn't she told him when he arrived that Bates wouldn't be in until later today? Calm down, he quickly warned himself; she probably didn't know . . . she hadn't done it on purpose.

"I'll call Mr. Bates for another appointment next week." Feeling humiliated, impotent, he walked out of the office to the elevator. He looked up at the dial. The hand indicated it was coming down from the eleventh floor. His head was pounding. God, it was hot. The perspiration was rolling down his face. As he reached for his handkerchief, he remembered leaving it on the bench. Rushing back, embarrassed, he opened the door of the office, apparently unnoticed, and for the first time heard the sound of the bookkeeper's voice as he bent over his ledgers.

"Well, you've got to give those Jew bastards a little credit. They've got plenty of moxie, they don't just give up. He could have sat here till hell froze over if you didn't get rid of him." The secretary laughed as the typewriter carriage came to an end and the bell rang.

"Over my dead body," she said.

The bookkeeper went on, "Those kikes ought to be locked up in a cage."

Someone had hit David between the eyes with a hammer. He jumped over the low railing, grabbed the bookkeeper by his tie, choking him, lifting him off the stool and hitting him so hard he swayed back and forth like an automaton, then fell to the floor in a heap. David stood over the man; his face was swollen and blue, red blood seeping out of his mouth. Teeth clenched, David shouted, "This is one Jew bastard you're not going to forget in a hurry, you son-of-a-bitch."

The secretary sat in stunned silence in her swivel chair, not able to move or call for help. David's fists were poised, wanting to beat her until she cried out for mercy. What he did was to say, slowly, deliberately enunciating each word, "I'd kill you if I could."

He ran out of the office, down the stairs in back of the elevator to the last landing, his breathing labored. Putting the palms of his hands on the wall, he buried his head against the cold cement, so sick with nausea he wanted to vomit. He couldn't. He pounded his fists against the wall, the tears on his face. Grateful at least that no one had come up the stairs to see him, he wiped the tears away with his hands, then leaned against the wall and waited for some inner composure, which did not come. Finally he walked out into the street toward the station; pure instinct guided him, and he felt empty, sick that he had given way to such violence, outraged at what had provoked it.

By the time he reached the station his acute anger was spent and he had regained some outward composure, but inwardly his stomach still churned and the heat of the day made it even worse. There were large half-circles of perspiration under his armpits. His shirt clung to his body as the sweat ran down his back.

He dropped a nickel in the box and picked up a newspaper, hoping it might distract him, and boarded the train. He seated himself near the window and opened the paper. Four times he read the same thing, "*The New York Times,* Friday, May 11, 1934." It was no use; he folded the paper again and let it lie in his lap as he turned his face to look out the window. All he could see was his own reflection. All right, what made him look so different? Did he have horns or a grotesque nose that was a caricature of all Jews, or whatever it was that Jews were supposed to look like? So far as he could see there were no characteristics in him or his family that shouted they were Jews. So what it all came down to was his name. If he had been Bill Jones, would he have seen Mr. Bates today?

All Jews had the same problem, one way or another, but why didn't they strike back? Why? Because Jews weren't expected to, they were supposed to take life without protest. The world apparently felt it was charity enough that they were permitted to survive on this planet at all.

Why else did that bastard hate him so this morning? *Why?* Not once had he looked at him that entire morning. He would never have recognized David if they passed one another on the street, and yet he despised David for no other reason than that he was Jewish and his name was Rezinetsky.

The rejections of the past came back to him. He thought of the times he had uselessly answered ads. No matter what time, no matter how early in the morning it was, the job had been taken or they came right out with no apologies offered. "No Jews wanted, no Jews need apply." How was it possible to feel lower than a leper, less than a man? What was there, he asked himself, down deep in him that prevented him from being able to resign himself as most other Jews in the ghetto did? Well, there was no anti-Semitism for them. They lived among Jews, the butcher was Jewish, the tailor, the baker, the candlestick maker, all Jewish. There was no need to venture outside. Here everybody was the same, all locked together in common bond. There was no language barrier. You needed a dress, you went to Bloom's; a second-hand suit, to Cohn's.

Of course there were problems, but anti-Semitism was not one of them. But for him—so many of his generation—it *was* the problem. Where did he belong? It wasn't here, of that he was sure; and it wasn't there, of that he was more sure. But how did he break the chains? Abe had managed, and had found a good life; more important, he was able to cope. What had happened today, David realized, had happened to many others, including Abe, but somehow Abe was equipped to handle the world outside. Why, he asked himself over and over again, why Abe and not him?

Abe's family had come to this country together with Isaac Rezinetsky, from the same village in Russia, but there was a difference. Mr. Isaac Rezinetsky labored as hard as Mr. Dov Garfinckel; but Isaac poured his labor into perpetuating the word of the Lord. He thought that a man endowed with the responsibilities of anything as spiritual, lofty, and important as God's law could not reconcile himself to doing anything as lowly as manual labor. It would be like desecrating the very image of God himself. So while Isaac prayed and studied the Torah and the Talmud, he left to his sons the work of man, and to provide for him in his old age. Mr. Dov Garfinckel also loved God—God who had given him the opportunity to reap the harvest of his efforts. Who else but God had made it possible for him to prosper in this blessed country? Dov wondered if he didn't love God even more than Isaac did, because Dov felt so loved by God. It must have been God that invented America.

When Dov Garfinckel arrived in this country he came with the same worldly goods as Isaac Rezinetsky, which consisted of a wife. He also brought with him a shrewd mind and tremendous determination to succeed. He would not allow his family to live in the poverty that he had been subjected to and his father before him. America was a rich plum to be plucked, if one took advantage. He got himself a job at the Ace Paper Box Company, and through frugal living and careful saving within ten years he owned the Ace Paper Box Company. True it was a very small factory in the beginning, but he thanked God and praised the Lord and the Lord rewarded him. The harder he worked the larger his factory grew. First he moved his family uptown. By now there were additions to the family, a young son, Abe, and a lovely daughter, Edith, and through the years Mr. Dov Garfinckel became a man of substantial means. Eventually he bought a home out on Long Island where he invited his friend Isaac many, many times, an invitation Isaac refused because he didn't think it necessary for a man to succeed in business if he lost his soul, and how could a man keep his soul if he spent all his time making money. The accomplishments and vanities, as Isaac viewed them, of Dov's luxuries impressed him not at all. In fact, served more to reinforce his own certainty that he had chosen the better way. David and Abe, however, had remained friends since childhood.

But just as there were differences between Isaac and Dov there were also differences between David and Abe. David saw his father's whole philosophy as the outgrowth of fear, which he had visited on his four sons: fear, and rejection, of life; fear of God; fear of father; fear of punishment and retribution—and when you cut your eyeteeth on that you were hardly equipped with the kind of courage needed to succeed as a Jew in a gentile world. Out there you had to be smarter, you had to prove you were better in a world that said, "Go back where you came from." This was supposed to be his home, the home of the free and land of the brave. His father had come here to escape Russian tyranny, and thought he had such escape and freedom because he could chant the Torah as loud as he wanted to without being stoned and walk down Hester Street without a black arm band and a Jewish star. But how free was Isaac when they lived in a ghetto without fences, without even the dignity he had in the old country? All that gave meaning to their lives was their heritage, but what good was it if one was not welcome.

Then again, David considered that maybe this was just an excuse to justify his failure to have ventured out of the East Side. His best friend Abe had done it, but for Abe, instead of a personal legacy of fear, there was one of love, love of God, love of father. Instead of punishment there was understanding. Abe had been blessed with an adoring father who not only loved him, but respected and understood him, and taught him that geography had nothing to do with the challenge of life or a man's response to it.

Isaac justified his wife and children often struggling without the necessities because of his unwillingness to work—how he argued, could he justify abandoning his duties toward God. Besides, sacrifice was good for the soul. And so, in the service of a higher calling, he allowed his sons to keep him when they now had families of their own which they could hardly support.

Why should Judaism burn so deeply in his soul, what had it brought him? What did it mean to him? That he could sit on a special bench in heaven? He would live and die in that stinking hovel and never give it a thought that maybe he also owed his children something—if not worldly goods, a man who lived with God as intimately as Isaac should have been able to offer some understanding and compassion to his sons. Surely his God would grant him a few minutes for that . . . David could never forget how his father had criticized him for his worldly interests in trying to better himself. Thinking about himself and Abe, he realized the only similarity in their lives was that each had been born and each would die, and the difference was all the years that lay between.

Judaism . . . what was this thing that it should be held over them so? Suddenly, right at this moment as he sat on the train leaving New Jersey, he felt acutely what he'd never before allowed himself to think. He tried to push it back, but it refused to be dismissed. "Face it, David, *face it,*" the voice kept saying relentlessly with the rhythm of the wheels upon rails . . . "You despise being Jewish. Admit it, you despise being a Jew . . ."

He broke out in a cold sweat, grew weak and slumped down in his seat . . . shaken, he deeply resented having to sit on this train and question whether or not it was worth living as a Jew. Living itself was difficult enough, even here in the land of the free and the home of the brave where any boy could grow up to be President unless his name happened to be Rezinetsky.

But his name *was* David Rezinetsky. And, of course, it was the centuries behind the name that, as he sat thinking of his past and of his father, pulled at him so strongly in another direction. Relinquishing his heritage wasn't so simple. It was like a fixed habit. Like it or not, he had been steeped in a tradition, he had heard and heard again the psalms chanted before he could walk; before he could talk it had been drummed into him that if he failed to obey God's commandments the wrath of God would come down upon him. He felt as though at any moment he might turn into a pillar of salt as Lot's wife had done.

And now the fear took him over . . . he must not think these things, he could not renounce Judaism—it was unthinkable, unbearable . . . Dripping wet, completely drained he ordered himself to stop thinking these thoughts. Stop thinking, stop thinking, stop thinking, the wheels echoed.

Picking up the paper, he tried to read once again, scanning the words without really seeing them as the small voice again intruded . . . "David," it asked hauntingly, "how long have you been unwilling to face the truth? How long have you known? It's really been a long time, hasn't it? Maybe back to when you were nine? It wasn't expressed then, but try to remember. Think back, David. Think back to that day." . . .

In his entire universe Miss Thompson was the only one he truly loved in the painful way that most small boys of nine fall in love with their teachers. She was soft and pretty and smelled of flowers. Her hands were delicate, her hair was blond like the silk that came out of the husks of green corn he'd seen in schoolbook pictures. She was kind and soft-spoken and David would have done anything she had commanded him to do. If only she would ask. There was a mystery about her . . . she was the only gentile he had ever known. From September to December of that year were the happiest three months David had spent in his whole life.

On a Friday, Miss Thompson had given the class a weekend assignment and on Monday night got around to correcting her test papers. When she came to David's she looked once again at the name to see if she had the right one. Over half his answers were wrong. She was shocked. On Tuesday morning all the papers were returned. David couldn't wait to get his. Excitedly, he looked at it, then suddenly felt a heavy pain in his chest. He put his pencil between his teeth and bit it hard. At least he wouldn't cry.

At one o'clock the class resumed with the usual spitballs, hitting on the back, passing notes back and forth.

"Open your geography books." Down came the heavy ruler on her desk. "Be quiet," she called out sternly. "I mean I want everyone to be quiet."

Suddenly she glanced toward the door as it was being closed gently; it was David. She hadn't even noticed he was absent. What's happening to you, she chastised herself, you didn't call the roll to see if anybody was missing. Don't excuse yourself by saying the class is too large. It's your duty to know if a student is missing. She motioned David into his seat.

"David Rezinetsky, take your geography book and turn to page twenty-four and start reading aloud at the second paragraph." He could hardly say the words, being sure she hated him, and especially now that he was late. He read so quietly he could barely be heard. Hymie Kerinsky called out, "Hey, turn up the radio, we can't hear you." Quickly Miss Thompson came down with the heavy ruler on the desk. "That will be enough from you, Hymie." The class began to laugh. Again the ruler came down, and they were quiet.

"Thank you, David, that was very good." . . . What an afternoon, it seemed endless. When the bell rang at three o'clock, nothing had ever sounded so good to her ears.

"Goodbye, class. Now please, no shoving, no pushing as you go out," she shouted above the chorus of children's voices. "And David Rezinetsky," she called out, "I'd like you to stay a few minutes." The class filed out, pushing and shoving. Shutting the door behind them, she leaned against it, closed her eyes for a moment, blew a strand of hair off her forehead, and returned to her desk. When she said, "David," his heart pounded hard, but the softness in her voice made tears come to his eyes. He twisted the cap even harder. He couldn't disgrace himself more than he already had done by failing the test, and on top of that he had been late, and now to stand in front of her and cry like a girl—if only she had been angry with him, he could have handled that. Tears now rolled down his cheek.

His embarrassment became unbearable to her. "Please, David, come up here." He walked slowly toward her. "Take a chair and sit down next to me." As he did so she reached in the drawer, took out a handkerchief and handed it to him. He wasn't sure whether he should use it or not, it was white and beautiful with blue forget-me-nots. He wiped his eyes.

"David, why were you late this afternoon?" she asked gently. He didn't look at her as he twisted the cap in his hands into a corkscrew.

"I wasn't going to come back to school today."

"You weren't? Why, David?"

"I didn't feel too well."

"Is that the only reason? You seemed all right this morning."

"I got sick this afternoon."

"Was it from something you ate?"

"No," he said, still twisting the cap and still not looking at her.

"Well then . . ."

How could he tell her how bad he felt over the low grade? He could expect that from anybody else, but not from *her*. He'd worked so hard on Sunday. It was the only day he was able to study because on Friday nights he was not allowed to read anything but Hebrew so that on Saturday he would be ready for Hebrew class, cheder, which he attended until sundown.

"David, I think we can be honest with each other. Why are you so upset?"

He looked up at her hesitatingly. "Because of the grade you gave me."

"David, it wasn't that I wanted to but I had to. Don't you understand that if I hadn't marked you according to your work it would have been like cheating? And all you would have had was a good grade, but then you really wouldn't have had to understand the problems, would you?"

"No, but I tried, I really tried, Miss Thompson."

"I know you did, and you don't know how sorry I am." He looked at her in amazement, she was sorry! Apologizing to him? Adults weren't supposed to do that to children. It would never happen with his father or at cheder with Reb Epstein, who hit you over the knuckles with the ruler if the accent was in the wrong place on the *aleph, baiz,* or *gimmel,* the first three letters of the Hebrew alphabet. Whoever said they were sorry?

"David, is there anyone at home who could help you with your work?"

He shook his head. He just couldn't tell her that his oldest brother, Harry, had not gone beyond the sixth grade, that his other brothers had to drop out of school to go to work, that his mother couldn't speak a word of English, and that his father was busy all day and evening praying. There was no one.

"All right, David, I have a plan. You stay after school every day and I'll help you." No wonder he loved her so much. But he couldn't stay, and he was afraid to tell her so . . . she might think he'd rather be at cheder than stay here with her every day.

"I can't," he said, averting his eyes.

"Why, David?"

Should he lie, he thought for a moment, and say he had to go to work? He felt confused . . . and somehow ashamed to tell her about cheder. But he couldn't lie and so he said, "Because I have to go to cheder after school every day. That's Hebrew school." Now he felt enraged . . . and of course couldn't know why.

"Well then, we'll just do the best we can and I'll help you in class as much as possible."

Nervously, he glanced up at the clock, it was getting late. If he didn't get to cheder on time he would encounter the wrath of Reb Epstein. "Good night, Miss Thompson, I'll try hard to do my best, thank you for being so nice . . ." He wanted to kiss her, to hug her . . . somehow touch her. He'd always hated and been afraid of the strictness of Reb Epstein;

cheder and Reb were synonymous, and today even more so as they became the hated thing that kept him away from Miss Thompson, the only one who really cared about him. He wasn't going to go to cheder. No matter what the consequences, he wasn't going today. Instead he went behind the Reicherts' Fish Market, sat on a barrel of unopened herrings, and cried until he had no more tears to cry. . . .

That childhood mingled fear and hatred had festered into his adulthood—a time that should have freed him, but under the injunctions of his father only hardened his resentments. Blind obedience was still the law. No opportunity was given to explore the meaning of his religious studying. No questions asked; to question was a lack of faith and a lack of faith was next to blasphemy. He had mouthed the words that had no meaning, his natural curiosity, his desire to understand frustrated and punished. As he grew older he began studying, in secrecy, everything he could about Judaism.

If he were Jewish he had to know why, from where he had come.

In the end, he recognized there could be beauty and comfort in Judaism, but he could never accept the orthodox, blind faith demanded of him. And, for that matter, what difference did his refinements make anyway? If you were born a Jew, whether you embraced Judaism or not, the world still considered you a Jew. The world said it was a stigma regardless of your personal feelings and history—a stigma applied in the cradle and visible at the grave.

David knew how it felt to be a Jew in a world that seemed to have been made for gentiles only. He knew it especially today. But how, he now began to wonder, how did it feel to be a gentile living in Eden. How did it feel? How did it feel to walk into Bates' office without any fear of how you would be received, to put your card down and say, "I have an appointment this morning." No need, he was sure, to wonder if one was accepted, to care what someone thought.

With new certainty, he knew now what he didn't

want—to live his life without the kind of freedom and dignity that no Jew seemed to have in the eyes of the world, and with the constant personal outrage that had happened to him today. He must finally be absolutely honest with himself—never mind the price. His whole life depended on it. What had Judaism brought him? Mostly anguish and loathing for himself and the world that apparently found his Jewishness so offensive. If he changed his name, moved elsewhere and took up a new way of life, would he be able to let go of all the things he had been brought up to believe in? It would mean a total break with his family—all of it, not just his father. And, what would he do in a gentile world? And once there would he find the peace and freedom he wanted so desperately? This moment was almost like conceiving and giving birth to oneself. No doubt about it, gentiles had more chances. After all, his life belonged to him. He hadn't *chosen* to be Jewish—it was an accident of birth, like being born a Rockefeller, the Queen of Spain, rich or black, just one great big accidental coincidence of birth. And he wasn't so stupid that he thought just being gentile gave passport to paradise. Everyone had to find his own salvation, find his own way in the world. Everyone walked alone. Yes, all right, he had come into the world a Jew, but by God, he was not going to die a Jew.

The train jerked and came screechingly to a halt. Now he was back in New York. As he got off and stood on the platform he looked around and decided it would be the last time he would ever stand here. He didn't want to be here at all. It was like gall in his mouth; it held no sweet memories for him.

His head still pounded. Leaning against a pillar, he lit a cigarette, which made him dizzy, as though he were looking at people through a kaleidoscope walking sideways. Small wonder, except for coffee this morning he hadn't eaten for some sixteen hours. He went to the refreshment counter in the station, sat down and ordered a sweet roll and coffee. So much had happened to him today in such a short time. He put his elbows on the counter and rested his head in his hands. Never had he felt such fatigue before. If only his mind would stop working . . .

If he truly were no longer to be Jewish . . . Well, the first thing he must do was change his name. To what? David—he repeated it over and over again. Of course, it was Hebrew, but in the second generation, gentiles had begun to give their children Biblical names like David, many girls were Sarah or Deborah; and—fair's fair—Jewish names were now Pamela and Susan and Sheldon and Geoffrey, with even an occasional Michael, which to David's ear sounded incongruous with a last name like Ginsberg. So David would be all right. But a last name, what? He paid for the untouched coffee and sweet roll and went to the phone book. Automatically he turned to the "R's." His finger ran down one page and then another: Razini, Ryan . . . His finger stopped at Reid. David Reid, David Reid . . . When he got settled and had the money he would have it made legal.

But where to live was not so easily solved. It could not be New York; it was too near the past, would be a constant and threatening reminder. But where? He would love to go to California, but that was out of the question, it required too much money. It occurred to him that his father had had less trouble coming here from Russia than he had trying to find his own promised land. So, what could he afford? It would have to be within a relatively short distance, and yet far enough to feel like a new world. Maybe Chicago . . . he could probably get enough money together for the fare. It was a large enough city for him to lose himself in and where there would be no questions asked. Chances of getting a job were pretty good . . . So Chicago it would be until the day when he could go all the way . . . to California, with his wife and child.

His wife? With a shock he thought of Katie. Oh God, what would she say? What if she said no, she wouldn't go with him? He doubted he could do this alone—he needed her. He'd be able to reach her; he knew he could . . . he had to. She'd see it his way and one day thank him for sparing Mark the trauma of discrimination.

But something worse lay ahead of him. His father, the thought of whom made him brace himself against the post. Never mind that he'd never had the kind of love for his father that he wished he'd felt, David had been a Jew for a long time. And a Jew found it impossible to turn his back brazenly upon his father. He would like to have been able to say, "Look, I don't need you, you never gave me anything, we never talked together, you wanted me to believe in something I don't even know the meaning of. You wanted me to be like you and shut out the world until they buried me in my tallis and put the coins over my eyes." Why did you come to America? he wanted to scream out. If you wanted that kind of a life then the persecution of Russia should have been like honey in your mouth. There at least you could have died a martyr. But he wouldn't say that. What he would say he didn't know, but whatever he said, it would be the worst ordeal of his life.

He wanted to go home. He had to go home and see Katie.

CHAPTER FIVE

Katie heard the door open and called out, "David, is that you?" He didn't answer. She had been baking a challeh for Shabbas. Wiping the flour from her hands she came out into the narrow hall and watched David go into the bedroom, following him as he stood facing the window.

"David?" He didn't respond. "David, is anything wrong?" He remained silent. She walked over and stood in front of him. His face was drawn, he looked haggard and dazed. Frightened, she asked again, "David, what happened? Are you ill? Please talk to me." He sat down heavily on the edge of the bed, staring into space.

She pulled the covers back. "Lie down, dear, I'll get you something, a cup of tea, you'll feel better."

"No, that won't help."

She was bewildered, "Why, David, what happened?"

He shook his head. "Oh, God, Katie, how can I tell you, how can I begin?" Abruptly, he got up and began pacing the floor, his hands behind his head, his thoughts moving back to that office in New Jersey where he looked down at the bleeding, disheveled bookkeeper lying on the floor. "In a cage . . ." reverberated over and over again until the loudness of the voice deafened him. Then, talking aloud to himself, without being aware that Katie stood watching him, he ground out, "I should have killed that bastard, hitting him wasn't enough—"

"My God, David, tell me, what happened today?"

He braced himself against the wall, stared at the ceiling and deliberately, in cold fury, began to recount the events of the day—piece by piece, step by step, until, exhausted, he slumped down on a wooden chair. Katie stood in stunned silence, looking in utter disbelief at her husband. Scarcely finding her voice, she said, "David, I can't believe that such a thing could have happened in this country."

He looked up at her and thought how naïve she was, that somehow life had protected her from the obscenity of anti-Semitism. "How little you know, Katie . . ."

"Perhaps, but the one thing I do know is that violence terrifies me—"

Quickly he got up and said, "Don't you think I should have hit him?"

"I don't know, David. I only know that you could have been hurt too. Please, David, I'm sorry, I know how you must have felt, but this is something that probably will never happen again. Please try to forget it. I know they have hurt you deeply, but in a few days you'll forget about it—really dear."

His look cut her off. "Katie"—he spoke as if to a child—"you don't know what it's like out there. You've never had to contend with bigotry and prejudice. The only world you knew was your protected special one in London. And who have you met since you've been here? All Jews. You haven't ever really lived among other kinds of people. You don't have to make a living; I do." His voice crescendoed. "If I don't get off Hester Street and out into the world I'm going to live and die hating myself. Katie, I'm not going to do that."

"David, please darling, you'll wake the baby. I can't bear to see you so upset."

He looked at her. "You have no idea what I'm talking about, do you?"

Quietly, taking his hand, she said, "David, sit down for a moment. I have something to tell you." She led him to the edge of the bed and they sat down together. It was as though a ten-pound weight were on his head.

"I've never told you how my father died, not because I wanted to keep any secrets from you but because I could never think about it." She began tentatively. "It was in Poland at Easter. I was a little girl at the time. My father had gone with my two young brothers into a small town near our village to buy food for Passover. They were in a horse-drawn wagon, and on the way home a group of Polish boys began to taunt my father, calling him terrible names. One got in front of the horse and held the reins while the others threw stones. My father took his whip and started to beat them; my brothers were too young to defend themselves. One boy grabbed the whip out of his hands and beat my father unconscious, then beat the horse; it ran wildly until it came to a large rut in the road, upsetting the wagon, which rolled over and over. When they found them, my father and brothers were dead. There were men in our village who saw what had happened, but they were afraid of retaliation. Always at Easter the pogroms started." Softly she said, "So you see, David dear, I do know about such things."

The awfulness of it only fueled David's outrage—even more intense now that he knew his Katie had suffered too. This monster reached out everywhere; there was no escape. Holding out his hand, he drew her down on the bed and stroked her hair. He held her close and whispered, "Katie, I love you. I want to protect you. No one will ever hurt you again, I'm going to see that you and Mark are safe." He held her, rocking her back and forth in his arms. It was a moment of communion, of trying to shut out the ugliness of the world.

After a while, he left her to walk to the window and look out on the scene below, a scene familiar since his childhood. He turned and faced Katie. "Do you know what I did all afternoon? I spent it thinking about my life, how a man must not allow the past to destroy his future, even if he has to hurt others. Katie . . ." He had to get to it, no more delays; he prayed she would love him enough . . .

"I decided today. I no longer want to be a Jew."

She stood up. Madness . . . this thing that had happened to David had bedeviled him. She held onto the wooden chair.

"David, you don't know what you're saying—today was a terrible ordeal, I know. But in a few days—"

"*No.* Today only made me know something I've felt for a long time."

"I don't know what you're talking about"—she was frightened by the sound of his conviction—"what do you think Judaism is, something you can throw away when you're through with it . . . listen to me—you're too upset to realize what you're saying—"

He spoke quietly now, with sureness. "Katie, I know how it is for you, my coming home and telling you this. I wish there was some other way, there's not. Darling, try to understand. This decision is something I've been thinking about for a long time but never had the courage to admit to myself. . . ."

"David, I only know this. You are Jewish. Nothing you do can change that." She was on the edge of hysteria.

"I'm going to change my name, and we're moving to Chicago."

"To Chicago?"

"Yes, it will be a chance to begin . . . to find out where I belong, who I am."

"Don't you know who you are now?"

"No, I want a chance to live my life. I'm not afraid to—"

"David, I love you, but I must say this . . . you've been afraid of too many things in your life. You were afraid of falling in love with me, and now you're afraid of your heritage—"

"You're right, I am afraid, afraid of the wall between me and what I want—money's only part of it—I want that too—but above all it's the freedom to live anywhere I choose, to join anything I wish, to make out of myself whatever my abilities will allow—"

"But David, what about who you really are—your heritage?"

"My heritage? . . . Judaism? I didn't start out feeling as I do. The world has taught me. The world treats it as though we should be ashamed of it. Why should I have to be ashamed of what I am?"

"My father died for it, and my mother didn't curse God, or give up her religion, or become bitter because she thought that life had been unfair or—"

"I'm not your father or your mother, may they rest in peace. I'm me, David, but their tragedies strengthen my feeling."

Bewildered, she repeated his words. "Strengthen your feelings?"

"Yes. *Why*, Katie, why should your father have died so violently for something he believed in—and your mother, why should she have suffered so because of it?"

"But people don't give up their religion just because they've suffered."

"I'm not telling anybody else to do this, I'm saying it happens to be right for me."

Biting her lip, she said, "You didn't ask if it was right for me."

"Katie, you're my wife. I love you. I believe what I'm doing is right for you too—and especially for our child. I don't want him to live with a stigma all his life. I don't want any of us to . . . I'm not asking you to feel the way I do now, but in the long run I believe you will. I want us to live with some dignity and respect and, dearest Katie, I no longer think that can be done as a Jew."

She was beside herself. "It's not as simple as that, believe me."

"I'm not saying it's simple, but the burden of being a Jew in a world that doesn't want us—"

"I don't find it a burden."

"I *do*, and I'll say to you what I told myself today: I was born a Jew, but I'm not going to die a Jew."

"You've thought out the consequences of this?"

"Yes, I have."

"How will you raise your son—as a Christian?" She said with defiance, "David, I'll never do that."

"That's not what I want. I have no intention of

giving up Judaism for Christianity; I wouldn't give them the satisfaction of that."

"Then how will you raise Mark, to be godless? Is that the heritage you're going to give your son? And you think he'll thank you in the end? No, David, you cannot do this. It's madness—"

"You're assuming if I am no longer a Jew that that automatically makes me an atheist?"

"Well?"

"God isn't only Jewish or gentile. I believe God can love me as much whether I go inside a temple or a church or neither one." He paused for a moment, then went on, "As for raising Mark, there are many people who have no formal religion and they don't become monsters or criminals. They lead good lives, as I know we can."

"But, David," she said, beseeching him now, "I love my life now. I don't need wealth. I'll love you no matter what, David, but please don't do this, I beg of you."

"Listen to me," he said quietly, "I need you in my life. Without you, well, life is unthinkable. But Katie I have to do this. I've come too far. I died a thousand times today before I decided. I can't turn back now. Katie, I'm not good at begging, but I beg you to stay with me and—"

"This will kill your father. Have you thought about your family?"

"Of course I've thought about them. My father loves the Torah more than his son."

"I doubt that, David, but what about your mother? You're her youngest, she loves you the best."

He nodded his head.

"You realize it also means cutting yourself off from everything, everybody that's been important to you? David, look at me and tell me, can you really do this?"

"I will have to do without them. They will have to do without me. I won't let myself feel guilty. I don't want to hurt them, but if they are hurt, remember they have lived as they wanted. I want the same right."

Katie made one last attempt. "David, I once told you there are some things we don't have a choice about. One cannot live his life as though he didn't owe anybody anything. We do owe, from the time we are born; we're born owing."

"I'm sorry, I don't believe that. I believe first a man owes himself. He has a right, a birthright, to choose the way he wants to live." . . . He had no more fight left in him after the grueling day, and now he turned away from her. "Katie, if you don't understand, nothing more I say will help . . ."

Listening to him, she wondered, why had Jews shed their blood for five thousand years, what had her father died for? She thought of the ageless Jewish struggle for survival, and now her beloved husband's obsession to deny that struggle and all it represented. Jews had died for centuries so that she and David and their son could retain a Jewish identity in the world. It was a covenant from birth that they had made with God, so strong it defied their enemies to destroy it. Their heritage and their culture had sustained them through centuries of trial. How wrong David was. Rather than reaffirming his decision, the Jews of history and the Jews in their lives should have been his evidence of courage in the face of suffering and doubt. Jews too had lived and survived their Sodom and Gomorrah. For five thousand years Jews had worshipped at the shrine of the one and only living God. When the cry of the Shema was heard, "The Lord is one," every Jew knew in his soul the bond between himself and his God.

What David was going through was not as special as he thought. So much of the beauty, wisdom and truth of the generations was between the pages of these scrolls of man's struggle within himself—the pages of this holy book that a human hand could hold, this book that taught the way for a man to be what he wanted to be, just a little lower than the angels or just a little above the beasts . . . this book expounded the conflict of good and evil that man was capable of; and offered a choice, a choice to be made by man out of the core of his selfishness, and selflessness. Above all, Judaism never flattered a man; it pointed out all his frailties, his deep seed of lust, his appetite for power. It showed him what he was in the full light of his conscience. It also taught that man could lift his eyes and feel exaltation, depending on how deep were his spiritual reservoirs.

Could David, in honesty, forget what he had been taught? Did David really believe that running away from what he had been born would bring him something better? Did he honestly believe that by changing his name and living elsewhere he would find peace and contentment? In his determination to be true to himself, did he realize the irony of his choice —that he would be living a lie?

And could *she* throw all this away? If she went with him, wouldn't she also be abdicating, wouldn't she be as much to blame, just as guilty? If she found this thing so unreconcilable, why was she debating with herself at this moment? True, the unexpectedness had caught her unprepared, but if her religion had given her the spiritual substance she had always thought she possessed, then why didn't she say no? Why didn't she say, No, David, I cannot build my life on a lie, a deception? I owe it to my son not to deprive him of his birthright. Instead, here she stood in the empty cocoon of herself, filled with indecision. She could not bring herself to say those things. The memory of what life had been without a father, a child raised alone, was still too vivid. To deprive her son of his father—did she have the right to make the decision for him? *His* father was alive; would she be able to justify their separation to him one day?

She also knew her own weaknesses—her fear of loneliness, of being alone as her mother had been. The thought was agonizing. To whom could she turn? Not even to poor Uncle Max, who was now dead and buried alongside her mother. To whom could she look here for comfort, for advice? She now had a child; she could no longer in fairness go even to Malka. She had chosen to be a woman, to take on the trust of motherhood and marriage. No, Malka could not share this with her. Nobody could. It was hers, hers alone to deal with. Above all, she loved David as she knew she could never love again. He *was* her life, all she had, no matter what life he chose. Could she eventually reconcile herself to living the way he proposed? Maybe not, but what meaning would life have without him, recalling in her marriage vows that she had said "forsaking all others." If those vows were sacred then her place was with David: he was her husband . . . A spark of hope occurred: how sure was she that David would give up Judaism once he had tried living a lie? Time was a wonderful teacher . . . perhaps David would realize that he had made a great mistake. There was nothing irrevocable about what he was doing, they could come back if . . .

"David, why don't you give yourself a little more time to think? Today was a great ordeal, you are hurt and angry. Tomorrow, next week, you might feel differently. Please, I beg you, at least don't tell your father tonight."

"No . . . It must be tonight."

"Why, what difference can a few days, a few hours make?"

"Katie, you don't seem to understand, this is not impulsive. I've made up my mind. It will be just as difficult whenever I have to come face to face with my father. To put it off would be worse. I must face it, and the sooner the better. It's got to be tonight. To wait would be unbearable. You talk of honesty. Knowing how I feel, could I in all honesty go on Friday nights and sit at his table? I ask you . . . no, it must be tonight. It must be done once and for all." There was a silence between them.

Taking up her husband's hands in hers, she said, "David, I ask you again, for all our sakes; have you searched your heart that this is what you want to do? Remember, once you break with your family, your father will never forgive you. Never. Not even if you change your mind later, as I hope and believe you will."

"Will you come with me?"

He had brought it to that. She had, finally, no choice.

"Yes, David."

Shabbas, Friday night, was the one night that the family was together. By the time David and Katie arrived, the rest of the family were all present. The women were in the kitchen watching the pots, cutting up the chicken, slicing the homemade challehs and coffee cakes that smelled of fragrant yeast and cinnamon and that Sarah had begun at six that morning. She lived from one Friday to the next. When she looked at her children and grandchildren she thought, who had ever been as blessed as she? When they had left the old country there had been only the two of them and from these two there were now four handsome sons, three beautiful daughters-in-law, and six grandchildren. To have accomplished so much in one short lifetime. When she saw them all sitting around her dining table on Friday nights she counted her blessings—they were her diamonds, her jewels, her riches. This was her naches, her pride, here was her world; she needed nothing else—only God, Isaac, and her children.

Isaac ran to hold his newest and youngest grandson. He took the child from his mother's arms and looked down at him.

"How long was it, David, since I held you like this? Like yesterday, and now I hold your son." Just like his mother he looked, and he was glad the child did, because of all his sons' wives he loved Katie the best. She understood the ways of the past, born in Europe as she was. The others were American-born, a difference. Since marriage, it seemed to Isaac there had been a change in his son; he was less defensive, less turbulent, more content now that he had become a husband and a father. All, he knew, was thanks to Katie.

Gerald, who was three years old, walked to his grandfather and looked at the baby. Isaac sat down so that the little boy could get a better look as he stood by now, watching, observing this ball of putty wrapped in a blue blanket with raisin eyes. Gerald stood for a moment very quietly, without moving. Then deciding to explore whether they were raisins or not, he put his finger in Mark's eye and the infant began to cry. His grandfather pushed his finger away and his mother picked him up and scolded him.

"Don't ever do that. It's your baby cousin, it's a *baby*," Esther said as she slapped him on the hand.

Harry, the oldest son, said to his wife, "O.K., Esther, cut it out. He's only a baby himself; he didn't do anything so terrible." Gerald was crying, his nose running. Harry grabbed him away from Esther and wiped his nose, kissed him and said, "It's okay, now go play with the other kids."

Katie looked around at this family and thought how David was going to give all this up. The Shabbas candles burned brightly in the silver candlesticks that Sarah Rezinetsky had brought with her from the old country. She had whispered to Katie one night that when her day came she wanted Katie to have them because the other girls had mothers whose candlesticks they would have. Now there would be no need, Katie thought. David had worked out the itinerary of their lives so well, but he had forgotten some things, small things, things incidental, like an ancient melody, a lullaby sung to one's child in a tongue to be perpetuated from one generation to the next, a recipe handed down from mother to daughter; little things that meant so much to a woman. How could she endure the pain of this loss? This was the place to which she had come as a stranger and they had all held out their hands to her to make her feel one with them. This was the last time she would see them, the last time she would be here. Oh David, please don't do this. Stop before you break them and yourself into little pieces. God, please don't let him do this . . . and then she heard Isaac saying, "Come, children, we will sit down and eat," and she was terrified as she anticipated what was coming.

"No, papa, we're not staying."

Isaac handed his youngest grandchild back to his mother and looked at David in amazement, "What do you mean, you're not staying? Why not?"

Sarah was bringing in an enormous tureen of chicken soup. Bertha was helping her mother-in-law by getting all the children seated. Esther was pouring the wine. David's brothers, Harry, Maurice and Ben were just going to sit down at the table. David looked at them, and for a moment his courage left him; this was even more difficult than he had imagined. He wavered and began to have second thoughts, but against them was another, inner voice reminding him . . . No matter how you say it, with all the diplomacy in the world, with all the attempts to justify it, no matter, in the end it will be the same . . . You cannot have your life and them too. . . . If you think you're hating yourself at this moment it is nothing as compared to how much you will hate yourself for the rest of your life . . . Say it now, get it over with or you'll curse yourself for being weak at the most important moment of your life . . . If you don't do it now, this opportunity will pass and never again will you have the courage you have right now. . . .

"No, papa, we're not staying." He paused, looked at his father and said, "I wish there were some other way to say this. I wish you and I could talk together, just you and me, but, papa, I've got to get away, I've got to start—"

The old man disregarded him and lightly said, "So you've got to go and start tonight, right now? Sit down, first we eat. This is Shabbas. Then we will talk if you go."

"No, papa, not 'if I go.' I'm leaving tomorrow, the next day at the latest—"

"Sit down," the old man shouted.

"No, papa, I can't stay."

Isaac stood up and faced his son. "What is this craziness about going away? Leaving the family? You think I'm going to let you take my youngest grandson away, I should never see him? No," he shouted excitedly, waving David into his seat. "First we eat, then we talk."

"Papa, listen to me, I don't know how to tell you this, I wish I did, but we're not only moving . . ." He looked at his father, clenched his fists and plunged ahead. "I've decided to leave Judaism . . . I'm going to change my name—"

The old man held onto the table for support. Sarah dropped the tureen, the soup spilled and splattered on her legs; she didn't feel the burning liquid as it spread out over the threadbare rug. The wine that Esther was pouring overflowed the glasses. A hush hung over the room; the children stopped laughing. David's brothers just stood staring. The only sound that was heard was Isaac's breathing. He straightened up, kicked the chair away. It toppled over on its side, one leg broken. Nobody picked it up. He came face to face with his youngest son. "You don't want to be a Jew? Let me understand, you don't want to be a Jew? You think running away will make you less a Jew?

Then, as he had for all of David's memory, Isaac directed his conversation and his emotion toward God rather than his son. His face like chiseled granite, his eyes dark and deep set, standing there in his skullcap, a shock of silver hair showing, the narrow prayer shawl around his shoulders, he indeed looked the role of an ancient patriarch. He now also proceeded to sound like one as he spoke . . . "Oh God, never have I questioned your goodness, but I stand here before you humbly your servant and beg my petition. Why have you cursed me with a devil for a son? Have I fallen so low in your eyes? Have I not always lived according to your law?" Like a man possessed, bereft of his senses now, he unleashed his thunderbolts on his son as though reliving the past, which he would now revenge as though it were yesterday—the pulling of beards, the calling of names, the wearing of black arm bands, the unspeakable indignities. As though for all the suffering of thousands upon thousands rotting in unmarked graves, this convinced avenger began to beat his son with the backs of his hands, first to the right side of David's face and then to the left, back and forth and side to side. David's nose bled. Isaac's hands were stained with David's blood.

David fell to the floor. "Get up, stand like a man," Isaac demanded, and pulled him up by the back of his shirt and leaned him against the wall. "It says that when the Meshiach comes he will raise the dead, cure the sick, help the afflicted, but for the fool there is no cure," Isaac told him. "Have you forgotten the words, 'Oh Lord, whither shall I go from Thy spirit? Or whither shall I flee from Thy presence? If I ascend up into the heavens, Thou art there; if I make my bed in the nether-world, behold Thou art there. If I take the wings of the morning and dwell in the uttermost parts of the sea, even there would Thy hand lead me and Thy right hand would hold me and if I say: surely the darkness shall envelop me and the light about me shall be night, even the darkness is not too dark for Thee.' . . . From whom do you run, from whom do you think you can escape? From God?" He slapped David again. It was the only sound in the room. His mother ran and stood in front of him.

"No, Isaac, no more! This is our son—"

"No, we have *no* son. He is dead." Isaac picked up a knife and cut the lapel of his jacket in the traditional gesture of mourning, took off his shoes and sat on the floor, turned to his other three sons. "We will sit shivah, but only for tonight. He does not deserve the honor of seven days."

And he began the Hebrew chant of mourning, his sons, uneasily, joining him,—"*Yis-gad-dal v'yis-kad-dash sh'meh rab-bo.*"

With the infant in her arms and tears blinding her eyes, Katie ran out of the room and down into the street. How could they . . . David so cruel to his father, and seeing his mother weep, this gentle woman, did he owe them nothing? But how awful was David's humiliation, in front of his brothers and their families, asking for all their understanding. David had suffered so much today. Why couldn't Isaac have tried to talk to David, to understand, to persuade him in some way. David was not just any man—David was his son. Was what happened today entirely David's fault? Who was really to blame? Who should bear the guilt? A world that had warned David not to fight against it? A father so steeped in thousands of years of tradition, a tradition that went beyond his understanding that a son of his could have been possessed by anything as blasphemous as the renunciation of Judaism? If they could have spoken together . . . But if David had been able to do that through the years he would not have found himself in this unbearable position now. If only they had said nothing and simply disappeared, but how could they have done such a thing . . . David's family would suffer even more from not knowing, from believing them dead, as though the earth had swallowed them up. She wished it had.

David went out of Isaac's house, holding onto the wall for support, walked down the dark narrow hall, and retreated to the bathroom. The door was open. He stuck his head under the faucet and let the cold water run. He hung onto the basin and finally looked at himself in the mirror. His face was swollen; the blood had been washed away but nothing could wash away what had just happened. He walked back past Isaac's door without a glance, down the stairs to where his wife and child were waiting for him. He took Katie's arm and they walked the rest of the way home in silence.

Slowly they climbed the five flights of stairs to their flat. Katie went into the front room, undressed the sleeping child and put him into his crib. She pulled the rocker near and sat down wearily, resting her head against the chair, rocked back and forth, remaining near her child all night.

The only light in the room came from the street below. The thin lace curtains swayed gently in the breeze, forming patterns that danced on the ceiling. David lay on his back, looking up, hearing Isaac's voice. Why couldn't his father have spoken to him as a father to a son, as Dov would have with Abe? But he knew that was too much to ask . . . If his father could not speak to him about things less important, how should he have been able to understand *this*? But still, David thought, he was his son, no matter what he had done. People stood by their children even if they had committed murder . . . which, in Isaac's eyes, he had done. But, David told himself,

Isaac was cut from different cloth. He was a father who expected obedience and respect without question, retribution without end. Well, if it had been Isaac's wish to see David go down in sackcloth and ashes, to extract his pound of flesh, he had succeeded. But did he have to disown me, to say I was dead? The chant echoed . . . *Yis-gad-dal v'yis-kad-dash* . . . Enough. He put his hands over his ears as though he could shut out the sound. It did no good. Rolling over with his head in his pillow, he waited for exhaustion to bring him sleep.

CHAPTER SIX

It had taken David two days to put his affairs in order. Saturday he phoned Abe and borrowed a hundred dollars, telling him he was going to live in Chicago—no explanation given or asked—and that he would return the money as soon as possible. He sold his household furnishings, such as they were, to the peddler Chaim for thirty-five dollars. On Sunday he came to pick everything up.

As David helped him down the stairs with the kitchen table, Chaim asked where they were going. David didn't answer.

"I hear you're going to California . . . well, I don't blame you, everybody goes to California. Why not? There everybody gets rich, the climate is better. What, it's good to freeze here in the winter and die of heat in the summer? It's best for the *kind*. Oy, if I could only go I would, but for me it's already late."

After they loaded the last of the things on the wagon, Chaim gave David the thirty-five dollars, counting it out very carefully, each dollar as though a fortune. He untied the reins that were wrapped around the telephone pole and slipped them over the sway-backed horse's head. As he did, the horse urinated, splashing Chaim's shoes. When he climbed back into the wagon he said, "Oy vay, Bessie, have you got manners!" As he rode off he said to David, "Well, I hope someday you'll come back a rich man. *Mazel tov*. Take care of yourself and God bless you. Say goodbye to your beautiful young wife and be careful she don't go in the movies. Come on, Bessie, now we go home."

For a few lingering moments Katie sat on her suitcase in the center of the kitchen while David waited out in the hall with the baby. She got up slowly, lifted the suitcase, walked to the door and never looked back.

When they reached the second floor she paused in front of the Hesslebergs' door, listening. Behind that door sat a boy of eight playing Mozart. His father worked overtime binding books far into the night to make enough money to pay for an old upright piano; his teacher taught him for nothing. She heard David saying, "Come on, Katie, we have to catch a train."

When they reached the bottom hall, Mrs. Feldman was waiting for her with a bag of mandelbrot she had just made. Mrs. Feldman who through all the months of Katie's pregnancy had sat at her bedside when there was a possibility that she might lose her child. She had cooked soup and brought it to her, barely able to climb the stairs with her arthritic legs. She had consoled Katie that the first was always the most difficult. Her face etched like delicate lace, her back arched, she smiled and embraced Katie, then watched as they walked out into the bright sun.

The streets were filled with people. A water hydrant had broken and half-naked children in bare feet ran back and forth, slipping, getting up again, laughing and shouting to each other. A woman was leaning out of a window, drawing in a clothesline festooned by a pair of her husband's long underwear hung out to dry. As she loosened the clothes pegs to gather them in they dropped out of her hands and a boy of eleven grabbed them and ran down the street happily ignoring her shouts of "Come back, you *goniff*, in hell you should only go . . ."

Sticking out his tongue and thumbing his nose at her he shouted back, "In hell I wouldn't need them. I'm gonna give them to my old man."

The carnival-like atmosphere, the whole panorama had become a familiar sight that Katie loved. It was in this place they were leaving, that had embraced her, that she'd found security for the first time in her life. Now she would become a wanderer against a world of the unknown. Here she had found the promises of her tomorrows. Now the beloved ghosts of her yesterdays would walk among these people and down these streets. No matter what might happen to her, no matter where she might be, the memory of this cherished place would be taken out and looked at a thousand times to ease the loss. The sun had reached its zenith. The day was hot. Katie felt cold.

The train ride had been long and exhausting, especially with an infant—Mark had cried most of the night. While David sat up in the coach, Katie spent the night in the ladies' room. As soon as the child cried she took him to her breast; it was the only way to appease him. It was hot and stuffy, smelling of fumes, and there was a strong odor of urine. Each time the train stopped to take on passengers or freight it would lunge forward, almost pushing her off her seat as she sat on the built-in bench against the wall. She had not cried up to now, not because she was strong nor because she was afraid of showing her emotions, but because, despite the awfulness of it, until now it was as though this really were happening to someone else, that she would wake up to find it all a terrible dream . . . But now, sitting here, holding the child in her arms while other children slept in their beds, she knew that this was not a dream. It was a nightmare whose reality came rushing at her like a torrent. At last, feeling as though she literally were falling apart, she gave way to a flood of wracking tears . . .

Finally they reached their destination. They stood on the platform watching the other passengers going their separate ways with the families and friends who had come to greet them. When they had dispersed, Katie and David stood alone; they had no place to go.

"Let's have something to eat," David said.

They went into the dining room in the station, sat down wearily at a table, completely spent, and ordered coffee and toast. They sat silently, each with his separate thoughts, David's most immediate was where they would live.

Buying a newspaper, he turned to the want ads. There were vacancies all over the city, but he had no idea where these were located or which part of town would be most convenient. Not knowing where he would work, and considering the small amount of money he had, he really couldn't be too choosy anyway. So he looked for those that were the least expensive and came to the one that seemed attractive: "Large sunny room with kitchenette, furnished, $27.50." He asked the waitress if she was familiar with that part of town and the approximate address. Born and raised in Chicago, she more or less knew where it was and wrote down the instructions for him. David thanked her as he paid the check. They took a streetcar, transferring three times, and at last found themselves looking up at 2267 Huntington Street.

At one time in the early 1900's this had been a street where some of Chicago's best families had lived, but the city had undergone many changes and these beautiful large homes, which at the time of their glory were intended as one-family dwellings, were now shabby rooming houses in a dilapidated neighborhood. The green paint on the front door had peeled off leaving the original mahogany showing, so that it looked the texture and color of a python, and the broken stained glass was patched with paper tape. As they went up to ring the bell, the stairs creaked. The door was opened by an enormous woman with dyed red hair and a dirty housedress that matched her dirty hands. Two of her front teeth were missing and when she opened her mouth she looked like a pumpkin at Halloween.

"Yea?"

David took a few steps backward, revolted by the liquor and stale cigarettes on her breath. He wanted to leave without looking at the room, knowing it could be no better than she was, but fatigue and the realization that he had to get Katie and the baby settled, if only for a day or so, persuaded him to say, "I read in the paper you have a room for rent."

"Yea, that's right."

"May I see it?"

She pointed her nicotine-yellowed finger at the baby. "Is that your kid?"

David wanted to say, No, I just found it on your doorstep, but instead only nodded.

"I don't rent to no kids."

"Why, what can a baby do, ruin the place?" David had to laugh to himself at the stupidity of this conversation. "Let me just take a look at it."

"Listen, I don't want no brats in the house. We got workin' people here that gotta get their rest. My old man works all night, and I don't want no bawlin' kid keepin 'em awake."

She was ready to shut the door in David's face, but he put his foot in the door. "Look, we've got to have a place to live. Let me look at it, if I like it I'll give you five dollars for yourself, and I give you my word the baby won't make any noise."

She mulled it over. Five dollars? Enough money for a week's food and a couple of bottles of booze. "Okay, but if the kid squeaks, out you go—even if it's in the middle of the night, understand?"

They followed her into the dark hall. The red flocked wallpaper that looked as though it had been up since the house was built was now stained and discolored, its beauty long since gone. On the newel post of the banister stood a gilded cherub with one broken leg, holding in its hand a lamp which dimly illuminated the stairs. The odor of cabbage and bacon permeated the walls, and the smell of liniment became even worse as they made their way up the stairs to the second floor.

Breathless by the time she had climbed the two flights with David and Katie after her, the pumpkin opened the door to a dingy back room that had never known the sun. Facing them was an iron double bed with a thin, lumpy mattress that sat on squeaking springs inside a metal frame, alongside it a rickety night table and a lamp. A golden oak dresser with an oval mirror attached by two arms stood against thc opposite wall, and in front of the window was a small round table with a wooden chair. In the center of the black painted floor was a piece of old carpet, its torn corner deliberately slipped under the bed. Separated from the bedroom by a pair of greasy, floral draperies was a closet with a small window that had now become a kitchenette. On top of a wooden cabinet in the lefthand corner stood a two-jet burner and next to it was a stained sink, the enamel worn off in parts, exposing the cast iron.

David looked around in disgust at the wallpaper hanging away from the walls as though they were mortal enemies, and the ceiling plaster that was broken in one corner. The thought of bringing Katie here was like poison for him, it was worse than Hester Street.

"Well, Katie, what do you think? Shall we take it for a month or so?" He meant a week, but didn't dare say so in front of the pumpkin.

Strange, she thought, he asked her about something as unimportant as this when he alone had made the decision that had brought them here.

"What difference does it make? It's as good as anything we can find, I'm sure, on a moment's notice."

The pumpkin had been leaning against the dresser, her huge bulk overlapping the edge.

"You people gonna be here for only a month, forget it. The owner don't like to spend money for ads in the paper, they're damned expensive."

David shot a glance at her and said sarcastically, "No, we're planning to make this our permanent home." Ignoring her he turned to Katie, "Shall we take it, or do you want to look around?"

What did it matter, she thought, "Take it; it's fine."

He paid a month's rent in advance, and the pumpkin showed him the bathroom facilities, shared by the other six roomers on the second floor. Then he followed her as she waddled downstairs to get the receipt.

By the time he returned Katie was asleep, her coat

around her, and the baby alongside. He left a note that he was going to buy some food and would be back soon, propped it against the mirror, then took one last look at them and left, closing the door behind him quietly.

David discovered a shopping district a few blocks away where happily he found a used furniture store and bought a second-hand crib for three dollars that would as part of the deal be delivered. Then he went to the grocery store and found that prices were much higher here than at home. Home? New York was no longer his home, this was home now; he would have to stop thinking of the past. It was all so new, like the first time he had given his name as Reid to the landlady today, he felt as though he were doing something unlawful. He would get over it. He would have to . . .

Coffee was twenty-seven cents a pound, so he bought half a pound, six eggs and the balance of the groceries which amounted to five dollars, leaving him with thirty-five dollars to tide him over until he got a job.

Holding the box of groceries in his hands he walked past the row of merchants, observing the stores, which were quite attractive, and stopped in front of a men's clothier. He had never owned a brand-new suit, wearing either his brothers' hand-me-downs or a second-hand suit which he bought from Gittleman on Fourth Avenue. He looked in the window at the handsome Harris tweed with wide lapels, extended shoulders, and cuffed trousers, but it was the fly that intrigued him most with its zipper instead of buttons. What a terrific suit, David thought, and for one brief moment the name Bates came back to him. Wasn't that what he had promised himself he would do—buy a new suit if he got the policy? But immediately he pushed it out of his mind. Looking down at his baggy trousers, he decided he must have a new suit for his new life; it would be like a good omen. If he wanted a decent job then he couldn't go looking like a slob; a new suit gave one the kind of confidence a well-tailored man had when he walked into a place feeling that he was really somebody, even if all he had was beans in his pockets.

Putting the box of groceries down to one side of the entrance so that they would not be in anybody's way, he walked into the store. Perhaps it was David's imagination, but the shop seemed to smell of lovely aged leather and masculine cologne.

The moment he entered, David was approached by a dapper man in his middle forties, well manicured, clean-shaven and dressed in a gray worsted suit, a white-on-white shirt with French cuffs and fancy cufflinks, a pure silk, hand-painted wide tie, a white handkerchief billowing out of his pocket, ending in points, and highly polished brown oxfords. Not much like Gittleman.

"Is there anything I can help you with?" he asked pleasantly.

Suddenly David became aware of his own clothing. His first impulse was to say that he had arrived in Chicago only that morning and that someone had stolen his luggage . . . but why did he have to make any excuses at all? He would have to develop more confidence in himself. Abe was right, what the hell did he care what this guy thought of him? He knew who he was and that's all that mattered.

"Yes, I'd like to see something like the suit you have in the window, the tweed."

"Step this way, sir, and I'll show you what we have."

As David followed him he asked, "Incidentally, how much is it?"

"Forty-two fifty."

Oh my God, he thought, he had a whole thirty-five dollars left after the fares and all the expenses as of this moment. "Do you have anything cheaper?"

"Yes, of course. What do you need it for, business or dress?"

"For work."

"Step right over here. We have a wonderful buy on some things that have just been reduced; $25.50 reduced from $37.50. It's a really terrific buy, why don't you try it on. What size do you wear?"

How did he know what size he wore? Every suit he had ever bought Gittleman either pinched in at the back, or lifted the shoulders up so that David could get a fair idea of how it would look when it had been altered. "I don't know, I've put on a little weight lately and I think I take a different size now."

The tailor measured him and the right size was selected. David viewed himself in the triple mirror and found it impossible to believe how different he looked, like another man; he'd had no idea how well good clothes could become him. It was a gray herring-bone, cut very much like the one in the window, and didn't cost $42.50. But if he did buy it he would be left with only $9.50 until he got a job. On the other hand what kind of job could he hope to get if he didn't have the clothes?

"I'll take it."

Katie lay somewhere between the valley of consciousness and deep sleep. Attempting to arouse herself, she found she could not move; her eyes seemed glued as she tried to open them. When finally she did she was unable to orient herself. She shook her head to try to throw off the heaviness of sleep when the knock on the door that had disturbed her in the first place was repeated; it was as though the sound was coming from an echo chamber. Without the window open, the room had become extremely hot and her clothes stuck to her body. Hanging her legs heavily over the side of the bed, for a moment she felt bewildered and light-headed from too deep a sleep and too little food; she had eaten nothing all day. The room now lay in semi-darkness at that precise moment that hovers between dusk and twilight. It seemed to linger as though it refused to die, as though it wanted to remain and not become a yesterday.

Quickly she rallied her senses, got out of bed and groped for the light switch, while the knocking became louder. She called softly through the door, "Who is it?"

"I got a crib here," the voice on the other side responded.

A shaft of light invaded the room as she opened the door slightly. "Yes?" she said, peering at the man as he stood holding the small bed, then let him into the dark room. Embarrassed, she told him, "We just moved in today and I don't know where the light switch is."

"Try the lamp over there on the night table."

"Oh," she said, "I hadn't even noticed it." She pulled the chain and the lamp gave off a yellow glare through its glass shade, hand-painted with grotesque birds that seemed to fly out at her.

"Where do you want the crib?"

"Are you sure this is for me?" she asked, surprised.

"Your name Reid?"

She was taken aback. This was the first time she had heard the name spoken. It sounded awkward, it had no connection with her at all. She was tempted to shout out, No, that's not my name, my name is Rezinetsky . . . she answered, "Yes, it is."

"Well then, I guess it's yours. Your husband bought it today. Now where do you want it?"

She looked around the room and decided to put it against the wall opposite the window, sure it would not ruin the decor.

As the man was leaving, David returned home from exploring the neighborhood. When he walked into the room with the groceries in his hands, wearing his new suit, she could only stare. She watched him as he went into the kitchen, as he put the groceries on the floor, then stood in front of her, smiling as he looked down at her sitting on the edge of the bed. The smile was pure bravado; he felt guilty as hell, then chastised himself, you've got to get over this feeling of guilt. It was a wise decision, the only way you'd get a job, remember?

Katie continued to stare. "How do you like it?"

Shaking her head, she said, "It's beautiful, but, David, do you think you should have with our small amount of money?" And then immediately was sorry she had come out with it so flatly.

"Yes, I do, or I wouldn't have bought it. I think it's going to be the most important investment I'll ever make," he said with more confidence than he felt—though he could hardly afford to let Katie know any of his feeling of uncertainty.

She would not ask what it had cost, did not want to sound petty, but as she started to take the groceries out of the wooden box she couldn't avoid thinking how they needed an ice box for the milk, the half-pound of butter and other perishables, not to mention a tub to bathe Mark in, or a baby carriage. And then she reminded herself that David had gotten them a crib. She tried to be grateful for that, without complete success.

Putting the staples on the exposed pine board shelves above the sink, she said, "David, would you go down and ask the landlady if she can let us use a hammer and maybe have a few nails, please?"

"What do you need them for?"

"We'll have to nail that wooden box outside the kitchen window as a cooler to store the milk and other things."

It wasn't lost on him.

That night Katie slept poorly. The room seemed strange and forbidding; the bed was lumpy and the metal springs stuck into her flesh through the thin mattress; the cotton comforter smelled of stale liniment, and she developed a terrible headache from the pillow that was hard as rock. Even in those moments of half-sleep she listened for any sound from Mark, fearing that if he cried they would be evicted and thrown out into the street in the middle of the night. David, on the other hand, slept like a man drugged, without moving or turning once. Slipping out of bed in her bare feet, without turning on the light, she adjusted the gas burner and fixed herself a cup of strong tea. She sat in the dark at the window and stared out . . . and there she remained, mind blank, feeling like a stuffed animal, sipping the tea. It occurred to her that if someone stuck her with a pin, she doubted she would even wince. Feeling, blessedly, had at least momentarily fled. It—and reality—came back with Mark's cry of hunger. Stumbling in the dark as she hurried over to him, she picked him up and took him to her breast. When he had finished, she put him on her bed and, still in the dark, changed his diaper, got back into bed, and fell asleep with the child in her arms.

David awoke with the light of dawn. Never had he slept so well; all the fatigue and exhaustion of the last few days had disappeared in that blessed sleep, as though the debris of the past had been washed away and in its place was left a renewed hope and promise. Turning on his side, he watched Katie and the baby asleep; it was the most beautiful sight he had ever seen. In fact, he thought, she looked more beautiful in repose than when she was awake, if that were possible. The baby was changing so; he was beginning to look more like a baby instead of a small doll that might break. Then his eyes wandered to the second most beautiful sight he had ever seen, his gray suit hanging carefully over the chair.

Getting out of bed quietly so as not to disturb them, he slipped into the bathrobe Katie had given him as a wedding present and went down the hall to the bathroom. When he returned Katie was awake. Mark had wet so badly she was soaked from head to toe. Changing into another cotton nightgown she put the water on for coffee, as David came up behind her, lifted her off the floor and kissed her.

"Good morning, Mrs. Reid. I feel great, how do you feel?"

She wished he hadn't called her that; it sounded so foolish, like they were playing some kind of game. Nonetheless, she told herself to get used to it, and answered him, "I feel fine, David, just fine. Now put me down."

"Boy, I slept like a rock, I didn't hear a thing. They could have set off a bomb and I wouldn't have heard it. I feel great and raring to go."

She managed a smile for him.

"I'm glad you do, David. What can I get you for breakfast?"

"Just toast and coffee."

"I'm sorry but I can't fix toast. We don't have anything to toast it with—"

He shrugged it off.

While she prepared breakfast, David put on his new suit, and sat down at the round table while Katie sat on the edge of the bed with a cup of coffee in her hand and watched him eat. She thought how handsome he was, that suit was indeed beautiful. She went to him and stood looking down at him. Somewhere deep within her, along with her love, she had not forgiven him, but she said, "David, may I sit on your lap for a moment?"

He smiled up at her. "If you promise not to crease the pants."

She sat down gently, put her head on his shoulder and for one brief moment they sat holding each other tightly. Then he spanked her on the bottom lightly and said, "I've got to get going if you want me to make a fortune for you." Putting on his straw hat, he thought maybe he should have thanked that son-of-a-bitch bookkeeper because . . . if it weren't for him he wouldn't be here at this moment, waiting to take his place in the world. He kissed Katie good-bye, and she whispered, "Good luck, David dear, good luck." Glancing at his son, he left with the distinct feeling that he could, indeed, lick the world with one hand tied behind him.

The want ads tucked under his arm, he adjusted his hat just slightly to one side and couldn't resist, trying all the while to appear casual, a quick check of the knife-edge trousers, down to his polished shoes, which he had worked over earlier that morning. No doubt about it, he looked like an executive . . . hell, a tycoon . . . like David Reid. Then, for the first time in how long he couldn't remember he whistled a tune as he walked jauntily to get the streetcar that would take him to his first interview.

He was given a form to fill out in the hiring office of Marshall Field's department store. As he looked at it he realized the first major consequence of his change of identity—that he would need references —previous jobs, how long he'd lived in the city, homeowner, or renter, experience in selling plus a dozen other personal questions—and of course David

Reid was unable to answer any of these. He would try a small concern less likely to check than a store like Marshall Field's. Hc tore up the application on his way out.

The rest of the morning he walked about trying to familiarize himself with the city. At noon he sat at a counter and ordered a sandwich and coffee, took out the want ads again and studied them with great care. There were not too many jobs for which he was qualified; in fact there were not too many jobs advertised at all. For a moment his confidence wavered, but he told himself he could least of all afford the luxury of self-pity, not for one half-second. This was his first day out, so why was he worrying? Except when he had paid the fifty cents for his lunch he was worried . . . a little . . .

He went from one haberdashery to another; there were more salesmen than customers.

Over the next two days he ran the gamut from shoes to hardware. No one was hiring. On the way home early one evening, waiting for the streetcar, he stood in front of the East Bay Realty Company. There was a salesman seated behind one of the six desks in the office. David looked inside and saw the man finishing up his work ready to go home. Impulsively he opened the door and went in. As he did so, the man looked. "Is there anything I can help you with?"

"I'd like to know if you need another man in the office. I'm looking for work."

"You've got to be kidding. We're having a hell of a time. You like to eat? Well, take it from me—this is the worst business you can get into."

"Can I ask you a question?"

"Sure, but—"

"How do you get to be an agent?"

"Well, you start out as an apprentice in an office, but you're really on your own. Then after two years, if you study, you can become a broker. Naturally, you work on commissions."

"That doesn't sound too difficult."

"Well, it sounds easier than it is. With all the competition, it's a rat race and unless you've got plenty of connections you can die between commissions."

David glanced around the office. "Can I ask you another question?"

"Shoot."

"How come you're in it if it's so bad?"

The man laughed. "Because this was my father's business. We've been here for thirty years. Real estate is all I know, that's why. But believe me, I wouldn't start this business now with conditions like they are." The man got up from his chair, reached in the closet to take out his jacket. "Take my advice, get yourself any kind of a job until this blows over. Who knows, maybe with this new president we'll see some changes . . ."

David thanked him and left.

That night the sounds of sensual laughter leaked through the thin walls from the room next door. Katie moved closer to David, seeking comfort as they lay quietly together in the darkness. Later they both awoke with a start to the screams and loud cries coming from the flat beyond. Holding him, Katie said, "Please, David, you must do something—that poor girl's being beaten."

But David had met their next door neighbor in the hall, and doubted that Dolly Swan would appreciate his intervention.

"Go to sleep, honey," David whispered. "She doesn't mind . . . she's being paid for it." He could feel Katie blush in his arms. And the pumpkin worried about a baby's cry, he thought bitterly before he drifted back to sleep. . . .

The next day he went to the employment agency. It was packed with men out of work, all jammed together waiting to get anything they could lay hands on, never mind, steady or not. At the end of the week he had thirty-five cents left. It had been coming on gradually, but now he really panicked. What was he going to do now that the food was beginning to run out? Come Monday they would have been here a week. Now he was beginning to leave the room in the morning earlier than before to be at the hiring hall ahead of anybody else, knowing all the while that there was really no reason to be early. The answer would be the same as the day before and the day before that. 1934 found the country feebly picking its battered head up from the onslaught of the great depression and the newfound confidence David had brought with him, all his resolutions, was becoming a casualty of the times. His feet were killing him from pounding the pavement, and by Friday afternoon he was beside himself. Finding a bench under a tree he sat down and wondered what he was going to do. He looked at the sandwich he'd brought from home, not really sure he was hungry. Only one thing was he sure of—he had to get some money; the rent was paid for another three weeks, but he wouldn't even have carfare for next week. Who should he turn to? Abe, he could always go to Abe, but he immediately dismissed that idea. He already owed him one hundred dollars. He would rather starve than become a leech. On Hester Street they had been poor for so long he didn't know the difference. Whether there was a depression or not, life was always the same. Here he'd thought, there would be a place for him, but in that wavering moment he began to feel that there was no more need for David Reid than there had been for David Rezinetsky. On Saturday he pawned his suit for five dollars.

Monday he heard they were hiring at Frank's Shoe Company. When he got there lines were already two deep and by the time he reached the hiring desks the jobs would have been taken. Always too many men for too few jobs. They stood around like vultures, and he was no different. What did they say, that survival was the first law of nature; that necessity was the mother of invention? He got out of line and observed the men standing, waiting. His eyes stopped on an enormous man who was probably a longshoreman, certainly long on brawn. David went up to the man and tapped him on the shoulder. He looked down at David.

"Can I see you for a minute?" David said.

"Sure, pal, what can I do for you?" he said, following David as he left the line.

Quietly David said, "How would you like to make three dollars?"

The man looked at David suspiciously, "Who do I have to kill?"

David laughed, the man was reading his mind. "You don't have to kill anybody . . . just start a fight, but I mean a real good fight. Will you do that?"

"Let me see the green first." David peeled off three one dollar bills, held them in his hand as though they were playing cards. The man looked at the money, decided he probably wouldn't get the job anyway, a bird in the hand . . . he shrugged, grabbed the money and said, "What the hell, it's an honest day's work."

David walked to the front of the line but stood aside. He didn't have long to wait. The big man, for no apparent reason, said to the man in back of him, "Hey, cut the pushing, you bum."

"Who're you calling a bum?" said the other man, and hauled off and hit the big man, who was poised and waiting and easily managed the first blow. Soon everybody had gotten into the fracas. The fists were flying as David walked quietly into the office and was hired.

For almost a week they had lived out of a suitcase, Katie putting nothing away for fear they might not be able to stay, but now that David had a job she unpacked the suitcase that had become her constant companion. The first thing she took out was the red satin heart box which she cherished, the chocolates long since gone. How well she remembered that Valentine's Day, the first one after their marriage, when David came home and made her guess what he had hidden in back, switching the box from one hand to another, teasing her until finally she gave up. When at last he had put it into her hand he'd said grandly, "It's more than candy, it's my heart I lay at your feet." Laughing, he said, "See, you didn't know the poet that lurks. This guy Shakespeare's got nothing on me." He picked her up, held her in his arms, and they laughed as though they were children.

Now she took off thc top and inside lay the remnants of all her cherished memories; a picture of her mother and father taken together on their wedding day, her father sitting on a chair dressed in a black frock, the bottom of his trousers tucked inside his black peasant boots, the black hair under the hard-topped peasant cap with a visor. She looked at his eyes; they were kind and gentle. Even the moustache, so carefully trimmed for the photograph, made him look no older than his nineteen years. Behind him stood his bride, with one hand poised on his shoulder, dressed in the dirndl skirt and the embroidered blouse with the full sleeves and a coronet of fresh flowers in her lovely braided hair. A bowl of artificial roses stood on a pedestal in the background before a pair of parted satin draperies. Katie looked down at the inscription in the right-hand corner—"Minsk, Poland." She kissed them both. Putting this possession aside for a moment she took out her marriage license and inspected it. She would try her best in this new life. Time healed all wounds, even those of death. Perhaps time would heal this.

Now she looked at the birth certificate of her son. He was the future that would sustain her. She prayed that God would deal fairly with him, this innocent child, and let him not inherit all the sins of the fathers. Let there be an end to that lugubrious legend. She put back the top and placed the box in the dresser drawer, took the rest of the things out of the suitcase and slid it under the bed along with the box that contained her white dress, then got on with the business of trying to make a home.

She scrubbed the black painted floor until it shone. The sink was so stained and rusted that it was impossible to get it white. She washed Mark's diapers and David's clothes, as well as the dirty gray curtains that fell apart in the process, then realized after she'd finished that there was no place to hang anything. When David came home from work the room looked like a Chinese laundry, everything strewn around—

over the crib rail, on the chair-back, and over the pole that had held the flowered draperies she had washed. They would have to put up with it until David was paid on Friday and she could buy a clothesline and washboard.

Each morning, after the baby had been bathed in the sink, Katie would feed him and put him down for his morning nap. Then she would go to the backyard and pull the weeds that had grown knee-high in one corner of what had once been a lovely garden. David had stretched the clothesline there from one fence to the other. To her delight, she also discovered what was left of a gazebo grown over with weeds and shrubs.

Their lives had now taken on a pattern, one quite different from what she had known in her earlier days as a young bride. She recalled how adept she had become at the recipes Malka had given her. How she longed to make the stuffed derma as Sarah had taught her, she could still taste the chicken soup with the succulent matzo balls light as a feather, fat brisket baked crisp on the outside and tender and juicy on the inside, swimming in its own natural rich juices, with potato pancakes that would win the heart of a gourmet. She recalled Sunday morning breakfast with bagels, lox, and onion rolls fresh and hot from Lipkin's Bakery. She could almost savor now the strudel, paper thin, that she had learned to make after a dozen disasters, priding herself, almost better than Malka's. All that had changed, without an oven she could no longer do any of these things; on the two burners she cooked either stew, soup or potted meat balls. For Katie, Hester Street had become home, but this place of exile had become an outpost in a cold wilderness. On Hester Street there were loved ones to share even the poverty with. As poor as they were, they managed to eat well. Their larder, far from being full, at least never seemed empty. Life for Katie had been good there.

She reprimanded herself at these thoughts. She had consented, she had to forget.

As the summer wore on, the weather changed from soft spring breezes to excruciating heat. The milk soured, the butter became rancid and the eggs rotten; she begged David to buy an ice box. The color was bilious green and it smelled foul. She scrubbed it with Fels Naptha soap and baking soda until the skin of her fingers shriveled from the excess water, the nails were brittle, broken and split. She painted it a cheerful yellow, stood back and admired it. When it had dried, David went down and bought a quarter's worth of ice, of which half melted on the way home. The David Reids at home. . . .

As September drew to a close the heat hung over the city and everyone took to their porches, fanning themselves and drinking beer. During the day Katie found relief for herself and Mark out in the backyard in the gazebo. The lattice had rotted away and the post that held it up was termite-ridden, but she had pulled the weeds away from the entrance, swept it clean and washed the benches. She brought down a blanket and pillows and there she lay Mark, who made contented noises while Katie either read or darned. Here she found solace.

But this morning, after Katie had settled Mark, she took a writing pad and pen, knowing that she could no longer push aside writing to Malka. She explained as best she could the events that had suddenly taken her away from their love and the reasons for David's sundering himself from Judaism, at the same time trying to preserve for them the image of the young man they had known. She feared that this would go beyond Malka's understanding, but at least she hoped they would realize how truly she loved them, that they were in her thoughts constantly, and that she missed them desperately. They would always be a comfort to her, and for that her gratitude was overwhelming. She would never forget them to the very end of her life. . . .

The summer had at long last gone. Nobody mourned it. Then suddenly, like a mighty whip, the winds came lashing off Lake Michigan at the beginning of fall and made it impossible to walk in the street without holding onto some available sturdy object. As the weather changed, so did Katie. Her milk had dried up and the hungry child sucked at the nipples until they were tender and raw. She paced the floors all night with him in her arms to comfort him, but also for fear that they might be evicted. Then one morning, dressing him warmly in a blanket, she put on her thin coat and exerting great effort against the elements, she got on the streetcar, transferring three times until she reached the free clinic across town. She waited and waited along with dozens of other mothers to see the doctor. When one child started to cry the others took it up, and soon there was a chorus of screaming children. At long last Katie was summoned into the cubicle where she saw the doctor. After a brief discussion with him she was given a formula and sent home. They could afford almost no food that week because Katie had to buy a large pot for sterilizing the bottles and nipples. The dextrose was expensive, in fact all the necessary ingredients were costly, so she added a little more water to the already thin vegetable soup they ate with stale bread. They survived.

After a week the baby developed colic. Again she walked the floors with the same fear of eviction. Once more she went across town to the free clinic. In all, the formula was changed four times until at last the doctor found one that was good for Mark, and relative insurance against being turned into the street by the benevolent landlady. . . .

The cold, long winter had settled in among them. Now Katie had no place to hang her wash, the baby was confined, and the weeds grew up around her summer retreat. After David left for work she did her washing, including the bed sheets and the pillow cases, David's work socks and shirts and the baby's things. She asked and received permission to hang them in the basement. Unable to carry the whole load at one time, Katie put as much as she could in one of the crib sheets, folded the corners together, then put the neatly tied clothesline and hooks on top of the pile and went down to the damp musty basement. There she turned on the bare exposed globe that hung from a cord which swung back and forth, making eerie shadows on the ceiling and down the wall. Katie shuddered at the sight; it was like a crypt, a cavern deep in the bowels of the earth, dirty and cobwebbed, webs that had been spun for fifty years and left untouched.

The silence was broken by an enormous rat that came bounding out of the woodwork toward her. Dropping the clean wash on the ground, she ran from the place, up the stairs to her room and slammed the door behind her, standing against it, her heart pounding and her body trembling, then fell onto the bare mattress and sobbed uncontrollably. When David came home from work she sent him downstairs for the wash. That night they slept without sheets, with the comforter only. From then until summer the room was littered with the wash.

In spite of the burners that were left on constantly the room was bitterly cold, and during the day Katie wore David's work socks, large enough to cover her flat shoes, while at night she slept in her coat over her night gown and kept the baby in bed next to her to provide warmth for him. The days passed slowly. At times she barely got out of bed; there was really no need to do so, no house to be cleaned, no chores to be done, no family to visit, no Mrs. Feldman to bring her soup, no Malka to comfort her, no Birdie to protect her. Each day she would lie in bed with only the past to occupy her thoughts and dreams of what life perhaps might have been. Dear Uncle Max, you wanted so much for me, but here—and she almost smiled to herself at the thought—there is no need for music and French . . . Perhaps, she thought, she might get a job after the dreadful winter, but then what would she do with the baby? Who would she be able to leave him with? After all, her child had a mother and a father, and wasn't this one of the reasons she had agreed to go with David? In all honesty she admitted that was not the only reason, of course. There were others, but this was one of the most important and when she thought of leaving him with someone like the pumpkin downstairs she became frantic. When he grew older and was at school, then she could think of doing something outside, but now her place was here with him.

Finally the snow melted, blossoms burst forth from their long winter sleep. Spring had come once again. By April the weeds had grown up, and Mark was one year old. Through it all he had become a chubby, pink-cheeked little boy, fed by the love, the adoration, and attention of his mother. He was amazing, having gone through teething with a minimum amount of discomfort for which David and Katie were grateful. It was almost as though he knew they needed his cooperation in order not to be thrown out into the streets or left to look for another place that would be as bad or worse.

Each morning he stood up in his crib soaking wet, laughing, making delicious gurgling sounds. He would shake the crib and look across the room to his sleeping mother and father, then plop down and play with the rubber toy David had bought him.

Again by adding a few more vegetables and a little less meat to the stew, they managed to buy a playpen they left in the small summer house in the backyard.

Summer came once again, and David found himself still in his detested job at the shoe factory, at payday waiting in line with the others like one big glob of fish roe that would separate into its tiny component eggs, and reform once more back at work on the line. Nonetheless, the memory of the man behind that desk at the East Bay Realty Company stayed with him, and he knew that when the depression was over . . . he was going into the real estate business. How, when, where—he didn't know, but in his mind's eye he imagined himself sitting in that man's place behind that same desk. He was sure real estate was for him; no boss, your own man. He knew what he wanted and, by God, he was going to have it.

He began to study so that when the day came he would be more than an apprentice. On Sundays he would hide away in the summer house and read until dark, buying and selling, wheeling and dealing with clients born of his fantasy. Monday morning . . .

The days seemed to melt one into another until Katie sometimes didn't know the date, or care. At night she would lie in bed beside her husband and pray that he would not touch her, lying very still after they turned the lights out, hoping he would fall asleep soon. The intimacy of one room drew them apart. When the doctor had told her there would be no more children, she had cried, grateful for the one she had just given birth to and thinking she had betrayed and denied her husband. At that time it was more than she could bear, but now she was grateful there would be no more. How wise God was. . . .

And so they spent their days and lost their years. Mark was two years old now. David grew sullen and spoke very little. The heat of the summer was once more on them. The room was oppressively hot, and at night Katie would sit at the window anticipating the winter that lay ahead. All too soon the snow would fall and once again there would be a time of overwhelming loneliness. Shut away in this cell, the prospect of another winter depressed her so that she could hardly bear the thought of it. They were at the crossroads . . .

David lay in the dark half-naked, staring up at the ceiling. He turned on his side and studied Katie's silhouette against the window, not speaking at first, knowing how she felt and what she thought; but then life had not turned out exactly as he had wanted either. Wasn't he suffering also? But this would not be forever, couldn't she see that? Couldn't she see that it was only a question of time until they would be out of here? The night and the dark were choking him. Katie's depression cut through him like a knife.

"What's wrong, Katie?" He asked the question already knowing the answer too well.

"It's too hot, I can't sleep . . ." Meaningless small talk, small evasions for two people trying not to face what lay between them.

"Katie, let's talk about it. . . . Really talk. Not about

the weather or apologizing for the soup being too thin or the meatballs too hard, or that Mark's getting too big for the bed. Let's talk about you and me."

"There's nothing to talk about. We said everything that had to be said two years ago. You know the saying, David . . . we made our bed, we'll lie in it."

He switched on the light and sat on the edge of the bed. "You think I've done something terrible to you, don't you? Well, say it, don't you?"

She bit her lip to keep from speaking.

He continued, "What did you have before that was so great? We lived in a hovel as bad as this. So it had two more rooms in it—"

"It's not the *rooms*, I never wanted rooms. I wanted to build something in our lives, David, but what are we building here? Please tell me David, what are we building?"

He got up abruptly. "What do you want? I'm trying to do the best I can. I can't give you luxuries." He paced the floor then turned to her. "Do I have and not give you, do I indulge myself and deprive you?"

"Darling, we're not talking about the same things."

"All right," he said, "what are you talking about? Tell me please so I'll understand."

"It's the loneliness, the deception, the strangeness, being cut off from everybody and everything. I want us to have some happiness in our life—"

"Who the hell is it I'm deceiving? Who the hell cares if my name is David Reid or Joe Blow, who gives a damn? And as for happiness . . . what do you call being happy? Living on Hester Street for the rest of your life, waking up one day to find you're a shriveled-up old lady who doesn't have the price of a proper burial?"

He took a deep breath and shook his head. "Let me tell you what this is all about. You can't forgive me because I deprived you of your precious Birdie, and your stove, and going to the fish market with all the rest of those yentas. I've seen the condemnation in your eyes get deeper and deeper each day." He braced himself against the dresser, and his voice was tinged with anger. "You've managed what my crummy job couldn't do . . . you've torn me down without a word, with just that look, condemning, accusing . . . I'm not going to settle for what we have now and you should know it. You should but you're too busy missing Birdie and Malka and Hester Street . . . If you loved me as much as you seem to love all of them we'd have had a chance." His voice rose as the anger took over.

"David, you're frightening the baby. Please don't shout . . ."

"Well," he said, breathing hard, "I'm not going to shout or frighten you or the baby anymore. I'm through with feeling guilty, I've paid enough for the terrible thing I've done to you. I don't owe anybody my soul . . . not even you."

She watched, stunned into silence, as he dressed, then reached in his pocket, took out all the money he had and threw it on the bed.

"Go back to your ghetto and be happy." He slammed the door behind him as he went out.

CHAPTER SEVEN

Summer, 1936

Esther Rezinetsky grabbed onto the drainboards for support, got up from her knees after scrubbing the kitchen floor and laid a row of newspapers across it from the sink to the door. With the bucket of dirty, sudsy water, she went into the bedroom, opened the window which looked out into the alley below, swirled the water around and heaved it out so that it hit the building opposite, running down the side like a small waterfall until it reached the broken concrete. She blew back the piece of hair that had fallen into her eyes and went back into the kitchen to get lunch ready for Harry. Only eleven o'clock, she said to herself—it was so damned hot and she was so damned pregnant, and she wondered if she could make it through the day. When she heard a knock on the door she picked up the clock and held it to her ear to see if it were going; it had not stopped. Angrily she thought, for God's sake, he had to come home so early for lunch, it would have killed him if he'd grabbed something to eat out? There was another knock.

"Open it, open the door," she called out, wiping her hands on a towel. The door didn't open. Probably Harry had brought home the sack of potatoes and was holding it in his hands. She turned the knob, pulling the door toward her, and let out a scream. "Oh my God, Katie, I don't believe it!" She could say no more, unable to find words as they stood facing each other.

Katie felt like a beggar without pride. Awkwardly she said, "I'm so happy to see you, Esther."

"I wish I could say the same about you. . . . That isn't what I mean . . . I'm glad to see you, but I can't ask you in. I'm afraid Harry might come home and he'd kill me if he saw you here."

She knew she should never have come here and put Esther in this position, but desperation had replaced logic. "I'm so sorry, Esther dear, I should have realized that this was wrong. Believe me, I don't blame Harry, or you, or the family for feeling that way; you have every right." Looking down, she said almost in a whisper, "I don't even know why I came here."

Esther looked at this young girl whose eyes told too much of her story. She knew in her heart that Katie was not to blame for what had happened. She asked herself, if Harry had been crazy like David, would she have followed him? Wasn't that what a woman was supposed to do? Wasn't that what made marriage, that whatever road a man took the woman's place was with him, for better or for worse? What did a young girl know when she married a man? If he became rich she became rich, if he remained poor she remained poor. If he were ambitious, it wasn't necessary to push him to become successful. If he wasn't ambitious, then all the pushing in the world did no good. If he became sick, she didn't leave him. These were the risks a woman took when she married; the risks Katie had taken when she married David . . .

"Forgive me, Esther, don't say anything to Harry." Katie picked up the suitcase and took Mark's hand and started down the stairs until Esther called out, "Wait a minute, don't go."

Katie turned and looked up at Esther. "No, really darling, I must. I should never have come—"

Esther reached out her hand to Katie.

"Listen, Katie, I'm glad to see you, but you can imagine how surprised I was to find you standing there. I thought it was Harry with a sack of potatoes

. . . oh, never mind that . . . it's early yet, come on in for a few minutes at least . . ."

Katie shook her head.

Esther insisted, "Come on, Katie, please." She waddled back up the stairs with Katie and Mark trailing after her.

"Do you think it's all right?"

"Sure, Harry won't be home till twelve."

Katie seated herself at Esther's kitchen table with Mark alongside her and watched while Esther fixed the tea and cut up a challeh she had made that morning. Katie's eyes wandered around the room. The kitchen walls were dirty gray and the linoleum was badly worn in spots and would not be replaced till who knew when? But there was a smell of cinnamon and sugar and yeast . . . They sat across the table, one from the other, Katie barely drinking her tea.

"Katie, I'm so shocked to see how big the baby is . . . Baby?" Esther corrected herself, "He's a big boy and so beautiful."

"Thank you, Esther. He's such a good child, I feel blessed. And you, when are you expecting?"

"It could drop any minute now." She laughed.

"You look so well," and hungrily she added, "I'm so happy to see you. How are the other children?"

"Fine, thank God, growing up, getting fresh, wearing out their shoes."

"I guess you want a girl after the two boys?"

"Whatever it is, I got news for you, I close the barn door. That's it, I got enough. Harry either uses something or he can get a shikseh and sleep with her." She laughed and added, "As long as he comes home for supper."

The tone of Esther's voice changed as she asked Katie, "How come you're in New York? I thought your fancy husband never wanted to come back."

Katie lowered her eyes to the table. "He didn't. I'm here without David."

"Just you and the baby?" Esther frowned in disbelief.

"Yes," Katie said, in a voice almost too low to be heard. "David thought it best that we separate for a while."

"Don't kid me, Katie, you left him, right? I don't blame you. You're damn well rid of him—he's no good."

Katie bit her lip. Talking about this was making her ill at the pit of her stomach. She couldn't stand talking about David this way behind his back; it seemed so disloyal. And still she should have known that it was inevitable Esther was going to ask questions. She wouldn't say that David had told her to go . . . Not without also saying she had become derelict in her obligations toward her husband, that she had been unwilling or unable to accept what he had given her in return for what she wanted, which it seemed was to be sitting in Esther's gray kitchen with the newspapers on the floor, sipping tea and talking about trivialities. Wives don't choose the time and place to help their husbands and to stand by them . . . Chicago had been the test of her fidelity. She had been found wanting. The opportunity had been there. She had failed. She knew that David needed her badly, that he never would have told her to leave if it weren't that he felt she'd already abandoned him.

"Please, Esther," Katie said, looking up now at her, "please don't say things like that about David—"

"I shouldn't talk about him? Say, listen, if I saw him on the street, I wouldn't spit on him after what he did to those two old people."

"I know, Esther, he hurt them terribly, but what does a man do when he finds he simply cannot accept what he was born? Didn't David have that right?" The words sounded false to Katie as she said them.

"Listen, I'm not a philosopher—I'm not educated like you and him; I only know that what he did was terrible and the family will never forgive him. I'm not even supposed to be talkin' to you, but what the hell, you're not responsible for that louse."

"I know you don't want to hurt me, but please don't call David that, and as for me I'm as much to blame as David. I'm his wife. I'm not justifying any of this, but what could David have done? How could he have broken with his tradition and his family without hurting them?" She was pleading now for Esther's understanding, and at the same time realized it was useless.

"Esther, please tell me. What could he have done?"

Esther didn't hesitate. "He could have gotten lost, or committed suicide. Which in the eyes of his parents he's already done . . ."

"Oh my God, what a terrible thing to say. Be honest, aren't they surviving without him? I survived the death of my whole family—surely you can survive this?"

Esther got up from her chair, walked to the sink and leaned against it, looking at Katie. "He really got to you, didn't he? With all his fancy words . . . Listen, I got one thing to say about him. He knew how to talk and you sound just like him. I'm sorry to say it, but you do. Now let me tell you something," she said, shaking her head. "I'll never forget that Friday night. When you left, mama got a stroke. We all took turns taking care of her and papa. Finally, last year, she got worse and Dr. Goldberg put her in the nursing home. It's hell, plain hell . . . Papa sits in her room all day. He never leaves until Ben or Harry or Maurice goes to pick him up at night. He eats and sleeps here one night, or at Bertha's house, and with all her kids it's tough. But he can't find a place for himself without mama.

"Remember how proud he was? Well, you'd never recognize him, he's so old and bent over. We can't get over it. Half the time he doesn't shave or take a bath. He looks worse than mama, if that's possible. He doesn't even pray as much anymore. It's like Harry says, he thinks that the old man's ashamed in front of God that he had a son like that. He tried to keep it a secret from the neighbors and the friends what David did; and if he's ashamed for them, so how can he stand before God? Do you know what I mean?"

Katie couldn't answer. Esther was right when she said that they should have gotten lost; maybe better still not to have been born at all. She felt vile; what they had done was unpardonable. They did not have the right to break the lives of others. There must have been another way that David could have had his fulfillment without leaving all this devastation behind them. No longer could she think, all she could feel was revulsion for herself, confusion, conflict; and a resentment toward David that he had not been able to find a different way . . .

She got up slowly and said, "I really must leave now. Thank you for your goodness. I love you. Although I have lost the right to say it, I love you all."

"Stay, sit a few more minutes."

"No, I really must go, and besides, Harry might come home and find me here. That wouldn't be pleasant for you, and I don't think I could face him after what you've just told me." She lifted Mark off the chair and walked to the door. Esther gave Mark a bag of homemade cookies, bending over with difficulty to kiss the child, admiring him again, and followed them out into the hall.

"Where are you going now?"

"I don't know, but I'll find a place for myself and then I'll go to work. Right now I can't think."

"Listen, Katie darling, why don't you go back to Malka? I'll try to find out where they're living now."

Katie looked up in surprise and said, "What do you mean, where they're living now?"

"Of course, how would you know? Solly got a good job as a manager in a movie house somewhere in Brooklyn. I don't know where, it's so far away. And Birdie moved the whole family out there with them."

"You mean they got married?"

"Sure, and you didn't even know."

"No, how long?"

"I'm not sure. Katie, go to Malka. I'll try to find out, okay?"

"No, thank you, but I can't do this to them. Every time I'm in trouble I run to them. I won't use them this way, it's wrong. Their lives must be complicated enough without me *and* Mark."

"Listen, Katie, it's none of my business but as one

woman to another, maybe it's best you should go back to Dave." She put her hand to her mouth. "May God forgive me for using his name, I was never supposed to say it, but he never loved anyone the way he loved you. I know a lot of things must have happened the last couple of years—you don't want to talk about them, it's okay and I'm not gonna ask, but listen, he loves you, you love him, you've got a baby so . . . you must have gotten over the toughest part already. You got nobody else," she said. "Go back to him. I don't understand why he did what he did, but you're a smart girl. You try to understand him." Then as though the walls could hear, she whispered, "Between us, Katie, it should go no further, I can't altogether blame him. I try because of the family, but really I don't. I wouldn't say this to another living soul except you, but you know what his problem is? He should have been born in a different family. That's really what his whole problem is . . ."

Katie looked at Esther for what she was certain was the last time, wanting to remember her as she stood with her bulging stomach, the red hair, the freckles, the kind blue eyes and the faded blue dress for a dollar ninety-five. If Katie had missed her before now, she would miss her even more for the shared warmth of this moment, painful as it was. What she had missed most in these last years was the sharing.

They kissed and embraced, each with her separate thoughts, Esther wondering what life would be like, to face the world alone, without a husband . . . and Katie not having to wonder—she knew. One last look, then Katie, her child's hand in hers, descended the stairs as Esther stood watching them from over the banister until they were lost to sight.

The air reeked of fruit rotting on the pushcarts from the strong summer sun. The streets were teeming with women shopping for Shabbas. Tomorrow they would be at home or in the synagogue, but today was Friday and suddenly Friday became significant to her. Slowly, aimlessly she walked along with

Mark at her side. She had become a nomad since the day they had left, and now she felt as though she were floating between the disarray of both of her lives, each one being a tangled skein of disorder. It was as though there were no beginning, no end, no past, no future, just limbo, suspension in mid-air. She walked through the pandemonium, feeling out of place; she didn't belong here, she didn't belong anywhere, to anyone, to anything, and the chaos of her life closed in.

Mark had been so good, but now he was becoming very tired and tugged at his mother's coat. She stopped and looked down at the small child, taking him up in her arms and holding him tight. He was all she had, but wasn't he enough? Hadn't he made her life worth living? She leaned against a tenement. She wasn't a tower of strength; she couldn't cope with the prospect of being homeless, jobless and near penniless. In her arms the little boy pushed himself away from his mother, putting his hands up to her face and touching the tears. For his sake at least she must pull herself together and stop crying. She carried him for blocks, not knowing or caring where she was going. Above the cries of the street she thought she heard her name being called, but who would call her? Deciding it was her imagination, she did not respond, but the voice became nearer, clearer, and then there was someone behind her tapping her on the shoulder. She turned around. "Yes?"

"I didn't know if it was really you."

Chaim, the peddler. "You remember me?" he asked.

"Yes, of course I do. We bought our furniture from you . . . and then sold it back?"

"What's the matter, you're not feeling good?"

"I'm fine, thank you." Katie started to tremble. She thought she might drop Mark, and put him down. "You'll have to forgive me but I'm really not feeling too well."

"Maybe I can help?"

"No, no, thank you."

Chaim thought she was going to faint. "Listen, let me at least help you. Where are you going? You're sick, I can see."

Her teeth were chattering; even with the heat of the day she was chilled.

"Where are you going? Let me help you."

"I'm not going anywhere. I'm sorry, I'm afraid I have no place to go . . ."

Shocked, Chaim asked, "Where's your husband? I remember how beautiful he was, and you too; Where is he?"

"He's not with me."

"Not with you?"

"No, I must find a place, a room, something for the baby and me." She paused. "I guess I'm just tired and so is the baby—"

"You haven't got a room?"

"No."

"Listen, you wouldn't be insulted please, come to my place, I'll fix you something to eat, you rest for a while and then we go look for a room. Please?" He picked Mark up in his arms, walked for several blocks toward Rivington Street, turned into the alley between the rows of garbage cans and the tenements on either side to the basement where he lived, then down a long dark hall, at the end of which was a huge coal furnace with large round rusty pipes coming out of the top looking like the tentacles of some prehistoric animal. Excited now, Chaim opened the door to his room and helped Katie down the wooden steps, closing the door behind them. He sat Katie and the little boy down on the wooden chair that stood by the table, then went around the room picking up rags and old clothing, stuffing them into orange crates that he stacked upright, one on top of the other; then shoved some things under the bed.

"You know how it is, I bring all this junk home; that's why it looks this way. If I knew I would have such fine company I would have cleaned it up better. I'll fix some tea." He filled a pot with water, put it on the fire of a two-jet burner and sat down.

"You're hungry? I'll run out while the water's boiling and buy some rolls and cream cheese. I'll be right back."

As he started toward the door, Katie said, "No, please don't bother. I'm not hungry—really, the tea will be fine."

"How long will it take, a few minutes?"

"Please don't. I really couldn't eat, but thank you for your kindness."

"Just the tea?"

"Yes, thank you." She drew her coat around her, beginning to tremble again.

Chaim walked back to her.

"Listen to me, you're not feeling good; believe me, I can tell. Why don't you lie down on my bed? I'll bring you tea."

"Please don't bother. You're really so kind, I can't take advantage of you."

"Oy vay," Chaim said, "what kind of foolishness is this kind of talk? What, one person can't help another person? What are we put on this earth for, tell me? What are we here for?"

She submitted and lay down. Soon her eyelids grew heavy, and as though she could no longer resist her own will she fell into a deep sleep. Chaim held his finger up to his mouth and whispered to Mark, "We wouldn't talk too loud so your mama can sleep." Then he bent over the child, resting one hand on the table, and said, "Listen, young man, would you like a sandwich and maybe a little milk?"

Mark's vocabulary consisted of four words: mama, dada, dog and bye-bye. Perhaps there were a few other choice sounds not yet words, but they did not qualify him to carry on a long conversation with Chaim's broken English. Chaim was obliged to answer his own question.

"You would? All right, we'll fix a lox on a roll. It's not so fresh, I apologize, but I don't want we should leave mama alone and go to the bakery." He nodded to Mark and said, "So we don't care."

He went to the window to get the milk and smoked salmon that he kept in a box attached outside, then poured some milk into a glass and placed it with the sandwich in front of the child. Mark could hardly reach up to the table, sitting where he was, so Chaim put some pillows on the chair and seated himself opposite. He took a cup of tea and a sandwich for himself. The two ate.

"I knew you when you were a baby," Chaim said. "You didn't know that? Sure, you and me have been friends for years now." Chaim blinked his lively brown eyes above his full red cheeks and made funny faces at Mark, who put the glass of milk down, leaving a white moustache on his upper lip, and broke out into a broad smile.

"You see, you do remember. You know what we're going to do later? I'm going to introduce you to Bessie and Becky."

Becky was the mangy black alley cat for which Chaim put out a saucer of milk every day. He had become a grandfather by her four times since he had adopted her, and was confident he would be blessed again. He told Mark about Bessie, how she was a little sway-backed but, after all, everybody gets old, and that she wore a straw hat with artificial flowers, all different colors, and he knew that the three of them were going to be very good friends. What a little boy, Chaim thought, so well behaved, so beautiful, like a little prince. But why not? His mother is a queen, so he's a prince.

Katie lay awake with her eyes half closed and felt the covers over her. Her shoes were off but she was still in her coat, feeling warm and unusually secure as she lay here just returning from deep sleep. What a relief to let go . . . not to think . . . not to feel . . . Mark stood at the bedside observing his mother; he pulled down the cover and said, "Mama?" She opened her eyes, reached down, picked him up and held him above her head, her arms outstretched. His short legs straddled as she put him on top of her while she propped the pillow high against the wooden headboard. Mark smiled back.

"We're going to go for a walk, darling, and mama's

going to get up in a moment and find a place to live." Lifting the child down, she swung her legs over and sat on the edge of the bed for a moment.

"You had a good rest?" Chaim asked.

"Oh yes, I feel so much better, thank you. Thank you very much. What time is it?"

"Five o'clock."

"Oh my, I slept almost five hours when I should have been out looking for a place to live."

Chaim laughed happily, pleased with himself. "You slept for more than twenty-four hours, that's how tired you were."

She looked at him. "Oh no, did I really, Chaim?"

"Yes." Chaim shook his head. "So what did you lose?"

"Oh, Chaim, you should have awakened me. How did you manage with the baby?"

"What . . . it's so hard to change a little boy's pants and give him something to eat? I should have been his grandfather."

Which is what Chaim had happily pretended as he bathed Mark in a round washtub he found among his junk, scrubbing it until it shone; found clothes for the child in Katie's suitcase; fed him, after which the two of them went to get Bessie and, with Mark in the wagon alongside him, started out in the morning to buy and sell. The night before he and Mark had slept in a bed he had just bought from Stella Bloom, the widow who three months later was marrying her dead husband's brother, a relatively new arrival from Plinsk. Finding it repugnant to sleep where his brother had lain with a wife that would soon be his, and filled with the fear that she might be compelled to make comparisons in their ardor, he insisted she dispose of it. So Stella called Chaim in and sold it to him, and it was there in that former nuptial bed that he and Mark had slept.

"Chaim, Chaim, you're like a dear old friend," Katie said, holding out her hand to him. "What would I have done if I hadn't found you?"

"How could you not have? It was all arranged by fate; it was all meant to be."

She looked at him; was this the peddler that bought and sold junk? Then her eyes strayed to the stacks of books that lay in the orange crates, a volume of Shakespeare, Voltaire was there, *War and Peace*, Dostoevsky, and a *melee* of authors she had never ever heard of. Was it possible that Chaim had read these, or were they just discarded things that he had lying around the room, unable to sell to anyone? No, it was true, Chaim had read them. She then saw the phonograph with the crank attached and the large horn coming out at one side. There were records piled high on a table alongside it.

Chaim watched her as she looked and quickly said, "Would you like to hear the great Caruso sing Pagliacci?" Not waiting for the answer, he began cranking the machine. Lifting his finger in a dramatic gesture, he said, "I've got one of the oldest records there is."

But as he put the record on he thought better of it. Maybe it was too sad. "No," he said, "better an aria from *La Boheme*," and the concert began. As the phonograph played, he sang out in robust tones along with it. Although he didn't know a word of Italian, he pronounced each syllable as though he had been born in Rome, following all the phrasing and pausing at each and every nuance—he had, after all, rehearsed with the record so many times over the years. When it was over he played the Schubert Serenade on the beaten up old violin, accompanying the record of Artur Rubinstein on the piano.

Katie was fascinated with Chaim; she sat in wonderment as he performed without embarrassment, launching into an aria or reciting a verse from *King Lear*. He could have gone on all night, but suddenly she remembered she had nowhere to live. Almost two days had been wasted and reluctantly she said, "Oh, Chaim, that's beautiful. I loved it so, and thank you for sharing all this with me, but I must try to find a place tonight."

She put on her shoes, took out a comb from her purse and ran it through her hair as she asked, "May I wash up a bit?"

Chaim shrugged and said, "Why not?" Handing her a towel, he stood watching her sadly. When she finished he said, "Listen, I'm gonna say something but you must sit down first."

Katie seated herself at the kitchen table and Chaim sat opposite.

"I don't know how to begin . . . what I'm trying to say is . . . why do you have to look for another place when you and the baby could live here with me?" Eagerly now, he rushed on to convince her. "I got the room, it wouldn't cost you a cent in rent." He looked down at the table and began to play with the crumbs that were still left from the sandwich. "Listen, maybe this will sound funny—but from the minute I met you as a bride, I thought you were the most beautiful and lovely girl I ever saw, and if I had a daughter I would pray that she be like you." He clasped his hands together and held them to him, "I wish you were my daughter and the *klein kind* was my grandchild." The twinkle left his eyes as he looked up at her. "Listen, I'm a lonely old man; I've got no one. You would do me such a favor and if you don't like it here you could always move . . . except to tell you the truth I don't like the idea of a decent young girl being alone without anybody to protect her." He paused while she looked at him, "Nu, so what do you say?"

Katie was so overwhelmed at the thought of an utter stranger wanting to protect her that she could not answer, while Chaim took her silence to mean that although she did not want to be rude she would rather not stay.

"Listen, if it's because you don't have a private room I can take care of that. All I have to do is put up a big canvas across the ceiling to divide the room where the beds are and then you have a private room. And another thing, if you go to work, who'll take care of the baby?"

Finally, Katie heard herself saying, "Chaim, I don't know what to say to you except that I think I'm going to cry." Shaking her head in disbelief, she thought how good people have been to her when she needed them, and said, "How can I thank you for this?"

He shrugged his shoulders. "You can thank me by saying yes."

"Oh God, Chaim, yes, yes, yes!" And then she did cry, but they were tears of gratitude and relief.

Chaim had persuaded her not to look for a job right away, feeling she needed the time to relax and restore her spirits. She resisted at first, then happily submitted and so for the next week busied herself with the household chores. She cleaned the large basement room thoroughly, placed everything separately into neat piles, scrubbed the wooden floor, washed Chaim's socks, shirts and underclothes, the baby's things, the curtains; she pressed Chaim's work pants, darned his socks, turned the frayed collars of his shirts; cooked soup and boiled chicken, and then she did something she had not done for two years. On the first Friday night she lit two Shabbas candles and prayed for them all . . . for David too.

Against Chaim's protest she decided she finally must start to look for a job, and the following Monday was up much earlier than usual, unable to sleep as she fretted about finding work. She put some water on and when it boiled, mixed half chicory and coffee, then poured a cup for herself and sat down at the table to drink; the hot brew felt good as it went down. After roaming the streets all night Becky was meowing outside the kitchen window. Katie filled a saucer with milk and put it outside, watching as she lapped it up, and thinking, were it not for the grace of Chaim there go I—an alley cat. She went back to the table, finished her coffee, and waited for her family to awaken.

She did not have long to wait as she saw Mark's soft curly head bob up. It turned and he looked at her. Standing up in bed he held out his arms and she went to him quickly.

"Good morning, Mark, did you sleep well, my little curly top?" She changed him, brought him to the table, poured him a glass of milk and gave him a roll. Then she filled a cup for herself and sat down next to the child.

"You're getting to be a big boy, Mark," she said, and Chaim agreed as he stood in his long johns with his pants over them, the suspenders hanging at the sides.

"Is he a big boy, already a man! You should see the way he drives the wagon and Bessie. If I'm not careful pretty soon I'll be working for him." Chaim bent down to the child, kissed him on the cheek and continued, "Isn't that right, Mark?"

The child made marvelous, inarticulate sentences in response to the attention he was getting, and held out his arms to Chaim saying, "Chime, Chime, Chime."

Katie put down the cup and listened. At the look on Katie's and Chaim's faces Mark responded, repeating the word. "Chaim," Katie said touching his arm, "he's saying your name." Then she added quickly, "Say it again, Mark: Chaim, Chaim." Katie and Chaim laughed with delight at the sound of the word. Mark watched them with the white moustache of milk above his lip and laughed along with them.

"Oy gevalt, what a boy!" Chaim said, clasping his hands together. Then he went to Mark and gently pushed the little chubby cheeks together in his fingers. "What a boy. Now go eat and pretty soon we'll get Bessie and you'll sit on my lap and drive . . . O.K., nu, so eat."

"Chaim, what can I get for you?"

"What can you get for me?" He stood shaking his head. "What you can get for me I already got," he said, stretching out his arms wide as though to encompass them.

"Thank you, Chaim. When you say things like that I want to cry."

"If you wanna cry, so cry; that's all right. But first I'll take some coffee and I think maybe we've got a bagel? If so, with cream cheese and lox." Then Chaim peered at Mark and said, "Maybe you'll fix one for my boss over here. Maybe you'd like a bagel and lox? . . . Sure, fix one."

Mark was intrigued with the new word and the response it evoked. He said over and over again, "Chime, Chime, Chime."

"So why don't you take something?" Chaim asked Katie.

"I don't feel hungry, thank you."

"So force yourself a little. If not you'll get so thin nobody'll be able to see you except a thin shadow. Eat something, here, take half of mine." He handed her his plate and held the other half of the bagel in his hand.

"No, really Chaim, I couldn't eat it."

"Eat, it's good for you."

She smiled at him. "Chaim, *you're* so good for *us*."

Shrugging he said, "I'm not so good to you, I'm good to myself. You think I do these things from the goodness of my heart? No, I'm a very selfish man. Why, you ask? Because I need you more than you need me. This is no longer a cellar, a basement—it's a palace! I thank you, my *schön kind* . . ."

How easy Chaim made things for her, how poetically the words that came from his heart tripped from his tongue. Chaim, the poet of Hester Street, the benign missionary. In wonderment she shook her head. "What would I have done without you?"

"Listen, if it hadn't been me it would have been someone else. But believe me, I know that God planned this, and I thank Him that He should do this for me."

"Chaim, I think you're the most wonderful person I've met in my life, and I thank you for everything—"

"Listen," he said shyly, "if you think I'm the most wonderful person you ever met, I should tell you different, though I wouldn't." He smiled, his eyes twinkling once again.

"Chaim, I'm going to dress Mark and straighten up a bit and then I'm going downtown to look for a job. Are you sure he won't be too much for you to handle? He has to nap in the afternoons."

Laughing and shaking his head, pointing to Mark, he said, "Ask yourself the question, will I be too much for Mark to handle? You see, Mark, your Mama doesn't know so much about men. We can handle ourselves, am I right? Of course."

Katie took the subway downtown to the garment district and went from one factory to another receiving the same response, the same answer, "Not hiring, no work." They needed only skeleton crews. There were things that Katie did not know or had never heard of, in fact. America had added to its vocabulary the NRA, the WPA, the CIO and the AFL. The unions were beginning to get a little stronger in the industry and soon every factory would have to yield to their demands. One such factory had already begun to feel the pinch of unionism.

Nathan Bernstein had started his factory in 1924 with his wife, his brother, and five Puerto Rican women, all of whom managed a meager living from making curtains and draperies which he sold to small merchants in Harlem and on the East Side. In 1936 the one thing Harlem and the East Side could live without was what Nathan Bernstein produced. He had to fight and claw in order to keep his factory going. To survive he was eating into the small capital he had accumulated in twelve years, which he guarded avariciously, spending only what was necessary to sustain himself and his wife; no more, no less. He had somehow managed to survive the last two years and keep his business going, but now the unions were coming to see Nathan Bernstein a little more frequently. The NRA had been a thorn in his side which did not particularly endear Franklin Roosevelt to Nathan Bernstein, but the unions were more than he could tolerate. He could hardly keep his doors open, and now they wanted him to organize and pay union scale when it was almost impossible to make a living. Every time he saw the agent come into his office, he would look up and mutter to himself that they wouldn't be happy until he went broke. "In hell I'll see them first," he told his wife.

After ulcers and what he thought was a mild heart attack—it turned out to be indigestion—Nathan found a plan. It was like Columbus discovering America. The first thing he did was to fire the five Puerto Ricans and put an advertisement in the paper for women who wanted to sew in their own homes. The same five were advised to apply for the job; he rehired them and farmed out the work. Which was how Nathan Bernstein stayed in business.

When finally Katie came across the advertisement in the newspaper, she could hardly wait to be interviewed. This job was sent to her from above; now she could work at home, take care of Chaim and Mark and still earn money.

Katie stood in front of Nathan Bernstein's desk while he sat smoking a black stubby cigar, wet and soggy at the tip that he never took out of his mouth. As he spoke he shifted it from one side to the next while some of the saliva dribbled on his chin, which he did not bother to wipe dry. Today neither his ulcer nor his indigestion disturbed him because the response to his ad had been so gratifying. Katie heard herself saying eagerly, "I came to inquire about the advertisement."

The advertisement? To inquire?

This one he wouldn't hire with an English accent yet. Immediately he knew she would be no good, he simply knew it. Such a lady couldn't sew drapes, doilies maybe but not heavy drapes. He could afford to be choosy. What he needed was those ignorant people willing to sew their guts out for the survival of Bernstein's. "Leave your name. If I need you I'll call you."

"Please, Mr. Bernstein," she said, "I don't have a phone. There's no way for you to call me and I do need the job. I have a little boy to support and I can sew very well, if I say so myself . . . Please, don't misunderstand, I'm not bragging, but really I can. I need the job so badly."

Nathan sat back with his felt hat tipped back on his head, swiveled from side to side with his hands on the arms of the chair, chewed on the cigar, rolling it around in his mouth, and appraised her. She was so thin, but when he took a better look at her he saw the desperation in her eyes. Shaking his head slightly he asked, "You ever sewed drapes and curtains before?"

"No," she answered quickly, "but I've worked in a large dress factory. I'm sure that I can do it, and I did make some curtains for myself once."

He got up from his desk and walked out of the glass-enclosed office into the workroom, motioning Katie to follow him. He sat her down in front of one of the sewing machines and handed her a length of fabric.

"All right, so let me see how good you can sew."

She looked down at the material and wondered what to do with it. Then looking up at Nathan with the unmade drapes in her hand, she asked, "How do you want me to make them?"

"A teacher I'm not," he said impatiently. See, he said to himself, I was right in the first place. She was good for making doilies. Still . . . He walked back to the finish table where all the draperies lay stacked, ready for delivery, and brought one to her as a sample. Handing it to her he said, "All right, so sew."

Katie studied it carefully, the hems, the pleats at the top, the way the edges were tucked back. She picked up the material again, laid it in her lap, threaded the machine, folded the first pleat at the heading, slipped it under the sewing foot and peddled nervously until she had done four pleats.

Nathan examined the finished pleats; they were perfect, meticulously straight as an arrow. Under his hat he scratched his head in amazement. Who should know? Go be smart, he would have sworn she couldn't sew herself into a sack.

"All right," he said, "you got the job. I'll give you the specification of how big to make the hems and the pleats and how many I want you to make a week. The job pays $5 a hundred for drapes and $2 a hundred for sheer curtains. Here's a card; fill it out, and I'll give you the material."

She held the card in her hand and said, "Thank you, Mr. Bernstein, but I don't have a machine." She paused and added, thinking of Chaim, "I could probably get a small one—"

"You ain't got a machine? You come for a job and you ain't got a machine? I take time out, I show you how to make a drape and you ain't got a machine? From this I never heard, such a thing. You think maybe you can sew drapes on a calliope?" Oy vay, his ulcer bothered him.

Apologetically, she asked, "I'm sorry, Mr. Bernstein, but couldn't you lend me one?"

Shocked, he said, indignantly, "Lend you? Who loans me? I should loan her a machine yet." He chewed on the unlit cigar more vigorously. Gradually he calmed down as he looked at her again closely. What the hell was there about this girl he felt so sorry for, what was she to him anyway? Loan her a machine, he said to himself, such chutzpa. Then he asked, "You a Jewish girl?"

"Yes."

"You said you had to support your baby?"

"Yes."

"So where's your husband?"

She bit her lip, then answered quietly without looking at him. "We're separated."

"Oy-oy-oy, in America," he said, shaking his head. Finally: "Listen, I'll tell you what I'm going to do. I'll rent you the machine for $2 a week. You gotta have someone pick it up and anything goes wrong, you gotta fix it." As he waddled to the back of the workroom to get the fabric he mumbled to himself, there's no fool like an old fool . . . He'd have to learn to be tougher.

She came home with the two large bundles tied with heavy string and placed them neatly on the floor, hardly able to wait for Chaim and Mark to return. After cleaning the room and changing the bed sheets, she went to the kosher butcher where she bought a pound of fat chuck steak which she pot roasted and made kasha with browned onions. While it bubbled away in the two pots she ironed Chaim's shirts, washed the sheets, and set the table. This should be an occasion to celebrate so she ran down the street again and using her last dollar, she bought two roses, a piece of fern and a bottle of celery tonic. Then, clutching the change in her hand, she hurried home and waited for her family. When she saw them turn into the alley, she ran to the door, opened it wide and met them in the hall.

"Chaim, I got a job." She kissed and hugged him, picked Mark up, twirling him around.

Later, while they ate, she told Chaim how she'd got the job, what an understanding man Mr. Bernstein was and how he had rented her the machine. Chaim almost choked on the kasha. Reaching for the celery tonic, he took a drink, cleared his throat and said with disgust, "That goniff! He gives you $5 for sewing 100 drapes and you pay him two dollars for the machine? You gotta sew 60 drapes before you make a dollar for yourself."

She looked at Chaim and started to laugh. "I'm not a very good business woman, am I?" Chaim's eyes twinkled. "No, you're not," he answered. "So you're excused, you can't be perfect in everything. You're almost an angel already. Anybody that can make pot roast from chuck and it should taste like pheasant must be an angel."

"Chaim, I'm so excited about the job, I'll just have to sew more drapes."

"No, you go back and tell that goniff that your father told you either he gives you the machine for a dollar a week or you don't work for him."

"I can't do that, Chaim darling. I already told him I'd take it."

"So he can sue you if you've changed your mind?"

She laughed, "Let me see how much I make this way. Then I can always go back and tell him I'm not making enough."

"All right, do it your way; but as far as I'm concerned, nothing is enough for you."

After dinner she bathed Mark and put him to bed, washed the dishes, scrubbed the pots, then sat down at the kitchen table across from Chaim and they read until she got tired. She kissed Chaim good night, pulled the canvas drape around her bed, slipped in alongside the sleeping child and for the first time in two years fell into a contented, exhausted sleep.

The next morning, Chaim brushed and groomed Bessie, adjusted her hat, hitched her to the wagon and took her downtown to get the machine while Mark stood at the window and cried, watching Chaim as he drove up the alley. He called out, "Chime."

"Don't cry, Mark, Chaim will be right back and he'll take you out later with Bessie. Darling, don't cry." She wiped the tears away, squatting down to his side. "I'll tell you what, if you help mama clean the house, I'll take you for a walk and buy some ice cream. How does that sound?" She took the pots from the shelf and set them down on the ground, letting him play with them, banging them together while she went back to straightening up the place. When she had finished she took Mark for a walk, proudly holding his hand as they walked up Ludlow Street, purposely avoiding Hester Street. The stores were not the familiar ones that she had known but they were much the same, and in the week since she had been back she had not wanted to venture far from home for fear she would see the face of someone she knew, particularly one of the Rezinetskys. It was as though Chaim's room was a haven; there she could shut out Hester Street and all its memories as though they were a million miles away. But today she felt buoyant with happiness and a new sense of assurance as she and Mark sat down at a small table in the candy store. She bought him an ice-cream cone and one for herself. Soon Mark's began dripping, getting all over his clean shirt. Oh dear, this was not a good idea, she thought, and she asked for a saucer and a spoon. She started to feed him, but he took the spoon from Katie's hand, saying, "No, mama." Smiling as she watched him feed himself, she thought how independent he was becoming, so grown-up . . . He seemed to thrive in the most difficult circumstances. The way he had adjusted to his new environment amazed Katie, but then perhaps all children did this;

perhaps, but so far as she was concerned he was exceptional.

Quite suddenly she was overcome with a feeling of sadness as she observed her child and saw David in him—he must have looked like this at Mark's age. Her feelings of loneliness came back with the thought that she and David were lost to one another, that he would miss . . . no, rather, be deprived of seeing his child grow up. She had spent the last few weeks living in a fool's paradise, so shocked and numbed that until now she had not been able to accept the real impact of what had happened. As though wearing blinders, she had looked neither to the right nor to the left—only straight ahead, and without seeing. She would never see David again. He had asked for her understanding and forbearance, and she had withheld it. When he needed most to share with her his own despair, she had withdrawn. No man could be expected to take such a woman in the night and hold her close, and would she have respected a man who pleaded for what was his right as a husband? And now she would lie in her bed alone and have the rest of her life to remember, covered with the veil of her tears.

She wiped Mark's hands and face and took him home.

The first thing she saw when she entered the room was the sewing machine and Chaim grinning broadly.

"Nu, so what do you think?" he asked.

"I think it's wonderful," she answered, hoping not to betray her mood to him. "Did you have a hard time getting it downstairs into the wagon?"

"What hard time? That goniff helped me down with it. Listen, I'll tell you what I did . . . that is, if you don't mind." Katie shook her head. "Once I had the machine in the wagon I said to the goniff, 'Listen, my daughter wouldn't pay you $2 a week. What, a dollar isn't enough for a machine that should sit here and rot from not being used? You'd lose money?' And the goniff said, 'Rich I wouldn't get either.' So I said, 'You either take the dollar or back the machine goes.' " Chaim laughed happily at the great coup that he had masterminded. He hesitated a moment and then admitted, "To tell the truth, happy he wasn't, but he took it. Nu, so you see, you do need a Papa."

She went over to him and put her head on his shoulder. He was a moment in the goodness of man, he was today, he was the world; in him was the rejoicing, in him was the solace and the need. She said, "Oh, Chaim, you will never know how much I need you." He put his arms around her like a father, a father who loves his child, with Mark standing alongside saying "Chime." Then he put his curly head on Chaim's knee and stuck his thumb in his mouth. And the three of them remained so, for one brief, close moment in time shutting out the world around them.

That night after dinner, when Mark had been bathed and put to bed, Katie started to sew while Chaim read and played "Moonlight Sonata." Mark slept, accustomed now to the sounds of soft voices and music.

Katie had been pensive and withdrawn all afternoon and during supper. More concerned than uncomfortable, Chaim looked up from his book, observing her expression. He questioned himself whether or not he had the right to invade her privacy, to share the thoughts she was living with at the moment. Since she had been here he had asked no questions, she had not been prepared to talk about her problems; but tonight it hurt him deeply to see her so disturbed. Hesitatingly he said, "Katela, what's wrong? Let me help you. Talk to me, that's what I'm here for."

Not sure that she could discuss this, even with Chaim, she kept on sewing without looking up.

"Chaim, I would tell you anything, but there are some things that are too painful to talk about."

"I know, but if you talk sometimes it stops being so painful."

She put the sewing aside.

"I feel ashamed of so many things, Chaim."

"You think you're alone? What person ever lived a life without feeling regret or shame, but what could you have done to feel such shame? Tell me?"

Leaving the machine, she walked over to the sink and put up some water for tea, then turned back to Chaim—his thick silver hair and his moustache, fit for an archangel, resplendent in the glimmering light of the exposed globe that was suspended by a cord above the kitchen table. Could she tell him about David and herself without earning his contempt? Dare she reveal her own weaknesses to him without losing his admiration? Would she destroy his love, his respect? This was a religious man whom love of God has sustained and whose soul was nourished by faith. Dare she risk this? He held out his hand in trust for her to take. Could she accept it? But hadn't she accepted the bed he had given her and the roof with which he had sheltered her and the board he had shared with her so willingly? If she accepted all these things, did she have the right to deceive him? For that was what she felt she was now doing.

"Chaim, would you like a cup of tea?"

Understanding the difficulty she was having, he answered, "Yes, with lemon if we have some." She poured the tea for both of them and cut up the lemon wedge, put it in a large glass for Chaim and took a cup for herself, poured milk and sugar into it, then brought them to the table and sat down opposite him. Sipping the tea through a lump of sugar held between his teeth, he waited for Katie to speak as the sugar lump melted in his mouth. She took the tea to her lips, then put it down without touching it, picked up the spoon, stirring the tea aimlessly. She began tentatively. "You remember when we left?"

"Yes," he answered.

"But you don't know why. You thought we were moving to California because we didn't like it here. Well that's not the reason." She bit her lip hard, hesitated, and then continued. "We left . . . because . . . I don't know how to say this," she said, looking up at him.

"Say it, whatever it is, I'll understand. You didn't kill anybody, you didn't rob anybody, you just left. Millions of people do that."

"Yes, but not for the reason we did." She moistened her lips, "Chaim, people can rob other people without taking their possessions. Yes, we did rob, we robbed people of their trust and their health and even their sanity."

He did not answer, allowing her to talk.

"Yes, Chaim, that's what we did, David and I." Very softly she said, "We left because David no longer wanted to be a Jew."

They sat in silence for a while. The silence was broken as Katie began again, and now that she had started it was as though a dam had broken loose.

"We went to Chicago and lived there for two years. Chaim, during those two years I thought we would die, being cut off from everything and everybody. I made no friends, there was nothing to hold on to. Life just seemed so empty, and yet, here I am living with you in a basement, cooking on two burners and making a home when I had the same thing there. But I couldn't do it with David. If he were here living with me in this same place I would be happy, but not living as an alien, not living a lie. You see, Chaim, the whole thing just seemed so meaningless, without reason. Life was just as difficult there as it had been here, but there were no compensations there. If you give up one thing there needs to be something else to replace it. I love being Jewish. The most security I ever had in my whole life was in this place." She paused, hoping for his understanding. "Two people have to agree on something as important as this, and when they don't the result is what we have."

The record was no longer playing music, only grinding noises as Chaim got up to turn it off. Not sure that she had finished, he remained silent.

"I'm afraid you hate me now—"

He reached over and took her hand. "Oh my dear child, how could I hate you? First of all, is it for me or anyone else to judge you or David for something he was unhappy with? It must have been very hard for him too. Giving up something like Judaism doesn't come easy."

She looked at him in amazement. "Chaim, who are you? You know so much about people I find it frightening."

"Who am I? I'm a man who's lived a long time and seen many things, a lot of people, and a lot of suffering. Who am I? I'm nobody, that's who I am."

"I feel so guilty about everything. If I hadn't gone with David I would have felt guilty, so I consented to go. But there were times I hated him for being unable to accept what he had been born, to live his life as other Jews do. I went through so many different feelings sometimes I thought I would go insane. I loved him, I hated him, I felt sorry for him, I pitied him; then I pitied myself, I hated myself, I went through all the same feelings for myself as I did for him. But the guilt I feel most keenly was for not having been woman enough to stand by my husband when he really needed me, and I'm paying for it now. He'll never have me back again."

They remained silent until Chaim asked, "This is a foolish question, but you miss him very much, no?"

"Yes, in spite of myself. Today is my worst day. Chaim, the thought of never seeing him again is more than I can bear."

Chaim hesitated for a moment, then said, "Listen, I'll tell you what I think you should do. Write him a letter. You know, between two young people who have different ideas, until they can agree on the same things they fight. Because you're not together now doesn't mean it's forever. Only death is forever. Take my advice, write a nice letter."

"Do you think it will do any good?"

"Harm it can't do. Believe me, David is just as sad as you are, he misses you as much as you miss him. What do you think, a man is like the rock of Gibraltar? He's a man, nu, so he's got fears and pride." Shaking his finger, he said, "Pride, that's the worst of all. When a man's pride is hurt, he acts like a wounded lion. You think that you can walk away from him and he won't worry about you and the baby? Don't be foolish; write a letter."

"Chaim, may I ask you something else?"

"Me you can ask anything and I wouldn't think it was foolish."

"Somehow or other I can't quite make myself understand why David found it so impossible to be a Jew. He told me the reasons, over and over again, but somehow I can't find them enough. When you think of Jews with all their suffering who never thought of giving up their Jewishness, why was it so unbearable for David? Why, Chaim, why?"

"Oy, *mein teueres kind,* I suppose you would have to go back a thousand generations to find out why a man turns out to be the way he is. What is a hardship for one man, another finds easy. What one man hates, another loves. So who can say why? But one thing we do know, David wasn't happy being a Jew. To say that I don't think it's very sad, I do, but to condemn him for that I couldn't. But Katie, you must realize that it would be as much a lie to live being a Jew and hating it as what you think he is doing now. To be something and not also to believe it is a lie." He took a sip of tea, cleared his throat and continued. "One important thing you must remember, whatever David was when you married him, he is now. The same person that you thought you could live with all your life is there. If you loved him then, you should love him still—he's the same person."

"Oh, Chaim, how did you come into my life? I feel as though I had known you forever—"

"Maybe you have. Who really knows about these things? Whatever the reason I thank God that we found each other. Now go to sleep. Don't sew any more tonight; tomorrow is another day."

Katie was left alone with her thoughts, staring down at the writing paper on the table. She picked up a pen and tried to say the things she was feeling but the words would not come. She started one sentence but it seemed all wrong. Crumbling the paper into a ball, she started again. Should she begin with "Dearest David," "Dear David"? Should she appeal to him, tell him about her loneliness, that life without him was meaningless; should she be casual, aloof? How do you write a letter to a husband who no longer wants you? If she said, please David, let's try again, and he meant absolutely what he had said, that he no longer wanted her, would she be able to live with that? True, what he had said was in a moment of extreme anger, but if after living by himself these last weeks he found life more satisfying, more tranquil without her; then what? If her letter evoked pity and he was willing to take her back only for that reason, how secure would their future be together? She was so confused, she wasn't thinking clearly. But the letter had to be written; Chaim was quite right. David ought to know where his son was. She could not allow him to think that she was living with Malka, and she knew he would naturally assume that. Should she tell him she was living with Chaim and the circumstances in which she had come to be with him? Would he be able to understand her living with a stranger, even if he knew the truth? She decided not to say anything. She felt he would be deeply hurt that his family had turned away from her, and above all, she would not hurt him further by telling him about his mother and what had happened as a result to his father. In the end, she thought it best to be brief, and prayed that this was the right thing to do.

Dear David,

When I arrived in New York I learned that Birdie and Solly had been married and that they had moved to Brooklyn, Malka and the family moving with them. In view of the fact that I had not been in touch with them over the last two years I felt it would be wrong to impose myself upon them, much as they undoubtedly would have wanted me to do so.

Fortunately I have found work and I believe that I will be able to support myself and the baby. I have a place to live and things have turned out better than I expected. Life is not what I would have hoped for, but it is tolerable.

I hope life for you is good and that this letter finds you content and in the best of health.

Love,
Katie

She examined the letter. It was not what she had wanted to say at all; she wanted to say, David I love you, I miss you, come take me home, let's try once again. This time I will try harder. But this she could not say; she was finding things out about herself, too, that pride was not David's shortcoming alone. It was hers, as well. She folded the letter, placed it inside the envelope, sealed it, wrote David's address, turned it over, put her address on the back, and stamped it.

Later as she dropped the letter into the mailbox, she wanted to retrieve it, certain she should have said more.

CHAPTER EIGHT

David fit the key into the lock and let himself into the room. The heat of the day hung heavily in the stagnant air. Going to the window, he pulled it up as far as he could. The room was full of flies, and a large miller flew from the lamp to the wall and back again. He swatted flies with the evening newspaper and was about to attack the moth when it flew out of the window. Walking to the kitchen, he struck a match on the wall and lit the two burners. He put the coffee left over from breakfast on one of them, then opened a can of beans with a sharp knife, took a small pot out of the sink where the dishes had been left for days, rinsed out the remains of food that had accumulated, examined the inside, scraped it out with a spoon, emptied the beans into it and put it on the other burner. He washed his face and hands in the sink, groped for a towel and dried himself. He sat on the edge of the unmade bed—the linen had not been changed for ten days—and let his right shoe fall thump to the floor, then the other, and smelled the beans now scorching at the bottom of the pot and the coffee boiling and sputtering through the lid. Turning off the gas, he grabbed the pot handle. It was hot and he burned himself. Cursing, he dropped it back on the stove. He let the water run cold on his hand until the stinging subsided. Taking up the pot again, this time with a towel around his hand, he poured the beans into Mark's cereal bowl, leaving the burnt part at the bottom. He turned on the radio he'd bought since Katie had gone. It helped keep him from going mad in the silence she had left behind her.

He lay down on the bed, crossing his long legs out in front of him, leaning against the pillows, and finally took a taste of the beans. They were also burnt but he ate them anyway. Bending over, he picked up the coffee cup, took one sip and spat it out; it was stale and bitter. He got off the bed, went to the icebox and took out a bottle of warm beer—he also hadn't bothered to buy ice since Katie left. Holding the bottle close to him, he worked at prying off the cap, which came off so abruptly that the beer spewed out like a geyser and hit him in the eye. For God's sake, he couldn't do anything right. He threw the glass into the sink. It broke. To hell with it. Back on the bed, he lay staring at the ceiling, his hands behind his head, while Carmen Lombardo sang "When whippoorwills call and evening is nigh, I hurry to my blue heaven . . ." He wanted to strangle Carmen Lombardo—instead was forced to settle for the knob on the radio, which he wrenched viciously to "off." As he got back onto the bed he spotted an envelope under his door. For a moment he could only stare down at it. Katie . . . it was from Katie, who else?

Excitedly he ripped open the envelope, took out the letter and sat on the edge of the bed, his hands trembling slightly as he held it. As his eyes scanned the paper and he read, "Dear David," he knew again how much he had missed her. When he finished, he read it again, hoping that the second time he would find something that he had not seen before. Wasn't it brief, he thought, but she had ended, "Love, Katie." He let it lie in the palms of his hands. He picked up the envelope and looked at her return address, trying to picture exactly where she lived. Although he was familiar with the general location he just couldn't place the building. Putting the letter back into the envelope, staring ahead, his eyes moved to the empty crib, and suddenly he wanted to hold Mark and hear his voice as it now sounded from memory in his ears, childish sounds echoing in the silence of the room. His temper had possessed him when he had told her to leave that night, and he'd regretted it the minute he got to the bottom of the stairs. Damn it, why hadn't he gone back the way he'd wanted to do? He'd been halfway up the stairs on his way back to her . . . it was his damned pride . . . He thought now how he'd walked the streets half the night, debating with himself about going back. He wanted her to love him so that no matter where he went or what he decided to do he would be enough for her. Maybe he wanted too much from her . . . and maybe their problem was she'd never fought with him openly.

She loved him up to a point, stayed only because she thought eventually he would realize he had made a terrible mistake . . . well, on that score, at least, *she* couldn't have been more mistaken. He hated it here, but to go back and kiss their asses and plead with them that he had been misguided . . . Katie could not seem to understand that when he had made this commitment it was final. Why couldn't she have loved him enough to let go of the past?

But sitting there with her letter in his hands, it was he who couldn't let go of the past. He'd turned her out, alone, and with their child. How manly had that been? How much understanding had he given her in the last few years? Of course it had been a terrible thing for her, being cut off. For the first time she'd had people who loved and wanted her. She loved his family. Maybe he hadn't eased her into this gradually enough. Maybe it had been too soon after their marriage, she was just beginning to take hold of her life when the rug was pulled out from under her . . . But what the hell good was all this now? He'd done the best he could at the time. You can't think of everything, can you? Otherwise, you'd be the smartest man in the world, and tonight he thought he was anything but that.

Still, he was getting damn tired of feeling so guilty. . . . Taking the letter out of the envelope again he walked back to the radio, switched it on and sat on the edge of the bed to reread the letter. Pretty damn short, wasn't it? . . . not a word about whether she'd seen Bertha, or Esther, or his mother. . . . They surely would not have condemned her for what he had done. . . . It was his decision, they knew that, and knowing it, they must have been damn pleased she'd left him. He could see them now, rubbing their hands together, saying, See, he's got exactly what he had coming to him. And you, dear Katie, we understand why you went, you were only showing your wifely devotion and loyalty, we knew how you disapproved of what he'd done and we forgive you. After all, you were so young and innocent and now you've come to your true senses. Good, let him rot alone, it's the best thing you ever did . . . Bravo!

And he could see them at the Friday night dinner as they passed the matzo ball soup and the roast chicken, Esther screaming at the kids, his father playing the grand old man while the rest of the family gathered dutifully around. He could see the holy man holding *his* son, playing with him, telling Katie, You did right . . . And if papa said so it must have been so, because papa had a direct line to God, and there was only one God and he was on the side of Isaac Rezinetsky. If papa said so, then God despised David. That's the kind of terms the old man was on with God . . .

David lit a cigarette and walked around the room, inhaling the smoke deeply into his lungs, conjuring up the images that did not exist, and the more he thought, the larger became his fantasies. He could just hear the women huddled around the table when dinner was over while papa and the boys sat in the front room debating about who said what in the Midrash while the kids ran around playing tag. He could just hear them asking Katie what happened in Chicago, what was it to live like a goy? He could just hear Katie telling her terrible experiences to all of them. He could just hear it . . . and when she had finished, she would be crying and his mother would put her arms around her, saying everything was all right now that she had come home, and the others would whisper among themselves as they pulled him limb from limb. And especially he could just see his father now, hearing the tail-end of the story and screaming out, *"From this night on we never speak of him in this house."*

"Okay, papa, okay," David screamed back in the

silence of the room. "Okay, Katie, talk. Who needs you? Not a word in the letter about anything. It's like you really want to show me, like I'm out in the cold and you're in, you're beloved and welcome. Well, *fine*, that's fine, I don't *need* you. Remember, I kicked you out, you didn't leave me, tell them *that*." He crushed out the cigarette. The letter, what the hell did it really say? Not a damned thing, not a word about Mark, not a word of regret, not a word of love, not a word that she'd like to come back. . . . Fine, he wouldn't take her back if she came on her knees. . . . She had them, they had her . . . good luck to all of them.

He tore up the letter and threw it on the floor, turned up the radio, took off his shirt and pants, put on his robe, took a bath towel he'd used more than a few times before and walked down the hall to the bathroom. He tried the knob. The door was locked so he walked back to his room, lit another cigarette and waited five minutes. He walked back and tried the door again. It was still locked. This time he knocked. The voice on the other side of the door called out, "Keep your pants on, I'll be right out."

He leaned against the wall, taking one drag after another. Finally he knocked on the door so hard he hurt his hand and yelled, "When the hell you coming out, how long you going to stay in there? There are other people on this floor, you know . . ."

In her own good time Dolly Swan opened the door and stood framed in the doorway, her bleached hair almost orange, the hazel eyes buried deep in the dark circles that surrounded them. The contour of her mouth had been drawn by bright lip rouge into a Cupid's bow. The contrast against her white skin was startling. Her body was slim, her pelvic bones limned into sharp peaks under the sheer nightgown and thin negligee.

David had never said one word to the accommodatingly skilled Miss Swan in two years when they'd met on the stairs, coming or going, but tonight she stood looking at David, figuring maybe she wouldn't have to go out after all. It was all so neighborly, and besides it was convenient, right next door. His little wife, that frump, had left him. She'd had her ear to the wall when he kicked her out. How long had it been, about two weeks or more? Well, she knew men, and this one was just about ripe. His room or hers, she wondered. Shouldn't take long . . .

"Hi, sugar, want me to scrub your back—"

"Please get out of the way—"

"That's not very neighborly . . . Come on, sweetie, let's be friends. You know, a friend helps when you're lonesome. I know your wife's—"

"Don't you ever mention her . . . I don't want her name to come out of your mouth. Now, please, get the hell out of the way."

Laughing, still toying with him, she said, "Make me."

He pulled her out into the hall, then slammed and locked the door behind him, not entirely unaware of the sanctimonious ring to his words. He washed out the tub as though she had leprosy, let the hot water run till it was half-filled, and got into the tub with the tap still running and the pipes banging. The water was a rusty color, but he lay back until the tub was filled and soaked himself while the steam became so thick he could not see the door. There he lay, trying to soothe his indignations.

That night he hardly slept. He smoked in the dark, the only light in the room coming from the glow of his cigarette.

The next day he went to the post office, a block from work, and mailed Katie a five-dollar money order. She had made her letter short. Well, he would do better. The money order would come to her without a word. He would do this every week from now on, and nothing more. Nothing. He was through with her, all through, his betrayal finally exonerated by her. She was out of his life for ever and ever, amen.

CHAPTER NINE

Katie was at the machine sewing a pair of sheer curtains when Chaim burst into the room waving an envelope in his hand.

"Look what I've got, see?"

Excitedly she took it from him, fumbling with it nervously. Smiling at Chaim, she opened it carefully. When she put her fingers in the envelope and took out only the money order, the smile faded. Once again she looked, but that was all there was. She sat stunned. Why hadn't David written a word? Was he really that angry? After all these weeks? She put the envelope down on the table as Chaim stood by in awkward silence.

"Maybe he'll send a letter still, maybe he didn't have the time . . ."

She looked up at him. "No, Chaim, this is his way of telling me he no longer wants me." She started to cry. "Oh, Chaim, I want to die." She lay down on the bed to cry her heart out. Chaim felt helpless and angry with himself because he had told her to write, and then thought perhaps it had been too soon, the time had been wrong. . . . He sat on the edge of the bed and stroked her hair and held her close, rocking her back and forth like a child.

"No, no, Katie, my darling little girl, don't cry. It must be a mistake. He'll write, you'll see."

Each week David sent the money order. Katie knew he would not write and still she opened the envelope with anticipation, until finally she no longer anticipated. She cashed the money order and took out a savings account for Mark, feeling this money was for him—she would never use it—and put the passbook inside the heart box.

As the months passed she submerged herself in her work, sewing sometimes into the early hours of the morning, until finally she succeeded in stopping thought. She would have to live without David. She steeled herself against hoping it would ever be different. She had her child and, thank God, she had Chaim.

The summer was now over. Each day she looked out to the gray, dismal alley. The room was becoming very cold, so Chaim got a small electric heater and she kept the kettle boiling. Mark could no longer go with Chaim and soon it would be impossible for Chaim to take Bessie out. Katie wondered how she would be able to get the draperies back to Mr. Bernstein, but she would not worry about that now. She didn't have long to wait though. It started to snow on the second of December.

She awoke on a Friday shivering from the cold. Getting out of bed she slipped into her coat, wrapped a blanket around herself and attached the plug to the heater. Striking a match, she turned on the gas jet and put up the kettle to boil. Looking out to the bleakness of the winter, to the snow, that lay like a blanket in the alley beyond, Katie heard Becky mewing. Opening the window she gently took the cat by the scruff of her neck and lifted her inside. As Chaim had predicted about the motherly Becky, she was pregnant again and Katie was afraid that her time had come as she held and petted her. Not quite sure how she could help Becky as a midwife, she put some clean rags in a box and lifted the cat into it gently.

When she heard Mark awaken, Katie pulled the canvas back as he started to jump out of bed.

"No, Mark, don't get up yet, it's still too cold. Stay tucked under the covers for a little while, darling. Mommy will bring you some milk." She opened the window once again and reached out for the milk, which had frozen solid through during the night. After putting it under the hot water to melt, she poured some into a pan and made hot chocolate.

Chaim was now up and came cheerfully to the table.

"Good morning, my little Katie. Oh ho, look what we have here. Soon we have a few more mouths to feed, I see." Chaim bent down, "Becky, Becky, what am I to do with you? Such a girl, tch."

Katie stood beside him. "I think her time has come," she said with a smile. "Chaim dear, what do you feel like having this morning, some eggs?"

"All right, so scramble me some with lox, if it's not too much trouble."

She smiled again and shook her head, "No, darling, it's not too much trouble." She went over to Mark. "Come on, love, let me change your pants under the covers, then you can eat with Chaim. Here now, let's put your coat on first."

He bounded out of bed and ran to kiss Chaim.

"You slept good, Mark?"

"Good," Mark answered. He was beginning to repeat everything.

"Oy vay, pretty soon we wouldn't be able to say a word without the professor saying it first."

"First," Mark said.

"Do you want an egg, Mark?"

"Egg."

Chaim laughed.

They sat down to breakfast and Katie said, "I'm going to call Mr. Bernstein. You won't need to take the things today if he can do without this order; otherwise I'll take them."

"No," Chaim protested, "I'm taking them. I'm not going to let you go out in this weather. So it's the first time I was out in the snow?"

"No, but you coughed last night and I think perhaps you're coming down with a little cold."

"What cold, so I coughed, that means I got a cold?"

"Nevertheless, I'm going to call—really, Chaim. If I don't have to go downtown and give the order back, what difference will it make?"

"Don't be foolish, it wouldn't hurt if I go out, believe me. How long will it take?"

"Please, Chaim, let me telephone."

"No, it's settled. I'll go get dressed."

"Me too, mommy," said Mark, scooting off the chair, ready to be dressed.

"No, sweetheart, you can't go with Chaim today. It's too cold."

He began to fuss and beg.

"No, love, you stay home with mommy." Taking him by the hand she said, "Come, say hello to Becky. Say hello, Becky." They walked to the box where she lay awaiting her grand event. Mark peered inside and started to pet her but she made funny noises and bared her teeth, so Mark pulled his hand away and just stood watching her.

After Chaim was dressed, Katie pulled his coat around him and put the muffler high on his neck.

"Are you sure you should do this, Chaim? It's so cold."

He smiled at her; how happy she made him. She cared so much . . . Nobody had done that since . . . he had long forgotten when.

"Don't ask foolish questions," he said.

"Are you warm enough?"

"I'm warm enough. Don't fuss over me," he said, loving it. He bent down and picked Mark up, looking into his eyes. "I'm going to bring you something, a present. Listen, you're the man now, remember you got two ladies to take care of and maybe you'll be an uncle today, so you wouldn't cry when I go, ha? . . . No, you wouldn't cry." He kissed the little boy and held him close for a moment, then bent down and picked up the two large bundles that became heavier each week with the burden of Katie's need to forget. Mark waved his hand and watched sadly as Chaim walked down the alley between the tenements to the street beyond. Katie dressed Mark warmly, took down the pots so he could play, washed the breakfast dishes, tidied up and then began to sew.

At eleven o'clock on December 2 Becky quietly gave birth to five kittens in that cold basement. She licked them and got them ready for life. Mark was present at the moment of birth and called out excitedly, "Mommy, Mommy, kitty, kitty."

Katie left her sewing and walked over to the box, smiling as she bent down and took Mark's hand in hers. "Well, Becky, aren't we lucky to have such fine sons? Look, Mark, aren't they tiny?"

Mark put his hand out to touch one, but Katie gently stopped him.

"No, darling, they're too young to play with today, but pretty soon you'll be able to hold them. You can stand here and watch, though." Katie poured a saucer of milk for Becky and left it outside the box for her. Then she went back to her sewing while Mark kneeled down and looked inside the box, his eyes large with wonder.

At noon Katie wondered why Chaim was not back, but knowing he would be home soon, she began to heat the soup and boiled beef for lunch. When she glanced out the window to the alley where it was snowing gently, she saw him trudging slowly toward the house and went down the hall to help him with the new material he had brought back.

"Oh, Chaim, you must be frozen, you poor darling. Come, let me take a bundle."

"Why, you think I'm too frozen to hold a bundle? Go open the door."

When he came in Mark ran to kiss him and said excitedly, "Chime, Chime, look, look—kitty, kitty," as he led Chaim by the hand.

Chaim looked down at the new mother. "Beckela, I don't mind being a grandfather, but to five all at once? I'm an old man, I can't stand the excitement."

Katie called out, "Chaim, come sit down and let me help you off with your galoshes." As she bent down to unbuckle them he stroked her hair. "You once asked me where I came from, now I ask the same question . . . where did you come from? But more than that, how was I so lucky?"

She looked up at him. "Oh, Chaim, be quiet and let me help you off with your overcoat so we can have a nice hot lunch."

"You know, Katela, I'm not so hungry. Maybe I'll just lie down for a while, then I'll get up and eat."

"Just a little hot soup, you'll feel better, please."

"No, darling, later, later. Now I'll snooze." He smiled and patted her on the shoulder, then went to his bed and sat down heavily. Katie followed him.

"I knew you shouldn't have gone, Chaim darling, I feel terrible. You're catching a cold, I just know it."

"Don't feel so terrible. Worse things than this I've lived through. Now do me a favor, go eat with the baby. If you don't take him away from that cat you'll see he'll marry one yet." They laughed.

"Don't laugh," Chaim said. "You'd like to be mother-in-law to a kitty? Go eat, darling, go eat." He leaned back, falling asleep almost at once on top of the bed, and Katie covered him with the blanket she had worn earlier that morning.

Chaim awoke at four in the afternoon and rubbed his eyes, but lay without moving. He really did not feel well. He forced himself to get up, though, so as not to worry Katie, and not wanting her to blame herself because he had gone out this morning. Hadn't he insisted on going? But women were like that, and somehow he felt suddenly like a child with a mother fussing over him, and he loved every delicious minute of it. He came to the kitchen table and sat down.

"How do you feel now, Chaim?"

"What, I felt bad before?"

"Tell me . . . how do you feel?"

"Fine. What, there's something wrong with me, I should feel sorry for myself? Maybe I should go to Miami and lie in the sun?"

Mark said, "Sun."

Chaim turned to him. "Mark, maybe you'd like to go to Miami and we'll all lie in the sun?"

Mark nodded his head and pointed to the box, saying, "Kitty, kitty."

Katie heated the beef and soup once again, put some into an old-fashioned soup bowl and set it down in front of Chaim. He picked up the large spoon, not really wanting to eat but forcing himself to do so. Halfway through, he put the spoon down. Katie understood, and worried.

"Chaim, I have some water on for tea."

"Ah, that's perfect—a big hot glass of tea and maybe a little schnaps."

Tiring of watching the kittens, Mark came over and wanted to get up onto Chaim's lap, but the old man said, "It's enough already, I kissed you this morning before I remembered I had a cold. It was already too late when I did. So you just sit over there across from me and we drink tea together.

"Waitress, bring a cup of tea, sugar, and lots of milk for my best friend." He pounded hard on the table, making tinkling sounds with the spoon. Mark seemed delighted, and Chaim kept it up until the tea came and he and Mark drank together, Chaim lifting his glass and toasting, *"L'chayim."* Mark imitated him, even trying to repeat the word.

Half that night Chaim coughed. In the morning Katie went to his bed. He looked as though he had a fever, and she felt his head.

"Chaim, you're not getting out of bed today. I'll go to the drug store and get some aspirin."

"No, no, I never took an aspirin in my whole life. At my age I should start now?"

"Chaim, it will help you. Please, let me go and get it."

"No, it's not necessary, believe me. No, don't come too close . . . that's all we need is for you to get a cold."

"Chaim, don't be afraid. I never catch colds."

"Never mind, don't be so brave."

She fixed some tea and brought it to him.

Mark awoke with a slight sniffle. Katie made him stay in bed too because the room was still cold. Perhaps he could get up later, but not now. She fixed him an egg and some hot chocolate, which he ate in bed.

Chaim called out from the other side of the canvas, "Nu, so how's everything with you this morning, Mark?"

Mark said, "Fine," then added "thanks," at Katie's prompting.

"You saw the new family this morning, the kitties?"

"No," Mark answered, shaking his head.

"Oy vay, Mark, I forgot to give you your present yesterday. Katie, look in my coat pocket."

Katie handed Mark a coloring book and some crayons, then whispered in his ear. He repeated, "Thank you, Chime."

Chaim called out, "Play the Chopin waltz so that Mark can have some inspiration. You'll see, he'll be a great artist yet. Go make a picture, Mark."

Mark colored while Chaim slept most of the day, refusing supper.

The next day Mark's cold grew worse, and he started to cough the same as Chaim. Now, despite Chaim's protests Katie got dressed and went to Faverman's drug store. She asked Mr. Faverman what he could suggest for both Mark's and Chaim's cough.

The medicine in hand, she ran home as quickly as possible on the slippery pavement. Crushing half an aspirin in a teaspoon, she filled the spoon with milk and gave it to Mark, then poured some cough syrup into a small glass and held Mark's chin rigidly as he squirmed. Once it was in his mouth he swallowed it, shaking his head back and forth, making dreadful faces as it went down. But when it came to Chaim, the patient was more vehement than Mark.

"Now you listen to me, Chaim. You're going to take this aspirin. Open your mouth."

"Leave them on the table next to the bed with a glass of water and I'll take."

She looked at him dubiously.

"I'll take, believe me, I'll take."

"No, Chaim darling, you're going to take them now and in front of me."

"Oy vay, like a regular policeman. You don't trust me?"

"With everything else." She smiled. When she poured the dark red syrup into a large tablespoon he put up his hands in protest. "That I wouldn't do, not even for you," and turned his head away from her as she followed him with the spoon, cupping her free hand under it to catch any spills.

"Chaim, you're being worse than Mark. I'm just shocked. Now you please take this, it's really very pleasant—"

"Nu, so if it's so pleasant, please, you take it."

"Oh Chaim, I give up. I didn't know you were such a baby, so stubborn."

"Listen, I got plenty of other faults too."

The next day Chaim began to wheeze and she became truly alarmed. Mark had slept badly all through the night and his breathing this morning was labored. She felt his forehead; he was burning up with fever. When he opened his eyes they were glazed. He just lay there looking at her. Seized with panic, Katie got whatever she could find and covered him, then went to Chaim. His false teeth were in a glass of water that made them appear doubled in size. Opening his eyes, he tried to reach for the glass but couldn't, attempting to hide his toothlessness from her. As he lay in his bed gasping for air, he thought wryly, vanity, vanity, all the world is vanity. Including a sick old man's . . .

Katie soothed him. "Just rest, Chaim dear. I'm going to get a doctor." Barely able to conceal her dismay, she dressed as quickly as she could and left.

Her breath steamed against the cold morning air as she made her way to Faverman's. There were old newspapers strewn about in the snow, and as she walked they clung to her shoes. Trying to free herself by shaking her foot but unable to separate them, she walked on. Pounding on Mr. Faverman's door frantically, she peered through the glass, wiping away the steam formed by her breath. Soon a door opened and she saw a light as Mr. Faverman came from the back of the store, his bathrobe around him. Unlocking the glass door, he let her in.

"I'm not open yet," he said.

"Please, Mr. Faverman, you must help me, Chaim and the baby are very sick and I don't know of a doctor. Can you help me, please?"

Seeing how distraught she was, he said gently, "I'll

call, you just wait. Maybe it's not as serious as you think."

"It's very serious, I just know it is. Thank you for being so kind, Mr. Faverman, but I'm terribly alarmed."

As he waited for the call to be completed he said, "Listen, everything will be all right, you'll see." Their conversation was interrupted by someone answering the phone. "Yes, this is Mr. Faverman. Can I speak to Dr. Goldberg?" Katie tried to control her nerves as the druggist waited for Mrs. Goldberg to wake her husband.

Finally the doctor came on.

"Bernard? Faverman speaking. I hate to call you so early but I have here a mother who says her child is very ill. Can you see her soon as possible?"

"All right, what's the name and address?"

Mr. Faverman asked Katie the address and she gave it to him along with her name. He relayed it and hung up.

As she left Katie said, "Thank you for your kindness. I appreciate it more than you know."

"Think nothing of it, they'll be all right—I'm sure they will," he reassured her as he let her out into the street.

She could hardly wait to get back, running as best she could. Once inside the room she went to Mark and felt his head; it was hotter than before and he hardly moved. Grabbing a dish towel, she put it under the faucet and let it run cold, wrung it out and washed Mark's face with it. She did the same for Chaim. The stubble of the two-day growth, minus the teeth, made him appear even more ill than she had supposed, frightening her.

"Oh my God, if anything happens to either one of them I can't go on living," Katie murmured. Pacing the floor while waiting for the doctor, she kept looking out into the alley as though by doing so she would hasten his arrival. What else could she do? Wearily, she fixed a cup of coffee and sat down at the kitchen table, but took only a few sips. Over and over again she said half aloud, "Please, God, don't let anything happen to them. I love them so. They're my life. I beg you, better me than my child . . ." And then she thought, as though we can arbitrate with God. Feeling helpless, all she could do was to keep her vigil. She looked at the clock; it was two hours since Mr. Faverman had called. Maybe Dr. Goldberg had forgotten, maybe he wasn't coming. At last, watching still at the window, she saw a form approaching the tenements in the dismal shadow of the alley. She ran to the door and opened it.

"Thank God you've come."

"I'm Doctor Goldberg," he said. "I understand that we've a sick child here—"

"Yes, and my father is very ill too," she answered, without realizing how she had referred to Chaim.

"We'll look at the child first." He examined Mark, and when he had finished he said, "Now I'll see your father." She directed him to Chaim's bed. He's with Chaim for a much longer time than he was with Mark, Katie thought, her heart pounding. She sat at the table, trying to compose herself.

When Dr. Goldberg had completed his examination of Chaim, he came to the table and sat down.

"Mrs. Rezinetsky, your son has tracheobronchitis, and your father has double pneumonia. It's very serious. I don't want to alarm you, but both of them will have to be hospitalized." Shocked, she appeared to receive the news calmly; she neither cried nor screamed, nor pulled her hair nor beat her breast. She just sat quietly without a word.

"Do you understand what I'm saying, Mrs. Rezinetsky?"

Nodding her head, she said, "Yes," and then cold, white terror seized her. "What will happen?"

"If we're lucky, your little boy may not need a tracheotomy . . . there's a new drug that just might work . . ."

She stared blankly at him, not even inquiring about the medical terminology. Shaking her head, she said without comprehension, "A few days ago they were fine, just colds. How could this have happened so quickly?"

"Unfortunately these things sometimes do come on quickly. Now . . . this is very difficult to say to you, but your father really is seriously ill."

"How seriously?"

"Well, I wouldn't want to predict at this time . . ." He shrugged his shoulders. "He is not a young man. We'll do everything we can."

She didn't hear a word he said. Nothing could touch Chaim, so full of living. She needed him so; he was going to live to see Mark a grown man. Nothing could happen to Chaim or the whole world would drop into darkness, the universe would fall apart. She would not allow anything to happen to him. Vaguely she heard the doctor saying, "I'll order an ambulance from Bellevue Hospital to come out as quickly as possible."

She started to tremble, her teeth chattering.

"Now, Mrs. Rezinetsky, calm yourself—they both need you. Come, sit down and drink your coffee." He paused for a moment and then inquired gently, "Do you have relatives, a family?" She shook her head.

"Well, no matter, we'll do the best we can."

He hated himself for having to take the money as she handed him the two dollars fee. Then he picked up his bag and left, closing the door softly behind him.

As she waited for the ambulance, Katie mechanically replaced Becky's dish of water, put out sufficient food for a few days—not knowing when she would be back—and opened the window a little way so that Becky could get in and out.

She sat at the edge of Mark's cot in the ambulance. Chaim lay unconscious in the opposite cot, an oxygen mask over his face. Listening to the harsh sound of the siren as they made their way through the snow-covered streets of New York, Katie couldn't feel that this was actually happening to her. It was as though she were in a play; that the performance would soon be over and she would take her bows, go backstage, remove her make-up and go home. Except this was not a play—everything was much too real as they wheeled Mark down the hall to the children's ward and Chaim to a private room. Private rooms were only for people who were dying. She went with Chaim.

Katie sat beside him in the straight wooden chair and watched the intravenous tube drip slowly, drop by drop, all the while listening to Chaim's distorted breathing through the oxygen mask, unable to see his face.

Where are you, Chaim, as you lie so quietly, the life ebbing away so slowly? Are you a child as you lie at this moment between life and the absence of life—a child, carrying your shoes tied together by their laces over your shoulder so as not to wear out the leather as you run through an orchard on your way to cheder in some village in Poland? Where are you, my dearest Chaim, my friend, my mentor, the father I never knew? She looked about the clean white room. Chaim should only have seen where he lay, in so immaculate a place. Better in the vigor of your life for you to have this . . . Sitting in utter stillness, oblivious even to the nurse who came in from time to time, she did not once take her eyes away from him for fear he would slip away, unnoticed in death as he had been in life. Again she thought of the suddenness as she sat quietly, waiting. How long ago was it since his beauty had surrounded her? A day, two days—she couldn't remember, she couldn't be sure. Then . . . the mask was silent. Chaim was lost to her forever. Taking off the mask, she put her face very close to his and whispered, "Sleep well, Chaim, sleep well, my beloved."

She pushed the tiny knob inside the bell that flashed on a light outside the closed door, then left, but not before she looked back once more. The hospital would take care of Chaim's funeral arrangements . . . now she must go to find her child.

Mark's condition had worsened through the night. Sitting at his bedside with only his labored breathing to fill the deafening silence of the room, she prayed to God to hear her. Finally a nurse tapped her on the shoulder and asked her to leave, saying she could wait outside but that they had to get on with their duties. Even mothers were in the way. Katie walked through the long row of beds. Not all of the children slept—some were crying; some were dying; some would survive.

Finding a small waiting room appointed with wicker furniture, she sat down on a settee, closed her eyes and tried not to think. But the days of sitting up with Chaim and the loss of him had taken their toll of her. Involuntarily she fell asleep. Twenty minutes later she awoke startled, as though something had nudged her not to sleep too long or too fast. Pulling her coat around her, she shuddered, perhaps from the cold. She walked out into the hall, where she watched the large clock on the wall as it ticked away the minutes.

Chaim had been gone only a few hours now; soon they would be getting him ready for his last journey. But life never stopped, not even for a moment—not even for Chaim. From the window she looked at the world outside. It was just beginning to get light as a new day opened its eyes to the world. Down the corridor the cry of a newborn could be heard. Two floors below workers in starched white performed their duties, unaware of the last rites being administered by a priest or a rabbi beyond closed doors. She wondered what this day would hold for her.

Katie went back to the ward and looked through the round window of the swinging door, hoping to see Mark. He was too far away. For hours she paced slowly back and forth in the corridor, at last looking, bewildered, at the clock. It was now seven. The waiting was unbearable. Returning to the window, she saw a coffee shop across the street. Her mouth felt dry and stale; perhaps a hot cup of coffee would revive her. She left the hospital and made her way across the street.

The shop was full of interns discussing their last case or the next. Katie sat down and soon a waitress came to take her order. She brought Katie coffee. For no good reason the girl made her remember Mr. Bernstein. She had all the material at home; how would she get it back to him now? She would not leave the hospital until she was sure Mark was out of danger. Mr. Bernstein and his work seemed so unimportant at this moment—like a cup of coffee?—she decided to telephone him sometime later in the day and explain what had happened, hoping he would understand.

Somewhere in her consciousness she realized that she would have to go on working for him . . . she would think about all that later. She sat drinking her coffee.

"Good morning, Mrs. Rezinetsky, how are you feeling?" She looked up at the face of Dr. Bernard Goldberg. What a nice face, what one hoped a doctor would be like. But he had asked how she felt. How did she feel? She had no idea how to say it.

"I'm well, thank you, doctor." The words seemed to be spoken by someone else.

"I heard about your father. I'm very sorry. It was too late."

"Thank you."

"May I sit down and join you for coffee?"

"Yes, please do."

The waitress came to their table and addressed him by name. He usually had his morning coffee and often ate lunch here when the food at the hospital was impossible to eat. It was becoming even worse lately.

"How are you, Doris?"

"Great, Dr. Goldberg. What are you gonna have today?"

"I'll take one of those sweet rolls with the raspberry jelly and coffee." He turned to Katie. "Wouldn't you like one too?"

"No, thank you. I don't think I could. Just coffee, please."

"Are you sure?"

"Quite sure, thank you."

"Okay, Doris, just one." He laid his napkin across his lap, then took a good look at her. Lovely young woman, he thought, too bad so alone to face all this by herself. He was a doctor but he was also a man, a father, a husband, and he never chastised himself for becoming at least a little involved.

"Have you seen my little boy this morning?" Katie asked, breaking into his thoughts.

"No, but he'll be the first I see on my rounds."

"Tell me how he is."

"Well, I've been in touch with the hospital and I saw him at about eleven last night. His condition has become a little worse but we have to give the medication a chance." He saw her become rigid, biting her lip so hard it began to bleed.

"Now, look, Mrs. Rezinetsky, I know what an ordeal this is for you. May I make a suggestion—that you get in touch with a friend or a relative? I think it's necessary."

She shook her head.

"There must be someone." Hesitating for a moment, he decided he must probe. "What about your husband? Or are you divorced?"

Strange, she thought, not once had it occurred to her to ask for David's help. The brutal events of the past few days had been so swift she had thought of nothing else but Chaim and the baby, but now she began to realize better the awful reality of the situation. It was his child, too, whose survival was uncertain. David had to be told. He had a right to know the seriousness of Mark's illness. She shuddered at the thought, but if anything did happen, would she be able to live with herself knowing she'd deprived him of that right? What they felt for one another was of no importance now. Self-pity was an obscene indulgence. There'd been enough of that. No matter if he thought this was a trick to get him back. She knew she must tell him.

Looking directly at the doctor, she said, "Dr. Goldberg, it is very serious, isn't it?" and prayed he would say no. But he answered, "Yes, very serious. I wish I could tell you otherwise. That's why I think you must try to contact your husband." He looked at Katie. "I take it you're estranged?"

"Yes."

"May I suggest you get in touch with him? He should know how serious this could be." She looked away. "I'm trying not to alarm you, but I think he should be here with you now. You simply cannot go through this ordeal alone."

She looked up at him again and asked, "It really is that serious?"

"Yes, and the responsibility is too great for you to

handle alone." Pausing, he added, "Will you do that?"

She nodded, then allowed him to help her across the street.

"I'm going to make my rounds now. I'll talk to you as soon as I've seen your little boy." Watching him as he went inside, she stood in front of the hospital and felt the crisp, cold morning bite at her cheeks. Then she went up the stairs and walked to the telephone booth. It was now almost eight o'clock. David would probably just be leaving for work. Praying that he would be there, she picked up the receiver, inserted a nickel in the slot, and asked for the long-distance operator. She was connected quickly.

"Yes, operator, I want to place a call to Mr. David Rez—I mean Reid, in Chicago. The number is Michigan 4792."

"Do you want this person-to-person?" the operator inquired.

"Yes, please."

"Deposit three dollars and seventy-five cents for the first three minutes."

"Can you hold on for just a moment, please?" Katie asked while fumbling in her coin purse, dropping the change as she took it out. It rolled over the floor of the small cubicle. She picked up the receiver. "Can you please hold on a little longer? I dropped my money —hold on." When she let go of the receiver again it thumped against the wall. She managed to gather the money together, and counted it out—she was short twenty-five cents. Desperate, she spoke into the mouthpiece, "Can you hold the phone while I get some change?"

The operator, in annoyance, told her, "I'll keep the call. When you're *ready*, ask for Operator 2 and the call will be completed."

Katie hung up, ran down the hall to the business office, and asked if someone could change a dollar bill. It seemed an eternity before the girl returned with the money. Running back to the phone, she replaced the call. "Please be there, David, please don't leave." Finally on the other end she heard a receiver being lifted. "Yeah, hello?" The operator answered, "New

York calling. I have a person-to-person call for Mr. David Reid."

Oh, for Christ's sake, the pumpkin said to herself at the thought of having to climb the two flights of stairs. "Wait a minute, I have to see if he's in." She let go the receiver, waddled up the stairs, and cursing under her breath banged on David's door. He was still in bed recovering from a bad cold and a touch of the flu, having lost almost a week of work, which he could ill afford. No work, no money.

"Who's there?"

"A phone call for you, from New York," she hollered through the closed door. He bounded out of bed, opened the door wide and said breathlessly, "What did you say?"

"Didn't you hear me? I said a phone call—"

"From where?"

"From New York, I already told ya."

He ran past her and down the stairs two at a time to the hall phone, picked up the receiver, and said nervously, "You have a call for me?"

"Mr. David Reid?" the operator asked.

"Yes, yes."

"One moment, p . . . lease, while I complete the call."

He took a cigarette and matches out of his bathrobe pocket, lit the cigarette while he held the receiver tucked between his chin and his shoulder, and waited, his heart pounding with fright. It had to be serious or Katie never would have called him, not after all these months. My God, what was it? He broke out in a cold sweat, bracing himself against the wall, and thought of how many times he had said to himself that if he saw their blood running in the gutter he wouldn't stop to spit on any of them, the way he had been treated. . . . He saw them in the fantasy of his mind's eye, especially his father, begging for forgiveness for wronging him so, and saying no, he should never forgive them, just as they had sworn never to forgive him . . . But as he stood in the dark hall with the cracked, gilded cherub watching him from across the room, he felt sick with fear—perhaps he had spoken his innermost feelings so loudly God had obliged him, and now something was really seriously wrong. Maybe his father was dying, or his mother. Or Katie . . . ? God only knew what must have happened or she would never have called him. Come on, you son of a bitch, complete the call, complete the call already.

The operator said, "I have your call now. Go ahead, New York."

For a moment there was silence, and then David heard Katie's voice say, "Hello, David, this is Katie. How are you?"

"I'm fine. How are you?"

"Fine . . . David, please try to get hold of yourself . . ."

His father was dead. Why hadn't he made friends with the old man and asked his forgiveness? "What's *happened*, Katie?"

She hesitated, then said, "David . . . Mark is seriously ill. They may have to operate."

Silence, as he braced himself against the wall, growing weak, thinking his knees would buckle under him. He felt old hostilities slip away, past anger was put to rest as he stood looking at the phone, unable to speak. My God . . . he never dreamed the baby . . . one only thought of the old being seriously ill . . . no, not the baby, my God, not the baby.

Finding his voice at last, he said, "When did it happen?"

"I brought him to the hospital the day before yesterday."

"The *hospital*? What hospital?"

"Bellevue."

"What's wrong with him?"

"He has tracheobronchitis."

"What in God's name is that?"

"He can't breathe properly—" She tried to explain but the operator interrupted.

"Your three minutes are up, deposit another twenty-five cents for each additional minute."

David said, "Hold on for a minute, Katie. Charge it to this number." The operator intoned, "I can't do that, sir, once the call has been completed."

He screamed through the phone for fear they might be disconnected. "Do you have the change, Katie?"

She answered, "Yes," then fumbled with the change in her hand and made the deposit.

"David, are you there?"

"I'm here. Listen, I'm taking the first train I can get out of here and I'll be there as soon as I can. . . . I love you, Katie, I love you," he heard himself say, and realized that he had unintentionally spoken his thoughts. Unintentionally?

"Oh, David," Katie said delightedly, "and I love you . . . I'll be at the hospital in the children's ward. And David . . . ask for Mark Rezinetsky."

They hung up. David stared into the silent phone, slowly replacing the receiver, then rushed up the stairs to pack everything he owned, which fitted into one small suitcase. He glanced quickly around the room, noting the dishes in the sink, the cough medicine bottle on the nightstand; ran down the stairs with the key in his hand, gave it to the pumpkin and told her he was giving up the room for good. He had just paid a month's rent in advance on the first. It was now only the sixth, and she was quick to tell him as he handed her the key, "You ain't gonna get back any rent, you know."

He felt as though he had been waiting a lifetime for this moment. "I didn't ask you for it, and you know where you can shove it."

He ran out into the street then, knowing he would never come back. Not to this place. Not to Chicago. . . .

At ten o'clock Dr. Goldberg found Katie waiting in a small room across from the children's ward, huddled in a corner of the settee, her arms across her chest for warmth, her eyes closed. But she was not asleep. Hearing his footsteps as he entered, she stood up and looked intently at him, hoping not to read into his eyes what she feared to hear him say.

"Mrs. Rezinetsky, your little boy is a remarkable child. Really, he's so good and cooperative, you can be very proud. His condition is about the same, which is actually a very good sign at this time. If it stays this way for the next twenty-four hours we may see a change for the better."

"You mean he's getting better?" she said, putting words into his mouth.

"No, no, I don't mean that. He's just holding his own."

"But you don't think surgery will be necessary?"

"I didn't say that. I don't want to build your hopes up and then find we do have to operate. I just think at this time we'll have to wait and see."

On his way out he turned back and asked, "Did you get in touch with your husband?"

"Yes, and he should be here tomorrow."

"That's fine. Now you get some rest and eat a little today. We don't want you as a patient. Take care of yourself and I'll look in on you this evening."

The hours seemed endless. She looked at the clock, didn't it ever move? What seemed a half-hour was only five minutes. The hours dragged by. At two o'clock in the afternoon she saw Mark, held his hand and touched his face, hardly able to keep from taking him in her arms; he looked so small, so helpless with the breathing apparatus attached to his mouth.

"Mark, love, mama's here. I'm going to stay right outside all night. Your Daddy's coming, everything will be all right." And then the bell sounded; visiting hours were over.

"I'll see you tonight, sweetheart." Mark's eyes followed her as she left.

Numb, Katie walked across to the small room again. Finally she allowed herself the indulgence of tears, burying her head in her arms until she could cry no more, and finally fell into an exhausted sleep. At five she awoke, went to the rest room down the corridor, and washed her hands and face in cold water. Somewhat revived, she returned to her vigil. Seeing a nurse come out of the ward, Katie asked hopefully if there had been any change, but was told that Mark's condition was the same. She knew she couldn't see him when she peered through the door-window, but she looked anyway. Somehow it made her feel closer to him.

Once again Katie crossed the street to the coffee shop, where she ordered a bowl of soup and a cup of tea, taking very little of the soup but drinking the tea as she sat observing the faces about her without seeing them, and hearing the sound of voices making small talk without listening to them. Thank God the minutes were ticking away, she thought, as she looked up at the clock. It was now six-fifteen, and each moment brought her closer to the time when David would be there. It had taken the tragedy of death and the fighting for a life to bring them back together again. God indeed worked in mysterious ways, and she hoped that from this bitter lesson she would realize now, as never before, that she belonged with David, that it was, simply, her destiny to be with him. This time she would accept him, unequivocally, because life without him was meaningless. Her heart and her soul would be given without reservation. If before she had suspected a mysterious overall scheme in life, she was certain of it now. How else explain that so many lives had been spent—Chaim's, Uncle Max's, her mother's, her father's, and others before them—so that she could stand on a ferry boat one night with a young man who was to become her husband, the father of her child, her life . . . her fate? She was convinced that their reunion was born out of more than circumstances—that their lives had been woven into the tapestry of a larger plan. No longer would she question David. Whatever his needs, they would also become hers. Without him she was lost. . . .

She paid her check and went to the drugstore to purchase a toothbrush and a small tube of toothpaste, then returned to the small room near Mark's ward, where she nervously awaited the doctor. He came at last.

"Mrs. Rezinetsky," he greeted her warmly. "Mark's breathing is somewhat better. He's still very ill, but even a slight improvement is a good sign. Now, when you see him this evening, don't be alarmed; we have him in an inhalator. It looks like an oxygen tent but it isn't. I'll see you in the morning. Good night."

When she saw Mark that evening she couldn't help but be alarmed, for she could barely see him through the fogged-up tent; but then quickly she reminded herself—Dr. Goldberg had said there was a slight improvement. She just had to trust him, she would trust him. Quietly, she sat beside the bed, putting her hand inside, lifting the tent up just far enough so that she could slip it under to touch Mark. He was asleep, but she stayed until the dismissal bell rang.

Thank God, she thought, as she looked out the window into the street below. The gray shadows of dawn were gently receding. The long night had passed and though every fiber of her being ached, she had managed at least so far to survive this ordeal. We can live through anything, she told herself, when there's something to live for. Now she had more to live for than ever.

With a new sense of purpose, Katie went down the hall to the rest room, where she washed her face and brushed her teeth. Coming out, she glanced up at the clock, saw that it was seven-thirty, and decided to go to the cafe across the street for coffee. If she were lucky perhaps she would meet Dr. Goldberg. As she stood waiting for the elevator, the doors suddenly parted—she was face to face with David.

He was *here*. Thank you, dearest God, he's here. There was no hesitation as they went into each other's arms and stood together, without a word, as people milled around them. This was where she belonged, this was where she would stay.

She led him down the hall to where Mark was, telling him, "David, we can't go in until visiting hours—"

"That's what they think," he said. "I'm going to see my son."

He pushed the doors open and went in, holding Katie's hand as he did so. David was shocked when he looked down into the tent, his eyes filling with tears. "How could I have let this happen?" Standing there, bending over his son, tears now streaming down his face, David felt Katie put her arms around him. She was talking to him. "Please, David, please darling, you're no more to blame for this than I am. It would have happened if we had been together. Our being apart didn't make Mark sick, it just happened. Please, David, it breaks my heart to see you like this."

Taking the handkerchief from his back pocket, he wiped his eyes and turned to her. "Katie, I promise you, this will never happen again. I know I'm to blame for letting you go, for sending you away, and I'm going to use the rest of my life to make it up to you, and the baby." He held her face in his hands. "No matter what, we're going on together because that's where we belong, together." He put his arms around her and kissed her.

Dr. Goldberg approached them as they stood in the corridor outside the children's ward.

"This is my husband," Katie told him.

The two shook hands and David asked, "What about my son? I don't quite understand what his condition is."

"Well, Mr. Rezinetsky, he has acute laryngo-tracheobronchitis."

"What does that mean?"

"That he can't get enough oxygen into his lungs. But he may respond to the medication and treatment we're giving him now."

"May? And if not?"

"If not, it means making a small incision into the trachea, inserting a tube. However, let's not think about it at this time because he seems to be showing a slight improvement and if we have no further complications we may be out of the woods very soon."

Then, looking at Katie, he smiled. "Please let me do the worrying. I can tell you I feel more confident today than I did when I first saw him." Turning to leave, the doctor shook hands with David once again.

"Thank you for everything," David said as the doctor patted him on the shoulder.

"I'm glad to have met you. You take good care of this girl of yours. Now get some rest, both of you." He smiled and walked off down the corridor to turn into another ward.

"David, you must be very tired from sitting up all night. Have you eaten?"

He smiled. "How nice to have you worrying about me . . . It's been a long time, hasn't it? But what about you? When did *you* eat last? And from the looks of things you haven't had much sleep either." He touched the dark circles around her eyes.

She smiled and took his hand. "There's a cafe across the street. Would you like a cup of coffee?"

They sat across from one another as though they had never been apart, no distance, no time had divided them. Here they were together and nobody existed in all the world except the two of them, and their child. How wonderful, how indestructible, how resilient people were in times of stress, and how thin was the line between love and hate. He ordered for both of them over Katie's refusal to eat anything, and when the waitress brought the sweet rolls and coffee she ate for the first time in days.

After they'd finished, David sat back, pinching himself that he was really here looking at her, hearing the lovely soft voice that he had first fallen in love with. Hesitatingly, he said, "I don't mean to complicate things, Katie, but how is the family going to feel when they see me at the hospital? You told them I was coming?"

She looked at him. He didn't know, of course, that she had seen none of them except Esther in that brief encounter. She had not mentioned it in her letter. Should she tell him everything here and now, or just part of what happened? She decided to tell him later about Chaim. For now it would be enough to hear about his family. Reaching across the table, she put her hand in his. "I haven't seen them since I came back, except Esther, and I spent only a few minutes with her."

"You haven't seen them?"

"No."

"I don't understand. Didn't you see my mother?"

She squeezed his hand, hoping to ease the shock. "David, your mother's been very ill. She suffered a stroke shortly after we left."

"Oh my God, no."

"Yes, dear, and your father, from what I understand, is not well either. I hate to have to tell you this now, what with Mark and all."

He sat, shaking his head, then asked, "But what do you mean, you spent only a few minutes with Esther?"

"David, I know that sounds foolish, but try to understand."

"I'll try, but why wouldn't Esther want to see you? She always liked you."

"Well, after we left, Harry and the others said that if we ever came back they wanted nothing to do with us, so poor Esther found herself in a very difficult position. She couldn't befriend me."

"Those ignorant bastards—to turn you away, you and the baby—" He caught himself, listening to what he had just said. Hadn't he done the same thing, turned her away? He would not defend what he had done; but at least they were husband and wife, and in the lives of two people there are differences and sometimes the differences become so great that they tear one another asunder. She was not their wife, she was their daughter-in-law and sister-in-law, a young girl with a child seeking refuge. Shouldn't they have understood enough to know that she had only gone with him because she had no other choice at the time? When she returned, they should have embraced her—the victim of a circumstance. Well, they could all rot in hell as far as he was concerned, it deepened his convictions even further, he was well rid of them, they were diseased with a malady that left no room for compassion. With all Isaac's love of God he saw to it that they would even turn away his own grandson. She hadn't betrayed him after all; he should have known that. Even if she had spoken to them she would never have betrayed him. In fact, he felt it was he who had betrayed her, and in doing so, himself. The only regret he had was hurting his mother; but if Isaac had only spoken to him that night, if they had been able to come together as father and son and talk about *his* feelings, *his* reasons, *his* fears and hurts, perhaps then his mother would not be where she was now. Only the feelings of Isaac were sacred. No one should have the temerity to question Isaac's beliefs. Isaac's beliefs were enough for all of them. The hell they were! They weren't enough for him. Isaac was no more in his heart. His brothers were only Isaac's pawns. It was Isaac who made them turn Katie and his child away. They were only the disciples; it was the almighty Isaac who was responsible for it all . . . his mother's illness—and his hatred.

Hatred . . . Katie could see it plainly now in his eyes. "David," Katie said, pressing his hand, "please, darling, try to understand . . . they're no more to be blamed for the way they feel than you are for your feelings. We're starting our new life together. Let's try to forget what happened; let's wash it away from our minds like debris and not allow it to haunt us. Let's forget the past's unhappiness and mistakes. Please, David, let's forget and forgive, even ourselves."

He looked at her without speaking. Nothing was revealed now in his face. But that didn't matter. It was his heart that concerned her.

Walking out into the clear winter day, her arm in his, they went back to the hospital. It would be hours until they could see Mark, so they went into the small waiting room and sat together on the settee. David asked where she had been working and where she was now living, what kind of a place she had and what she had done in the months since they had been apart. It was easy to tell him where she was working, but when it came to where she was living . . .

She got up and walked to the window, then seated herself on the wicker chair opposite him so that she could look directly into his face. She began from the very beginning, from the moment that she had knocked on Esther's door until she met Chaim, and the circumstances in which she had come to live with him. At the end of the story, she related the most painful experience of all, the death of Chaim.

David sat there unable to speak. It was unbelievable. Chaim so profound. Chaim with the capacity for such understanding, such compassion? People lived together never knowing each other, their lives never touching. He couldn't imagine Chaim with such traits, knowing him as he had since he could remember. The peddler, the clown of Hester Street that people laughed at, driving down the street with his horse decked out in the straw hat trimmed with colored fake flowers, and talking to her like she was his child. One almost expected Bessie to answer him. Chaim with the ready joke, making light of the things people took so seriously. After hearing him, a person might well think, nu, so if it's so funny, how come I'm not laughing? Chaim with the antidote—whether it be about the sages, the prophets, or what Mrs. Finckelstein should give her husband for his gout. This was the Chaim that David had known, but how much more there was to a human being that most people never knew about, or cared. No one had wondered whether Chaim had a life of his own, whether he had Shabbas, or sat at anybody's table at Passover, or had dinner on Yom Kippur. He was faceless, a nothing nobody belonged to, that belonged to nobody. He was just Chaim the peddler, who sang out in robust tones like a star of grand opera as he and Bessie rode along the street. He could remember his mother pointing to her head and touching her temple and saying, "Such a shame, the poor man is meshuggener."

But this was not the Chaim that Katie knew and adored. David got up now and walked to her, picked her up in his arms and sat down with her in his lap, kissing her hungrily. How much pain he had caused her while a total stranger had befriended her. How little he knew about this frail girl he miraculously held in his arms. He would learn, though, he promised himself, he would learn.

They fell asleep sitting in the chair, David with his arms around her, and slept for hours. When they awoke it was time for them to see Mark. Walking along the rows of cribs, they tried not to notice the children who were critically ill, or their parents who stood alongside and wept. To Katie's relief, the tent at Mark's crib had been removed. Mark was still wearing the breathing mask, but he could look at his mother and father, his eyes telling Katie how happy he was to see her. As Mark reached out his hand for hers David realized, with a stab, that the child had no idea who he was.

"This is your daddy," Katie said almost in a whisper. She took David's hand and Mark's and put them together while the two looked at each other. David bent over the crib and kissed the child, holding him under his arms, thinking how much he had changed, how much time had gone by . . . For as long as they could, they remained admiring the child that had been born of their love.

Katie's hopes were high for the first time in a week. Out in the corridor she told David, "I just feel he's better. His color was different."

"I'm sure you're right, but remember I hadn't seen him until today. I think maybe we had better have something to eat. Let's go across the street." Anything to get her away from the hospital.

Yesterday, Katie thought, I felt I would go mad with the waiting, today the hours are ticking away just as they did then but the difference is we're together. They talked in the small anteroom, grateful that it was rarely used. Most parents came only during visiting hours, so Katie and David had the place to themselves. They talked about what life would be when they brought Mark home, where they would live. David had no plan in mind, except he was firm they would not go back to Chicago—that had been a mistake, that was where they had almost lost each other. Now that they were together what difference did it make where they settled? They might go to upstate New York, even to New Jersey—his new name no longer bothered him. There was no need now to go away simply to get lost. He would find a place when Mark got better. While in Chicago, he had been able to save a little money and what he had now, after buying his ticket back to New York, was about $100, give or take a little for today's breakfast and lunch, and it did not bother him, not one damn little bit—not this trip.

They looked up as Dr. Goldberg came into the room, smiling at them.

"Well," he said, "I have some good news. I can say with certainty that your child has shown marked improvement, his lungs are much clearer, his breathing is improved, and we've removed the breathing mask." He looked at his watch, it was ten of seven. "I think you can go in and see him."

Katie went to Dr. Goldberg and hoped her eyes spoke what she felt more than whatever words she had to thank him—for bringing her child back to her, and for bringing David back.

"Thank you for everything," she said.

David shook hands with him and thanked him as well, and Dr. Goldberg left the room with a feeling too infrequently justified in the day-to-day defeats of his profession.

They were jubilant at seeing Mark looking more like himself, the only sad moment coming when Mark asked, "Where's Chime?"

"He's sleeping, darling, but Daddy's here with you," Katie told him.

"Daddy," Mark said, and David answered, "Yes, I'm here and that's where I'm going to stay."

After visiting hours they stood in the corridor, each sensing the other's relief and gratitude. It was overwhelming, there were no words for what they felt. David glanced at the clock. It was five after eight.

"There's no need to stay at the hospital now that Mark's out of danger. You know, we're going to have to find a hotel round here. I'll get my suitcase, you wait here." Soon he was back and they walked out into the night where the snow was falling gently to find a small, second-rate hotel four blocks away.

Katie bathed first—she'd almost forgotten what a delicious luxury it could be, not having bathed in days. Time had ceased to exist since Chaim's and Mark's illness, but lying back after soaping herself she decided heaven would be incomplete without a big, beautiful bath tub. Having no fresh clothes with her, after the bath she wrapped herself in a towel and walked to the bedroom, where David lay on the bed waiting for his turn. But when he saw her he knew the bath would come later. She slipped in under the covers, with him now beside her. He switched off the bed lamp, took her in his arms and held her very close. It was as though he were taking her for the first time. The feel of her body against his made him newly alive, so that he felt as though there were a pouring out of every sensual joy he had ever known. He had abstained for so long—happy now that he had done so—kissing her with a force and intensity he had not known his passions could carry him to, for David was a gentle lover, and she responded to his every move, his touch, the rhythm of his body, and soon they were one in a beautiful, ecstatic moment of union, both feeling that nothing and nobody existed outside this moment uniquely their own. When they had spent themselves they lay back quietly, David's arm around her, her head on his shoulder.

The only light in the room was from the neon sign on the bar across the street and the glow of David's cigarette as he smoked contentedly. They talked about everything . . . their first night, laughing now at the remembrance of how shy she had been, about how wonderful it was that out of this great enormous world they had somehow found each other. The past was mentioned but—only the good—and the future, how bright it looked! There would be less than $100 when the hotel was paid and Mark finally came out of the hospital, but it made no difference.

Silently, they lay very close together, no longer talking, just listening to one another's breathing, and soon he became warm in his desire for her and took her once again, but this time quietly, slowly and gently, as the snow fell softly against their window.

Katie awoke earlier than David and lay looking at her husband while he slept peacefully, not believing he was here, still filled with the warmth and indeed ecstasy of the night before. Slipping out of bed she started to dress when David stretched, rubbed his eyes, and looked toward her. She walked back to the bed, sat on the edge, bent down and kissed him as he drew her close. "You'd better not kiss me like that or you'll find out you're married to a sex maniac." They laughed and then he said, "I wonder what time it is?"

Katie picked up the phone and asked the desk clerk for the time. It was eleven o'clock.

Getting out of bed, David went to the bathroom, turned on the tap to shower and called out, "Better phone the hospital and find out how Mark is."

Lifting the phone off the hook, she was shocked that this was the first time since she had lain in David's arms that Chaim had come into her thoughts. Dear Chaim, I've not forgotten you . . . the beginning of life had overcome the end of it. . . . Her thoughts were brought up sharply as the desk clerk said, "Good morning."

She asked to be connected to Bellevue Hospital. After many delays, a nurse told her that Mark was much better, had slept well and taken a little nourishment that morning. Katie thanked her and hung up. Continuing to dress she called to David in the bathroom, where in front of the mirror he stood with a towel around his middle and shaved, telling him about the good news.

After he dressed, they went to breakfast in the coffee shop across from the hospital.

When they had finished, they went to the drugstore, where David bought Mark a stuffed animal and a newspaper for himself; then they crossed the street and walked up the steps to the hospital to wait until two.

When David gave the animal to Mark his eyes grew large. Hugging it he said, "Kitty, Kitty, Becky." They looked at one another and then at Mark and, although he was still very weak, the color had begun to come back to his cheeks and he chattered softly.

Visiting hours over, they went to the small room and sat down, she across from him, her mood having changed from one of jubilation to reflection.

"What's wrong, Katie?"

"David, I have to go back to Chaim's for my things." With the feeling that she shouldn't, she said, "I've been so happy these last few hours, being together, I had almost forgotten. And, incidentally, I must go to the bank; I hadn't remembered it until now but I saved all the money you sent me."

"You didn't spend any of it?"

"No, I wanted to keep it for Mark. I got by, thanks to Chaim, without it. We have about $210."

"But I didn't send you that much."

"I know, David, but you see I was able to save most of the money I earned because Chaim would never allow me to pay for anything."

How right Katie was when once she had said that lovers bring each other luck. She was the luckiest thing that ever happened to him in his whole life and the only thing that made any sense in this world. "I'm going with you," he said. "We don't have to be back 'til seven."

"No, darling, please try to understand. I want to be alone, I can't explain why."

"Are you sure?"

"Yes, David, I'm very sure." She was unable to explain the reasons completely to herself, but she knew it had to do with the fact that David had not been a part of her life while she was with Chaim, and so this was something that she could not share with him; this moment was between Chaim and herself.

She stood framed in the doorway of what had been her refuge, Chaim's room. Her glance wandered to the night table, where Chaim's teeth were still in the glass, to the coffee cup that remained on the kitchen table, to the rope where the canvas hung, to the unmade beds, the orange crates with the volumes of dusty old books, the phonograph with the oversized horn, the records that lay stacked on top of the small table. It was almost as though she could hear the Moonlight Sonata once again as the music wandered through her memory. All of this remained the same, nothing had changed since that day, and yet so much had happened. As it often did, again the sense of fate, sometimes terrifying, overwhelmed her. The patterns of things, the mosaic of circumstance. That Chaim had to die, that her child had to be near to death to bring David and her together, was that so? . . . Or was she really reading more into the mysteries of life than were actually there?

Closing the door gently behind her, she stood in the center of the room, feeling the presence that was Chaim as all the poignant moments filled the room with his memory. Suddenly she was taken by the realization that Chaim was really gone, gone forever, and that here was the visible sum total of his life. Chaim had no friend to mourn him except herself, and there would not even have been her if she had not walked down that street, that day, at that precise moment. He would have lived and died unloved and unknown, when he possessed the gift of delight, in giving that was born out of the soul. How many people were capable of that, to give without reward? He had lived unnoticed and he had died unnoticed and no one but she knew what he was. She could hear him saying to her in this silent room, "So they don't know who Chaim is? What difference does that make? If a man is noticed by others, but within his soul is a stranger, a forgotten man, then he is indeed not noticed. To love is more than to be loved. People think that love is only for the young. You see, *mein kind,* this is not true, because the heart has no wrinkles. No matter how old we get, or how long we live, the heart can still love." Dear Chaim, beloved Chaim, I remember you and I will remember you all the days of my life. You should have been born to a gentler age, life should have dealt more kindly with you.

Briefly she wished she had not come back, wanting to run from this place that was Chaim; instead she picked up the kitchen knife, cut the rope and watched as the canvas fell to the ground. Then she folded it neatly, took the bedding off and placed it on top of the canvas, took Chaim's teeth out of the glass, found a small box and put them into it. She could not throw them away. She would bury the box in the ground as a part of Chaim; nothing of him could be discarded. She washed the stained cup and placed it on the shelf about the sink. Becky was in her box with her kittens around her, trying to keep them warm. Katie heated the frozen milk until it was tepid, poured it into a saucer and put it alongside Becky as she mewed with expectation. Katie bent down and Becky looked up at her, as though scrutinizing her.

"We've lost our best friend, Becky."

She went to the dresser, where Chaim kept his clothes, opened the top drawer and took out the heavy work socks she had darned so carefully, for which Chaim had kissed her hands, put them into a wooden crate, took out the two wool shirts and placed them on top. The drawer now empty, she opened the second and took out the long underwear, the woolen scarf, several handkerchiefs and a pair of old suspenders. She then tried the third drawer, where Chaim kept a bulky sweater, but the drawer was stuck. Pulling hard but unable to open it, she tried again with all her might; still it would not budge. Examining it more closely, she found it was not stuck but locked. Getting the kitchen knife she pried it open, took out the woolen sweater and a cigar box. Inside she found a letter. Dropping the sweater, she walked over to the kitchen table, sat down and took out the envelope, on the front of which was written:

"My Dearest Love"

Carefully she reached inside and unfolded the letter. It was in the hand of another time, another world; the scrolls painstakingly inscribed. She could almost hear Chaim's sweet voice whispering in her ear as she started to read. It began,

> My dearest Child, My Katie,
>
> How can I begin to tell you of the great love I have for you and your child? Words seem to fail me, nothing that I can say would be enough to describe the happiness you have brought into my life. Where my life had been an empty, barren desert, you made the blossoms of spring bloom, you brought springtime to an old man who thought he would die childless. How will I ever be able to thank you for so much? Please listen to what I have to say, and forgive the ramblings of an old man.
>
> We spoke little of my life when we were together and you must have thought that life had

passed me by. It was not always so. Once I was a man like other men. I loved and I was loved by a young girl very much like you. We married and a child was born, but I was not to know the fulfillment of that love. They were taken from me in death on the day of my son's birth. When that happened I despised the Lord, I despised life, my own existence. How could I believe in a God that would punish me so? I asked what I had done that he should have taken out His wrath upon me.

When the Rabbi said it was God's will I thought, if this be God's will then I renounce Him. How could God have wanted the lives of two innocent children? What kind of God was it that made me suffer so? I left Poland and came here.

But life teaches us many things if we listen. After the torment and the struggle within myself, I realized a very important lesson—that a man must have something to cling to, not only people, but something to believe in, although I believe in the goodness of man. Because we are men we are weak and frail and, being weak, men do many things that offend God. You see, it is true that the meek shall inherit the earth, ah yes, but not the weak. So after walking alone down the long dark hallways of my life, searching, I realized that I had within my reach the very thing I was seeking. I found God once again, but this time I had come to terms with myself. I knew I had been wrong. Nothing is ours to keep.

She stopped reading. Her tears fell on the letter making it impossible to see. She wiped her eyes and sat still, aware of the sounds of her own breathing. She continued:

I have saved $1,500 through all the years, hoping that someday I would return to Poland and be buried next to those I loved and not be alone in death as I had been in my life. But this was a fantasy, the crazy notion of an old man, for what difference does it make where a man is buried, when it is God who owns the whole earth and all that dwell in it, and He will be with me wherever I am? I know little more than I knew when I was in my mother's womb or why I was meant to walk on God's good earth, but this I do know, the money was never intended for death. It was meant for life.

Please, Katie, my child, go back to David. With your help and your love he will find his way back as I found mine. Perhaps he feels that God has turned away from him, but someday he will find that this is not so. Please take the money and find a way for you, your husband, and your child. May God help you, keep you, and love you as I do.

With my greatest devotion,
Chaim

She had read, hanging onto every word as though it might disappear were she to allow her eyes to wander away. She sat staring down at the letter in her hands. She looked at the money tied together with a red ribbon. How long had it been since she was almost penniless; how long had it been that if she had found a sum, to be sure much smaller than this, she would have reeled with intoxicated happiness? A few days ago, a few weeks ago, a few months ago? But there was no joy in this moment, for inside this small casket lay the remains of a life filled with deprivation, denial of love, renunciation of affection, and a small dream that had once looked homeward. No, she would not count out the money, she would not even touch it.

Putting the letter back into the envelope and the envelope into the cigar box, she closed the lid and sat, unseeing, caught up in the flow of time. How long she sat there she had no idea.

It was the damp cold of the floor beneath her thin-soled shoes that brought her out of her bittersweet reverie, and to a realization that here, in this old basement room, she had, thanks to Chaim's final tutelage, at last become a woman, and at last would be able to face whatever the future might hold for her.

The gray winter day began to give way to shadows just before evening. Pulling her coat around her, she took down the suitcase that had accompanied her to unknown places and wiped away the accumulated dust; she packed her belongings and put the cigar box alongside the red satin heart, then snapped the locks closed. She walked slowly to the door, opened it and once more, and for the last time, looked at this room that had been her home, that would be her shrine.

It began to snow, a gentle drift that made everything look unreal, almost enchanted, as it lay covering the ground in the alley with a lovely white blanket. She looked up, finding pleasure in the soft white petals that fell caressingly against her face.

Then she walked through the shadows of the tenements to the street beyond.

CHAPTER TEN

Winter, 1937

"Look, daddy," Mark said excitedly, "look, the birdies . . ." He pointed to the seagulls perched on the rail of the ferry boat that would take them from Oakland, California, to San Francisco. They walked down the gangplank then up the stairs to the upper level, went inside and looked out of the window, seeing for the first time the panorama that lay before them. The bay, the sky, the city itself lay clothed in delicate soft winter blue that seemed to turn to mauve as David thrilled to the sight of the distant San Francisco skyline. It was more beautiful than he had ever imagined anything on God's earth could be. Standing here at this moment, he knew he had fallen in love as one does with a desirable woman, listening to the sound of the waves as they coyly slapped against the bow. The boat swayed gently from side to side as though the two shared a secret. The refreshing smell of salt water excited him as the huge iron arms began to turn over, and as he heard the sound of the engines starting he thought his heart had skipped a beat. He held Mark up so that the child could see this promised land for the first time.

"Look out there, Mark, that's going to be our home. That's where we're going to live forever."

Mark looked at David and nodded vigorously. "Forever." He liked the word so well he said it again. "Forever, daddy, forever."

Katie hung onto David's arm. She, too, was caught up in the moment.

The train ride from New York had been a more exhilarating experience for David than for Katie. He had always dreamed of California. He had never been anywhere except Chicago, and had seen very little of that city. In fact, he realized that even though he had been born and raised in New York, the greatest mecca of all, he really knew very little even of that place. Katie at least had been to Paris and seen the best of London, thanks to Uncle Max; and although she was fascinated by the scenery as they came across the desert and the farmlands that looked like giant patchwork quilts, she was not able to share completely David's electricity as he came across this so different world.

It would be snowing and bitterly cold in New York today, he thought as he walked out to the deck without an overcoat and felt the cool sea breeze in his face. As they began to dock, he decided he had reached Utopia.

They stood in front of the ferry building, looking up Market Street and watching people hurrying to get streetcars or taxis. David instantly sensed this city was like an old friend, a family to whom he had come home, whose arms were held out to embrace him.

He asked the Negro porter where the hotels might be and what streetcar he should take. The porter's manner was unhurried and pleasant as he instructed him. They were to take any streetcar up Market Street and get off at Powell. In that vicinity they would find many hotels, from the St. Francis Hotel, which was one of San Francisco's oldest and finest, to the Manx, which was clean but not expensive.

They rode up Market Street, then got off at the corner of Powell and Market and for the first time saw the cable car. Eyes wide, they watched with great curiosity as the conductors revolved it around on its turntable.

Mark called out to his father, "Daddy, take the train, please daddy, the train."

"It's not a train, honey, it's a cable car, but we'll take it later. Let's walk now."

He insisted, "Please, daddy, the train."

Katie took him up in her arms and said, "We'll go later, darling, I promise. Daddy needs to find a place for us to stay."

They walked up Powell Street and found a small hotel just off Geary Street. David registered under the name of Reid, this time without qualms. The bellboy took them up to a nicely furnished room overlooking Powell Street, complete with a white-tiled bathroom for three dollars a night. Mark struggled onto a chair in front of the closed window and looked out. He heard the clank of the cable car as the conductor rang the bell vigorously and it came to a stop almost in front of their window; people then got on and sat outside in comfort, even though it was winter. Soon it was lost from Mark's sight as it started its climb up toward the top of Nob Hill.

They refreshed themselves, went downstairs, found a restaurant on Geary Street and ate a leisurely meal. After lunch Mark became tired from all the excitement, so Katie took him upstairs. Soon they both fell asleep to the sounds of the cable car.

David walked across the street to Union Square and gazed up at the statue of the Winged Victory, deciding that he felt much the same as she did. He browsed up one street and down another, looking at all the shops, the most impressive of which was Gump's on Post Street. He went inside and looked around at the lovely antiques. He went to the Jade Room and was overwhelmed by the display. Not taking the elevator, he walked up the stairs to the second floor and paused in front of the portrait of Mr. Gump the First. What must a man have been like who had the desire to create such a thing of beauty? Scrutinizing the face, he said to himself that one day these were the things he would surround himself with. He climbed higher until he reached the art gallery, and realized how hungry he had been for beauty such as this. He could hardly wait to bring Katie here. A little different fror Chicago, he thought with satisfaction.

Feeling he had just come from a magnificence fit for a cathedral, he walked unhurriedly down Post Street to Grant, looking at the jewelry in the window of Shreve and Company, then crossed over and down past Podesta-Baldocchi, the florist, back to Stockton Street and Geary, amazed that the shopping area was so condensed. Standing on the corner of Geary and Stockton in front of the City of Paris department store, he looked at the small flower stall and shook his head in wonderment, as he watched the elegantly dressed women with their stone martin fur scarves draped around their elegant necks, their leather gloves, their expensive hats, their tailored suits. The depression seemed very far away—if this were illusion, he indeed wished to make the most of it.

David next turned down Stockton Street toward Market and found himself looking into the windows of Roos Brothers, Men's Clothiers. He found his way to the suit department and after considering several, decided on a harris tweed—this one he would not pawn, not with the inheritance and Katie's savings he carried in the money-belt around his waist.

Leaving Roos Brothers, he walked to the corner of Stockton and O'Farrell, and there in the window of Joseph Magnin's he saw a coat that would be perfect for Katie. He looked at a number of coats, discussing the size and color with the saleslady, who advised him to take the pink pastel with the silver buttons.

"Pink?" David asked.

"Yes, we're showing the new spring lines now, sir."

David shook his head. In New York even a fur coat wouldn't have kept you warm this time of year.

He bought it and said, "Show me a dress to go with it." He was shown a lovely print dress which was to his liking and which he bought, along with a pair of black patent leather shoes. If they didn't fit his wife, could he bring them back for the right size? No problem. How nice they were, how accommodating. To complete the ensemble Katie needed a new bag and gloves. The saleslady suggested a small pillbox hat with a veil that just covered the eyes.

Loaded with boxes, David crossed the street to O'Conner and Moffit, which was just kitty-corner from Joseph Magnin's. He found the children's department and bought a new coat with a matching cap that had a small visor. Deciding on the camel color instead of navy blue, he bought a pair of short pants in plaid and a white cotton jersey. Quite a fashion expert . . . he had to laugh at himself. It was a heady experience, though, and he was enjoying himself.

Striding along the street as though he were a native, he could hardly wait until he saw the expressions on Katie and Mark's faces when he gave them their gifts. Opening the door to their room he found Katie sitting in a chair near the window watching the sights below. When she heard him, she got up to greet him, her face lighting up. "David!" she wanted to scream delightedly, but spoke softly because of the sleeping child. "You look gorgeous, darling. Let me take a look."

Holding the boxes, he turned around, then came face to face with her, handing her the packages. She looked down at the boxes and asked, "What's this?"

"For you and Mark," he said with a big wide grin.

"No, David, I won't take it. You needed the suit to get a job, but I don't need anything now until we get on our feet. Really, David—no, darling."

But he insisted, taking them from her and putting them on the bed. Holding her in his arms he said, "Listen, we're starting a new life and I want us to begin this way. I think we all deserve it. Let's be frivolous this one time and not think about the cost. We'll have to do without plenty later, but just this once let's not think about it." He kissed her. "Now try them on. That, madam, is an order."

Excitedly she took the coat out first and, slipping into it, said, "David, you're so good to me, it's beautiful. Thank you, darling, thank you for being you." She tried the hat on, and he lifted her off the ground and kissed her.

When Mark awoke Katie dressed him, and the two of them stood back admiring the little outfit. Then they walked across the street and waited for the cable car. They sat inside near the door so that Mark could see the motor man pull the brakes toward him, then release them again. He rang the bell as they made their way up Taylor. From there they walked to

Fisherman's Wharf, and for the first time in their lives they had fresh crab for dinner.

The next morning David left early to look for an apartment. As he sat having breakfast at Foster's Cafeteria on Geary Street, he looked over the house ads, eliminating them according to price, finally getting into the range he thought he could afford. There were many in the Mission, the Marina, out in the Sunset, in the Avenues; which to take he had no idea. So after finishing his coffee he walked down the street to a real estate office and spoke to a young woman seated behind a desk. He explained his particular problem—that he was taking up permanent residency in this city, that he had a small child—would there be any difficulty? She suggested the Marina and wrote out the instructions for getting there, telling him as she did so that it was a nice new district with families and small children. It was near the bay on the other side of town.

In a little more than fifteen minutes David was getting off the streetcar at the corner of Fillmore and Chestnut. Imposing Spanish-style apartment houses and beautiful two-story flats lined the sparkling clean streets. Knowing he could never afford these rents, he decided the real estate lady must have gotten the wrong impression—surely the suit he wore had fooled her. There were many vacancy signs in the windows, but he was afraid to inquire inside, thinking they would be out of his reach in any case. Nevertheless, he proceeded on down to Marina Boulevard.

The beauty of the bay delighted him, and he felt the urge to throw his hat in the air and roll on the Marina green, where mothers wheeled their children and people walked their dogs. Magnificent yachts lay anchored alongside each other in the harbor, while across the wide boulevard sat imposing two-story mansions that varied from formal French architecture to homes with red-tiled Spanish roofs and stairs that led up to oak doors studded with large ornamental nailheads in unique designs. It was a sight to behold as he looked down at the farthest end toward the entrance to the Presidio with its clumps of eucalyptus trees standing in rows silhouetted against the sky. Just before receding into the horizon, the sun was reflected against the buildings on the hills overlooking the Marina, and the windows looked like a mass of red and orange glitter in the strong winter sun.

Finally he turned off Marina Boulevard and walked up the side streets, inquiring at one building after another, each more desirable than the last; but the rents were too high, starting at $65 to $85 for five- and six-room flats. He walked further up Chestnut Street, which was the main shopping center. Away from Marina Boulevard, the buildings became somewhat less imposing but still were lovely, the streets still clean and the houses well cared for. On Cervantes Boulevard, a wide street that angled off from Fillmore back to Marina Boulevard, he found a furnished one-bedroom apartment. It had a fairly large living room; the bedroom was a good size; there was a tiled bathroom off the small foyer and a large closet with a wall-bed that could be rolled into the living room at night and back during the day; a breakfast room that was divided by two narrow built-in cupboards on either side from the kitchen. It had a refrigerator and a gas stove with an oven and four burners. The rent was $47.50 a month, a palace compared to what he had in Chicago for only $20 less.

Apprehensively, he asked the Italian landlady, who spoke with a slight accent, if she accepted children. Of course, no problem, and they could move in any time. Giving her a five-dollar deposit, he said that he would be back with his wife and that if she liked it, they would move in tomorrow. If not, she told him, the five dollars would be refunded. She actually smiled when she said it. No pumpkin, she. Thank God!

Impatient to tell Katie the good news, he telephoned her, telling her excitedly, ". . . and it's got a stove with four burners and a big oven."

"David, you sound so happy, why don't you take it, and perhaps we can move in tonight, that way we don't have to pay for another day at the hotel."

"No, I want you to see it first. If you like it, we'll

move in tomorrow. Let's make this a honeymoon for another day."

That afternoon he showed her the apartment. She loved it, unable to believe that they were really going to live in anything as luxurious as this. She looked at the green velour sofa, the matching chair, the lamp and the table to one side, a pastoral print on the wall above the sofa with the coffee table in front of it. In the center of the room was an imitation Oriental rug in multicolors.

"Can we afford it?" she whispered to him in the bedroom as Mrs. Francetti waited in the living room.

"Yes. If you like it, this is where we're going to live. I'm going to get a job, I just know it, don't you worry. Now, do you like it?"

"I love it, I love it," and she threw her arms around his neck.

He paid the balance of the rent and proceeded to take Katie and Mark on a guided tour of the district as though he had been there for years. With memories of Chicago, he said as he looked at the Marina green, "Just think, you can bring Mark here and he can play all year round. It's unbelievable."

That night they walked through Chinatown and had dinner at a Chinese restaurant where they were seated at a table near the window in the corner overlooking California Street and Grant Avenue. When Mark heard the clanking of the cable car as it chugged down California Street, he jumped up on his chair and looked out; he already loved those cable cars. After dinner they walked for a while, bought Mark a toy in one of the Chinese bazaars, then took the cable car up California Street to Powell, transferred to the Powell cable down the hill once again, got off at Geary. Finally back in their rooms, Katie and Mark were asleep before David could switch off the lamp.

The first day they occupied their new home, the joy they felt was an unspoken shared thing. That afternoon, shopping for the bare necessities to establish themselves, Katie had found Woolworth's five-and-ten on Chestnut Street a source of treasure, selecting carefully four crockery dishes with yellow flowers on a white background. They were cheerful and she adored them. She bought the same number of forks, knives and spoons; a saucepan, a frying pan, a pot for boiling soup, a small enameled roaster; a tea kettle and a coffee pot; the minimum amount of bath towels and sheets with matching pillow slips, and although they were scratchy heavy muslin she knew that after she had laundered them a few times they would lose their rough texture. They came home with five dollars' worth of groceries and David noted again that the dollar bought more here than in Chicago.

For her first special dinner Katie had placed two yellow candles in little holders that matched the plates on the table. In the center she arranged a small bowl of yellow chrysanthemums. The three ate romantically by candlelight. It was perfect.

After putting Mark to bed, Katie and David lined the kitchen cupboards with white and yellow paper they had bought at the market. Once in the roller bed, David fell happily asleep with the thought of tomorrow, knowing exactly where he was going and certain he would find a job. They had been asleep for a very short time when they felt a small body creep in between them. By the time morning came, David was almost on the floor and Katie was on the extreme edge of her side. Mark slept contentedly across the bed.

After breakfast David left, to slay his Goliath, which looked to be the Rogers Real Estate Company on Chestnut Street, where he spoke to a Mrs. Rogers who was in business with her husband. He talked to her about working out of their office; he told her that he knew a good deal about real estate, that he had studied it, and that he had worked for a firm in Chicago, name of Bayview. Part of the story was true—he had studied—he had never sold. David figured they would never check. Besides, why should they? He would be working for commissions only. As for his own self-confidence, the last two years had been spent in extensive study so that now he felt far better qualified than any beginner. The Rogers' had nothing to lose and everything to gain with a bright newcomer. If he didn't sell, he didn't get paid.

Lela Rogers' shrewd, discerning eye took the measure of him. He sounded convincing and self-assured.

"I think you'll do well in this office," she said. "Tell me, how familiar are you with the Marina?"

"I just moved here, but the little I know about it I already love. It's the most beautiful area I've ever seen."

She smiled, pleased at his enthusiasm; that was always a good sign. "Well, let me explain. This is one of the districts in the city where there are really good real estate values. However, houses don't sell quickly, and sometimes you can wait on a house until the cows come home and then it doesn't sell; but on rentals there's a waiting list. In fact, the best rentals in the city are in the Marina because it's accessible to downtown, the weather's good and it's a marvelous area for children. Now just to brief you, the houses sell for about $7,500 to $10,000 and the flats for approximately $22,000 to $28,000."

David interrupted, "What about the houses on the Boulevard?" He was fascinated by them.

"Yes, the houses on the Boulevard sell for about $20,000 to $30,000, give or take. Now that gives you a fair idea of prices." The prices staggered him; he couldn't get over it, a house that cost from $20,000 to $30,000. Why, if he had $10,000 stashed away in the bank, he would think he was a millionaire. But he did his best to give the impression he was aware of and even accustomed to prices like this.

"Well now, Mr. Reid," he heard her saying, "I want to be perfectly honest with you. I don't know how things are moving in Chicago, but here they're slow. Now if you're prepared to support yourself for about three months until you develop a clientele and the commissions start coming in, I think you'll be fine in this office."

"Well, that's no problem," he said, with the security of the money belt around his middle. "I'd like to start tomorrow if I can."

"Good. You'll have to bring your license in and let

us sign it. Now good luck," she said, winking at him. "I have an idea you have what it takes to sell." She smiled as David left the office and thought, a good-looking kid like that's going to do O.K., unless she missed her bet.

The next day David went down and filled out the application for the real estate license. He was given a temporary, the permanent would be sent to him from Sacramento. In 1937 it was about as difficult as getting a dog license. He had done his homework well and the test was a breeze.

Seeing his nameplate sitting on the desk that was to be his made him feel big as the king of Siam. There it sat, all spelled out in white letters on a black background. Seating himself behind the desk, he waited for the phone to ring. For two days the other agents rented and sometimes sold while he sat. On a Sunday afternoon, all by himself in the office, he finally broke through and rented two flats and an apartment. After splitting half the fee of five percent with the office at the end of that week, he took home $20. It was less than he had earned at making shoes six days a week, nine hours a day, which was $25, but he wouldn't worry—the rent was paid for a month. If they could only manage on the small amount that he earned until his income improved . . . He refused to touch the money he had now deposited in the bank, even if it meant skipping a few meals or doing without—no matter what.

After two months his earnings gradually rose from about $80 a month to $150 and in the third month he sold his first house. The house went for $9,500, plus the rentals on two large stores and several flats; and although he had to split the commissions, to David this amount of money seemed enormous. He had never thought there was that much money in the world. The thing that excited him even more than the money he himself received was the dealing in what he considered large sums, which gave him a vicarious sense of wealth and well-being. The poverty he had known had so influenced him that when people spoke of how bad the real estate market was, he laughed, smiling every time he made a deposit—never mind how much—clutching the bank book in his hand. This was better than anything he'd ever known. Never had life treated him so well. When David cashed his commission checks, he spent money only when and where it was completely necessary—the rent, the food, an occasional dinner out at an inexpensive restaurant in North Beach called Luca's, where the food was good, plentiful and cheap, about a dollar, give or take. It was family style with all the spaghetti you could eat, not to mention antipasto, pot roast, salad, and enough petits fours left over to take home.

On Sundays they spent the day either at the beach, where they indulged themselves with hot dogs and soft drinks, or took a picnic lunch and went to Golden Gate Park, where Mark ran on the grass. They loved walking the city. After living a year in this magnificent place that jutted out and caressed the bay, with the sights of Chinatown, whose streets they often walked, the Súndays on the Embarcadero still remained a thrilling experience, as though they were seeing San Francisco again for the first time.

They lived frugally. Whatever they could do without, they did, except for Mark. David budgeted himself down to the bone, never charged, paying cash for everything, refusing to get into debt. He would deny them now, so as eventually to buy them the moon.

He pursued his career according to a studied plan, and almost with a vengeance. Not content just to sit in the office and wait for someone off the street to come in and inquire about a flat or an apartment advertised in the newspaper, David called people on the phone, following up every lead, leaving nothing to chance, making contacts with the merchants in the area so they came to know him on a first-name basis. Of all his contacts the most important was the manager of a small branch bank, a man whose friendship he encouraged on a personal basis. He made it a point to take Jim Fowler to lunch at least once a week. For himself he ordered carefully, but the sky was the limit for Jim Fowler, such an invaluable contact that he did not count the cost . . . not too much. And he tactfully persuaded his clients to secure their loans from Jim's branch, knowing that in time he would return the compliment. Jim Fowler had worked himself up from an ordinary clerk to bank manager, and although the job didn't pay very well, it had considerable prestige. He was 31, with a great future, a future David considered essential to his own, and in time the two became not only business acquaintances but also good friends.

David had decreed the past out of existence. His mind was only on the future, to which he dedicated himself, grateful he'd accomplished what he had in so short a time but not yet content. A small bank account fell short on at least two counts—it could not buy him peace of mind—not that he felt especially aware of its lack—and it surely couldn't buy the life he would need to go on in his bright new world. And if he were to make big money he had to get a broker's license. So he not only studied real estate technique in every free moment and far into the night, but also real estate law. He listened to everything that went on in the office and on the Sundays when it was his turn to keep the office open, he systematically noted from the files every name he felt could be of future value to him.

Eventually he knew he had to buy a car, finding it impossible to use the clients' any longer, and so he bought a shiny new bottle-green Chevrolet, which he took out on time for 36 months, his only debt. The payments were nominal enough, but it was the interest he hated. He would not, however, touch that small capital he had stashed away in the bank. Who knew, maybe a good buy on a house would present itself?

Jim was a friend who had a few faults, but one had to accept that nobody was perfect. You put up with some things you didn't like for the sake of the big future; maybe you turned the other cheek, but for a change it was at least in good cause—yours. All in all Jim was a sincere and affable young man with a very bright future . . . too bad he was anti-Semitic. He didn't much care for Italians either, tending to find them, in general, somewhat rough and crude, making their money in such things as booze and the garbage business. "Those characters can turn garbage into money," he would say to David. Of course, on the other side of the coin, the founding fathers of the bank that paid Jim's salary were originally from Sicily. Jim's mind, however, was sufficiently sophisticated to handle what to some might have posed a dilemma, having a talent for perceiving and separating the wheat from the chaff.

When he and David lunched together, he was there with a ready joke, the names always the same, the accents contrived and sounding artificial with the Anglo-Saxon overtones. Jim Fowler made David feel exceedingly uncomfortable, to say the least. He remembered all too well that day in a New Jersey office —and in more ways than one swallowed hard each time Jim told these jokes that disclosed feelings that were not only anti but also unlike those of any Jew David had ever known. Actually he wanted to spit in Jim's eye, but realized he would accomplish nothing by such self-indulgence except the loss of a steppingstone. Jim Fowler's bigotry was mindlessly obscene. He would leave it behind as soon as possible.

Meanwhile, he learned of a foreclosure on a house that would go on the auction block the next month. The house originally cost $7,500 and the outstanding loan was $4,200. It was on Francisco Street, and David could assume the present mortgage, paying it off like rent, with no gratuity to the owner. All the bank was interested in was securing the loan. If it went up on the auction block, chances were it would be sold for less than the mortgage, which meant Jim's branch would lose money. Naturally Jim hoped David would take it. It seemed David's uneasy relationship with Jim was about to pay off—Jim, his "good friend," was going to make some money for him.

David showed the house to Katie, who asked, reasonably, "David, can we afford it?"

"We can afford it. How would you like to live here?"

"It's beyond my wildest dreams, but, well, we don't even have any furniture."

"Don't worry, maybe I can make a deal for this man's furniture, and if not, we can at least buy the bare necessities for now."

They went through the house room by room. It was a stucco bungalow with two bedrooms and a sun room that looked out to a tiny backyard with dahlias planted around the fence. There was a kitchen, a breakfast room that opened to a dining room, which in turn lead into a living room with a lovely fireplace made of composition marble in the Italian style. Down the central hall was a bathroom. Not only was it a good investment which David could not turn down, but above all, this truly would be the home of their dreams. Never in the world did they think they would achieve anything so grand. And imagine—they could pay it out as rent; indeed, the payments would be almost the same. So they bought the house, and paid Mr. Martinelli $400 for his furniture.

Now Angelo and Rosa Martinelli waited in the living room for their son Tony to pick them up in Uncle Victor's Ford. Angelo cursed his sickness, this damnable scourge that had brought such a hardship on his family. They had spent their last dollar trying to cure the incurable thing in his belly. He had lost the barber shop, and now he was leaving his life's blood, his sweat, behind for someone else to enjoy. And in the end nothing would save him—not the dollars, not the house, nothing. Rosa stood at the window behind the curtains and watched Tony drive up to the house.

"Come on, he's here," she said, taking her husband's arm and helping him down the stairs. He descended very slowly; there was no hurry, he was going nowhere important, and where he was going could surely wait. By the time he reached the car, the lump in his throat had turned to bitter tears.

"Come on, papa," said Tony, helping his father into the back seat of the car. They drove away, never having met the new owners . . . their tragedy a private matter to be shared with no one.

That night David and Katie went to see the house,

and when David opened the door he carried Katie over the threshold, saying with a flourish as he put her down, "Here, madam, is the key to your castle. It is all yours."

"Oh, David, aren't we the luckiest people in the world?" She hugged him, then went to explore the rooms, opening one door after another. She examined every closet, every cupboard, figuring as she went how they would paint and fix up the garden, neglected since Mr. Martinelli's illness. Two days later they moved in. And, much as he hated to spend money on that bigoted bastard, David nevertheless sent "good friend" Jim a case of California champagne.

Now their Sundays were spent in painting and gardening, and the joys of their life were indeed supreme.

Shortly thereafter via accommodating—and self-serving—Jim Fowler, came news that on Union Street there were two stores that the owner was about to lose. David assumed the loan of $12,000 for a small, two-storied wooden structured building, vintage about 1925. He rented out the upper story to a young couple for whom the flight of rickety stairs was no problem and who took it as it was, no repairs. The rent was very cheap. David and Katie painted the inside of one of the stores on Saturday night and all day Sunday, and then David placed an advertisement not only in the leading newspaper but in all the ethnic papers around town. He got as a tenant in one store a Chinese laundry, in the other, an Italian grocer, renting them as quickly as possible to avoid paying the mortgage out of his own pocket. His concern was to cover the loan payments, the taxes and the insurance, and he was content with just a few dollars at the end of the month for himself because, above all, he wanted to own the property.

So now David was a property owner; he had a small bank account, a car, furniture, and a conviction that this was only the beginning. He had accomplished all this in two years in this, their Promised Land, and was now ready to take the examination to become a broker. Laughing at how elementary it was, he showed it in seeming embarrassment to the Rogers, who decided he was being too modest—David had learned in a very short time how to appeal to "friend" and friend alike.

Now when he took Mark for a walk on Sundays, he would stand on the opposite corner of Union Street, from which vantage point he could look across and admire his works. What, indeed, a wonder to behold! And in so few years.

In 1939 there was a war going on in Europe that few people talked about. It seemed to have very little to do with their immediate lives. People went about their business as the boots of the Nazis trampled the vineyards of the Rhine Valley, Poland was overrun, France fell to her knees, and England fought for her very existence. America was sending bundles to Britain along with a few implements of war to be sure to keep it over there. Few concerned themselves, or believed, that six million Jews were being exterminated. Six million? Jews? Really? Well, what could Americans do about it . . . except be sure to look out for any direct attack on themselves. Survival, after all, was the first law of nature.

Such, in any case, was the attitude of Henry and Viola Burns, who about eleven o'clock one night were awakened out of a sound sleep by the blast of a cannon going off in the Presidio near their home on Marina Boulevard. Viola Burns just knew that the Germans had landed and that they would soon be murdered in their beautiful beds. She sat up nervously and switched on the night lamp. "Do you think we've been attacked?" Henry looked wide-eyed about the room as though he could tell whether or not that was the case. Picking up the phone, he asked for the police department immediately. When he was connected, Henry explained what had happened. The desk sergeant knew nothing about the episode, but had it been important he surely would have been alerted. His advice was to go back to sleep and call the Presidio in the morning or now, if they would feel better. He was sure, though, that it had been a mistake. That did not satisfy Viola, not one bit. They're keeping things from us, she thought, as she climbed into Henry's bed and snuggled close to him. Viola insisted that if there was a war with Germany or anyone else, the Presidio might well be the first place to be hit. There and then she decided they were not going to phone the Presidio; they were going to sell the house and move down the peninsula where they would be safe. The next day the house went on the market.

It originally cost $30,000. David made a deal with them for $16,000. He bought it with 80% financing for 25 years, and agreed with them that they were fortunate to be able to sell and get out, in view of the threat of the impending invasion; it was only because he was in the real estate business that he was prepared to take the risk. The rugs and silk draperies remained as a part of the deal. The moment the house was out of escrow David rented it to an engineer with three children from Seattle who had been transferred to San Francisco. David insisted they take a lease for only two years—he would either sell it or move into it himself, not yet being sure of his plans. Perhaps they could renew it, he would see. He asked for the first and last two months' rent in advance, which was unheard of in those days, but the engineer agreed, the Burns house being one of the few exceptional properties for lease anywhere in the Marina.

As the Burnses moved into an equally lovely home with an acre of ground in Atherton on Selby Lane, where the Germans would never be able to find them, David deposited in the bank the three months' rent plus the security bond, from which he would harvest at least two years' interest. And everybody went happily home, respectively safe, content, and—in David's case—richer.

CHAPTER ELEVEN

Winter, 1941–42

As Katie prepared the waffle batter, Mark came into the kitchen and seated himself at the table to watch his mother drop the eggs into the bowl and whip them into fluffy whites that stood like snow-capped mountains above the rim of the bowl. Then his mother did something she called "folded." He never quite understood why it was called that because you folded your clothes or the napkins, or the towels, but not eggs. How could you fold eggs? She turned to him and asked, "Did you brush your teeth, darling?"

"No, not yet."

"Go do that and get ready for breakfast. Daddy will be up in a few minutes."

He kneeled on the chair with his elbows on the table, cupping his face, watching her.

"Before I go, mom, tell me, where's Pearl Harbor?"

Katie laughed. Wasn't he bright? He was only eight and asked the most difficult questions.

"I don't have the slightest idea. Wait until your father gets up and ask him."

"Mom, don't you know where Pearl Harbor is?"

"No, Mark, I don't. Why do you have to know this minute?"

"Because the man on the radio said Pearl Harbor was bombed."

"Oh that," she laughed, "that's only your Sunday morning programs. Go and brush your teeth now, dear, and breakfast will be ready soon. Go along."

"Mom, it's not a program, there's a lot of noise on

the radio and the man's saying Pearl Harbor was bombed today."

She put down the bowl and looked at him. He was so serious. Smiling she said, "Come on, I'll help you get a different station and you can listen to another program." They went back to Mark's bedroom, where he had a small radio David had given him for his birthday. Katie changed the station. In the middle of a sentence, the voice said, ". . . there's much confusion and disbelief here in Hawaii that something of this magnitude . . ." Katie switched the station and again, "Pearl Harbor was attacked this morning in a sneak attack from the Japanese. It occurred while all of . . ." She switched to still another station. It was the same. She went in to awaken David with Mark at her side. She shook him gently.

"Dear, wake up, I think something is terribly wrong."

He sat up in bed, startled. "Wrong? What do you mean—wrong?"

"It's something about Pearl Harbor. Where is that?"

"It's in Hawaii. Why?"

"Because it was bombed this morning."

He pulled back the covers, got out of bed, ran into Mark's room and switched on the radio, listening in disbelief. My God, maybe that blond was about as dumb as a fox, selling the house on Marina Boulevard.

"What is it, daddy?" Mark asked.

David told him to be silent as he sat motionless on Mark's bed, finally saying, "I don't believe this. Those damned Japs were in Washington talking about peace while all the time they were getting ready for this . . . ?"

Katie told Mark to brush his teeth. While he was in the bathroom she said, "David, please don't talk like that in front of Mark. He picks up everything."

"You're worrying about him hearing a few cuss words at a time like this? When the whole damned world has gone insane?"

"It's not that, but . . . I don't want to seem insensitive, but it's so very far away and why should we frighten him?"

He looked at her and shook his head. "I don't think you really understand what's happened. Hawaii belongs to the United States and that means we're in a state of war. You don't want to frighten Mark? Well, it's a hell of a lot closer to San Francisco than you think." He paced the floor. "And me with that damned house sitting almost in the Presidio. Now do you know what it means? It means we could be bombed. I don't mean today, but if they could get as far as Pearl Harbor, they won't stop at anything. Now do you see what I'm talking about?"

She was frightened. When Mark had finished brushing his teeth, she fixed waffles for him and for herself, which she could not eat. Instead, she sat in the breakfast room next to Mark and read aloud the funny papers to divert him. She brought coffee to David in Mark's room, where he sat listening to the radio.

David stayed glued to the radio all day without getting dressed, switching from one station to another. In the afternoon Katie took Mark to a movie. When they returned Katie found David still in his pajamas and in the same place where she had left him.

"Now, David, please, that's enough. I know it's terrible, but you can't do anything about this." She paused, then added, "Have you eaten anything?" He shook his head, hardly hearing her.

"Come and have some dinner, please."

He watched her as she left. Yes, it was terrible, all right. And for them in particular it could be disastrous. She had no idea . . . he would lose everything he'd fought so hard for. She also didn't realize he would have to register for the draft and that the prospect of being called up, in spite of having one child, was imminent. There was a war in Europe, so whatever allies America had could not be depended upon, preoccupied as they were with their own problems. America was in this thing alone. And when it filtered down from America to David—well, he'd never legally changed his name. So now he would have to register as Rezinetsky. If "friend" Jim Fowler found out, he would be finished. For that matter, what would the Rogers' say? The Japs had bombed more than Pearl Harbor. . . .

Early next morning, David went to an attorney in the Phelan Building on Market Street to draw up the necessary papers to change his name legally. That, however, would take some time before it became effective, and Uncle Sam wasn't about to wait. There was nothing for it but to register under the name of David Rezinetsky, tasting like gall in his mouth. David Reid didn't exist legally—and he had no desire to be stopped on the street without a draft card and be adjudged a draft dodger. He decided to register immediately, though this would still put him out in left field. How the hell could he explain to the draft board why he had changed his name without going into the whole past? He perspired; this would be tough. Maybe they'd think he was a fugitive from justice or a foreign agent—God only knew what. He grew sick to his stomach; there was so much to think about. There were undoubtedly things that he wasn't even anticipating. Damn it, it could all have been avoided if only he had changed his name legally. Well, it was a little late for all that. He wasn't as smart as he thought he was. Today he decided he was still pretty damp behind the ears.

Every district in the city had set up a draft board, so David was obliged to go to the one nearest him. That afternoon he stood across the street and looked through the window at the inductees waiting their turns. He had not closed his eyes the night before. He gave up at four in the morning and listened to the accounts of the bombing and the state of affairs in Hawaii on Mark's radio, which was the same as yesterday . . . still, with many other Americans, hoping it had been a gigantic hoax.

He thought about what his status would be with one child. He was only 31 years old, strong as a bull, and even with one child, if this thing got really bad, he would be eligible. He felt sure they would take him. Why not, he shrugged. Life was getting to be too good to him; it was as though the gods were jealous, or disapproving, of his success. . . . He could well imagine what he would get as a private—maybe $50 a month. . . . The lease on the house on Marina Boulevard, which David had renewed at six-month intervals, was coming due now, and there was a possibility that property values so close to the Presidio might drop. Chances were he would lose the house —if he couldn't sell it, he would stand not only to lose the house, but also the $3,200 he had paid into it as well. He doubted if he could even afford to live in a small house on a private's pay, and of course Katie would have to go to work to supplement their income; he wasn't going to dip into the savings he had struggled so to accumulate. Furthermore, the stores on Union Street were rented from month to month, and, anyway, the rent from these was far from sufficient to support the family. A dismal situation altogether . . .

The day was cold but David was dripping with perspiration as he crossed the street to the draft office. Waiting his turn, he finally heard himself say to the chairman sitting behind the desk, "I want to register for the draft," and then—more important—"may I ask you if all of this is private information that only the Army has on file?"

"Yes, that's right."

David cleared his throat. "You see, I've been living in California for several years under the name of Reid, which is not my legal name . . . my real name is David Rezinetsky." Before questions he added quickly, "The reason I changed it was that it was a difficult name in business, people were always mispronouncing or misspelling it. Reid seemed easier. For business purposes, so I'm having it changed legally but that won't be for some time."

"Well, you'll have to register under the name of Rezinetsky."

When the form was completed, he handed it back as the chairman said, "I'll give you the name and address of the examining physician."

Standing outside the draft office, he studied the certificate of registration. He passed over the lines that said "Place of Residence," "Has been duly registered this day," "The Registrar of local board," as well as the number, city, state; *all* he saw was "First name—David" and "Last name—Rezinetsky." What's in a name . . . ? Enough to come back to haunt him. After the war, he decided, this would be one memento he would never keep.

David sat on the examining table while the doctor listened to his heart, his lungs, and checked all the vital signs, looked into his eyes, his nose and his throat, handed him a paper cup and asked him to leave a specimen. Then he was told to dress. David returned to the consultation room where he sat nervously waiting for the report. Soon the doctor came in and seated himself behind his desk, adjusted his glasses and wrote down the findings while David waited for the verdict to be returned before sentencing. The doctor looked up and asked him, "Has there been any heart disease in your family?"

"No, not that I know of."

"Any kidney, diabetes, or any other disease that you might know of?"

"My grandfather and my mother had diabetes."

"Well, Mr. Rezinetsky"—the doctor paused—"we found two-plus sugar in your urine."

"What does *that* mean?"

"It means that you have a mild case of diabetes; it's incipient, what we call *diabetes mellitus*."

"What kind is that?"

"It's not serious and can be controlled with a special diet without having to take insulin."

"But I've never been sick."

"That's the strange thing about this type of diabetes. You really have no clear-cut symptoms except frequency of urination and sometimes that's not really enough to warn the patient."

"Nothing else?"

"That's about all. However, if you take good care of yourself and eat properly, there's no reason why you should have any serious problems. I would suggest that you see your own doctor, however."

David sat shaking his head. "I can't get over this, Doctor."

Sympathetically the doctor said, "I can understand your surprise. However, this will undoubtedly change your draft status."

"What do you mean?"

"Well . . ." the doctor said slowly, "I'm really not at liberty to say what classification you'll be given, but the chances are—I'm only saying the chances are—that you will not be 1-A." Then, more cheerfully, he said, "I'll have to send my findings to the Presidio, and they'll take a blood test to confirm my diagnosis and notify you when to appear before the examining board."

The doctor got up from behind his desk to indicate that the examination was over and started for the door. David sat rooted in his chair. For a moment he could not believe what he had just heard. The gods weren't jealous after all; they were, apparently, not only benign but positively smiling.

The good doctor walked over to David and patted him on the shoulder. "Don't feel too badly about this, it could be worse." David looked up and thought the doctor was indeed in the business of saving lives—the man had just saved his.

After the army examination and findings were substantiated, he was classified 4-F. But the scare had served its purpose: David would never again take anything—especially his good fortune—for granted. He would have to be doubly on guard to protect his small but growing nest egg. And he would have to work harder and longer than ever to make the most of the golden opportunity that now loomed.

The day started out warm and lazy, one of those wonderful days that San Franciscans uniquely know . . . not a cloud on the horizon . . . not in the sky . . . and not in David's life since he had apparently become exempt from the special threat of his own personal war. Today the beaches would be crowded and David hated crowds, so he took Katie and Mark high above the San Francisco hills overlooking the bay and stood at the parapet that surrounded Coit Tower. David looked out to beyond the East Bay and the Berkeley hills. Turning, he gazed at the Bay Bridge that joined Oakland to San Francisco, that magnificent structure of steel and concrete which spanned the bay like the wings of some giant eagle. Mark adjusted the telescope as he looked out to Alcatraz.

"Are there really convicts there, dad?" Mark asked his father who, being dream-worlds away, hardly heard him. Still peering through the lens, Mark continued, "I don't see why they couldn't escape. What do you think, dad? Would it be hard?"

David answered with a grunt, "Uh huh."

Mark looked hard, absorbed with the idea of escape. "You know what I'd do if I were a convict?"

David answered, "Uh uh."

"When the guard wasn't looking, I'd dive off and swim. I bet you could do it, dad, if you really wanted to."

"Sure."

"Do you think you could, dad?"

"Sure." David was preoccupied with his own thoughts. If he was, for the moment, a sort of destiny's darling, he'd damn well better not sit back on his haunches and fail to take advantage of his good fortune. The war had created new frontiers to conquer that were previously unheard of. If he continued to work for Lela Rogers, the most he could accomplish was commissions. That would be foolish, he reasoned, because of all he earned, he got only half; secondly, what could he hope to accomplish working in an office for her, or for anyone, for that matter—even if he sold a great deal of property, which he had begun to do? He was not really his own boss; besides, what Lela Rogers could do, he could do better. He now had a broker's license and why shouldn't he make half the commission of agents working for him, plus 100% of his own? If he had a firm of his own, he could pick and choose the listings and sales. He had learned a good deal from Lela Rogers and he was grateful. But she'd made her money on him, and if she didn't like the idea that he was going to take the store next to hers, well, that would be understandable but unavoidable. Fortunes of war.

As David saw it, a lot of things were going to happen in real estate over the next few years. Materials were already allocated to the government, so property would be at a premium, especially with the influx of people to the bay area. The times had dictated the tune, and he again determined that he was going to take the location on Chestnut Street right next to Lela Rogers. The next few years would be the test of his foresight. . . . If he were in the right place at the right time, and if he took advantage of it, he could become a very rich man indeed. He had to take the risk of striking out alone, on his own . . . if he missed this golden opportunity, he almost surely would never get another. . . .

Katie had walked to the other side of the viewing platform to look out to the Golden Gate bridge. She stood there, basking in its beauty, the rolling green hills of Marin to one side like a diamond in a magnificent setting and the blue Pacific beneath, the white foamy waves washing against the shore. It was impossible on this Indian summer day to believe that just beyond the Golden Gate raged a war where untold millions were being slaughtered. But at this moment the war seemed very, very far away, very far away indeed. After a while she walked back to where David and Mark were, slipping her arm into David's and feeling so secure standing next to him, as though he could keep them safe no matter what the world said or did.

"Isn't it peaceful and calm, darling?" she said.

"Uh huh," David answered.

"It's so beautiful."

"Uh huh."

"David."

"Yes."

"You're a million miles away, darling."

"Was I?"

She smiled. "You know you were. What are you thinking about?"

"That I'm going to try it on my own."

"What? When did you decide that?"

"Couple of days ago. That is, I started thinking about it, but now I've decided I don't want to spend my life working for Lela Rogers."

"What will you do?"

"Open my own office. There's a location on Chestnut Street, and I'm going to sign the lease tomorrow."

"Is this a good time to do it—with the war and all?"

He had not really asked for her advice or opinion, he had merely told her that's what he would do; and for one brief moment he resented her questioning his decision. But the moment passed and he appreciated, though was somewhat surprised at, her obvious interest. He explained, "Yes, this is the right time, *because* the war is on." In convincing Katie, he became more certain himself that he was right. "I'm sure."

"And I'm sure you're right, dear. You usually are," Katie said.

If there was a tinge of sarcasm, indeed anger, to her last words, she doubted that David, caught up in his enthusiasm as he was, would take note of it. Still, Katie realized the implications of David's owning his own business. On the one hand, it was surely a dream come true for this man who had struggled so hard all his life, both with his inner demons and with the harsh world outside. Though he seemed unwilling—or unable—to share the problems or satisfactions of his working life with her—after all this time, David still had not been able to break down his instinctive barriers, still keeping so much locked up inside himself—their life together in the last few years had been very close, truly rewarding. In spite of the disastrous consequences immediately following his renunciation of Judaism, which still hurt Katie, David had made all the decisions, and at least on the worldly level they had turned out to be sound ones. They lived comfortably in a virtual paradise, and best of all, they had each other. She didn't regret her vow, made so many years before in a New York hospital, to follow her husband without question—the awfulness of separation had been object lesson enough.

Here was another momentous turning point in their lives. David's venturing out on his own would be risky—to him, the man . . . her man. He was already working very hard, very long hours, and this step would undoubtedly mean more work for David and less time together with the family. With her.

If only he weren't such a loner . . . if only he would let her help him in some way! An idea was taking shape in Katie's mind. If David wouldn't—couldn't—bring his worries to her, then maybe she could help him in a more practical way. Katie knew that starting up a new office would be rough going, at least until he found and hired people he could trust: How would he react to the idea of *her* working in his office until he found the people he needed?

She took her arm out of his. But how would she manage? Besides the fact that she had no clerical skills, there was Mark to consider. Even though Mark was in school, he only went until two in the afternoon. He came home to lunch every day, and on Saturdays, who would be with him?

"Katie?" David asked, interrupting her reverie.

"Yes?"

"Now who's a million miles away?"

"Well, I was just thinking . . . David, do you think you might be able to use me in your new office? . . . I mean, just until you find the right people to work for you?"

David looked at her in amazement. He kept forgetting that Katie was something more than a simple wife and mother—that she was ingenious and capable—a survivor. The thought of her participating in his business both troubled and intrigued him. He had been careful to keep his professional and private worlds separate until now; but practicality also demanded consideration.

He thought for a while, his mind quickly running

over the pros and cons, and then said, "I suppose . . . but what would you do in the office?"

"Be a receptionist."

"Yes. I've got to make a good impression, and I won't be able to afford a girl in the office right away." He paused for a moment, finding the idea more and more appealing. It seemed too good to be true. Suddenly, he said, "But Katie, you know you don't type."

"Well, how long does that take to learn?"

"You mean, take a course?"

"Why not? In the meantime I could do a lot of things for you until you got started." She hesitated, then mentioned her single reservation. "I'm a little worried about Mark, though. He's so small—"

David answered quickly, "He's not so small; he's more grown up than you give him credit for."

Mark overheard the conversation and said, "I can take care of myself, Mommy."

Looking down at him she said, "I suppose you can, sweetheart."

"After all, Katie, it'll only be for a while," David said enthusiastically.

She thought carefully and, pleased that after all David needed her, she made her decision. "Oh, I'm going to love it, David. We'll work it out somehow and—"

"Look, dad, there's a big ship out there. Boy, is she ever big?" Mark called out as he looked through the telescope, following the ship as it passed Alcatraz, slipped out through the Golden Gate and seemed to drop off the horizon. It was a large army transport with all the paraphernalia aboard, including anti-aircraft guns. It was in olive drab, right down to the men as they stood at the rail waving their goodbyes. David and Katie, arm in arm, counted their blessings.

David stood back from the curb and watched the sign painter. For one dark moment he wondered how Rezinetsky would have looked, but dismissed the thought quickly as though from the devil, especially when he thought of Jim Fowler and his ilk. With the baton in one hand and a thin sable brush in the other, the man finished the last letter of Reid, outlining it in black. When it was dry, he brushed away the gold leaf, turned to David with a flourish of his hand, and said, "Well, there it is, all finished. I hope you have a lot of luck."

They stood side by side now, one admiring his handiwork as though he were Rembrandt just finishing "The Night Watch" to hang in the Amsterdam Museum, the other feeling like a man newborn.

DAVID REID
REALTOR

The older man felt pride in a finished piece of work; the younger man knew his work had just begun. He could hardly wait, a cavalier swashbuckling, brandishing his sabre at anybody unwise—and unlucky—enough to stand in his way.

For example, Lela Rogers, who came in the next day to wish him well, and felt some jealousy tinged with resentment; after all, she had been the teacher and he the pupil, whom she'd taught so well that he might now become her best adversary. David had anticipated her sentiments . . . "Hire a Jew and he winds up your worst competitor" he could hear her thinking, and then quickly dismissed the thought, annoyed with himself for still reacting defensively at crucial moments, like some ghetto Jew who couldn't get over what he was, or where he had come from.

All the merchants came to wish him good luck. With his arm around David's shoulder, acting like his patron, Jim Fowler said, "I'm very proud of you, David, and very happy that I was instrumental in helping you achieve all this." The arm felt like a snake. He would have been pleased to stomp it to death.

"Thanks, Jim," David said.

Laughing and squeezing David's arm, Jim added, "We're looking for big things from you, and I expect you to be able to send the bank's way at least a million dollars in loans every year." David smiled back, but in his heart he believed that what Jim Fowler had just said in jest would one day be a real prospect

—and Jim Fowler would not get a damn red cent of it then. Now was a different story.

For the first time Katie was able to show her artistic flair as she and David selected the office furniture. When you did something to show the world, you went first class, David decided. Appearances were the ticket—especially in the beginning. They continued to live frugally in a style to which they had become accustomed, but the office had to be the most spectacular on Chestnut Street. He allowed Katie to express her taste freely, which she had never had the chance to do for him before. The walls were cocoa brown grass cloth, the rug matched, the desk was shiny black lacquer, the Danish modern chairs were done in robin's egg blue, and there was a large-scale wallpaper mural of San Francisco on the far wall. The effect was handsome.

The contrast between the office and their home, with Rosa and Tony's heavy Italian furniture, found David almost reluctant to leave when he closed the office and went home at night. And within only a very short time the office attracted not only clients, but also ambitious young women who longed to become associated with an office as chic as this, especially since the young men were away at war.

Katie's efforts at working in the office were less successful than her attempt to decorate it. She completed her course in typing, but she hated it with a passion. Her loathing was impossible to keep a secret, no matter how she tried. She made one mistake after another, embarrassed by her own clumsiness. At first David's irritation with her was minor, but soon, under the pressure of the business day, his tolerance raveled, and the more his impatience, the more dreadful her performance. And as she increasingly exasperated David, he began with his outbursts to humiliate her in front of others, from whom she would retreat in tears to the ladies' room. Still, he knew she was trying hard for him, and kept telling himself she just had to improve . . . she couldn't get worse. He knew his wife had real talents, but in his business she became another worker—unpaid, in her case—who couldn't be singled out from the obligation he put on himself and his other associates to meet top standards in *their* world.

Gradually, in self-defense, though hardly the world's champion secretary, she did learn to type up leases and made fewer mistakes. But she was also beginning to spend more and more time in the office typing bills of sale and answering mail—she showed special talent in composing, for example, business letters, which David admitted were far better than his. Now Katie no longer picked Mark up at school and was unable to take him on Saturday outings; he spent the day in the park or by himself, and there were some nights when she had to stay to help David by typing up a lease or an offer on a house by a client who came back to the office with him. All the time, however, her mind—and her conscience—were at home with Mark.

When she returned home, he would usually be sitting in his room alone, listening to the radio, eating a peanut butter sandwich he had made for himself. "I don't mind, mom. I know you're busy," he would say, and she would hug him, thinking she was beginning to mind it very much—especially now that it seemed David could afford to get someone else and pay her. Her resentment grew, in spite of herself. She was Mark's mother, this was where she belonged. If anyone knew how a child felt waiting for his mother, surely she did. She remembered only too well standing outside Rosalind's back door waiting for her mother to come. But why should Mark have to feel this way? There had been good reason for her mother not to be there, but was there for her? She reminded herself that it had been her idea, not David's, that she work in the office. Fine, but it had gone beyond its original purpose, and now from a shared beginning it had become . . . face it, Katie . . . too one-sided, unfair to her—and especially to Mark. First things came first.

The breaking point occurred one day while she sat alone in the office. Two of the agents were home with colds, a middle-aged man who had recently joined the staff was out showing property, and David was negotiating a deal on a house on Broderick Street. Unexpectedly it began to rain, hail pelting down on the windows. If it continued until Mark got out of school at two, he would have to walk home in the rain without his overshoes or yellow slicker and fisherman's hat.

Picking up the phone, she called the school and left a message for Mark to wait for her to pick him up. Then she called the cab company, wrote a note saying the office would be closed for thirty minutes and taped it to the door.

When she arrived at the school, she asked the cabbie to wait and ran up the stairs with her coat over her head. When Mark saw her, the look on his face was as though the rain had stopped and been replaced by a rainbow. She felt the same way. She knew she had been right to come.

"Mommy, I'm glad to see you."

"Me too, darling. There's a taxi waiting for us. Here, get under my coat. Okay, now let's walk fast, but be careful, don't slip."

They got into the cab waiting to take them home. Mark felt terribly important; he had never been in a taxi before. He was glad it had rained. Katie had the taxi driver turn into the driveway, open the garage door, and drive in. After paying the driver, Katie and Mark went up the inner stairs to the kitchen with their arms around each other. She fixed hot chocolate and put out a dish of cookies.

"Thanks for picking me up," Mark said as he drank the chocolate, leaving the best for the last—his favorite cookies, vanillas with cream that he separated, licking the cream first. It was really nice, with the rain and all and his mother sitting right across from him. He'd missed not seeing her after school. Now she was here, and it was keen.

"Mom, do you have to go back today?"

Who would come to the office on a day like this? She doubted if there would be anyone. Why not? Mark wanted her to stay as much as she wanted to be here with him.

"Yes, Mark, I'll stay."

He got up from his chair, came to her and hugged her. "Thank you, mom."

She smiled a little uneasily, but Mark didn't notice. He wasn't supposed to.

He asked, happily, "Would you like to play cards?"

"I couldn't think of anything I'd rather do."

Running to his room, he got the cards, brought them back to the kitchen, and sat down across from her.

"What do you want to play?"

"Anything you want to play."

"How about Go Fish?"

"Well, you'll have to show me how."

"Okay. I deal you four cards; then I go first. If you have the same one in your hand, you take it. If not you have to say 'go fish.' Understand?"

"I think so, but if I make a mistake, will you tell me?"

"Sure. You want to deal?"

"No. You deal."

"Okay." He shuffled the cards, some of them spilling on the table. Then with his pudgy fingers he dealt one to her, one to himself, until they had four apiece. He won all the games.

"You're too good for me, Mark." They laughed. The phone rang and Katie got up to answer it.

"Where the hell have you been?"

Shocked at David's outburst, she began to tremble inwardly. Her eyes grew dark, but her voice was composed, for Mark's sake. She would not let him see her cry and answered with false calm. "I picked Mark up after school. It was raining so hard."

"He couldn't have waited?"

"It rained most of the afternoon, David, he had no overshoes or raincoat—"

"It would have killed him if he had to walk a few blocks in the rain?" David was speaking louder now.

"David, is there anyone in the office with you?"

"Yes."

"Why are you shouting at me this way in front of other people?"

"Why? Listen, Katie, what kind of an office do you think we run here anyway, with that phony sign on the window like a drygoods store." He almost said, You're not on Hester Street, but realized in time not to say it. He did not think of the real irony—that it was he who feared he was back on Hester Street, which held terrors for him, not Katie. "Mr. Dickerson brought back a client to sign a lease," David continued, "and he couldn't get in, he doesn't have a key. You should know that."

"Oh, David, I am sorry. I really didn't think of that. I'm sorry—"

"Sorry! That does a lot of good . . . he had to wait in the car until I came back."

"I'm coming back right away," she said.

"Don't bother." He hung up, slamming down the receiver.

She stared at the silent phone. Mark looked at her. He had not heard the sound of his father's voice, and though his mother had spoken softly, he knew by the sad look on her face that she was upset. Going over to her he asked, "What's wrong, mommy?"

"Nothing, dear . . . nothing at all. You deal the cards."

They played for a while longer, but all the joy was gone from the game. Finally Mark went to his room, while Katie fixed dinner, not knowing when David would be home. She tried to dismiss David's apparent lack of understanding that she owed her child something, not only him. Why should he have spoken to her as he had, again embarrassing her in front of others . . . would he have acted the same to a hired girl in the office . . . to be honest, the answer was he probably would have—he was consistent in his rigid standards. Her hurt feelings began to give way some . . . she felt in a way she *had* let David down . . . but should she have stayed in the office and let Mark go home in the rain? He was still a little boy. Was she being overly protective of him? It wasn't so easy to sort out the answers.

When David came home that night he went into his room and shut the door without a word. He had already eaten. For one solid week he did not speak to her, either at home or at the office. And the bouts of angry silence—they felt that way, like blows that wounded as much as anything physical—began to repeat and, indeed, extend themselves.

Finally she decided she was going to tell David she could no longer work in the office. She geared herself for the outcome.

After putting Mark to bed she sat in the living room trying to knit while David read. She had difficulty starting the conversation, but finally, putting the knitting in her lap, she began guardedly.

"David?"

He answered without looking up. "Yes?"

"David . . . I don't think you really need me in the office anymore, you're doing so well now—"

He stopped reading and looked at her. She was not sure if he was angry; she was not sure what he felt.

"Of course I need you, what brought that up?"

"Well, David . . . I think Mark is getting to the age where I should spend a little more time with him. He's really a very lonely little boy."

"What do you mean, little? He's nine years old."

"That's still a little boy."

He got up from his chair and stood before the fireplace. "When I was nine my mother didn't worry so much about whether I was a lonely little boy."

"Mark isn't you and I'm not your mother. Aren't you happy Mark is more fortunate?"

"You bet he's more fortunate, thanks to a father who worked his tail off here on earth instead of sitting on it talking to his one and only God. Listen, you coddle him too much. I really believe that. What the hell do you think's going to happen to him if he's exposed to life a little? Give it a chance and it just might make a man of him."

"Oh, David, he's just a child." She got up and went to the bedroom, but David followed.

"It seems to me you're running true to form. When things are tough, when *I* really need *you*, you run away. You did it in Chicago, you're doing it now. Then it was my family you were so worried about.

Now it's Mark. You don't approve of me, but you don't mind accepting my money or the house I provide for you, and you won't mind what I manage for us in the future, either. All right, fine, I don't want you to come back to the office, you're no damn good there anyway."

He slammed the door behind him as he left the house. Katie sat stunned, she simply did not know David any longer. What had happened to their lives? Is this what success did to a man? Now she would be at home with Mark, a small victory won, she feared, at the cost of undermining what she had tried so desperately to hold onto, what she knew in her heart she needed and wanted above all else . . . the respect and love of David—David, her husband.

Fortunately she could not know that Mark lay in his bed crying, the pillow over his head to shut out what he had heard through those thin walls. Otherwise her heart would have broken.

Fortunately, too, in the days and the weeks that followed, the anger, like most things, spent itself, and once again they spoke together, they smiled, they even laughed a little. She cooked his meals and did his shirts and ironed his underwear and, to all outward appearances, they were a family with a family's ups and downs.

But David would forever after keep his own counsel in *all* matters. And always there remained the residue of hurt and resentment stored away, waiting to be conjured up to work its mischief.

On a Sunday afternoon in 1942, Katie packed lunch in a small wicker hamper, then took Mark by streetcar out to Golden Gate Park for boating on Stowe Lake. Stowe was an artificial lake in the middle of the park, where one could rent a tiny boat whose throttle was adjusted to propel it at about ten miles an hour as it floated along lagoons and under bridges that looked as though they might have come from some medieval castle. The weeping willows bowed gracefully and spread their lacy branches out into the water while the white swans glided proudly, their heads erect in regal splendor. Mark paddled his feet and steered the boat while Katie sat alongside, taken with the sight. It was quiet and tranquil as she put her hand into the water, making small ripples as the boat moved along. All that could be heard was the putt-putt of the motor and the quaint sound of ducks swimming along, dodging the swans, and the chirps of birds fluttering in the trees.

On this lovely day at the end of August, Katie's bemusing reverie was abruptly ended when Mark, steering the boat without looking at her, asked, "Why couldn't dad come today, Mom?"

"Well, dear, you know how busy daddy is, his business keeps him working so hard . . ." It was difficult for her to say because it was a lie. David worked the way he did because of what he had to prove. The demon lived inside, not in the exigencies of the office.

"Why does he have to work so hard?"

"So that we can have all the nice things we do."

"I know, but why can't he ever take us out like he used to?"

"He hasn't had the time lately, dear."

"Can't he ever get the time?"

"He will. It's not that he doesn't want to. Look how lucky we are to be here while daddy has to work."

"I know, but it seems like, well, we're not together much anymore." Which, she silently agreed, was becoming truer all the time. The more David acquired, the less he had for his family. Katie tried to justify the whole thing, but somewhere in her mind she wondered if it was worth giving up *so much;* immediately she stopped herself in her mental tracks and thought, if it took a little loneliness—which had always been part of her life. . . . She shut out the thought. It was worth it because David was accomplishing what he'd set out to do. And when he had all that he wanted, needed, and they were as secure as David thought they should be, then he would find the time and once more they would be a complete family. . . .

As the small boat skimmed along, David was signing the papers on a pair of flats on Jefferson Street that belonged to a doctor who had just been commissioned into the Navy. On the pay of a Navy lieutenant, he could no longer keep up the payments. Fortunes of war.

In April of 1942 the Office of Price Administration had been signed into law and the United States added to its vocabulary another bit of alphabetic Americana—the OPA. It meant gas rationing and food stamps. Suddenly people began to realize how tough the war was really getting. And some, like David, realized the attendant opportunities if handled with brains and hard work. His timing had been right, his instincts had whispered in his ear, and he had listened. He had worked hard—diligently and sometimes far into the night, pulling down the blackout shades and working through an occasional siren alert.

At the end of the year David bought a building on Market Street. It was a three-story structure with an enormous store that he would subdivide. He raised the money he needed from the sale of the house on the Boulevard, which he sold to an engineer who knew that he'd have to remain in San Francisco now, at least until the end of the war. The engineer paid $42,500 for a house that David had bought for $16,000 in 1939 because an agitated blonde had convinced her husband that the Germans or the Japanese were going to land in her living room. David invested the minimum amount required from that money as a down payment on the building that cost him $85,000, on which he got a 90% loan at a low interest rate of 4½%. There was one small item in the deal that stuck hard in David's craw—he still needed Jim Fowler.

Jim, too, had let no grass grow under his size twelve shoes. He resigned from the Italians and became chairman of the board for a new savings and loan company backed by Jewish capital. Jim—skilled at facing facts when they added up to the color green—shrugged. . . . What the hell, they were the ones that seemed to have all the dough and the brains. He hated to admit it, but those were the facts. However, there were, thank God, some limits. He belonged to a country club that excluded if not all the wops at least all the chosen people. Besides, when all was said and done, it was *his* name that was out front. He was the man who put his stamp on whether or not a loan passed at the Sentinel Savings and Loan Company on Montgomery Street, pretty as it could be down there among the giants in the heart of the financial district.

He could even tolerate putting his arm around Sam Lesser at the cocktail party that was held the night before the official opening. But tonight was for only the very important people—the mayor, the hotel and restaurant owners, important merchants, lawyers, investors. Anyone and everyone who was important was there, surrounded with the exquisite flower arrangements and plants from the best florists in town—some large, some not so large, depending on how valuable Jim Fowler was going to be to the sender.

Jim weaved in and out of the crowd with a glass of just-right chilled champagne, catching up with David, standing against the wall in a tailored black mohair suit from Bullock & Jones.

"Well, we really showed them, didn't we, Davie?" Jim said, putting his arm around David's shoulder.

Jim's arm still felt reptilian to David, who hated being called "Davie." Jim was just ever so slightly tight from his success, and David also thought he saw in Jim's eyes that night the ever so slight signs of fear. David had been among those who had sent the largest floral contributions—his was one which when the flowers died the plant would nonetheless continue to grow taller each year, a constant reminder to Jim.

Jim repeated himself, "We sure showed 'em."

"We sure did, old buddy," David answered, smiling.

And it was so. David had become a war baby, nurtured by an era. Low interest rates, big loans, small down payments in a country sprung from a deep depression into a war economy . . . if a man were in the right place at the right time, and had the wit, ambition and capacity for hard work—yes, for David especially the blessedly all-consuming hard work—well, such a man found himself just where David was. Riding on the crest of the wave.

CHAPTER TWELVE

1945

In 1945 David sold the building on Market Street for $156,000: just as the war came to a close. He now had more money than he had ever thought possible in his wildest dreams. Not even at the height of his most extravagant visions did he ever think that life would take him so far, in so short a time.

Still, when he sat back and looked down from his lofty peak and viewed the situation, he arrived at one important revelation—that he did not know how to live. The fear of poverty had burned deep within the marrow of his bones, and even now that he had more than he had bargained for, he was still afraid to spend some of it. One thing he knew for certain: that a man had to progress, to expand his horizons. So he took the only road he knew was open to him, and that was the road down the peninsula.

It was a small piece of real estate that jutted out from the bay, where land and the opportunities were plentiful, and the trends were going south away from San Francisco, south to suburbia. As the bird flew, so did David.

A man of means is compelled to live up to his position in life, and David had emerged on the scene like Halley's Comet across the sky. In certain circles there were people who knew that David had arrived. It seemed only reasonable that there should be further tangible proof of it. So one day in early spring David drove down the Bayshore Highway in his shiny, new, yellow Buick (which he paid a premium for because automobiles were still on allocation) to Hillsborough. Driving to Rosehaven Road, he parked the car in front of an imposing English home set on an acre of cultivated garden with blue-green Kentucky grass that rolled gently up to the wide brick steps. He stood now in front of a heavy oak door with solid brass knocker, waiting for it to be opened. As he waited, he looked around at the garden that was in bloom. The yellow and purple pansies that bordered lush green lawn seemed to lift their faces in welcome. His eyes followed as the lawn sloped back to the road and stopped at a wide section of black earth where a line of hawthorn trees surrounded the property; in the back was a high privet hedge that secluded the owners from the road. He observed the graceful gate, tall and slender, imposing in its stylish way, and seeming to say, however politely, do not enter, dwelling within are the chosen few . . . "the chosen"? Ironic, considering the life decision taken so many years ago by the new owner.

Alice McFee showed David through the house. Poor Frank had talked himself hoarse making the deal with David and now was resting, exhausted, upstairs. Frank had finally succumbed and sold the house for $36,000. Alice had told David that if he had not loved the garden as she did, she would not have allowed poor Frank to sell the house to him—or to anyone who would not take care of her beloved garden, especially her roses. Now she led David along the wide brick path that led to the gate, that led to the road, that led to the car, that would lead him home to see Katie, whom he could tell he had just bought a home in Hillsborough.

David got into the yellow convertible, proceeded up Summit Drive until he came to a clearing off the narrow road. He parked the car on the knoll, got out and stood near the edge looking down at the property he had just bought. From that lofty peak in this pastoral countryside he reveled in the sight that lay before him: this house of his with the heavy slate roof; below it, the dormer windows; the green plush lawn surrounding it; the flagstone terrace; the garden; the huge oak trees and the rhododendrons that lay snugly sheltered beneath them. The hydrangeas were in bloom. From here it looked even more beautiful than from down below—he had missed the vista as he had walked down the garden paths with Mrs. McFee just a few minutes ago. He'd been so excited at having made such a good deal with poor Frank that many of the aesthetics had gone unnoticed; but standing here now, alone in the quiet of this meadow, he felt keenly the impact of what he had really accomplished. In spite of all the money he now had, and except for the feeling of security it gave him, he had to admit that there was nothing very beautiful or aesthetic about the sight of a bank book and the paper detailing his mortgages and loans. But this was something of subtler dimension, indeed a beauty to behold. All his wealth could never excite him as this sight did at this moment, and it took on even greater dimension when he considered whence he had come and how he had come here.

Up until a very short time ago, Hillsborough had been anti-Semitic. There existed an unwritten covenant among the inhabitants and the fathers of that unincorporated, bucolic township that all but excluded Jews. The country club, for example, never accepted Jews, no matter how illustrious or influential. With this in mind he felt he had further reason to applaud himself and the steps he had taken. His judgment had been *right* on that arduous train ride between New Jersey and New York, and no matter what problems he might encounter from here on, at least he was exempt from the hazards of Rezinetsky. Perhaps poor Frank McFee and dear, gracious Alice might not have been quite as happy for a Jew to be tending Alice's precious babies.

Thoughts of what he had been and from where he had come laved over his mind, bringing in their wake feelings of self-appreciation, pleasure and, by God, flat-out pride. Well, why not? He'd been born into abject poverty, a nobody, a nothing. Had he remained, he knew he would still be running down Hester Street hustling a 50-cent policy. He had escaped. He had fought and hacked his way out of the jungle, his own self-will his only weapon . . . he had fought and he had won. He had fought despair and loneliness, fear and prejudice, family, friend and enemy alike. At this moment he felt quite like a Roman soldier returning home from the wars . . . the conquering hero. All hail.

The external evolutions of man from his mother's womb to the eternal womb of the earth are easily visible to the naked eye; less obvious are the gradual, subtle evolutions of the heart, the mind and the soul. These aren't so easily detected by others. At what precise moment does a man become aware of passions that make him reach out for sensual love? At what moment does he realize the needs of the heart—realize he is more than flesh, blood, marrow and sinew?

It would be difficult to say. It would not be difficult—or inaccurate—to say that at that precise moment, standing there surveying his domain, David Rezinetsky-Reid had become sufficiently taken with himself to be unaware that such of his qualities as compassion and tenderness were in danger of losing out to his heady sense of victory. It was as though the heart, mind and soul had not taken him into their confidence, as though the trinity demanded that David Rezinetsky-Reid find out for himself that the soul could be rejected, the heart become bitter, but memories were not to be dismissed so lightly.

As David looked down from that plateau, the smell of spring all about him, his thoughts once again went back to another day in an earlier May, to an office in New Jersey; he still clearly saw a young man standing awkwardly with his straw hat in his hand, eager but frightened that his purpose for being there would not be fulfilled. And once more he realized that had he *not* gone back into the office that morning and heard the conversation taking place there, he likely would not be here at this moment. His mind's eye took in the form of the bookkeeper sitting on the tall stool, hunched over his high desk, his green eyeshade over his eyes and saying, "They ought to be put in a cage."

He did indeed owe that bigot s.o.b. more than he'd ever know. Those words helped spring loose courage to face what he felt. From that moment he began to garner the will to follow his dreams. . . . Memory wandered on, to stop at Hester Street, and he thought of his mother in the hospital, as Katie had told him. . . . He felt the sadness wash over him, and willed it away, banished it to the limbo of what was . . . and would never be again. No recriminations, no guilt allowed . . . until suddenly he knew the presence of Isaac standing alongside him, Isaac with the eyes deepset in stone-chiseled face; Isaac in skull cap, with the prayer shawl around his shoulders, whispering, "For this you gave up your soul, for this your heritage? Fool, you fool. From whom do you think you can escape?" David nearly put his hands to his ears as once again he heard the mournful chant, "*Yis-gad-dal v'yis-kad-dah. . . .*"

Ghosts of the past. But what of the present? What of Katie, who would always remind him of Hester Street? Katie who, though surely she would never betray him, nonetheless knew his secret . . . and what of Mark, his son, who had no heritage . . . ?

The armor he had so skillfully constructed and fortified throughout the years, how vulnerable they made it! In spite of anything he achieved in this gentile world, he would still be David Rezinetsky—to at least one person. Suddenly the flaw, the fact of it seemed enormous, and sensations of fear, guilt, and—admit it—even momentary hatred overwhelmed him.

He hurried away from this place and down the narrow winding hill, past the house, past the lush green lawns behind the privet hedge. He drove as fast as he could along the highway until he reached the house on Francisco Street.

He slammed the door to the car, ran up the stairs to where Katie and Mark waited for him, and for the first time told Katie about their new home—which she had never seen. She did not even know where Hillsborough was. She withdrew into silence. For the moment . . .

David sold the house on Francisco Street to a family

with three children; the sale price of $15,000 was nearly half of the cost of the infinitely more palatial home in Hillsborough. Again the times called the tune. The homes in Hillsborough Oaks up to then were all two-story dwellings, but with the shift of people who'd worked as servants before the war, in defense plants during the war, and now had no intention of returning to the status of domestics, it was becoming difficult for people to staff their large homes with appropriate domestic help. Most of the mistresses of these mansions were unaccustomed to managing their household affairs on their own. A dish towel was a foreign object and scrubbing a toilet an unheard-of chore. Adrift in a domestic crisis, many of them were giving up their palatial homes and moving to smaller dwellings, often back into the city apartments on Nob Hill. Also beckoning were the new tracts now being developed with rambling one-story homes on choice country club estates—the two-story houses were left for someone else to climb the stairs.

David also began to sell off smaller commercial holdings and acquire large parcels of property, one after another. In the process he sold the building on Union Street to a fellow entrepreneur, the Italian grocer Guido—all cash—leaving Guido to wait impatiently for the OPA to drop dead, after which he could evict the tenants upstairs along with the Chinese laundryman, remodel the building and sit pretty on the subsequent high-rental proceeds for the rest of his days. Crossing himself, Guido would say Hail Marys to good fortune while periodically counting out his money in the small private room at the bank after opening and peering inside his very own metal vault box.

David had driven Katie and Mark down to the house on Rosehaven in the morning to wait for the movers, saying he would return as soon as he got things under control at the office. Katie walked now from one room to the other in the empty house while Mark ran outside and climbed the giant oak tree. When he heard the moving van drive up, he jumped down and ran back into the house. Opening the door, he called out excitedly to Katie, "Mom, the movers are here!"

Katie came into the entry. "Say, lady, where do you want these things?"

She hesitated before answering. "As you bring them in I'll tell you."

The McFees had sold the house with the draperies —they had been handwoven by Dorothy Liebes in beige with bands of light turquoise blue at the bottom to match the walls—since they would be no earthly good to them in the house in Palm Springs, although Alice did love them so, almost as much as her roses, bird bath, potting shed and greenhouse, which was at the farthest end of the property.

When Rosa and Angelo's couch, covered with the heavily embossed deep green brocatelle, and the armchair in red velour were carried in, Katie stood in the center of the room in a state of shock. The sofa was heavily carved walnut from Grand Rapids, Michigan. The day Rosa and Angelo brought it from Delucchi Furniture Company on Columbus Avenue, they cried with nostalgia, looking at each other and shaking their heads—just like from the old country. But in this place . . . to begin with, the sofa looked too small and out of place in the lovely large living room with the hand-pegged, dark oak floors and the high-beamed ceiling, the Tudor mantel, the three double French doors that opened onto the terrace and the garden beyond. When the imitation Oriental rug in strong reds and blues was put in the center of the floor, it looked like a postage stamp—the rug was nine by twelve and the room was twenty-eight by fifteen feet.

She might be less than ideal in an office, Katie thought, and less than sophisticated in the ways of finance, but in matters of taste, decoration and style, well, at least here she felt she had some talent and right to speak up. How could David have bought this house without considering they had no furniture? Surely he must have intended to furnish this house as it should be. He would see the incongruity. But when he returned, peacock proud, and went through the large living room across the square foyer to the dining room with its leaded-glass bay window, it was as though he were seeing it for the first time. He apparently hadn't realized the size and beauty of the room. His eyes lingered on the brass Georgian chandelier, the globes hidden by tiny silk shades—so awestruck that he had no eyes for the ornately carved dining room set, so out of place with the hand-painted English mural that sat above the wainscot. Katie followed him into the breakfast room to the butler's pantry, then to the kitchen and out to the main hall, at the end of which was the library with the large leaded picture window providing a view set off by a gnarled oak tree branch, the terraced rose garden, flagstones separated by thick green English moss, and a birdbath. To the right were beautifully molded bookcases the width of the room; between them was a stone fireplace, and opposite were a pair of French doors leading to the outdoor dining terrace. What appointments would they use here?

David turned to his wife. "Well, what do you think of this?"

"I think it's beautiful, just beautiful." From the sound of her voice, David wasn't so sure she meant it. He shrugged it off.

"What do you think of the garden? I'd think you'd love it—"

"I do, it's just lovely," she replied nervously.

"Just like an old English country estate," he needled.

"Well, not exactly, but it's lovely, David," she added quickly.

He swung around sharply. "What's wrong, Katie?"

That tone always made her nervous and now she backed down completely. "Nothing, David, *really*."

"Don't start that, damn it. If there's something on your mind, let's hear it."

She knew he didn't really want to hear, that it might even sound frivolous to complain about furniture at this point—but of course, that was only a part of it, the tangible thing of the moment that represented David's failure even to tell her in advance before buying this house . . . surely she was entitled to that. It wasn't furniture, it was David and Katie she was so upset about. But how to solve that now? And so what she said was, "We just don't have enough furniture, David—"

He didn't take his eyes from her. "Is *that* what it is? Well, we've just moved in and when I can afford it, we'll furnish—"

She was almost on the verge of tears. "But what we have looks so . . . wrong, and we don't have any furniture for this room—"

"You never complained about furniture before."

Of course, she hadn't, and she wasn't now, even though she answered, "It looked all right in the other house—we were poor and happy to have anything, but in this house—"

One word led to another. She had said none of the things she wanted to. They were not really speaking their minds. She dared not. Finally, she said, "I'm sorry, David. I do love it, and when we can I know we'll furnish it . . ." Better this than bringing matters to an ugly boil. Cut it off, at least for a while. . . .

That night after David had fallen asleep Katie slipped out of bed quietly, walked downstairs to the living room and sat down on Rosa's sofa, listening to the echo of the empty rooms. What had she wanted to say to David? So many things . . . why did he still need to show off to the world, to prove something? She welcomed good things too, but David seemed obsessed with façade, with symbols of success to wear across his chest like campaign ribbon. And no matter how impressive the façade, her own instinctive identity as Katie Kovitz-Rezinetsky was in the way of his believing his own self-creation. Oh, David, I am a threat to you, aren't I? You almost came out and said as much tonight. As for the other side of the façade, where Mrs. David Reid lived, Mr. Reid seemed rather less concerned. His war was outside, and it seemed to have a duration even greater than the one between nations just recently concluded.

She still had only the vaguest notion of what he was worth—he'd never really told her, not even when it was important for her to sign the papers he brought home to her (politics, religion, above all, money . . . some things a man just didn't discuss). Obviously, though, it must have been considerable. How much, she wondered, did David *need?* How much did the person David had become need? She was beginning to accept that perhaps she knew David less well than she'd thought. David? Which David? Had he really been this way when she had married him? They had been too poor to know, and their poverty had seemed so natural. Had he changed this much? Success did things to people. Or were these latent traits coming to the surface? Rosa's furniture had looked fine in the house on Francisco Street. So had their lives those first few years. . . .

She never brought the furniture question up again —especially since it was hardly the point anyway, just a small part of a bigger picture. She did buy a sewing machine and some bolts of English floral linen and began to make slip covers for what they had. She put the imitation Oriental rug in the library, scrounged about second-hand stores for odds and ends which she painted or refinished, bought a second-hand couch that an upholsterer did for her at a price. Gradually the house began to take on the semblance of a home. Using the third garage, she bleached the dining room table and chairs to a lighter color—with apologies to Angelo in his grave. Ironically—she couldn't resist the thought; why should she?—she was well equipped to have assumed the full role of a rich and prominent Mrs. David Reid, even though she had no real interest in it. And her mind turned briefly to the house of dear Aunt Rosalind. Oh my, this was indeed a day for looking inward, and backward . . . to times and feelings perhaps better left alone but which refused to go away.

Else how to avoid the question? Why did she stay? Why? She wasn't certain she really knew the answer. But she did know and still lived the memory of being a woman completely alone. For some it might be tolerable, but not for her, not for Katie who had waited for her mother in a fancy home whose mistress openly detested her, not for Katie who had come alone to America to be taken in by strangers who shared their family with her and even made her part of it, not for Katie who had exchanged that family's love for the love of David—husband and then father of her child. If only he could remember the truly lovely and private things that they'd shared in their marriage instead of fighting the memory of Hester Street—his demon, her refuge. Still, with it all, in spite of it all, this had become a way of life . . . she had made a choice. Could she deny it?

CHAPTER THIRTEEN

1947

By 1947, with all of his other investments and property that he had acquired through the years, David had at last become a millionaire.

The morning his son graduated from Hillsborough Grammar School, David was not present at the graduation because he was in Los Angeles negotiating a deal on a property in upper San Mateo County that belonged to a widow, now living in the South, who had been left the property by her husband.

What does a boy of thirteen think when he stands staring out at the group of parents and friends, mothers and fathers sitting together, each sharing the rich satisfaction of seeing his and her child receive a diploma, certificate of a time that spelled the end of all innocence? When a boy sees his mother sitting alone among the others, tugging at the white handkerchief in her hand, he knows her loneliness as he knows his own. And what he wishes at that moment is that the plane his father is on would crash and then his father would be sorry. But he wishes it only for a moment, trying to swallow the hard lump in his throat and hold back the tears. He would have felt even worse could he have read his mother's thoughts.

More than David not being here with her, at her side where he should have been, much more, was the fact that today was even more significant to her than to all the other parents sitting there. Mark had become 13 this year and should have taken his place among the people to which he had been born. He should have stood among the elders in the temple, proclaiming his covenant with God, blessed be He. As she looked at her son, Katie closed her eyes and saw him standing in another place, at his Bar Mitzvah, with the white satin skull cap, a narrow prayer shawl over navy-blue suit, reading from the Torah, "Praised be Thou, oh Lord, God of our fathers, God of Abraham, Isaac and Jacob, great, mighty and exalted, Thou bestowest loving kindness upon all Thy children, Thou rememberest all the devotion of the fathers. In Thy love Thou bringest redemption to their descendants for the sake of Thy name. Thou art our king and helper, our savior and protector." . . . David, how could you have taken so much from your son? I hope you hear me, David, wherever you are. Your father was right; you are a fool; but I, too, am a fool. Chaim, you gave your life's blood to fools.

At first when Mark looked across the courtyard and saw his mother sitting there on the gilded Vienna chair he thought she was shielding her eyes from the strong sun. When she opened them and looked at him again, he knew he could not cry and disgrace his mother . . . she was unhappy enough over his father's absence. Instead, he stood erect and at the end of the exercise shook hands with the principal as he accepted his diploma and seated himself with the other children graduating from the small, almost rural school and listened to the principal addressing the graduating class.

The principal began his inspiring speech with "And now you boys and girls stand on the threshold of a new . . ." Mark hardly heard those opening words, or the rest of the speech. Threshold of a new life? He was wondering why his father thought he was so unimportant, why he didn't feel he had to be here, like the rest of the fathers, on what was one of the most important days in his life. He adored his mother, but he also loved his father, wanting more than anything in the world for his father to be there, to praise him. His grades were so good . . . Mark loved and admired his father enormously. Katie had helped build a myth around David—after all, David Reid could not exist in a void, not for his son.

"Well, what happened after dad left the orphanage?" Mark would ask, trying to conjure up the image of his father as a small boy. And, at another time, "Well, what happened to dad's parents?"

Katie did not look at him when she answered, "They died."

"How old was he when he became an orphan?"

"A very little boy, Mark."

Mark would put his arms round his mother and say, "Boy, I'm sure glad I'm not an orphan."

What could Katie have said to her son? That she wasn't certain but it was possible he might have grandparents still living in New York, that his father had become obsessed with an idea that even at this moment she could not reconcile herself to? When Katie told Mark the lie about his father being an orphan, he did not take it as a simple explanation and stop there. Like most children, he was imaginative—and so he translated his father's childhood into terms of Oliver Twist. The images loomed large in his mind as he saw his poor father at the age of five or six begging for another crust of bread. And Mark grew to thirteen with a sense of pity, of compassion, and even protectiveness about David. Yes, David, his father. But today, for one split second, he had wanted his father to die. His father who wasn't there, who couldn't, he decided, really love him. And then the feeling turned inward, into guilt and self-hatred as he remembered what his mother had told him just that morning:

"Mark, dear, I know how much you're going to miss not seeing Daddy at the graduation, but darling, he's going to feel much worse, not being able to see you stand there today. He'll make it up to you."

Not convinced, but desperately wanting to be, as he stood tucking the white shirt into the navy-blue trousers, he said, "I know, Mom, but I don't see why he couldn't have come home today and gone back on Monday."

"You know how your father's business is—his time's

not always his own. He explained it to you. A man can lose a great deal by putting off something that should have been done today. Believe me, Mark, if it were possible, nothing could have kept him away."

As he slipped into the jacket, buttoning it while Katie adjusted the knot of his tie, he looked for the truth in his mother's eyes; he wanted to believe her but somehow, somewhere, without his wanting to doubt her, he did, even as he fought against disliking his father for not coming home on this day. Again the feeling was there as he recalled the conversation around the breakfast table and his father saying, "I never had it so good when I was a kid. I sold newspapers when it was ten degrees below and delivered meat in a wagon when it was so hot you thought you'd die—and I didn't have a nickel to buy an ice cream cone. . . . Kids today have something to complain about, it's so damned easy for you. You've got to be strong in this world . . ."

Listening, Mark thought then of his father as the strong man in the circus who lifted the 200-pound weights. And remembering, and looking now at his mother, he wanted to tell her that it was okay, that he guessed his father would have been home if he could have been. He would have told her that, because he so badly wanted to believe it.

David looked out of the window and saw the landing strip that extended out into the bay. From above, it looked like a narrow piece of brown ribbon, and as the plane began to make its descent the ribbon widened until finally the plane jerked to a landing, then seemed to glide for a minute before it stopped at its destination, the San Francisco Airport. He got out of his seat and stood in line as the other passengers moved forward, bowing his head slightly to avoid the cabin door height. He looked at the young stewardess as she smiled, exposing a mouth of very white and very young teeth framed by softly curved pink lips.

"Thank you for flying with us. Hope you had a very nice trip, sir."

As David looked at her, he also thought of Mark,

perhaps because she was so young. What was today? Sunday? My God, Mark had graduated yesterday, and he had not even called home to congratulate him. He supposed Mark would feel terribly hurt that he had not been there. But then again, he and Katie were so close that he wondered at times if Mark really knew he was around. Besides, Mark would have to learn that he could not always have things his way; there had been little disappointment in his life so far, and when David compared his life at thirteen . . .

The differences in their lives were staggering. Because of him, Mark was never going to know the poverty, the absence of love he had known. Mark would be spared because of his father's determination to become someone in the world; he would never have to claw himself up and hack a way out of the jungle; there was no anti-Semitism for *him* to contend with. He doubted Mark would ever appreciate these differences. Everything came easily to him. So what if he couldn't have been there yesterday? He hadn't exactly been on a vacation, he'd been working his tail off . . . just as he'd been doing all these years to give his son a big, beautiful house and the opportunity to go to Hillsborough and graduate alongside the kids of the richest and most prominent families in the area, maybe in the country. And he'd made all this possible not only for Mark but for Katie as well. Well, one thing he promised himself—Mark wasn't going to have it all served to him on a silver platter. No, he was going to learn the value of a dollar. Mark wasn't going to be a spoiled mama's boy.

As David walked through the corridors of the airport, he passed a gift shop and hesitated, then went in and looked about until he spotted a camera. He asked the price; it was $17.50. He decided to buy it and a roll of film as well. Waiting for it to be wrapped, his thoughts went to Isaac. And for the same reason that Katie had thought painfully of the symbolic number, the age of thirteen kept coming back to him, too—a time of Bar Mitzvah, a time of Isaac. He had tried to force himself to forget that day, standing there on the knoll, but Isaac would still not go away. He saw himself at thirteen in a small *shul* on Hester Street, reading the Torah alongside his father, the look in Isaac's eyes, a look of admiration, of pride, of love. He never saw that look again after that day. David knew anger at the next thought, that maybe his father did know him better than he knew himself, anger at allowing himself to be shaken in *his* faith—a self-created faith that went beyond Isaac's, a faith in himself (and, as an ex-associate once put it, in the holy trinity of money, property, and small down-payments). With a faith as strong as this he ought to have been able to tell anybody—including Isaac—to go to hell. Ought to have been . . . but my God, if Katie knew the thoughts about the past that still flooded back to him . . . he would have died if he thought Katie had known the dreams from which he awoke, drenched and spent. . . . She would never know, he would never let her know, that in moments of weakness he remembered Isaac. Get out of my life, Isaac, get out of my life, old man.

He took himself in hand now, straightened up, and was David Reid once again; his thinking was straight, with full command of his mind. As he was handed the gift, he took it carefully in his hands and walked out with it. A camera for graduation—his father didn't even offer him a word of praise when he came home to that tenement, the diploma in his hands, and showed it to him with such pride. David had been the only one out of Isaac's four sons who had graduated from high school. It was as nothing to that holy man whose only favors were for his God. . . . He picked up his overnight case and walked to the valet service where the new Cadillac he had bought a few weeks before had been parked for the last five days. As he headed out, he tried to concentrate on the beauties of Rosehaven Road and his rhododendrons. Their welcome was at least assured when he got home. His wife's and his son's was another matter.

Mark heard the sound of David's motor as the car turned into the driveway and called out excitedly to

Katie, "Dad's home!" as he ran down two stairs at a time.

David had just come from the garage with the present in one hand and his suitcase in the other. Mark ran to him and kissed him on the cheek.

"Gee, dad, I'm really glad to see you."

"Me too, Mark."

"Let me carry your suitcase, dad," Mark said, taking it from David. They walked to the side of the house off the terrace, through the French doors into the library. The room always excited David—he looked out the picture window to the garden in bloom, rhododendrons in a profusion of color under the large oak trees that sheltered them from the summer sun. It was just as Alice McFee had promised. He too had kept his promise and had not stinted on spending money for Takahashi, the Japanese gardener; it was worth every penny of it when David saw what the gardener and mother nature in collaboration could bring about—with some help from Katie who, each season, put up seventy to eighty flats of plants from seedlings nurtured in the greenhouse.

Katie came out of the kitchen into the library and kissed David—a rather pointedly unenthusiastic kiss. "How was your trip, David?" she asked, also without enthusiasm.

He caught the tone as he answered, "Fine, the deal went off as I had hoped. We own thirty-two acres. We're going to build a shopping center in San Mateo."

"Oh, really?"

"Yes, they're the biggest thing down south, all centralized . . ."

Katie stood looking at her husband as he rambled on. We, David had said, we. . . . What "we" was he talking about?

Her thoughts were interrupted as she heard David say, "Here, Mark, I've brought you something for graduation." He handed him the present, and Mark whipped off the ribbon and fancy paper, opened the box hurriedly and took out the camera.

"Gee, dad, this is really keen. Thanks a million."

"I'm glad you like it. How was the graduation?"

Katie went back to the kitchen rather than hear the rest of it.

"I got all A's, let me show you," Mark said, running upstairs and then down again so fast that David didn't have time to take off his tie and unbutton his collar. Mark proudly handed the report card to David. He had really worked hard, he wanted his father to be proud and admire him, and to give him something he guessed David never had a chance to give *his* father, being an orphan and never even knowing his father . . . David looked the report card over and handed it back to him.

"That's a good card, Mark. Now you keep up the good work and someday you're really going to amount to something and then you'll take over when I'm gone. . . ."

Didn't he amount to anything now? What did his father mean by someday? He didn't want to take over his father's business, he wanted to go to the Florida Keys and buy a fishing boat like Captain Kingsley had done in the book he'd just finished reading, or maybe be an airplane pilot. And what did David mean, when he was gone? Was his father going to die, someday, really die, and be dead? The thought was too much for him to handle. He went to his father, forgetting he was thirteen and just graduated from grammar school ready to stand on the threshold of a new . . . and put his head on David's shoulder, barely able to hold back the tears, while David had no idea in all the world why. He sat, uncomfortable, with the boy in his lap. After all, Mark was thirteen. Now he was a man. . . .

They sat at the table in the breakfast room and ate in silence, except for a word now and then from Mark, who told David, "Jim Parks is going to Black Fox Academy in southern California, but I wouldn't want to go away from home." Besides, he thought, his mother would miss him and his father would feel real sad if he was in a place sort of like an orphanage, sort of.

David nodded, agreed and continued eating.

That evening Mark lay in bed listening to the radio, conjuring up images of Union soldiers in combat with the Confederates; and when the South had lost, the Union Jack was raised as the North rode off from the battlefield singing the "Battle Hymn of the Republic." He lay staring out at the stars beyond his dormer window, thinking about the summer that lay ahead of him, hoping that maybe his father would find enough time between now and the new shopping center to take him and Katie to Lake Tahoe.

Katie had gone up to bed, leaving David downstairs in the library to read the Sunday paper, which he had not had time to do. For a few minutes he looked out of the French doors and saw the garden by moonlight. The scent of daphne in bloom was intoxicating. The garden was more beautiful, if possible, by night than by day. He did love this house. He walked up the stairs in the dark, past Mark's room, past the two closed, empty bedrooms, into the room he shared with Katie. She did not look up from her book as he entered. Holding back his anger, he said, "You're a little peeved at me, aren't you, Kate?" She left the book and looked at him. Kate? She repeated the name to herself, Kate—that was the first time he had ever called her Kate. Was the sound of Katie a little too Jewish, like Birdie, perhaps?

Tonight she was hurt and angry, which was hardly unusual. Having the courage to speak up was. "Yes, David, I'm very peeved indeed."

His jaw tightened. "Because I couldn't come home for Mark's graduation, right?"

"No, not because you couldn't. You didn't even think it important enough. You didn't even remember to call."

"You don't know what the hell you're talking about."

"David, I know exactly what I'm talking about. Remember, I've lived with you long enough."

He walked to the edge of the bed and looked down at her, narrowing his eyes. Damn her, who the hell did she think she was, taking that line with him. Who the hell was she when he met her on a blind date, and who the hell would she have been without him? *Where* would she have been . . .? "I don't have to take this from you, nobody is going to talk like that to me . . ." It was Chicago all over again, except in a more elegant setting.

She got out of bed. "You don't care who you hurt, do you? That little boy in there loves you and you don't give a damn, do you?" She screamed for the first time in her life.

David stood above her. "Let me tell you something. He's got a lot more than I ever had, and if it wasn't for me, just what the hell do you think his future would be?"

Standing up, she answered back, "Well, you're not God, David, so you don't know that. Where, by the way, would you have been without Chaim's money?" She hadn't thought she would ever be angry enough to say it.

His face turned red. She thought he was going to strike her as he clenched his fists together. Instead he started to pack his clothes, first taking them out of the closet and throwing them on the floor.

David moved out and took a suite of rooms at the Fairmont Hotel. He sent Katie the $1,500 by registered mail. She tried to pretend to Mark that David was away on business, but Mark grew silent. His animated talk at mealtimes subsided. Katie understood why. Walls have ears.

Two days later Katie locked the house, got into the station wagon and drove to Lake Tahoe. After registering at Cal Neva Lodge, she placed a call to David's office in the City and left word where they were. Chicago, Chicago all over again. Oh dearest Chaim, your money has been so badly used. I'm sorry . . .

David moved back into the house during their absence, bought a bedroom set and moved in directly across the hall from the room he and Katie had shared. He had never been any good at bachelorhood, remembering too well the burnt fingers and the burnt can of beans—and after a month of living in the city even the French cuisine and the fine food at the Fairmont no longer tasted like anything. Besides, he had to be careful of his diet if he were not eventually going to have to give in to insulin—Katie had always taken pains to be sure that he ate properly. The house quickly became dusty, so he hired Takahashi's wife, who not only charged plenty but couldn't come in every day. Damned inconvenient. And then it occurred to him—what if Katie was serious about leaving him? He couldn't gauge how angry she really was. What if she intended to live alone? That could be very expensive. This was no longer Chicago; he was a very rich man now, and in the State of California there were community property laws. If she got a smart attorney, he could get David right by the balls. Besides, the lending companies necessary to his business tended to frown upon divorces—like it or not, he still couldn't afford to do without Jim Fowler. And, also like it or not, it felt peculiar not having Katie at home. . . .

He picked up the phone and called Tahoe. It was Mark who answered.

"How are you, Mark?"

"Dad," Mark screamed with joy. "Dad, where are you?"

"I'm home, but I just wanted to see how everything was going."

"Keen, dad. It's so beautiful up here. I go boating every day with the man who owns a boat. It's so keen, and Mother drives me to a place nearby and I go swimming. You should see me dive." He paused and quickly, without thinking about whether he should or shouldn't, asked, "Dad, why don't you come up? You'd love it, and we could go boating on the lake. You should see it. We could go swimming too. Would you, dad?"

"Well, I'll see. How's your mother?"

"She's fine. Do you think you could come up?"

"Is she there?"

"Yes."

"Can I speak to her?"

"Just a minute . . . Oh, and dad, I took a lot of pictures to show you. You should see all the pine trees, it's really beautiful." Mark screamed through the phone as though David were in Outer Mongolia.

"Not so loud, Mark. Let me speak to your mother."

"Oh, I'm sorry. Okay, dad, just a minute." He

handed the receiver to Katie. "Dad wants to speak to you, mom."

Katie felt the receiver in her hand and hesitated.

"Talk to him," Mark said pleadingly. "It's . . . long distance." Katie held the receiver, looked at it, then at Mark's eyes. She tried to smile at him.

"David?" she said softly.

"How are you, Kate?"

"Fine."

"Are you having a good time?"

"Yes, just lovely." She heard his breathing, and then his words, "Can I come up? I really miss the two of you, the house is pretty empty without you . . ."

She didn't answer immediately, instead listened to the by now so familiar thoughts—thoughts that had been with her through the years, always vacillating between the love and the hate, the need and the resentment. By now it was like a litany . . . they had been through so much together, they had a child who loved and needed his father, their lives were woven into tangled skeins that at least had survived the past, if she could only learn to look away maybe Mark would become the beneficiary of it all—it was his life that was at stake here, if Mark could be happy . . . And after all the long weeks of separation, she too was feeling the pain of loneliness. People said extreme things to one another in the heat of an argument, trying to annihilate each other with words, not really meaning it . . . besides, she admonished herself, she was not totally without fault. She had hurt David's pride—where he was so vulnerable—with her comment about Chaim's money. After all, it really was insignificant, even if essential at the time, in terms of all that David had gone on to earn . . . maybe she *was* too protective of Mark, remembering too much her own fears in childhood. . . . Finally, "Yes, David, come up."

She was right about David being a proud man. He didn't say he was sorry; only, "I'll be there tomorrow."

CHAPTER FOURTEEN

Summer, 1947

Mark didn't go boating, but waited for his father to arrive. He went into the Lodge where he was permitted to watch the gamblers playing at the dice tables. For a while it held his interest as the players spoke a new kind of language. "Crap," one said, while another shouted, "Come on, baby, come to papa," and the croupier calling out, "Eight's the point . . ."

If his father were here, he could have won every time. His father could do anything he wanted, and for a moment he heard again David saying to him, "You can do anything you want, if you've got what it takes. You've got to be up earlier than the next guy, you've got to take a chance on yourself and believe that you're better than the next man, you've got to be willing to gamble on your own abilities, that's the big secret, Mark. Remember . . ."

Tired of watching and itchy to see his father, Mark left the casino and walked across the wooden bridge that separated the main casino building from the small luxurious cottages that lay nestled in the pines on the lake front, built on stilts, their sundecks jutting out over the blue water.

As Mark approached the cottage and saw only the station wagon out in front, he became apprehensive, afraid that David wasn't coming after all and had decided to remain in the city. Maybe something important had come up. . . . By the time he reached the cottage and saw his mother sitting on the sundeck reading a book, he was more than a little worried. Katie put the book down as he approached.

"Are you having a good time, Mark?" she said, noticing the look in his eyes.

"It's okay. Did dad call? He's late. It's almost four and we won't have time to go boating." He had looked forward to going out and showing his father how well he could steer the small cabin cruiser, with the captain at his side.

"He'll be here soon, I'm sure, or he would have called," she said, knowing too well that David might not make it if "something" had come up between last night and today. She at least, though, ought to try to sound convincing. "He'll be here, Mark, I'm sure. Now why don't you let me order you a sandwich while you're waiting?" But Mark no longer felt hungry, only disappointed by his father's absence.

At seven o'clock they were in the dining room, seated on the California side of the room. This arrangement intrigued Mark, for just under the floor of Cal Neva Lodge was the dividing line between California and Nevada.

There was a new *maître d'* in the dining room. As Katie was seated, he slipped the napkin across her lap with a practiced gesture and bowed slightly from the waist. In accented English he said, "Enjoy your dinner, madame."

Katie had neither heard nor spoken French since that so long ago fairy tale trip to Paris with her Uncle Max. Suddenly the whole glorious event came into focus as though it were yesterday. She wondered if she still could make herself understood, and impulsively tried the obvious, "*Est-ce que vous êtes français, Monsieur?*" How exciting the sound was to her ear. The *maître d'* smiled; he had not spoken French for a very long while either. To whom would he speak, was his thought, accompanied by a Gallic shrug. To the croupiers in the gambling casinos, the American busboys, the cowboys turned waiters for the big summer season? So to hear his mother tongue spoken on the California side of Cal Neva Lodge made him enormously happy and piqued his nostalgia—indeed, for a brief moment his mind flashed back to his father's restaurant in Marseilles.

"*Ah, Madame, vous parlez français très bien.*"

"*Merci, Monsieur. Je ne parle pas français depuis longtemps, depuis l'énfance.*" She smiled diffidently but was obviously delighted.

"*Vous parlez magnifique,*" Marcel said lavishly.

"*Oh, comme vous êtes gentil.*" She nearly giggled. Marcel pursued the conversation in French. Could he order madame something very special, could he suggest the wine, *et pour le garçon,* what was his pleasure? He looked at Mark.

"A hamburger."

Marcel, betraying nothing, bowed as though being given the most gourmet of requests and made his way back to the kitchen, leaving Katie in a glow of remembrance.

She remembered how Uncle Max had taken her on the steamer across the channel so long ago, could still hear the sound of the water against the ship and see the white, foamy waves as it cut through, parting the channel on either side. They had docked at Calais, where they took a train which sped them across the French countryside to Paris. Speaking perfect French then, she now heard the voice of her youth ordering from the French menus as Uncle Max admired his niece's accomplishments. How far the distances were between that time in Paris and now. Looking across the table at her son, she felt all too strongly what he was feeling—it was all too apparent from the look of disappointment in his eyes as he kept them on the entrance to the dining room. Katie knew that Mark knew David was not coming.

Mark hardly touched the hamburger but toyed with it anyway, reluctant to show his mother how he felt, feeling she must be disappointed, too. Katie tried to make small talk. How would he like it if they went to Carson City tomorrow? Or they could get an early start and drive to Reno, or spend the day on the south shore.

Suddenly Mark jumped up from his chair and was

across the dining room. David. He'd come after all. Mark hugged him—it made no difference to him whether anybody saw or not—and kissed his father on the cheek. He had learned love from his mother, and felt no need to apologize for showing honest emotion, even if he were 13 and on the threshold of a new . . .

Exhilarated, he said, "Dad, when did you get in?"

"Just now. How are you, Mark?"

"I'm great, dad. We waited all day. Why were you so late?" He was too happy at the sight of his father to remember the earlier hurt.

"I had some business to take care of this morning and got a late start."

They crossed the dining room to the table and Katie. David looked down at her and smiled awkwardly, remembering the cruel things they'd said to each other, being careful not to allow his voice to betray him. As always, it was conditioned to reveal as little of his feelings as possible.

"How are you, Kate?" he asked, smiling now his best, most engaging smile. She knew that smile.

"Fine," she answered, remembering their reunion in New York after *that* long separation. But he was not the same and this was not the same. That was a different time, a different age, a hundred years ago. "And you?" she asked.

"Fine." He sat down. Marcel came over to take his order.

"Monsieur?"

Katie interrupted. *"Mon mari, il ne parle pas français."*

"Ah, Monsieur Reid, you 'ave a very charming wife. You are most fortunate."

David nodded. "Yes, thank you, I'm a lucky man." The flat tone in his voice tended to deny his words. Mark didn't notice, didn't want to. For him—for a while, at least—it was enough that his mother and father were together, and he was with them.

That night Mark fell asleep more content than in many months, and dreamed of boating with his father tomorrow.

There was less content elsewhere. There were no apologies offered by either one of them. Who had been right, who had been wrong? Did it matter? Katie lay beneath her husband, waiting for the climax. Was it a reconciliation . . . or an arrangement?

The next morning Katie had breakfast sent to the cabin. It was served on the sundeck while David looked out across the lake. He had never seen it before in all the time he had been in California. He'd missed a good deal, he thought. He had worked so hard without taking time out to enjoy the fruits, and for the first time was struck with the realization that there was indeed more to life than just making money. A man needed to refresh himself, and where better than in this marvelous place?

Mark sensed his father's pleasure as he looked out to the gorgeous blue lake.

"Isn't it great, dad?"

"It is that, Mark."

"Aren't you glad you came now?"

"You bet I am."

"When you get through, we'll go boating, okay? I called Andy Andrews this morning and told him we were going out."

"It's a date," David said, sipping his coffee.

"Did you ever hear a name like Andy Andrews, dad?" Mark asked, eating rapidly, and then noting the suddenly annoyed look on his father's face—and, of course, not understanding—hastened on to say he hadn't meant to make fun of Andy Andrews' name, he just thought it was sort of funny, "having your first and last names the same. Honest, that's all I meant—"

"I know you did, Mark," Katie interrupted, understanding very well David's reaction and thinking it interesting that David was still so sensitive on the subject. She suppressed an impulse to say aloud "What's in a name . . ."

The top of the convertible down, they proceeded to drive around the lake toward the boat landing. Riding along leisurely, taking in the beauty and observing the home sites for sale, David speculated on the cost of property up here. The further they went, the more beauty he observed, the more tranquil he felt. The usual tensions seemed to fade away. And an idea began to form in his mind.

"How would you like it if I bought a lot up here and built a house?" he said to Mark.

"Dad, do you really mean it?"

"Sure, I really mean it."

"Could it be down by the lake and could we have our own boat like some of the houses over there?" He pointed to the homes that stood snug and cozy among the pines at the lake's edge.

"We'll think about that later, but right now, would you like to spend your summers here? And," he added somewhat hesitatingly, "do you think your mother would like it?"

"And how! Wait till we tell her! Boy, that would be just great, dad . . ."

They were just about to turn into the dirt road at Andy Andrews' pier landing when a bee stung Mark on the arm. He bit his lower lip so hard the teeth marks showed momentarily. Frightened, he held back the tears, as he had the day he graduated. If he could do it then, with the pain he felt inside, he could endure this. After all, his father was here this time.

By the time they'd finished boating Mark's arm was quite swollen and the lump enlarged to twice the size; he was in agony. Hardly able to stand the pain, he rode back in awkward silence, thinking that he should make conversation with his father, worrying that David would be bored with him. He flipped on the radio, then, biting back the pain, he asked, "Did you enjoy it, dad?"

"Yes, very much. First time I've ever been on a boat like that," he said, remembering another boat on another day that he and Katie had first met. . . . He was sure he couldn't live without her then; wasn't sure he could live with her now. Their worlds were so apart. He'd grown, he'd gone on. She still clung to the past. . . .

David's silence made Mark again feel that his father was bored with him. Trying to ignore his arm, he said, "Would you like to go out again tomorrow, dad?"

"We'll see. Maybe."

"Would you rather go swimming. Mother could come along then and—"

"We'll see."

Again the silence.

Katie lay stretched out on a canvas chaise with her face to the sun, her eyes protected by the rose-colored glasses. She was coming to a decision—while they were away—about her life and Mark's that had increasingly been on her mind. Soon the summer would be at an end and September would be here before they knew. The more she thought, the more she was convinced that Mark should go away to school. It would be the first time in his life that he had been separated from her or, in fact, away from home. David had objected to the cost of camps and "all that kind of foolishness." He'd never gone to camp and he had managed to grow up, and not, by a long shot, in a place like Hillsborough. . . . Well, whatever his protests, if she decided it was better for Mark to go away to school, then she would see to it that he went. For the first time in her life she had some money of her own—Chaim's money, returned to her by David, the money that was to be used for a new life for the three of them. Well, David no longer needed it, but Mark did. Besides, it rightfully was Mark's legacy from Chaim—who saved his life as he saved hers. And who had loved him so. Am I right, Chaim? If he were here, he would have told her so. For her own reasons, she knew it was so. David seemed to resent Mark's having a father to provide the necessities and comforts of life, whereas Isaac had hardly done so for him. He also seemed to resent that Mark was closer to Katie than to him, going to her for advice and help in his emotional needs and not to David. Well, Katie thought, David couldn't have it both ways. He couldn't keep Mark at arm's length, give so little of himself and still have Mark feel a strong and abiding closeness with him. How ironic, she thought, that he seemed to repeat at least the emotional pattern with his son that he'd known with Isaac. Like Isaac with his son, David hadn't begun to know his son.

Mark had developed into a young boy with forbearance, with an intuitive understanding, which Katie had watched develop. If Mark had felt the rejection David had from Isaac, then Mark should have been hostile, belligerent, and hateful to David, but lucky man that David was, he had a son who at the age of thirteen not only very much loved his father but could ride over the aloofness—as though it were not there. Lucky, and yet so unlucky . . . David, it seemed, was simply unable to give love—at least to show it—anymore; it was as though the well had run dry, its contents lavished elsewhere. . . .

She lay smelling the scent of pine needles that had fallen onto the sundeck. Perhaps, she thought as she had before, David was right about one thing—perhaps Mark *was* too attached to her. Good reason in itself for sending him away to school. There were others. If anything happened to her or to David, Mark needed some greater sense of himself to survive such a blow. Who knew better than she the shock of a loved one's unexpected death—was it ever really expected? Not her father's, not her mother's, not Uncle Max's, not her young brothers', especially not Chaim's. Living apart from her for a year might be a great boost in developing strength and independence. It would also give Mark a respite away from the bickering and uneasy silences she tried with uneven success to avoid in his presence. Whatever the reality of David—she wasn't certain she always knew—Mark still needed a father to look up to. Given the state of things at home, that would be easier to manage with Mark removed from the scene. David might even still care, she reminded herself, but he no longer seemed to know how to show it—by now it was more like a tactic in closing a deal; method from another context seemed to have overwhelmed conviction and feeling on the human level. Success had had its way with David, just as he had had his with it—only he was paying the piper. If it were a myth she were building and perpetuating about David, she still would have succeeded in her purpose with Mark.

At first when David had returned the $1,500, she actually felt guilty, not really knowing why she should, except old habits tend to linger unaccountably. She immediately considered buying a piano, but she'd survived without one up to now and could continue to do so. What was it Chaim had said? *That* money was not meant for death—the past—but for life. Well, dearest Chaim, it now will be used for life, just as you willed it. Yes, she would invest the money in school tuition. Carefully she thought about where he should go. If he went east or down south it would be an expense she could not afford, considering the cost of transportation. There was a school on the peninsula, close to home, that she would investigate on her return, if her funds were sufficient, he would go in September to Menlo School for Boys, even though she undoubtedly would only be able to afford one year. This vacation Katie would not pay for out of Chaim's money, as at first she thought she would. David would pay, and when she got home there would be some other changes. It might be a battle—at least a modest opening salvo—but she was going to hire a full-time maid. Façades were not David's province alone. She would begin to live more as Mrs. David Reid should. She would try to keep the family together for all their sakes, but she would no longer deny her love for Judaism. She would say *Yahrtzeit* and light memorial candles for all her dear ones, even if she had to do it in the attic or some other place where David never went—she would find a place. There would be six. If need be, she would steal money from the household, but she would plant trees in their names in the soil of Israel, whose roots reached out to Canaan whence they had all come. And she would not have him dole out every cent he gave her. She laughed at her great emancipation. Dear me, hadn't she changed from that shy frightened girl who first came to David all tremulous with love. She had pretty well learned to live with her loneliness, her aloneness. Maybe David would still learn to open up . . . someday. No matter, she must finally learn to deal with the now in her life, with today. Understanding that David was a man living the most painful of charades, and a father who in his son seemed too often to see himself and the relationship with *his* father, was no longer grounds for her persistent submergence of her own and Mark's welfare. She wished it were not so. It gave her no pleasure . . . but there it was and, to survive, she'd have to face it. Survival—Katie was an expert at that. . . .

She heard Mark's voice as they entered the cottage and came out to the deck.

"Thanks, dad, for everything," he said as he went to his room to shower.

Drinks were sent up and they sat quietly sipping them, looking out at the blue lake. David asked, "How would you like to buy a house up here?"

Oh no, he had found a house? He was ready to buy a summer place before he'd settled the one on Rosehaven Road. Still, for Mark . . .

"I think that might be fine. Mark would have somewhere to go in the summer."

David tensed. As usual, he thought, she was thinking of Mark, not of him. He answered calmly, "Yes, I know he'd like it."

"Did you see a place you liked?"

"No, but I'm going out to look tomorrow," then added, "you want to go along?" remembering her reaction last time when she had not been consulted before he'd bought the house in Hillsborough.

The invitation sounded like an afterthought to Katie. "You find one you like and I'm sure it will be all right." She leaned back against the canvas chaise, lifted her face toward the sun again and put on her rose-colored glasses.

David was predictably angry at the response, understanding its source and resenting it. He was a damn good provider. He not only gave her a country mansion but now she would have the privilege of spending her summers in a lovely house overlooking the lake. Not so bad for a young girl who had come to him without a dowry, as a matter of fact he had even paid for her wedding dress. If he hadn't married her she could have wound up like Birdie, marrying another Solly. The odds dictated it, Hester Street was full of Sollys. . . .

Oddly enough, Katie too was thinking of Solly and Birdie, and David would have been astonished if he could have read his wife's mind—or had read anything more in the papers than the business section and headlines. Katie had indeed clipped an item out of the Sunday paper about Mr. Solomon Obromowitz, the noted Hollywood producer, who was going east with his lovely wife to be given a special award for having produced one of the ten best pictures of the year. Katie's first instinct was to show it to David, but she would not flaunt it in his face. She had to look twice, three times, at the picture to be sure if it was Solly and Birdie. How thrilled and excited she was, feeling that Solly deserved his success, and she only wished she could have shared Birdie's happiness. Observe, Mr. David Reid—formerly Mr. David Rezinetsky of Hester Street—Jews can make it without the elaborate deceptions to be someone in a gentile world. Imagine . . . someone with a name like Solly Obromowitz. Little Solly. Some joke, huh, David? But on whom? The clipping would take its place with other souvenirs of her past in the red heart box.

The next morning David and Mark set out right after breakfast along the Alpine Highway. There were some "For Sale" signs along the road, but David didn't like the houses, they were too close to the highway. As they drove further on he noticed that his gas indicator was almost empty, so he turned in at the first gas station he came to, parked beside the pump and got out, as he always did when he bought gas, to watch the service station attendant pump it into the tank.

"Good morning, Mr. Reid."

It was Andy Andrews, who had just driven up to fill his Ford pickup truck.

"Good morning," David said, irked at the young man's cheerfulness. He was in no mood for small talk.

When Mark saw Andy, he got out of the car, delighted to see him. Andy had become a very dear friend to Mark. It was the first time in his life that he had spent a period of time—a month—in the easy company of an adult male. He'd have liked it to have been with his father—the summer's excitement he'd had with Andy, the thrill of boating on the lake, but, of course, that hadn't been possible. Andy had become the summer replacement. But now his father was here, and Mark was proud to show him off.

"Where are you off to, Mark? Showing your dad the sights?"

"No, we're looking for a house and then I'll be up every summer and we'll go boating. Wouldn't that be great?"

"Sure would be, Mark. I'll look forward to it. You're a pretty good skipper, you know." He turned to David. "So you're looking for a place up here, Mr. Reid?"

David wished Mark hadn't mentioned it this way, could drive the prices up. He liked to poke around quietly first, sizing up things before he showed his hand. Besides, what business was it of this Andy's? Everybody wants to know your business. . . . "Maybe," he answered shortly, got into the car and shut the door.

"Listen, Mr. Reid, if you want to see a knock-out of a house, I know where there's one just coming on the market."

David looked at this blond handyman and wondered what the hell he would know about a "knock-out of a house." So he had a boat he rented out in the summer, so that made him an expert appraiser?

"Thanks very much, but we're really just out to show me the sights."

Not put off, Andy persisted. "I'm telling you, Mr. Reid, you ought to see this house. It's right down at the lakefront, secluded from the road."

"That's what my dad's looking for," Mark said, proud that his friend was so knowledgeable.

"Hold it a minute, will you, Mark," David said more sharply than he'd intended. Mark turned pink as a lobster, the embarrassment written on his face as he got back into the car. Andy felt sorry for the kid, being snapped at that way. Turning to get into the truck, he said to David, "Okay, Mr. Reid, just thought I'd mention it. So long, Mark. See you soon, fella."

Mark just waved goodbye.

David paid for the gas, started up the motor and they drove off in silence, David feeling more than somewhat uneasy as he saw Mark from the corner of his eye staring out the window, sitting close to the door, as far away from David as he could. Mark's feelings were badly hurt. He had no idea why his father had spoken to him in such a manner, and in front of his friend Andy. And what would Andy think of his father now? He'd been so proud that David was with him. . . . David knew he had hurt Mark, but didn't know how to tell him. He just couldn't come right out and say he was sorry. Katie, of course, could have gushed it all over the place; words were easy for her. He even tried to form them, and they literally stuck in his craw. What he managed was, "Mark, would you like to stop and have a coke?"

Mark shook his head without looking at his father. "No, thank you."

"Come on, Mark," David said, trying to act as though nothing had happened. "I'm going to have a soft drink. There's a place over there. I'm going to stop." He stopped the car and waited for Mark to get out, but he stayed as David opened the door on his side to step down.

"Come on, Mark, don't be like that. Don't be a sorehead."

Mark stole a glance at his father. Sometimes his father scared him, seemed really to hate him and he had no idea why. Maybe, though, like his father said, he *was* being a sorehead; maybe his father hadn't meant anything mean . . . maybe he *had* talked out of turn. Maybe that was the way adults were when they discussed business. Maybe he talked too much anyway. Maybe mothers and fathers were just different—one was soft and the other harsh . . . maybe that's the way men and women were . . . maybe it was his arm that was bothering him—God, it really did hurt. Maybe he'd misjudged his father. . . . He opened the door and went to David's side. Feeling ashamed and sheepish now, he smiled to show he really wasn't a sorehead, hoping his father understood, and feeling that in just the last few minutes he'd grown up a lot. He wasn't such a kid that his old man had to worry every second about his hurt feelings. He understood these things . . .

Looking at his father, trying to read his mood as they drank their sodas, Mark hesitated but decided to risk the subject of Andy and the house again now that things had calmed down.

"Dad," Mark said guardedly.

"Yes, Mark?" His father was no longer angry from the tone of his voice.

"Dad, I hope you won't mind if I suggest something, but why don't we take a look at the house Andy told you about?"

"Why would he know about houses, Mark?"

"Listen, dad, Andy's lived here all his life. I mean, around here; he really lives in Reno, but he knows about everything and he's got a lot of friends. Why don't we, dad? It might be just the place."

David wondered at Mark. A few minutes ago he seemed terribly hurt, sitting in the car like a wounded rabbit, and now here he was speaking as though nothing had happened. He got over things just like that, thought David. If Isaac had spoken to him that way, he wouldn't have talked to him for a week, which had happened so many, many times in his growing up, and even after. Mark was pretty tough, maybe he was more his father's son than he'd thought . . . when he wanted something, like a new house for his summers and maybe a boat of his own, he knew how to go after it. Well, well . . .

"Okay, Mark, we'll drive over to the landing and see if your friend's there."

"Hello again, Mr. Reid." Andy was cordial, but cool.

David nodded. "Look, tell me about that house. Do you think we could see it today?"

"Tell you what, I'll go back to the boathouse and telephone and see if the owners are there."

Mark went with him, praying that they would answer as Andy called and waited for the response. Then he heard Andy say pleasantly in a businesslike manner, "Hello, Mrs. Fleming," having, of course, no idea that Andy had more than a nodding acquaintance with the lovely mistress who lived there. In fact, for the last year and a half he had spent most of his evenings in her bed, which her husband shared only on the weekends, attending to business from Monday to Friday in San Francisco.

"Hi, sweetie, just couldn't wait to call? You'd think that after last night you'd be too weak to pick up a phone."

"Yes, well . . . we can talk about that another time. Mrs. Fleming, I have a man who wants to see the house, is it okay to bring him up?"

"When?"

"Right now."

"Do you have any idea where I happen to be?"

Andy cleared his throat. "Yes."

"Where?" she purred.

For God's sake, didn't she know that he couldn't talk? You'd think she would have guessed. She was going to find herself in plenty of hot water if she didn't take it easier. If her husband found out about them, she would never get the new house at Squaw Valley, where she wanted to spend the winters skiing (and where Mr. Fleming wouldn't be able to plough his way through the snow so readily and come up as often), while still being able to go boating in the summer. He didn't like the loose talk, not one damn bit. *He* ran the risk of being shot by a jealous husband, a prospect that struck him as distinctly unglamorous. Even a little buckshot in the rump could be damn painful. He winced as he pictured it. . . .

"Is it all right if we come up, Mrs. Fleming?"

"Tell me first where I am and what I've got on."

"I won't be able to do that, Mrs. Fleming."

"Mrs. Fleming?" she teased.

"That's right," he said.

"You afraid to say naked?"

"That's right."

She laughed. "Say it."

"I can't do that, Mrs. Fleming."

"Say naked."

"Well, I guess it won't be convenient for you after all. Thank you—"

Mark's heart sank.

"Wait a minute, don't hang up," she said, thinking about this afternoon.

"I'm sorry, Mrs. Fleming, these people are here and they wanted to see the house now, but . . ."

"All right, I won't tease anymore. I'll hop out of bed and get dressed. Give me about fifteen minutes, but stay after they leave."

"That will be fine, Mrs. Fleming, and thanks for your consideration."

It was a little sarcastic, she thought as they hung up, then quickly ran into the bathroom, showered and rubbed herself down with expensive cologne.

"Okay, Mark, I think we can go. Tell your dad to follow me."

Mark ran to the car and got in. They drove slowly back to Alpine Road for a few miles with Andy in the lead, then turned down a winding dirt road off the highway until they came to a house in the clearing.

David couldn't believe the sight that lay before him. The front of the house had a pair of heavy, rustic hand-hewn double pine doors that opened to an enormous living room–dining room combination. A portion of the floor in the entry was of smooth flagstones that angled off to meet plush yellow-green carpet. The house was all windows except for one stone wall with a huge two-story fireplace; the roof then sloped back to the bedrooms. It opened to a large sundeck that cantilevered out above the lake as though it floated on top. The furnishings were simple elegance. David was more than impressed. The door had been left unlocked. Andy opened it, and the three of them walked into the living room to wait for madame to make her appearance. Patricia Fleming didn't keep them in suspense, quickly making her grand entrance upon the scene, her perfume preceding and trailing.

She was about thirtyish, but one would never guess.

She was five years older than Andy, yet did not look as old as he. Her hair was light chestnut brown and fell softly across one eye as she pushed it back with a practiced gesture. She looked even more slim in the well tailored capri pants and the casual sweater that had cost $75 at Saks. At first glance David thought she had to be the daughter—nobody that young owned a place like this—but he soon learned otherwise.

"Mrs. Fleming, I would like you to meet Mr. Reid and his son Mark," Andy said.

She acknowledged the introduction in her best Vassar tone, from which college she had been expelled for being caught in the bushes one night with one of the young gardeners, and apprehended, in appropriate storybook fashion, by none less than the dean. Nothing was said of the incident but she was compelled to leave immediately, in the middle of the spring semester, telling friends she was sick of school and was going off to Europe with her family, which turned out to be true. If nothing else could be said of Patricia Wells Fleming, she never lied—except on those rare occasions, such as when Charles Fleming called in the middle of the week and asked what she was doing, to which she would say something to the effect of "Nothing, except missing you," as Andy lay nude, his legs spread over her, his head on her shoulder so that his heavy breathing could not be heard, thinking if he ever got married he would kill his wife if she deceived him as the lovely lady Fleming was doing.

David was not only in awe of the house, he was also in awe of Mrs. Fleming. He had never met such an elegant, gracious, well groomed woman in his whole life. Breeding and culture, you couldn't deny them.

"I'm very happy to meet you, Mr. Reid. Andy tells me you wanted to see the house. Feel free to wander about," she said as she and Andy walked out to the sundeck.

God, what a place! Never, but never, had he seen anything like this. Damn, he was going to have it, no matter what it cost. He'd work on the price, but he'd pay if need be. It wasn't necessary to look any further, he knew a good thing when he saw it, and to think he'd come by it through someone like Andy Andrews! Imagine Andy Andrews even knowing someone like Patricia Fleming. The chances were he'd just taught her how to sail or did repairs on her boat, and so naturally he'd heard of the house being on the market. Otherwise he'd never have gotten past that front door. Mrs. Fleming would never have invited him in if he hadn't brought them over.

Soon Patricia Fleming and Andy came back with a pitcher of martinis and a tray of chilled glasses. David watched as she graciously poured them. A lady! David accepted his and the three of them sipped.

Nobody noticed that Mark had walked from the deck to the boat landing, praying his father would buy the house.

When David finished his cocktail, Lady Patricia poured him another, wishing he would say something and quickly leave, now that he had seen the house. Did he like it, did he intend to buy it? Was he interested? Say something, instead of just sitting there. She wanted to get rid of him and that kid, whatever his name was. She and Andy needed to get on with the rest of the day.

"Well, Mr. Reid, I'm so happy Andy brought you over, and thank *you*, Andy, it's nice of you to remember me. I'll have to make it up to you somehow." She put down the cocktail, extended her hand in an unmistakable gesture of goodbye, and took David's. The lady's hand was so soft, so delicate.

"I'm sorry, Mrs. Fleming, that we stayed so long," David said.

"Not at all."

"Tell me, what are you asking for the house?" It was a question he ordinarily waited much longer to ask. But nothing was ordinary in the company of Patricia Fleming.

"Oh, Mr. Reid, I'm really terribly stupid about money." She laughed, making the subject sound so vulgar. "You'll have to speak to Charles about that. I never interfere in money matters." She smiled her helpless smile.

"I can understand that. How can I get in touch with your husband?"

She could hardly wait for them to leave. "Charles will be here this evening. It's Friday, you see."

"What time should I call?"

"Oh, let's see . . . about eightish?"

"It won't be inconvenient then?" he said, still pressing her hand gently.

"Not at all," she said, still smiling. If you called this afternoon, that would be inconvenient, she thought, but this evening—please be my guest. She walked them to the car and said good-bye.

David got into the car before he realized Mark hadn't come back yet. Andy said, "Let me go back and get Mark. He probably went down to the pier landing."

Pat said goodbye and, keeping proper distance, she and Andy walked back to the house. Once inside, she held him close, ran her fingers through his hair and whispered, "Come back soon. I haven't got a thing on under this. I'll be waiting."

He shook his head and wondered how she could stand getting laid so soon after the strenuous night that they had had. Thursdays were always "the most" because she wouldn't have him again until Monday.

He went out onto the sundeck and down the planked stairs, where he found Mark, then walked him back to the car without going through the house again. David took out three one-dollar bills and handed them to Andy. He was in a good mood, and remembered that on another occasion three dollars had bought him a job. Andy looked down at the money. Who the hell did David Reid think he was? A big shot because he had a Cadillac? Was he kidding? Why, his father could buy and sell him twice over—he owned one of the oldest and biggest hotels and gambling casinos in Reno. Which was why Andy could afford to be a skipper for hire on a boat that had cost $45,000. It had been a whim of his to live the simple life, and Mr. Andrews had said, "Okay, if that makes you happy, go to it, Andy, my boy."

He looked back at David. David assumed he was being humble; a nice trait, humility. Andy wanted to spit in his eye as he handed the money back to Mr. Reid, saying, "Thank you very much, but I just couldn't accept your generosity." David took the money back and thought, pride, that's a nice quality too. Andy had gone up in David's opinion. He might not have much else, but he had pride. David understood *that* very well.

CHAPTER FIFTEEN

David waited for the *maître d'* to seat them at dinner.

"Good evening, Monsieur Reid et Madame. I have your table ready."

David grunted good evening under his breath, while Katie smiled and said, *"Comment allez-vous ce soir?"*

"Très bien, merci, et le petit garçon?" looking at Mark.

Mark said, "Fine, thank you." Katie had decided it wasn't a crime to talk a little French around the house, and teach Mark in the process.

Marcel bowed slightly and seated them at their table.

It annoyed David that Katie was being so friendly with a waiter, or whatever the hell he was. Patricia Fleming wouldn't have. But that was Katie, speaking to everyone, no matter who they were—butcher, baker, waiter. A woman in her position . . . after all, she was his wife.

Silently they sat watching the other diners, each with his separate thoughts. David thought about Katie's lack of reaction earlier in the day when he had come home and told her about the new house and what it was like, while Mark had given her a room-by-room description, especially about the private pier where maybe they could have a boat next summer when dad could afford it. And all she had done was smile and say casually that it sounded delightful. And she was going to live there. . . . One would think she at least would say something like "Thank you, David," or "I'm so thrilled, David."

David, of course, missed the point of the matter. When he had told her about the house, she was not enthusiastic because she felt it was mostly a new testimonial for *him.* It was another monument to his success in an unkind, alien world, another testament to his wisdom in outsmarting that world for the last thirteen years. Yet he made himself believe—and would have Katie and Mark believe—that he was doing it for them. David's growing proficiency in deceiving the world was spilling over to himself and his family . . . And how, she wondered, could he ever be made to see it . . .?

"Dad, what time is it?"

David looked at his thin Patek Phillipe watch and answered under his breath, "Eight o'clock."

"Aren't you going to call Mr. Fleming?"

"When I've finished eating. When I'm ready—"

"I know, dad, but you said you were going to call at eight." A promise was very much a promise to Mark.

"When I'm *ready,* I said." His voice was tight. Looking at Mark, David said, "Never show the next guy you're that anxious, you lose a lot of edge that way. Let Fleming sweat, let him wonder if I'm going to call."

Mark stopped eating, toyed with his french fries so his feelings would not be too obvious, remembering this morning; but hard as he tried, tonight he just couldn't dismiss his father's attitude toward him. It wasn't his imagination, not this time.

"May I be excused?" he asked, his voice low.

"Of course, Mark, here are the keys," Katie said.

"Thanks for dinner, dad," he said. He walked across the floor, not sure whether his father had said okay or not, going as fast as he could through the casino and over the wooden bridge to their cabin. Once there, he threw himself on his bed. His father hated him, and he couldn't understand why.

Marcel looked down at the half-eaten, succulent chicken and the small artichokes in the delicate French sauce that hadn't been touched, a dish fit for a baroness. He removed the plate unhappily, knowing he had failed madame.

Leaving the table, David went to the phone to call Mr. Fleming as Katie sat stirring her black coffee. How inconsiderate David had become, she thought. How does one learn to deal, to cope with a mixed-up man who isn't aware of how he hurts or whom? She had asked him so many times before to be kind to Mark; it wasn't necessary to scream or to speak harshly. Mark responded to kindness, but David was so ready with his answers. How many times he had said to her, "That's what's wrong with him, you mollycoddle him, he's becoming so damn sensitive that the least thing you say to him his tender feelings are hurt . . . I'm warning you, if you don't stop you're going to make a girl out of him. . . . In this world you've got to be tough; I've got to make a man out of him." . . . But she knew as she sat here, projecting the vision of her son ten years from now that he would be stronger than David, because Mark had already begun to show signs of having the strength to forgive, to love even when he felt unloved by a father who confused himself with his son. It was as though David were punishing Mark now instead of Isaac. She knew that what Mark needed most right now was to be alone for just a little while to try to figure out the rebuffs for himself. Time enough to comfort him as soon as David left and she could tell him—and herself—that David hadn't meant it, that he would be sorry, that deep down his father was really a very good man. . . .

Meanwhile, David had arrived at the Fleming home. Turning off the lights, he sat in the car for a few minutes drinking in the scent of pine and watching the moonlight play on the water. How peaceful it was here, a place for a man to renew his spirit. Lighting a cigarette, he watched the gray-white smoke dissipate into the perfumed night air, then got out of the car, walked to the front door and rang. It was opened by a young man; David wasn't sure of his age as he stood shaking his hand and introducing himself. Perhaps 28; no, he had to be older than that. Nobody could own a house like this—for the summer, no less—and be that young, he thought.

He was right about the age. Charles Fleming I, grandfather of the present thirty-five-year-old heir to the throne, held a seat on the New York Stock Exchange which Charles II had inherited; and Charles III had been presented with his seat as a wedding present by his father the day he married the lovely lady Patricia Wells. The letterhead on the stationery of the brokerage firm that Charles Fleming chaired read, "Fleming, Fleming, Hadley, Morley and Fleming."

David followed Charles into the spacious living room and sat down on the large bronze linen velvet chair across from Charles. He felt the texture of the material and by touch knew it was expensive, just as expensive as the casually studied clothes that his host wore. David felt more than a touch of jealousy at the young man's wealth, his attire, and the easy manner as he sat lighting his pipe. No denying, breeding like this had to come from genteel—gentile—forebears. He must look "new rich" to Charles in his plaid slacks and silk shirt that undoubtedly cost as much or more than Charles Fleming III's—as though he still had the mark of Hester Street on him. For a moment he had an antic thought . . . saw Lady Patricia and Lord Charles in bed together, both so elegant, lying side by side without betraying a drop of perspiration, so elegant, she so ladylike, so charming, and at the end her saying, "Thank you so much, Charles, it was indeed lovely."

"What will you drink, Mr. Reid?"

Charles's question snapped David out of his boudoir fantasy. And then made him feel even more like a Hester Street push-cart peddler. Tell the truth, he didn't quite know what to drink in the presence of this elegant man. Since he had left New York, no one had made him feel so uncomfortable or inadequate, and he despised Charles Fleming III for making him feel this way. He found himself unable to make even that small decision, and answered, offhandedly, "I don't know. What are you going to have?"

"I drink Scotch myself after dinner, but have anything you like, brandy, bourbon. . . ." David hated the sureness of this bastard, and he hated Scotch almost as much as he hated Charles.

"Yes, that's what I drink—I'll have Scotch, thanks."

"Over the rocks or with a dash of soda?" Charles asked from behind the bar, which was complete with tiny sink and small refrigerator under it.

"Same as you, thanks," David said with his special smile. He heard the tinkle of ice being dropped into the tall, Waterford glasses, then the squirt of siphoned water.

"A twist of lemon?"

"Yes, thanks." At last he found himself holding the glass in his hand. The cold felt good against his sweating palm.

"Well, Mr. Reid, Patricia tells me you're interested in buying the house."

David was out of enemy territory; now Charles was in his camp.

"I'm interested in anything if it can be bought at the right price." And the minute he had said it, David thought he should never have tried to show his shrewdness to someone like Charles Fleming; for a moment he hated himself for sounding like a cocky Jew trying to bargain. He should merely have said, "What are you asking?" Well, he had never bargained with royalty before.

"As you know," he heard Charles say, "the house is not officially listed as yet. To be honest, I'm not so anxious to sell, but my wife wants a different kind of house, some place where she can ski in the winter and still be in reach of the lake during the summer. She doesn't like the skiing as much here as in Squaw Valley. So we've been sort of debating."

Charles twirled the glass casually in his hand, revolving the ice, but David wasn't buying it for a minute. Charles knew whether or not he wanted to sell the house, who was he kidding? This stalling didn't fool him. He was speaking David's language now.

Proceeding now on a different tack, he said casually, "You do intend to sell, though, eventually?"

"Yes. As a matter of fact, Patricia is rather anxious to buy a house that she had just seen, and this being July, she would like to dispose of this one before the end of summer. I happen to like this part of the lake, but she spends most of the summer up here while I commute back and forth to town. I come back on Friday for the weekend. It does seem wrong to have a place she's not happy with if she has to spend the most time in it."

That was why Fridays were significant. Suddenly Andy flashed through his mind. Andy and the Lady Fleming?

"Well, Mr. Fleming, I have to go back tomorrow myself. I happen to be in business in San Francisco too, so I thought if you were interested in negotiating a deal, it would save me a lot of work. The only reason I'm interested in buying at all is because of my son. He's thirteen and likes to go boating, and he rather took to the place. You do a hell of a lot of things for your family," David said as he took a sip, "even if it takes a little sacrifice on your part. After all, what do we live for if it isn't to make our wives and our children happy?" Lighting a cigarette, he said confidingly, "I don't even know when I'll be able to spend time with them myself, I'm sorry to say."

How right the man was, Charles thought, especially when he remembered Patricia and how restless she had been in the city, living from one cocktail party to the next, one social event to the other, never able to find what she wanted. And in the last three summers she had become a different person, so calm, as though she had found herself in this rural atmosphere. At least here he always knew where she was and the four days' separation made each weekend seem like a honeymoon, as though they were more mistress and lover than husband and wife. If this was what it took to keep their marriage together, it was a small price to pay. A short separation each week for three months; better that than to come home each night and find a discontented wife. Look what this man was doing for his son and his wife. What good was anything if your marriage was uneasy . . . ?

"I must be honest with you. I really have no idea what I want for the house."

"Well, Mr. Fleming, you know what you paid for it," David said in his most agreeable tone.

"Yes, I do, because we built it ourselves; but two years ago I put a lot of extra money into the boat landing and a lot of other things which I would have to consider."

"If you will forgive me, Mr. Fleming, we're both businessmen . . . now, let's be realistic. This is strictly a home of luxury. It has a very limited market and if you don't sell it this summer, it will sit here all winter and maybe by the time you do get around to buying, you might lose the other house because you can't sell this one. That's the way it is with real estate."

"You sound like you know a great deal about it."

"I do. As a matter of fact, that's my business. Now the second thing is, and mind you, I'm merely suggesting, if you put it in the hands of an agent it means paying a commission which cuts down your profit." David took a sip of the Scotch and now Charles followed his suit. "And here again I'm only going to suggest, but if you want to sell, I'm a prospective buyer right here, right now willing to negotiate a deal with you; and believe me, Mr. Fleming," David said in his most sincere voice, "I've seen people turn down a deal when they should have sold and they sat with a piece of property for years and finally had to give it away because their timing was off. Now that might not happen to you, but, on the other hand, I could turn around and buy another house tomorrow. Those are the hazards of the trade."

David let Charles mull it over for a few minutes. Then, "Now, as you know, I'm a businessman and when I get back I have an enormous chore ahead of me. We're starting a large shopping center"—David thought that might impress even Sir Charles Fleming, at least let him know he wasn't dealing with just anyone—"so my situation may change and, who knows, maybe in a month I won't be in the market for a house such as this."

Charles thought for a moment. He still wasn't ready to commit himself, so he said, not having made up his mind, "Here, let me freshen your drink, Mr. Reid."

Oh God! David wanted to say no, but he had to reach this young man and thought he was beginning to see signs of weakening. He'd drink poison if he had to and take an antidote later. Charles III was a very big fish to him. It was very important that he land him.

"Sure, I'd love another."

Charles poured the drinks, and while he stood behind the bar, he decided he really should sell it. It would make Patricia so happy to have the new house and what the hell difference did it make if he liked the lake front? And maybe, maybe, you can't keep this and her, too. The house will sit here all winter and she'll be unhappy because she didn't get the one in Squaw Valley, and then the problems will start all over again with the restlessness and the never knowing where she is . . . As Charles poured the Scotch, squirted the siphoned water and dropped the ice into the glasses, David didn't know it yet, but he had just bought himself a house. Not to mention, for a change, all the furniture in it.

The deal concluded an hour later, Charles Fleming walked David to the car, shook hands, and waited until the car disappeared. He stood alone in the pine-scented night and thought what a fine man David Reid was; that he had helped him come to a decision about what he had known all the time; that things can't be one-sided: there were always compromises that one had to make with life and if Mr. Reid was willing to do this for his son, then it also made Charles feel good to give up a house in which he would have loved to raise a son of his own.

It was 12:30 by the time David returned to the cabin with the sales agreement clutched in his no longer sweaty palm. In those few hours he'd found out a lot about Charles Fleming. Maybe he wasn't a Harvard graduate, but he had emasculated the scion of the House of Fleming. The smart guy with the background and loaded with all those stocks and bonds hadn't outsmarted David. David had bargained every fine point with the man until he was like a punch-drunk fighter asking for the knock-out. Of course, the third, fourth, and fifth Scotches did no harm. David had not only outwitted him—in fact, David had even outdrunk him, even though he detested Scotch. Hester Street had some advantages, after all. A goy, is a goy, is a goy. Wait a minute . . . what the hell was wrong with him, a goy? *He* was a goy, wasn't he? He must be having a delayed reaction to the drinks. He had never been drunk in his life, but he was drunk now, especially from the feeling of power.

Walking into the cottage, he found Katie and Mark asleep. Damn it, no one to share his great moment with. He was indeed drunk now, more drunk than he realized, as he stumbled ever so slightly out onto the sundeck and sat down on the canvas chair in the moonlight. We showed 'em. We? *I* showed 'em. A goy, is a goy, is a goy.

David woke a little later than usual. He felt *good* this morning. What a day! As he brushed his teeth, shaved, and combed his hair, observing himself in the mirror, he decided he compared more than favorably with Charles Fleming—was better built, had more character written in his face and was smarter. At thirty-seven he was trimmer, in better shape than he had been at twenty-seven. Like other good things, he improved with age. Damn right . . .

Clad only in his shorts, back in the bedroom, he picked up the checkbook and looked at the amount he had written for the deposit on the house and glanced again over the purchase agreement. Boy, hadn't he made a deal, the deal of the century, and all because he knew where Charles was most vulnerable. The clue became all too obvious as soon as Charles mentioned that Patricia wanted the mountains while he wanted the shore. David knew he had him right there. If Charles had been strong he would have said to his Lady Patricia, "This is where we live; this is where we stay. If you don't want it, you're welcome to leave. It's as simple as that." So David thought . . . but it wasn't that simple for Charles Fleming. Charles just happened to be so in love with Patricia Wells Fleming that he would try to hold her no matter what the cost. David sensed this and knew it was the man's vulnerability. What he didn't realize was that it was also the man's strength.

David carefully selected an expensive silk sports shirt and a pair of matching slacks, then appraised himself after he'd dressed. Feeling on top of the world, he walked to the sundeck, where Katie and Mark were already having breakfast.

"Good morning."

"Good morning, dad," Mark said, trying not to remember last night—the talk he and Katie had later had done much to soothe his feelings, but he would not risk another rebuff by asking about the house and whether his father had bought it.

"Good morning, David, you got home late?" Katie said. She said it pleasantly.

"Yes, I did. I'll have a cup of coffee if there's any left in the pot, and tell you all about it."

She lifted the lid of the coffee pot and found that there was some left, poured a cup, handed it to David and said, "Before you begin, don't you want me to ring and have some breakfast sent up for you?"

He was bursting to tell them, but decided it could wait now until after breakfast since she hadn't been interested enough to want to know right away.

"Beautiful day, isn't it, dad?"

"Yeah, great."

"What do you think we should do today?"

Mark was learning—no more "Let's go boating."

"We're going home after breakfast."

"Dad, you just came up." Mark's disappointment was impossible to mask.

"I know, but I have a lot of business at the office and a lot of phoning to do and besides, I want to get in touch with Jim Fowler before Monday."

"But, dad, couldn't it wait for a few days? We hardly ever get any time together . . ." Mark hesitated, then cautiously went on, "I thought . . . now don't get mad, dad . . . I thought maybe we could go boating just once more. Could we?"

"I'm sorry, Mark, I have to get back. It's just one of those things."

Mark got up without further word and left.

The waiter brought the breakfast and David ate heartily, relishing it.

"David," Katie said, "don't you think this one time you could make an exception? This is such an important time in his life, he's going into high school this year and will be growing up so fast from now on that his demands on us will be very little. Give him these few days, you won't regret it . . ."

David pushed the plate away. The day that had begun so perfectly was now clouded with her nagging. She was making him look the heavy, herself the concerned mother heroine. What about *his* feelings, how hard he worked? If he had led a life of fun, of ease and vacations, he wouldn't be where he was today, and they wouldn't either. Even with last night's triumph, he'd momentarily felt guilty about oversleeping this morning, like a child playing hooky. Discipline, the long years of denial, were his ever-present companions, the fear of poverty his close kin, and here she stood, acting as though he were doing something so terrible to a deprived Mark. Why didn't she say, *you* need a vacation, David? No, she never seemed to think about the way he worked, the hours he put in, how bone tired he was. And never did she, or anyone else, know how bad things really could be for him. . . . He answered firmly, "No, we're going home. I told you I have too much to do, can't waste any more time. He's been up almost a month now. I think that's being a pretty good father, don't you?"

She didn't answer.

"I bought the house," he said, almost as an afterthought. "I'm almost sorry I did, my efforts seem to be so taken for granted. I'm going to pack now and I want to leave as soon as possible." He got up abruptly, and she sat holding back tears.

They packed their suitcases. Mark called the bellboy to put them into the car and directed which case went into which car. He went back to the sundeck to take one last look at the lake and turned away, hating to leave, especially without saying goodbye to Andy; feeling too a deep unhappiness that he and his father had somehow just not been able to make it. He did not know who had failed whom, or the answer to the more important question—why there should be a failure at all. It made him afraid.

Katie got into the Ford station wagon. David got into the Cadillac and started the engine, wondering if he should suggest she see the new house. After a moment, he turned off the motor and went over to her car.

"Would you like to see the house before we leave?" He said it like a formal invitation.

"All right, if you want to."

"If you want to." It would kill her, of course, to say, I would love to. God forbid she show a little enthusiasm.

"Wait here. I'll call and see if the Flemings are at home." He returned soon to tell her it was okay.

David got back into his car, started the motor once again and drove off as Katie followed with Mark. He drove down the dirt road until he reached the house, *his* house, stopped the car and got out. Charles opened the door dressed in blue denim shorts, a simple T-shirt and tennis shoes, looking even younger, taller and leaner than last night. You wouldn't know he had a quarter, rich bastard. Didn't come up the hard way, no lines of poverty written on his face, no lines of hunger written in his gut.

Well, it was David's house now and one day soon he would have that no-sweat look of the rich. Soon he would have enough not to need to impress *anybody*. What an incredible relief *that* would be . . .

"Mr. Reid, how are you today?" Charles Fleming said, smiling.

"Fine, and you?" David smiled, too. You could light a building with the smile power, he thought ironically.

"Fine, thanks. And I take it that this is Mrs. Reid and your son? So nice to meet you," he said, looking to Katie and Mark. "Come in."

They entered the stone foyer, from where could be seen the sundeck and Patricia lying on a chaise lounge in the sun, one leg arched, the other extended straight. She did not bother to move.

"Come meet my wife, she's on the sundeck," he said to Katie. "You've never met, I understand."

He led the way through the wide open glass doors as Patricia stood up, displaying a scant bikini that barely covered the one strip of white flesh on her otherwise bronzed body where the bikini had slipped ever so slightly below the umbilicus and the pelvic region; and although her bosom was just ample, just, still the bra held little even of that. She was barefooted, her toenails well pedicured and delicately painted pearlized summer pink, the same as her tapering fingernails.

Extending her hand to David, she threw back the heavy chestnut hair that fell over one eye to hang softly to her shoulders.

"How are you this morning, Mr. Reid?" she said in that same Vassar tone he remembered from when he first met her.

"Thank you, and you?" David replied warmly.

"Patricia, I want you to meet Mrs. Reid and their son, Mark," Charles said.

"Mrs. Reid, happy to know you and . . ." damn it, again she couldn't remember what that child's name was. She was really paying no attention to the introduction anyway; Charles could have been introducing her to a piece of liver for all she cared. She was concerned only with the fact that David had bought the house so soon, delighted that he did, fearing that she would go back to the city without it being sold. Thank you, Mr. Reid—a girl's best friend. Her thoughts were interrupted as she heard that child say,

"Mark—" his voice cracked; it rose and fell in squeaky resonance—"my name is Mark Reid," he repeated, embarrassed over more than the sound of his voice. He had seen girls at the beach or in pictures, he'd seen his mother, but never had been so affected as he was when he observed Lady Patricia's bronzed body in the bikini. Thoughts and feelings came rushing at him so rapidly he began to grow weak. Although sex was not a forbidden topic, and he had learned about conception and birth from his mother, Mark still found it a curious, confusing, and embarrassing thing. For example, childbirth happened to other ladies, not *his* mother . . . And he had certainly never been exposed to such blatant eroticism as now confronted him. To hide his unease, he walked down to the lake front, grabbed up a handful of pebbles and proceeded to throw them one at a time into the water as hard as he could.

The Flemings proved to be early drinkers, a large pitcher of martinis standing on the table by eleven o'clock in the morning.

"Would you care for a martini, Mrs. Reid?" Charles asked.

"No, thank you very much."

Charles thought, what a lovely lady, but such sad eyes. He looked again—no, not sad . . . tender and, well, soulful. "How about you, Mr. Reid?" he asked.

"Thank you, but I think I'll beg off. We're driving back this morning," David answered, sounding most friendly and sure of himself. Not so bad for Hester Street, just as smooth and easy as Harvard. "We're driving back to the city. Got to keep your wits about you, especially when you have your family with you. A man can't be too careful." He smiled his can't-be-too-careful smile.

Lucky man, thought Charles, lovely devoted wife, exceptionally well-behaved son, especially in this day and age, shook hands like a man, handsome, poised and well-adjusted. Some men are so lucky, everything just seems to fall in place for them. Lucky people. He would have given up not only the seat on the stock exchange but his share in heaven if he had this. Charles looked at David. "Mr. Reid, why don't you show Mrs. Reid through the house, just the two of you? Take all the time you want; we're not going anywhere."

"Thank you, Mr. Fleming, that's so kind," Katie said.

David took Katie from room to room as though he were Louis XIV conducting a guided tour through the Palace of Versailles, showing a commoner the palace for the first time.

"Well, what do you think?" David said, forgetting how aggravated he had been with her this morning, so excited at the deal he had made and the prospect of having this that for the moment he even forgave her. Today he had reached the zenith; he could overlook almost anything. For the moment . . . His thoughts were interrupted when Katie said, "It's absolutely beautiful. This is the loveliest, most unusual house I've ever seen," and she meant it, even though as she said it she felt she did not belong here. It was not her house. It never would be.

Patricia Wells Fleming adjusted the back of the chaise, seated herself in a reclining position and put on the large sunglasses—mustn't let the sun play around the eyes, it wrinkles one so badly before her time. She toyed with the toothpick in the martini glass, twirled the green olive at the other end and considered Mrs. Reid, so plain, so unglamorous, though admittedly with possibilities. Wouldn't you think, though, that with money, even *nouveau riche* money, a woman would be more careful about herself to make sure her husband didn't stray, which she had no doubt in the world the attractive Mr. Reid did. Probably had some adorable love nest on some little hill somewhere in San Francisco. And why not? People made mistakes in their youth, married when they were young, and lived to regret it. God, she ought to know. Of course maybe—unlike decent, gentle, ineffective Charles—Mrs. Reid was the kind who was prim-proper in the drawing room and a tiger in bed? Maybe . . . but not likely. She suspected that, like herself, David Reid took his business elsewhere, and that—also like herself—with him business was good.

She had, of course, no idea how right—and how wrong—she was. And it was unlikely she cared—her inclination being to find fellow-sufferers to justify her own behavior.

"Well, now, Mrs. Reid," Patricia heard Charles saying in that irritatingly gentle voice, "I hope you found the house to your liking."

I bought the house, David thought. Why the hell doesn't he ask me?

"It's the loveliest house I've ever seen. I only hope we'll be as happy as you've been."

Oh, my God, Patricia thought, this is all I need today, little Mary Sunshine. She got up abruptly and said, "I hope so, just as happy," then, adding "Nice knowing you," she dismissed them all by entering the house, heading straight for the bar, pouring herself a double Scotch on the rocks and disappearing into her bedroom, finally slamming the door hard behind her.

David watched as she made her dramatic exit. A lady—even in the revealing bikini. He looked to Katie, thinking how she might look and act under similar circumstances, and feeling at once a renewed sense of discontent—and a new sense of excitement he neither understood nor, at the moment, recognized for what it was. . . .

David called to Mark that they were leaving, and Mark met them at the car, opting to drive with David as far as the Nut Tree Inn, just past Sacramento, where they would have lunch. Mark and David got into the Cadillac, and Katie into the Ford station wagon. Charles Fleming stood in the driveway watching the cars leave in a small cloud of dust as they made their way to the main highway, thinking again how lucky some men were. That fine little boy, that lovely, serene wife. How lucky can you get?

Mark wanted to drive back to the city with his father not only because he had spent the last weeks with Katie and wanted to be alone with David in the car, but also because he wanted to show his father how much he appreciated that David had bought the house so he could spend the summers here. It took quite a father to go to such expense. He really would have something to tell his friends, not just about his first exciting vacation and that he might even have a boat of his own but also about what a really great guy his father was after all. However, there was another reason he asked Katie if it were all right to drive with David: he needed a man's advice about the things that had happened to him today, the strange sensations, the disturbing feelings.

As he drove along the road heading for Sacramento at his father's side, the more miles they covered the more difficult it became for him to launch into the subject. How did you say to your dad you felt guilty because you had thoughts about your mother having been in a compromising position, the kind of position that he heard kids discuss at school about what girls and boys did in the bushes and parked cars? How did you say that you had compared your mother with the bronzed lady in the bikini with the triangle of hair beneath the panties, and that you even knew what there was beyond that, and that your mother had the same, well, things? He resented Patricia Fleming for having evoked these feelings in him, and he was vaguely ashamed of himself—as well as being confused about what he felt. So, as the mileage went up, his courage went down. In the end he decided it would be impossible for him to ask after all, so he tried to shut away the whole thought and erase the awful mental pictures he had had earlier today. He decided to speak to his father about something else, but what? Real estate, that's it, real estate; he was as uninformed and ignorant about that subject as he was about sex. But this was his father's favorite topic, so he could ask the questions and then sit back and listen. It would be better than the silence between them now.

"Dad, how do you make a deal with someone?"

"What kind of a deal?" David asked as he sped along.

"I mean like when you bought the house from Mr. Fleming. What do you say?"

David was surprised, but pleased. It was the first time Mark had shown an interest in his business.

Maybe he wouldn't be such a loss after all. David began as though he were a lecturer speaking to a group of young students interested in how to buy and sell real property, launching into the subject of how to make a million dollars with the investment of a few. He started by explaining the fundamentals —financing, interest rates, where to go for the best bargains; how to buy, when to sell, what to invest; to watch the trends, to go along with the big buyers because if they invested it was likely the risks were fewer. He instructed Mark, emphasizing the fact that the adage "A fool and his money are soon parted" was crazy. If a man had a lot of money, he couldn't be a fool to begin with—unless he had inherited it from his father, thinking of Charles Fleming—he was talking about the man who anteed up his wits and ingenuity against the odds. On and on went the lecture.

By this time Mark was more confused about the real estate business than he was about sex, and wished he'd never asked his father about how to make a deal. Bored stiff, he wanted to turn on the radio and drown out his father's voice, for David had been carried so far afield from the simple question Mark had asked, awash in his own rhetoric, that he had nearly forgotten Mark was in the car.

Mark kept turning around to see if Katie was behind them, but she was lost from sight, having lagged behind a truck, and he began to panic, wondering if maybe she had a flat tire. He asked David to slow down and wait until she could catch up with them (that is, if nothing had happened) but David continued right on with the challenges of his business. It wasn't as simple as it looked, this was only a business for people who believed in themselves . . . Mark kept watching, hoping that Katie would catch up with them. Finally he saw her swerve around another car; now she was in back of them and he was more at ease. Mark was no longer listening to his father. One thing he knew for certain and one thing he was wondering about—for certain he knew he was definitely *not* going into the real estate business; he wondered about what he was going to have for lunch, being almost tired of hamburgers and french fries.

God finally granted him a reprieve as they came to a stop in the parking area in front of the Nut Tree Inn. He could hardly wait to get out of the car. The two experiences he had had today were the most exhausting he could remember, and he hoped he could drive the rest of the way home with Katie. He and David went to the men's room and washed up while Katie went to the ladies' room. As they walked back to the table, David said to him, "I hope you learned something today, because what I've just told you I had to learn the hard way. I mean, the hard way. I wish there had been someone to advise me when I was coming up. You're luckier than I was and don't you forget it."

He wouldn't forget it. He wouldn't be in real estate. As they approached the table Mark decided to have the hamburger and french fries after all. No more major decisions wanted just now.

They sat at the table, each with their separate thoughts.

After lunch Mark switched to Katie's car. She followed David, speeding along the highway toward the Golden Gate Bridge, which would take them across to San Francisco, where they would turn off the Bayshore Highway to home. Suddenly Mark was happy he was going home, to things at least familiar and so somehow more safe.

"You know, mom, I'm glad we're going home," he said as he peered out the front window to see if they were still following David.

She nodded. "Are you happy about the new house?"

"I sure am. We're going to have a great time next summer. I can hardly wait."

"Did you have a nice drive with your father?"

Gosh, how did you tell your mother that you hated every minute of it, especially when your dad had just bought you a place for the summer? How did you say that you'd asked your father a question and he had provided you with a whole bible, complete with chapter and verse on how to succeed in the real estate business on small capital, how to go from rags to riches in one very long lesson? How did you tell her that what you really wanted to do was talk over with your father yourself, why you felt as you had today, about being so affected by Mrs. Fleming, about being bothered most of all by the realization that your mother was made the same way as Mrs. Fleming, and that she was no longer quite as *different* as she had been earlier that same morning.

"We talked about a lot of things."

"That's nice." After a pause, she said softly, "Mark . . ."

"Yes, mom."

"Mark, I've been thinking."

"About what?"

"I've been thinking that it might be very nice for you to go away to school at Menlo next year."

"What?" His voice rose in shock. "I don't want to go away from home."

"Well, you know it's not really like going away from home as Jim Parks did. It's so close it would hardly be like going away at all."

"Well, what's wrong with Burlingame?"

"Nothing at all, Mark, it's a lovely school."

"Then why, mom?"

"Well, Mark, I think it might be nice for you to have some contact with other boys in a closer way than you might have at Burlingame." (She couldn't say, have a kind of family feeling, though that's what she meant.)

"Why do I need that?"

"Well, you'll make a lot of close and lasting friends at private school." She couldn't really answer his question.

"Oh, mom, I'll make just as many friends at Burlingame, and close ones, too."

She wasn't handling this as she had hoped. Her arguments seemed weak because there was no way to tell your child that the relationship between you and him is so close that now was the time to break not just the bonds between you but the umbilical cord; for him to cut loose the apron strings, not the family ties; that she wanted him to develop a sense of independence while still feeling he could turn to her whenever he wanted or needed her advice; that she was not abandoning him, but giving him a chance of freedom—freedom to be able to fortify himself with his own strengths, his own personality, without living in the shadow of his father's domination, his father's image so strong that he felt constant pressure to live up to it. How could she tell him that once a very wise and extraordinary man who had loved him as much as she had said that nothing was ours to keep, and that not until we learned to give up what we loved best in the world did we really know what love was, that giving someone to himself was the only way we could love him. How could she tell him that this was the greatest test of her own strength that she had ever been called upon to make; that this year without him would be the most painful one she would have to survive in her life—that if she could conquer her own loneliness without his presence at home, then she would have conquered herself. He was the reason for her existence; life without him would be meaningless. God, put the words in my mouth.

"Mark, this really has nothing to do with making close friends or lasting friendships—it has to do with *you.* I thought very carefully about this next year and what it would mean for you. You're really on the threshold of a new life, this is a whole new world opening up. I want you to have the opportunity to make up your mind about things without your father, or me, influencing you. That doesn't mean that when you need us or want an opinion we won't be there—we always will be. You see, darling, I want to give you your chance to find your own . . . self. When we're very close with our parents, we find ourselves caught up in their opinions and their ideas, and sometimes we become overwhelmed by them. We have to be able to find out who we are and what we want. Do you understand what I'm saying, Mark?"

He turned away from her. Through the window he saw the old cars heaped up, wrecked and demolished in the junkyards off the highways, the factory smokestacks belching billows of gray smoke in the distance. Although he could not have said what his mother meant, he thought he understood what she had said and he tried to sort it out. If she wanted him to make up his own mind, then why did he have to go away and do it? He wanted to stay at home, wasn't that making up his own mind? If she really loved him, why would she want him to go away? And why hadn't his father mentioned it to him in the car today? Why had he kept it a secret? His mother must have discussed it with him. Something like this must have been talked over between his parents. They must have agreed then, and his mother was the person who was supposed to tell him about it. Well, he could only assume that he was in the way, that they didn't want him. But he couldn't accept that. No—he supposed they really thought this was best for him. But there were so many confusing things his mother had said. His mind was working furiously to sort it all out, and the only conclusion he could reach was that life was impossible to understand, at least life such as love, sex, parents . . . and real estate! . . . Well, he would go to Menlo, not because it was *his* wish, not because *he* had been given the freedom to make his own decision, but because *they* had decided. And right now, *that* was what really counted, regardless of what he felt. Later . . . ?

"Okay, mom, I'll go if that's what you want me to do." He would have been surprised if he'd known his mother knew so much of how he was feeling, as well as the reasons. It was like cutting the moorings loose, and he felt adrift on a sea he could not navigate. She could only hope that what she was doing for him was best. But if it proved to be wrong, then all she could do would be to cope with the consequences, and all she would have to console herself with was that she had done what she did because she felt it was right at the time, fair and honest. She could only hope that her judgment had been wise. Please, God.

CHAPTER SIXTEEN

Fall, 1947

The anticipation of the unknown world of boarding school left Mark with a feeling of anxiety so great that when September came he was almost relieved that it was actually time to leave home. He had spent the month of August vacillating between sorrow, unhappiness, wretchedness, distress, despair, anger and boredom. Not wanting his parents to know his private feelings, he had tried to hide them—an obviously impossible task since he had undergone a metamorphosis from a young boy who had been animated at the breakfast table to a silent adolescent answering questions in words of one syllable. He stayed in his room with the shades drawn without leaving it for hours, listening to the radio, unable even to read. He thought maybe he'd call some of the boys he had gone to school with, hoping that they'd be home, but they were still away with their parents. They had either gone to Hawaii or Europe, or were visiting their grandparents in the country. That was the trouble when you didn't have grandparents who were alive—when both your parents were orphans. And then he was given to gnawing feelings of guilt because he had so much more than either of his parents had at his age.

Katie had watched the transformation take place, and was uneasy for having cast the die, but she couldn't turn back now, it would only confuse Mark —she'd seemed so certain of her decision at the time.

There'd been an awful row with David when she

told him about Mark going away. He exploded, carrying on so that she was physically frightened and shaken in her belief that she was doing the right thing. Most of all, David was angry that she'd made her decision without consulting him. How dare she do a thing like that? Who the hell did she think she was, treating him as though he were only there to be used in case of emergency? And in the process he became more antagonistic toward her and even Mark, because of their apparent conspiracy.

What had seemed the best solution to Mark's problems and hers, sitting on the sundeck that sunny afternoon in Tahoe, did not seem quite the same sitting on the edge of her bed here in Hillsborough. But wasn't it her determination to have Mark avoid just such situations and scenes as these that had made her decide in the first place? Nonetheless David was right that she should have discussed something like this with him; it had to do with his son as well as hers. In all honesty, though, it never entered her mind that David would object so strenuously. He seemed so preoccupied all the time, so basically uninterested in Mark's activities. After all, he hadn't come home or even called when Mark graduated. . . . She could reassure herself only up to a point. Perhaps she had misjudged him in this. Now when she examined the situation carefully, she acknowledged that she had wanted for years to have some control of her life. Her son had become just about her whole life, for better or worse, and with Chaim's small legacy to her she felt she finally had the combination to make at least this step toward asserting herself. But now she wondered if it were as much for Mark as for herself that she'd made her decision. And if she hadn't, unknowingly, made him a part of her on-going contest with David. My God, she hoped not. Or if so, that regardless of her motives, the consequences would still be best for her son.

Katie almost smiled to herself. Being a mensch, a person, even the tentative first steps toward it, certainly brought its complications. Black and white suddenly began to go gray. . . .

All week she sewed nametapes into Mark's clothes and prepared for his departure without joy. Sunday finally arrived and with it came an overwhelming depression. Although Mark didn't have to be at school until one o'clock that afternoon, she couldn't sleep after five and got up to fix coffee.

As if the day weren't momentous enough, David was leaving for Los Angeles that same morning, taking an early flight for a business conference that afternoon, one of the most important of his career. It was time to bring another dream, this one the biggest of all, to reality, and he was going down to hire an architectural firm in Los Angeles, having studied and approved their plans and the renderings for his two large shopping centers. Jim Fowler was flying down with him—they would be met at the airport in Los Angeles and driven to the Ambassador Hotel, where there would be the gathering of forces.

Katie heard David's footsteps as he approached the breakfast room. He was dressed in a gray, impeccably tailored suit. As she set the table she was still taking stock, continuing the self-questioning begun when David had reacted so strongly to her sending Mark away to school. She wondered what part of the trouble between herself and David was because of her lack, and why she couldn't solve it. . . . Knowing how strong-willed and defiant he was, she realized that, instead of tempering his anger, at times she inflamed it. And yet she felt she must refuse to submit completely or David, even unintentionally, would break her spirit. Wasn't that really it? . . . Oh, dear God, she had so many doubts today, she felt so many failures. This morning, seeing him seated at the table, she wondered what she could have done to preserve the young man David had been when first they had met and married. She could hardly remember what he had looked like then. When had the true changes occurred in him—not only in him, but in her? Perhaps if she'd seen the changes coming and not made constant excuses for him—and her—there wouldn't be the chasm that lay between them now.

Oh, Katie, if only you had accepted him totally,

down deep in your heart . . . instead of—face it—often resenting his bravado, if you had praised him more . . . and if you had come to him first with the suggestion about Mark, maybe he would not have been so opposed and this one conflict at least could have been avoided. And so might another if you had not made him feel less a father—and so guilty—when he returned from Los Angeles that evening after Mark's graduation. She didn't see herself as being a very strong determined person, but it occurred to her that perhaps that was the way David saw her. And what was it they said . . . that ninety percent of any marriage depended upon the woman? She had loved him so much, and had to admit that she still did, even now. If only she understood how to live with him, how to make him happy, and herself too. Yes, herself too . . . Or was it already too late for that?

"David," she said in a conciliatory tone, anticipating his mood, hoping that she could perhaps break through the barrier of his coldness, "what can I get you for breakfast? I know you have an important meeting—"

"Nothing," he said, still angry, reading a notebook he had propped up in front of him.

Again she tried, disregarding his tone. "David, couldn't I get you anything?"

"Just coffee, that's enough."

"How long will you be away?"

"I'm not sure, maybe a week. I'll be at the Ambassador Hotel."

"Can I drive you?"

"No, I'll park the car and leave it," he added, his voice cold, "like I always do."

"Hi, mom, dad," Mark said, not looking at them.

"Hi, Mark. Well, you all set to go off today, all packed?"

"I suppose so. Mom did it last night."

"You happy about going?"

Katie felt ill, her heart pounding. That was cruel. Mark avoided David's eyes. Didn't his father know how he felt?

"Sure, real happy," he said, going along. "You're coming down with us today, aren't you, dad?"

"No, Mark. I wish I could, but I have a very important business meeting in Los Angeles this afternoon, otherwise, nothing could have kept me away, believe me. But it won't be long before I see you, son. You'll be home every weekend."

"But you won't always be, so if I don't get to see you, will you call?"

"Of course, what a question!"

"Thanks, dad." Mark thought his father seemed more upset than his mother about his going away, which for some reason pleased him.

"Mark, darling, what would you like to have for breakfast? Eggs? French toast?" Katie smiled, trying to be casual, an attempt which, considering that she felt like an outsider as well as an ogre at this point, was not exactly successful.

"I don't feel hungry, mom." Fortified by the large box of cookies he had stashed away in his nightstand, Mark was able to resist all temptation. His refusal succeeded in compounding Katie's guilt.

Oh my God, always the Jewish mother with the food, David thought as he observed Katie's reactions. Finishing quickly, he kissed Mark on the cheek, said goodbye to Katie and left through the pantry, letting the screen door slam behind him.

Mark could no longer keep up the game of pretense the adults played. Running out to the garage just as David was stepping into the car, he put his arms around his father, holding him close, his cheek buried in David's chest, and swallowed back the tears. He wanted to cry out to his father not to let him go, that he wanted to stay home with him and Katie . . . instead, he clung to David in silence.

Damn it, David thought, touched in spite of himself, why the hell was she doing this? Mark could just as well have gone to Burlingame High School. Damned if he could understand her. She wasn't proving a damn thing, just making her son unhappy. The school was only twenty minutes away from home. Try to figure her out . . .

David found himself with his arms around Mark, and finally said, "I have to go now, Mark. Be a good fellow and make me proud of you."

Mark broke the embrace, but looked intently at his father. "I will, dad, I promise you. Wait and see . . . I love you, dad."

David nodded his head, wanting very badly just then to say I love you, too . . . except he really didn't know how to say the words. Mark didn't expect the words to be spoken, but it was one of those rare moments when he felt what his father meant. David took out a ten-dollar bill and handed it to Mark, who accepted it, thanking his father. He watched David get into the car and head up the driveway, waving once again and saying, half aloud, "Don't forget to call . . ."

David waved back. Mark's voice, unheard, had been drowned by the motor.

Katie and Mark walked up the stairs to see his room. Mark hesitated before going in, knowing he was going to hate it even with the pictures his mother had suggested he bring to hang on his side of the wall. He was going to share the room with a boy called Bruce Abbot whom he had met earlier that day in the hall downstairs. Bruce had gone all through school at Menlo and to him it was like home away from home. From the beginning Mark disliked Bruce —his cheerfulness irritated him . . . he didn't want Bruce to give Katie the impression that this school was anything more than a glorified prison—and he was annoyed with his mother when she said, "I'm so glad you're going to have such a nice boy to share your room with. I'm sure you and he will get to be very good friends." NEVER!

They inspected where he would go to classes, met his teachers, and then walked silently around the spacious grounds, Mark noting the pleasant camaraderie between the boys. He felt like an outsider and hated it. The next few hours were unbearable to him, soon his mother would leave and he would be alone. At four o'clock everyone went in to early dinner.

There were mothers and fathers together; Mark sat next to his mother, feeling awkward glances, positive that all eyes were focused on him, worrying that they would assume he didn't have a father, or something. The moments ticked away all too rapidly. He knew that the minute Katie left he would go to his room and stay there until it got dark, then bury his head in the pillow and hope that Bruce, that smiling hyena, wouldn't make fun of him. He clung to every second, but the clock would not stand still and before he knew it, the time came to an end even more quickly than he had feared. Walking to the car with Katie, he would not allow her to see how he felt, trying to make her think it didn't matter. She would be sorry she had done this to him. He wouldn't forgive her for this, at least not for a long time. He wouldn't even kiss her goodbye, he decided. But when she got into the car his stomach fluttered. His courage was not up to his angry promise to himself. He looked at her as though he would never see her again in his life. He hurt.

Covering his hand with hers, Katie asked, "Mark, would it embarrass you if I kissed you goodbye? I know I shouldn't ask but, darling, I'll miss you terribly. I know it's the wrong thing to say, but forgive me for being a silly mother . . ."

All his resolutions to make her suffer were gone and, not caring who was looking, he threw his arms around her. He wasn't going to apologize no matter what his father said . . . Be a man, learn to take it, boys don't cry. His mother had said something else . . . never apologize for being honest about how you feel.

"Mark, try to understand why I wanted you to have this, please? I love you, Mark, good luck, darling. I'll be here on Friday to pick you up."

He watched the car until it disappeared, then ran to his room. He didn't wait until dark to throw himself down across the bed and, thankful only for Bruce not being there yet, let the tears come as though they would never stop.

CHAPTER SEVENTEEN

How she got home without an accident, Katie would never know. She parked the car in the garage and went in by the back door. The house was silent, the house was empty. She heard only the sound of her own breathing as she wandered from room to room, not knowing what to do or where to go. She found herself in the library looking out at the green garden. Sitting down in the chair that David usually sat in, she felt as though she had just had an arm or a leg amputated. Her loneliness was unbearable. This was the first time she had been entirely alone since leaving England—that was a million years ago —and suddenly she felt as she had that day in the cemetery, staring down into the abyss, holding a small piece of earth in her hand. Only God must have known what she felt that day, the lonely despair. Now she was seventeen again with the same void, the same emptiness she had then. It seemed she always lost those she loved. There was no one to whom she could turn now. They had come to her as strangers, strangers who had given freely of their love, and all of them were lost to her . . . Chaim, Birdie, Malka . . . and David?

Why *did* David seem to hate her so? Had she really been such an unworthy wife? What did other women do that made them loved by their husbands? What was the secret formula that made them seem worthy? Hadn't she struggled along with David? Hadn't she submerged her own love of Judaism? In what way had she been demanding? What did she ask for herself except that David be understanding of what he had called upon her to do? To divorce herself from her heritage, the place and people she'd come to love. He still remembered Chicago; she still remembered Hester Street. He never forgave her for either memory.

The silence was deafening. Her gaze wandered about the room and fell on the whiskey decanter on the table across from her. Getting up, she poured herself a drink, holding it up to the light; it was a lovely deep warm amber. She drank it down fast. It burned as it went down. She grimaced and shook slightly, but began gradually to feel lightheaded and sat down with the empty glass in her hand, letting the whiskey take hold of her emotions as her head rested back on the chair. It finally released her from all thoughts. Curling up in the large chair, she feel asleep.

When she awoke it was dark, and now the dark frightened her. She switched on the lamp. There was no one here, only Katie, and memories, and aloneness. She shuddered at the thought of being alone. When David was away on business, which, as now, he frequently was, there was Mark to protect. She had never really been frightened with him in the house because he distracted her from herself, from the old fears, but now . . . She went about checking all the French doors leading to the terrace—there were so many of them—then the back doors, making sure that they were locked. Her better judgment told her that there was nothing to be afraid of, that this was a well guarded, well patrolled community, and that nothing had ever happened here to justify her feeling this way. But still she could not shake off her anxiety; it was almost forbidding tonight. Her mouth felt dry. She went to the kitchen, fixed a cup of strong tea, left two lights burning downstairs and took the tea to her room. Locking the door behind her, she switched on the bathroom light and left it burning all night, with the door open so that a shaft of light came into the room; in spite of all her precautions, she was still apprehensive, imagining she heard noises downstairs. She realized she had always been afraid of the dark and of lonely rooms. . . .

Her mind strayed to her room when she had been a little girl, a room with a large round window, a room on the third floor of Aunt Rosalind's house. Dear hateful Aunt Rosalind, you did your work well —one frightened, insecure little girl . . . and woman, who, as before, still seems to have nothing of her own . . . first I lived in your house, then I lived in Malka's, now I live in David's. The only home I ever knew that I felt truly was mine was a three-room flat on Hester Street where David Rezinetsky carried me over the threshold, and that was taken away from me by David Reid. I've been frightened all my life of everything, everyone. I'm afraid of you, David. I was afraid of bringing up something as ordinary as keeping a maid for company because you were angry about my sending Mark to school. I'm afraid to live with you, and I'm afraid to live without you. *I had to send Mark away because I had begun to substitute him for you, David.* I don't feel I have a husband, and I have to have someone to love. I was afraid of what you were doing to him, pushing him away when he needs you, never mind if you knew what you were doing or why. You could destroy him, break his spirit. Why were you really so upset? Does Mark mean that much to you, or did you do it to hurt me? I hope it's the first reason, but I wonder . . . you seem to turn on anyone who wants to love you. You want to show up the world like a little boy trying to prove something. I have no friends—you saw to that. After all, *I'm* Jewish.

My God, why, why is he punishing me so? When did his hatred begin and what feeds it so well? Surely the memory of Chicago couldn't have made such a deep impression on him that he would hold it over me for the rest of my life? I was only a young girl. It was such a new world. How much did he really expect of me? I was cut off from everyone I loved. I loved being Jewish. I found it no hardship—I loved being Mrs. Rezinetsky. I still would.

In the silence, a veil was lifting. The puzzle was coming together. She understood reasons she had suspected but not enumerated, causes she had in fact underestimated. They became a litany . . . David sees me as a constant reminder of his past. I stick in his craw like a morsel he can't spit out and can't swallow, I'm the sound of pushcart peddlers. I'm Birdie, and Solly, and the sound of his mother's weeping. I'm his father standing over him, beating him, demanding, "Get up, stand like a man." In me he sees Isaac cutting his lapel, sitting shivah for his living son, *Yis-gad-dal v'yis-kad-dash.* He sees Mark born and conceived from that past—Mark, his son, whom he owes a legacy that he'll never deliver. I'm six million Jews who must have screamed in his brain, Jews who were sent to the gas chambers and yet he, one of them, profits from the war in which they were slaughtered. He fights, but he is a condemned man, condemned *by himself.* He knows down deep in his heart he can't break me of thinking, of feeling, I'm a Jew. I am a Jew. I'll never be anything else. He can't forgive me because I am his guilt. He can't destroy me because I am his penance. Oh God, if only I could be his understanding . . . most of all, his wife. Perhaps . . .

When we came here from New York with Chaim's legacy he still loved me. I was all that he had, there were really only the two of us. But when he went into the other world, I was also the only obstacle in his way—his success in a gentile world was threatened by his Jewish wife. Never mind what *they* knew . . . *he* knew. Well, David, I'm not so frightened anymore. Do you hear me, David? I'm going to stay and fight you, David, and *remind* you. For now, I'm going to be your guilt. I'm going to be your father's voice, I'm going to be your comeuppance. And in time maybe you'll realize the only way to rid yourself forever of the ghosts and the guilt is to be true to yourself, and to let us be true to ourselves. Mark and I are your family; we love you and we'll stand by you. Maybe one day you'll understand, and forgive me. And then forgive yourself.

It was a moment of insight and resolution that terrified her with its clarity, and consequences. Thoroughly shaken, she jumped out of bed, unlocked the door and ran down the stairs into the library to pour herself another drink, this time even larger, and went back upstairs. As she walked past Mark's room, she hesitated for a moment at the open door, wanting to go in and touch his things, sit on his bed, then told herself not to be maudlin. Looking straight ahead, she went past the bedroom that David had furnished for himself, punishing her, and walked into her room. Although still afraid of the silence, she did not lock the door behind her; got into bed, let the strong amber liquid trickle down, slowly this time, and waited for the release of sleep.

She had passed the night sleeping fitfully, at times straining to hear if someone were in the house. Fears grown over many years did not loose their hold easily. She heard the mice, which got in from time to time between the shake roof, running across the eaves in the attic. When, to her surprise, morning came, she felt that God had kept faith with her—somehow she had survived the night alone, she hadn't died. Tonight would be bad, but not quite as bad as the one she had just lived through, and perhaps tomorrow would be less so until finally she learned to conquer herself. But she could never do it alone . . . help me, dear God, please help me.

She heard the sound of the gardener as he rolled the lawnmower along the expansive lawn, the aroma of newly cut grass wafting through the open window. It was a hot September morning and she had no desire to get out of bed: what was there to get up for? She lay on her back just listening, and wondered what kind of a night Mark had spent. Her longing for him this morning was unbearable. What would she do with herself now? David would be away most of the time, but even when he might be home, how different would that make her life? It was more lonely when two people who were estranged lived in the same house than when one lived alone. How would she spend her days? Would she garden? Yes, but she couldn't do that all day. Maybe she would take up painting. But that would only take care of the days—what about the nights? Oh God, the nights.

Suddenly she knew what she was going to do this moment. She was going to get up, take a bath, get dressed and go to the city. She was definitely going to buy her longed-for piano, paying it out on term with the one hundred dollars a month allowance she had fought so hard for. The maid could come later—she wasn't even sure that she wanted one now. She wasn't accustomed to being waited upon, unlike the fine ladies she had met at the PTA. How charming they were, and how cliquish. You see, David, even with all your money, Mrs. David Reid was not accepted. Suddenly the whole idea of a maid seemed so silly. She would not compete with David in maintaining a façade she cared nothing about. She would not condemn him. She *would* be herself. Katie, David, for better or worse.

Excitedly she walked along the rows of pianos at Sherman Clay. It was all she could do to restrain herself from sitting down to see if her fingers still worked, if she could recall anything of what she had been taught. Her eyes wandered to one particular grand piano which transported her back to a diminutive flat in Chelsea with its English floral wallpaper, where the sun filtered through the imitation Brussels' lace curtains that hung to the floor making marvelous patterns on the flowered carpet, and the picture of Queen Victoria in an oval gold frame suspended by a rose-colored cord with the tassel at the top, dear Albert in another frame beside her. Each time Katie had gone there, she thought what delightful company she kept, royalty and all! Vividly she recalled the scent of verbena that was Miss Trevellyan. How whimsically fey she was as she made sweeping gestures to the sound of Katie's arpeggios, tapping her foot rhythmically, keeping pace with Katie's rendition of a Chopin waltz. Then, just short of the forty minutes, Miss Trevellyan would say, "Come on, love, time for tea."

She was brought back sharply as the salesman told

her that the piano was one of their most expensive. Since Katie knew it would be impossible for her to keep up the payments, she settled for the spinet, thinking as she signed the contract how ludicrous it was, all the questions she was being asked. Here she was taking the piano out on time while her husband was a millionaire. She laughed, not without pleasure, to herself.

When could the piano be delivered? Not until Thursday, so sorry, Mrs. Reid. Oh dear, Thursday. But she had waited so long, a few days more or less wouldn't matter that much.

Standing in front of the store on the Sutter Street side looking up toward Grant Avenue, she saw the noonday throngs and observed their faces, wondering where they had come from and where they were going, thinking how little could be read in the face of a passerby. Who noticed her, knew what she felt? She was sure nobody did, but if they had noticed at all, would she have suggested the average hausfrau, a woman rushing home to put on supper for her working husband? Probably. How absurd—sad?—that she would soon be going home to that empty mansion in Hillsborough. The mood of anticipation, which had been sparked by her defiance, had darkened. She had longed so for the piano, but the wanting it was more than any satisfaction in having bought it; somehow the joy of the moment had been dissipated.

She wandered aimlessly down one street and then the next. She recalled how happy they had been when first they saw these streets; how long ago it now seemed they had made their promises to one another. He had most of all wanted to live his life in dignity, he'd said. Wasn't that why he renounced his heritage? So you said, David, darling.

For no reason at all, certainly not from hunger, she turned into a delightful restaurant called Townsend's on Geary Street. The room was filled with charming, elegantly dressed ladies waiting to be seated, having already made up their minds what they would have for lunch. The enchiladas were marvelous, or then again perhaps the creamed spinach with a little white and yellow egg that floated so nimbly on top. There were either two's or four's at the tables, so Katie decided she would sit at the counter.

Order, please? Oh, let's see . . . perhaps a tuna or chicken sandwich and coffee . . . or how about a lox and bagel or a hot pastrami and a kosher dill . . . ? What? Yes, the chicken sandwich and coffee would be fine. It was *some*place to sit down and look and hear the sound of human chatter that spilled from the rouged lips of intimates exchanging the "events" of the day—"Oh yes, the sales at Saks were stupendous," "Have you seen the new collection of Chanel?" The conversations were lost as the waitress placed the sandwich in front of her. My, the coffee was nice, hot, marvelous aroma. She took a bite of the sandwich, tried without success to wash it down with the coffee, and failed. She paid the check, got off the stool, which somebody occupied immediately, walked out of the pleasant atmosphere into the street once again; then down to the Union Square garage, where she waited for her car to be brought to her, observing the women carrying their boxes and packages from I. Magnin. Let's play a game: guess what's inside the box. A lovely frock to be worn to the next party? Bravo, guessed right! With a husband who said, my dear, you look lovely? Right, absolutely right! She felt impoverished.

By the time Katie arrived home, a feeling of heavy weariness had settled over her. Slowly she walked up the stairs to her room and lay down on the bed, staring up at the ceiling. What would she do today . . . tonight? She glanced at the clock; it was only three. Changing into blue jeans, a white blouse that she left hanging out, and tying a red bandana over her hair, she ran to the garage in her stocking feet, put on the pair of sneakers she kept there, then walked up the slight incline to the potting shed.

She reached up for a flower flat, placed it on the work table, picked up the large trowel and thrust it quickly into the mulch of fertilizer, peat moss and topsoil, filling the flat; then she took down another until six had been completed. Carrying two at a time into the adjacent hothouse, she spread them out on the slatted workbench and began separating the seedlings, working until it grew dark. Time for supper? She turned on the tap, ran the cold water over her hands, her thumbnail digging out the dirt, wiped them on the paper towels that she kept nearby and walked back to the big house. In the garage she took off her sneakers and went to the kitchen, where she switched on the light and put up a kettle for tea. On her way to the refrigerator she glanced up at the kitchen clock. Eight o'clock. God, she did miss Mark. She must at least hear his voice. She went to the library, picked up the phone and held the receiver in her hand for a moment, and put it down. Mark would never adjust there if she didn't give him the chance. She went back into the kitchen to fix herself a bite. . . . She would worry about tonight later.

The first day Mark was exhausted in class, hardly able to keep awake. He had slept so badly the night before. The bed was strange, the room was strange, Bruce Abbot was strange, more strange than Mark could comprehend. Bruce couldn't wait for school to begin after the long boring summer—being first with his mother, then with his father, who had remarried. He loved Menlo. He hated his parents; they were a pain in the neck as far as he was concerned. Bruce had been shockingly outspoken about them, telling Mark, a total stranger, about his father's escapades, his mother's broken promises that were always accompanied by a gift, her junkets to Europe with some other man; and how each played him against the other—he knew their game, all right—saying terrible things about one another, trying as hard as they could to get him to despise now the father, now the mother, depending on which one he happened to be staying with. He told Mark he knew they didn't love him or give a damn whether he was happy or not, they just used him, one against the other. What they could not supply in love they bought with money. How hard was it for his mother to send him an expensive gift from Spain on his birthday, or his father to buy him any old thing he wanted. But he didn't want anything at all, except to be old enough to be able to tell them they could go screw themselves, and be free of them.

He was much more sophisticated than Mark and knew more about a lot of things, including a vast amount of fascinating carnal knowledge. Mark didn't really want to hear about all this, but he forced himself to listen, not wanting Bruce to think he knew nothing about such things. He couldn't give Bruce the idea he was a sissy, and besides, it was interesting. . . .

Mark lay on his bed and observed Bruce as he thumbed through a magazine looking for a picture he wanted Mark to see. When shown the page, Mark looked at the nude model, embarrassed for both Bruce and himself. He looked first at her legs, feeling hot all over. He handed the magazine back to Bruce. Casually, he hoped.

"You ever get fresh with a girl?" Bruce asked. A quiz from the man of experience.

"What do you mean, fresh?"

"You know what I mean—feel a girl down there."

Now he *was* embarrassed, thankful that the only light was from the lamp in Bruce's corner because he felt himself blushing.

"No," he said, hoping he would give the impression that he too was worldly, but unable to think of what to say.

"Never? You mean you never played with a girl?"

"Well . . . not exactly."

"What do you mean, not exactly. You either did or you didn't. Did you?"

"Yes," Mark said, thinking of Patricia Fleming.

"Did you ever screw?"

God, why didn't Bruce go to sleep, or change the subject? Talk about football or something. Bruce made him feel like a damn kid.

"No," he finally answered, trying to sound as if he had had the opportunity but decided not to take it.

"I did," Bruce said.

"Really?" Mark tried again to sound casual, as though such experience were routine for all thirteen-year-olds.

"I sure did." Bruce didn't wait to be asked who or how. "We had a Swedish maid this summer and she showed me how. I think my father screwed her too. I'm almost sure he did. He screwed every other maid, why not her."

God! His *father!*

Bruce continued, "You want to try it on the weekend?"

"No," Mark said, shaking his head in the dark.

"Why?"

"We don't have a maid."

"I mean mine, stupid."

"Oh, well thanks, but I have plans this weekend. Some other time." He rolled over onto his side and pretended he was going to sleep as Bruce elaborated some more on the subject, but the strong, dramatic cadence of Mark's breathing, signalling—Mark hoped—that he was drifting off into deep slumber, convinced Bruce he had lost his captive audience. He turned off the lamp and fell asleep almost immediately. Mark lay awake for hours and wondered if Bruce were really telling the truth. He doubted it.

He thought about his mother and wondered if she were lonely and missed him, and thought about her being by herself in the big house. His own loneliness became physical as he felt a sharp pain in his chest.

The first week away from home was misery. Mark was sure he would never survive it. He couldn't pay attention in class. The window seemed to be in his way as he constantly stared out of it, and the food was inedible, not like his mother's at all. But what upset him most was that he had expected a phone call from David, which didn't come. He brooded over this, but he called Katie every night except for the first few days, when he was still punishing her for ever sending him here in the first place.

When Friday finally came he could hardly wait to get into the car and hug Katie. Had she missed him? Yes. Yes? Was that all? Not *very much?* Maybe she had not missed him at all, maybe she had gotten used to his not being home this week, maybe she had become accustomed to being without him. God, the pain in his chest. . . . He could hardly wait to get home. Maybe once there she would realize what a terrible mistake all this had been. Maybe after being together again this weekend she would say no, no you're not going back to that prison. Maybe nothing . . . the weekend passed, and Katie drove him back to school.

The next week proved even more painful, for both of them. Katie's loneliness had grown so it was even greater than the week before, and as for Mark, he decided not to go home at all the next weekend because leaving Katie last Sunday night was just more than he wanted to go through again. He made a lame excuse that he wanted to spend the weekend at school with Bruce, which of course he wouldn't think of doing—he had enough of him five days and nights a week. The boys who stayed were all friends with each other while so far he knew none of them. It turned out to be more miserable than ever. He wished that he would get an attack of appendicitis; then Katie would have to come and get him and maybe by the time he recovered the school semester would be over. Maybe . . .

The week in Los Angeles had been fruitful for David. He had selected the best architects in the country for what he needed. They had come up with a basic idea that more than met with his approval. He was told the blueprints would be complete within eight months to a year.

The day had been difficult, terribly hot and exhausting. He was happy it was over. How he would welcome the cool breezes of San Francisco. He went back to his room and showered, letting the cool water pelt his body for a long time. Refreshed, he changed into clean clothing and went down to dinner without Jim Fowler. He needed to be alone. He had been confronted with so many people. What a week this had been, being confined for seven days, cooped up in that office. After dinner he decided what he needed was a little exercise, and walked for blocks. How good it felt to use his legs instead of his brains for a change. As he strolled along Beverly Boulevard, admiring the buildings, he realized he had never really seen Los Angeles, although he'd been here many times. It wasn't San Francisco, to be sure—nothing was like that magnificent lady—but Los Angeles was interesting. He walked on, observing the shops and large stores, until he found himself on Fairfax Avenue. Without realizing it, he had happened into a Jewish district. It wasn't shabby, this was no ghetto, there were no Hester Streets. Just a pleasant middle-class area where Jews, by their own choice, lived because they wanted to live among themselves. The awareness brought him up short. It was the first time he had been this close to anything Jewish since he had left New York. But here he was, standing in front of a large delicatessen store with a bold neon sign above it that nearly blinded him: "Cantor's." He could not look at the name. Instead, his eyes wandered down to the windows where huge displays of Manischewitz matzos in boxes and Mogen David wine took up so much space that there was little room for any other foods. . . . His mind moved back to when he was a boy, and as though through the lens of a camera the scene of the seder came back. He could not even compel himself to turn away from the face of his father sitting at the head of the table, with his black skull cap and tallis, giving the blessing. He saw it as though it were yesterday. Being the youngest, he was called upon to answer the four questions. He heard his father's voice resounding solemnly in the hushed silence. Propped up between the pillows surrounding the huge chair in which he sat, his father asked, Why is this day different from any other day? How sweet and simple it was, with the whole family sitting at Isaac's table. A time of joy, and a brief moment in life, to keep alive the memory that Israel had broken free from the chains of bondage, a thing never to be forgotten. A time that would not allow itself to be willed from memory. A time of innocence, and for this moment at least he indulged himself as he recalled scenes which had been stored away for so long.

Somewhere, deep within David there was a longing to go back and relive that one moment of his lost childhood. So he hadn't really conquered himself after all, not really. He could not dismiss it all, no matter how hard he tried, and suddenly he felt the tears. Immediately, he reached for his handkerchief and, erasing all traces of grief, he quickly turned, hurried away and hailed a taxi that took him back to his room. Tomorrow, when he returned to San Francisco, his old resolve and determination would be intact. He would make sure of that. But this night, David could not sleep. Isaac was there, beside him. Tonight there was nowhere to hide.

David's work had just begun. On the thirty-two acres, only the shopping center and the complex of 28 two-story apartment house dwellings would be erected, while the rest of the acreage would be held in abeyance for homesites, which would be developed at a later date. To expedite the project, David felt that he should divide the work between two firms. The Los Angeles firm would draw up the plans for the shopping center, while a San Francisco firm would do the blueprints for the apartment houses and the office building. He had already contacted the San Francisco firm. The office building would be the only building on the site for some time, but David had to have offices on the peninsula. After that he would turn to the leases on the proposed stores. Business could go only one way and that was south, with the influx of new people into the area all the way from Burlingame to Redwood City. In fact, the population was growing so rapidly that contractors couldn't keep up with the demand and David was right in the middle of it all. Once the big names came in, the smaller merchants were sure to follow. David's property was a natural. . . .

Katie was in the living room when she heard the car come into the driveway. She arranged herself at the piano, where David found her. He said nothing, walked over to her and gave her the customary kiss on the cheek.

"How are you?" he asked, grateful for the first time in a long while to be in the familiar surroundings, but unsure of his reception. He had been through such an emotionally exhausting night that there should be no danger of his reconstituted defenses slipping today.

"I'm fine, David. How are you?" Katie, too, was proceeding cautiously, the resolutions of the last two weeks still fresh in her mind.

"Good."

"Well, did you accomplish what you wanted to?"

She got up from the piano and waited for him to say something about it. He did not.

"Yes, and more," he answered.

"That's wonderful. I take it everything went smoothly?" They were strangers talking about the moon. Was it really made of green cheese?

He elaborated, "Even better than I'd hoped."

"That's marvelous, David. When do you plan to start?" Should she add . . . "Mr. Reid"?

"We figure about June next year we'll break ground. I'm hoping, though, the office building will be up by about April."

"Oh, you're going to have an office building down there . . . I should have realized. Isn't that stupid of me?"

It had been said without apparent sarcasm, but David felt it was implied. As too often between them . . . the worst of what they meant was the best communicated. The rest, the good and honest . . . it had miles to go, mountains to climb . . .

"Well, David, I'm so happy for you, I really am."

He walked to the library and flipped through his mail. She followed, asking, "David, did you call Mark?"

"No, I'll call today." She knew damn well he hadn't, and she knew why, that he'd been so busy. . . . As he sorted his mail he asked, "How is he?"

"He's fine, except . . . well, it's natural, he misses us. He also was disappointed you hadn't called."

"Why did you ask me if you knew?"

"I meant today." That wasn't what she meant, she just wanted to embarrass him. "Have you eaten?"

Katie's standby question. "Yes, I had lunch at the airport in Los Angeles." Without another word, he walked out through the French doors and took a turn around the grounds.

Katie, suddenly hungry, fixed a small salad, took some biscuits from the tin of English Bath Olivers, and ate by herself in the breakfast room, thinking . . . well, wasn't she growing up.

She heard David come back into the library and make several phone calls. Then he left, saying he was going up to the city on business and not to wait dinner for him, chances were he'd be tied up with some people this evening and would have dinner in town. She continued eating, looking up at him only once. After David left she went back to the living room and began playing a Bach fugue. She was terribly out of practice, not having touched a piano since she was sixteen. Her fingers were stiff and she could no longer read notes so rapidly. No matter. It was nourishment for her soul—a place too long starved.

CHAPTER EIGHTEEN

David worked all morning in the San Francisco office of Ron Bordini, who was head architect of the firm he'd retained. The two of them went over the blueprints with a slide rule, the plans having advanced to a point where Ron had recommended to David that they begin to work in terms of interior as well as exterior. Did David have any preference about whom he wanted to do the interiors of the office? No, as a matter of fact, he hadn't given it a thought. Ron recommended Maggie Kent, his favorite specialist in interior design. In his opinion, there was really no one in all the world like her. Ron would arrange for a meeting of the three of them at their next session.

David arrived a little earlier than expected on the afternoon of their conference and was going over the plans on the drawing board when the door opened and Maggie Kent walked in. Her hair, light golden-brown streaked with sun, was worn in a simple page-boy; her wide-set eyes were amber shaded to green, the delicate peach tones of her skin gave her face a subtle glow. She was dressed in a cream-beige two-piece dress with a small turquoise and diamond pin near the shoulder. A pair of gold bangles made an enchanting sound as she moved her hand. Her shoes were brown alligator, matching her handbag, and she wore discreetly an expensive perfume.

Ron turned to greet her warmly when she closed the door behind her. "Maggie, come in."

She walked over and kissed him—no cutesy peck—on the cheek.

"You look delicious as usual," he said.

Her generous, neatly rouged lips parted as she smiled. "Thanks. How are you, Ron?"

"Fine, I want you to meet Mr. Reid. David Reid, meet Maggie Kent."

She extended her hand and said cordially, "I've heard good things about you, Mr. Reid."

"Likewise, Miss Kent." My God, what a lovely looking woman . . .

"Now tell me, Mr. Reid, what have you in mind for the office?" Her professionalism also impressed him—she got right to it.

"I really hadn't thought about the furnishings until now, to be honest, but Ron thought we were at a point on the drawing board where we should work with a designer."

"In that case, let me tell you what I've come up with after going over the plans with Ron." She had brought a portfolio with her and opened it up onto the large table in front of them, revealing paint chips, samples of wallpaper, swatches of fabrics for the different offices, photographs of furniture and tiny squares of floor covering, as well as a colored rendering of David's private office. It would include a large piece of sculpture and several good paintings, and she had suggested to Ron a built-in bar, the interior all mirrored; at the touch of a button, two doors would separate and the bar would open. David looked and was indeed impressed; but my God, what was this going to cost? There was a limit to what he was going to spend. "I think it's very nice, Miss Kent, and I know it would be beautiful, but isn't it going to be quite expensive?"

She looked up at him with a pleasant if unrevealing smile. "Almost anything, Mr. Reid, that's beautiful and exciting is likely to be expensive."

He didn't care who she was, he didn't like Maggie Kent, not one damn bit—a little too wonderfully sure of herself. She was also putting him in the position that Charles Fleming had that evening a while back, making him feel as though Hester Street were still written all over him.

Maggie continued, "However, Mr. Reid, you're under no obligation to hire me. If you want to compare prices, don't hesitate to do so."

She was still smiling and he still didn't like Maggie Kent. Maybe she knew her business, but so did he. He would not be intimidated by her.

"I'd like an idea of how much this will cost."

Maggie appraised David. "I haven't broken down the figures, but if you're looking to do this on a budget—"

"I wasn't thinking about a budget, but there's a limit to what I'm going to put into furnishings."

"That's entirely up to you, Mr. Reid." Still smiling, she nodded, took the renderings and put them back into the portfolio, laid the samples and swatches down very gently, closed the portfolio, and picked it up to indicate that as far as she was concerned the case was closed.

"Look, Miss Kent, can't you even give me a *general* idea what this is going to cost?" He had a right to know. After all, it was his money she would be spending, and here she was playing the prima donna.

She looked at David again. "Do you still think you'd be interested?"

"Yes, of course," wondering why the hell he'd said so.

"Well, in that case," she said pleasantly, "I'll have the estimate for you in a day or two. Is that all right?"

"Yes, that'll be fine," he said coolly.

She extended a gloved hand. "It's been nice meeting you, Mr. Reid. When I have the estimate I'll send it along, with my fee for consultation." Then, with portfolio in hand, she walked toward Ron.

"Wait a minute, Miss Kent," David said. "Would you mind if I kept the layout for a few days?"

"Not at all," she said, handing it back to him. "Goodbye, Ron, I'll talk to you." She smiled graciously and dispensed another goodbye to David.

Spoiled independent bitch, David thought as she walked out. No doubt born with the silver spoon in her mouth. Didn't know a thing about money except how to spend it—after one look at her, he'd bet she'd graduated with honors in that department. Probably had a rich father who indulged the hell out of her and this designing thing was just a hobby. What the hell did she care how she'd spend his money? Well, he'd worked too hard for that. And suddenly he became a little suspicious of Ron Bordini. Why had he recommended her? Did he get a kickback?

In his room that night he went over the rendering and the layouts. He'd have to pay a bundle for them whether he used them or not. God only knew what her fee was going to be for this, damn it, whether he liked them or not. She *had* intimidated him, which was why he hadn't pressed harder for a figure. He decided he wasn't going to have any part of her and went to bed, but even after he'd turned out the lamp at his bedside, he lay awake thinking how talented she obviously was—the rendering was like a work of art, beautiful down to the most minute detail. Well, he supposed he could wait to see how much she actually wanted.

When he received the estimate a few days later, he was staggered. She must have thought he was John D. Rockefeller, for God's sake. Well, forget it. He didn't need an office like Sam Goldwyn, and anyway, she wasn't the only one in town. But he kept going back to the renderings . . . Damn, they were gorgeous.

David called Ron to express his annoyance. Ron laughed and said that if David needed any further proof of Maggie's enormous ability, seeing her home would surely convince him, and that perhaps he could arrange it. David scoffed at the idea, but Ron was serious, certain that David would not be able to resist the appeal of her style when he saw the house. David grumbled but promised to consider the suggestion. Well, what the hell did he have to lose if he at least took her to lunch, if they had a few drinks and relaxed and he turned on the charm as he'd done with Charles Fleming and his grand Lady

Patricia. And maybe he would take a look at her house, just for curiosity's sake. So he called her.

"Miss Kent, this is David Reid," he said, with his charm at full sail.

"Yes, Mr. Reid, how are you?" she replied, as though he were calling for the weather report.

"I'm fine, thanks. Look, I've been going over the layout. Why don't we have lunch and discuss it. How about tomorrow?"

"I'd love to, but I'm doing a house in Pebble Beach and I'll be down there until next Tuesday."

"Look . . . can't we go over this before you leave?" In business, at least, he was accustomed to having things done on his terms, and the delay made him both impatient and uneasy.

"I'm sorry, Mr. Reid, but I don't have a free minute until next week."

She didn't sound a bit sorry, he thought.

"What about next Wednesday then?"

"Let me check and see if I have any appointments." He waited for what seemed longer than necessary. At last she said, "That's fine, Mr. Reid. At your office or mine?"

"No, at lunch. How about twelve at Piero's on Montgomery Street?"

"Yes, I know where it is. Very good, Mr. Reid, see you then." She hung up first. He held the receiver in his hand for a moment, then hung up. He had a good idea to call her back and tell her to go to hell.

But Wednesday came, and she walked into Piero's looking like something out of *Vogue*. The *maitre d'* bestowed the full treatment.

"Ah, Miss Kent, as lovely as ever. I believe a gentleman is waiting for you at the bar."

"Thank you, Alfred."

David was seated at the plush bar; the dim lights and the background music made her seem even more enchanting than the first time he'd seen her. The whole atmosphere was a foil, embellishing her loveliness. David was annoyed with himself that he thought of her at all in this way. She was not, however, easy to ignore.

"Mr. Reid," she offered her gloved hand, "how are you?"

"Great, and you?"

"Thank you, fine. I hope I haven't kept you waiting too long. The traffic was terrible today, Christmas shoppers and all."

David motioned to the bartender, who came over. "Hi, Miss Kent, glad to see you."

"Thank you, Robert. How are you?"

David didn't know anybody, Maggie knew everybody. Funny, he thought he was taking her to lunch. Maggie was still in charge. The bartender asked David what he would like to drink and whether Maggie would have the usual, vodka over ice with two large green olives. David would try the same. They drank the first drink, then the second, slowly, David feeling it more than he would have liked. He figured, though, that he'd better at least ask Maggie if she would like another. That would be nice. Just one olive this time, Robert. The *maitre d'* came to carry their third drinks to the table, and they were seated at the red velvet banquette against the wall of the dimly lighted room. An enormous French menu was placed in front of David, which annoyed him. He always ended up ordering a simple salad or a plain breast of chicken to begin with, never anything exciting or different when he was out to lunch with business associates; but today he decided to be grand and asked the waiter to order for them, trying to appear as though he did this every day. He turned his attention to Maggie Kent. The approach was casual.

They talked about the new shopping center, his favorite subject, and the office building. He asked her about her job in Pebble Beach. When luncheon was served, he looked down at a large gold-rimmed plate occupied by veal Piccata swimming in butter and sprinkled with pine nuts, and small Jerusalem artichokes covered with *ménagère* sauce. To the other side, cradled in a bed of watercress, lay stuffed tomatoes browned and broiled with a crust of Parmesan cheese. David watched Maggie, from the corner of his eye, eat with gusto, finishing the meal almost entirely, leaving only the most minute portions on the plate. He thought for a girl her size (size eight, to be exact) she laid it away like a lumberjack. He scarcely touched his, remembering his diabetes.

After a proper time lapse, André removed first Maggie's plate and then David's. As he removed them, he bowed slightly and addressed himself to Maggie. Was the dish to Miss Kent's liking? Yes, indeed, André, as delightful as ever. He disappeared with the plates and then quickly returned. What was Miss Kent's pleasure for dessert? What would André suggest? French pastries perhaps? Ah yes, the strawberry tart and black coffee. And for monsieur?

"Nothing," said David.

Waiting for dessert, they spoke about . . . how long had Mr. Reid lived in San Francisco? Long enough to feel like a native. Lovely city? Simply beautiful. Dessert came. André poured the hot coffee into the gold-and-white porcelain cups, smiled *again* and finally, was gone. David would have liked to push bowing-and-smiling André's face into the French pastry.

After dessert, David motioned to André to refill their cups. *Encore, voilà,* merci. Stuff it. David asked if Maggie would care for another drink. Brandy perhaps. Brandy *à deux,* yet. As they sat lingering over their coffee and brandy, David wasn't feeling so well, but he continued trying to give the impression that he was ready for eighteen holes of golf, figuring that by now the incomparable Miss Kent should at least be in a reasonable . . . receptive? . . . mood.

He started, quietly but businesslike, "Miss Kent, I received your estimate and I'm sure for what you have proposed in the layout it isn't too high"—he smiled—"but frankly I hadn't thought of spending anything near that for furnishings."

He thought he'd managed that fairly well, until she said, also cordial but businesslike, "Well, Mr. Reid, everyone knows what they can afford."

"That's true, but I thought we might come to a compromise—"

"I never compromise, Mr. Reid."

David had to smile inwardly. This little size eight, a mere five feet three inches with a gargantuan appetite, sure as hell stood her ground. She was neither intimidated, frightened, nor impressed. "Never?" he nonetheless pressed.

"No, and let me tell you why. I built my reputation on preferring to lose a job than do what I think is wrong."

"That's admirable. Is it practical in all cases?"

"Yes, because in the long run people spend more money replacing their mistakes."

"Yes, Miss Kent, but that doesn't make much money for you, does it?"

"Indeed it does, Mr. Reid, because there are no bargains in this life: you get *exactly* what you pay for."

Maybe the drinks were affecting him, maybe it was Maggie Kent's perfume, maybe it was the unaccustomed atmosphere of dim lights and plush red velvet, but David was beginning to like her spirited, independent style in spite of himself. She was not Katie, she was not Jim Fowler, she was Maggie Kent. All right, let's see, here was a businesswoman, a smart bargainer. Also a woman. Well, appeal to her sense of womanly understanding.

"Look, Miss Kent, as you know, what we have is a terribly costly project, and much as I like what you propose, I just feel at this moment I can't afford it. Perhaps we could do something just a little less elegant for now, a little less exciting, to use your words, and later we can—"

"I don't think so, Mr. Reid. As I also said, your approach would really be a very poor investment because you'd be paying twice."

"Miss Kent, I've never really thought of furnishings as being a very good investment, if you will forgive me."

Taking a sip of the brandy, she looked him squarely in the eye, laughed, and said, "I find that almost unforgivable. In fact, no, I don't think I will forgive you. You're talking about the profession I love." They both laughed, and then just as suddenly her manner was all business once again.

"Mr. Reid, just what is a good investment?"

"Real estate."

"And?"

"And? That's about it."

"What kind of car do you drive?"

"A Cadillac."

"Do you think that's a good investment?"

"You don't buy a car because it's a good investment; you buy it because it's a necessity."

"That's true, but an automobile is the worst investment you can have."

"Really? Tell me why."

"Because the minute you take it out of the showroom, it depreciates enormously. Am I right?" She didn't wait for an answer. "Now you said a car was a necessity and that's true, but why do you drive a Cadillac and not a . . . Ford?"

"Because I like a Cadillac."

"Exactly. It's the same with furnishings, there are Fords and there are Cadillacs, and there are people who sell both; I happen to sell Cadillacs. I could no more think of doing your gorgeous building like a Ford than I could fly like a bird." She took a sip of the brandy, paused, looked at David. "I simply couldn't do it. A building like that, you don't compromise. One lovely thing demands another. Good taste can't go half way."

Beautiful, exquisite, feminine, with a mind like the proverbial steel trap. What a combination. She not only knew about money, she knew how to sell, and make you like it. . . .

"By the way," Maggie continued, "Ron thought you might like to drop by and see my house."

"I would indeed."

"Please be my guest," she said, writing him the address. "Afternoons would be best. Somebody will always be there. Just drop by."

"Thank you. And by the way, you're quite a salesman. Maybe I should learn more about your technique." He knew it sounded a bit forward, maybe corny. He hoped not—besides, she really *was* a salesman, and no baloney.

Smiling at him she said, "Take me to lunch some other time and maybe I'll tell you. I really have to dash, I have an appointment this afternoon. Thank you for the lovely lunch."

Outside in the parking lot the attendant said, "Bring your car right up, Miss Kent." While they waited, David promised to think on her proposal and she told him to take all the time he needed. The car was waiting now, motor running; she got into the red Jaguar and sped away in the gray December afternoon mist, as David stood watching the car disappear around the corner. The mist felt good, refreshing against his face. That's one gorgeous woman, he thought. And one damn smart one.

That night David was restless. Somehow he could do nothing but think of Maggie Kent. He truly had met no one like her. In no sense was he a promiscuous man. To have an affair with anyone had been unthinkable, or at least it was something he had never thought of. So as far as he was concerned, he had never been able to enjoy the act of sex unless it was with a woman he at least liked, and until now he had been so consumed with his business ventures that little time or energy was left for anything else. Maggie Kent was—on the surface—the sort of woman who in the past had put him off. Delicate, feminine . . . that was his style. That was what had at least partly attracted him to Katie in the beginning. But Maggie Kent was different. Maggie Kent was a combination he'd never met. Maggie Kent was, in a word, something else.

Maggie's house stood at the tip of a cul-de-sac, looking like a small French jewel box between two apartment houses on either side. The house had been built by an eccentric, near middle-aged *roué* in 1922, but the results of his imagination, which he could indulge because of the enormous wealth left by dear papa, still lived. This was his legacy to the world, along with a number of illegitimate children whom he had never acknowledged.

Leaving his car, David walked across the street, and looked up at the façade. He was totally captivated. In front of the French windows on the two floors above the carefully concealed garage were green, hand-wrought iron balconies that had been brought from a chateau near Versailles, the sea air having supplied a magnificent patina. The house was delicate soft-white brick. He looked upward to the roof and was fascinated by the heavy gray-mauve slate. At the entry was a pair of verd antique green iron gates; the off-white marble stoop ended at the front door, which was slightly higher than the street level; on either side was a pair of French stone dogs, sitting on their hind legs and holding flower baskets in their mouths.

Suddenly the front door opened, and a maid dressed in a blue-and-white uniform came out and removed the mail from the box, not yet noticing him. He walked up to her and said good morning. She smiled and returned his greeting.

"My name is David Reid," he said, tugging on his ear. "Miss Kent said that I could drop by and look at the house."

"Oh, yes, Mr. Reid. Miss Kent told me. I'll be happy to show you around."

"Thank you very much," he said as he followed her into the foyer and shut the door behind them. The floors were the same off-white marble that followed through from the entry stoop, and in the center was a small gem of an Aubusson rug. The walls were saffron silk, and going up the circular staircase were paintings in soft pastels. Standing at the bottom, he could see all the way up to the third floor and the oval of a stained glass skylight. His attention was diverted by a large marquetry commode with heavy French ormolu, above which hung a tall *trumeau* mirror, and against the opposite wall was a Venetian loveseat. Although he couldn't have identified these styles, he had a sense of this being right for Maggie.

"Would you like to take the elevator up?" the maid asked.

He looked around. Where was it?

"All right," he said, curious. She opened the door to what appeared to be a guest closet. When she did so, a filigreed grill moved slowly back, they entered, and rose to the third floor. The grill then cascaded back, and David found himself looking out through the expansive windows onto an unexpected, majestic view.

As they walked toward the hall, they stopped in front of a Louis XIV beige marble mantel. "That's a magnificent portrait."

It was Maggie. He was fascinated and more than a little affected as his eyes met those of the painting. So strong was the likeness he felt he could—and almost did—reach up and touch her. His eyes still on the portrait, he murmured, "She's beautiful."

"She sure is. And even better in person."

How right she was. Maggie was more than paint and canvas; she was soft ivory flesh, and he felt warm thinking of her. Turning from the portrait, he said, "This is certainly the most unusual house I've ever seen."

"It sure is. I just love working here, especially for her."

"Why?"

"Because she's the best person I ever worked for."

"How long has she lived here?"

"About five years now. That's when I came."

David was in no hurry to leave, walking leisurely toward the wide sliding glass doors. Beyond them was a terrace that ran the width of the house, and above it a scalloped awning. Here and there were enormous French stone urns, which Maggie filled weekly with fresh flowers . . . at the moment, yellow chrysanthemums. Just in front of the wrought-iron rail, planters of English boxwood bordered the house, and in the corners stood topiary trees alongside which were stone sculptures Maggie had bought in Paris depicting the seasons. The floor consisted of large black-and-white marble squares, and in the center was a white wrought-iron dining table and six chairs. Nearby was a chaise longue, waiting regally.

"That's really something, isn't it?" the maid said, coming up beside him.

David nodded.

"When Miss Kent bought the house she remodeled this whole section. Before, the windows were small" —she laughed admiringly—"if Miss Kent doesn't like something, she just knocks out a wall."

"Forgive me for staying so long. I happen to be in the real estate business, so I'm really very interested. I've just never run across anything like this."

"That's what everybody says. Of course, Miss Kent is an interior designer. Do you know her well?"

"I've met her a couple of times." He turned around, his attention wandering from one item to the next. The room was much larger than he would have imagined by what was suggested of it from the street. There were no partitions; Maggie had had them removed so that on the third floor there was only one large living room and a bedroom suite—which he decided he was going to see before he left. For the moment he concentrated on his immediate surroundings. All the furnishings were European antiques except for the modern paintings. The furniture was arranged in intimate, conversational groupings. The floors were marquetry and scattered around were area rugs. The walls were bleached poplar with *boiserie* moldings that enhanced the muted color of soft golden yellow in the fabrics so carefully selected. It must have cost a fortune.

Then he got to Maggie's bedroom and stood in the doorway; the room might have been reconstructed out of the pages of history—from the *Petite Trianon.* Without asking permission, he slowly walked in, followed by the maid, and stood for a long moment in the center of the room looking at the large *directoire* bed with its white silk coverlet and bolster . . . and wanting the feel of Maggie Kent's body next to his, wondering what it would be like, then dismissing as errant stupidity even having the thought. . . . Finally, realizing he was staring, he took in the dressing room, all mirrored from floor to ceiling, concealing the wardrobes, and on the skirted dressing table a profusion of oversized perfume bottles from Patou to Lanvin, Christmas Night, My Sin, Chanel No. 5 . . . the list went on. And in a pink marble bathroom were gold fittings, sunken tub, and chaise.

Almost literally filled with Maggie Kent, he began to descend the winding stairs to the second floor. The plan was the same as the one above, except for the huge modern kitchen. Here the furnishings were less formal. This room doubled as a dining room–sitting room. The house, for all its elegance, had a very lived-in look.

Maggie Kent was an exceptional woman with rare talents. And there was no doubt that she knew how to live, as he had seen today.

Back in his office next morning, David realized that he hadn't felt well since he'd had lunch with Maggie Kent and began to wonder if there wasn't something very wrong with him. Aside from the diabetes, which never bothered him, he had never been really ill in his life, and the idea that something might be amiss startled him. The only doctor he knew was Mark's pediatrician, so he called Jim Fowler and got the name of his family doctor, who agreed to see him late that afternoon.

After taking some tests in the office, it was discovered that his diabetes was the problem and he was advised to abstain from alcohol; a little dry white wine at the most. The conclusion was that his blood sugar was up slightly but not alarmingly so; and if he continued to eat sensibly, chances were he would have no more trouble, although he should be checked more often. No wonder he'd felt poorly at lunch with Maggie Kent.

A few days later David called her to ask if he could take her to lunch and go over the estimate once again. They met at Piero's. She was on time for their appointment, in fact, she was a bit early. He met her at the bar; she looked her usual elegant self.

"Have I kept you waiting?" he asked.

"No, not at all. I had an appointment nearby and I was through earlier than I expected."

"It's nice to know a woman who's on time—"

"One of my few virtues." She laughed.

"And vices?"

"I never volunteer information about my vices."

The bartender came over. This time he recognized David. "How are you, sir, and you, Miss Kent?"

David nodded as Maggie said, "Fine, thanks, Robert."

"The usual, Miss Kent?"

She nodded her head.

"And for you, sir?"

"I'll have a glass of dry white wine."

"Wait, Robert. I'll have the same."

David noted the change—it was as though she were making them more in tune with each other. And then, again, it could mean she was being cautious, wouldn't drink more than he and be caught off guard.

In time Alfred came over to them and said, "If you would care to go to lunch now, I have your table ready." They got up while Alfred carried their wine and seated them at the same table as the last time.

"Now what would you like?" David asked, still having trouble with the menu. "I'm sticking to something easy—cold chicken, and I guess asparagus."

"That sounds marvelous. I'll have the same."

"You're sure, now?"

"I'm sure. I hope I never have a more difficult decision to make than that."

My God, she was gorgeous. He decided the fight was over. Now the question was how to capitulate gracefully.

"By the way, I understand you checked out the homestead. I hope it met with your approval."

And there it was . . . she'd given him the perfect opening. "It certainly did. The renderings were pretty tempting, but I admit your home sold me. I've decided to go along with you, even though it still is much more than I wanted to spend."

"Don't worry, Mr. Reid, it's only painful when you write the check."

David laughed. If she were being clever at his expense, she at least was making it awfully pleasant. Maggie Kent, in all things, was easy to take.

As they ate their lunch David became more at ease with her. She was so open and honest, no contrived femininity or coyness. Between the wine and the atmosphere, David was completely relaxed. He simply loved being *here* with *her*. She had not, however, even once given him the slightest encouragement to feel that this was anything more than a friendly business lunch. She was warm and communicative, but never personal. He was fascinated with her and as his fascination grew he wanted to know more about her.

"How long have you been an interior designer, Miss Kent?"

"Oh, ten years."

"Have you always lived in San Francisco?"

"No, not always. I was born in Rhode Island. I've been here for eight years."

"Do you like it?"

"I love it—it's the most magnificent city I've ever seen, and I never want to live anywhere else."

"Strange, I felt that way when I first saw it."

"Yes, there's a magic about it, no question, I think most people just fall in love with this place."

She hadn't asked where he'd come from, which for a moment annoyed him, until he caught himself in time: no questions asked, no stories to fabricate. He would need to be more careful. Momentarily rattled, he pressed with a question he knew was too forward the moment he said it. "Do you live alone?"

"Yes, and happily . . . excuse me, but do you have the time?"

David looked at his watch. "It's one-thirty. Look, I'm sorry—"

"Don't be silly. I've really enjoyed it, but you'll

have to forgive me for cutting this short. I have an appointment. It's really been most delightful." As she began to put on her gloves she added, "I'll go ahead with the preliminary layout as proposed for now, if that meets with your approval?"

Disappointed, he said, "Yes, that's fine," but wanting to spend more time with her. She was still a mystery to him. Maybe it was all for the best. Maybe.

During the next few days, sitting at his desk, going over figures, wherever, whatever . . . his thoughts were on Maggie Kent. And the more he tried, the more difficult it became to dismiss her from those thoughts. Then one morning shortly after their last lunch together, while going through his mail, he found an envelope addressed to Mr. and Mrs. David Reid. When it happened he still had a most uneasy feeling. When he opened it, he found an invitation to a cocktail party Maggie Kent was giving on the 21st of December from six to nine. He looked at the calendar, it was the 17th. He assumed the party must have been planned far in advance and the invitations sent out much earlier; but he had met her only during the last week or so. That must be the reason for such short notice. (Did it really matter?) There was nothing personal in the invitation; why should there be? Obviously she sent them to clients as well as friends. Holding the card in his hand (feeling almost as though he were touching her), he immediately called her.

"Hello, Miss Kent, this is David Reid. How are you?"

"Fine, thank you, and you?"

"Fine. I received your invitation. I'll be very happy to come, but . . . Mrs. Reid won't be able to make it, she'll be away that week—"

"Oh well, I hope I'll have the pleasure another time."

"Yes . . . by the way, when do you think we might get together and go over the whole project?" Anything to keep the conversation going, just to hear the sound of her voice.

"It's so close to the end of the year, I don't have a free moment. But right after the first we'll get started. Don't worry about a thing, Mr. Reid. Once we do get started, things will hum along, I can assure you. The most important thing is the planning. After that it's pretty much a breeze until the installation."

"Yes, I know." Mustn't be too eager, David. "I'm in capable hands."

Maggie laughed. "I hope you'll say the same about me when the job is completed."

"I have no doubt."

"Well then, Mr. Reid, I'll see you on the twenty-first." She hung up.

David sat staring down at the phone, shocked by the feeling of loneliness overwhelming him. His impulse was to call her back, like a schoolboy, he thought, with his first crush. But he wasn't a schoolboy, and if he didn't forget about all this foolishness he could get himself into one Godawful mess. That was all he needed—to get himself involved with another woman.

Get involved? Where was his mind going? Aside from practical considerations such as Katie, Mark, and his own hard-won independence, what made him so cocksure that Maggie Kent would ever want to get involved with him. He reminded himself that she'd not given him the slightest encouragement along such lines. And as for the cocktail party, well, that was impersonal business too. Besides, chances were that Maggie Kent had a lover, or perhaps more than one. Just because she lived alone didn't mean she had no commitments. That's sensible thinking, David. Except that, not very sensibly, the idea of there being someone else made him feel even more lonely. As though he had lost somebody already very close to him. . . .

CHAPTER NINETEEN

Driving up to the City the evening of Maggie Kent's party, David still felt the uncomfortable embarrassment . . . guilt? . . . that had been with him when he'd said goodbye to Katie, as though he were off to a clandestine rendezvous. Katie thought nothing of it, assuming another business meeting.

David arrived about seven. Maggie had hired two parking attendants to take her guests' cars down the hill to a garage at the foot of Lombard Street. The narrow street Maggie lived on was originally designed for only two lanes of traffic as it led up Telegraph Hill. He got out of the car, walked to the front door and rang, remembering the first time he had rung that bell and never imagining that he would ever be entering this splendor socially. This time the door was opened by a butler hired for the evening along with other help provided by a catering company.

"Good evening, sir, may I take your coat?" the butler said as David slipped out of it. "Miss Kent is in the upstairs sitting room. Will you take the elevator?"

"No, thanks, I'll walk."

By now the party was in full swing and the guests had overflowed into the halls and were sitting on the stairs as David made his way up to the third floor. Finally reaching the upper hall, David came upon a breathtaking sight. The room was done in winter wonderland. Trees in huge tubs, brought in from the Podesta Baldocchi florist, were decorated with tiny Christmas lights. The room smelled of pine commingled with a French perfume. Candles glowed from the huge Baccarat crystal chandelier which hung from the high ceiling, and had been converted from electricity for the evening's festivities. There were candelabra on the buffet table and also on the mantel. David surveyed the room, impressed by the assortment of people, the likes of which he had never seen together in one place. To him it seemed that Maggie had invited the cream of the immediate world. High society was represented here, the ladies breathtakingly gowned, which was what he would imagine Maggie's friends would be; but looking about he also spotted a small group of beatniks, which he wouldn't have expected. Also on hand were a turbaned gentleman and his lady in a jewel-encrusted sari; two couples from Japan, the ladies dressed in traditional kimonos and obis; and near them a young black couple. An elegant melting pot, and David felt uncomfortable. Suddenly he heard his name being called above the din of voices.

"Mr. Reid, I'm so delighted to see you." Maggie seemed to float in a cloud of pink chiffon and crystal beads as she came to greet him. Her hair was piled high on top of her head.

"How are you, Miss Kent?" he said.

"Fine, thank you, and you?"

He nodded. "Fine."

Before he could say another word she took him by the hand and led him over to Ron Bordini. "Look who I have here," she said, releasing his hand. He didn't want her to let go of it. Then she was gone.

"How are you, Ron?"

"Great, David. I want you to meet my wife Sylvia. Darling, this is Mr. Reid."

"Nice meeting you, Mr. Reid."

"The pleasure is . . ." Before David knew it, he found a wine glass in his hand. What a fabulous woman, he thought. How had she remembered that he had drunk only wine that second time at lunch? He was so captivated by her, he hardly heard Ron talking to him.

"I'm sorry, Ron, what did you say?"

"I was saying what do you think of this architecture?"

"It's spectacular. I've never seen anything like it."

"Anything Maggie does is spectacular."

Sylvia laughed. "My husband is like the postman on holiday. When we were in Paris we went to the Folies Bergères, and what do you think he talked about on the way back to the hotel?"

"I'm afraid to ask." David smiled.

"No, not what you'd imagine, Mr. Reid. Not a word about the girls, just architecture."

"Well, I noticed you, didn't I?" Ron said.

"That's right, darling, but I'll never know how—the first time we met was in front of the Opera House." She squeezed his arm affectionately.

"How do you happen to know Maggie?" said David, startled to realize that he had called her Maggie for the first time.

"We studied together at the Sorbonne and have been very good friends ever since."

Somehow David couldn't imagine these two young women being *very* good friends, as Sylvia put it; in appearance, at least, they seemed opposites. Sylvia was only a little shorter than her husband, with dark brown hair that looked as though she had just run a comb through it and eyes of the same color; her manner was soft, with a lovely face to complement it, but she seemed rather prosaic amidst all the glamor, wearing a simple black dress. For some reason David visualized her in jeans walking through a meadow, her hair in braids. She was not only unlike Maggie, she was not really what David had expected Ron's wife to be. He supposed it was because having met Maggie through Ron he would have thought Maggie would be the prototype of the woman Ron would be attracted to.

"Oh, Mr. Reid, will you forgive me? I see a friend I want to say hello to."

"Of course," David said as she went off, leaving Ron and himself alone.

"Charming lady, your wife," David said, and he meant it.

"Thank you."

The two then began to talk about the plans, the blueprints, and so forth, but soon Sylvia was back, taking Ron by the hand.

"Darling, Eleanor and Roger want to say hello. She can't come over, she broke her leg skiing."

"Okay. David, will you excuse me for a moment?"

"Sure."

David knew no one else and kept glancing around the room, hoping to catch sight of Maggie; eventually he wandered about the room, hearing fragments of conversation . . . "Let me tell you about the rabbi and the priest . . ." David moved on. "I thought she looked perfectly dreadful. She's no right to wear a dress that tight since she's gained all that weight and I . . ." David moved on, until once again he found himself standing in front of Maggie's portrait.

"Do you like it?" Ron was behind him. David turned around to him.

"To put it mildly."

"Sylvia did that."

"Your Sylvia?" David asked in astonishment.

"Yes, she's a portrait painter and a damn good one, if I say so myself."

"I don't know why, but somehow I thought it was done by a man."

"I know," Ron said, looking up at the picture. "Sylvia has a power about her work that I think is very unusual. She captures the whole of a person, don't you think?" He stood alongside David, examining the portrait as though seeing it for the first time.

"She certainly does." David peered at the right-hand corner and noticed the signature for the first time. Kalish. Kalish? My God, she's Jewish! And, as always, he felt the shocked embarrassment, as though by cutting himself off he had managed to cause all Jews to disappear, thereby eliminating the trauma of their existence, and his. It simply had not occurred to him, although he'd not really thought about it, that Ron Bordini, who was of Italian extraction and undoubtedly Catholic, would be married to a Jewish girl who was also one of Maggie's best friends. Suddenly he felt slightly ill, which had nothing to do with the wine. Jews apparently could be accepted, and for a moment he was forced to wonder if he couldn't have accomplished the same things in his life had he remained a Jew . . . and then quickly amended his disturbing realization—*some* Jews were accepted, Jews who had the money and background that got them to Paris, that made it possible to meet people like Maggie Kent . . . not Jews like David, son of Isaac, dirt poor from Hester Street. And so thinking, he felt a little better, though still shaken, about the way he had chosen for himself, and his family.

Sylvia was back, to disrupt his thoughts, for which he was grateful. "Darling, I hate to break this up, but I think we'll have to be leaving. We're meeting the Feldmans at eight-thirty in front of the theater. It's been so nice meeting you, Mr. Reid. I hope I have the pleasure again."

"Thank you, Mrs. Bordini. I hope so." Even saying it, David hoped he never would. Ron Bordini shook hands with David and said something about seeing him right after the first of the year and going over some details, but David didn't hear. He was left standing by himself listening to all the chatter around him in that luxurious room filled with all those beautiful people who seemed so at ease with each other. Even the beatniks seemed at home here, one even reciting an unintelligible poem about the decay of American civilization, while David felt more alone than if he were on an island in the middle of the Pacific Ocean.

"A penny for your thoughts."

He turned around. Maggie had come up next to him.

"You'd get robbed if I told you." How the hell did he think in his wildest fantasies that she would ever see anything in him?

"I'm afraid I've neglected you badly."

His glass was refilled and then Maggie took him by the hand and led him to the buffet table. "Here, let me fix a plate for you."

The buffet was overwhelming: a whole salmon glazed with mayonnaise and truffles; curried rice salad; cold sliced chicken; *quiche Lorraine; paté de foie gras* in an aspic glaze; caviar and cucumber aspic; lobster cooked in brandy with toasted almonds; artichokes and shrimp; hot crepes filled with crab in an enormous chafing dish at one end, and at the other a ham *en croûte* and a beef baked in burgundy. Maggie hadn't eaten all day, so as she fixed a plate for David, she did the same for herself, and handing David his plate, she asked, "Are you having a good time, Mr. Reid?"

"Yes, it's a wonderful party."

"Thank you. You met Sylvia, isn't she charming?"

"Yes, very."

David felt so awkward. He looked for a table to put down his glass.

"Here, let me take that," Maggie said. At the moment she turned around one of the maids was in back of her still serving the hot hors d'oeuvres and the canapes, so Maggie handed the glass to her. Then they stood together, she devouring her plate and he scarcely touching his. When he had finished all he could manage, he looked around for somewhere to put his plate.

Taking the plate, she said, "You certainly weren't very hungry. Are you sure I can't get you something else?"

"No, it's delicious. I've had plenty, thanks." He certainly wasn't going to tell her about the diabetes.

"Well, let me get you some more wine."

Before he could object he found himself with another glass in his hand.

The guests lingered on, but by now it was well past ten and some of them were leaving. Maggie kissed one of the men on the cheek, and David once again listened to fragments of conversation . . . "So glad you could come, darling" . . . "We always enjoy your parties" . . . "Honestly, Mag, you're really so damned clever, I just hate you" . . . "See you at Theo's party, want us to pick you up?" "No," Maggie was replying, "Peter will be in town." . . . Now only a small group of Maggie's intimate friends remained. She returned to David.

"Well, now, Mr. Reid, how's your drink holding up?"

"Fine, thank you."

She checked; his glass was almost empty. "Here, let me have it refilled," she said, taking it.

"No, no more thank you. I really have to be going now."

"Do you really?" She put the glass down.

"Well . . ."

"Please stay if you can."

"Are you sure?"

"I never say anything I'm not sure of," she said. "Come, let me introduce you to my friends, but first I want you to meet my mother and Aunt Violet."

Maggie's mother was seated on one of the French *bergères* in front of the fireplace. She was a lovely, white-haired lady dressed in a long pearl-gray lace gown, which was almost the color of her hair.

"Mother, I want you to meet Mr. Reid." Before the introductions could be completed she was interrupted by the return of a maid who refreshed their drinks. Then Maggie led him to Aunt Violet, dressed in a cerise-colored Balenciaga, her hair carefully coiffed, looking as though the wind wouldn't dare to blow it out of place.

"Aunt Violet, I want you to meet Mr. Reid."

She extended a diamond spangled arm to David, shifting the cocktail glass to her left hand. "Well, now, look what we have here. You have the best taste in men, Maggie my girl. Who is this, a new suitor?"

"Mr. Reid is my new client."

But Violet, feeling her drinks, said boldly, "You know, my dear, in business you can make an enemy out of a friend, but you can make a friend out of a client, and Mr. Reid looks as though he could be a very good friend indeed," and looked him up and down.

"Oh, Aunt Violet, I think you need another drink, or else you've had too many." They all laughed together.

David noted the differences in the two sisters' appearance—not so much in their ages but in demeanor.

He could just see Aunt Violet taking out all her jewels for inspection—the ones she wore tonight as well as the ones David was sure she had stashed away at home. Maggie's mother seemed so much more subdued.

Maggie now led him off by the arm and said, "Let me introduce you to a dear friend. This is Peter Douglas. Peter, this is Mr. Reid."

The two shook hands, and David realized that Peter Douglas must have been the one Maggie had said would still be in town. They were probably very, very good friends, and suddenly David was angry with himself because he resented Peter Douglas more than he could tolerate, or justify. He knew when all the guests left, she would kick off her shoes, dim the lights, change into something else, and sit before the fire—prelude to their night together.

He was sickened by the thought that she would lie in Peter Douglas' arms and not his, and it was at that moment he admitted how much he wanted her.

Maggie was introducing him now to the rest of her friends; most of them couldn't have cared less, hardly acknowledging the introduction. Someone turned on the music and Lana Tate began to dance. More drinks were served, a few guests went to the buffet and refilled their plates, Amy Foster kicked off her shoes and began to dance in place, keeping time with her so slim derrière, her partner holding onto the tips of her fingers. David observed it all. He didn't even know how to waltz. Who had time to dance when all you thought about was filling your stomach? What the hell was he doing here in the first place, feeling like a wart on someone's nose. None of these people knew what it was like to be hungry. It was all so gay and comfortable for them; they were all out of the same mold. Okay, all his success and money didn't fit him into their self-indulgent lives. The only thing he knew about life was how to get ahead. He didn't belong here and, depressed, knew he never would. He thought of Sylvia Kalish Bordini; she belonged, Jewish and all. She hadn't signed Maggie's portrait with "Bordini"—she could have—but still she belonged.

And they were meeting friends by the name of Feldman. Well, they never had to scratch the way he had; they were the *goyisk* Jews you couldn't tell from gentiles . . . oh, the hell with it. Suddenly he felt threatened. He had to get the hell out of here and go home, to be safely in his own territory.

He found Maggie. "I really have to be going now, thank you for inviting me."

"Do you really? The party is just beginning."

"Thank you, but I really have to."

"Well, it was so nice of you to come. I hope that next time Mrs. Reid will be able to make it."

He walked down the stairs, the rhumba music following him into the entry foyer on the first floor, where the butler helped him on with his coat.

"I'll call the attendant to have your car brought around."

"Thank you. I'll wait outside."

"Good night, sir," the man said, opening the front door.

"Good night." He stood with his back against the wall and waited, feeling very alone.

He drove around for a while. It was only quarter of eleven. He didn't much want to face going home and going through the pretended amenities tonight, but finally he wearied of wandering aimlessly up one street and down another, gave up and headed for home, driving slowly.

The houses on Rosehaven Road were decorated with Christmas lights and inside, parties were in progress. He could sense the happy holiday spirit behind those doors and contrasted it with what he was anticipating. He came in through the back door and walked through the kitchen to the library, where Katie was curled up in a chair, reading.

"Hello, David, how did things go tonight?"

"Okay, I suppose."

"I assume you had dinner."

Always food. First we eat and then we fight. "Of course I had dinner. What did you do?"

"Nothing very much. Mark and I had dinner out, since you weren't here, and went to a movie."

"Where's Mark?"

"He's in his room wrapping his gifts."

"Oh? That's nice. I'm going up to bed, I've had a very tough day."

"Can I get you anything?"

If she asks once more about something to eat. . . . "No, I'm just tired. Good night."

David turned and left, switching on the lamp as he passed the living room. My God, how dour everything looked. Until now he had always thought of the inside of the house as Katie's and the outside as his, but after all he lived here, this was his house too. Why not have Maggie Kent decorate it? He could hardly keep on building offices for her to furnish just so he could continue to see her. At least the house would be a good excuse for him to get to know her a little better, and he would see to it that the job took a very long time.

Passing Mark's room on the way to his, he found his son sitting on the bed, watching television, with his gifts and wrappings all around him.

"Hi, dad," Mark said as David stood in the doorway.

"Hi."

"I'm awfully tired, Mark." It was the truth.

He and his father really didn't have much luck finding something good to hear about this holiday. It would be nice, though, to have his father's company for a while . . . "See you tomorrow, dad."

"Yeah, tomorrow."

"Good night."

"Good night."

David went into his room, shutting the door quietly behind him. He threw open the window to get a breath of fresh air, breathing the cold winter night into his lungs, then went into the bathroom and took a shower, turning on the hot first and then the cold, letting it pelt down on his back, making him shiver. He turned off the water and got out, huddling as he rubbed his hands, then dried himself, put on fresh pajamas, and got into bed. Lying in the dark, he thought about the evening. What a misfit he had been. What could he talk about? All he knew was real estate. Business talk was the only kind he knew, and business people were the only kind he came in contact with. When it was a matter of making a deal—a real deal—not the kind with Maggie Kent—he felt he had no peer. Likewise when it came to financing and banking. He knew the ways and now he had the means. But obviously there were other things in the world to talk about. Did his life always have to be so hard, so *serious?* All work and no play, David . . . He realized more than ever that while he was hell-bent on proving his survival by his success he had neglected to improve the quality of his life. It was as though he'd been born an old man. He had never been able to make small talk, yet that, he was coming to realize, wasn't necessarily something to be proud of. It happened to be a lack, not a mark of superiority. Part of getting along with other people was small talk . . . not business or big events of the day, but the everyday things that happened to people. In a word, living . . . He felt like a man who'd been in a cave so long that when he finally came out into the sunshine it was like a rebirth, and he had to learn how to adjust to the light. He took everything so seriously, he didn't even know how to relax. Well, how could he, when just living had been so tough? Besides, he'd married too young, he'd never sown his wild oats. How many women had he ever met besides Katie, and of those, he couldn't even stand sleeping with them. One thing he had to give himself—his taste in women was good, including Katie, who was hardly an ordinary Hester Street type. What had happened in later years was beside the point. At the time she was certainly the best . . .

Turning over, he closed his eyes, but he could not shut out the image of Maggie Kent, her graciousness tonight in knowing the needs of each one of that multitude of guests, remembering that he preferred wine. Her combination of spontaneity and order fascinated him. She seemed to enjoy her own party and friends, and yet he got the distinct feeling that she could find pleasure in being alone as well. There were so many sides to discover about this exceptional young woman. She had managed to make him feel as though he were the only guest who had been there tonight. She was capable of making anyone feel that way. She was genuinely interested in everyone and everything. Her vitality was contagious, and she seemed to have her life completely in hand. David had become so intrigued with her that he wondered how he could stay away from her. But, my God, there was so much involved here. He was a very, very rich man; he had a son; he was married; and, most frightening, he had no reason to suppose that Maggie Kent would ever return his feeling for her. Why should she?

Why should she, why shouldn't . . .? My God, he was acting like a damn schoolboy. Well, in matters like this he *was* a schoolboy. Face it, and face it that—schoolboy crush or something deeper or a combination thereof—he was obsessed with Maggie Kent and had to risk letting her at least begin to get the idea. So next morning he called the florist and ordered four dozen American beauty roses to be sent to Miss Maggie Kent, with a card saying, "Thank you for allowing me to share your gracious party." He waited until eleven, then, with his heart thumping, he called Maggie's house. Listening to the phone ring, he nearly hung up, worrying that Peter Douglas might answer. He couldn't take that. . . .

"Miss Kent's residence."

David recognized the maid's voice. It sounded uncommonly good to him at the moment. "Yes, may I speak to Miss Kent? Tell her Mr. David Reid is calling."

"I'm sorry but Miss Kent isn't here."

He was surprised. "When will she be back?"

"She's gone away."

"Gone away?"

"Yes, she left this morning."

"Left?" Left? He panicked but tried to stay calm. "I was told she would . . . I have some business to discuss . . ."

"She left for Pebble Beach this morning. I'm sorry."

Damn it, and he hadn't called earlier, thinking that she might still be asleep.

"How long will she be away?"

"She won't be back until after New Year's."

"Thank you, thank you very much," he said, and hung up, staring at the phone for a very, very long time.

The Fowlers had included the Reids on Christmas day along with family and a few very close friends, but it was a bad day for David, preoccupied with thoughts of Maggie. Having no excuse to talk to her until after the first of the year, when they would begin working together, left him with a feeling of frustration and despair.

The week between Christmas and New Year's Day found him with a variety of external remonstrations. First he was withdrawn and silent, then he snapped at Mark; whatever Katie said, he argued with her. The most ordinary things sent him off into a rage. He was disgruntled, caustic, impatient. Mark complained to Katie, who explained that David was under great pressure and really didn't mean to be the way he was. Mark would be happy to escape his father's tirades when the holiday was over.

On New Year's Eve, David and Katie had been invited to a party given by one of David's attorneys. He stood in a corner and watched all the people assembled, with their crazy hats and horns and noisemakers, listening to their conversations and jokes, wishing he could escape. Thank God the sirens finally blew at midnight and everybody kissed and hugged each other. Another year. HAPPY . . . NEW . . . YEAR . . . Hurray! Katie wished David a happy New Year as she reached up to kiss him. He mouthed the words, happy New Year. His thoughts were with Maggie Kent, assuming that at this moment she must be in the embrace of Peter Douglas, or maybe someone else.

The second of January, 1948, finally rolled around and none too soon for David. He was crawling the walls.

Maggie was seated at the desk in her studio when her secretary rang the intercom. "Miss Kent, Mr. Reid for you."

"Put him on." Taking off her tortoise-shell rimmed glasses and holding the receiver to her ear under her chin, she lit a cigarette.

"Good morning, Miss Kent. Happy New Year, plus one."

"Thank you, Mr. Reid, the same to you."

"I hope you had a nice holiday," he said, hoping that the sound of his voice would not betray him.

"Yes, delightful. And you?"

"Yes, the same."

"Now, Mr. Reid, what can I do for you?"

What could she do for him? "I wonder if we might get together and go over a few details on the project?"

"Well, let me see how I am on appointments."

He waited impatiently.

"How about Tuesday next?"

He meant *now*. "How about today for lunch?"

"I'm going to be all tied up with a big installation. I'm sorry."

He couldn't bear to wait until next week. "Can't you somehow make it tomorrow?"

"I'm sorry, the job will take all my time this week. It's a large hotel and I must be on hand to see that everything goes smoothly. I know you're anxious to get started, but we have loads of time, really—"

He interrupted, "Yes, I am anxious."

"Well, I can understand, but, Mr. Reid, you have no need to worry at this stage, especially since we've decided on the theme and know more or less where we're going."

Maybe you know where you're going but I don't, he thought. Reluctantly, he said, "Well, next week then. And, Miss Kent, when we get started I hope you'll give me a little more of your time." He risked a laugh.

"Don't you worry about that. You'll get so tired of seeing me, you'll probably scream. You know, I can be very difficult when I'm opposed. It goes with the job—the temperament, I mean."

"I can't imagine it."

"Wait until you get to know me a bit better."

He would wait, impatiently. "Well, shall we say noon at Piero's on Tuesday?"

"Tuesday it is. And for heaven's sake, stop worrying —it ages one so, you know." They both laughed, she a little more than he.

"Oh, and Mr. Reid, thank you for those beautiful roses. They happen to be one of my special loves—"

"Well, thank you. It was just my way of saying that I enjoyed your party." And have been crazy to see you ever since.

"Thank you again. See you Tuesday. . . ."

She arrived precisely at twelve, David having gotten there earlier and waited. They had the usual wine before lunch, sat at the usual table and said the usual things. David waited to tell her about the house until after lunch . . . in order to prolong their being together.

"Miss Kent, I'd like you to redecorate my home."

"That sounds interesting . . . I'd have to see it, of course."

He cleared his throat. "I'm almost embarrassed to show it to you. Don't misunderstand, I'm not criticizing my wife—"

Maggie smiled. "I'm sure she has excellent taste, but you know what happens when people live with the same things for a long time. They become so accustomed to them that they grow a bit weary of seeing them year in and year out. I suspect that's why you feel as you do."

Perhaps she should have substituted people for things. . . .

"Anyway, I'd like you to see what could be done."

"Fine, we'll make an appointment and I'll run out and take a look."

"How about today?"

"Today?"

"Yes. I'll drive you down and back to the city."

"I must say, Mr. Reid, when you want something done, you don't leave room, or time, for doubt."

"Then you'll come?"

She hesitated, presumably reviewing her schedule. "Look, Mr. Reid, let me make one phone call and I'll see if I can put this client off until tomorrow. I'll be right back."

Pleased with himself, David poured more wine into their glasses while she was gone and took a few sips, feeling the glow. Soon she came back and sat down.

"It's fine. I took care of everything."

"I hope it wasn't too much bother," he said, delighted at the prospect of being with her.

"Well, just a little. I'm starting to redo this friend's office and I think he was a bit miffed. You remember Mike Brooks from my party?"

"There were so many new people I don't remember. Describe him."

"Well, anyone meeting Michael Brooks usually never forgets him. He was the handsome attorney with the shock of silver hair, tall. Do you remember now?"

"Yes, I think you asked him if he had an appointment with a blonde or something?"

"A good memory; that's a virtue *I* admire."

He was more than rewarded. She began to get up.

"Wait, this is so pleasant, let's just finish the wine."

"All right, but I must have enough time to go over the house, and I have to be back in the city before five, I'm expected for early dinner."

"We'll have plenty of time." They finished the wine and when they were on their way, David drove slowly down the highway to his home, wanting to draw out to the maximum their time alone together. As they walked up the brick path to the door, Maggie stopped and admired the garden, saying the house was simply gorgeous, authentically country English.

"Has Ron seen this?" she asked.

"No."

"Well, you'll have to show it to him. Whoever designed this certainly meets with my approval."

And then the moment David worried about arrived. All too soon he put his key in the lock and opened the door to the foyer, taking her arm as he led her into the living room. He hoped Maggie would not mention that she was sorry Mrs. Reid had been away and unable to attend her party, and realized she was hardly likely to . . . a woman of experience. He also realized Katie would be furious at him for not calling her in advance—Maggie no doubt assumed he had—but he hadn't dared risk Katie's refusal . . . not with what he really had at stake here.

"Let me find Mrs. Reid," he said as he left Maggie in the living room and went to see if, hopefully, the Ford station wagon was gone; there it was, bigger than life. Obviously she was home, probably up at the greenhouse. He'd get her.

While Maggie waited for Mr. Reid to return with his wife—he certainly seemed apprehensive—she looked around. Good Lord, it really was pretty awful, gloomy and somehow empty-feeling, as though nobody lived here. Well, everything needed to go, everything, or she wouldn't take it on. Mr. Reid seemed to understand what the problem was, so there would probably be no conflict with him, but what about Mrs. Reid? If she put up any opposition, well then, Mrs. Reid could just go to hell, much as Maggie disliked turning down the money.

Katie was out in her potting shed separating tiny seedlings into larger flats. Wearing a pair of denim pants (the back pocket slightly torn) and a red-and-white checked shirt, her hair was in disarray, fresh dirt was under her nails, and there was a distinct aura of fertilizer and peat moss about her.

Without preliminaries—it seemed the best tactic—David said, "Kate, I'd like you to come up to the house and meet Miss Kent. You remember her, she's doing the office, and I thought as long as she was down this way she could take a look at the house." He emphasized, "I know how much you've always wanted to do it, so please come up and meet her."

Katie stood staring at David, the trowel in her hand and dirt smudges on her face, too angry for a moment to say anything. But she could think, and furiously . . . wanted to do it? *She* do the house, for *me*? And when had David done something like this because she wanted it? Why hadn't he ever asked her, Katie, would *you* like to do the house over . . . *you*? I believe this is my house too, don't I have a say in choosing who should decorate it? In fact, I don't want a decorator, or need one. I think I'm capable of expressing myself in my own home. David forgets that long before I met him, I lived in a house such as he's never seen, probably never will. Likewise for Miss Kent . . .

Finally she found her voice. "David, I can't meet anyone looking like this. You should at least have called and told me you were bringing Miss Kent home."

She was, of course, right. And so was he, damn it, in his reasons for not telling her. He'd better temporize, though, for the moment. "You look all right. Besides, she's just a decorator. You don't have to put it on for her. You look fine."

Still furious, but not wanting a scene, Katie went along and allowed him to introduce her to Maggie Kent—glamorous, beautifully groomed Miss Maggie Kent, alongside whom Katie felt like the hired help. No, just plain and simple humiliated. Finally composing herself, she said coldly, "Miss Kent, I'm happy to meet you. Sorry I didn't have more notice, I'd have managed to be a bit more presentable. I've been gardening, as you can plainly see."

"Of course, Mrs. Reid. Now, do you have any ideas about what you'd like to achieve here?"

Katie felt like saying, yes, I want it to look exactly like the Taj Mahal, but instead she said, "No, not really . . ."

"I see," Maggie said, thinking no wonder the house looks this way. How the hell did he ever marry her?

"Well, do you have a preference for English furniture?"

"Yes." Silence.

"Well, fine. . . . Now let me ask you this, how functional do you want the house to be? I mean, do you live formally or informally?"

"Informally." So informally, Katie thought, that they'd never had a guest to dinner since they'd lived here.

"Well, then, that gives me an idea of what we're looking for. May I see the rest of the house?"

"Yes, of course," David spoke up, as he led the way through the house while Katie excused herself and went into the kitchen to fix herself a cup of tea—she'd forgotten about lunch until that moment.

After Maggie had seen all she needed, she and David came back downstairs and he left her waiting in the living room while he went to look for Katie, who was sitting in the breakfast room drinking her tea.

"Miss Kent is leaving," he said.

Without a word she got up, followed him into the living room and stood facing the decorator.

"Well, Mrs. Reid, you have a perfectly charming house," which Maggie meant. "I feel a great deal can be done here," which she also meant, then added, "but of course I'd need to, well, start from scratch. I believe in having these things understood and agreed on from the start to avoid misunderstandings. I certainly mean no offense, it's just the way I have to work to feel I'm giving you the best I have to offer. So . . . I'm afraid that means everything would go, even the piano. It's very nice, but a spinet in that lovely large room just seems incongruous."

The piano had saved Katie's life, her sanity, and she had deprived herself to have it. She would, by God, keep it.

Encouraged by Katie's silence, Maggie went on, "I've taken the liberty of suggesting to Mr. Reid that we do some remodelling upstairs where the sundeck comes off the master bedroom. I'd knock out that wall and incorporate it into the bedroom area so that you'd have a bedroom-sitting room. It could be quite lovely, overlooking the garden."

"That's very interesting, Miss Kent. I have no objections. The piano, however, stays. Oh yes, I'll also decorate my own room. The rest of the house is yours." She looked directly at Miss Kent. "Now, if you'll excuse me, I was in the midst of separating some seedlings." Katie turned and left Maggie staring after her.

Maggie picked up her bag and put on her gloves as she walked to the front door, then opened it and walked down the path to the car. They drove back in silence, David wanting to kill himself, not to mention Katie.

As they approached the outskirts of San Francisco, Maggie said, "Mr. Reid, I must be honest with you. I really can't take this job."

He'd been expecting it, and wanted to die. "Listen, Miss Kent, I know how you feel. I really want to apologize for—"

"Look, please don't apologize."

"Then please say you'll do the house."

"I couldn't possibly."

"Why?" Knowing the answer.

"Well, obviously it would be a mistake."

"Please don't say that."

"I'm sorry, but I must. When there's a conflict of personalities at the very beginning, the job can never be a success, and I'm not foolish enough to take a job that I feel in advance I can't be successful with."

"If I ask you to do this for me, will you?"

"It has nothing to do with you, believe me, Mr. Reid. But I just couldn't work in a, well, an uncooperative atmosphere. I'm sorry."

"I'm the one who's sorry."

She looked at him and saw the genuine misery in his face. Then, still maintaining her professional attitude, but with the anger gone from her voice, she said, "Maybe someone else would be more acceptable to Mrs. Reid. After all, I'm not the only decorator in town. In fact, I'm sure there are better." Which she didn't believe for one moment. And she was right.

David persisted. "No, I don't believe you. Look, do this for me as a special favor. Please reconsider, I promise you won't be interfered with."

Quietly she said, "Let me think it over. I'll give you my answer in a few days."

"No, Miss Kent, please. I want your answer now."

She looked closely at him. Seriously. Finally she said, "Did you ever do something you knew you were going to be sorry for, but you did it anyway? Never mind answering. I'll do it."

"Thank you," he said softly, and the world was on again.

But qualifying her agreement she said, "Remember, I'll only take the job if I really can do as I think best. I tell you in advance I won't tolerate any interference once the job has been started. Understood?"

"Definitely, and thank you."

They were in the city now, in front of Piero's. It was quarter to five. David parked, switched off the ignition and turned to her. "Miss Kent, please let me buy you a cocktail. To celebrate . . ."

"No, really, I simply have to dash." She looked at him, her arm resting on the back of the seat. "You certainly are a persistent man." She smiled, shaking her head.

"Please?"

"Just one," she said, holding up her finger with the look of a woman who meant it, adding, "I can be very persistent, too."

David felt like turning handsprings.

They sat at the bar. Dim lights, soft music, a room filled with the comforting murmur of pleasantries exchanged by people wanting to be together after a long day. Sipping wine with Maggie, he experienced a feeling he'd never known before in his entire life—he felt young and gay and mischievous, all the special things a man feels when he is with the woman he wants to be with. Too soon it was time for her to go.

It was unbearable, watching her drive off in the little red Jaguar, watching it turn the corner and disappear from sight. He didn't know what to do with himself, but he did know that he simply could not go home, not yet. Somehow it meant losing the sense of Maggie. He needed to be alone to savor what he felt.

He went back into Piero's to have dinner. Afterward he went to a movie by himself. Something he never did. Too guilty-making, such a self-indulgence. When he came out, he couldn't, if his life had depended upon it, have told anyone what the picture was about.

CHAPTER TWENTY

Winter, 1947

Maggie unzipped the back of her dress and stepped out of it, slipped off her bra, sat on the edge of the bed and took off her stockings. She put on her terry robe, went to the bar, poured some vodka over ice, started the phonograph. Coincidentally it was the same record that had been playing when they'd said goodbye. She hummed along with the music, "Begin the Beguine," sat down with the drink in her hand and looked around the room. It was perfect. Clarice had fluffed up the pillows and filled the bowls with the flowers that were sent each week from the florist. She was a true gem, and Maggie hoped she would never leave. Her life was so very much as she had planned it—she had money, success, and enormous recognition as one of the very best designers in the city. She had worked hard and she had acquired a good reputation for herself. She had many friends and acquaintances and knew the joys of a small coterie of intimates. She was almost never lonely and she believed her life was exactly what she wanted it to be.

So if she had all of this, why had David Reid disturbed her so today? There were men she had turned down who were better looking—grudgingly she thought, if not better looking, at least "as good." The fact was that Peter Douglas had been pursuing her for a long time, asking her to marry him. She had slept with Peter and adored him. She did not love him. Yet she was having most extraordinary feelings about a man whom she had never, she suddenly realized, even called by his first name. She hadn't even *thought* about it until today. . . . Pouring herself another vodka, she said aloud, "Oh come now, Maggie, this is ridiculous." She went into the bathroom and showered, rubbed herself all over with Chanel cologne, dressed hurriedly, and called for a taxi. She was having dinner with Sylvia and Ron, after which they were all going to the symphony.

All evening she had difficulty keeping her mind on the conversation; the symphony went almost unheard, and she barely managed to applaud in the right places. Afterward the Bordinis suggested they go somewhere for a drink but she begged off, hoping that they wouldn't think her impolite. Driven back to her home, she thanked them and Ron got out of the car, took her key and opened the front door. As she went in she kissed him on the cheek, then called out, "Thanks again, Sylvia, for the dinner and all. We'll have lunch together one day this week."

She walked upstairs to her bedroom, undressed and slipped into a printed silk gown with a matching peignoir, then went back into the living room, turned on one lamp, poured herself a drink and switched on the phonograph. The same record was playing. She went to the window and watched the automobiles as they crossed the bridge. Maggie's batting average for handling her emotions was in the big leagues; tonight, however, she simply couldn't get Mr. Reid off her mind. . . . She was startled to hear the doorbell.

Clarice buzzed, her room being just off the main foyer. Maggie picked up the house phone and heard Clarice say, "Miss Kent, there's someone at the door. Do you want me to answer?"

"No, Clarice, I'll see who it is. Go back to sleep. I'm sorry you were disturbed."

The bell rang insistently. Maggie picked up the intercom phone in the hall just off the living room. "Yes. Who is it?" she asked.

"David Reid."

She didn't believe it. As she buzzed to let him in,

knowing her own present unaccustomed emotions, she became nervous—also something Miss Maggie Kent rarely experienced.

David took the elevator to the third floor, where Maggie was waiting for him. When the door opened, their eyes met and David said, uncomfortably, "I know this is ridiculous, but I just had to see you."

To break the tension she laughed and said, "I hope it's not about my neglecting your job."

"No"—David smiled—"hardly that."

"How did you know I'd be alone? I might have been entertaining a gentleman." Her tone was good-natured, not suggestive or sniggering.

"I knew," he said.

"Oh? That's not very flattering, Mr. Reid."

"No, I just knew that you were alone tonight."

"And how did you know that?"

"Because I've been parked across the street since ten."

"Well, you certainly are persistent. Anyway, come in. We're standing here like two kids with egg on our faces. Come in and let me get you a drink."

He followed her into the room and sat down.

"Wine?" she asked.

"Please."

"I'll stick with my vodka. Now tell me, Mr. Reid—"

"I've come to tell you straight out that I'm in love with you."

She blinked her eyes, but David, his feelings having taken on a life of their own, was not to be put off—couldn't stop himself if he'd wanted . . . "I don't think that comes as a complete surprise. And you know something else, Miss Kent?"

"No, please tell me, Mr. Reid."

"I think you more than like me."

She really was stunned. Had she done anything to give away what she might have felt? She didn't even realize it herself until a very short time ago. Confused—also a feeling that was foreign to Maggie—she tried quickly to review her actions.

"I'm going to have another drink. How about you, Mr. Reid?"

He said he'd had enough.

"Oh why not, Mr. Reid? You're among friends." She looked at him. "I hope I am too," and filled his wine glass. "Do you know what I think, Mr. Reid?"

"No, but I'd sure as hell like to, Miss Kent."

"I think this has got to be the most unbelievable thing that's ever happened to me in my entire life." She took a large swallow and added, "*That's* what I think, Mr. Reid."

David put his wine glass down, took hers out of her hand and placed it on the table in front of them, took her in his arms and kissed her so forcefully that when he released her, Maggie was literally breathless. Not quite recovered, she reached for her glass, took a swallow, cleared her throat, took a deep breath and said, "You know, this is never going to work, Mr. Reid."

"Please call me David."

"Okay, David, I'm Maggie. But this still is never going to work; you must know that."

"I only know that I love you, and I don't fall in love so easily. In fact, I tell you here and now that you're the only woman I've ever felt this way about."

"Well, we know how we feel, but I'm not going to say that you're the only man I've ever felt this way about—I certainly can't say I'm in love with you. Except what I feel comes damned close to it and that's why I'm going to let you finish your glass of wine and take the first elevator out of here and forget this whole crazy mixed-up business . . . I'm sorry but I'm not going to mess up my life—"

"You think my taking that elevator down is going to be the end of this?"

"It's got to be, do you understand, David? It's got to be, before we both get in so deep we can't get out and—"

"What makes you think I want to get out?"

"Because, if you don't mind, I'm not thinking just of you at this moment, I'm thinking about Maggie Kent and Maggie Kent's life."

"I love you, that's all I know."

"Listen, my friend, you don't know the first thing about me."

"So I'll learn."

"You'll be sorry for the day you ever fell in love with me, David."

"All right, tell me about Maggie Kent."

"Well, to begin with, she's an egotistical woman who always has to win, always has to be first and always has to be best. Now that's just for openers. She's also the most possessive woman in the world when it comes to love; she's selfish, she can be ruthless and heartless, and she likes herself well enough to feel no guilt over any of these things because she knows she's human, with the same frailties and shortcomings that other people have who refuse to see themselves as they are. But she's perfectly honest with herself and accepts what she is because she knows that she's also more than those things. They're only part of her. She's also just about the most loving, loyal, devoted friend anyone could have. She doesn't give—or take—herself lightly. That's why, David, I ask you to go home. I feel a great deal for you. I had no strong idea of it until today. I feel a great deal for you and I'm not coy. I don't know how it happened or when, but I would rather get over it now than cry for a very long time afterward."

"Maggie, I can't accept that. Sometimes I ask myself how I was crazy lucky enough to find you—"

"Sad that you did, because I'm not very good at playing backstreet wife waiting for the phone to ring. When I love someone, I have to share everything with him, not just part time—all the time. I can't live in a way that I'm not free to be seen with the person I love, hiding in a car or stealing away for a weekend. That's not for me, David, which I suppose is another way of saying I'm not going to get involved with a married man."

He took her in his arms. "When did they abolish divorce?"

She released herself, walked across the room and stood in front of the writing table. "Now slow down,

David. We've only just discovered each other. You have to be very sure to do a thing like that."

"I don't have to cross-examine myself. I've thought this out very carefully—look, I'm not exactly a schoolboy, you know."

"But this happened to me very suddenly, and I haven't had a chance to sort it out . . . we don't even know each other—"

"I know you well enough to want to get a divorce. It's the first time—"

"But *I* have to be sure too, because if people don't love each other, a license isn't going to be worth a damn. Forgive me for saying it, but your marriage seems to be an object lesson. No, love is *more* than just marriage—it's love, not only marriage, that should be till death do us part. It has to do with sharing. Not only bodies—for that you can sleep with anyone. It has to do with two people who share their thoughts with no deceit between them; two people who can say to one another, 'I don't like you today,' because they don't own each other body and soul; two people who want to be together just because there would be no world out there without one another; it has to do with being so in love that you love someone else more than yourself. And I think, David, a person needs time to develop such a love. It can't be done on a part-time basis, and divorces can get messy and involved and take up a great deal of time."

"Maggie, will you trust me? What you talk about, I've wanted all my life."

Very slowly and quietly she said, "David, are you sure what you feel for me is so positive you'll never regret this? Because once we live together and share each other, we won't be the same again. I have to be very sure, very sure."

He took her in his arms. "When I couldn't think of an excuse to get in touch with you during the holidays I thought I'd go crazy. And you may think this is crazy, but on New Year's Eve I felt so close to you I asked you to love me, just as though we were together, and if I were some kind of a mystic or something,

I'd think that you heard me. Maggie, I'm still asking you to love me . . ."

"Oh, David, you're very lonely, aren't you?"

In answer, he held her closer to him. Turning off the lamp, he kissed her, and then, both filled with their need of each other, he carried her into the bedroom. She let her gown fall to her feet as he kissed her. He undressed her and they lay next to each other and, disbelievingly, he took her for the first time. Never, never again, he was certain, would he *feel* the happiness spreading through his body, pervading him as he was lifted to exalted heights from which he wanted never to return.

Later they lay clinging together in the dark, not speaking. Finally Maggie asked, "What are you thinking of, David?"

"That I can't believe this has happened."

"I feel the same."

"When did you begin to know how you felt about me?"

She smiled. "That's a new lover's favorite question, isn't it . . . ?" She thought for a moment. "I don't know, not really, but it might have been when you so wanted me to help you today. I think it was more than your home you wanted me to redecorate. I don't know, it's difficult to tell. But I'm surprised I gave myself away so easily. I'm usually too clever for that . . ."

"You never had me to get clever about," he said delightedly. "Anyway, when you left me this afternoon, you weren't so clever that you could disguise a look in your eye that told me you didn't want to leave. But it was even before that, I think, in the car when I was trying to convince you to help me. You sensed how I felt, and you took my hand and I was sure you at least felt something for me . . . enough of this ancient history . . ." He kissed her gently and held her, very close. "Maggie, I love you so much."

They lay silent while he stroked her hair. Then, unable to keep down the question that had been nagging him since the night of her party, David ventured,

"Did . . . Peter Douglas stay over the night of your party?"

"What difference would it make if he had?" Her tone was suddenly matter of fact.

"Don't answer a question with a question. Did he?"

"No."

"I know this sounds a little crazy, but that night I felt you ought to be with me, and I was jealous—"

"Jealous?"

"Very. He did want to stay . . ."

"Yes, but for some reason I wouldn't let him. Don't ask me why, I don't know—"

"What's there been between you, Maggie . . . ?"

"Well, I've known him for three years and we've been very good friends since the beginning."

"How good?"

"Well, he's been after me to marry him."

"And you?"

"Well, obviously I didn't want to or we'd be married by now."

"Why didn't you marry him? He seems like the kind of man that would appeal to a woman—young, desirable, a gentleman." He laughed. "I wonder why I'm being so damn generous to him?"

"You know why," she said. "Because you know I don't love him. However, all the things you say are true, and what's more, he absolutely adores me. But, as we found out today, love picks us. We seem to have very little to do with it. If there's anyone that I should be in love with, if love were logical, I should be in love with Peter, and I suppose if I were smart I would have married him long ago. You know, David, practically speaking, in most marriages there's one who loves more than the other, and in fact it's very nice and comfortable to be loved without any demands on you. It just doesn't happen to work for me."

"I'm glad, or else I wouldn't be here holding you tonight."

"That's right, I play for keeps. I can't cheat anyone, not in business and not in love. I could no more sleep around being married, as so many of my friends do, than I could fly to the moon. In fact, I can't think of a better reason not to be married than not loving someone. I've often thought how impossible it must be to make love in the afternoon and to sleep with your husband that night. Anyway, it would be impossible for me." David loosened his hold on Maggie. "What's wrong, David?"

"Nothing."

"Now, darling, let's not start like that. What's wrong?"

"Well, I'm doing exactly what you just said you wouldn't do."

"You also talked about divorce. You intend to leave your wife. I was talking about a man or woman who has no intention of leaving a marriage and still has one affair after the other."

He didn't answer. She knew he was having a difficult time.

"You know, David, this has been something new for me too. I would never have thought of even beginning with a married man. I think I must care very much for you. Look, David, please let's not have unnecessary feelings of guilt. This is going to be difficult enough without that . . . guilt can be a very corrosive thing. It destroys love."

Getting out of bed and slipping into the peignoir, she said quietly, "David, are you the least bit in love with her?"

He couldn't answer.

"All right, David, tell me this. Am I the first woman you've slept with since you've been married?"

"Yes."

"I think *that's* the answer, don't you see? Could you think of our living together without marrying?"

"Never. I couldn't do that, not to you, or myself, or . . ."

"Or your wife? . . . You know what I think, David?"

"What?" He reached out for her.

"I think we'd better go very slow on this."

"What are you saying to me?" He was afraid she was having second thoughts, that she was backing off. "Please, Maggie, don't test me. I'm selfish enough to want a kind of happiness in my life I've never had. I just can't think of living without you, not now." He held her close to him, her head was on his shoulder and he was stroking her hair.

"Oh, David, please. I only meant until you come to terms with yourself. Let things stand as they are and say nothing to your wife about the divorce yet. I'm finding out things about myself too, David, so that I'm willing to wait even though it's going to be difficult being apart, and very much against my nature. But I want you to have as few problems about this as possible when the divorce comes—it'll be better for both of us that way . . ."

He let go of her and sat on the edge of the bed, head in hands.

Coming to his side, she said, "Look, David, this isn't anything we wanted to happen but it did, and I'll have to learn to be patient even though I've never been very good at that sort of thing. I'm like you, I want what I want now, but I'm betting with you on something bigger than the moment."

Taking her in his arms, he said, "I don't want to hurt you, darling, or make things miserable and difficult . . . although I admit that hasn't always bothered me so much in the past—I mean, hurting somebody to get what I want . . . I can be a selfish son-of-a-bitch—"

"Don't worry about hurting me, I'm pretty good in the clinches myself." And to prove it she pulled away and gave him a very solid, if loving, cuff on the arm.

He laughed and pulled her back to him. "This is the worst part . . . you know that I have to go home tonight—"

"I know, David. Of course you do."

"It's funny, I've been away on business for weeks at a time but I've never stayed out all night when I've been home. No point in getting her suspicious until we're ready to tell her, just harden her and make her more difficult . . . She's not a fool, you know—"

"Go home, David, and we'll meet for lunch and talk and—"

"God, I almost forgot. I have to be in Los Angeles tomorrow with the architect. I wish I didn't have to go but I can't put it off." He hesitated, then taking her hand he said, "Please come with me."

"Darling, I wish I could, but I have a million things to do this week, and I've got appointments like mad."

"Of course, that was selfish—I told you—but I'm going to try to learn."

"What time are you leaving? Maybe I could come to the airport and we could have breakfast together."

"No, don't be silly. I'm taking the earliest flight out. I'll call you every day. I'll be at the Ambassador."

"All right, David, now go home." He lingered. "Go home, darling."

He got up and went into the bathroom with its faint scent of Chanel No. 5, washed up and combed his hair, then observed himself in the mirror. God, he felt he'd aged a hundred years. He hadn't even left and he was already beginning to sense the return of the loneliness that was always a part of him. Dressed, he went back into the bedroom and saw Maggie with a fur coat over the peignoir standing near the rail on the sheltered terrace between the sculptured cherubs. He went out and put his arms around her. "Come in, darling, you'll catch cold out here." Taking her by the hand, they walked to the elevator. There was no need for words as they stood looking at each other; all that needed to be said was in their eyes. What could they say? I'll miss you? I'll wait for the next moment? There's nothing without you? Wish you didn't have to go? And then David got into the tiny enclosure and the grill closed behind him while Maggie stood staring at the silent door. Then she did something she hadn't done for a very long time. She lay on her bed, touching the place where David had lain beside her, and cried until there were no more tears.

As David sat on the plane in the morning he wondered how long he could keep up the pretense, and this was only the beginning. He felt guilty as hell, never mind Maggie's earlier attempts to offset it. When he saw Katie over breakfast his heart pounded, he was sure the night before was written all over his face. He was afraid to bring anything up. The strain was dreadful. Katie's coldness of the day before went unchallenged, and he mentioned nothing about the house being furnished. For the most part he had lain awake during the night, wondering if he should make a *point* of changing. He needed Katie to come to the point where she would give him the release he wanted . . . and not turn Mark against him . . . He was not accustomed to subterfuge, and, after all, how does one suddenly, overnight, make an outward show of being an understanding, sweet husband without arousing comment, and suspicion . . . He wondered if he could manage it, and realized he would have to change gradually. So that morning his voice was somewhat more pleasant, he was less abrupt. When Katie asked what he would like for breakfast, he simply replied, "Nothing, thanks, except coffee." When she said, from inevitable habit, she hated him to go without anything to eat, he accepted it with no visible rancor. He also kissed her quickly on the cheek and told her he would be at the Ambassador Hotel if she needed him for any reason. And got into the car and drove away.

After he'd left Katie indeed marveled that David hadn't upbraided her for her behavior to Miss Kent—she'd expected a scene over her show of defiance. She even allowed herself to believe David had decided he was wrong—but, being David wasn't able to apologize—for bringing a decorator to their home without consulting her. For the first time in . . . how many years . . . she began to hope things were changing, that perhaps he was at least beginning to mellow. To her astonishment, she found herself humming, and all afternoon she practiced a lilting waltz.

David had worked very hard all day. Things were not going well with the blueprints. There were engineering difficulties and the electrical plans had to be altered and rerouted. Between that and not having been able to reach Maggie that day, he was utterly exhausted and frustrated when he finally returned to the Ambassador about five-thirty and called Maggie's home, knowing she would not be at the studio at that hour, and was even more upset to learn she still wasn't home. Damn. He called room service to send up a bottle of his favorite wine, went into the bathroom, turned on the water tap, undressed, and with the tub filled lay back and soaked himself. While steam filled the room he smoked, and his thoughts were of Maggie, how tender yet sensible she was, how understanding she had been, how crazy he was about her. He wished so much that he could have spared her this waiting, but how? There would be so much to lose from an immediate divorce, even assuming it were possible. Right now he needed all the cash and the financing he could get in order to build, and a large divorce settlement on Katie could strip him and certainly set back all his plans. Maggie would wait, he was sure; she would understand—she'd already shown that. . . . He decided to have dinner sent up to the room; he couldn't eat out—he just couldn't stand seeing anyone this evening.

The phone rang as he got out of the tub and he ran to answer it, dripping wet with a towel around his middle. He picked up the receiver anxiously.

"Hello."

"Darling."

"Maggie! Where the hell have you been all day, I've been going crazy trying to get you on the phone—"

"I know, but I've been so busy I'm not sure which end is up—"

"I wish to God you'd give up that damn business so we could be together—"

"David! You'd have to support me. Anyway, how'd your day go, darling?"

"Terrible, everything went wrong, the worst of it being not able to get you on the telephone. I hope they told you I kept calling?"

"Yes."

"Where are you, at home?"

"No."

"Where?"

"In a phone booth."

"In a phone booth?"

Maggie paused, then said, "Yes. I'm waiting to see a friend."

Silence.

"Now after all, David, I do have friends."

Peter Douglas? And then aloud, "I know I'm a fool to ask, so I'm asking . . . who's the friend?"

"I don't think I'm going to tell you. You're being entirely too inquisitive." She laughed, and even without her being here, he could see her face light up in that special way it always did when she laughed. He changed the subject.

"Do you have any idea how much I miss you?"

"Yes, and it cuts two ways."

"Will you be home by ten, eleven?"

"I'm not sure. Why?"

"Because I want to say good night."

"I'll call you when I get in. Incidentally, do you have a date tonight?"

"Yes, with a blonde."

"I'm glad, it'll take your mind off things."

"You'll be sorry. I might even try for a redhead."

"I don't think so."

"Don't be so damned sure—"

"Listen, darling, I've really got to go. I love you."

"Don't hang up, keep talking."

"No, darling, I really must. My friend is waiting. I'll speak to you later." She hung up, leaving him sitting on the edge of the bed. He was still wet from the bath and the bed was damp where he'd sat on it. He went back to the bathroom and was drying himself when room service knocked at the door. "Wait a moment," he called out as he put on his robe and, barefooted, went to the door. Thank God the wine was here. He'd need it . . .

He opened the door, to face Maggie, holding the bucket of wine.

"Did you order this, sir?" she said, a napkin draped over her arm.

"Oh my God! I don't believe this!"

She laughed delightedly at the expression on his face. He took the bucket from her and put it on the table.

"Damn you, you wasted all that time downstairs when you could've been up here." Scooping her up, he kissed her and twirled her around until they fell on the bed laughing. He slipped out of his robe and she out of her clothes and they made love in the hungry, excited way of new lovers, discovering, the experience heightened by the sudden intimacy with someone still, in so many ways, a stranger.

And, face it, especially for David, tinged with guilt. . . . Afterward he said, "I can't believe this. What happened?"

"It's quite simple. I spent the day on the phone canceling appointments and politely putting people off until next week. I want you to know, Mr. Reid, I've *got* to be in love to do anything like that. I confess, I just couldn't stand another hour without you, at least until the newness wears off just a bit and we simmer down. It's like having the groom go off to the wars the night after the nuptials. The lady cries—she wouldn't tell him that she actually had—and moves in with the family. Well, not *this* lady . . ."

He hugged her. "You're wonderful."

"I agree . . . now let's get dressed and get out of here unless we want the house detectives evicting us."

"Where will we go?"

"I made reservations at the Beverly Hills Hotel early this morning under the name of Mr. and Mrs. David Reid. Do you mind?"

"You bet. I hate it . . ." Taking her face in his hands and kissing her he added, "You really think of everything. You're not only wonderful, you're perfect—"

She nodded sagely. "Try not to forget that, darling."

Their room was beautiful and they felt like honeymooners at the luxurious Beverly Hills Hotel, which catered to the cream of the entertainment world and specialized in pampering its guests with superb if unobtrusive service.

"Now, what would you like to do?"

"David, do you know what I think would be fun?"

"What?"

"Have you ever been to Ciro's on Sunset Strip?"

"No, among a few other places I've never been."

"Would you like that?"

"I'd love it, but you're in for a rotten surprise."

"What's that?"

"I don't know how to dance."

"Well, now, that's no problem." Maggie switched on the radio, adjusted the tuner until she got the right station. The tune was a rhumba. "Okay, David," taking him by the hands. "Now stand with your feet together facing me."

He looked down at his feet.

"No, don't look at your feet. Look up. That's good. Now put your arm just casually right here on my hip."

He let his hand drop to her backside and gently pinched her.

"Now stop that, David. Do you want to learn to dance or not? Listen, for all you know your whole future may depend on it—you may want to become a professional dancer, how do you know?"

He threw back his head and laughed. He'd never laughed like that in his life. "All right, enough of this foolishness."

Acting like a top sergeant, she said, "Now, feet close together, right hand on my hip, left palms touching." She waited. "No, David, on my *hip!*" They giggled like children. "Okay, that's great. Now for the intricate stuff. You make a box." She showed him how, doing it by herself. "All right, now you've got that? Okay?"

He shook his head, still laughing.

"David, you've got to take this seriously. Where would Arthur Murray be if he acted like that?"

"All right, I'm serious." He tried, still grinning like the happy idiot he felt.

"Good. Now, let's do the box. I'll count. Okay, feet together, head up, eyes level, right hand on my *hip*" —laughter—"palms together, all right? Now here we go, one two three four, one two three four, make a box, one two three four. That's wonderful, David. Now all you have to do is swivel your hips just a little. Let me show you how with the rhythm." She went through the dance by herself. Then, still dancing to the music, she placed David's hands in the right position and they began.

"That's marvelous, David. Now just a little more relaxed. One two three four. There, you've got it, you really are marvelous!" Her compliments were interrupted as he stepped on her toe, slightly.

"Did I hurt you?"

"Forget it, now just concentrate on the box step. A little more with the hips." They continued until he became rather good. His sense of rhythm, in fact, astounded her and she told him so.

"Of course. I'm a born dancer, except that I have two left feet."

"Now, now, none of that. I'll not allow my favorite protégé to run himself down."

When the music stopped, David wanted to continue, but she was out of breath. "That's enough. I think I've created a monster. That's all you're going to want to do, dance."

He lifted her off the floor and held her to him. "Don't worry, I'll force myself to have other interests."

Ciro's was filled with dramatically turned out women and a gaggle of movie stars, but nobody turned more heads than Maggie. He couldn't wait to get her on the dance floor as the music began to play, "Begin the Beguine." They had dinner, and the moment they were finished, David wanted to dance every dance until she finally said, "David, I'm not going to be able to walk for a week."

"Well, in that case I'm going to get myself another dancing partner."

"All right, come on, but you won't be happy with another partner, I've spoiled you for everyone else." She whispered in his ear, "Because I can at least keep up with you in other areas. Right, Mr. Reid?"

They got their coats and took a taxi back to the hotel. David unlocked the door to their room. The bed had been turned down for the night. The night lamp was on and the room smelled with the fragrance of four dozen American Beauty roses; there was champagne in a wine bucket and two champagne glasses tied with white ribbon and a sprig of lily of the valley.

Maggie ran to the roses and almost embraced them, then she turned to David. "David, when did you do all this?"

"As we left the hotel, I told the desk clerk to have them sent up."

"Oh, darling, *you're* worth waiting for. I'm beginning to realize what really counts is the time we'll have together . . . darling, I love you," she said as she put her arms around him and kissed him.

David never in his life thought he would experience the feeling of that moment. It was as though he were two different people—He was finding within himself a capacity for a tenderness, a love he would never have believed possible. Life seemed new. It was as though there had never been anything before she came into his life, as though his life had begun with her. She kissed him again, went into the bathroom and undressed while he undressed in the bedroom. He put on his robe and waited for her to come back, lying on the bed looking up at the ceiling and listening to the soft music, thinking how good life was and how precious this moment, and how miraculous that she was here with him. When Maggie came out dressed in a sheer white gown and peignoir, with blue satin slippers, David slowly rose to his feet.

"You look more lovely than anything I've ever seen."

"Thank you, David. I've never felt quite this way before. Promise if I tell you something you won't laugh?"

"Promise."

"I went to I. Magnin's today and bought this. And I said to the saleslady, 'Show me a peignoir for a bride.' That's the way I felt all day when I made my mind up I was coming down. I knew this should be the most important day in our lives. I didn't want to wear anything I'd worn before you, David. Oh, David, I love you so much."

They drank to their future and toasted one another, then with the music ever so soft, they took each other eagerly, making the experience linger. The world had stopped, time had stopped, leaving only the two of them together.

The next morning they had breakfast in their room, both of them rising early. As David sat across from her, he remembered he had not called Katie and realized he had better do so. What if for some reason she had called the Ambassador and found he had checked out? Nervously he said, "Maggie, I've got to call and tell her I'm not at the Ambassador . . . I forgot to call before I checked out yesterday." His face was drawn.

"Darling, don't let this be spoiled. I love you for *not* taking this casually, for worrying even though we know that to be hasty would be foolhardy and even, perhaps, more cruel. . . . You know, David, somebody always gets hurt—no matter where or how bad the marriage is . . ."

He nodded, then picked up the phone and called. For a moment when the operator asked for the number, he actually forgot it, and then remembered, but when Katie answered, he had to control the sound of his voice and Maggie discreetly stepped into the bathroom and shut the door.

"Hello," Katie said at the other end.

"Hi, Kate, how are you?"

"Fine."

"I'm checking out of the hotel today."

"Oh, are you coming home?"

"No, I have to go to Santa Barbara and look over some property, but I'll call you."

"Oh, well, how long do you think you'll be gone?"

His voice was pleasant if casual, he hoped. "A day or two longer. I'm not sure."

"Then I'll see you when you get home."

"Well, I wanted you to know. Say hello to Mark."

"Why don't you call him at school? He'd like hearing from you."

"If I get a chance. I've been so damn busy . . ." They said goodbye. David wondered if he'd ever get over the guilty feeling.

Katie was left, wonderingly, with an unaccustomed good feeling. Dared she trust it?

Maggie came back into the room. She said nothing for a moment, then: "More coffee, darling?"

"Yes, please. What are you going to do today while I slave?"

"Well, as long as I'm down here, I'll do some buying. In fact, I do come down here fairly often. You know this is a mecca for decorators."

"Good. I just didn't want you to be lonely—"

"How could I be, knowing we're together?"

He smiled at her and suddenly felt as though they really were back together again. Each would go their ways until five, when they would meet back at the hotel.

Maggie returned before David. She'd bought a new gown for the evening and held it up admiringly as she looked at herself in the full-length mirror. It was a two-piece velvet dinner suit. The short jacket had jeweled buttons down the front and was trimmed with white mink on the collar and cuffs. She especially loved the sleeveless dress with the high, demure neckline and the back cut down to her waist. She would wear black sheer hose and silk pumps. When she heard the key in the latch, she hung it quickly in the closet.

"Hi, darling," Maggie said as she stood on her toes in her stocking feet to kiss him. She led him by the hand to the large chair, where she sat in his lap. "Good day?"

"Well, better than yesterday. We got a lot of kinks worked out, which helps, but there are still going to be plenty of problems. Look, I don't want to talk about it now. And how did you do?"

"Well, I did some shopping for clients but I felt like playing hooky so I mostly went shopping for me. By the way, I'm very glad to see you."

He kissed her in answer.

"You know, I find myself thinking of you right in the middle of something supposedly very important. . . . Do you think I'll ever get over that?"

She snuggled up to him. "No, and please don't."

"Yes, ma'm. Now, what's on for tonight?"

"First let me get some wine and then we'll decide." She took the wine out of the ice bucket, poured it into their glasses, gave one to David and kept one for herself, then seated herself on the small divan opposite David. He got up and joined her.

"Why don't you decide where we'll go? I'm really pretty green when it comes to something like this. . . . Remember the first time I took you to lunch?"

"Yes."

"Well, I thought you'd be impressed with how sophisticated I was taking you to Piero's, and when I found out everybody knew you, well, I was crushed."

She laughed. "Poor darling, were you really?"

"Yes, but that was the afternoon I began to fall in love with you." It also occurred to him at the moment that he had fallen in love with Katie the same way, the first time. He dismissed the thought immediately, refusing to dwell on it.

"How different we are . . . I didn't think about you at all—"

"Not at all?"

"Well, not that way, as a client only. You'll probably laugh when I tell you this."

"I can stand a laugh. Tell me."

"I thought you were inclined to be rather penny-pinching."

"You were right. I've always had a terrible fear about money. I still do, except with you."

"I'm not so different, though I try to make a point of being good to myself and the people closest to me. I guess it depends on one's conditioning."

"What do you mean?"

"Well, I've known what it is to do without."

"That's hard to believe—"

"For your information, Mr. Reid, we were as poor as the proverbial church mice. I mean literally."

"I still can't believe it."

"Believe it. My father was a Presbyterian minister in a small parish church in Rhode Island."

"And I assumed you were born with a silver spoon in your mouth."

"Well, it only proves how little we can tell from appearances."

He thought about *that.* . . . "The first time I met you in Ron's office, I figured you for a spoiled rich man's daughter. I thought all this was just a lark to you."

"A lark nothing. I'm a pretty tough business woman. I'm ambitious. I love money and what it can do for me."

"There's a lot I'm finding out about you. I'd like to try for your life story."

"I warn you, David, you've asked me about my favorite subject—aside from you, that is. This could take hours."

"I wouldn't mind if it took years."

"Being a minister's child isn't easy—you've heard the term 'p.k.,' preacher's kid . . . well, you grow up in a congregation where you're at the mercy of the parishioners. Everything is contributed to you: you wear discarded dresses, you're treated as if you were on charity. Young as I was, I resented being poor; I despised the smell of poverty. I always felt like an outsider when I was invited to parties. All the other girls had new dresses and I looked like Little Orphan Annie. I suppose it was then that I decided to be rich and famous—well, if not famous, at least important. But I was fortunate in other things. Oh, you would have loved my father, David, he was an exceptional man. When I graduated from high school, my father decided that he should send me to the Sorbonne, which, of course, he could ill afford. With my mother's consent he cashed in his life insurance policy, which meant she'd be penniless if anything happened to him.

"At first I wanted to be an artist, but didn't have the patience or, probably, the talent. When I came home to the States I lived in New York and went to work for a very large decorating firm. Talk about luck of the Irish, from almost the very beginning I made money, not large fees at first, but after a year or two I began to get referrals—" She stopped talking suddenly. It seemed difficult for her to go on.

"Maybe you'd rather not talk anymore about it now?"

"No, I guess I can take it if you can. Besides, I want you to know everything about me . . . my father died—David, unless you've been through it, it's impossible to know the feeling of losing someone you love—and it was then that Aunt Violet, who was married to an enormously wealthy man in San Francisco, insisted that we come to live with her."

"Did you work for a firm in San Francisco?"

"No."

"Well, how did you get started?"

"I refurnished Aunt Violet's house, and she gave a big party introducing me to all her friends. I was in."

The room was in semi-darkness. Maggie got up and switched on a lamp, switched on the radio softly and said, "David, did you know that I was married before?"

"No. Everybody calls you *Miss* Kent."

"That's true, but you know how it is in business."

"Are you divorced?"

"No . . ."

"What happened?"

Not really hearing him, she went on, "Shortly after coming to San Francisco I met Richard Kent and we fell deeply in love. He was a successful attorney with an exceptional future, and we had more in two years than two people have a right to expect in a lifetime. . . . David, I think I'll have some more wine. How about you?"

He watched as she got up and filled their glasses, handed one to David, lit a cigarette and sat down. Holding up the glass, she looked at David through the light yellow liquid and sipped it.

"He was killed crossing the street on his way to meet me for lunch one day. . . . Drink up, David."

He put down his glass, took hers, and held her tight, as though to say he would never let the world hurt her like that again. They sat quietly for a while, then David asked, "And you'd never thought of marrying again?"

"No, I never thought I could love anyone again like that. I've been a widow now for six years. I guess I was waiting for you."

He felt grateful that she had shared the intimacy of her painful inner feelings with him, and yet with the gratitude was a sense of misgiving as he debated whether he should reciprocate. Dared he? But could he afford to leave any subterfuge between them? Well, he'd need to think more about that, have to gear himself up for it; but not now, not tonight.

"Some more wine?"

"No thank you."

Maggie had apparently learned to live with the loss of Richard and had accepted that part of her life, had returned the past to where it belonged, recovering herself. Once again she was Maggie Kent. And, he noted gratefully, she did not press him for any contributions about his own past. . . .

"You know what, David, let's go to Romanoff's. I think you'd like it."

"Anything, with you."

"Thank you, darling." She kissed him, then went into the bathroom to shower.

David sat across the table unable to take his eyes off Maggie, off the black velvet so flattering and soft against her fair skin. He found himself saying and doing things he had never done before. "You look so beautiful—" When, for example, had he ever said *that* before?

She smiled up at him. "Thank you, sir."

He took a small box from his pocket and held it out to her.

"Oh, David, what's this?" Excitedly she took off the gift paper and untied the ribbons, finally managing to open the box. Inside was a saucer-sized cabochon ruby with diamonds.

"David, why—"

"Because you make me so happy, I'm bribing you not to stop . . . and besides it's your birthstone."

"But it's not my birthday—"

"It's mine, so far as I'm concerned."

"I love it, but really, darling, I don't think you should be giving me gifts—"

"It's not just a gift. It's so I can be with you even when I'm not. Because you're the only one in the world who could make me feel like this." He reached over, took the ring out of the box and slipped it onto her left hand. "The day I really want to see is when I can give you the most important ring of all."

She held his hand. "David, I'm going to cry."

She took out her handkerchief and blotted the tears in the corners of her eyes, then said, "We're going to be very happy, David. Nothing is going to come between us, I know it—I insist . . ."

"I feel the same. It will be a little while until I get this project all set and then we'll be together much more. And I can't wait for the whole world to see you, see us together."

"It will happen, I'm going to have to learn to be patient."

David paid the check and helped Maggie on with her jacket. "You know you're the most beautiful woman here," he whispered. "Anywhere, in fact."

"You're prejudiced."

"You're right," he said. "Now where to?"

"Anywhere."

"Well, you name it."

"There's a small club on Sunset Boulevard that has dancing. Do you think you can keep up with me?"

"Listen, you'd better have a little respect. I took lessons from a pro."

They danced until two and David felt as if he didn't have a worry in the world. He actually felt young for the first time in his life. When the music stopped, he wanted to keep going but there was no place to go, so they returned to the hotel, exhilarated from the evening. He undressed and got into bed, hardly able to wait for Maggie. After what seemed hours she was beside him. Switching off the lamp, he held her close. "Do you know what happens to me the instant I see you walk into a room?"

"No," she whispered, biting his ear.

"I want to make love to you all night. I can't get enough of you." Then he kissed her, hard. At the climax, he whispered, "Maggie, Maggie, Maggie." They lay very quiet afterward. She lit two cigarettes and handed him one. He took it, and the only light in the room was from the glow of their cigarettes.

"You know, I don't think there's anything that compares with really loving a woman."

"Unless it's loving a man. Oh, David, and I love you so. I wonder if I'll have the strength to go through being separated from you."

To divert her—and himself—from that thought he asked, "Tell me about your Aunt Violet."

"Oh, David, that's some story." She laughed. "She's really the most outrageous, outspoken woman you could ever meet, and with the greatest sense of humor of anybody I know. When she was very young she had dreams of being an actress. She had beauty and lots of that Irish which is, I suppose, in all our clan. Well, when she was eighteen, she left home and went on the stage. There was a road company playing in Philadelphia—that's where my mother and Aunt Violet were born. She left a dramatic note, which I gather my grandfather thought very funny. He said she'd be home when they discovered she had as much talent as a back fence. What my grandfather didn't know was that Violet Harrison wasn't going to need professional talent. Eventually, the company came to San Francisco and played at the Alcazar Theater in, I believe, a Coward play. I can't remember the name—and don't ask her or she'll never let you go. You see, Aunt Violet thinks to this day she's nothing less than Bernhardt.

"Well, on opening night, in the front row sat Harry Dorn, who fell madly in love with Violet from the moment she came out dressed in a maid's uniform and said, 'This is for you, Madam.' Her only line. He had never been married before, and although he was twenty-two years older than Violet, they were married within two weeks and she was introduced to San Francisco society. I'm not sure how they accepted her, but because Harry Dorn was a very important person, I suppose that whatever they said about her was behind her back. I'm sure it mattered not at all to him. They took her in and eventually her wit and charm won them over. Harry died last year a very old man, but Aunt Violet, trouper that she is, took it in stride."

"And how about your mother?"

"My mother is the most magnificent person I know. I adore her."

He silently compared this with his relationship with his parents.

"Now what about you, David? Tell me about my other favorite subject."

It was the inevitable moment he had feared, and it had come too soon. Again he asked himself if he dared tell her, dared risk her not understanding his feelings about being a Jew, why he had them, and had done what he'd done . . . including his family disowning him. With all the love that existed in her family, could she possibly understand? Would she be able to comprehend that in a family there could be such hatred, such venom? More than anything he *wanted* to tell her, but in the end he couldn't bring himself to reveal it all to her, not even to her. Not now. Maybe not ever . . . How ironic. When Katie had opened herself to him those many years ago, he had told her nothing about himself because he had nothing to tell. Now he could tell Maggie nothing because he had too much to tell, too much to hide.

"Don't be shy, young man. For a start, what kind of a childhood did you have?"

"Pretty bad, my family died when I was very young and I've pretty much been on my own ever since." The words came easily, but left him feeling guilty as hell.

"Oh, David, how dreadful. Then you know how awful it can be to lose someone you love—"

"Yes, and now to find someone I love. I guess it evens out. I'll tell you, Maggie, I'm going to have you no matter what it costs. . . ." His vehemence seemed to end the moment, and they lay silent. They would say no more that night.

When Maggie awoke she looked at David. How wonderful to wake alongside him. As she quietly slipped out of bed, David tried to encircle her wrist with his fingers, his eyes closed. "Where do you think you're going?" he asked.

She bent over and kissed him. "I'm going to the bathroom. Now isn't that romantic?"

Pulling her down he kissed her, then let her go.

When she came back, she called room service and ordered breakfast.

"What are you up to today?"

"I have to work until about noon. I was going to take an early flight back, but that was before you came down. Now we'll go back tomorrow. What would you like to do?"

"Some shopping and then we'll meet for lunch at the Brown Derby in Beverly Hills. How does that sound?"

"Great!"

As he got out of bed, he turned on the radio, put his hand on her hip and his palm against hers, and played the Spanish dancer. "Now how's that for fancy dancing? And from a beginner."

She laughed. "You're marvelous, darling."

He took off for the bathroom when the waiter knocked. After he left, she called out, "Don't shower yet, David, breakfast is here."

They sat across from one another. "You know something?" she said.

"What?"

"I feel like we've been married for years."

"So do I. It's amazing how close you can feel to somebody in so short a time, and how you can live with someone for years and be like . . ."

She put her finger to his lips and poured his coffee, buttered his toast and perched a soft-boiled egg in an egg cup. Strange, he thought, Katie could have done the same unimportant little things Maggie was doing and he would have been annoyed. It all depends, he thought . . . and realized that the simple phrase said it all. He thought, when you love someone everything they do is right, and when you don't, everything is wrong.

CHAPTER TWENTY-ONE

Maggie pressed the bell and Clarice answered on the intercom. "Who is it?"

"It's me, Clarice, come down and help with the bags please."

"Be right down, Miss Kent."

Maggie carried one, Clarice the other, as they took the elevator up to the third floor. Clarice followed her into the bedroom and put one on the velvet-covered luggage rack and the other on the floor.

"Any messages, Clarice?"

"Yes, your mother called, Mr. Douglas has been calling all week, and Mrs. Bordini asked for you to call as soon as you got in."

Clarice opened the suitcase on the floor and started to hang her things away. "You got a lot more calls too. I wrote them down, they're on your desk."

Maggie was taking off her coat when Clarice glanced over to her. "You feel okay, Miss Kent?" She stood with a hanger in her hand.

"Of course, why do you ask?"

"I don't know, you look tired, or sad, or something."

"I don't know why I should. I had a perfectly delightful holiday. Sad? Oh no, Clarice, you're imagining it. In fact, I feel just the opposite."

"Okay, Miss Kent, if you say so."

"Clarice, let me finish putting those things away."

"All right. How about a little dinner?"

"Oh, I don't know, I hadn't thought about it."

"Well, you'd better start thinking about it or you're going to be so skinny you'll be the only woman in the world who can take a shower and not get wet. An old joke, Miss Kent."

Maggie looked at herself in the mirror, holding her dress close to her in back. "Don't be silly, Clarice, I look my old full-blown self."

"No, ma'am, you look like you lost weight."

She went into the bathroom and weighed herself —110, same as before. And enough for someone with a small frame, five feet three, plenty of weight. She went back into the bedroom. "It must be the dress that makes me look thinner."

"Okay, if that's what you say, but you look awful thin to me."

"You'd like me to look like a nursing mother, right?"

"Right, and that's what you should be—a mother."

Maggie thought that was being a little too personal, but she said nothing. Clarice had been with her for a long time now and Maggie was truly fond of her, so she overlooked most of the annoying things that Clarice said.

Clarice pressed on. "I didn't know if you were coming home today so I didn't cook anything. How about some baked ham and a garden salad? Or some curried eggs?"

"Anything, anything at all, Clarice."

As she turned to leave, she said, "Don't forget to call your mother. I think she's worried about you."

Maggie wasn't in the mood to be hovered over tonight, and besides, why should her mother be worried about her? That was ridiculous. "Yes, I'll do that, Clarice, thank you." Maggie shut the door behind her, sat down at her dressing table and observed herself. Did she really look tired, or sad, or something? Of course not, why should she? Be honest, Maggie . . . you were damn sad when you saw David drive away, it's only natural, and so was he.

She got up abruptly. This was a new experience and she would have to learn to take it step by step. Starting to unpack the other bag, she took out the white peignoir, held it up to her, then quickly took out a satin hanger from the closet and put it away; she went back to the case, looked at the black dinner suit which smelled of Christmas Night, and decided not to bother to hang it up. Instead she went into the living room, seated herself behind the Boule desk, picked up the French phone and called her mother. She waited. Finally, "Dorn residence." It was Aunt Violet's maid.

"Hello, Eva. Is Mrs. McLeod there?"

"One minute, Miss Kent."

She waited. Her mother sounded frantic when she got on.

"Maggie, where on earth have you been?"

That wasn't like her mother. "I've been down south on a buying trip."

"I'd think you'd let someone know where you were. We all thought you'd been abducted, to say the least."

Oh, Good Lord, with all there had been to do the day she rushed off to David she'd forgotten to call her mother as she usually did before going away. Her mother was right; in case of an emergency, who would know where she was?

"Oh darling, I am so sorry, that was inconsiderate."

"Indeed it was, my girl. Suppose I'd died—you wouldn't know what cemetery I was buried in."

"Forgive me?"

"Forgiven. Now, how are you?"

"Fine, and you?"

"Couldn't be better. Aunt Violet's expecting you for dinner tomorrow night you know."

Oh my God, she'd completely forgotten Aunt Violet was having a dinner party, but she didn't want to go without David, and he could hardly escort her, well, could he?

"Mother, this *is* my night for apologies . . . I won't be able to come."

"You won't? Well, I think that's pretty impolite to let Aunt Violet know at the last minute. What about Peter?"

Oh no, Peter! "I'll have to call and tell him I simply can't go." Her voice seemed strained even to herself. "I just got myself all mixed up."

"In what way?"

"Well, I've had so much on my mind with all the new projects I've been doing that I forgot all about tomorrow night, and some clients are flying in from Los Angeles and I'm taking them to dinner—"

"Well, can't you cancel it?"

"No . . . I don't think so. . . . In fact I know it." Her hand was trembling as she held the receiver to her ear. She was just not good at deception, not even mildly, especially when it came to those she loved.

"Maggie"—her mother's voice was gentle now—"is there anything wrong?"

She couldn't answer immediately and then, trying to control the cadence of her speech: "Wrong? What should be wrong?"

"I don't know, dear, but I do know you, Maggie, and the one thing you're not is inconsiderate. You'd never do this to Violet nor to Peter if there wasn't something good and wrong."

"Good and wrong" . . . She almost smiled to herself at the combination . . . and at how, ironically, right it was. "Believe me, mother, there's not. I'd tell you if—"

"I hope you know that you could tell me anything, even if I disapproved."

Was it possible she was being so transparent that her mother had guessed she was having an affair? No, don't let your imagination run away with you. She tried to sound sure of herself. "Darling, there's nothing wrong. I'm fine. I simply got my dates mixed up and I committed myself without realizing it. Violet will have to understand I didn't mean to offend her. May I speak with her?"

"No, she's gone to dinner and the theater with the Blakes."

"Then I'll call her first thing in the morning, but better mention it to her tonight and I'll send her a gift of apology first thing tomorrow."

"You can't buy your way into heaven with gifts, dear girl. Maggie, I know it must be very important or you would be here." She paused for a moment, then added, "Is there anything I can do?"

"No, mother dear, but thank you."

"Well, as long as you're all right. I have to go back now, I'm in the middle of a hot cribbage game with Angela and I'm sure she's cheating while my back is turned."

"Is Angela there?"

"Yes."

"Well, give her my best."

"I'll do that. Now get some rest, you sound tired. Good night, dear."

"Good night, mother."

She put the receiver back on the cradle slowly. At another time she would have teased her mother when she said she was having a "hot" game, but tonight she was too worried about being so transparent. She got up and went to the bar, poured herself a vodka, took a sip, then flipped through the albums of records. They were all filed in alphabetical order: A, B, C . . . She reached for "Clair de Lune," put it on the stereo, adjusted the arm and soon the music began. Turning off all but one lamp, she sat on the velvet sofa sipping her drink and looking about the room. Her eyes came to rest on the pair of French bergères in front of the fireplace. Somehow they looked shabby tonight. How would she do them this time? Have the frames painted, or should she antique them? Maybe she'd leave them as they were and just redo the coverings, not that they really needed doing. . . . She got up, went over to her desk and looked at the phone messages. Priorities were Sylvia and Peter. She decided to call Sylvia tomorrow. Sylvia knew her too well—for tonight it was enough that her mother and Clarice had guessed something was up. Twice in one evening, the *first* evening, was sufficient. Peter was safer. She forced herself to wait out six rings. Well, she'd call later, grateful that he wasn't home.

She started going through the mail, ripping the envelopes with the letter opener. There was an advance notice from Saks; she looked through the items advertised then put it aside. She examined the invitation to a showing of a new collection of Dior's at I. Magnin's, and put that aside, then opened several invitations—one for a cocktail party in March, the others for dinner parties, and one from her good friends in Pebble Beach who wanted her for the weekend. She would send regrets as soon as possible, but for tonight she just could not sit down and answer any of them. For a moment she decided she knew how the heroine in Fanny Hurst's novel *Backstreet* felt, then quickly dismissed the thought as being entirely too loaded with self-pity. Besides, it wasn't accurate. . . .

Clarice brought a tray and set it down on the round silk-skirted table near the window, instructing her on the way out, "Now I want you to eat that, Miss Kent, hear?"

"All right, I will, thank you and good night, Clarice." She said that last sharply and just as quickly wished she hadn't. Clarice was really so good to her and for her most of the time, except tonight she could have done without her solicitude.

The phone startled her and she ran to pick it up so quickly that she almost spilled her drink reaching for it. She *knew* it was David.

"Hello, Dav—Oh Peter, how nice of you to call."

He hesitated, then said, "You sounded as though you were expecting someone else."

"Not really, I thought it might be some friends, well not friends, really, clients. Peter, can you forgive me if I beg off tomorrow? I don't think I'll be able to make it." She found herself trembling. Now, slowly, she said, "Look, Peter, I'm not going to go on with this stupidity." She cleared her throat. "Peter, dear, I wish that I could pick a better time and way to tell you . . . but I've met someone . . ." Silence. How cruel. If a man whom she'd been seeing for three years suddenly in effect said "I've replaced you," what would she have felt? She hated having to do this to Peter, who was probably the dearest friend she'd ever have, and here she was hurting him and he had done nothing except be wonderful to her.

"Peter?"

"Yes. . . . Well, I can't say that I'm not surprised. This must have happened pretty suddenly."

"Very, in fact so suddenly it sort of caught me off-guard—"

"Well, then I guess it must be the real thing because I've never seen you off-guard. I mean that as a compliment."

She didn't feel flattered. "Thank you, Peter."

"I believe the next question is, anyone I know?"

He was hurt. Well, what did she expect? "No, I don't believe so." She didn't want to say that they'd been introduced at her party.

"From San Francisco?"

"No, not exactly." The peninsula, she told herself, was not San Francisco.

"Forgive me for prying. If you'd wanted me to know you would've told me."

"Oh, Peter darling, forgive me for being so damned evasive . . . Peter, dare I risk committing you to a secret? I wonder if it's even fair."

"It is, if you want me to know."

"Peter, he's married."

Silence. Finally she heard him say, "Well, I guess you've thought that over carefully?"

"I don't know, I really don't know."

"Isn't that a bit unusual for you? You're always so level-headed—"

"I'm *not*, and besides, I'm a woman thinking with my heart, my head, level or otherwise, has nothing to do with it . . . I'm sorry, Peter, I didn't mean to sound so sharp. You know, I've thought about my being so brave and level-headed and all that and the truth is, when was I ever really put to the test? My father left my mother without anything so that *I* could become an artist—although in the end I didn't—so where was the decision for me to make there? Then I came to San Francisco and Aunt Violet saw to it that I was properly launched—no decision there. And when I met Richard, how level-headed did I have to be? So up to now it's pretty much been all my way, hasn't it? Don't you see? Now finally I'm beginning to re-evaluate myself and take stock. A lot of the things I used to think I was, well, I'm finding out I'm not."

"Maybe, but you made a decision about me, didn't you?"

Silence. He continued, "You made a decision not to marry me because you weren't in love with me. I wish you were, but you're not. So I suppose you know more than you realize how right this thing is for you; I hope it is and, Maggie, as someone who loves you and couldn't do otherwise if he tried, I really do hope it is because, as you've said, you've had life pretty much your way up to now and I'd hate to see you hurt if this doesn't work out. It could affect you more than most others. It would be a new and nasty shock . . . Well, enough of the philosopher. I give you my blessing—do I have a choice?—and may he be worthy of you and see all the things I see in you. I love you, Maggie. I always will. If you need me, *any*time, I'll be around because, you see, I'm not going anywhere. Now I'll say good night."

After she'd hung up she stared at the phone for a very long time. How uncomplicated it could have been if only she were in love with Peter Douglas. Finally she got up and walked out onto the terrace and into the fresh air without feeling the chill that came up from the bay. How long she stood looking out to the bridge with its shimmering lights she didn't know. All she knew was that now the phone was ringing and it had better be David or she'd die. She ran to it.

"Hello." She screamed it.

"Darling, what's wrong?"

"Nothing . . . Yes there is, I just can't stand this loneliness, David, I'll die if I don't see you. The few days we had together haven't given me enough strength, not one damn little bit." She was crying. She didn't feel brave, she didn't feel anything but desperate. "Being apart appears to be more than I can bear. I've never minded being alone but this is *lonely* . . . when Richard died I at least had my family to help me but I can't even tell them about us—"

"Maggie . . . Maggie, let me talk to you. Please, darling, don't cry, I can't stand hearing you cry."

She couldn't answer.

"Darling, you're unhappy already—"

"No, David, you've brought me nothing but the greatest joy. I know I've got to be sensible about this and I promise I will be. It's just tonight, I've sort of fallen on my face—but I'll be all right, I promise." There was a pause.

"I know, I hate being apart, but I have to take it easy with her, I can't just leave now. I can't change my routine or she'll know and then I'll never get a divorce and . . . please, darling, I love you. I wish there were some other way, but it's not forever. We have so much ahead of us, if we can just get over this right now—"

"You're absolutely right."

"Maggie, will you do something for me?"

"Yes, anything."

"Please believe me that this will work out, and the next thing is get some rest and don't cry anymore. Will you do that?"

"Yes, David. Will I see you tomorrow?"

"Damn right. I love you, Maggie. Now get some rest."

She sighed deeply as they hung up, then looked down at the huge cabuchon ruby on her left hand, turning it around to see the thin platinum underband. She took a deep breath and wiped her eyes, blew her nose, got up and changed the record to a rhumba. As it played softly she poured another vodka, took a swallow, put the glass down and walked quickly from the room to the stairs that led to the attic.

Turning on the light, she searched about, finally picking up her easel, the box of paints, and finding the size canvas she needed. Carrying everything, Maggie went back to the living room, got a dust cloth and dusted them off, went into her bedroom and put on a pair of capris and a loose blouse, tied her hair back in a pony tail, returned to the living room, took up the charcoal and began to sketch what would be the beginning of a portrait of David. She hadn't painted in three years, and it felt marvelous to have this old friend between her fingers once again. She painted all night.

By morning the tiredness had gone, disappeared. At six Clarice came upstairs with the morning paper, shocked to see Maggie with paint on her face and smudges of ochre yellow fingerprints on her navy blue capris.

"What are you doing up so early, Miss Kent?"

"I just felt like it." She threw her arms around Clarice and kissed her. "You're absolutely right, Clarice, I am too thin. I want orange juice, a ham omelet fried in lots of butter, English muffins and coffee."

Clarice looked at the untouched tray she had left the night before, and she shook her head as she left. Maggie went to the banister and leaned over as Clarice was half-way down the stairs. "Bring gallons of hot coffee and lots of marmalade." She went back to the easel and stood away from it. "This is the beginning of a masterpiece." She laughed at her own approving critique, then said aloud, "Okay, Maggie, I'm not going to worry about you anymore." Whereupon she went into the bathroom, took off her clothes and stepped into the shower. It felt marvelous.

The next few months found them content. Life for the moment had developed into a pattern. Maggie had so immersed herself in her work that there was little time to think about the fact that she and David were seeing each other only on occasion. They spoke on the phone four and five times a day, if only to say hello, very little conversation at times. But David never failed to call her and say good night, whether he'd seen her or not that evening. They managed to have dinner at her home a couple of times a week. The hours they did manage to spend together mattered and counted that much more because of their brevity. Each week David had a standing order with the florist for four dozen roses. After David would leave, she would lie awake and marvel at how much she had changed, and the adjustment she had made to her life found her liking herself—she had discovered greater depths within and a degree of forbearance that she didn't know she had. Not for all the world could she have imagined herself being willing to wait for a man, content to pick up a phone and just listen to the sound of his voice, content just to have lunch or dinner and never go out together with friends or family. She would have loved to tell Sylvia about them but realized that would be a mistake, would be too great a risk even though Sylvia was a good friend, so instead she found herself doing what she had thought impossible . . . she waited.

Sylvia Bordini called Meg McLeod on the telephone and asked her for lunch on Wednesday. They met at Meg's favorite restaurant in Maiden Lane. In the past, Maggie had taken her there frequently. Meg was waiting when Sylvia arrived; they kissed.

"Meg, I'm so happy to see you," Sylvia said.

"Me too, let me look at you."

Sylvia was five months pregnant. She was wearing a maternity dress, although she did not show at all.

"Sylvia, you look radiant—hardly pregnant, very radiant."

"Don't I look just a little bit?"

"Sorry no, but in that dress nobody would find it a surprise, my dear." She hugged Sylvia again.

They were shown to their table and ordered.

"I know it's so silly, Meg, but when I found I was expecting, I wanted to scream for happiness. I couldn't wait to rush down and buy this."

"Really? What was your hurry? Nine months is a long time!"

"Well, we'd just about given up. In fact, Ron and I were thinking seriously of adopting, but miracle of miracles, after ten years here I am. Meg, I just can't believe it."

"And well you should feel that way, it's the most rewarding thing in a woman's life."

"Oh, Meg, I just couldn't go through life childless.

No matter how much you love someone you have to have something that's a part of both of you, do you know what I mean?"

"Of course I do, and I couldn't be happier if it were Maggie, and dear God, how I wish it were." She ate her salad and continued. "I love this place, thank you for asking me. I couldn't think of a nicer thing happening to me today."

"Thank you for coming, Meg."

The waitress removed the salads and brought coffee.

"Meg, let's have dessert."

"I don't think I will, but you go ahead, please."

"Are you sure?"

"Yes, but no thank you, I'm putting a little weight on in the wrong places." They both skipped dessert but lingered over coffee.

"Meg," Sylvia hesitated for a moment before she said, "You know, I hate people who meddle and I've always prided myself that I never do . . . but when you have a dear friend, and you are truly concerned, is that prying?"

"No, it most certainly is not. So?"

"But for some reason you hesitate."

Trying to encourage her, Meg asked, "Why should you hesitate?"

"Well, what *are* the boundaries of friendship?"

"Many things, I suppose, but silence isn't one of them."

Meg looked across the table at this lovely young woman, the concern written on her face, and without hesitation she said, "You're referring to Maggie, aren't you?"

"Yes."

"What do you think is wrong?"

"Please believe me, I'm hesitant even now to speak to you about this, it seems so disloyal, but I've been upset about her for the last few months. In fact, I must admit that's why I asked you to have lunch with me."

"It's not at all disloyal if you have a friend and you know that they're doing something to hurt themselves.

In fact, you're not much of a friend to stand by and say, 'Well, this is not my business.' Now tell me, Sylvia, what do you think is wrong?"

"Well, Meg, in the last few months Maggie has refused every one of my invitations. She's begged off without any explanation, and it's not just me, it's all her friends." Sylvia took a sip of her coffee. "I want you to know, Meg, that I waited till now to bring this up because if something is wrong I felt that you should know . . . Will you forgive me?"

"There's nothing to forgive." Meg sipped her coffee. "However, Sylvia, you aren't telling tales out of school, because I've known something was wrong since after the first of the year. I haven't seen her for ages either. Maggie is simply not Maggie."

"I'm reluctant to mention this because I don't want to worry you but . . . do you think perhaps Maggie isn't well and is avoiding everybody so she won't have to tell them . . .?"

Meg sighed. "Well, there are all kinds of illnesses, my dear, and love can be one of them. I don't think it's because she's ill, physically I mean—she'd tell me if she were. I believe she is having an affair with someone. I know this will go no further, so let's think together about it for a moment, Sylvia. Maggie's too gregarious to be alone for long periods of time, it's against her nature, and it seems to me that she's leading a very isolated life. When a woman needs that kind of privacy you can come to only one conclusion—that she has something to hide."

"Oh, Meg, I don't think that's true. But I spoke to Ron about Maggie, and he thinks she's lost weight and that she's not her usual self—"

"And why would he think that?"

"He thinks it's because she's taking on too many jobs and running herself ragged. That's why I'm worried she might be ill."

"You could be right, but again, let's think about this. As you know, Maggie doesn't have to work that hard, not with the legacy Richard left her and what she has made on her own. Why, if she took four or five jobs a year, it would be enough to keep her in style, so why *is* she working so hard?"

"Well, Maggie has always loved money—please don't think I mean that in a derogatory way."

"The truth is never derogatory. She does have an appetite for wealth and luxury, and I can't blame her. But I don't believe that's why she's working so hard. I think she's involved with a man who's somehow wrong for her. Knowing Maggie's taste in men, I know he's not undesirable, so the only thing I can logically think is that he's a married man."

"Meg, I can't believe that. I mean not in Maggie's case—"

"Well, dear, you tell me why a lovely woman of thirty-one who's usually full of life and open to her friends and family suddenly turns away from all of them."

"I . . . I really don't know."

"I think you do, you're not naïve. And part of what bothers me, I admit it, is that I didn't go to her when I first realized something was wrong. Instead I hung back and conformed to what the image of the perfect modern mother is supposed to be. No longer," Meg said with vehemence, "the time has come for mother to have a long, long talk with her darlin' Maggie and see if she can do some good. I can't be sure about results, but at least I won't have to reproach myself for trying to be too modern to interfere, even if I saw my daughter jump off the Golden Gate bridge. Thank you, Sylvia, for making up my mind." She took Sylvia's hand across the small table and squeezed it. "What a lucky little one yours will be to have such a mother. You're quite a young woman, Sylvia Bordini, and a good friend."

That evening Meg called her daughter.

"Margaret." Maggie knew her mother was annoyed with her, she never called her Margaret unless she was, and she didn't really blame her a bit. She had neglected her and Aunt Violet terribly in the last months, but what else could she have done?

"Yes, mother, how are you, dear?"

"I'm fine. Margaret, do I have to make an appointment to see you?" There was sarcasm but no anger in her voice. Maggie wasn't offended—in fact, she was relieved. It made her feel like a child. At sixteen if her mother had spoken to her in that tone, she would have resented it, but somehow not at thirty-one.

"No, you don't. Come to lunch on Sunday." She didn't see David on Sundays until late afternoon, when he usually stayed for a very short time.

Meg rejected the invitation. "I'm afraid not. This is only Wednesday and I have some things to say to you, Margaret."

For the first time, Maggie was slightly annoyed. "What's so important, mother, that it can't wait until Sunday?"

"It's five days—*that's* what's important—and I don't think what I have to say can wait that long."

Oh my God, she knew! But how, hadn't they been discreet? They had gone nowhere together, been seen nowhere. Her stomach quivered. "All right, mother, when can you come over?"

"This evening."

She was expecting David for dinner. There had to be complications. For one awful moment she wondered what would happen if Mrs. Reid found out—her situation suddenly had a new reality. She took a deep breath. "All right, mother. How about nine, is that all right?"

"That'll be fine."

She hung up nervously. Now that's enough of that, Maggie Kent, you're not hurting anyone. Besides, her mother would understand when she explained how she'd become involved with David, although her mother definitely would not approve. Maggie hated having to hurt her, as she knew she would, but what else could she do? Give up David . . . ?

He arrived at five. They embraced, their need for each other more intense now each time they met. Maggie took him over to the divan, but before they sat down David held her at arm's length.

"Maggie, let me look at you. What's wrong?"

"Sit down, David. Let me get you some—"

"No, forget the wine. What's wrong?"

"David, I think my mother knows about us."

"How could she? Clarice is the only one who knows and she's loyal to you."

"Of course, but she wouldn't have to say anything. We know why you couldn't suddenly change your routine at home. Well, I know my mother suspects because I changed mine. She doesn't know it's you, but she's suspected something for some time now. I just know it. I know *her*. She's a very astute woman, David."

"Did she say she knew?"

"No, but she's coming to see me this evening. Oh, David, I'll just have to face her and try to explain."

"God, Maggie, I'm sorry . . . it's tougher for you than I'd thought. . . . Do you want me to stay?"

She put her head on his shoulder. "No, darling, it's just as difficult for you. I suppose I knew I had to face this sooner or later."

He walked up and down, pounding his fist into the palm of his hand.

"David, come and sit down now. Don't you get yourself all worked up. Remember, it's my *mother* who suspects, *not* your wife. And I understand why you can't get a divorce yet. We'll handle it."

He put his arms around her and held her very tight. Maggie kissed him, took him by the hand and sat down alongside him. "Look, David, listen to me, I was the one in the beginning who didn't think I could wait, but now I can. It isn't going to be forever. I can live this way for a year or so—"

"But you're losing all your friends and family—"

"My friends will all be there, if they're my friends, and if not, then I've lost nothing. And I think I'm relieved my mother will know now . . . she's the only one who really matters, except for Sylvia. I'd like to tell her if you don't mind."

"No, Maggie, please don't tell anyone else."

"All right, if you insist, but I could trust her . . . Sylvia's the best friend I have . . ."

Sylvia, his nemesis. Sylvia, who still made him uneasy for reasons he still couldn't let Maggie know. . . . "The fewer people we tell just now, the less chance that . . . she'll find out. Please, Maggie, just your mother—*if* she guesses."

"All right, darling. Now let me get you some wine, it's chilled just right, and then we'll go in to dinner."

After dinner they sat together and talked about the new project, how the house was coming along, and then at eight-thirty Maggie followed him to the elevator. Before he left he said, "Now you're sure you don't want me to stay and see your mother? I will, you know, like I said before."

"No, David, I really think it would be better if I saw her alone, but I love you for asking."

She waited until the front door closed, then went to the bedroom and opened the closet. Now let's see, something demure. Come on, Maggie, since when did you ever think you could fool Meg, and besides, would you want to do that? No, hardly—stand up and take the consequences.

The perils of Maggie Kent, she thought wryly, looking out the window as she heard Aunt Violet's Rolls come to a stop in front of the house. Paul, the uniformed chauffeur, got out, came round and opened the door to help Meg out.

"It isn't necessary to wait. I don't know how long I'll be," she told him.

Maggie had told Clarice not to bother to answer the door since she was expecting her mother that evening. She released the door at Meg's ring, then ran to the hall mirror, inspected herself, adjusted her dress, patted her hair in place, rubbed her little finger over her lips, removing some of the lipstick. Then she stood in front of the elevator and waited. The elevator stopped and mother and daughter faced one another.

"Mother, I'm so happy to see you," she said as she embraced and kissed her.

"I'm happy to see you too, Margaret," Meg said as she walked ahead of Maggie into the living room and seated herself on the sofa while Maggie braced herself against the Boule writing table, holding onto the edge.

"You look wonderful, mother."

"Thank you." No return compliment.

"How's Aunt Violet?"

"Just fine."

"Is she still peeved because I turned down her party?"

"You know that Aunt Violet recovers very well from things, and besides, she's very understanding. Remember, she's a woman of the world, an aging actress and that sort of thing—more modern, I'm afraid, than I am."

Meg settled herself into the sofa, sat up straight, hands clasped in her lap, legs crossed at the ankles. She cleared her throat as she always did when she had something important to say.

Maggie played for time. "Mother, what can I get you to drink?"

"Nothing, thank you . . . but you please go ahead."

No, she would not fortify herself with vodka, not in the face of a challenge. Later. "No, I don't really want anything either." She sat down on the bergère facing her mother, crossing her legs. She fought not to steady her hand as she lit a cigarette.

"Margaret, I'm sure you know this is not only a social visit." She hadn't expected a reply. "And I'm not going to embarrass or insult you with a lot of stupid preliminaries. I believe you're having a clandestine affair with someone."

"Well, that's certainly without stupid preliminaries." Maggie got up. "'Clandestine' seems like such a . . . what shall I say? Well, I just don't like that word, it sounds so . . . cloak-and-dagger . . . sneaky."

"Well, maybe you don't like the word but you do know what it means. Let's say 'secret' if you prefer. Does that sound nicer?"

Maggie didn't answer. She sat down again.

"Margaret, if I hadn't felt something was wrong I wouldn't have come here tonight. Let's get right to the point. What's happening to you?"

Maggie really did need that drink now and was

tempted to pour one for herself. Instead: "Yes, I'm having an affair, but more important than that, I'm terribly, completely in love. That's why I resented your saying it's 'clandestine.'"

"Thank you for your honesty, but let's forget about words for now. What difference does it make what we call it? The point is that since you've been seeing this man, whoever he may be, you've lost touch with your life. That's what upsets me so. It's simply not in your nature to live this way, isolated from everyone and everything."

"Mother, you'd be surprised what we can adjust to when the reasons are strong enough. You find resources inside yourself you never thought you had . . ."

How alike they were, Maggie and that handsome, brawny Scot Meg had fallen so madly in love with at eighteen—to her parents' dismay. "For a moment you sounded like your father," she said. "I'm happy you have his spirit, but however magnificent the spirit, I doubt your reasons. . . . I say that if this person is worth giving up your life for, then isn't it strange you weren't able to come and tell me about this great and abiding love? Are you ashamed of him for some reason?"

Maggie knew her mother was giving her the opportunity to tell her before she asked the question point-blank. "Not ashamed," Maggie said adamantly. "No, *not* ashamed, mother."

"Why, then?"

Maggie's voice rose as she said, "Because he's married. *That's* why." She lit another cigarette.

"And that's exactly what I thought." They were silent for a while, each with her separate thoughts, then Meg asked, "How do you expect to resolve this?"

"He's going to get a divorce as soon as possible."

"How long have you known him?"

"Since just before Christmas."

"Where did you meet?"

"I met him through Ron when he recommended me to do his office building. Yes . . . I might as well tell you that you've met."

"Oh?"

"Yes. I introduced you to him at my Christmas party. His name is David Reid. He's tall, has dark hair. He's the most charming wonderful man I've ever known, including Richard—and you know I loved Richard so much that I never thought of remarrying. Not until David. Do you know who I'm talking about, mother?"

"Surprisingly, yes, I do remember him, strangely enough, considering that galaxy you had here that night. I do remember him because I thought he was an extremely handsome man. But looks don't impress me very much, as you know. I've always said we should take no credit for what thc good Lord happened to be handing out that day. Everyone would like to be born charming, beautiful and all the other things you see in your Mr. Reid." Meg was getting angry now just at the thought of him, so she stopped at that point and checked herself.

She began again, more softly. "Do you remember, Margaret, when you were a little girl? Wherever we went people complimented you, talked about you. You always had the ability to attract people. Well, I realized the one thing I was not going to do was allow you to think that good looks were the only requirement for success, whether social or professional. You do remember that I tried to teach you that?"

"Yes."

"I'm glad. Perhaps you also remember that I said there had to be much more to a person than good looks. Good looks fail us, they fade. When that happens, underneath there has to be a person, a person of real worth. Now, Margaret, I think that your Mr. Reid is all the physical things that you say he is, but are you so sure of his character?"

Maggie stood up abruptly, facing her mother. "Now, mother, that's unfair. I cannot let you say things like that when you don't even know him. In fact, he wanted to be here tonight and face this with me. I'm really shocked at you. How can you say a thing like that?"

Meg disregarded her completely. "I can say it,

Margaret, because in four months this man should have considered the hardships he was subjecting you to. Now I ask you, how much character does a man have when he doesn't break off with his wife—the least he could do is separate."

"He isn't in a position to."

"Look, my girl, if you have the strength to hide from the world that's been one big playground for you, then I cannot justify his staying with a woman whom I'm sure he's told you he doesn't love any longer—unless, of course, this is simply a fling for him and you don't care—"

"Oh, mother, you don't know what you're saying and I resent it; really, I think that's going a bit too far. In all the years he's been married he's never had anything to do with another woman." Now—to hell with it—she did pour a double vodka for herself, took a gulp and paced the floor.

"Look, Margaret, you know how I feel about divorce, not because of my Irish ancestry and having once been Catholic. You know I'm pretty much of a renegade when it comes to that or else I wouldn't have married your father, a Presbyterian minister no less. But no matter what my feelings about the church, I still think marriage is sacred and it should be preserved. I know that people make no contract with life and that they fall out of love, and I feel it's wrong to stay married to someone you no longer love, in spite of my Catholic upbringing. Nothing should stand in the way of that, not man or the church. Now, if Mr. Reid loves you as much as he says he does, then why hasn't he made an attempt, if not to divorce his wife, at least to separate and not live under the same roof with her?"

"Because it's very complicated." Maggie's voice rose as she said it.

"Why is it so complicated?" Meg said evenly.

"Because he's a very rich man and has important holdings that he would no doubt lose under community property laws, and he can't afford the loss because he's also extremely obligated financially. In a year or so when he has the shopping center up, he'll be out of the woods on this thing and then he'll be in a position to make a settlement. You know, mother, love is a lot of things. He's not a twenty-year-old lovesick boy, and a divorce at this time could be murderous for him—"

"Oh, I see. And the money is all that important?"

"Well, I don't know about 'all that important,' but important, yes, although you know perfectly well nothing could induce me to marry a man for his money. Let's be perfectly honest. In the past seven years I've had plenty of opportunity to do that, now haven't I?"

"Yes."

"But we do have to be practical. I don't want this to hurt him. He's worked awfully hard for what he has. I'd be a stupid woman to risk being the cause of his losing everything he's gained, and have him end up resenting me for it." Listening to herself, she wondered if she weren't trying to convince herself as well as her mother. . . .

Meg laughed. "Maggie, Maggie, Maggie, your Scottish ancestry still always holds onto you. No matter how madly in love you are, you still think about money."

"I know that's hard for you to comprehend, but, mother, love stands more of a chance with it than without it—I know to you that sounds terribly materialistic—"

"You're absolutely right. I married your father when he had absolutely nothing, and remember, I came from a wealthy home. You remember your grandfather had a great deal of money at one time? . . . Anyway, I still found that what I had with your father was worth more, if I may say so, than what Violet had with Harry Dorn. The point, though, is what *you* intend to do with *your* life."

"It's simple, mother. I'm going to wait until the time when David can get a divorce, and then *everybody* will be happy—we'll be married and live happily ever after."

"And carry on behind people's backs in the meantime . . . I think that's indecent, Maggie."

"Well, mother, I must say you're not being very complimentary, are you?"

"I didn't mean to be complimentary."

"I know, you never did flatter me, now did you?"

"No, but I always praised you when the praise was due. I also didn't when you didn't deserve it. How else would I mean anything to you if I'd flattered you just to appease you?"

Maggie sat down. "Mother, I love you, and above all I don't want to hurt you . . . but please be fair with me . . . What choice do I have except to wait for David, knowing me as you do? I just wouldn't live with someone unless he was worthwhile and the person was tremendously important to me, now would I?"

"I'd always hoped that was the case, Margaret."

"Thank you."

Meg sighed, shaking her head. "Well, what do you propose to do while he's still not free? Have an affair with him?"

"Yes."

"I'm sorry, Margaret, but I find that unacceptable. I don't know how you can be happy hurting others."

"Who am I hurting?"

"Yourself, for one. But how can you and this lover of yours delude yourselves that he has no other responsibilities—"

"I tried to tell you that they haven't lived together as husband and wife for a very long time. It's not exactly a warm relationship, I gather. Of course, I haven't pressed him about that, and I don't intend to."

"I know, but—forgive me I still don't see how you can carry on together as if he had no obligations . . . no wife."

"Look, mother, no matter what I say, if you don't understand now, what good will it do for us to pursue this? I only know I in no way feel guilty where she is concerned. Indecent or not, I don't."

"Please listen to me, Maggie. Why not at least see some other men you've been friendly with? Don't pin all your hopes on this—see Sylvia, see your friends, go to parties—"

"Oh, mother, I'm not some fluttering maiden of nineteen that you send on a sea voyage to get over a temporary love vapor. Please . . . Besides, what do you think happens after a night out with most men? Do you imagine they shake your hand and say good-night? Every man who takes you to dinner wants to go to bed with you. I could become the most scandalous lady about town. Would you prefer that? I've always latched onto one man, a good man such as Peter because his demands were really so few, to spare myself that game. Now how can I see other men when I have a deep commitment? I ask you, how? . . . I'm in love, don't you understand?"

"I think I can, and I suppose you're right about seeing other men, but Maggie, I have to say the obvious . . . that this is something so much more than just sex. I'm not so puritan I don't know that these things happen. I don't approve, but, after all, this is nineteen forty-eight. Nevertheless, dearest girl, do you have any idea what can happen in this kind of relationship?"

"No, mother. Tell me."

"It can build you up, take you over, and then drop and destroy you."

"Now you are being a little dramatic and that's out of character for you, darling. Please trust me and believe what I'm doing is right . . . please?"

Meg looked severely at her, then finally smiled—if a little weakly. "All right, Maggie, I've never had reason to be ashamed of you before and I won't be now. I know that if you think this man is right, you must have your reasons; and even if I disapprove of what you're doing—and I do—you can still count on me. I'm not just your mother, I'm someone who loves you very much."

Maggie ran to her mother then, sank to her knees and, burying her head in her mother's lap, cried like a child. "I don't know if I'm *right*, I only know that I can't live without him." She looked up into Meg's eyes and said, "Please love me whether I'm right or wrong. Please love me."

Her mother stroked her hair, and neither spoke.

Finally Meg said, "I think I will have that drink now."

Maggie kissed her. "I love you. I love David. In fact, I'm a very lucky girl when it comes to love."

"I hope so, darling. . . . Maggie, at least call Sylvia —don't tell her if you feel you can't, but don't hurt her by pushing her aside. She loves you very much too."

Maggie got to her feet and went to the bar. "I will, I promise I will in the morning." Picking up a glass she poured a sweet sherry for Meg and a vodka for herself, handed the sherry to her mother then seated herself alongside her.

Meg toasted her child. "Here's to you, Maggie my girl. May the things you have in your heart be fulfilled in your life."

CHAPTER TWENTY-TWO

At the end of April the offices were completed and so was the Reid house. Maggie had outdone herself. David had asked her to arrange a cocktail party to celebrate the official opening of the office complex to coincide with a cocktail buffet at his home. He was anxious to show off what she had accomplished with both.

Ron Bordini had designed the building as though it were sculpture, and Maggie had carried through the theme, using large pieces of sculpture in David's private office, where she also hung large abstract paintings with vivid splashes of color; and yet for all the modernity there still remained a special warmth.

She managed the same taste, imagination and versatility in the house on Rosehaven Road. And, modern as the offices were, the house was traditional—warm eighteenth-century English with a studied air of informality, blocked linens, soft faded Oriental rugs . . . and the whole atmosphere country English. These were her priority projects—secretly, privately, she shared with David the fantasy—the dream—that she was doing it for herself (he had told her he would try to keep the house in any divorce settlement, hoping Katie would not want it). They had gone to Los Angeles, for a few days at a time, and had shopped for furnishings; at the same time he had seen his architects and viewed the progress on the plans.

Unbelievably, the day had come. That moment—a culmination of David's ambitions and the first link to his future—was finally here. When he looked around him, he realized that all of it had been formed out of his drive, his hunger to *show* what he could do. And now he would no longer be driven solely by the desire for wealth for its own sake. Now, with the future with Maggie as his goal, he felt he had a new and healthier goal to drive him on. Something for the future instead of the ashes of the past.

Everyone complimented Ron, but the decorating was so impressive, the building appeared to have been designed around the interior. In fact, they'd worked so sympatically that it seemed the work of one person. Sylvia and Ron were the first to compliment Maggie, and wherever she turned, she heard, "You're simply marvelous, Miss Kent". . . "You're just fabulous, Miss Kent" . . . "I'm redoing my offices. I'd like to have you help me, Miss Kent" . . . "Where can I reach you, Miss Kent?" . . . and on and on. David stood on the sidelines, and beamed. He could hardly believe that she was his—if only everybody could have known, if only he could have stood by her side. He watched her smile graciously and answer, "Thank you for being so kind" . . . "Really, you're too kind" . . . "I think I'll blush with all this" —she never did that in her life—"oh dear, you're embarrassing me"—she was never embarrassed when it came to a compliment, in fact Maggie thrived on compliments, like a kitten on milk . . .

From the corner of her eye, she saw her, as of course he knew she must. Katie.

"Miss Kent, may I tell you how lovely this is? I think my husband is very fortunate to have found someone as talented as you."

"Thank you, Mrs. Reid, you're being very kind."

"I mean it."

"Thank you, Mrs. Reid." Maggie felt no embarrassment or guilt. Katie didn't exist as David's wife. Maggie wouldn't allow herself to think of Katie that way. No, in fact much more real to her was herself as Mrs. David Reid. In the months that Maggie had worked on the house the two women had had little to do with each other. It was impossible, however, during those months for Maggie not at least to see

Katie, but she'd schooled herself not to be bothered, and when the occasion for conversation arose she was properly polite. Katie had neither interfered nor made suggestions, which for Maggie reinforced an early impression that Katie simply had no convictions in the matter—she didn't guess, so skilled was Katie at camouflage, that Mrs. Reid didn't much give a damn what was done in the house she no longer felt was *her* home . . . and so left Maggie a free hand, except for her bedroom, which she did secretly and away from the eyes of Mr. Reid's designer, secretly but with imagination and tasteful simplicity uniquely *her* hallmark. She even brought the spinet up into her new "sitting room." Maggie was indeed pleasantly shocked the day she crept upstairs out of curiosity while Katie was working in the greenhouse. She stood in the doorway of the room, thinking that somehow the two simply did not seem to go together—Katie in the jeans, the trowel in her hands, the smudge on her face and the dirt under her unmanicured nails, and this most tasteful creation . . . or maybe it was that she didn't want to think of Katie, David's clinging wife, in favorable terms. Maybe to do that would be to risk her own carefully constructed insulation from any feelings of guilt. . . .

David's certainty of feeling was also affected by Katie when he looked over to see her and Maggie together. Seeing them together dramatized uniquely the new-found joy in his life, and the threat to it. He wished he could tell her now that he was through playing a game. But he had managed to hold out for this long, and soon the shopping center would be finished and he could enjoy what he'd proudly achieved, face her and tell her he wanted a divorce without fear of losing it. He could hardly wait to make an end to this deception, to be rid once and for all of the whole past . . . Isaac, and Hester Street. . . . A world split apart. For good.

Katie came to stand near David as a good and devoted wife should. After all, wasn't she Mrs. Reid? People would want to meet the fortunate lady. One of David's attorneys said, "Congratulations, Mrs. Reid," while the charming, buxom lady in the blue suit said, "So nice meeting you, Mrs. Reid"; the mayor said, "A man of vision, a credit to the community."

"How nice, my husband will be pleased to know that you feel that way," Katie told them all.

"We're expecting bigger and bigger things from David," said the banker. She smiled. "We're awfully proud of David," said another.

"Thank you." She smiled.

"We feel privileged that Mr. Reid decided to develop this part of San Mateo," said the man from the Chamber of Commerce. . . .

"An exceptional man, you're a lucky woman," said the judge, who'd had a bit too much champagne.

She smiled.

His coming out as a man of affairs had been a smash. And now came the *pièce de resistance,* the showing to the world of what Maggie had created for their home—at least that was the secret they shared, the way they privately and intimately looked at it.

The florist had come early, appointing the house with giant bowls of spring flowers. The catering company arrived at eleven in the morning with a staff of six. Tables and folding chairs were set out under a striped tent just off the long hall that led to one of the terraces. The dining room furniture had been stored away for the evening in the third garage in order to make room for the buffet table, on which were placed tall crystal and silver epergnes with lilacs, tulips and pink roses. Maggie had even ordered a large point Venice cloth, which hung halfway down over the floor-length écru satin lining.

With all the activities going on in the house Katie worked in the greenhouse until one o'clock, then changed into a dress, took out the station wagon and drove to the beauty salon, which she seldom frequented. Sitting under the dryer, she tried to read but found it impossible to keep her mind on anything, remembering how David had told her that they, *they* were going to have a party. Who were *they* having, she asked. David said all the people in the firm, his business associates, his lawyers, accountants, Ron Bordini and his wife (she still made him uneasy), the mayor, prominent politicians, Jim and Nora Fowler, the investors; let's see, and, oh yes, Miss Kent, of course—about sixty, perhaps a few more, give or take. What would he like her to prepare—a buffet, or would he just like hot hors d'oeuvres and cocktails? And she could hire a few waitresses to help for the evening. No, thanks very much, there would be nothing for her to do in view of the fact that he had taken care of the whole thing, having already hired a catering company. That was considerate, but didn't he think he should have at least asked her, consulted her? One word led to another, and though David had put his best foot forward lately not to antagonize her, he became angry and said some things he later regretted. That was no way to act, especially when one was on the brink of asking one's spouse for a divorce. So he told her that he had arranged for it himself because he felt it would be too much bother for her and in the end he suggested she go down and buy something and charge it, which she indeed did. And for the first time in her life she bought a truly expensive evening dress. Maybe, she decided, it was time she became a bit more glamorous; perhaps too late, but nevertheless she bought special make-up and had the cosmetologist deftly apply it for her. She looked at herself. This was not Katie, she looked beautiful! She looked again—it *was* Katie! Try not to forget it.

For the rest of the afternoon she had nothing to do but wander from room to room, trying to keep out of the way. Finally at four she went up to her room and bathed, getting ready except for the dress—she would slip into that just before seven so as not to crease it. She wanted to lie down, but was afraid to do so because of her hair, so she practiced the piano until six. By ten minutes of seven she was so nervous she decided to put her dress on and go downstairs. Slipping into it, she told herself it wasn't surprising she felt this way, unsure: after all, this would be the first time any guest had crossed the threshold of this lovely house. She felt inadequate, especially after being shunned and moved aside all day. Nevertheless, she still wanted to be an asset this evening. She'd had some concept of how successful David was financially, but after the opening of the office building she realized for the first time how important he had become in the community, and despite what their life together had become, she still believed—no, more, wanted—a sense of decency about their relationship, and this also gave her a rare chance to play the role of mistress of *their* home. Caught up now in the spirit of the event, she could almost accept his reasons for keeping her out of the preparations. Besides, he did want it to be impressive, which she could hardly blame him for, and she had to confess that although she was an excellent cook she was certainly far from being an experienced manager of a gala affair.

The day he had mentioned the party she'd been rather surly and biting, which she now regretted. It was mean-spirited of her, and not a fair target for her resentment, she felt. Besides, in the last months his manner had rather changed, not radically or suddenly, but there was change. At times she almost allowed herself to wonder if by some miracle they might not find a semblance of . . . well, if not love perhaps companionship . . . no, that wasn't the word . . . friendship? Actually, it seemed more an armed truce, but after all the turbulence in their lives, it was a welcome stranger.

So now she could at last be the lady of the house, bathed, smelling fragrant, and rested by the time their guests arrived, which, since David was now a man of property and position, was only fitting. He could hardly have his wife dashing upstairs at the zero moment, perspiring from all the chores, getting into a dress, then rushing to greet her guests. Suddenly, added to these thoughts, was the conviction that in this instance, at least, she had wronged his intentions. . . . One last look at herself in the mirror. My, she did look lovely; in fact she was downright pleased with the way she looked this evening and hoped that David would not only be proud of her but *notice* her a little, as well.

Katie went downstairs, trembling slightly with the same feeling as the evening she had crept into her Aunt Rosalind's dining room at that grand *soirée* and was slapped for being there uninvited. Her heart raced. How the past comes back to haunt one. She dismissed it quickly.

David was already downstairs, checking with the caterers to be certain everything was going smoothly. On his way to the library, he passed Katie in the hall.

"David," she said shyly, holding out her dress slightly.

"Yes?"

"David—"

"Excuse me, I need to check on the bartender and make sure he has everything. I'll see you in a minute . . ." There was nothing harsh in his voice; it was not tender, but not harsh either.

"But, David . . ." He was already gone, he hadn't noticed her. She felt a flush of heat come up from her neck into her face and her eyes stung. Don't be so sensitive, she told herself—he's preoccupied, after all. God, she just couldn't seem to find the answers to her own feelings. He was really behaving quite decently. Damn, damn her, why couldn't she learn to react to what was happening, not always so much to the past . . . ? She went to the living room. Everything was so perfect. The flowers and their fragrance permeated the room. Wasn't this really what *she* had always wanted too? He had worked so terribly hard, and of course everything should be perfect.

A little after seven the bell rang. Katie and David stood at the front door together along with a member of the staff on the other side of the foyer to take the guests' wraps. They greeted Jim and Nora Fowler, who were the first to arrive.

"Katie, I'm so happy to see you. Let me look. You're lovely. Doesn't she look lovely, Jim? You lucky man,

David, to have such a charming wife." David smiled and nodded his head. Katie's transformation that night had in fact registered on him, and for a few minutes in the library he'd wondered whether he shouldn't have given her a chance to do this sooner.

Jim agreed with his wife's endorsement of Katie. Taking off her mink stole and handing it to the maid, Nora said, "This is simply gorgeous, Katie. I'm so glad we're the first ones here so I can take a real good look. Do you mind if I browse?"

"Please do, you'll excuse me if I don't show you around . . . Good evening, Judge Henderson."

"You just stay and greet your guests while I turn green with envy." Nora laughed as she went into the living room.

"Well, David, remember the first time we met?" Jim said, facing David. He never did let David forget, not for one moment.

"That's right, I certainly do," David said.

"Well, Kate, I knew this boy had it in him. I'm a pretty good judge." Jim looked back at his host. "Far cry from Francisco Street, eh, Davie boy?" He poked his index finger into David's ribs, then patted him on the shoulder. "Now, where's the bar?"

"In the library, Jim, make yourself at home. I'll be with you in a while."

Jim, who'd already had a few before leaving home, couldn't wait.

Then the guests really began to arrive, and suddenly the house was filled with people. David looked at his watch. It was 7:40. Maggie still wasn't there, and he began to worry. The bell rang again—it was the Bordinis, *with Maggie,* whom they'd driven down. She was elegant in a white tissue printed taffeta designed especially for her, the print the same color as the ruby. Sylvia, who was in her seventh month, looked it as Ron helped her over the threshold.

"Mr. Reid, thank you so much for asking us," Sylvia said. "And this is your charming wife?" Maggie had not mentioned her first encounter with Katie to Sylvia—in fact Maggie never discussed her clients with anyone—so Sylvia had no reason to be tentative as she extended her hand and said, "Mrs. Reid, how nice to meet you. I hope you'll forgive us for being late, but as you can see I carry my excuse up-front . . . In fact I was afraid I wouldn't be able to come at all, but here I am and delighted indeed."

"It's our pleasure, Mrs. Bordini."

Sylvia walked over to the maid, taking off her coat and handing it to her, while standing behind her, the next to be greeted, was Maggie smiling her most disarming smile.

"How are you, Mrs. Reid?"

"Fine, thank you, Miss Kent."

"And how are you, Mr. Reid?"

"Fine, thank you, Miss Kent."

The maid took Maggie's white mink jacket and she, Sylvia and Ron walked into the living room. Now the guests were assembled and the festivities began in earnest as the waitresses circulated among them serving hot hors d'oeuvres and canapés. Everyone had glasses in hand. Maggie was the center of attention and David was the perfect host, and Katie got lost in the shuffle. In fact, she wondered if anybody remembered that she was there at all. She knew none of them personally, except for the Fowlers, and many of her guests she had only been introduced to as they entered. That seemed to be the extent of her function. However, she did try to mingle, but what did she have in common with them? What could she talk with them about? How do you like the new fashions? How are the children? Don't you think we are having exceptional weather for April? I put up seventy flats of marigolds. How are things at the country club? Isn't it a problem with help these days? Would you like to see my own private domain upstairs, and would you like to hear a few Bach fugues? I'm very good, you know. My son? Oh, well, he isn't home this weekend . . . we, I mean his father, thought it best because of the party, but I miss him terribly. . . . Glad you could come, delighted you're here, shall we meet again, for lunch perhaps? Or better still, when my husband opens the next building and we have another party, or when the shopping center is completed. Wouldn't that be lovely, and then we'll be friends. She took a stiff drink.

Jim Fowler was getting systematically drunk. He sought David out. "David, I have to speak to you," he said, swaying slightly.

"Now?" David asked, irritated despite himself.

"Yes, it's damned important," he slurred.

"Later."

Turning away Jim put his hand on David's arm. "Now. I want to talk to you now." His voice was getting loud.

"I can't leave my guests. And Jim, I don't think I'd drink anymore if I were you. You're getting drunk, and I don't think it would be a good idea to pass out in front of all the investors. You know, they just might frown at having the president of Sentinel Savings passed out on the floor."

"Listen, David, I'm serious. I have to talk to you." He grabbed David's arm even harder and wouldn't let go.

Shaking his arm loose, David said, "It'll have to wait until Monday."

"It can't wait."

David looked at the man. His eyes were glassy but in them was unmistakable fear. "Okay, come on, but please, just for a few minutes." David was obviously angry at being taken away from the most important people in his life, but he led the way up to the bedroom with Jim Fowler following him unsteadily. David shut the door behind them.

Jim took a swallow of his highball and looked around at the newly decorated suite. The walls of the adjoining bedroom had been removed at Maggie's suggestion, and with Ron's help she had designed a bedroom-study which provided an enormous bathroom and wardrobe combination.

"Well, this is the cat's meow, that's some little decorator you got in that Maggie Kent, huh, Davie my boy?" He winked and stuck his elbow in David's rib, then turned around to view the room. "Yes, sir, she's sure okay." Another wink.

David wanted to beat the hell out of him. He knew

that Jim was trying to pump him about the relationship, that Jim suspected that it would be almost impossible to work with someone like Maggie and not be physically attracted to her. But David knew it was nonetheless just an assumption, nothing more; Jim could have no actual way of knowing anything about them. . . . He asked, sharply now, "Did you come to admire the decor or do you really have something so important to talk about?"

"Now, now, David, don't get mad. It only shows you got something going on when you do that."

"You're drunk, Jim. I'm going to get Nora to take you home and we'll talk in the morning." He started walking toward the door but Jim staggered after him and propped himself against it.

"No, David, please, I was just ribbing you. Please sit down, David, please . . ."

"No, you sit down, you look like you're going to fall down." He helped him to a chair. "Okay, now shoot. I have to get downstairs."

Jim took the last swallow and, bleary-eyed, he peered at David. "You've got to do me a favor. You know we've always been very, very good friends, you and me, right?"

"Yes"—you son-of-a-bitch—"yes, very good friends. Now what's the favor?"

"You've got to loan me fifty thousand dollars until next week."

David stared at him, then laughed. "You're more drunk than I thought."

"David, I wouldn't ask if it wasn't important."

"Well, you're not kidding. Fifty thousand dollars is always important."

"Will you do that for me, David?"

"Jim, for Christ's sake, how the hell do you think I'd get my hands on fifty thousand by Monday? You know everything I've got is invested—who knows that better than you?"

"Dave, I'm desperate, I'm really desperate." The liquor was wearing off slightly. "Dave, I got myself into a terrible mess, overextended myself on some loans, and the examiners are coming in on Monday to complete the audit. If they find the money gone, I don't have to tell you what will happen."

"What do you mean, 'overextended'?"

Jim hesitated, cleared his throat. "Not overextended exactly, I mean I invested with you when I didn't have the money."

Stunned, David looked at him. When he managed to find his voice, he demanded, "Let me get this straight: you manipulated other people's accounts!"

Jim nodded his head.

"Well, you crazy son-of-a-bitch, that's embezzlement."

Jim sat with his head in his hands, then looked up. "I've got to have another drink."

"No, no drinks. How long has this been going on?"

He moistened his lips with his tongue and when he spoke it was so quietly David couldn't understand him.

"Speak up, I can't hear you. What did you say?"

"I said for a long time now."

"Well, I'll be goddamned. How the hell could you live with that? Does Nora know?"

"No, I'd die if she knew that all the money that paid for the good times and the country club and the house was money . . . borrowed. Goddamn, I can't believe I did it."

"Why *did* you do it?"

"Because you get sucked in, because you see everyone else riding the gravy train and you want to get in on some of the action."

"Well, for God's sake, you make a hell of a big salary, why did you have to steal?"

"Oh, come on now, Dave, you know my salary was never big enough to be able to invest. By the time I got through just trying to live decent with all the taxes and the insurance and the college educations and the fur coats . . . what the hell did I have left over?"

"So you had to steal?"

He winced at the sound of the word. "I didn't think of it like that at first. You know, things can just sort of happen. First you take and jostle the accounts *just* a little. You put back, then you take over, and over again, until it begins to seem normal, even respectable, and you begin to believe that you're not doing anything wrong—"

"But my God, you have enough know-how to have made it honestly."

"That's right, I had the know-how, which, incidentally I taught you, didn't I, Davie?" he said with some bitterness. "But you were in a position to take advantage of it because you weren't tied to a job you were afraid of losing. I couldn't devote myself to real estate, I got seduced by a job. Titles can make the biggest prostitutes in the world. I made money for other people, but when it came to making it on my own, I was afraid to give up the security of being *president* of Sentinel Savings. Sure, I could have taken small sums and invested, but I wanted to be up there with the big boys. I got to have another drink."

"Okay, sit here and I'll go down."

He left and Jim Fowler sat in the midst of David's luxury. As his eyes wandered about the room, he thought, if it weren't for me he wouldn't have all this. I got him started when he didn't have a dime in his pocket; but, he admitted grudgingly, by God, once I showed him how he learned fast. He had something I never had—the guts to know or at least act like he couldn't fail. His thoughts were interrupted by David's return.

"Here's your drink." Jim drank like a man dehydrated from the sun. David sat on a straight chair and straddled it, facing Jim.

"Well, what are you going to do now?"

"I'm going to beg you to help me, David. It'll only be for a little while . . ."

"For a little while?" For a little while? Who the hell is he kidding? "Look, if you can't crack the nut now, when the hell would you ever be able to pay it back?"

"Just give me time to liquidate my assets, please?"

"Why didn't you do it before?"

"Well, who the hell knew? You see, they came down on me like a bunch of locusts yesterday, no warning."

"Who?"

"The bank examiners."

"Well, how come they never found out your deficits before if this has been going on for a long time?"

He took another swallow. "They found out through some damned little two-bit accountant who's been with us since we opened. That's loyalty for you, huh, Davie? That's loyalty." He was infuriated at the thought that he had been careless in one lousy little account, just one that he hadn't covered. "Well, they're coming in on Monday and they're gonna shoot my ass to the moon. I can't prevent that, but at least if I had the money I could at least protect myself somehow . . . Dave, you've gotta help me—like I said, just until I can liquidate."

David got up and paced the floor, then stopped to look down at Jim. "I'm sorry, but I just *can't;* not now, with all that's happening with me at the moment—"

Jim stood up abruptly and stood close to David, who, sickened by the smell of whiskey on Jim's breath, took a step back. "If you needed it I'd do it for you."

"Sit down and lower your voice. Someone will hear you."

He sat down. "It's funny, isn't it, the one person I thought I could count on was you." He scrutinized David's face. "I gave you deals you never dreamed of. Where the hell would you be now if I hadn't taught you how? You'd still be working for Lela Rogers."

"You know better than that. I'd have learned on my own—"

"Yes, but I did things to get you started that nobody else would have done. Do you remember when you developed Woodglen? I financed it. Not only with almost nothing down, but I had my appraiser jack up the appraisal so high that you had seventy thousand dollars more than the loan allowed, and that was all gravy—wasn't it, Davie boy?—for you to put in your pocket."

"Listen, I've had my bellyful of that kind of talk. You have no gripe coming. I kicked back my share, you made money with me, didn't you?"

"Sure I did. Sure, I made peanuts, you took the gravy—"

"Listen, Jim Fowler, I don't owe you a damn thing. We're even-up. I'm sorry you've gotten yourself in this bind but I'm not going to be an accessory to a crime, I'm not going to risk everything I've got on somebody who'd be crazy enough to do what you've done. I'm sorry, Jim . . ."

He buried his head in his hands, David watching. When Jim had spent himself, his eyes red and swollen from the liquor, once again he asked, "Please, David, loan the money to me. It will only be for a short time, I promise you, believe me."

"I can't do it."

"Well, will you lend me twenty-five thousand? Maybe I could raise the rest somewhere else? I only came to you because I didn't want anybody else to get wind of it, on account of Nora and the boys. You can understand that . . ."

"Yes, I can understand. And no, I still can't help you—you're too big a risk. You more than anyone should know I don't gamble, unless it's on myself." He walked to the door and opened it. "Now go home and sleep it off."

Jim steadied himself as he got up, brushed off his suit, picked a piece of lint from the jacket, adjusted his tie and ran his hands through his hair. As he passed in front of David, he looked him straight in the eye. "You know who's the son-of-a-bitch, don't you? I'm going to go to jail and you're not going to lift a finger to help me. But I'll tell you something, Davie boy—" and he paused—"I wouldn't want to be in your place—you must live in hell." Out in the hall, he turned around and smiled. "Oh yes, I wouldn't want to forget my manners, that wouldn't be nice now would it? Please give my best to your lovely wife who, incidentally, is much too good for you.

And for your sake I'll give you a little advice. I'd be careful when I whored around with that little filly tart downstairs. You might just get *your* ass bit off." He laughed uproariously. "You see, Davie, you just can't put the whole world on, now can you?" Then unsteadily he bowed, and in the gesture of the cavalier waved his hand and said, "Good night, dear and trusted friend, sweet prince. Good night and pleasant dreams."

David did not see Jim Fowler as he walked down the stairs, missing one or two as he descended, because he'd slammed the door behind him. David was breathing hard from anger now. When Jim brought up Maggie he had wanted to beat him to a pulp, but David had more at stake now than when he had responded to an insult by assaulting a bookkeeper in a New Jersey office so long ago. This David could no longer afford to indulge himself with such tactics. Nor did he need them. Life was dealing with Jim Fowler on its own terms.

From the beginning, he had despised Jim for being anti-Semitic—never mind the irony of that—and still recalled how he had squirmed when Jim told his jokes about Abie Goldberg, infuriating and making him feel so guilty at the same time. And then through the years his resentment had built as Jim always made him feel so damn beholden, as though he owed him something for life. He couldn't stand being obligated to anyone, *not anyone* . . . well, now he was finally rid of Jim Fowler. He needed only Maggie. . . .

Katie watched Maggie across the room. How scintillating she was, her magic wit captivated everyone. She was exquisite, talented, gregarious, and Katie was envious—and frustrated. Once she had felt there was no life outside David, and now it seemed very late to do anything about it. She looked across to another part of the room and observed her husband, who had just returned. How gracious, and how changed from that wistful, sad-eyed boy she had met on the ferry boat so long ago. She could feel the respect that was afforded him this evening, how important he had become. And she? She had a pounding headache . . . and now suddenly Maggie Kent and David had drifted to the same part of the room, were indeed talking animatedly with a circle of guests, and then they were split off by themselves, not even, so far as she could tell from this distance, speaking to each other but looking at each other in a way that mere professional associates didn't look at each other . . . and then she saw Maggie Kent's hand briefly on David's arm, a quick look from him and the arm dropped, and they were parted and lost in the room's swirl once again. Lost . . . oh, my God, yes, lost, but not to each other. . . .

And now she understood the change in David recently. And once again she was reminded how desperate she was still to find signs of hope. For a moment she thought she might pass out, and barely managed to make her way through the French doors at the far end of the living room, then around the front of the house to avoid the guests on the other terraces, racing through the side door until at last she reached the safety of her room. Slamming the door, she rushed into the bathroom, washed her face free of the make-up, then literally tore off the dress and lay down on her bed in the dark, trying not to listen to the sounds of gaiety that came from below through the open window.

During the evening Sylvia had been feeling poorly, so Ron went to Maggie, taking her aside. "Sylvia's not feeling well. I'm going to take her home. What about you?"

"Don't worry about me. Do you want me to go with you? Can I help?"

"No, thank you, dear."

"Well, you stay with Sylvia and I'll go find Mr. Reid." She found David at the bar with the mayor and his wife. "Mr. Reid, I hate to disturb you, but Mrs. Bordini isn't feeling very well."

"Will you excuse me?" David said to his guests, and taking Maggie by the elbow he escorted her out. "What's wrong?" he whispered.

"Sylvia wasn't feeling well when we came down

this evening. In fact, Ron didn't want her to come, but she insisted. Now they want to leave and I'm their car. I don't know what to do."

"You stay, and I'll see to it that you get home. Meet me under the oak tree when they've gone. I've been going out of my mind." David went ahead of her.

"I'm sorry, Mrs. Bordini, that you're not well. Is there anything at all that we can do?"

"No. Thank you for your gracious hospitality. I'm sorry if I've disturbed anything. Will you apologize to your wife for me?"

"Of course," David said.

"Maggie, what about you?" Ron asked.

"Mr. Reid has made arrangements for me to go back with someone from the city, so don't worry. Sylvia, would you like me to come home with you? I will if you need me."

"I wouldn't think of it. I'll speak to you in the morning. Again, thank you, Mr. Reid, and to Mrs. Reid. Good night."

By twelve o'clock the guests were beginning to leave.

"I've looked around and I don't seem to be able to find Mrs. Reid. Will you say good night and thank her for a delightful evening?" David heard the mayor's wife saying. He thanked them for coming. He looked around and went from room to room, out to the terraces, everywhere. Katie was not to be found. In the name of God, what the hell would people think? And then it occurred to him, could she possibly be out in the greenhouse? No, that was crazy. He rushed upstairs, opened the door to her room and through the shaft of light coming from the open door of the bathroom he saw her lying on her bed with her dress strewn on the floor. "What the hell do you think you're doing?"

She didn't answer. He walked over to where she lay and looked down at her. "We have guests downstairs."

She still didn't answer. Enraged, he shook her. "Damn you for embarrassing me this way," then walked quickly from the room, slamming the door behind him.

He stood at the front door as the guests were leaving. "My wife sends her regrets, she has a terrible headache, she suffers from these migraines . . . she hopes you'll understand," . . . and heard voices saying, "Of course, what a shame" . . . "We had a lovely evening, such fun" . . . "Give our best to your wife" . . . "Good night, Mr. Reid, and say good night to Mrs. Reid" . . . "Lovely party" . . . "Thank you for inviting us" . . . "Good night, David, thanks so much."

When they had all finally left he closed the door behind him and stood against it, staring up at the ceiling. Maggie and himself were the only ones left downstairs except for the catering staff, who were cleaning up.

"What's wrong, David, what happened?"

He turned around and faced the door so that she would not see his eyes, his anger. He pounded his fists on the door, then turned around and faced her, his face white. Quietly he said, "*She* is upstairs sulking. Now how do you like that? They'll probably think she got so drunk she couldn't come down. You don't think for one moment they bought that migraine, do you?" He clenched his fist.

"Perhaps they did, David, but in any event don't carry on so, you'll be ill. Please, it's hurting me."

The muscles in his jaw tightened, then he said quickly, "Go get your wrap, Maggie. I'm taking you home."

"Is that wise, David?"

"Yes," he said adamantly. "I'm driving you home. If she thinks I'm going to spend the night here, she's mistaken. Not even *she's* crazy enough to think that." Gone were his momentary second thoughts of the early evening. Katie was still Katie. He was a fool, even for a moment, to have thought differently.

CHAPTER TWENTY-THREE

Sunday, April 18, 1948

Clarice was still awake when they let themselves in. As they came into the foyer and waited for the elevator, she came out in a bathrobe over her nightgown.

"Miss Kent, Mr. Bordini called and said Mrs. Bordini was taken to the hospital."

"My God, when?"

"Well, he called about ten and said she wanted to see you."

"Did he say anything else?"

"Yes, that she's at the Children's Hospital and that they think she's going to have a premature baby."

"Oh my God!" She covered her face with her hands.

David held her close. "Are you all right?"

She looked up at him. "Yes, David, but I'm frightened. If anything happens to her, Ron will just die, and if she loses that child, she'll die. I'm frightened, David."

"Come on, darling, I'll take you."

"No, Ron would guess. I'll go alone."

"No you won't, I'm going. If he guesses, then he guesses, but I have a strong feeling he won't say a word. To hell with it, that's the chance we'll have to take. Come on."

"Do you want to change, Miss Kent? I'll help you."

"No, Clarice, thank you, I don't want to take the time."

They found Ron in an anteroom just off the main

corridor of the maternity ward. His face was expressionless, his eyes red. Maggie ran to him and put her arms around him.

"We came as soon as we could." She guided him to the settee and sat down alongside him, holding his hand. "What happened?" she asked quietly.

He couldn't speak; she waited. Finally: "We were in the car coming home and Sylvia said she had this excruciating pain. I think it all started today—you remember when we picked you up she wasn't feeling well? But you know Sylvia, she's like that, she was afraid to tell me earlier thinking I'd be disappointed not going tonight. Oh God, how I only wish she had." He buried his head in his hands and said, "I just can't lose them, I just can't. We wanted this baby so much. We've waited so long."

"I don't know what I can say to comfort you, but I know nothing is going to happen to either one of them; I just feel it." She didn't feel it at all. "Let's wait and see, dear."

David just stood by in silence, envious of these two very close and good friends, thinking how rewarding their friendship must have been . . . and, unwilled, thinking about Abe, remembering in this touching moment among friends that he had never returned the hundred dollars he'd borrowed, and felt guilty he hadn't, wondering how Abe was . . .

"Ron," Maggie asked, "can I see Sylvia?"

"No, the doctors are in there now trying to decide whether or not it's safe to do a caesarean." Again they sat in silence.

As the doctor came in Ron looked up. "Mr. Bordini," he said. As Ron rose, the doctor said, "No, please don't get up," and sat down opposite him, saying, "Mr. Bordini, we think it's best to do a caesarean."

"Oh, my God!"

"Now don't worry. Your wife is in excellent health, we don't anticipate any complications. In fact, we're having her prepared for surgery now. Would you like to see her before we take her up?"

He nodded and followed the doctor down the hall, with Maggie and David behind, to Sylvia's room.

She had been sedated and was half asleep when Ron bent over her; he would not cry.

"Ron, is that you?" she asked, her eyes half closed in the dimly lit room.

"Yes, darling, it's me."

"I'm glad you're here."

He didn't answer. He couldn't.

"Darling, this time tomorrow you're going to be a father, you know. What shall I give you? Tell me now while I still have time to make a choice." She laughed, a very painful laugh.

"Anything you give me is a gift."

"Darling, is Maggie here?"

"Yes, she's outside."

"Kiss me, and until I see you with our child, I love you, darling."

He kissed her, then went out into the hall.

David put his arm around Ron's shoulders and tried to comfort him, but Ron was inconsolable. He asked Maggie to go into the room.

Maggie bent over Sylvia, holding her hand.

"Maggie, I don't know what's going to happen, but if anything should, please don't let Ron be alone. You and I have been so close—"

Her tears falling on Sylvia's face, Maggie held her close. "Nothing is going to happen to you, it just can't. Now, darling, you're getting very tired; rest."

"Before you go, I want you to know that I've guessed about you and David . . ."

"Oh, Sylvia, I think I'm glad. . . . You know, I almost told you . . . how did you know . . . ?"

"This evening, when you two looked at each other, even the few words you spoke together, I just somehow knew. Be happy. When you find it and it's real, take it, take it. No one ever knows about life . . . I mean, no guarantees." She released her hold on Maggie, and fell into a deep sleep.

The night seemed endless. Ron became haggard, the black stubble of his beard now heavy, his eyes bloodshot, and he prayed much of the time. Maggie couldn't watch him; she hadn't been inside a church since her father had died and the sight of Ron made her realize how far away she had gotten from God. And David . . . whom should he pray to? . . . to Isaac's God? . . . It was a long night indeed, a dreadful night of waiting.

The dawn was just breaking on what promised to be a warm, lazy day in spring. The doctor, still dressed in his surgery garb, came into the small anteroom and said, "Well, Mr. Bordini . . . you have a beautiful daughter. Still a little red, but an absolute beauty."

Ron threw his arms around the doctor. "What can I say that I'm sure you don't already know? Thank you, thank you, thank you. Has Sylvia been told?"

"Not yet, but I don't think we'll have any problems with her when she learns it's a girl. Between the two of us, for seven months now that's what she said she secretly wanted."

Ron stood back. "How is she? Did she have a rough time?"

"Everything went smoothly."

"Thank God . . . and you."

Maggie kissed Ron. "Oh, darling, I'm so happy for you both. I only wish I could have done more—"

"You've done plenty, you and David—and let me tell you, David, I'm damn happy you and Maggie, well, know each other." He said it as though he had known for a while. Well, it was difficult to see them together in the office or on the job and not suspect. Or earlier this evening, when somebody else had also noticed.

David shook his hand and said warmly, "Congratulations to both of you, and as long as you've guessed about Maggie and me, my added thanks, Ron. I know this will go no further, but I have a great deal to thank you for."

"Now," Maggie said, "let's go find someplace to have breakfast. I think we all need some hot coffee."

"No, I'd rather stay and wait for Sylvia to wake up."

"That could be a long time yet, please come."

Ron hesitated.

"Please?" Maggie said. "This has been a very long night for you. The doctor does say she's fine—"

"Well, let me find a nurse and see when they think Sylvia will wake up—I want to be in her room when she does." He walked out and down the hall, and soon was back. "She said it wouldn't be for hours. I guess it's all right."

They found a 24-hour coffee shop on Eddy Street filled with ladies of the night just finished with their evening's work, sitting with their pimps, bus drivers, after-hours musicians, drunks sobering up. As Maggie seated herself in a booth with David beside her, one of the ladies said to her friend, "Get a load of that, will ya? I wonder what corner she's got."

Maggie overheard it and laughed; they all laughed as David said, "I guess we look like the most prosperous pimps in town, Ron."

"Are you kidding? I probably look like an Italian gangster with this stubble, like I just bumped somebody off." The laughter was a release for all of them.

Maggie said, "If I knew you were going to bring me to such an elegant place, I'd have dressed." They laughed again as they looked at her, dressed as she was and wearing the white mink jacket. The huge ruby on her left hand staggered the waitress as she took the pencil out from behind her ear and wrote down their order for breakfast, barely able to divert her eyes from Maggie's adorned finger. They ordered bacon and eggs, hash-browned potatoes, toast and butter, and lots and lots of coffee.

David still had to be careful of his diet, new baby or not, so he ate only part of his. Ron became silent as he sipped his coffee. Then he put the cup down and said, "You know, I'm sitting here, but my mind is at the hospital. I just can't believe it." And then, as though it had finally gotten through to him: "I'm a father, I'm a *father*, my God, I've got a daughter! There'll be no living with me after this." Then, like a cloudburst, he added, "I forgot to call Sylvia's mother and mine." He looked at his watch then said, "It's too early for Sylvia's mother and my mother is probably up praying for another grandson. Will she be surprised when she finds out she's got another granddaughter . . . Listen, sit here while I go phone the hospital. I'll be right back."

"David," Maggie said after he'd left, "you know I never wanted a child before, but after tonight I want one very badly."

David put down his coffee cup and looked at her, and what he felt he said aloud: "I'd love a child with you."

Laughing she said, "Do you think when we get married, I could get pregnant immediately? I mean immediately—I'm thirty-one, you know."

"I'll have you pregnant on the way up in the elevator to our honeymoon suite." But then his tone changed as he seemed to be momentarily disturbed. She took his hand in hers.

"Would you like a child?"

He responded immediately, "What do you think?"

"I don't know, you suddenly became so quiet."

"It's because we have to wait, that's the only reason, and it's things like this that make me realize how much we're really missing."

Lightly she said, "What difference? I still won't be over the hill in a year and a half or so."

He kissed her. "I wish it could be sooner than that."

What bothered David was not the fact that Maggie mentioned wanting a child, or even having to wait. At that moment what really had disturbed him was what Ron had said about calling his mother and then Sylvia's. Undoubtedly his mother was a very devout Catholic, while Sylvia's mother was Jewish, and still there seemed to be no conflict, or at least so it appeared. His thoughts strayed to Isaac. If he had brought home a Maria Bordini, his father would still have disowned him . . . Isaac, the terrible, the hand of God. Isaac, and his wrath, would not go away.

Ron came back and jubilantly said, "Mother and child doing well. Sylvia's still asleep. Damn, I can't believe it," he said, shaking his head.

David looked at his watch and said, "I think we'd better get moving, we're all tired." As he helped Maggie on with her jacket he said, "What are you going to do, Ron?"

"I'm going back to the hospital and wait for Sylvia to wake up."

"We'll drive you."

"No, I wouldn't think of it. I'll take a taxi."

David paid the bill and once again on the way out Ron said, "Maggie, you and David have been just wonderful. I'll never forget how you stood by me tonight. It would have been too much with two Jewish mothers there at one time"—he was laughing—"*my* mother and Sylvia's, two of a kind, both in hysterics. That's why Sylvia only wanted myself and Maggie there. Thanks, you're beautiful." He kissed Maggie, shook hands with David and hailed a cab, never noticing in his delight the bemused expression on David's face.

Exhausted, they lay in each other's arms; there was nothing of the flesh in this moment. Sleepily Maggie said, "David, I hope you don't mind them guessing about us."

He thought of Jim Fowler, then quickly dismissed it. "Well, I suppose it was impossible to keep it from Ron. After all, as casual as we've tried to be, a glance, a look, I suppose, can give you away to people who are around a good deal and know us well."

Maggie hugged David closer as she asked him softly, "David, do you suppose your wife suspects?"

"I'd say no. How could she? After all, she's never seen us together except the first time when you came to look over the house and last night, but I hardly came near you all evening. You were usually in one room and I was in the next, and I made damn sure I didn't look at you too much, and when I did catch a glimpse of you, you were mostly looking the other way. No. I really doubt it, but after this I'm going to make damn sure she doesn't see us together again."

They slept until one. When they awoke they were both refreshed. They had brunch and read the Sunday papers, staying in their robes all day. Maggie called the hospital, everything was fine. Sylvia was resting comfortably. Then she called and ordered flowers for both of them. By nine in the evening David was beginning to get a little apprehensive.

"Maggie, I think I'd better get home and try to make up, especially after what happened last night. I wouldn't want her to begin to wonder too much." He kissed her as he got up and went to the bedroom, took off the robe and slippers Maggie had bought him and hung them away in the closet, placing them alongside the other clothes that he kept there, while she dressed.

They left the house together and Maggie went to the hospital while David went back. Back . . . On his way to his room, he noted with relief that the door to Katie's was closed. He walked noisily enough and shut the door with such force that it would have been impossible for Katie not to have heard him enter. On his desk was a note asking him to call Nora Fowler. He picked up the phone, dialed, and waited. It was answered quickly.

"Hello, is Mrs. Fowler there?"

"This is she speaking."

"Nora, this is David. You called; I just got home."

"Oh, David." She was distraught. "Jim hasn't been home all day."

"Where did he go?"

"That's just it, I don't know. I thought maybe you might."

"No. When did he leave?"

"Well, you know he had a great deal to drink last night, so I drove home, and when we got here he said he wanted to go for a walk. I thought nothing of it, and since I was tired, I went right to bed. When I awoke this morning I realized he hadn't been to bed at all. I've been frantic, trying to get you all day. The boys are away at school and I didn't want to call and alarm them, but I'm beside myself now and I'm reluctant to call the police."

"Look, don't do anything. If something had happened to him, you would have been notified. He surely has identification on him. Maybe he just went off on a binge; remember, he's done that from time to time—"

"You're right, but not for this long. I'm very upset, David."

"I know you're worried, but nothing has happened to Jim. Now, do you want me to come up and stay with you?"

"No, thanks, David, you're a dear. I feel better since I've spoken to you and I know you're no further away than the phone. You're a good friend—no wonder Jim is so fond of you. If anything comes up I'll phone, or if you hear I know you'll do the same."

"I'll come up if you want."

"No, really, I feel better. Thank you for being so kind. Good night."

He held the receiver in his hand for a moment, then replaced it. Of course Nora had no way of knowing what David knew, and he wondered where Jim had disappeared to, exploring the possibilities that after last night Jim could have gotten it into his head simply to take off. Mexico, David wondered? Well, anything was possible, but he doubted if he would have let Nora and the boys face the consequences without him, probably he'd taken a room for the night downtown, bought a bottle and gotten stinking drunk, and he was now sleeping it off. If anything had happened, Nora would have known by now. Besides, Jim Fowler wasn't above a little hanky-panky, much as he seemed to love Nora and the boys, and when a man was that distraught, with all the problems facing Jim, he might feel it was a good idea not only to get plastered, but also to find a more basic kind of relief for a night. It wasn't a solution, but in Jim Fowler's case, what was?

On Monday morning, the janitor, rushing out into the street, announced Jim's solution to his problem. "Call a policeman, Mr. Fowler's shot himself!"

After Jim had kissed Nora good-bye on Saturday night, saying he was going for a walk, he drove instead to his office. Once inside, he stood in the dark for a few moments, then turned on the lamp, which cast eerie shadows on the wall, opened the liquor cabinet, took out a glass and a bottle of bourbon; then he seated himself behind his desk, poured the bourbon into the glass until it almost overflowed, and drank it down in large gulps, scarcely breathing inbetween. Images grew distorted in his mind as he recalled the great future promised when he started out as an eager young man, and so much in love. And the greed and fear and ravening hunger for wealth that went beyond his capacities that had also seduced him. He sat behind his desk now, the desk where he had signed his name over and over again to pieces of paper, merely paper, that would make millions for other people. Somehow when he dealt in large sums they became like so much candy, losing intrinsic value, so he stole from the rich to pay for Jim Fowler's appetites and laughed at himself as he waved his arm, almost like Robin Hood taking from the rich to give to poor little Jim Fowler. He swallowed the last gulp of what remained in the tall glass and took out the gun he kept in the side drawer, in case of robbery. Well, that was what it was going to be used for—robbery. That silent room would remember and reverberate the echo of his last words, "Oh, what the hell, nobody gets out of this world alive." Then he put the gun to his temple and pulled the trigger. It went off at almost the precise moment that Stephanie Bordini saw the world for the first time.

When the police came on Monday morning, they found what remained of Jim Fowler slumped over his desk, his head lying sideways in a pool of his own blood, the whiskey bottle overturned, the blood and the liquor staining the sides of the desk.

Nora Fowler's two handsome sons stood at the side of their mother and heard the voice of the minister saying those solemn words, "And now we commit unto Thee, O Lord . . ." Nora heard no more as she looked at the casket that bore so few tributes. The day was warm, the birds sang; but for Nora the air was filled with the sounds of dying. She looked down at the open plot and thought, how strange, the friends that one has in life very often desert one when there is no honor in death. Even then people stand in judgment. But at least some old friends were at the graveside to pay their respects, friends like Katie and David. . . .

After the funeral, the few friends and relatives who had attended went back to the Fowler home to be with the bereaved widow and sons. Naturally Katie had gone with David; Nora had been just about her only friend, and she genuinely loved and admired her. She was broken-hearted for Nora.

"Nora, what can I say to you?" Katie said.

"Nothing, nothing at all, my dear. Thank you for being here when I needed you." Then turning to David she said, "Thank you for everything. You know, David"—it was as though she were looking back into the past and hearing again the words of her husband —"of all the people Jim ever knew, I do believe he had the highest regard for you. I remember so many years ago he spoke of you as though you were his protégé. He admired your spunk, your determination. I think he felt a part of your success. He was so proud of you, David, almost like a father. . . ."

As they were leaving, Katie kissed her and David began, "If there's anything I can do—"

"Thank you." She closed the door gently behind them.

They drove home in silence. When they arrived, Katie went to her room and David to his. He went to his desk, took out his large checkbook, wrote a check for $5,000 to each of the Fowler boys, closed it; put it back neatly, then went to the phone.

"Maggie, it's me . . . I feel kind of rotten. . . ."

CHAPTER TWENTY-FOUR

It was the last day of school. Mark ambled over to the car where Katie waited for him. He was now saying his last good-byes to the many friends he had made. He even liked Bruce Abbot now, although he still didn't believe he was quite the operator he had pretended to be. In fact Mark had his doubts if there had ever really been a Swedish maid who had cradled him between her legs last summer. As he walked down the path with his gear, he heard, "So long, Reid" . . . "See you around, Reid."

Then he spotted Ralph Hansen, who like himself would not be back next year, but for different reasons. Ralph Hansen had been too eager, too innovative and progressive. He would sit casually on his desk, discuss by the hour all kinds of subjects without sermonizing, allowing the boys the exhilarating experience of making up their own minds. After being in Mr. Hansen's class, Mark realized he owed him a great deal, and so did Katie. But Mr. Hansen would no longer be on hand to do for other students what he'd done for Mark and so many before him. Mr. Hansen had been asked to resign. His major transgression: an inability to treat students as inferiors. A belief that his superiors meant what they said about "stimulating young hearts and minds . . ."

Even though Katie had seen Mark as recently as the past weekend, somehow today he seemed taller than some of the boys his own age and even a little more mature. The year had been difficult for both of them, but she had gained a great deal, and so had he. They'd managed even more than she knew at this moment, mostly thanks to Ralph Hansen. Mark was able to figure out certain situations with his father for the first time. He could see his father through his own eyes now. People, including his father, looked different to him now. Mr. Hansen had mentioned a word called "relating," that was the most important thing. But that didn't mean always having the same opinion—after all, if two people had the same opinion on every subject then one of them would be superfluous. Respect was another thing, respect for other people's opinions; but along with respect you wanted to be free to make up your own mind. And life wasn't a popularity contest. It wasn't only important to stand up for the things you believed in, you needed to speak out against things you were opposed to. "To thine own self be true," was still pretty good advice, Mr. Hansen told the boys. He also tried to live up to his own words.

Mark would never think of discussing his mother or father with anyone in a disparaging way as Bruce had done, yet one day after school he asked Mr. Hansen if he could speak with him.

"Of course, Mark, come in."

"I'm not taking up your time, am I?"

"Not at all, what's the problem?"

He began to get cold feet. It seemed disloyal to talk about his father to a stranger, even if the stranger was Mr. Hansen.

"Mark, I hope you and I are friends." He waited for Mark to pick up the lifeline.

"Okay, Mr. Hansen . . . you won't think I'm terrible for talking about my dad, will you?"

"Now, Mark, let's understand each other. First, whatever we say in this room is between you and me, and the next thing is that I'm not here to judge you. We're friends, which I assume is why you came here in the first place."

Mark looked at Ralph Hansen and if he could have wished for one thing, it would be that Ralph Hansen had been his father or that his father had been like Ralph Hansen. He made him feel like an equal. Apart from his mother, Mr. Hansen was the only one who made him feel that way; but still, coming from a man made it seem more important, gave *him* a sense of importance. He always felt so childish around his father, as though he didn't know anything.

"Mr. Hansen, I love my father, but I don't think he loves me."

"How do you mean?"

Mark hesitated again, then said, "My dad's a very busy man and I know it's not easy for him to get away, but he hasn't come up to see me once since I've been here, and I know when I go home in June he won't have anymore time for me then."

"And that bothers you a great deal?"

"Sure. I want to be close to my dad, but I just don't seem to be able to. It's . . . it's as if he doesn't like me."

"Well, I'll tell you something about parents. They take their kids for granted, and," he added, "kids take their parents for granted too. Still, I admit it's a little tough to say, 'Here I am, dad, look at me.'"

"Why should it be so tough? He's my father."

"Because fathers sometimes don't realize that their kids need them as much as their businesses do."

Mark mulled it over for a moment. "Are you saying my dad cares more about his business than me?"

"I don't know your dad, but I don't think that would be putting it quite right. He doesn't say, now let's see, who do I care more about? My business or Mark? Who do I choose, one or the other? I doubt it ever occurs to him to make a choice because most parents don't think they have a choice to make."

"Why, Mr. Hansen?"

"Because they take it for granted that their children will be there whether they fail in business or succeed. For the same reason, children think that no matter what they do their parents will always be there to protect them. In other words, they *expect* something of each other. And up to a point they have a right to."

Again Mark thought it over, then slowly said, "I think I see what you mean, but how do I get my dad to realize all this and let me get closer to him?"

"Okay, now here comes the most important thing of

all. Suppose your father never sees it and you don't ever have a close relationship, how would you feel about that?"

"Real bad."

"But if you were faced with the fact that you could never change him, what would you do?"

"I guess I'd feel real lousy . . ."

"Of course, and that's pretty normal, but don't you think it's also very negative?"

"What do you mean?"

"I mean that if we find ourselves in a position that we have no control over, instead of feeling bad forever, and ever and ever, that we accept the situation as it exists."

"You mean that my father might not love me?"

"Now, first of all, Mark, I'm sure that your father does love you; but I'm not so sure he'll ever have time for you, and right now I'm more interested in how you feel than in how he feels."

"That's nice of you to say, Mr. Hansen."

"It's true, and let me tell you why. You see, there has to come a time when young people like yourself start learning how to become a good parent, and the only way that you can do that is to know how to be a complete person and that includes learning how at least to know what your problems are and then how to cope with them."

"Such as, for instance?"

"For instance, if we do things because we're angry or because we're hostile, that spills over to the next generation, and the new generation passes on the same feeling, and it never stops because the old generation never knows *what* to give its kids or *how* to give it." He watched Mark's face.

"Now, Mark, let's not complicate this. Not everybody is born with the same abilities. Two people will take the same subject in school; one will excel while the other fails, not necessarily because he likes the subject better, but because he's born with a greater potential, a greater understanding, a larger ability to understand. Two people hear music and one is deeply touched; it makes him happy, sad, or feel like crying, while the other's not affected at all—yet it's the same music. Now the same thing is true of love."

"Love?"

"Yes. Some parents are able to show a great deal of affection to their children, others aren't. Now it's very possible for the parent who can't express himself to love just as much, but for one reason or another he can't show it—maybe he wasn't given love when he was young—but whatever *his* reasons, his child doesn't understand them and gets very unhappy over the way the parent behaves. Do you follow what I'm saying?"

Mark was trying to hold onto every word. "I think I do. What you're trying to tell me is that my father loves me, but he can't show it."

"That's right. Now what else do you think?"

"I don't know, Mr. Hansen. It's a little bit confusing."

"In what way?"

"Well . . . supposing my father does love me but can't show it. What does that have to do with him never finding time to be with me?"

"He doesn't realize how important it is to you."

Mark considered the answer, then asked, "Do you think I should talk to him about it—tell him how I feel?"

Mr. Hansen smiled. "Now you're cookin', Mark! That's exactly what I mean, because if you don't, he'll probably never catch on."

"He's usually not home long enough for me to talk to him."

"You'll find time."

"Mr. Hansen, suppose my dad doesn't change after I tell him, what then?"

"Then maybe you'll simply have to make up your mind that your father's one of those people who have a great deal of trouble showing love or understanding. I know it's no great comfort to hear that, or to accept it, but if that's the way it is . . . Remember, you have a life aside from him, and you've got to learn to live it for yourself."

"Does that mean I don't love my father anymore?"

"Of course not, it means you stop expecting him to

act toward you in a certain way. It also means you feel differently at fourteen than at fifteen or twenty. Feelings change, and the sooner we begin to handle them and our problems, well, the sooner we begin to grow up. It's not so easy . . . and neither is it for me to give you all this wonderful advice. Forgive me, Mark, if I seem to be preaching at you. Anyway, enough for now, but if you ever get a hankering for Mr. Hansen's cracker barrel of instant wisdom, just give me a call. I'll be around."

"Could we talk some more?"

"Of course, and I'm glad we had this opportunity to become better friends."

Mark shook his hand; his grasp was strong, firm.

"Thank you, Mr. Hansen, I'm going to think about what you said." And he turned and walked slowly from the room.

Ralph Hansen sat on the edge of his desk looking out the open window as he heard the sound of young voices coming from the tennis court beyond. . . . "It's your serve, Ken, what's the score?" . . . "Thirty-love, my favor," said the voice on the other side of the net. The ball whirred through the air and there was a dull thump as it was received by the racket. The sounds coming lazily to him from that court were pleasurable, but Ralph Hansen's thoughts were elsewhere as he recalled the conversation he'd just had with Mark. A really nice kid . . . he'd like to get to know him better. He'd like to know them *all* better, and realized, of course, it was impossible. They weren't really so different from anybody else. Like most people—men and women, parents and children, lovers, friends—they all seemed to live in a world of strangers.

CHAPTER TWENTY-FIVE

Summer, 1948

David awoke earlier than usual and for the first time that he could remember he was in no hurry to get out of bed and challenge the day. On this warm, inviting June morning he stretched luxuriously and gazed at the ceiling.

Yesterday they had broken ground for the shopping center. There had been an impressive ceremony—the mayor was there, the city officials were there, his wife, his son, his business associates, his bankers, his attorneys. They had all praised him lavishly—he had been given the accolades befitting a pioneer who had just opened up the Northwest Passage; and again the same speeches. The mayor spoke of him as a man of vision, of the center as a monument to "this man's imagination." Everyone agreed that if this were an indication of things to come, the community would long remember, and with pride, David Reid.

David also thought about Katie and remembered how she had looked . . . she seemed to have changed in some way he couldn't quite define, but she appeared less vulnerable, her face set and her eyes directly on him . . . and how unexcited Mark had acted, hardly the way you'd expect a son to behave at something as important to his father as *this* day. It started when Mark had gone to Menlo and was worse since he'd come home, this change in the boy. He was no longer the warm and wide-eyed little kid who seemed grateful and generally uncomplaining. Now he was friendly but also somewhat reserved as he shook hands with his father, no longer kissing him and holding him as once he would have done. And all he said after the ceremony was, "Congratulations, dad . . . I'd like to be excused now, I want to go home and pack . . ."

Well, both of them would be going up to the lake today or tomorrow. He got out of bed, went into the bathroom and inspected himself in the mirror. His hair was just a bit grayer at the temples, but it sort of made him look more distinguished. He hit his stomach —it was firm, not an ounce of fat; he flexed his muscles, they were firm. He looked sideways to see the flesh under his chin, it was firm. He washed and dressed and went downstairs, passing Katie's room. The bed was made. Then he passed Mark's room. They were already gone; must have left right after breakfast. He went into the kitchen to make coffee, which he hated doing, but he managed to measure out the water, put the grounds into the metal basket, and plugged in the electric maker.

For a moment he thought of Chicago and how he had burned his hands that time, and how lonely he had been. God, would he ever forget those days? Everything then had seemed against him—hell, it was, and she had deserted him. It was pretty tough to face self-imposed exile by yourself, and in a world that didn't seem to have a place for you, and you didn't have a quarter to your name. Too bad he hadn't been as farsighted as he was ambitious. She was older and smarter now; she wouldn't go off so easily or quickly this time. She had to be handled carefully even to get things to the point where he thought she would consider the divorce. And even then, what with community laws in California, she'd no doubt be awarded a substantial part of what he'd worked so damn hard for. They didn't even sleep together anymore, but those attorneys would get to her fast enough . . . And as for Mark, well, somehow he'd always seemed more *her* child than his . . . as if he somehow weren't good enough for his own son. His mother's son . . . What would it have been like if Maggie had been that mother? David saw the two women again as they stood together that day at the big office opening. Katie and Maggie . . . good God, and to think there was a time when he was sure he couldn't live without her. He'd compared her with his brothers' wives and people like Birdie and thought her the most gracious, the most charming, the most accomplished everything he'd ever dreamed of in a girl. Maggie was, literally, a godsend. He was crazy about her. And, in a way Katie never could, Maggie Kent would complete the transformation of David Rezinetsky into David Reid.

Thinking on it, the regrets diminished, to be replaced by the anticipation of being free at last to have three glorious months with Maggie while Katie and Mark summered at Lake Tahoe.

David packed and moved into Maggie's house. Their days were filled with the simplest of pleasures. They had dinner in small out-of-the-way restaurants, not only because they didn't want unnecessarily to risk meeting people but because this was also a lark, a sort of Bohemian adventure. One evening as they sat at Luigi's, with the checkered table cloth, the dripping candles, the fragrant smell of onions sautéing in olive oil and a bottle of Chianti on the table, David said, "You know, when I was poor I used to eat in places like this and I vowed that when I could afford it, I would never set foot in one again. But you," he said, reaching his hand across the table to hers, "make the difference. *All* the difference." Their evenings at home were spent like happily married people: he would sit reading the *Chronicle* or *Wall Street Journal*, looking up at her from time to time, watching her knit a sweater for Stephanie Bordini, whom she adored and whom they saw as much as possible. Maggie had, in fact, become so domesticated that she could hardly wait for Clarice to take her week's vacation so that she could pursue her culinary prowess with the same creativity that she applied to all things she loved doing, the most important of which just now was preparing David's favorite dishes.

Weather permitting, they would have dinner on

the terrace overlooking the bay amid the large tubs of marguerites in bloom, and lazily and lovingly they would enjoy whatever the moment brought them. On Sundays they would take long walks or stop in at the art galleries, and on weekends they would drive down the coast to Carmel, where they stayed at a charming little place called the Normandy Inn. The only time David became unhappy was when he registered under an assumed name so as to make sure that no one would be able to check later if anything came up in the eventual divorce. It made him angry to submit to hiding when he felt that now he was doing what life had intended for him. Somewhere the conviction returned, as it had once before—this was his life and he was entitled to it.

David called Mark every week without fail, in case Mark might want to contact him, taking no chances that Katie might become suspicious that he was not at home. He spoke to Katie only if she answered the phone, and then the conversations were always brief, to the point and superficial. He tried to dismiss the feeling the minute he hung up, but there were times, try as he might, after speaking to Mark, when he had feelings of guilt which he tried carefully to submerge so that Maggie would not suspect.

Maggie accepted no new jobs until September, completing the ones she had by the end of May so that she could be home when David returned or be free to go wherever he wanted, whether it be down the peninsula to observe progress on the shopping center or whatever else he might like. From this time until they were married, she decided to abandon her usual plans for going to Europe and New York on buying trips. She too was beginning to realize that there was more to life than a career, parties, friends and money for its own sake. What they had between them seemed more than any two people had any right to . . . except, as they reminded themselves, they were two people who'd paid their dues and deserved their happiness.

Maggie's birthday was in July and David anticipated it when he called Meg McLeod on the phone one morning.

"Mrs. McLeod? This is David Reid. I'm sorry to say I haven't had the pleasure of seeing you since we last met, but I wonder if I might have that pleasure by taking you to lunch . . . just the two of us?"

Meg hung onto the phone, unable to answer. David had caught her completely unprepared. She had been dreading the moment when she would have to come face to face with the man whom she thought was wrong for her Maggie. How could she bear seeing a man who slept with her daughter and was married at the same time? No matter how Maggie justified or rationalized it, so far as Meg McLeod was concerned, it amounted to only one thing—adultery—and, as she'd told Maggie, Meg was too old to feel differently. "I'm sorry, Mr. Reid, but I don't think that would be possible . . . Now I'm not going to be diplomatic about this and pretend some nice-sounding little excuse. I'm going to be blunt and come right to the point and tell you I don't like what's happening between you and Margaret."

"I don't blame you, Mrs. McLeod, and I can certainly understand it, because, believe it or not, I share your feelings. I don't like it anymore than you do, but the time is going to come when we'll have to face each other, and for the sake of Maggie, whom we both love, I thought perhaps it might be best to do that now. Understand, I don't expect you to like me . . ." He waited for a reply, and when there was none continued, "I wish you could, but what's important is that we try not to complicate things anymore than they are already. I wouldn't be calling you now if I didn't know how much Maggie loves you. Now, will you do it?" She still didn't answer. "Please let me have the pleasure of taking you to lunch? You might even find out I'm not as terriblc as you think I am."

Meg's own judgment told her that if she became openly antagonistic toward David that a breach could be created between Maggie and herself, and eventually, as he said, she was going to have to meet and face him. After all, this was the life her daughter had chosen, like it or not. Even the greatest love between mother and daughter could be altered by circumstances, and wouldn't Maggie choose David's love if she were forced into a choice, and wasn't that in reality the way it should be? Hadn't she done the same with her life when she met Alistair McLeod? Hadn't she defied her father and her church to stay with him? If she wasn't careful, she could lose her child.

"All right, Mr. Reid, where shall we meet?"

"At the St. Francis Hotel. Is that all right?"

"Yes, when?"

"Is today agreeable?"

"Yes."

"I'm very happy, Mrs. McLeod, thank you. Till noon then." He hung up, savoring the moment. How sensible and sensitive Meg McLeod was—no wonder her daughter had all the virtues David saw in her. It took a great deal of strength to do what she was doing today, facing her daughter's lover. His feelings for Meg McLeod went beyond mere liking; he admired her tremendously.

David did not wait for lunch to be over, but began to explain as they sat across the table from one another why he had asked her out today. He wanted them to be friends, but it was more than that. He wanted her understanding.

"Please try to see my position, Mrs. McLeod. I really don't want to hurt anyone else, but I find I can't live without Maggie. She's become my whole life. I feel as bad—or worse—about the deception as you, and so does Maggie. But both of us can only survive if we have freedom; you don't know how hard I've had to fight for mine, but you do know Maggie, her qualities, and the problems she's had better than anyone else." He paused, unsure of how to continue. "It's for our freedom that I'm working now. But please try, if you can, to understand how impossible it would be for us to be separated for the long period of time it will take before I can put my affairs in order. I have a great deal to lose by being impulsive, and Maggie understands my position. If you'll just try to be tolerant of our situation, if not happy, all I can tell you, with all the love and honesty in my heart, is I'm going to spend the rest of my life making Maggie happy when this is over." He looked into her face, seeking but not begging for her approval. Then he added, "I know that that's what we both want for Maggie, her happiness, isn't it?"

Meg McLeod looked down at the tablecloth without a word. David concluded his case: "I would like us to be friends. I know that seems impossible for you at this time, but I think you could learn to like me."

She could begin to understand what Maggie had seen in this man. He seemed to have all the things Maggie had claimed for him—warmth, charm . . . good sense. He already had Maggie, and still he knew how important it was that nothing should come between her and her child. It took a man of substance to know and follow up on that. He really needn't have bothered, but he had. She looked up at him.

"All right, Mr. Reid, I feel we can be friends."

"Please call me David."

She had difficulty, but then she said, "David, you know I came here today to do battle with you and to try to convince you how much you're hurting Maggie and how wrong I think you are for her, but somehow I just can't seem to, sitting across from you like this. In fact, reluctantly, I must admit that I can see how and why Maggie fell in love with you; and that, coming from an old, dyed-in-the-wool converted Catholic, is really something of an admission."

Everybody converts from something, David thought. "And I know why Maggie is what she is, after speaking to you," David said.

"Now, now, David, you've already gone far toward winning me over, but you'll find that I'm not very receptive to flattery." She smiled, and for one moment he thought he was seeing Maggie in her face.

"This will make Maggie very happy, as you can well imagine, but you've made me happier than you'll ever believe. Thank you, Mrs. McLeod."

"Well, I'm pleased, too. I came to grips with something I didn't think I could handle. And incidentally, call me Meg."

Now that they were at ease with one another, pretense was no longer necessary. David smiled broadly as he said, "Now, Meg, as you know it's Maggie's birthday on the sixth of July and this will be the first time I'll be celebrating it with her. I would have liked it to have been different, but under the circumstances, all I can do is try to arrange something a little special."

She smiled. Maggie's birthday was three weeks away, and he had already thought of it. "Yes, David. What would you like to do?"

"Well, I thought perhaps we could surprise her by having dinner at her house, which I could arrange with Clarice, and I'll keep Maggie away all day. And, of course, we'll include Mrs. Dorn and the Bordinis. Do you think that would make her happy—"

"David, I think that would be perfect."

They talked over plans and arrangements. Meg would order the cake and go over the menu with Clarice, and David would spend the day down the peninsula with Maggie. Then, on the pretense that he was going to take her someplace special, perhaps to Marin, they would come home and dress, making sure they would be ready by 7:30 when the bell would ring and Meg, Violet, Sylvia and Ron would get off the elevator and sing out with "Happy Birthday! Surprise! Surprise!" and David would give her a French poodle he had already picked out. She was a beautiful apricot color, soft as down; and her name was *Cadeau,* which appropriately enough meant "gift" in French. She was now three months old and house-broken, and the one surprise that even Meg would not know until then was that he had ordered a cabochon ruby and diamond bracelet for Maggie that would be attached to a pink ribbon and tied around Cadeau's neck.

The party turned out to be the sweetest, most wonderful and memorable day in Maggie's life. She keep saying over and over again, "And to think you've all kept this a secret!" She laughed like a child, and when she saw David and her mother together, her cup did indeed run over. She had dreamed that eventually they would become friends, but not so soon. David, she thought, could do anything, even this; what magic he could weave. She stood up, raised her champagne glass and toasted them: "To the people in my life who mean the most to me, all of you right here, I love you all beyond words."

"Oh David, David my dearest," she said later as she lay in his arms after they had made love, "my life is so full of you."

Time had ticked itself away, the days had turned into weeks, the weeks into months, and like the sands in an hourglass, the summer had run out, and once again they would go back to what they had before—Maggie to waiting and David to living his life on the periphery of Katie's with all the old feelings reinforced. And for Mark it would be the end of the best summer he had ever had with friends from both Hillsborough school and Menlo who had come to the lake, the best time of all being the weeks that Bruce Abbot had spent with him. He had learned to water-ski with Bruce steering the boat. He had seen a lot of Andy Andrews, who had taught him a great deal about boats, and on the Fourth of July Katie had had a barbecue.

She had developed her own little world. She tried not to think of David at all. Mark had missed David less that summer, partly thanks to the sane words of Ralph Hansen. He'd asked David to come up to the lake a couple of times, and of course David had said he was busy with the shopping center (partly true), needing to devote all his time to it if it were going to be finished by next summer. For now, Mark was happy to be going home to start his sophomore year at Burlingame High School. Katie, meanwhile, braced herself to return to her happy . . . terribly happy life.

Next summer would be momentous indeed—for everybody. For David it would mean the beginning of his life with Maggie. For Mark, it represented the hope that when the project was finished, his father would find some real time to come up to the lake and he could show off his swimming and water-skiing. And for Katie . . .

September had brought many changes to the community of Hillsborough. Side by side with the Gentile population were now living a few Jewish families in that small, bucolic neighborhood. They apparently held no threat for anyone—except, it would seem, to David Reid. In the house adjacent to his a Doctor and Mrs. Silverman, along with their two daughters, had moved in. When David discovered that the doctor was living next door, he became so incensed that he seriously thought about selling, then reasoned that had he known the house was on the market, he would have bought it. Should have. He decided to make the best of it and ignore the Silvermans.

If David felt threatened, Katie felt pleasure and, indeed, relief to have Jewish neighbors next door. Not that she could become truly friends with them—how could she?—but she found private satisfaction in the thought that the son of an immigrant delicatessen operator from McAllister Street in San Francisco could achieve what Dr. Silverman had achieved. And she wondered—secretly hoped—if perhaps David didn't think on Dr. Silverman's career and wonder if he too might not have achieved without denying who, and what, he was. In fact, Dr. Silverman was one of the outstanding surgeons in San Francisco. Katie was delighted.

Her satisfactions, it turned out, were short-lived.

Dr. Silverman, being not only an exceptional surgeon but also very enterprising, had invested his money soundly and carefully. When he purchased the house next door to the Reids, he did so with the intention of subdividing the acre on which it stood, planning on selling the old house and building a new, much smaller one for himself. He called in the engineers to take off a topographical map and a line was drawn right through the middle of the property, which would eventually leave the old house on a half-acre facing Summer Drive while the new house would face Rosehaven. By the end of August the bulldozers were brought in, and within a week the site was ready for construction. The big house had already been sold, but the Silvermans would continue to live there until the new one was completed, which would be in approximately four months. This was going to be the house of Mrs. Silverman's dreams. She had anticipated it for a very long time. In fact, she had worked on the plans for years, so now when the time came the plans were almost perfect for this particular site—actually, this was why they'd gone to all the bother of buying the property in the first place. For years she had collected hardware and fixtures and stored away fabrics that she had found in her travels. Then one day in the mail she received a letter saying that the city engineers had surveyed the property and found that they were building on an illegal lot. Nervously she called her husband's office.

"Monroe, you simply have got to come home."

"Now, darling, I can't do that. What's wrong?"

"I don't know, Monroe, but we've got a letter here saying that we're building on an illegal lot."

"Say that again."

She repeated it.

"Well, I don't know what this is all about, but I'm going to find out right now and I'll call you back." He hung up and phoned the city engineer's office.

"Yes," Mr. Wills said.

"This is Dr. Silverman speaking. I received a letter from your office saying that we're building on an illegal lot. Now I know there must be some mistake."

"Let me get a copy of the letter." He left the phone and when he returned he said, "You're on Rosehaven, right? That's the new lot?"

"Yes, that's right."

"Hold on for a moment." His voice was pleasant.

Monroe Silverman was outraged. Here he had sold the big house; the foundation on the new one was already complete; in the next day or so they would begin to erect the first uprights; the entire, expensive garden had been ripped out to provide for the house site—if the lot did prove to be illegal, he would stand to lose not only a great deal of money but the lot would be useless to him. Above all, it would be a terrible blow to Vivian and the girls.

"Yes, Dr. Silverman, I have your survey here. Now it seems that when you posted your intention to build, nobody objected except, well, except one of your neighbors. He claims after having his own survey taken, that where the property slopes back to Rosehaven it narrows, and that although your setbacks are fine at the furthest end of the property, you're two-and-a-half feet off on either side as it slopes down to Rosehaven Road. Do I make myself clear?"

He had not. How could this have happened when it had been surveyed? "I don't understand all this."

"Well, apparently what happened was that your architect didn't provide for the irregularity of the lot. In other words, it becomes sort of pie-shaped toward the front of Rosehaven, and what's happening is that you're encroaching on Mr. Reid's property."

"Well, what right did he have to survey my property in the first place? You never said anything about it; why him?"

"Because he does have that right. When you post your intentions to build, anyone has a right to make certain all the boundaries are correct."

"I'm going to fight this, you know."

"Well, you certainly have the right to take it up with the city council, doctor. Find out when they meet and go down and see what you can do. But I can tell you right now you are off on those boundaries."

"Thank you very much." Dr. Silverman called his attorney and explained what had happened. The attorney told him that if what the city engineer had said was so, then he wouldn't have a chance of beating the case—boundaries don't lie. So who could he sue? City Hall? What happens in cases of this kind, the attorney told him, was that everybody passes the buck. The architect claims he took the plot from a survey, and the surveyor claims he gave the map to the architect, who gave it to the builder, who claims that he built according to the plan. So that's exactly what Dr. Silverman would do—sue city hall. Building on the house stopped.

The next day Katie was up at the greenhouse working when Mrs. Silverman looked over the hedge. "Mrs. Reid," she said. "I'm Mrs. Silverman."

Katie smiled. "I'm *very* glad to meet you, Mrs. Silverman."

"Thank you. I was looking forward to being your neighbor, but now it looks as though we may not be able to build our home."

Katie put down the trowel and came closer. "I'm sorry to hear that."

"I'm simply ill over the whole thing, and so is Dr. Silverman."

"What happened?"

"Don't you know?" she asked, trying to keep her voice calm.

"No, I really don't."

"Well, I would have imagined that your husband would have told you."

"No, as a matter of fact, he didn't, but what has he to do with it?" Her heart began to race.

"Well, he's the one who filed the complaint."

"About what?"

"That we're off on the boundaries, or rather the setback from your fence. He could have said something about it before the foundation was completed."

"Oh . . . I'm sure he didn't mean it deliberately . . ."

She looked at Katie, her eyes disbelieving. After all, wouldn't Mrs. Reid know, wouldn't Mr. Reid have discussed something like that with her? All right, if she wanted to pretend she knew nothing, so be it.

"Yes, and if Mr. Reid had only done the neighborly thing and come to Dr. Silverman and told him what the problem was instead of complaining to the city engineer, it could probably have been corrected. Now we'll have to rip out the whole foundation." She was on the verge of tears.

"Oh, my dear, I'm so sorry, but I'm sure Mr. Reid didn't do it to inconvenience—"

"Well, maybe," Mrs. Silverman replied, but she felt

offended, for all Katie's graciousness. "We've already sold the big house, and the people we've sold it to are going to move in on a set date, and now we can't go ahead with the new house until this thing is resolved. In fact, our architect doesn't think the plans we have will adapt to another lot."

"Oh, what a pity—"

"It's more than that."

It certainly was, Katie thought.

"I can't tell you how sorry I am about this, Mrs. Silverman. I don't know what to say—" It was the truth.

"Can you talk to your husband? Dr. Silverman has tried calling him at his office, but he never returns the calls."

"Talk to your husband." What a joke! This good lady had no idea she was dealing with a man obsessed by a demon long buried, yet seemingly forever alive to him. She said, "Of course I will, Mrs. Silverman. I don't know how much good I can do, but I will speak to my husband this evening."

Mrs. Silverman smiled. "You know, Mrs. Reid, I wonder if the world would be an easier place if the women could take over more of its problems. . . ."

All day their conversation rankled. The episode had built itself up in her mind so that by the time David came home for dinner her anger was barely controlled.

Since he'd not seen them all summer, David had begun to spend more evenings at home, especially with Mark being there, and although they had little to talk about, at least he felt his presence in the house would help divert suspicion. Whether it was guilt or cleverness on his part that made him feel this way, he preferred not to question—perhaps it was a little of both. In any case, for whatever the reason, he would follow his instinct until the memory of last summer could be put to rest without Mark saying to him, "Well, dad, what did you do every night? Gee, it must have been lonesome without anybody around. . . ."

He felt he should remain at home, deprived of seeing Maggie for the next week at least, painful as it might be for both of them.

This afternoon Mark was up in his room doing his homework while Katie busied herself with dinner, and as she looked through the kitchen window above the sink, she saw David turn into the driveway. He parked the car in the garage and came in through the back door, offering the usual greetings. She said nothing, but her heart was pounding. As David started to his room to wash before dinner, she followed him out into the hall.

"David, I want to speak to you."

He swung around and looked at her; he had never seen her face so set, and the anger showed in her eyes. For one awful moment he wondered if she knew. . . . "Yes, what would you like to talk to me about?"

"Come into the library. I don't want Mark to hear; he's in his room."

"I'm tired, I've had a big day. Let me wash up first."

"No, David. I want to speak to you now." She walked into the library and waited. He shrugged and entered, closing the door behind him. This was a new Katie.

"Sit down."

"I don't feel like sitting down. Now what's the problem?"

"It's about our next door neighbors—I hesitate to mention their names in this Christian house."

He held back the anger, his jaw tightening. "All right, what about them?"

Katie paced back and forth and then turned to face him. "David, how could you have done such a despicable thing to people you don't even know?"

"Listen, don't use that tone of voice to me—"

She was frightened—yes, frightened . . . one didn't shed a lifetime's conditioning so easily. She was not nearly as sure of herself as she wanted to appear. She tried to stand her ground, even though her anger helped less now.

"How else can I talk to you? Mrs. Silverman came to see me today and told me what happened. Why did you do this to them?"

"It's interesting you heard what she had to say but you didn't think that maybe you should just come and ask me what happened. But you've always done that —taken sides against me—and, damn it, don't use a word like despicable to me, not ever again. I don't have to take that."

She began to back off, afraid for one moment that he might actually strike her.

"But you had no right—"

"No right? Do you have any idea what you're talking about? They were encroaching on this property. I have an investment here. I have a *right* to protect it—"

"Couldn't you have talked to them before they got so involved?"

"Gone to them? For God's sake, it's his responsibility to know what he can and can't do—"

"Well, if you had the lot measured, or whatever it is that you did to find out they were doing something wrong, couldn't you have done it before he got so far ahead?"

"He's supposed to know."

"I still think you could have been more considerate—"

"Considerate? Oh yes, it's true. I'm guilty of not being considerate. Except may I ask what . . . and where . . . was the last time somebody considered my feelings?" . . . Momentarily the doctor who'd saved Mark's life came to him . . . "Do you think he would have behaved differently if things had been reversed?"

"Yes, I do."

"Wake up, get out of your dream world for a change."

"You're wrong but it doesn't matter—I know why you hurt them." The accusation hung there, unbidden, but it was too late to withdraw.

He stopped, his fists clenched, knowing what was coming, the threat she held over his head. "Why?" he challenged her, "*why?*"

She hadn't meant to say it out loud. She didn't answer. Finally: "I don't know why. I'm just upset—"

"*Why?*"

"Because they're Jewish, damn you!"

He turned and walked away from her . . . from himself . . . got into the car, and, tires screeching, tore up the driveway and around the bend to Rosehaven Road.

Mark had heard everything, and understood nothing. How could he? Except he understood that he hated to hear them going at each other like that. God, why did they always have to fight? Why, why, why? It was the word of the moment, all right.

David let himself in, then went up the stairs two at a time to the third floor. The anger, the guilt, were still with him. As he approached the top of the stairs and stood in the hall, Cadeau, the scene-stealer, went into her routine. She ran around in circles, stood on her hind legs and begged David to pick her up, then, impatient, in one giant leap was in his arms, licking him. When Maggie tried to come near David, Cadeau barked at her. She stepped back and laughed.

"I suspect I could compete with most any female for your affection except that one. Okay, enough, Cadeau, I knew him before you did."

David put the poodle down and took Maggie in his arms, holding her close to him without saying a word, then, very quietly: "Oh God, Maggie, you make the world go away. What the hell would I do without you?"

"You'd come to an instant bad end, of course. I'm so happy to see you darling, but I know your coming here like this means something's happened—"

He sighed. "That's right . . . as soon as I walked into the house she started—I don't want to talk about it, okay?"

"All right, darling. You are, as they say, the boss. Well, let's see, have you had dinner?"

"No. I'm not really hungry—"

"Nonsense. First we'll have a drink and then I'll get

a tray and we can have it right up here, and afterwards I'll beat you at a game of dominos—"

"You will not."

"That's what you say, I'm too good for you and you know it."

"That's right, you're too good for me, except at dominos."

"Well, the grand master speaks." She kissed him and poured the wine. They drank leisurely. Finally he was relaxed, in the one and only place where he had found peace.

"Darling," Maggie said, "I've done something I hope you're going to like."

"I'd like anything you do. Out with it."

"It's your birthday next week."

He'd forgotten. "You're right, by God, it is."

"Well, I decided that one good turn deserves another. We're going to celebrate, really celebrate. I bought tickets for the opening of the opera and I've asked mother, Violet and the Bordinis, and I've made reservations at the Blue Fox for dinner. I wanted it to be a secret, but how could I? It'll be such fun, David. Would you like that?"

"I'd love it, but I'm not going to let you pay for all that—"

"Oh yes you are, Mr. Reid. You know, I'm not as poor as I look." She waved the ruby-ring finger. "I can always pawn this."

As she went to prepare dinner, David played with Cadeau, who amused him by doing her repertoire of tricks. Maggie had taught her how to roll over, jump and tumble, do somersaults; she sat up on her hind legs and caught little tidbits in her mouth. She "threw" her doll to David, expecting him to throw it back. In spite of himself, he found himself treating her like a child . . . He thought wryly of his own . . . Mark seemed a little off-hand these days, come to think of it, since he'd come home from that school. He was beginning to detect an independence in him, even in the little time he'd seen him since he'd come back this summer. Maybe it was a good sign, maybe he was finally beginning to grow up. Maybe, but unaccountably, it bothered him, made him uneasy. . . . He tried to shrug it off. Just as he did the momentarily gut-tightening thought that conceivably Katie was angry enough at him to tell the Silvermans that the Reids were Jewish occurred to him. No, she wouldn't do that, not if she hadn't for all these years. But she might well do something else . . . He forced himself not to think about it.

Maggie sent the tray up on the dumbwaiter and David carried it out to the terrace. It was a magnificent evening in early September, and as they sat having dinner, David looked out to and beyond the bridge and the bay that was spread before them. "You know, Maggie, the first time I saw this city I fell completely in love with it. This may sound funny, but somehow you and the city seem like one person to me—you're both very beautiful ladies with jewels in your eyes. You make everything so right for me. No matter what happens I can close that front door and shut it all out. I'm so different when I'm with you, it's as though I were two people. I suppose I am. You make all the magic happen in my life."

Maggie got up and sat in his lap. "David, what beautiful things you say to me. I hope I'll always make you happy. Well, we'll be together soon, but it's not getting easier, you know, I mean being separated . . ."

"Yes, how well I know it. But I'm getting things in order. In fact, I was at my attorney's today. I'm going to fight like hell for the house in Hillsborough—you know how much I love it; she can have the flats in the Marina. I have an apartment house I acquired a long time ago which will bring her in a good income. We figure that with a small cash settlement as well, *maybe* that will suffice, if we can keep it out of court. Oh come on, that's enough business for one night." He kissed her, then picked her up and carried her into the bedroom. "And now, madam, it's time to get serious." Whereupon Cadeau jumped up on the bed, started barking in his face and running all over the bed. "Get that damned dog out of here," roared the frustrated lover, and Maggie, laughing so hard she couldn't stop, said, "Don't call her a dog or you'll hurt her feelings."

"Get her out of here or I'll call her something a damn sight worse."

"Come on, Cadeau, you know when you're not wanted," Maggie said, and picked her up, put her in the living room and shut the door.

Over sounds of Cadeau scratching and whimpering, David said, "Let me tell you something, if anything comes between us, it'll be her." And then, moving to resume what they'd started, he added, "If you don't mind, I'd like to get back to the business at hand."

"Don't mind at all. Not at all . . ."

Fortified with the anticipation of his birthday party as planned by Maggie, and sobered by the memory of the dangerous argument with Katie of the night before, David now realized he would have to call Katie and mend fences. He also realized he'd been wrong to provoke her, and yet welcomed the unintended release for his long pent-up feelings. It was a relief, however temporary, that he badly needed. Now, though, on the phone to Katie, he told her that he'd been wrong to be so harsh with her, that he could see why she might have felt his treatment of the Silvermans was too rough, but that he really had looked on it as a business matter, and, anyway, he was sorry and he also wanted to tell her that a snag had come up in the shopping center construction and he'd have to be away for a few days. As he hung up, excited at the prospect of a week of uninterrupted time with Maggie, he thought wryly that in a way it was the consequence of making up over his unwanted neighbor—thank you, Dr. Silverman.

Finally the time arrived. He and Maggie spent the whole day together. They went to Marin and had lunch in Tiburon in a charming restaurant called Sam's on the wharf overlooking the harbor and watched the sailboats out in the distance and the yachts anchored at the wharf, basking languidly in the sun. Contentedly they arrived home at five. While David showered, Maggie went to the telephone, spoke to her secretary, and checked with a few clients she felt she'd neglected that day. She poured two glasses of wine and took them into the bedroom as David came in dressed in his robe. She handed him his glass, kissed him, and said, "Happy Birthday again, darling. Today you are one year old in the age of David and Maggie." Whereupon she saucily presented him her backside as she went off to her shower.

Dressed now, he considered himself in the full-length mirror. He had become comfortable within himself, inside his own skin. No longer did the Charles Flemings of the world make him feel self-conscious. And it was Maggie who was largely responsible. His self-esteem was heightened by so many things she did for him, including not questioning him about his past—his parents, his religion . . . She seemed to accept him for what he was, as he was. And if she wondered, as she must, from time to time, she never indulged her curiosity to the extent of prying. Among other things, she was too smart for that. She admired his ambitions, his admitted appetite for luxury and wealth. Love was so good between them, too, and when it was over they could lie in the dark and talk about things that interested them both. Their lives with each other had only really begun. No past, only the present and the promise of the future.

In the living room, waiting for Maggie, he filled his eyes with the elegance that surrounded him. Pouring another glass of wine, he looked out beyond, loving the City even more because he was seeing it through *her* windows. He saw Coit Tower in the distance and remembered another day in September, when he surveyed the City from that lofty perch, debating with himself what next steps he would take. A prospect beyond any imagining was that just across the plateau from where he stood that Indian summer day was a woman who would allow him to enter her life—and change his so completely. . . . He turned as Maggie entered the room dressed in a long satin Trigère, the bodice encrusted with crystal beads that moved slightly as she walked, the day-ending sun picking up the iridescence so that they shone like prisms. The soft ivory tone of the gown enhanced the blood-red of the ruby necklace.

"Maggie, you're so damn beautiful. I don't want to share you with the world."

Pirouetting around and smiling she said, "You know, David, I think you may do after all. Just keep talking that way."

He kissed her gently so as not to muss her. She put on a long matching opera coat and took a side view of herself, noticing the way the coat flared out in the back, falling with soft pleats to the ground.

Aunt Violet was in her Rolls-Royce in front of the house at precisely six. Meg sat alongside her, dressed in the same gown she had worn to Maggie's Christmas party; Aunt Violet was wearing a long French brocade Patou, and over it her floor-length sable coat.

The Bordinis were already at the Blue Fox when they arrived.

They toasted David with champagne. The intimate dining room was filled with beautiful people all headed for the opera. With dessert Maggie presented David a magnificent pair of jade and diamond cuff links she'd had made up months ago. A grand setting and indeed, one he frankly reveled in as he realized again how unimportant one's origins were if one could only learn to forget them, to leave them behind. In the past, where they belonged.

The Rolls came to a stop at the side entrance of the opera house, and Paul opened the door for them. As he collapsed his silk hat and checked it, David was conscious of the shiny patent leather shoes, the crease in his trousers, the white waistcoat, the white bow-tie. As he walked back to join the ladies, he recalled another day, in Chicago, when he'd bought a different outfit, the first suit he'd ever owned, and remembered having to pawn it in order to buy a job.

By now most of the audience had arrived and people were standing about in the Great Hall visiting and greeting their friends, many not breaking up even when the overture began. For Maggie it was an evening of special excitement. She was seeing her friends for the first time since her party in December.

"David, would you be offended if I left for a moment? I hate to, darling, not being able to introduce you and all, but I don't want anyone to think I'm snubbing them—"

"Not at all," he said, caring, in fact, very much. He felt rejected for a moment, but she was right, regardless of his feelings. In fact, it was the only thing that she could do if no questions were to be asked about the extra man.

"I'll be right back." She excused herself, turned and walked away toward Jane Bowman. As she did so, a photographer called out to Maggie; she waved to him and remembered the years her picture had appeared in the society section as one of the best-dressed women of the year on opening night. Suddenly she had to confess to herself that she missed it all. . . . Soon there were people around her, friends she hadn't seen for nine months. How good to see everyone! She was barraged with questions. Where had she been keeping herself? "We thought you got lost." "Lynn said she'd heard you were living in Europe." . . . Rumors, rumors, don't believe everything you hear . . . "We missed not seeing you."

David stood between Meg and Violet with the Bordinis opposite and heard only the voices of camaraderie among old friends around him exchanging flatteries, and for a moment he felt like an outsider. Just as quickly, though, he checked his thoughts, trying to concentrate on what Sylvia was saying about her Stephanie . . . how chubby and precocious she was becoming, and how positively fascinating it was to see the personality she had developed in five months, and that she had her father eating out of her tiny hand . . . David's attention strayed as he glanced over to Maggie.

Soon the lights dimmed, the bell rang and all went to their seats, where some men would be content to fall asleep while their wives yawned in the dark. Maggie walked down the aisle with Sylvia and Ron while David escorted Meg and Violet. The seating arrangement was such that David sat between Violet and Meg, Ron next, Sylvia and Maggie next to each other. David looked down at the program in his hands and tried to keep his feelings controlled, but he found it difficult with Maggie at the other end. And although he knew that she had been purposely subtle in the seating arrangement, his logic had nothing to do with what he felt. He tried to divert the feeling by concentrating on the libretto.

After he'd finished he kept his eyes on the program, his memory now moving back to a day when Abe had asked him to hear Rubinstein play. He hadn't wanted to go that day because he didn't have a suit to wear and he recalled the frustration until his spirits were lifted once the music began. What would Abe say if he were here tonight and could see him in this splendor, dressed in this get-up, accompanied by these people? The reverie was interrupted as the maestro tapped the baton and a hush fell over the crowd as the overture began.

When the first act came to an end the applause was enthusiastic, so much so that the man in front of David woke up, and as they were leaving their seats to go downstairs for refreshments David overheard him say to his wife, "What did you say the name of the opera was?" . . . "Read your program, I've forgotten," and then, as she adjusted her gown . . . "Oh my God, Henry, that woman's wearing the same dress I am. Saks is going to hear about *this* . . ."

Downstairs they ordered champagne. Maggie came to David and asked, "Have you ever had such fun, darling? Oh, David, just think, next year we'll be sitting here next to each other." She wanted to take his hand but refrained from doing so, standing at a proper distance. For a moment he had to fight down the impulse to reach out and pull her against him and kiss her in front of all of them. Sometimes the play-acting got to be more than he could handle. . . .

"Yes, darling, this is a great evening, thanks to you." Well, part of it had been. And then he saw Peter Douglas coming toward Maggie, on his arm a stunning blonde dressed in black chiffon with ropes and ropes of pearls. David was instantly threatened. Jealous. In spite of himself, he suddenly conjured up Maggie and Peter kissing, making love. He simply could not stand the idea that anyone had ever possessed her except himself.

"Maggie, you look lovely. Let me introduce you to Mrs. Adams."

She noticed that Mrs. Adams wore no wedding ring. Peter then introduced the newcomer to Maggie's family and friends. He and Maggie, David thought, looked at each other like two people who had shared a great deal. Peter looked and smiled at David as Maggie introduced the two once again. "Yes, we met at Maggie's," he said. He looked back at Maggie, and in that one glance she knew that Peter had guessed David was the man she'd told him about. The current was broken as Peter said, taking Meg's hand, "So nice to see you again, how have you been?"

Smiling, she said, "Fine, Peter, just fine. And you?"

"Busy." He turned to Violet. "And how is the most glamorous lady of them all?"

Violet laughed in that marvelous deep husky voice and said, "Oh, Peter, no wonder I adore you. I'm going to call you and you'll have dinner with me, soon." She pretended to whisper, "And then you and I can get down to a little serious drinking. How would you like that?" They all laughed except Maggie and David. Maggie could have shot dear Aunt Violet as she looked at David's face, knowing he felt that Violet's allegiances should be with him, not with a man who was obviously still in love with her. She would speak to Aunt Violet.

Peter, not unexpectedly, responded quickly, "I couldn't think of anything I'd rather do."

And Violet: "I'll be in touch next week. You still live in the same place, I assume?"

"Yes. I don't make many changes in my life, dear Violet. Now let me look at the madonna. Sylvia, if possible you look more beautiful than ever."

"Thank you, Peter, and incidentally, I had Stephanie's picture taken in the dress that you sent. It's simply beautiful. In fact, I'm going to do her portrait in it. I'll send you one of the photographs."

"I'll treasure it. And you, Ron, I'm afraid to ask how fatherhood is agreeing with you."

Before Ron could answer Sylvia said, "I beg you, don't ask him, he'll have you down here the entire second act."

"You're just jealous of the other woman in my life—"

"Yes, because I'm not nearly as chubby or lovable. I certainly don't get the attention she does." They all laughed as the lights dimmed and the bell sounded for act two.

Aunt Violet suggested that they all go back to her house and have champagne, which she always kept on ice "just in case of an emergency like this," but Sylvia begged off, saying she had to be up early with Stephanie. So they said their good nights and thank you's as Violet looked to Maggie and David, feeling that perhaps she shouldn't insist, that the lovers no doubt would prefer to be on their way. She knew that she preferred that there be somebody in *her* bed tonight. After all, fifty-eight wasn't exactly over the hill. Well, maybe this spring she would go to France and get in touch with one of her old admirers, but only for the season. She wouldn't think of leaving Meg for too long—after all, this was the only family she wanted and needed—and she knew that Meg wouldn't want to go. However, with Harry now gone almost two years she needed a change, and a little harmless fling . . . Of course she'd get back in time to be here when Maggie was married in July after David got his Mexican divorce. Goodness, what would papa say to this new generation? Well, she would go home with Meg to a little cold champagne and to her cold little bed.

David held the champagne bottle firmly as he popped the cork, then poured the bubbling liquid into the crystal, hollow-stemmed glasses. Maggie held hers up as the bubbles merrily danced to the top.

"May this be only the first of many wonderful firsts together." She was exhilarated from the evening's excitement.

"Thank you, darling, but next time I hope we can be sitting next to each other," he said, a slight irritation in his voice in spite of himself.

They clicked glasses, then Maggie put hers down and put a record on the stereo, took David's hand, and they danced.

"David," she said as they held one another, "were you annoyed tonight?"

Still dancing, he said, "Yes."

"Why?"

"Because I had to be separated from you, for one thing. Look, God knows it's not your fault . . . but remember once telling me that true love is when people can say to each other, 'I don't like you today?' Do you remember that?"

"Yes. Why?"

"In other words, you were saying you wanted me to be completely honest."

"Didn't you like me tonight?"

"I was, I am, I always will be crazy about you . . . which is also part of the trouble. It makes me damn jealous of Mr. Peter Douglas."

"You know you needn't—"

"I know I needn't have been a lot of things, but the fact was that I had a rough time trying not to think, to remember that he'd slept with you—"

She stopped dancing and looked at him in amazement.

"David, I'm shocked at you, and for the first time I'm disappointed."

"Why?"

"Because what I did with my life before was my own business; what I do now is yours. So if you were jealous for that reason, I assure you I'm not flattered."

"I'm sorry I said it, I know I shouldn't—"

"No, the fact that you said it doesn't make me angry

but that you must have imagined us in bed, making love, does."

He took her by the hand. "Please don't be angry, Maggie. I just can't help it. Anything about your life that I wasn't a part of makes me feel left out."

"Now isn't that ridiculous and childish?"

"Don't ask me to make sense—"

"Why not?—especially knowing how I feel about you. As far as not sitting together tonight, I arranged it that way on purpose and you know it, and you know why. In fact, one of my friends asked who you were in spite of my precaution."

"What did you say?"

"I said you were a very old friend of the family." She removed her hand from his, picked up the glass of champagne and drank. Still holding the glass in her hand, she said, "Now let me tell you something, so long as we're about it. Do you have any idea how *I've* been fighting with myself since those too brief months this summer? Mostly the time together makes being apart even worse. I hate being lonely, and I've had a bad case of it. In fact, the closer we get to next June the farther away it seems." She took another sip, put down the glass and lit a cigarette. "Do you have any idea how much discipline it takes for me not to accept invitations, not to see anyone, David? It isn't natural for me to be alone so much, but I made a bargain and I've never griped or complained about it, so why should you?"

This was the first time since they had been lovers that there'd been a moment of anger. Maggie went into her bedroom, unzipped her back and let the heavy satin dress fall to the floor. She picked it up and hung it away, then reached for a robe and put it on. David came in after her.

"Darling, I'm sorry if I said or did anything to offend you or to spoil the evening. I could shoot myself."

She looked at him for a long moment, and when she saw the solemn expression on his face she smiled and said, "Please don't do that. I won't have anyone to play dominos with." They laughed, and all the anger and tension was gone; but David learned once again that Maggie Kent was not a person to be taken lightly, or dealt with unfairly. . . .

As though nothing had happened, they went back into the living room to finish their champagne. He drained his glass, picked her up, carried her into the bedroom, and onto the bed. He turned out the light. The best part of their evening had just begun.

CHAPTER TWENTY-SIX

The months passed, David and Maggie each trying as best they could not to think in terms of time. Suddenly December was on them. Maggie said nothing to David about not having her annual party which had become a tradition among her friends on the Saturday before Christmas. They all had standing invitations to her house. As she sent out notes of regret to them, she had to fight down the feeling of deprivation; but send them she did, realizing that if she had the party, it would just mean a continuation of the invitations to parties and affairs that she had already turned down until gradually they had begun to taper off. Then, just before Christmas, a feeling that definitely was not familiar came over Maggie. She developed the most dreadful melancholia, which she rallied herself to fight against, reasoning that it was all a result of being shut away from everybody and the period of waiting would be over soon; but since that night at the opera, after having seen her friends again, the feeling had grown.

There were other problems. As the completion of the shopping center became imminent, things began happening so rapidly that, for reasons that were beyond his control, David saw even less of Maggie, and he was so busy there were days he barely managed to call. When she found herself depressed, she painted furiously, and the evenings he was not with her, she invited her mother and Violet to dinner or Ron and Sylvia, or she would dine with them, all the while missing David terribly; and at the end of a short evening, she would find herself so restless she simply had to go home. The Bordinis did not accept too often because of Stephanie, and besides, none of them could be with her constantly. So on the nights that she was alone she would have dinner on a tray in her room; and when she could no longer endure the sounds of silence, she would have Clarice come and play gin rummy with her. But by eleven Clarice would yawn and go off to her room, leaving Maggie alone with only Cadeau to keep her company in her bed.

On Christmas Eve, David came at seven laden down with boxes not only for Maggie, but for Meg, Violet and Clarice. Cadeau performed her antics, and Maggie, looking at David, thought how impossible it was going to be for her when he left this evening. She steeled herself against it as he kissed her. He was having the same difficulty, but he too said nothing, each sensing the same thoughts, the same feelings, the same needs. As they sat and talked about inconsequential things, David took a box out of his overcoat pocket and gave it to Maggie. She opened the velvet jeweler's box. Inside was a pair of ruby and diamond earrings. She held the box in her hands, unable to take them out.

"David, I don't know what to say—these are the most exquisite things I've ever seen."

"Try them on."

She did so, and he said, "They look lovely on you. Wear them with all my love."

"Thank you, David, but my, how I've changed! Much as I love them, I can think of something I'd rather you'd bought me." When she looked up she had tears in her eyes. Then, not being able to hold back any longer, she said, "I'm a greedy lady, please buy me June, David."

"I will, darling, I promise, and thank you for being so patient. Fact is, I'm just about set with everything. The day we have the official opening, which is scheduled for the fifteenth of June, I'll buy you the moon."

"I don't need the moon—just you, darling."

He took her face between his hands. "*That's* the day I'm going to tell her."

"Oh, David . . ." She went to the hall closet, returning with a beautifully wrapped package, almost as large as she was. David got up to help her with it. "This is for you, darling."

He propped it against the wall and took off the ribbons, then the Christmas wrappings, the corrugated cardboard, and there before him was his likeness. He stared at it, finally looked at her, then back to the portrait and shook his head. It was so startling a likeness he could find no words. She had selected the frame so as not to detract from the subject matter, which had been carefully planned, with David standing at the summit of the mountain with Coit Tower dwarfed in the background, the bay stretching out behind him. It was David as she saw him. It was the face of paradox. On the one hand it was the image of a man who had won the battle of self-mastery as he stood strong with all that he had resolved, a man capable of malevolence, yes, but the eyes spoke with love and devotion. It was the eyes that Maggie loved best.

"I don't know what to say . . . when did you have time for this?"

"Oh, David, that's the one thing I've had lots of—time. I worked at night, sometimes well into the hours of the morning. In a way, it was like having you with me."

"I just have no words—it makes me ashamed to have given you a piece of jewelry. How easy it is to buy something—"

"You see, that's what I tried to capture in my painting—the thing you just said now. A man who would let precious little stand in his way to accomplish what he wants, but still has such tenderness. When something basic touches him, he responds. I love you, David, beyond words." She kissed him tenderly. "Come, help me hang it. I took down the other painting and hung it in the hall."

Afterward, sitting across from one another at dinner, Maggie thought about herself and Christmas. Only once had she experienced Christmas alone, and that was the year she went to the Sorbonne. She missed her family so much she wanted to die; and from that time till now, she had made this the happiest time of the year. But tonight she was not completely joyous.

David looked up from his plate. "You're going to Aunt Violet's tomorrow?"

"Yes."

"Then will you take the gifts I've bought them, and I'll give Clarice's to her on the way out." On the way out—that was the moment she would dread tonight.

"David . . . I'm going away for a week with mother. We're driving down to Pebble Beach. The Swansons have asked us and I've accepted. I just can't stand being in the City this week, knowing we're so close and not able to be together—"

"Please don't go."

"It will be easier for both of us, believe me darling, just until we get over the holidays . . ." She wanted to cut off the possible argument she felt coming, and changed the subject to something she'd felt she should have said to him earlier. "David, I've been thinking that perhaps you should spend a little more time with Mark."

David was startled. It was one of the few times she'd ever mentioned his name. "What made you think of that?"

"I'm not sure . . . I'm really not. Who knows when an idea really happens or why? Maybe it's because of little Stephanie, maybe because I've had a lot of time this year for thinking about things instead of always being in motion. Maybe it's because I've begun to think that without your knowing it, he'll grow into manhood and you may just regret not having been closer to him. Maybe it's because I want him to like me."

"Well, I have to tell you, we've never been close—"

"I know that, but there's something strange. When you get the divorce, it could be the severing even of your friendship with him. Face it, how will you feel if you never see him? He's only fourteen now, but he's going to grow up and I think you'll have many regrets later. Perhaps it's the time of the season. I don't know, David. Maybe it's because I don't want him to think I've taken his father away from his mother. I'm not nearly as sure of things as I used to be . . ." She got up and walked to the window, looking out at the city, which tonight looked like a gigantic Christmas tree. "I don't know, David, I just have a very odd and peculiar feeling tonight."

He came to her side and said nothing for a while, just looking out with her.

After David left, Maggie packed her bag, took Cadeau, got into the red Jaguar and drove to Aunt Violet's. She simply had to be with her mother, and once she arrived there, she gave in to the needed relief of crying on that stalwart woman's shoulder.

Katie had never been able to respond fully to Christmas, but every other year she had at least been enthusiastic about the holiday season in general, if only for Mark's sake. Nobody knew what feelings of isolation and sorrow she experienced during this time every year, missing all the people she loved more than at any other time. But this year there was no joy whatsoever to be found within herself, nor could she manufacture any for Mark. She would not even allow herself to think about what was happening to them. It had been a year in which hope had flickered—hope that with David's successes and apparent thawing toward her there could still be a better time in their marriage. But the hope had been brutally set aside by such as her own terrifying enlightenment on the very night of Jim Fowler's death; and the episode with the Silvermans that had raised again, so nakedly, the painful spectre of Judaism, of a heritage, denied. Their heritage denied . . . all of them, including her son. So Katie had retreated . . . into the care of the house, to her books and her music, and to the observation of her son's gradual maturing—and her husband's deception. Love was frozen in her heart this Christmas, and there was no merriment in the Reid household.

In fact, each lost in his own thoughts, not a single word passed between the lord and lady of the manor all Christmas Day.

Christmas was a miserable time for Mark. All his friends were away for the holidays, some in Hawaii, others in Palm Springs, and those who stayed home found lots of things to do with their families. So on Christmas Day he brooded in his room and thought how odd it was that his mother and father had no close friends. They were never invited to places as the parents of his friends were, their lives were lonely and today Mark felt terribly sad, especially remembering last year's Christmas Day with the Fowlers and the Fowler boys. They had talked about girls and cars and school and what they would do when they graduated from college. He recalled Bob Fowler saying, "I'm going into banking like my dad," and Doug Fowler had said, "Who wants to do that? Not me. I'm going to be a doctor. What are you going to do, Mark, go into real estate, I suppose? Boy, are you lucky, you've really got it made."

"No, I'm not, not ever," Mark had said vehemently.

"What are you going to do then, made up your mind?"

"I don't know."

This Christmas he felt the loss of his friends and the loss of his father's old friend—the thought of all the gruesome details he'd read in the newspapers had disturbed Mark. Among other things, for the first time he realized that something could happen to his parents. He slept fitfully for weeks after it happened, waking up in the middle of the night unable to fall back asleep, and today he could hardly wait for this Christmas to be over so that he could get back to school, where he was really happiest. He loved Burlingame and had begun to make many friends. There was only one thing that he didn't like about school, and that was the fact that Katie had to drive him there and back every day because there was no transportation available from where they lived. To make it less embarrassing for him, Katie dropped him two blocks from school in the morning and met him each afternoon in the same place, unless someone else drove him home. But in March he would be fifteen, and although he had a whole year ahead of him before he could drive, he had already made up his mind what kind of a car he wanted.

Mark had developed into quite a self-sufficient adolescent. Although he and Katie were still close, he now spent most of his free time with boys his own age, leading a normally active social life of movies, sports, hobbies, and long talks with his friends. If there was one source of discontent in his world, it was his relationship with David. In spite of Mr. Hansen's advice and encouragement, Mark had not really had the opportunity to have the long heart-to-heart talk with his father he had anticipated—David never seemed to be home long enough for Mark to get around to it. But Mark had learned to cope with the situation, and he no longer brooded so much over his father's attitude.

The first indication of a possible breakthrough occurred, oddly enough, when Mark most expected to feel his father's rage. It was the first time he had ever asked David for anything that meant so much to him—it was the biggest dream he'd ever had. Somehow he just assumed it would mean a lot of trouble. Nevertheless, just before his birthday, Mark hitched up his courage and asked his father for money to build up from its shell an original Model-T Ford, vintage 1924. A real classic . . . To his amazement, his father seemed interested, and they had the longest conversation Mark could remember.

David thought Mark was crazy for not taking him up on his offer to buy him a new car, and even, for one irrational moment, considered turning down the boy's request completely for his seeming ingratitude. He tried hard to hold in check his usual impatience, remembering Maggie's advice and warning. Grudgingly, he had to admit that he really didn't know very much about his son—who would have believed that he'd soon be old enough to drive, never mind build his own car? He hadn't noticed how tall Mark had gotten until now, or that there were the beginnings of dark, fuzzy hair on Mark's face. He actually seemed quite mature to David, almost a man. But at this moment he wished Maggie had never given him her advice—he was so much more confused now than ever before about his feelings toward Mark. Before it had all seemed so cut and dried (of course he'd hardly considered it before, which, of course, tended to make things simple).

"What will it cost to build this jalopy?" David asked, feeling awkward in this unaccustomed role of temporizing with his son, actually *talking* to him.

"About five hundred dollars," Mark said, his eyes lighting up.

Look at that, he was almost as tall as his father—he also smelled a little gamy after basketball practice.

"Mark, do you use a deodorant?"

"Of course I do, dad. What a question to ask me."

"Well, you'd better take a shower, Mark . . . Okay, okay, Mark, go and buy the thing, but let me tell you this—if you don't build it you don't get another car. Remember, I was willing to buy you one, remember that."

The threat sailed high over Mark's head, he was so excited with the go-ahead. He wouldn't press David for the money now—just reaching his father and winning his point was too overwhelming.

David almost fainted when he saw Mark directing his friend down the driveway with a trailer attached to the boy's car, the classic body strapped on top.

"Okay," Mark called out, "a little more to the left. Wait a minute, you almost hit the tree. Okay now, come back easy, that's okay. Great, you almost got her backed into the garage. Come on back, easy, easy . . . okay, she's *in*." Mark jumped up in the air, then ran inside and got Katie and David to come and see his masterpiece. The other boy had just taken the strap off and there Mark's magnificent classic lay nude in the third garage, which would become its natural habitat from now on forevermore. Mark promised himself he would never part with this beauty.

"Well," Mark said in reverence, running his hand tenderly over the body, "what do you think?"

Neither David nor Katie could answer. It was a beat-up hulk of a shell, battleship gray and rusting, once a Model-T Ford that had cost all of $350 new, chassis and all, tires included. So far as David was concerned, it was ready for the first junkyard that would accept it, and he had his doubts that they would even buy it for five dollars. This was what Mark had conned him into buying? Katie, not knowing what to say, finally stammered, "I think it's very nice, Mark, and I know you must have great plans for making it into something . . . very nice." She also was certain, looking at it, that it would be impossible. For once she found herself in sympathy with David about something Mark had done.

"Gee, mom, thanks, I knew you'd appreciate it. Isn't it great, dad?"

"Can you get your money back?"

Mark was stunned. Could it be that his father didn't understand the aesthetics of this treasure? "What do you mean, get my money back, dad?" Mark's friend stood by and listened. He quickly put in, "Hey, I'll buy it from you, Mark."

"You will not, I'm not selling it, even if I could make a profit. You don't understand, listen, this is rare, probably left from that year. All I need is a loan, dad, I'll get a job. Anyway, I'm *not* going to sell her." He left his friend with his mother and father standing in the garage, ran into the house, up the stairs and into his room, slamming the door behind him. Remembering Maggie, David controlled himself. Besides, in a way you had to admire the kid, the way he stood his ground. . . .

CHAPTER TWENTY-SEVEN

Summer, 1951

The months stretched out before them and Maggie and David began counting the weeks that eventually dwindled into days, and now June was theirs. Together they stood in hushed silence as they looked out of the window of David's private office and saw the lights of the shopping center turned on for the first time. The enormous neon sign that said, "San Madale" streaked across the sky. The center was jammed with people, and there was an atmosphere of carnival in the air. At the furthest corner flew large banners. Children were given free ice cream and balloons. There was a marimba band that played up and down the inner mall, with the children following them like the Pied Pipers they were, passing the small specialty shops that looked like gems in a setting as fountains danced merrily, spouting up water as the different spotlights changed color. Off the main highway were enormous spotlights that shone for miles. At nine o'clock there were fireworks.

Mark had come with his friends from Burlingame High, who didn't resent him because his father was the owner of all this; in fact they admired him even more because he acted like any other kid, accepting the free ice cream. He was excited, same as they, but not especially impressed that it was his father who had done this. Mark didn't especially feel like the son of a rich potentate, he didn't feel rich at all. To be honest, he didn't feel much of anything so far as his father's accomplishments were concerned, and he didn't want to be judged by his father, he wanted to be judged for himself by his friends—he made a conscious effort to play down that he was David Reid's son. He need not have made the effort, because arrogance was not a part of his nature to begin with. He would have been as happy if his father had been like a lot of the fathers of his friends from Burlingame High School. Happier . . .

Katie did not come at all.

It was ten o'clock when David got the chance to be alone with Maggie and take her in his arms. "Well, by God, we *finally* made it," and as he said it he felt as though the world had been lifted from his shoulders. "And now, Miss Maggie Kent, may I ask you to marry me?"

She could hardly speak, realizing that now the waiting was actually behind them. "Oh David, David, my dearest, for all my life and with all my heart."

The closer David came to Rosehaven Road the more difficult became the prospect of facing the ordeal he'd put off for so long. He did not park the car in the garage tonight; instead he left it in front of the house, turned off the engine and sat thinking of what he would say. After all, they'd been married sixteen years. What had she actually done that was so bad? Nothing really, nothing of such great importance, mostly the same kinds of things most people do in marriage. So he became annoyed at the sound of her voice, so he became annoyed at the way she swallowed at the table, or nagged him about breakfast; actually she'd never been demanding of him. . . . They were simply misfits, but he had loved her once—which maybe was why he was having these feelings . . . Except one thing he knew for certain, he no longer loved her. He was going to end this marriage and take the happiness he now finally was ready for. . . . Getting out of the car, he walked up the front path to the door and looked up at her room. The rest of the house was in darkness. His heart pounded as he put the latchkey in the lock and turned it until the door opened. He switched on the hall light, climbed the stairs slowly. Outside her door, his fist poised to knock, he hesitated. Then he tapped softly on the door.

"Come in," Katie said.

She was in bed, eating an apple. She had on her reading glasses and a blue silk bed jacket around her shoulders; her face was sunburned from working in the garden and there was a transparent layer of vaseline on her nose.

"Yes, David?" she asked.

He stood awkwardly, not knowing how to begin, and for the lack of anything better he said, "You wouldn't come to the opening tonight. Why? You might have enjoyed it."

She smiled. "Why? Oh, I don't know, David. I guess because I knew there would be so many people there I really wouldn't be too interested in seeing, and vice-versa."

He remained standing.

"Why don't you sit down?"

He really wanted to get it over with, but easy, now easy, don't rush, no fights tonight; remember your damn temper. He sat down on the chintz-covered chair, impressed again that she really had done this room with all the grace of a seasoned decorator.

"Well, David, you must be very happy that it's finished," she said agreeably.

"Yes, very happy about that"—it was the opening he needed—"but not entirely happy about other things."

"Really, David? I'm sorry to hear that. What other things are you not happy about?"

"Well, believe it or not, I do worry about you."

"You do?"

"Yes, I do."

She took off her glasses and folded them, placing them on the bed alongside her and looked at her husband. "I'm sorry that I'm the cause of your concern, but why should you worry? I have everything I want, you've given me everything a wife could want —a magnificent home exquisitely furnished—something I've always dreamed of having—a successful husband, a lovely son. I don't know why you're worrying."

She was baiting him, of course, but he'd play along with her. "Katie, let's be honest with each other, let's not act any longer."

"All right, David, let's not."

"We haven't been happy or compatible for a very long time now, I'm sorry to say, and maybe the things that we've gone through leave people drained, like after any long battle. Now, be honest with me, will you?"

"Yes, I will, David."

"You never accepted me, and you feel I've done a lot to hurt you, don't you?"

"Yes, I do."

"Thank you for your honesty, because that's really what I'm talking about. A wife has to believe in and support her husband without any reservations, especially on the most important decisions of their lives. You never did that—"

"You're right, David. And I made mistakes. I made the mistake of thinking that the love I once felt for you would be enough. Or that our son would be. Or later, that I would be your father's presence, reminding you of who you were, waiting for you to grow up and accept yourself. Of course, I never accepted in my heart what you had done—how could I and not destroy myself, but you see, David, I'm like most human beings, I have my weaknesses, just like you do. Mine, I'm afraid, haven't brought me the satisfactions yours apparently have. . . ."

That last went over him as he fought to control himself, to not react and strike back at her. "All right, damn it, Katie, think what you want. Anyway, I agree I've put you in a position that's made it impossible for you to have a life for yourself and find some happiness of your own—"

"That's very decent of you."

He pretended not to notice the sarcasm. "This is no life for you, living alone most of the time. You're getting older and so am I." He hesitated, timing the moment, hoping it was finally the right one. "Katie, I want a divorce."

She closed the book, picked up the glasses and toyed with them, opening and closing the frames until David wanted to grab them out of her hand and smash them to bits, but he sat outwardly calm and composed. At last she looked up at him and, quietly and slowly, summoning up more dignity than she felt, she said, "David, I think this is very kind of you to consider my life . . . but you see I don't have any intention whatever of divorcing you."

He sat there, stunned, unable to speak. She watched him for a few moments, the silence hanging there between them, the room this warm June night filled with the fragrance of blossoms from the garden. Then she said, "Since you have been so kind, I'll try to tell you why. You know, David, there was a time in my life when I needed love more than you can ever imagine. Well, as you know, I've had too little of that. I needed the companionship not only of a husband but of friends. And when I saw other women and their husbands together, I knew I had neither, so I made a world of my own. The thing you failed to remember is that from my very earliest childhood I have never lived without loneliness. Do you know what loneliness really is, David?"

He couldn't answer, and she continued. "Loneliness destroys the spirit, but even loneliness reaches its peak and then levels off. Once I reached to you for love, but when you began not to respond, the urgent need began to disappear, and eventually I learned to live with it . . . not that one ever becomes *entirely* accustomed to that kind of living alone." She paused and studied the expression on David's face. She got out of bed, went into the bathroom and drank a glass of water. When she came back, she sat on a chair, facing David.

"You see, David," she said, "life has prepared me for these things. At this point, I'm very settled. I have nowhere to go, I'm not going anywhere. So you see, my dear, you needn't have worried about me." She got back into bed, opened the book, picked up the glasses and just before slipping them on, she looked directly into David's eyes and said, "Besides, David

. . . I don't happen to have a lover who's waiting for me."

She knew. My God, how long had she known? His shoulders slumped. Still, he was unable to move. My God, she *knew*. At this moment he was too confused to even think about the hows, the whens. Later—but at this moment, all he could think of was Maggie waiting. God, what could he say to her? He didn't know. He only knew that he felt suffocated, that he had to get out of there right now, this minute, or he would die . . . or commit murder.

Maggie stood in the hall waiting for him as she heard the elevator rise. This was the moment. Thank God, the waiting was over. The lights were dimmed, the champagne was chilled, their favorite song was on the record player. Finally, the elevator door opened. Maggie ran into David's arms, but as she held his face in her hands there was pain, not pleasure written in his eyes. All her deliciously nervous anticipation was gone. Releasing herself, she took him by the hand and led him to the sofa and sat quietly alongside him. He couldn't speak, not yet. To break the tension she poured him a glass of wine, and one for herself too. No champagne. It didn't seem to be a moment of celebration. Poor David, she thought, the ordeal must have been more than he'd expected, the scene must have been dreadful. There'd probably been name-calling and even Mark might have been present. David just sat with his head back against the sofa cushion, his hands over his eyes. His face was colorless. To see David like this was more than she could bear. "David, darling, drink your wine. It will help." He opened his eyes, moistened his lips and took a large gulp. Finally she said, taking his hand gently, "It must have been terrible for you—I'm sure these things are never easy—but thank God it's over with. At least, at long last, she knows."

"Yes, she knows."

The way he answered frightened her. Trying to compose her inner feelings, she repeated, "It must have been terrible for you, darling. Was there awful bickering—"

"No . . . none of that." He took another sip of the wine.

Now she was frightened. Why was David acting so withdrawn, so silent, so evasive? She had to know. "Well, tell me, David, what happened?"

He looked at her, then quietly answered, "She knows about us."

At first she couldn't respond at all. When she found her voice, she asked, "But how . . . when could—"

"I wish I knew, but what difference does it make? She does."

Maggie got up and paced the floor, then stood in front of the marble mantel, her voice tight. "Tell me, David . . . just tell me what happened!"

He hesitated for too long. He could not find the courage to tell her.

Finally, almost shouting, Maggie said, "What *happened*, David?"

"She said she will not give me a divorce."

Maggie thought her mind was playing tricks on her and that she had not heard him correctly. "What did you say? I don't think I heard you."

He repeated it as if by rote. "She said she would not divorce me."

She looked at him, unable to accept it. "My God, this can't be true. It can't be true, we've waited for years, now this? All for nothing . . . ? Go away, David, I have to be alone. *Please.*"

She slumped down in the bergère and wept out of control. He came to her side, held her head against his shoulder and stroked her hair. After the long fit of weeping had subsided, she stayed motionless, without a word. She stared up at the ceiling. Finally: "You know, David, I guess there must be a law of retribution after all, and mine has caught up with me. In a way I wonder if we—at least I—haven't helped bring this down on ourselves. Maybe I'm more my mother's daughter than I ever suspected. When I think of it, it really isn't so surprising that she should find out, or at least suspect. She is, after all, a woman, and her husband, never mind all the plausible reasons, was hardly ever at home, and for all his careful behavior he may even have made her more suspicious. I'm sure there must have been a time or two when she saw us together, noticed or at least thought she noticed something. From suspicion to certainty is not much of a distance for a woman in her position. It didn't have to be anything dramatic or anybody telling her. I should have known this could happen. I guess it was just that I just didn't *want* to admit the possibility to myself. I was too afraid of it, of the consequences. . . . Well, what do we say now? It's been nice knowing you but the party's over, ended, finished, *fini*—"

"Oh *no,* not quite. Yes, I was shocked, too shocked at first to think straight, but don't think I'm going to take this as final. Do you hear me? Now I'm really mad and I'm going to fight her. Believe me, I'm going to find a way—"

"Don't underestimate a woman scorned, David. She doesn't have to give you a divorce."

"She will . . . I'll make her—"

"And how long will that take? I can't go on this way any longer. There's a limit—"

He took her in his arms and held her tight. "Listen to me, Maggie. I love you too much, too much for her or anybody to keep us from having what we're entitled to. We're not criminals, for God's sake, we're two people in love who want to get married and live together. What the hell's wrong with *that?*"

"But she said she would not give you a divorce."

"Don't be frightened by that. Tonight was only bravado. Okay, she wanted to hurt me by letting me know she knew about us. That was all it was, a threat. Listen, I know her better than you do—"

"But if she means it, David, we can't go on like this."

"Now, please hear me out. First of all, trust my judgment. I'm not going home for a week. Let her cool off; she'll have second thoughts about this. I know something about human nature and I know her. I'm asking you to have confidence in me. Will you, darling?"

Quietly she said, "I have no other choice. It isn't you I'm afraid of, it's her. You see, David, *I* know about women."

"But you don't know *her*. After she cools off, I'll go home. And I can assure you, this time I'll be ready for her."

In the week that followed, Maggie could not sleep. She could not eat, her weight dropped drastically. She took no phone calls, not even her mother's. She could not keep up a positive attitude for all of David's reassurances, and a heavy depression took hold of her. She could not get rid of the fears, even at those moments when David made love to her, which made the lovemaking almost unbearable. All she wanted was for Sunday to come so that once and for all, the uncertainty would be at an end.

Finally, nine o'clock, Sunday night. She had a sense of foreboding as they held onto each other and kissed just before he was ready to leave. The fear in her eyes was unmistakable. "Trust me, please, Maggie."

"I do, David, wonderful David, of course I do. But as soon as it's over, call. I love you so, David."

"Just trust me, Maggie. This time it really will be all right."

"I know, my dearest." And for one moment, she believed it.

David knocked softly at Katie's door. When she responded, he entered and found her in bed, reading as usual. He was counting on his strategy. By now, and if he behaved, she would be feeling uneasy at her mean-spirited behavior earlier—she would be ashamed of feelings she herself felt spiteful . . . "Sit down, David. I suppose you've come back to try and work out our marital problems?"

She sounded pleasant, reasonable. The strategy was working. "Yes."

"All right."

"Kate, I'm sure that during the week past, you must have thought things over and—"

"I have indeed."

"And?"

"And I hold the same position now that I held then."

Holding back the anger, he asked, "What do you feel will be accomplished by holding on to a marriage that was over a long, long time ago?"

"A great deal."

"What? Except for punishing me, what will you gain, Kate?"

"Please don't call me Kate . . . my name is Katie, a little too Jewish perhaps, but that's it, Katie. . . . Yes, you are absolutely right, I want to punish you as you have punished me for never having given up my heritage . . . and while we're about it, I want you to know something about how very Jewish I've been. I sent money to Israel for trees to be planted in the name of those whose memories have sustained me through all the years, including the members of the Rezinetsky family. I have lighted my memorial candles in their behalf each year. I know how much it pains you, but try to think back to a little flat on Hester Street. Do you remember that day when you said all you wanted was to live a life of dignity and you couldn't do it being a Jew? I don't know, maybe you honestly believed it then. I know I wanted to believe you did. I loved you. But the truth was you didn't really abdicate Judaism for dignity, you despised being born a Jew. I'm not sure of all the reasons, and I no longer care . . . by the way, speaking of dignity, did you know that Solly—Solly Obromowitz—has become one of the most important and respected men in the movie world?" She gave him a chance to digest that, then continued, "Imagine—with a name like that. Dignity? Solly's got dignity. You cheated your son out of his heritage to save him from a life of prejudice. What a joke, what a despicable hoax."

"Then why have you waited all these years to tell him?" He heard himself shouting. Well, what difference could his outburst make now—except for the slight matter of pushing her to tell not only their son but the whole world what he'd spent years denying. . . .

"Because," she answered with deliberate calmness, "it would have served no purpose. It would have only confused him, and it would have given him a coward for a father. A child needs to be born into Judaism from his mother's womb. You decreed otherwise for our son." She took a deep breath. "You see, David, as you may have noticed, I'm no longer the shy little eighteen-year-old girl you manipulated, nor the frightened and so terribly lonely and abandoned young wife from Chicago days any longer. I'm not afraid of you, or of losing you. You've already left, and I'm all grown up."

"Then in God's name, why won't you give me a divorce?"

"In God's name?" She laughed sardonically. "Which God would that be? Yours? Mine? Yourself, perhaps? . . . You know, David, you've played God too long. Up to now it's all been *your* way, everything *you* wanted . . . well, this is one thing you're not going to have. Not your lovely American Protestant shiksa mistress to live with in blessed matrimony, rid of Katie, helping you finally to get rid of the past and all your ghosts. You can live with her, you can do anything you want, but one thing you will never do is marry her, because never, *never* will I give you a divorce."

It was her victory. His face became flushed and hot; his jaw tightened; his hands were clenched in the pockets of his jacket. He stood up, came to the bed and looked down at her. God, what was holding him back from killing her? The room was choking him and he rushed out, slamming the door behind him with all his might and walked across the hall to his room, where with a grand sweep of his hand he shoved everything off the desk—the inkwell, the lamp—everything went crashing to the floor. He banged his fist against the wall until his knuckles bled.

My God, how was he going to tell Maggie? His head pounded. Well, he still couldn't give up. Not yet. In his heart, he knew he had no grounds for divorce, but he would call his attorneys in the morning. Maybe he would think of something. . . . It was now twelve o'clock and Maggie was waiting impatiently. Oh, my

God. He went into the bathroom and washed his face, the soap stinging his raw knuckles. He sat on the edge of the bed. He couldn't think of a damn thing to say—God, he just couldn't lose her now.

Finally he went downstairs, poured a stiff drink, drank it down and brought the bottle back with him. He didn't care what it did to him, he needed it. He dialed the number, and when he heard her voice he wanted to die.

"Hello, David," she said quickly.

"Yes, darling," hardly able to speak.

"Has everything been . . . resolved?"

Silence. Then, scarcely above a whisper: "There are a few things we have to work out—"

Silence, then: "What do you mean, David? You don't sound very sure of yourself. What did she say?"

"I'm coming up to the city right away."

"No, David, before you do that I want to *know*. What did she say about the divorce?"

"I'm coming up to the city."

"No, David, no." She almost screamed. "I have to know."

"Maggie, I want to come up and see you. I'm starting right now."

"No, not until you tell me. Are you going to get a divorce, or not?"

"Now, Maggie, please don't take this too seriously—"

"What do you *mean*, David?"

It was like listening to himself from an echo chamber. "She says she won't divorce me, but I'm not taking that as final." He could hear the awful sigh. "Maggie, are you there? Darling, answer me, please. My God, I didn't expect anything like this—"

"I'm here, David."

"I'll be there in about twenty minutes."

"No, David, please, don't come tonight. I couldn't bear it."

"Don't say that, darling, please don't say that."

"Not tonight, David. I'm going to hang up, I'm sorry."

She stared about the room. It was like the refusal to

face his wife's ever finding out. She had also refused to consider the possibility that finally, in spite of all his careful efforts, she would refuse to give him the divorce. The prospect was just too dreadful to think about. She wanted to cry, but no tears would come. Some things, like death, were too deep to cry over. David and Maggie. Dead. A death in the family. Suddenly she felt very cold. . . .

David paced the floor all night, refusing to believe there was nothing he could do. He would speak to Katie tomorrow. She was Katie. After all, he'd known her for a long time. He'd simply have to try a different tactic, he'd convince her, break down her defenses; she couldn't mean to be this cruel. Tonight she'd wanted to punish him . . . hell, he'd even give her the damn house—what did it mean to him now anyway? He could hardly wait for morning to come. The whiskey had made him feel even more miserable. By eight he was on his way to the city, arriving at Maggie's house by eight-thirty. Letting himself in, he ran up the stairs, not waiting for the elevator. When he got to the third floor, he found Clarice was in Maggie's room tidying up.

"Where's Miss Kent?"

"Mr. Reid, you'd better sit down."

"What? I said where's Miss Kent."

Clarice hesitated. She was fond of him and he looked like a man who had already suffered a great deal. His face was waxy and pale, and his hair looked somehow more gray this morning.

"Mr. Reid," she said almost inaudibly, "Miss Kent left for Mexico this morning."

"For Mexico?" Why hadn't she told him or waited for him? . . . "I don't understand. Did she go with her mother or aunt—"

"No, Mr. Reid. I hate to have to be the one to tell you, but she left with Mr. Peter Douglas."

"With Mr. Douglas?"

"Yes, she told me, her mother and aunt too, that they're going to be married. I guess you know that he's always asking her and one time she came close . . .

She wrote a note for you, it's on the desk. Shall I go and get it?"

David shook his head slowly.

"Is there anything I can get for you, Mr. Reid?"

"No."

"Can I do anything for you?"

He did not answer, just shook his head, dazed. She decided he wanted to be alone and left him standing in the middle of the room by himself. How long he was there with his thoughts, he could not say. Nothing seemed important, only the empty, sickening realization that he had lost Maggie, his life. He went into the living room, took the keys and placed them on the desk, picked up the note, put it in his pocket unopened—he would have the rest of a lifetime to read it. On the way out he paused in front of his portrait. He wondered if Maggie, seeing him now, could have altered the face to show what was behind. Beside the misery, he wondered what she would find. Maybe she would send it to him. . . . He looked for the last time at this room that once had held all his dreams, and now represented all his despair. He turned and walked down the stairs for the last time, shut the door behind him, got into his car and drove away.

CHAPTER TWENTY-EIGHT

June brought its changes into their lives. For Katie, an end to the subterfuge, the waiting for the moment that would be as sweet as honey to her taste. At long last it was over, David had not had his way. She felt free. Now she would try to pick up a part of her life; if not whole, at least it would be more rewarding. She would work at the hospital as a volunteer in the children's ward, doing whatever she could to relieve their suffering. She decided to take piano lessons. . . .

For David the pieces were so fragmented that there was nothing to pick up. It would have been utterly impossible to return to live under the same roof with Katie again. In fact, he was afraid of what he might do in a fit of anger. And in the end, he realized, the ironic part of all this was that it was Katie and Peter Douglas who had won, mostly by waiting things out . . . something neither he nor Maggie had much talent for.

He took a suite of rooms at the Huntington Hotel in San Francisco. Lying in bed alone that first night, remembering the touch of Maggie, he looked at the still unopened letter on top of the dresser. He'd not been able to bring himself to read it up to now. Finally, hours later, his hands trembling as they had once so long before when, alone in Chicago, he'd gotten the letter from Katie, he got up and took it in his hand. Afraid to read it, afraid not to; hoping that somehow this was all a grotesque hoax, knowing damn well that it wasn't . . . he looked down at his name written by her hand. Carefully, as though it might explode from careless handling, he opened the envelope, slowly removed the letter and began to read:

June 15, 1951

My dearest David,

I have no idea where I'm getting the courage to sit here and write you. Even now I have terrible doubts and misgivings. After speaking to you tonight I thought I would die. I felt cold all over. I was scared to death. I realized the hopelessness of our situation. I told you once before about the feelings of a woman scorned, and it's no joke. I know it's how she felt, and how she will always feel. After you hung up tonight I realized she either loved you so much or hated you so much —they're close in some ways, aren't they?— that she would never let you go. I was forced not to underestimate her, however much I would have liked to, and however much I think I may have before.

I don't know what we could have done to have prevented this from happening. Maybe the trouble is we shut our eyes too often to what we didn't want to look at. I don't know, but I do know there could be nothing for us without the divorce. And I must have something in my life, David. I must. I need to get on with life again, right away, or I'm afraid I'll die. I mean that. My darling, I'm going to marry Peter. I don't have any choice. It goes without saying that life without you won't be the same, and that I will never love anyone again, not the same way. But my life with Peter will be a good one. He is a good man, and I think he has enough love for both of us.

David got up and poured himself a drink, took a large gulp and lay down once again to finish the letter:

I don't really know everything I'm saying tonight, but what I'm doing does seem the only thing to do. Somehow I know I'll adjust to my life. But I worry about you. Oh, I suppose we could have gone on living together, but eventually you would have hated me. Your son would never have seen you and would eventually have hated you for leaving his mother for me. How else could he have felt? And my family, my mother, she's made a great many concessions, but she would never have forgiven us forever, and that would have added another burden for us. I don't believe you could have been content to live with me without my being your wife, and we could never have had children. We just had too much against us. If we had stayed together, in the end we would have destroyed the only thing we have left for ourselves now—our lovely memories. And, David, my memories will sustain me the rest of my life.

Your portrait will remain where it is, and I will look at it when my life seems to reach out to you, as I know it will. I love you as I always have, as I always will.

Forgive me, but I would not have had the strength to tell you this if you were standing here at this moment. Just remember I love you, dearest. And try to forgive me.

Maggie

After that David, feeling intolerably lonely and without real friends, took to calling his son. If Katie happened to answer the phone, he would hang up. After a while he had a private phone installed in Mark's room.

For Mark the month brought a combination of sadness and joy. The joy was that he and David were becoming closer, and also that he had made a new and good friend. The sadness was that his father had left his mother and he didn't know why. Although he questioned Katie, she said quite frankly that she was not prepared to discuss his father with him because their problems had to do only with the two of them, apologizing that she couldn't take him into her confidence. But he insisted that no matter what their personal feelings were toward each other it certainly made him unhappy that now the small family they had been was broken up. In fact, he was embarrassed to say to his new-found friends who had just moved in across the street that his mother and father were separated. It was true that many of his friends' mothers and fathers were not only separated but divorced; but he knew only too well the troubles they had in getting accustomed to this, remembering how Bruce was split between his mother and father. The only good thing was that now that his father had moved out of the house, for some strange reason he seemed to have time for him that he never had before. Mark couldn't, of course, know why.

The key was David's sudden, total aloneness, and especially the reasons behind it. Without Maggie, knowing there could never be another woman for him, he needed some human being to reach out to. David also had no close friends, in fact no friends at all to whom he could go. He had wondered about calling Meg and then Ron, but thought better of it. After all, they were Maggie's family and friends, not his. The only friend he could have turned to would have been Jim Fowler . . . Ironically, the most available was his son, whom he'd known and understood so little in the past. He'd been wondering more and more of late what Mark thought of him. Did he know about him and Maggie? Had Katie told him? Would she want Mark to hate him as much as she did and try to poison Mark's mind against him? He doubted it, but after what she'd done he couldn't be sure. It was late, he realized, but Mark was making him aware as never before how much he had missed and how little he knew about his son. He recalled that the business with that crazy jalopy was just about the first time he'd noticed that Mark was no longer a child but an adolescent well on the way to manhood. They'd lived in the same house, Mark was of his flesh, and they were strangers. In a way his whole life had made him a stranger. The success, the great wealth meant so little now—he'd heard other men say such things and never believed them. Even his organization could get on without him. He needed someone to share what was left. He wondered if Maggie realized how prophetic she'd been that Christmas Eve when she'd encouraged him to know his son better. . . .

Mark had decided not to go up to the lake this year. Now that David and Katie were no longer together, he felt the coming summer would be meaningless without what he'd at least been able to look forward to last summer—that when the shopping center was finished the three of them would be together at their terrific lake place. He decided to stay home and try to be near both of them. And there was another reason for his not wanting to go. He would work on his car so that it would be ready by next March and his fifteenth birthday.

Jeff Wallace had moved in across the street. His father was a prominent attorney in San Francisco from an equally prominent family. Greg Wallace had bought the house because not only did he and his lovely wife Linda think it time for Jeff to go to a coeducational school but also because they felt their nine-year-old Cherry ought to know the wholesome atmosphere of a good public school. The city had undergone tremendous changes since the war, and Greg and Linda found the school situation in the city of San Francisco no longer much to their liking.

Mark and Jeff became friends immediately although they were a year apart in age. When Jeff saw Mark's 1924 classic body for the first time he wanted to ask his father to sell his little MG, but he knew his father would never let him do that since they'd bought it in London and gone to all the trouble of bringing it home. Boy, what a lucky guy Mark Reid was to have a father who would let him have a great thing like that. The boys worked on the body all summer. By the end of July the chassis was ready. Katie rented a trailer and several of Mark's friends came over that morning to help lift the body onto the trailer. Cherry was there every day. She begged to go along with Mark and Jeff to the body shop. Jeff refused, telling her to get lost, but Mark said to let her come. So she sat with Katie, who had fallen in love with her, freckles, pony tail, braces and all. She was an adorable little girl, a bit on the plump side, mildly precocious, extremely bright, moderately spoiled not only by her doting parents but also her big brother (even if she did get in his hair).

They arrived at the garage and learned the shell would have to be left overnight, so the next day Katie drove them back and picked it up with the chassis now attached. It could have been the launching of the Queen Mary as Mark and Jeff laughed delightedly at the sight of their creation no longer supported on the wooden saw horses. The boys decided to ride in the trailer. Cherry wanted to stay with them but Jeff adamantly said, "No, you ride up front with Mrs. Reid."

"Can I, Mark?"

"Gee, Cherry, I wouldn't mind, but you'll have nowhere to sit. We have to stand."

"I don't care. I want to."

"No, Cherry, you can't and that's that," Jeff said impatiently. He wanted to get back so that they could really get down to doing some serious work.

"I'm going to tell mother," she said with her hands on her hips.

"You do that," Jeff said, taking her by the waist and sitting her alongside Katie, who smiled at her as she slumped down in the seat, crossed her arms and grimaced. Katie switched on the ignition and off they went. Cherry got up and kneeled on the seat, looking out back. When they came to a stop light, a hot rod pulled up alongside them. The boys in the other car called out to Mark, "What year is it?"

"Nineteen twenty-four."

"Where'd you get it?" But the light changed and they were away again.

When they arrived home and undid the hitch, they got the chassis back into the garage and immediately started to assemble the parts. Soon they were up to their eyeballs in grease, there were parts strewn all over the garage, and from time to time other boys would come to see the progress, envious of poor little rich kid Reid. They would stand in silent envy, then drive away in their brand new convertibles.

Every time Jeff turned around Cherry was under foot; always handing them the wrong tool, axle grease on her face. Mark would say she wasn't in the way, but Jeff would say, "Will you get outa here? You're getting to be a regular pest." She would put her hands on her hips and talk back to him. "I have just as much right to be here as you. It's a free country."

"Listen, Cherry, get lost, you hear?"

"Okay," she would say in defiance. "I'm going home and tell mother."

Jeff would say, "Please do." After waiting for him to relent, she would finally go off in a huff. All she wanted to do was to be next to Mark, that was all. He was her first real love. Billy Haynes didn't matter any longer, he was her age, but Mark! If only he'd notice her. After her bath she would hold her nightgown around her middle, wondering if she should go on a diet. That's just what she would do—go on a diet and become a glamorous woman. But when she observed the silver caps and braces on her teeth, she would shut her mouth and try to figure out a way to talk without showing them. She began to practice speaking through her teeth with her mouth almost closed, but when she found how hard it was—it made a person's jaws ache—she gave up the idea. She would ask her mother to tell the orthodontist to take off the shiny silver caps and braces in front and substitute a halter that had to be worn only at night.

At dinner Linda began to notice that Cherry was eating less, which was almost unheard of since she was usually the first to sit down and the last to leave the dinner table, always taking the last potato, the last cookie, the last of anything. Up to now she had been very content to be on the plump side. It had never bothered her before, but then this was the first time she'd ever been truly in love.

"Finish your milk, Cherry," Linda said.

"I'm full. I can't eat any more."

"It wouldn't hurt her if she skipped a meal," Jeff said.

Cherry stuck her tongue out at him.

"How's the car coming, Jeff?" Greg Wallace asked.

"Great, dad. It's going to be the end, it's so fabulous, and the ideas that Mark's got are just too much."

"Yes, and they won't even let me help," Cherry complained to her father, hoping he would reprimand Jeff.

"Dad, you've got to talk to her, she's always in the way."

"Are you, Cherry, in the way?"

"No, I'm not, but big potato over there doesn't want me to have any fun."

"Now, Cherry, don't speak like that to Jeff," Linda said.

"Well, he is," leaning over the table and glaring at Jeff.

"She wants to be a lady mechanic . . . look, Cherry, why don't you play with girls?"

"All right, now, that's enough from both of you," Greg said, and a truce was called.

Toying with her food, Cherry said, "Mom . . . how do you feel about a girl marrying an older man?"

Linda looked at her, then realizing how serious she was, said, "Well, it all depends on the people, I suppose."

Jeff asked, "You have anybody in mind?"

"No, I don't, Buttinsky."

"Now, Jeff," then turning, Linda said, "Why do you ask, Cherry?"

"Oh, I was just wondering."

Jeff couldn't resist. "Why? Are you thinking of getting married?"

"No, I'm not, fresh." She turned red.

"Well if you do, send me an invitation."

She ran out of the room and up the stairs.

Greg was annoyed with Jeff. "Now, Jeff, I don't know what this is all about, but I resent your teasing her; she's no match for you. After all, you are a little older. Sixteen is quite a challenge for nine, wouldn't you say?"

"I wasn't, dad," he said, sorry that he had.

"Yes, you were, and I want this to stop."

"I know, dad, but honest, she's such a pest. She takes over at Mark's every minute of the day, she's into everything. You just can't pry her loose. She's leaning over his shoulder, or handing him the wrong tools. Honest, dad, today she just drove me nuts."

"Really?" Greg said, and then looked at Linda, who was looking at him.

"Are you thinking the same thing I'm thinking?" Linda asked.

He nodded his head. "I'm afraid so."

Jeff looked at one and then the other and asked, "What's the big mystery? Clue me in."

"You haven't guessed?"

"Guessed what?"

"That our little Cherry is in love," Greg told his son.

Jeff started to laugh. "In love with who?"

"In love with Mark."

"Come on, dad, you've got to be kidding."

"I wouldn't kid about anything as serious as that, would I?"

"Now I've heard everything."

"Not quite. You seem to have forgotten that one year when you were eight, you were so madly in love with one of your counselors at camp, we thought you were going to join the Foreign Legion."

"But Mark?"

"Why should that surprise you so much? He's just at the age where Cherry thinks of him as a Greek god. In about a year or two she'll have a dozen crushes, but this is her first real crush and that can be very painful. All of us have to be very understanding about it. Now I'll tell you what I want you to do. Treat her as though she were one of the boys. Let her help. Make her feel important, and you'll see that by the end of the summer, she'll even stop dieting."

"Okay, dad. I guess it was stupid to get so mad at her."

"Well, I don't think there was any permanent damage done."

After dinner Jeff went upstairs to see Cherry. He

walked in on her unexpectedly as she sat at the skirted dressing table in her room, all ruffles and ribbons, applying lipstick and making amorous gestures to her image. She had on a pair of Linda's high-heeled shoes. Jeff backed off, went part way down the hall, then coughed out loud so that she could hear him, giving her sufficient time to take off the shoes and wipe away the lipstick before he entered. When he knocked on the open door, she was lying across the bed like the death scene in *Camille*, waiting for Armand to appear.

"Cherry," Jeff said straight-faced, "would you do me a favor?"

She put her chubby arm across her eyes in a dramatic gesture, too weak and wan from all the years of suffering in exile. It was, in fact, difficult to breathe after having been told by her doctor that she had tuberculosis, and the thought of losing Armand was more than she could bear.

"Yes?" she said, the effort of speaking taxing her so.

"Would you come over to Mark's tomorrow and help? We're going to take down the armature and have it wound."

She leaped up in bed, forgetting Camille for the moment. "Would I? And how!" Then attempting to recoup, "That is, if you really want me."

"We couldn't do without you, are you kidding?"

She rushed from the bed, threw her arms around Jeff's neck and said, "You're the best brother a girl ever had." And then suddenly Camille appeared again as Jeff left—she stumbled back to the dressing table, barely able to make it, put on Linda's shoes, applied some lipstick with trembling fingers, and wondered what an armature was.

The first week in August found Mark missing Jeff terribly. Mr. Wallace had taken him to Baja, Mexico, for ten days' fishing, and Linda had gone with Cherry and her parents to Coronada. They would be gone for two weeks in all. Jeff had asked Mark to come with him and his father, but Mark declined, giving a lame excuse that he was so far along with the car. But he would not think of leaving Katie alone.

The night before Jeff and his father left, Mark lay awake in the dark with the radio playing softly and thought about how Jeff and his father were. Greg found time to do things with Jeff in spite of his law practice. The two of them went to ball games, played tennis on Sunday mornings, and every Wednesday during summer vacation they golfed. And then for one week each year at Easter time the whole family would fly to Hawaii. But the thing that impressed Mark most was the Wallace *family*—there was a sense of belonging in it that he had never experienced. Mark was frequently invited to dinner and he would sit back and take in the conversation and the closeness. They spoke at the dinner table with hardly any gaps in the conversation, it just flowed free and easy. Greg was not only interested in the car, he was interested in everything about his family, and for the first time in Mark's life he was really envious of somebody. How he did envy the Wallaces, their family, even little Cherry, a cute thing with the freckles, braces and all, her family never knowing who or what she'd be from one day to the next.

In the morning Mark called David. "Dad, how are you?"

"Fine, Mark. How are you?"

"Okay, dad. What are you doing today?"

"Nothing, just sitting here reading the Sunday paper."

"How would you like me to come into the city and maybe we could go to the ball game?"

David thought, God, how he hated baseball, but he did want to see Mark—he hadn't seen him in over a week. "Okay, Mark, that would be great. What time?"

"Well, it's ten now. I can be up in about an hour."

"How will you come up? On the bus? I could meet you at the station."

"No, mom will drive me up."

David winced even at the mention of "mom," but he said, "Okay, see you then."

Mark came into the city only about once a week for a few hours on Sunday to have dinner with his father. Afterward, David would put him on an early bus and Katie would meet him in Burlingame. Today especially he did miss Mark, although when they were together the strain of making conversation usually left him emotionally exhausted and edgy: he simply did not know what to talk to the boy about. Still, he longed for Mark to stay with him for a few days from time to time, but Mark refused, not wanting to leave Katie alone, thinking she might need him—well, in a way he *was* the man of the house. . . .

David was bored at the game in spite of all the shouting and action going on. It didn't communicate itself to him, but when Mark got up and cheered and waved his arms, David went along and did the same. At least he could make an effort to pretend to like what his son liked. After the game was over, and none too soon for David, he took Mark to a restaurant mostly patronized by men, where there was very little atmosphere but the food was excellent and the service good. He marvelled as he watched Mark consume salad, veal scallopini, spaghetti, dessert, and a big glass of milk *after* all the hotdogs, peanuts and soft drinks he'd had a few hours ago. Still, Mark was as straight as a stick without an ounce of fat. In fact, he was now as tall as David, and as he looked across at his son, he noted that his upper lip sported considerably more hair than a week ago. And the thought of Maggie flashed through to him. . . . Knowing Maggie, he was sure she could have won Mark over in time, and that Mark would have eventually accepted her. He might even have decided to live with them for a time. Why in God's name did he let himself go on like that? . . . He drank his wine.

After dinner Mark said to his father, "Dad, could we go back to your place? I'd like to talk to you."

David worried that he was going to bring up something about Maggie, maybe Katie *had* told Mark why he left and now Mark had decided to ask questions he'd been holding back. . . .

David seated himself in the large chair opposite

Mark, who began to tell him about the Wallaces in the house across the street—that Mr. Wallace was a very important tax attorney; that he smoked a pipe and wore a tweed jacket with suede patches at the elbow and walked his terrific cocker spaniel by the name of Keeper; that Mrs. Wallace was just beautiful, tall and slender with sort of sandy blond hair; and that they had a little girl Cherry who looked like her name, sweet and plump. The thing Mark did not tell his father was how he wished they were like the Wallaces, and that he longed for a sister and a brother. He said that Jeff had become his best friend, that he owned an MG—with four shifts no less—and that Katie would no longer have to drive him to school because he would go every day with Jeff. Mark told David how close they were as a family, about the things they did together and what fun they had. . . . Listening to him, it also occurred to David that whenever he was away there seemed to be a house sold on the street. He was surprised the Thompsons had sold that marvelous house and wondered why. And, despite himself, he thought about Dr. Silverman, who after much aggravation and expense finally sold the subdivided lot to the people who had bought the original house for practically nothing, and finally purchased a piece of property on the other side of Hillsborough in the Brewer tract, where Mrs. Silverman could build the house of her dreams. Well, at least that had worked out all right . . .

His thoughts were refocused when he heard Mark say, "Dad, I think I better call mom and tell her I'm taking a later bus. May I use the phone?" David pointed to it, then left, unable to bear the thought of being in the same room with her, even on the other end of the line. Looking out the window that faced California Street, he saw the cable car chugging along, and for a moment recalled the first day they had arrived in the city, remembering how Mark had looked out another window and called, "Train, train." How much had happened since that day. How long ago was that? A century? An eternity?

He turned around when Mark came to the doorway

and said, "It's okay. Mom will meet me when I call from the Burlingame station."

David walked back into the living room, impatient for Mark to get on with whatever it was he wanted to talk about. Suddenly he wanted to be alone.

"Okay, Mark, you said you wanted to talk to me?"

Mark's face grew tense, unsure of what David's reaction would be. Although David couldn't have been nicer these days, still Mark was like the little boy who had been burned and was afraid of fire, in this case the fire of his father's temper as he remembered it. Still, the thing he wanted to say pressed heavily on him. He studied his father's face, which looked haggard and tired; he couldn't remember his father ever looking quite this way, and he felt at once uneasy and sorry for this man who now sat opposite him.

"Dad," he began slowly, "I know you and I haven't spent a lot of time together"—adding quickly, "Not that it was your fault, I understand that, I know how hard you had to work and that your time wasn't always your own, like last summer not being able to come up to the lake and all. I didn't used to understand when I was a kid, but now I do. I still missed you a lot, but I understood . . ." He wanted to add thanks to Ralph Hansen, who gave him the idea to teach himself not to miss his father so much. He looked into David's eyes again and thought how difficult it was to talk honestly with your own father. "Dad, what I really wanted to say was . . . can't you and mom try to make up whatever happened between you?"

David winced, got up and walked to the window, not wanting Mark to see his face. Still looking out the window, he said, "No, Mark, I'm afraid that's impossible."

Mark got up and went to his father, standing behind him. "*Why* is it impossible?"

"You wouldn't understand."

"I know I don't understand a lot of things, but it seems to me that if you're a family you ought to try to stay together—"

"I'm sorry, Mark, I just can't go into it."

"Well, just tell me why can't you and mom find out what's wrong, why you fight? Isn't that what the psychologists are saying about kids, you're supposed to try to understand *them?* Well, then why can't grown-ups help kids understand them . . . ?"

David turned around and went back to his chair. "Because things happen with married people that you couldn't understand—"

"Okay, then tell me, dad. Maybe I will understand."

"Some people find that after they're married for a long time, they simply aren't right for one another."

"Does it take sixteen years to find that out?"

"Yes, sometimes it does and sometimes you know it before but don't do anything about it."

"You're right, dad, I don't understand, I really don't. I'd think that after all that time you'd get to love each other better."

"That isn't always the way it is. A lot of things happen in that length of time that can pull people apart."

"Don't you think mother's nice anymore?"

"This has nothing to do with your mother being nice or me being nice. It has to do with two people who are complete opposites."

"That doesn't happen to all people. Look at the Wallaces. They love each other."

"They're very lucky, but all people aren't the same."

Mark wasn't through. "Dad, you must have loved mother once. How can you stop loving somebody, especially when you're a family?"

"I wish I had the answers. I don't."

"You did love her once though, didn't you?"

It was almost more than David could do to bring himself to admit it, but he had to answer. "Yes, I did . . . once."

"And you don't love her at all anymore?"

David hesitated, then: "I wish I did, but I don't."

Mark bit his lip, he felt like he was going to choke. Finally he said, "Mom still loves you, dad, I know she does—"

David got up and began to pace. He realized now that Mark had no idea at all what had happened between his parents. She obviously had not mentioned his affair with Maggie after all. But Maggie wasn't the problem. Maggie and his falling in love with her was a consequence of what their life together had become. She'd never really gone along with him, had condemned him without words. How much better if she'd just come out with it—"I hate you for what you've done"—and have an end to it once and for all. . . .

He looked at Mark. "No, you're wrong, Mark. I know your mother doesn't love me and I know she hasn't for a long time."

"But that's not true, dad, it's not true. She cried at night when we were at Tahoe last summer. I used to hear her. She must have missed you."

"Sit down, Mark, and let me tell you something."

"Okay, dad."

"I know how tough this must be for you, a growing boy without his parents living together, but believe me, it's better for us to be apart than having you live with the two of us bickering all the time—"

"But it doesn't *have* to be that way, honest it doesn't. All we have are the three of us, that's all. Please, dad, please make up with mom, she wants you to come home." He had tears in his eyes.

"Did she say that or are you saying it?"

"No, she didn't say it," he snapped back, "but I know her better than you do. She's lonesome."

"Mark, please understand, I can't do that."

Mark's voice began to crescendo. "You could if you wanted to. You just don't want to because of your pride—it's just selfish pride, that's all it is. Why don't you think of someone else for a change?" He began to cry now, the tears streaming down his face. Then, with no more words, he threw his arms around David's neck and sobbed. "Please, dad, please come home and make up with mom so we can be a family again."

David felt awkward, strange with this man in his arms who stood as tall as he. Not knowing quite what to do with his hands, he finally put them on Mark's back and held him.

"We'll see, Mark." What else could he say?

Finally the tears subsided and Mark sat down, feeling sure he'd failed. They would never be a family. When Christmas came, his birthday, his graduation, he would want to be with both of them, and would have to make a choice that would never be the one he wanted—how could he *not* miss the one he couldn't be with? Sitting here in his father's apartment, he knew that this wasn't a home and that the house on Rosehaven wasn't either. They were just places where people lived. He looked about the room, hearing the clank of the cable car outside and suddenly he wanted to go home.

"Dad, I think I'll go now." He stood up.

David heard the words and suddenly, if it was possible, was filled with a feeling of complete emptiness.

"I'll drive you back," he said.

"No, dad, I can take the bus."

"No. Come on, Mark, I'll drive you."

"Are you sure you want to?"

"Of course I'm sure."

They spoke little on the way home. When they arrived and Mark got out of the car, he wanted to kiss his father good night but thought better of it. There'd been enough of that sort of thing for one evening. "Good night, dad. I'll call you during the week, thanks for everything."

"I'm glad you came."

"Me too. Well, good night."

David waited for Mark to disappear behind the tall gate, then drove up Summer Drive. He parked the car and looked down at the outline of what had once been his home, bathed now in the August moonlight. He remembered the day he bought it. He would never live there again. He loved that house more than anything in the world, except Maggie. Now they were both gone.

Maggie. All the way back to his apartment and once there over drinks that he knew he shouldn't have, he thought of her, gave in to thinking about her. He remembered those first days after she'd left, and days after that, when he'd be walking the streets and suddenly be sure he'd seen her, or that she was just up ahead, and then stealthily, like a thief trying to steal back the past, walk faster until he would be abreast of the person, and after a quick sidelong glance know what in his heart he knew anyway, that it wasn't Maggie. It wasn't going to be Maggie . . .

Still feeling anything of her was better than nothing, he took out the letter and reread it for . . . how many times? And no matter what he brought to it, it always read the same, said the same thing. Maggie was gone. Maggie was gone . . . Was he going to brood for the rest of his life. He still had a son, damn it, and he'd at least better get on with trying, the way she'd said, to be a father.

He poured himself another drink, picked up the phone and called Mark on his private line.

When Mark left his father he went into his mother's room; she had been reading, and now put her book down and looked up at him.

"Mark, dear, did you enjoy the game with your father?"

"Yeah, it was great."

She waited for him to say more, but he seemed withdrawn so she said, "I have a chocolate cake I baked. Could I get you a piece and a glass of milk?"

"No, mom, we ate at a swell restaurant." He wanted to add, I wish you had been there, but instead, "I think I'll go to bed now, mom, I'm a little tired, it was pretty hot out at the game today, sitting in the sun and all." He walked over to the bed and thought how beautiful his mother was. Why couldn't his father see how beautiful she was, and gentle and loving. He bent down and kissed her on the cheek, then left.

He lay in his room in the dark and thought about Jeff and his father, knowing they probably hadn't arrived yet but closed his eyes and saw them standing together, casting their lines out into the blue water and waiting for their catch.

The phone ringing startled him. "Hello."

"Hi, Mark, are you asleep?"

"Dad . . . no, I'm just lying here daydreaming."

"Same here. Mark, I've also been doing some thinking . . . How would you like to come up to the lake for a few weeks?"

His first impulse was to say, and how, dad, just the two of us? But just as quickly he thought of Katie alone in her room, and quietly, not wanting to seem to be turning down his father, said, "I'd love to, dad, I really would, but I just can't leave mom . . ."

There was a pause. Katie. Still in the way, as she would always be. Katie and *her* beloved Isaac . . . was there to be no relief from them? "Well, your mother's been alone before, hasn't she?" He could hardly say the word "mother."

"Yes, she has, but, well, it wasn't like now. You know what I mean. I'm sorry, dad, I'd really like to—"

"Okay, Mark, I understand. It's okay. We'll do it some other time."

"Sure, and I'll see you next Sunday. Thanks for asking me, though."

Placing the phone on the cradle, David wondered if there were any place on this green earth where he could find a little peace. He made up his mind right then he was going to sell the house at Tahoe. It was only an expense and besides, Mark wouldn't go up this year and who knew what would happen next year? . . . Let next year take care of itself. It was tonight he worried about. If only he could go to sleep tonight, and not dream.

From that Sunday evening until the end of August David increasingly thought about what Mark had said to him that night. Maybe what they both wanted couldn't be solved, but maybe there was something in between that would at least partly work for them both. Mark was asking for, begging for, David to be together with his mother again as husband and wife. David needed relief from the awful loneliness of his life, his strange apartment, his separation from *everything*—good and bad—that had made up his life. All right, Maggie was out of his life forever, where did he turn to make a life of his own? It was almost three months and he could foresee no change for him, no relief—how could there be without friends and without desire to seek them out? A woman would certainly not be the answer. But being alone without anything familiar was like being cut off from humanity. How much could a man read, how long could he remain alone? The days were at least filled with people and decisions. It was the nights, those damned long lonely nights. Katie had everything—the house, Mark. He provided for them and wound up with a fat zero. He didn't begrudge Maggie her way out, and hoped she would be happy, at least have the contentment as the years went by, that she said Peter would give her. And Peter Douglas, well, at least he loved her, and he'd been there when she needed him most. For him, her love wasn't necessary—it was enough for him to have her at all.

At first David refused even to consider going back to living under the same roof with her, but as the weeks and months passed slowly, so very slowly, his opposition began to crumble. Was it maybe worse to live the rest of his life like this than to go back to a life that was not much better? After all, it was easier to live with things that were familiar. Besides, he loved that house, he could at least walk on Sunday mornings among his hydrangeas and stand outside savoring the physical beauty of what he had worked so hard for. And there was the presence of Maggie in that house too. It was she, really, who had given it its special personality, and left something of herself in it. And there would be Mark. Why should Katie have the constant companionship and he be left out in the cold? He hoped Mark would one day come into the business.

He would teach and train him. The more he thought on it, the more logical it seemed that he should go back to what was rightfully his. And even if they could never be reconciled, at least they could appear to be a family and Mark would have a big part of what he wanted so badly. He would establish a life apart from her, and they would try to avoid each other as much as possible . . . and he would also be able to keep his eye on things. He never forgot that Katie could finally destroy him by exposing his true background, either to Mark or to his business associates. . . .

He called Mark on Labor Day, recalling, as the phone rang, that it was Mark who had brought them back together the first time. Of course, this coming together would hardly be the same; but still it would be through Mark that it would happen. He would not lie to himself that it was all for the sake of his son, even though that would have to be the way he made it appear to Katie. He was entitled to *some* face-saving, wasn't he?

It had been a fine Labor Day weekend for Mark and Katie. Mark worked all day Saturday and Sunday on his car, which was progressing nicely with the exuberant help of his friends, especially Jeff. Saturday night he had some of the guys over for games of cards and Jeff Wallace spent the night.

Katie spent a lot of time in the greenhouse and visiting with Mark, although being careful to stay out of the way of the busy workers. She felt at peace, the first real contentment she had known in many years.

On Labor Day they went to a barbecue at the Wallaces'. It was a beautiful day, there was plenty of food, and the group was in boisterous good spirits—more than one person ended up in the pool involuntarily.

Katie enjoyed herself thoroughly and returned home that night in a state of delicious exhaustion. As they came through the front door they heard Mark's phone ringing. He raced upstairs to answer it.

"Hello," Mark answered.

"It's me, Mark, how are you?"

"Fine, dad. I'm really glad you called. What a great day we had!"

"I'm glad to hear it. . . . Mark, how is your mother?"

Mark heard the question in amazement. His father had never mentioned her name once in all the months he'd visited with him. He also sounded strange when he asked, but Mark immediately answered, "Okay, dad, she's okay . . . I guess," adding that last to tell him she really wasn't okay, that she would only be okay if he came home.

He'd at least begun. Now he'd need to go easy, feeling his way into the right approach. "What do you mean, 'you guess'?"

"I mean she misses us . . . being a family."

"You mean she misses you when you're with me."

"*No*, us."

So far, so good. "Oh, come on, Mark, you know better than that. Did she ever mention my name to you in all these months?"

Mark cleared his throat. He couldn't lie about something like this, even though he was very tempted. "Well, she maybe doesn't actually mention your name, but whenever she asks me about how you and I spent our day, she always does it so that I know she still misses you, dad."

"Really? In what way?"

"Well, for instance, she'll say, 'Did you have a good time with your *father*?' and I can tell she would have liked to ask more, it's the way she says it . . . I just know she's not mad at you. Believe me dad, I *know* it."

"You really think so, huh?"

"I know so, she'd want us to be a family again too." Mark paused and wondered if he dared bring up again the idea of his father coming back home. It had seemed so hopeless a couple of weeks ago, but maybe he'd made a deeper impression on his father than he thought . . . maybe if he were tactful and didn't push his father too much, and if they could avoid an argument, maybe, just maybe . . . "Dad . . . have you thought over what we talked about a few weeks ago?"

"What about?" David asked. It really was going well, he thought.

"About us being a family, and you and mom trying to make up, no matter what happened before?" Mark gripped the phone nervously.

"Oh, that . . . well, as a matter of fact, Mark, some of the things you said did get me to thinking, and you're the one who did it. Now, Mark, you want me to be honest with you, don't you?"

"Yes."

"Okay. I thought carefully about our conversation after you left that Sunday and began to realize, like you said, how tough it can be for a boy growing up without both his parents. Well, to get right to it, I decided—after a lot of debating with myself, mind you—that I haven't exactly been the greatest father in the world and that, seeing how you feel, the least I could do was be willing to give it another try."

Mark's reaction surprised both of them. He didn't want to be the only reason his father came home. He didn't want *that* much responsibility, it scared him. He wanted his father to come back because he wanted to, because he wanted them to be a family again, too, and because in some way his mother still meant something to him down deep. Mark was sure she must. He just couldn't bring himself to believe that parents who were once in love, and had had a child, could ever just stop loving each other. Especially these two people, whom *he* loved so much.

"Is anything wrong?" David asked, worried by Mark's silence.

Mark was not sure how to answer, but hadn't his father said that they should be honest? "Well, dad, you know how much I want you to come home, but . . . I want it to be because *you* want to as much as me—"

"Well, Mark, sure I do. You know, we've seen each other enough for that, you know I haven't exactly been having a great time myself. But this could all be beside the point . . . what makes you think your mother would be willing?"

Quickly Mark blurted out, "Oh, believe me, dad, I know she would—"

"How can you be so sure?"

"Because I do—"

"All right, I'll tell you what. You go and speak to your mother. Now be honest and tell her that *you* were the one who brought it up in the first place, and let's face it, Mark, although I may want to come, you still are the main reason. It does mean a lot to you, doesn't it?"

"Yes, it does . . ." He only wished it meant as much to his father, but he'd settle for whatever he could get at this point—it was far more than he had dared hope for and maybe after being separated from his mother for three whole months, when he saw her again maybe he'd realize how good she really was and . . . maybe.

"Okay, Mark, you tell your mother I'm willing to try again if she is. But we've both got to be willing to give it a fair chance. She's got to be as much for it as you and I are . . ."

"Dad, I'm so glad. I just know it's going to work out."

"Okay, Mark, let's hope you're right—"

"I know, I'm sure she'll go along when I tell her what you've said." He wished he were as sure as he sounded. He really had no idea how she would react. Well, at least half the battle was over.

The conversation had gone on for nearly an hour. When they finally said good-bye and hung up, Mark flopped on his bed, totally wrung out.

After the lovely day she and Mark had had with the Wallaces—really a nice family, she thought—Katie had taken a bath and refreshed, was propped up in bed, relaxing with a book. She smiled at Mark when she noticed him standing in her doorway.

He walked into the room and sat down on the bed next to her. Once he'd recovered from the exhausting conversation with his father, he couldn't wait to talk to her.

"Mom, will you be honest with me?"

"I always try to be."

"I know, but this is very important."

"I promise."

"How do you feel about dad? I don't mean about all the fights, I mean about him as . . . a person."

This was one thing she couldn't be honest about. She couldn't and wouldn't say she thought him deceitful and selfish, and that the most peaceful time in all the years of her marriage had been the last three months, living without dissension, subterfuge and tensions. No, she could not be honest. "Your father's very smart, very ambitious, and he's become an important man. I can understand your liking to be with him. These last few months have brought you closer, and I think that's good."

"That doesn't answer my question, though. What do you think of *him*?"

"Well, my dear, I've just told you."

"No, you haven't. You didn't say how you felt about him as, well, your husband."

"Well, that's very difficult because a man can be many things. He can be the things I've just mentioned, which are very appealing to the world. A man can also be a father, and his children see him a certain way. And then again as a husband he can be something entirely different—"

"You're not answering me. I don't care about the world and children. I'm asking how *you* feel—"

She hesitated. "All right," she said, "but you're going to have to let me tell it in my own way, because nothing is black and white, or cut and dried. You're going to have to learn that—"

"That's okay, just tell me."

"When I married your father I loved him, very much, but as the years went on he began to fall out of love with me. I don't condemn him, I was partly to blame. But as we continued being together I began to find it almost impossible to show my love to a man who didn't respond to it—I reacted like any other person. Now please, Mark, I'm not talking against him—"

"You're still not answering me."

"What do you want me to say, that we haven't been very happy together for a long time? What do you want me to tell you? You know that."

"You can tell me if you still love him, no matter what happened between you."

Why was Mark bringing this up? She had finally reconciled herself to her life as it was, had found some peace and a small place for herself. Did she still love him? No, she didn't think so. Or at least she couldn't forgive him for the unforgiveable. But somewhere, down deep, she guessed she did still love the boy she met on the ferry boat that day, the one who knocked at Malka's door at eleven o'clock that night, who brought her the red satin heart box of candy. Even now, in spite of everything, she still loved that small part of David that had fathered their child . . . but what was this sudden interrogation all about? And how was she going to answer her son without really answering him? He was no longer a child . . .

"Mark, darling, please try to understand, this is important at your age. I don't want you to think that all marriages are the same, or that all love is the same."

"Tell me honestly, mom, do you have any feelings at all for dad?"

She wasn't getting through to him. "Yes, I suppose I do, but in a very different way than I think you mean. After all, he is your father, and there were many good things in the past—"

It was as much as he was going to get from her, he'd better not wait any longer to take advantage of it. "Mom, dad and I had a long talk—that was dad on the phone—and I'm going to be honest with *you*. I asked him about trying to start over again, I mean the two of you, so that we could be a family. I can't remember all the things that we said, but dad wants to come home—"

She stared at him, shook her head in disbelief. "Did *he* tell you that?"

"Yes, he said that both of you should try . . . for all our sakes."

"He said that?"

"Yes, especially for me and besides, he loves you, mom, and he's unhappy and very lonesome—"

"He told you he *loved* me?"

"Well, no, not exactly, but then you didn't say it about him either. I don't care what's happened between you—if you'll both try, then maybe you'll find out that you still do love each other, at least more than you thought. . . ."

Katie lay in her bed unable to move. The years came rushing at her, all the things they had said to one another . . . How could she go back . . . ? Of course he wanted to come back now that he had no place else to go.

"Did your father bring all this up?"

"No, I told you, I'm the one who did. Somebody had to."

Mark was angry. If she didn't go along, Mark would blame her and she knew it. David had cornered her. She would lose Mark, and he'd never be able to understand why.

"Mark, dear, please listen to me, will you?"

"I'm listening."

"There are a great many children whose parents don't live together, and many of them learn to live a good life. I wish you could believe that I am considering you, but this won't work for your father and me. I wish it would, but it won't, please believe me—"

"It would if you wanted it to, you're just being selfish. At first I thought it was all dad, but now I'm beginning to see he was right to move out. You're the one who stopped loving him, you just said so. Just like you've stopped loving me. Well, that's okay, because I don't love you anymore either and if dad wants me I'm going to live with him. At least he cares about me." He slammed the door as he left, then ran across the hall to his bedroom.

She was shaken, and trembling with rage. Oh yes, David, congratulations. You've won again. Either I give in or I lose my son. Not much choice, I'd say. Well, no use putting it off.

Doing her best to compose herself, she got out of bed, walked slowly to Mark's door and knocked.

"All right, Mark," she said evenly, "I'm shocked by some of the things you've said, but we'll talk about that later. You can tell your father that I'm willing. But don't expect miracles."

She started to turn and leave, then stopped as she felt his hand tentatively on her shoulder.

"I love you, mom, and I'm sorry for what I said. I could never stop loving you, no matter what. I just want us to be a family, that's all. We belong together. We don't have anybody else."

CHAPTER TWENTY-NINE

In the beginning they found it impossible to meet each other's glances, avoiding one another whenever they could, but for Mark's sake what recriminations were felt, they tried to hide. On the surface they seemed decent enough, polite, but they spoke to each other only when necessary. For Katie, David's presence was a constant reminder of Maggie Kent—of the lie; for David, the sight of Katie was like a knife in his heart—she was between him and Maggie. But he showed little of it. At least, as he'd planned, he was living among the things, the possessions he loved. This house *was* Maggie, and instead of it being a painful recollection of what might have been, it was as though she had left him this small part of herself. Katie's most rewarding compensation was that she had kept her son's love and respect, the total reward of her life. Mark was happier than ever before. He had what he wanted: his parents, his home intact; school was a joy, he was finding he was very good at track, his grades were A's. Jeff drove him to school and after class—Mark had a driver's permit—they would go up to where the traffic was very sparse, up to Skyline Boulevard, and Mark would take the wheel of the MG, whose right-hand drive felt strange to him—strange but exciting.

As the months passed David moved his affairs further south to San Jose, and again was completely immersed in plans and blueprints and trips to Los Angeles. He continued to miss Maggie unmercifully, but the trips gave him the relief he so desperately needed.

The seasons changed. Thanksgiving. And then the spirit of Christmas was in the air. All the houses on Rosehaven Road were decorated—except one, the Wallace home. It did seem strangely out of place without the festive outdoor lights. Almost, in fact, forbidding. When David arrived home one evening, he slowed in front of the Wallace house, and he began to wonder. With two children, especially a small girl? He asked himself why, and suddenly, of course, understood.

Upstairs, the door to Mark's room was open. Christmas paper and ribbon was strewn on his bed.

"Hi, dad," Mark said as he continued wrapping packages.

"Hi, Mark, what's new?"

"Lots. Right after the first of the year we're going to be ready to take the car down and have the great painting. Bet you never thought we'd make it . . ."

"Bet you're right . . . You said 'we.' You mean the kids across the street?"

David's voice had an odd sound in it, and Mark looked up in surprise.

"Sure, that's who I mean . . ."

"Tell me about them—I mean, what sort of people are they . . . ?"

"What? They're the greatest, dad—"

"Well, they don't seem to care much about their kids . . . here it is Christmas and they don't even have any decorations or—"

"They're Jewish, dad, that's why. Jeff explained to me why he isn't going to give me a Christmas present —they don't give presents at Christmas but they have something where they give presents every day for a week, I think Jeff said. It's called something like Hanaka, I'm not sure. But I'm going to give him one—"

David looked suddenly very drawn.

"Dad, what's wrong?"

"Nothing, son, nothing at all." He paused. "Mark, something's happened that I can't discuss with you right now, but I'm going to tell you something you might not like, but you must still obey me—"

Puzzled, Mark asked, "What's that, dad?"

Quickly David said, "I just don't want you to be friends with Jeff—"

Mark dropped his scissors and looked, dumbfounded, at his father. "I don't think I heard you right—what did you say?"

"Yes, you did. I don't want you to be friends with Jeff."

Mark got up slowly and looked at David, trying to comprehend. "Dad," he said, "you've *met* Jeff. What could you have against him?"

"Listen, Mark, I don't want you to question me—"

"Well, why not? Jeff's my best friend." Mark was very angry now. "You come in here and out of a clear blue sky tell me you don't want me to be friends with him, and you don't want me to ask why?"

"That's right—"

"Well, you gotta give me a reason. What have you got against him? Did he do something you didn't like?"

"No."

"Well, then you just can't tell me you don't want me to be friends with my best friend—"

"Yes, I can. I happen to be your father, and as your father it's up to me to be concerned about the kind of friends you have—"

"What are you talking about?"

"You heard me."

"No I didn't, because you didn't say anything. Jeff's the best friend I ever had. I love his whole family—"

"Look, Mark, I don't want an argument about this."

"No argument?" He looked at David incredulously. "You're the one who always says let's be honest. Okay, let's. *What do you have against Jeff?*"

"Just calm down now, let's not have any temper tantrums."

Mark snapped back, "Well, how do you want me to act? You want me to stop seeing a boy who's my best friend, you don't give me any reason and you want me to be calm?"

"Okay," David said, his anger now showing, and feeling panicky in his desperate need for an excuse that deep inside himself offended him without his being willing or even able to acknowledge it. . . . "Okay, Mark, I'll tell you but I don't expect you to understand completely, which is why I tried not to—"

"Then tell me, give me a chance to understand."

"Well, Mr. Wallace has been known to be very unethical in some of his business dealings, Mark, and this is hard for a son to know about his father so I beg you don't talk about it to Jeff, it would just make things harder, but you can't always tell about somebody by the way you see them at home or just on a social basis. Matter of fact, even though I haven't met him personally, his firm and he personally have been involved in something that's caused a serious business problem for me, Mark, and that's as much as I'm going to tell you, except to repeat that hard as it may be for you right now, I have to ask you—no insist—that you do not see Jeff anymore—"

Mark slumped down on the bed in disbelief. "But how can our friendship affect any business deals you have with his father?"

"Mark, that's it. I've told you all I intend to. You're going to have to learn someday that maybe I know just a little more than you do, and that if I say somebody isn't desirable—"

"Not desirable? Who said so? Jeff is one of the best-liked guys at school—so what do you know?" His voice was getting louder as he talked.

"Listen, I'm not going to stand for you raising your voice, do you hear me?" His eyes were hard, but Mark stood his ground.

"You don't have the right to tell me what friends I should have."

David came nearer to Mark, looking into his face, and in a low angry voice said, "Oh, yes I do, I have every right."

Mark met David's glance. "No, you don't."

"I'm warning you, don't talk to me like that." David's fists were clenched. He wanted to slap him, but controlled himself. "Listen, it's a damned funny thing, you don't mind going along with me when it's for something you want . . . like the house in Tahoe where you had a ball all summer, and the boat, and when you asked me to come home I did, didn't I? But when I ask you to do one thing for me, and tell you it's important for you not to associate with people like that, you fight me."

"What's all that got to do with Jeff—a house, a boat, and your coming home? You wanted it as much as I did."

David took hold of him by the front of the shirt, started to speak, got control of himself just as Mark pushed his hand aside, ran out of the room and down the stairs into the garage. He looked to see if the keys were in David's car—they were. He jumped inside and started the engine, drove out the driveway, up the hills of Summer Drive toward Skyline Boulevard full throttle. He wanted to smash the car. The sweat was pouring out of him. God, how he hated his father! And thinking it, felt a chill of terror . . . a guilty chill. . . . But at that moment he wished David had never come home. Faster, faster he drove around the sharp turns until he hit a chuck hole in the road and suddenly came to a stop. He turned off the engine, his breathing labored from anger, then put his head down against the steering wheel. What was he doing? He must have gone out of his mind for a while. He thought of his mother. If anything happened to the car, she would get the brunt of it along with him; matter of fact, if anything happened to him, she'd be in bad trouble. He had to face it, there was something just plain wrong with his father. He acted crazy sometimes and who knew why? Well, as far as he was concerned, after tonight, whatever he and his father had built up between them was not going to be the same. He wouldn't take anything from him again; he'd earn the rest of the money for his car on his own. Maybe Mr. Wallace was giving his father some kind of business problem, but Mark thought his father could learn a lot from Mr. Wallace when it came to being a husband and a father . . .

David had not heard the car being started. When

Mark ran down the stairs, David went to his room, and Katie followed him. She stared at him. "I think that's the most unforgiveable thing you've ever done, and you have done some damned unforgiveable things in your life. How *dare* you deprive your son of a friendship that means so much to him? I heard every word. You couldn't stand him having a Jew for a friend anymore than you could stand Dr. Silverman living in the next house. You couldn't stand the living proof that there are Jews in this world who are able to live as well as David Reid, that what you did wasn't even *necessary* to get what you wanted . . . and now your son might discover it too . . . Oh, damn you, why did you come back?"

"That bothers you, doesn't it? You'd like to have punished me, right? Kept me in some kind of permanent exile for all my sins. Well, you're the one who's going to be punished. You're going to have to live with me in the same house. You wanted me so much you wouldn't let me go. Okay, here I am . . . Now, if you don't mind, get the hell out of my room."

She stood her ground. "I'm going to get the hell out of your room, as you so delicately put it, but you're going to get the hell out of this house. I don't want you here."

"I'll see you dead first. If you don't like it, *you* leave."

"Oh no, not this time. This is not Chicago. This is my house, and you're not welcome."

"Your house?" he shouted. "Why, damn you, just where the hell would you be if I hadn't bought it for you and your son—"

"It's my son I'm thinking of." Her voice was icy calm now. "You're not a good influence on him."

"Oh really? Well, what do you propose to do?"

"I don't have to do anything, you've already done that. I doubt Mark will ever forgive you after tonight. What do you think he'd say if he knew the truth . . .?"

"Why don't you tell him? And while you're about it, tell him you lived with me all these years knowing this awful truth, let's see how much he thinks of a mother who sold out her beloved heritage herself for a little security." David paused, caught his breath. "Now, you listen to me and listen carefully. Don't ever threaten me again, do you hear, because if you do, I'll take Mark away from you."

Frightened, but still trying to keep her voice calm, she said, "Take Mark away from me? In what way do you think you could possibly do that?"

"Don't you worry, I can do it."

"No, you can't, not after tonight. Mark won't even talk to you—"

David laughed. "Don't you worry about me and Mark. Tonight won't mean a damn thing—I'll see to that. He's my son, do you hear me? He and I have things together you can't share and never will. He's angry now, sure, but he'll come around. He'll have . . . I'll see to it. And unless you want him to really hate you, there's not a damn thing you can do about it. Now, once more, get the hell out of my room."

Katie looked at David and realized he was capable of anything. There *was* no way to justify herself in her son's eyes for having stayed all these years. She could think of no way he would not hate her for telling him the truth. . . . She turned and left, knowing she had buried herself in the coffin of her own revenge.

Later that night, after he'd calmed down enough to get into bed and try to get some sleep, Mark began to think about what had happened. It still just didn't make much sense, except . . . he remembered his father's big deal about Jeff and the Wallaces came right after he'd told him the Wallaces were Jewish. It was hard to believe that could have anything to do with it, not for *his* father, and yet he remembered now another argument—a real bad one between his mother and father about something awful his father had done because, she had said, *the people were Jewish*. . . . It was hard to understand it, or to accept it, but thinking about it Mark was pretty sure he knew, finally, what his father's real reason was for not wanting him to see Jeff, God . . . *why?* And the question was overwhelmed almost as soon as it surfaced by the more immediate—and important—one for him of figuring out what he would tell Jeff. They were just too close for him not to tell him the real reason instead of trying to pass off his father's senseless excuse. At first he thought of not telling Jeff anything and seeing him anyway, but that wouldn't work . . . not at home, where his father would know about it and might actually say something to Mr. Wallace or Jeff. . . . God, he'd die. No, he'd have to go along, but he'd tell the truth. After all, how could he say, Listen, Jeff I want us to be friends but my father doesn't want us to be . . . I don't understand why, but I can't do much about it and if I don't go along it will only make things worse for us all . . . He simply couldn't drop Jeff without a word, without an explanation, and when he thought of little Cherry, he cringed. Could he say, Look, Cherry, you'd better leave because you're not desirable! He thought of speaking to Katie in the morning, but the more he thought on it the more he realized she didn't seem to have much more influence with his father than he did. He had encouraged his father to come back and start again, and now that they had at least sort of made up he would be the cause of another rift between them—he was already feeling the weight of it on his fifteen-year-old shoulders. If he spoke about his father's unfairness, arguments would be the result, and his mother would be more unhappy. He couldn't do that to her. . . . So he lay awake half the night trying to work out the most important decision in his life: how to tell his best friend they could no longer continue their friendship. When he thought about it, about how he wouldn't be able to ride to school with Jeff any longer and work on the car and be over at the Wallaces' . . . he wished he were dead.

Exhausted, he got out of bed at six, dressed and hurried down the stairs and across the street, went around the back of the Wallace home and sat in the garden, waiting for Jeff to wake up, knowing it was still too early for him.

"Good morning, Mark." Willie Mae let the cocker spaniel out. She stood by the open screen door as the dog leaped up on Mark, who hugged and petted him, holding him close.

"Now get down, Keeper," Willie Mae said.

"No, he's okay, really." Mark held the dog even closer. Mark wondered if Keeper knew how undesirable his master was.

Willie Mae asked, "What are you doing out here so early?"

"I'm waiting for Jeff to get up."

"Well, for heaven's sake, you can't sit out here in the cold. Come into the kitchen."

He followed her inside, feeling guilty in spite of himself because he was already defying his father. Besides, who knew, he thought bitterly, maybe seeing Jeff would corrupt him in some way, maybe the undesirableness would rub off on him—

"Did you have breakfast yet, Mark?"

"No, I'm not hungry, thanks."

"Oh, come on, have a cup of coffee—here, I just fixed a pot."

"Thanks, Willie Mae," he said, not wanting to hurt her feelings.

Cherry came into the kitchen in her long robe. When she saw Mark she was embarrassed. "Hi, Mark," she said, wishing that she had known he would be here this early in the morning; she must have looked like a mess.

"Hi, Cherry, is Jeff up?"

Wanting to seem sophisticated she said, "I don't know, I'm sure."

"Good morning, missy. What's it going to be today?" Willie Mae asked.

Cherry shot a glance at her, treating her as though she were just a child. "I'm going to skip breakfast this morning, thank you."

Willie Mae put down the frying pan on the stove and looked at her. "You feeling all right?"

"Of course," Cherry said with irritation. "Why shouldn't I?"

"I don't know. This is the first time you ever skipped breakfast since you had the measles."

Without another word Cherry turned and fled from the room.

Mark felt very uncomfortable, thinking that perhaps he was in the way. "Maybe I'll leave and come back?"

"Oh, don't be silly, just sit still. Shirley Temple will be back in a few minutes asking what we got for breakfast." It was about eight-fifteen when she said, "Why don't you go upstairs? I think Jeff is probably up by now."

"You think it's all right?"

"Sure, the family will be coming down soon."

"Thanks, Willie Mae," he said, leaving the room.

He knocked on Jeff's door.

"Yeah?" Jeff said, sounding half asleep.

"It's me—Mark. Can I come in?"

"Sure, come on in."

Mark opened the door and found Jeff in bed lying on his stomach, rolling over as Mark stood near the bed. He sat up, stretching, and said, "What's cookin'?"

Mark licked his lips. Plenty, he thought, but he said, "Nothing much."

"What are you going to do today?"

"I don't know."

Jeff looked at him. "Hey, what's wrong? You look like you're mad or something."

Mark turned away and faced the window, he could see his father's room through the shutters; then he turned and sat down on the straight-backed chair and straddled it.

"What's wrong, Mark, did you have a fight or something?"

God, how would he get through this, how was he going to begin and, more important, how could he tell Jeff what had happened without having him think his father was some kind of a nut or something? Boy, this was going to be tough, but there seemed no way out so he answered, "Yeah, I had a fight with my father."

"Well, what's the big deal? It happens to me too sometimes," Jeff said as he yawned, flexing his muscles and putting his hands behind his head.

"It does?"

"Sure. You think we always agree on everything? The only thing is, my dad's a lawyer, so by the time he gets through he usually convinces me he's right, and I guess he usually is. I don't let him know I think so, but I got to admit he puts up some pretty strong arguments—"

"Hey, I didn't think you ever argued with your dad."

"Sure, every kid does. So what? It's not the end of the world."

"Does your dad ever tell you you can't do something, no good reason, you just can't?"

"No, not really. We usually talk about it and sometimes he leaves it up to me."

"Hey, that's great."

"Yes, but he puts up some pretty stiff opposition and sometimes it's plain no. Anyway, I'm going to be a lawyer too, so I use some of his own arguments against him." Jeff laughed as he turned on his side and looked at Mark, realizing he was bothered by something between his dad and himself. (And Mark, listening carefully, could find no parallels between his father and himself and the Wallaces.)

"What's the problem, Mark?"

He shook his head.

"It helps, Mark, really, when you've got a problem. I know, that's when I go to my dad."

Mark looked across at his friend and at that moment Jeff seemed so much older than he, even though there was only a year's difference in their ages. He sat there feeling like a little tongue-tied kid.

"Listen, Mark, I don't know what the problem is with you and your dad, but I'm sure if you sat down together, you could work it out—"

Mark turned his eyes away—if only Jeff had an idea how impossible *that* was. He began slowly, "Listen, Jeff, if you had a very good friend, in fact your best friend, and your dad said he wanted you to stop seeing him, what would you say?"

Jeff thought carefully. "Well, the first thing I'd do is ask my dad why."

"And suppose you asked and the reasons didn't make any sense to you at all?"

"Well, then, let's take it another way. Suppose the father was convinced that the friend wasn't the kind of a boy he thought was right for the son, then I guess the son ought to listen and take a good look."

"Even if the boy thought the father was wrong?"

"Well, I said listen and think about it. I don't know, maybe the father had some information that was really bad and didn't want to tell the son—"

"And what if he didn't? What if the father was just way off base, then what?"

Jeff thought for a moment, then said, "Well, Mark, then I think that the only thing the kid could do would be try to put up the best argument he could and take it from there . . . Let me ask you, Mark, do you have that kind of a problem?"

Mark placed his hands over the top of the chair, holding on so tight that the knuckles showed white. "Yes."

Jeff shook his head. "Well, it's hard to know what to say. I really don't know the story . . ." He waited for Mark to answer. Finally to break the silence Jeff said, "Okay, let's put it this way. Is this kid the kind of a guy your father doesn't want you to pal with?"

Mark just looked down.

Jeff continued, "All right, at least ask yourself what's wrong with—"

"Nothing is wrong with him," Mark snapped back, looking at Jeff.

"Okay, don't get steamed up, I just asked."

"I'm sorry." Mark cleared his throat, but before he could begin again Cherry was knocking at the door.

"Can I come in?" she said, opening the door, not waiting to be invited.

"What do you want?" Jeff asked, irritated.

"You're to come right down to breakfast," she said like Mother Superior.

"Tell Willie Mae to skip it, I'll be down later."

"She'll be mad if you don't come down now."

"No she won't."

"Then can I stay?" Her hair was combed and she'd changed into another robe, her very best, which was used in cases of emergency such as when she was recovering from the mumps.

"No, Cherry, you can't."

"I'm going to stay. Mark doesn't mind, do you, Mark?"

"Of course not, Cherry." He was in fact grateful to Cherry for having given him this moment of relief before going on with the ordeal.

"See, Mark doesn't mind," she said, sitting herself on the edge of the bed.

Jeff threw back the covers, jumped out of bed and towered over her. "I do," he said. "Now please leave."

She stood with her hands on her hips and said, defiantly, "What will you do if I don't?" That should certainly prove to Mark that she was mature, standing up to Jeff, that she was a woman to be reckoned with. Nobody had the right to talk to her in that tone of voice.

"Okay, I asked you in a nice way, I said *please*, now I'll show you what I'm going to do." He picked her up around the waist and stood her outside the door.

Narrowing her eyes on him, she said slowly, deliberately, "I'll never forgive you—never, never." After all, a woman did have some pride, and she ran down the stairs to the kitchen, where she instructed Willie Mae to fix breakfast for her immediately.

"Sorry about the pest—"

"Well, I suppose she feels left out. That can be a pretty bad feeling, Jeff."

"I know, but sometimes she gets in my hair."

God, how he wished he had a sister to get in his hair—he'd even settle for a Keeper.

"Okay, Mark, where were we?"

Mark took a deep breath. "Jeff, I'm going to tell you about this because there doesn't seem to be any other way out." He hesitated, then quickly said, "This will sound crazy, Jeff, but my dad doesn't want us to be friends anymore."

Jeff looked at him in surprise. They had been talking about *him*? "Why, did I do something he didn't like?"

"Not exactly."

"Well, then, what?"

"I don't know how to say this, Jeff, without hurting

your feelings. If we hadn't been such good friends, I would have just dropped it there—"

"All right. So what's the problem?"

He swallowed hard. "God, I know this is going to hurt your feelings, Jeff."

"So my feelings will be hurt—it won't be the first time . . . Now why?"

Mark asked hopefully, "Is your father suing my father, or something?"

Jeff laughed. "I doubt it. My father doesn't even know your father, and he really likes you and your mother. I'm sure he'd never do anything like that—at least, without talking it over with all of us and your family first. Why?"

"Because that's the reason he gave me. But something like this happened once before, so I know the real reason."

"And what's that, Mark?"

There was a long pause, then Mark said without looking at him, "I'm pretty sure my dad doesn't want us to be friends because . . . you're Jewish."

At first Jeff couldn't answer. Then he said quietly, "And that's the only reason?"

"Yes."

"Wow," Jeff said shaking his head, "I guess there's a first time for everything." They were silent for a while and then Jeff said, "Look, Mark, this has nothing to do with you, you're not responsible for your father. I think it's stupid, even if he has his reasons for feeling that way. But that doesn't change my feelings for you. You're still my friend, and if you want to be mine we can at least see each other at school."

"But this means we can't . . . you know, like work on the car together."

"Well, it's too bad, but it's not the end of the world."

"Maybe I can still talk to him."

"No, even if you convinced him now, I could never come to your house knowing I'm not welcome. I'm sorry about this, Mark."

"Me too."

"But please don't let your father influence you about something like this."

Mark couldn't say any more. He felt ashamed for his father, and horribly embarrassed. It was a first for Mark too. The first time *he* had ever experienced anti-Semitism, and it had to come from his own father . . . He had never even known a Jew before—if he had he wasn't aware of it. He just couldn't see where the Wallaces were in any way, shape or form different from the Reids.

"I wish I could understand all this, Jeff, but I can't. I'd like to think maybe I'm wrong about his reason but I know I'm not. There just isn't any other . . . All I can say is I hope you will still be my friend and, well, thanks for being so really great about everything . . ."

Jeff put his arm around Mark's shoulder. "It's okay." The two boys walked downstairs. As Mark left, he said, "Do me a favor."

"Sure, Mark, what?"

"Please don't tell your folks about this, all right?" He paused. "I don't want them to know. Just say we had a fight or something. Will you do that?"

"Yeah, I'm glad you feel that way, because I'd rather not tell my folks."

Jeff took Mark to the front door, remembering what a nice guy Mr. Reid had seemed when he'd met him. He was obviously rich and successful, had a great kid like Mark, a nice wife . . . What in the world, he wondered, would make a man like that feel the way he did?

All week long David had thought about his behavior with Mark, feeling increasingly unhappy about it and somewhat less certain about his ability to recoup his ground with Mark than he'd blustered to Katie. She was right in a way, of course. Mark wasn't going to forgive him overnight, but David was determined that eventually he would. Part of it was that he was going to make sure that never again would he leave the field so clear and easy for Katie with their son. Just the opposite from now on. It was his son too, damn it, and if he'd been less than a perfect father—he had no great illusions there—he at least had been changing that some already and would continue to do so with even more effort. It had begun with the lonely days in the apartment in the city when Mark had come to visit him and they had begun to be around each other and talk enough to feel as though they weren't such strangers—maybe not exactly ordinary father-son (though that was emerging more too, he thought) but in a way sort of friends. And best of all, as friends he discovered that he actually *liked* Mark more, and thought that Mark was beginning to feel the same about him.

The fiasco with Mark over the Wallace boy—damn it, the past seemed always intruding on the present just when he'd thought he'd finally buried it—was a setback, no question about it, but he wouldn't let it lie there to get worse and for Katie to point to as one more transgression of the wayward father. No, not this time . . .

"Yeah?" Mark called out from his room in answer to the knock on his door.

"Can I come in?" David asked.

Mark's heart began to pound. He just couldn't look at his father; in fact, he didn't want to talk to him at all. He wondered if he would ever be able to face him again, and yet he couldn't bring himself to say, "No, I don't want to see you." "Okay," he said.

Mark was lying on the bed with his hand behind his head, staring at the wall, noting that the picture was askew. He didn't look up as he waited for his father to speak.

"How are you, Mark?"

Mark wanted to say, How do you think I am—you should know. "Okay," he said.

"I'd like to talk to you. Why don't you come on into my room and—"

Mark said, "I'm tired."

Quietly David persisted. "Mark, I'd like to talk to you about a few things if you don't mind." His voice was friendly, casual, but Mark wanted to say, Why? Do you want to find out if I've met any more Jews? Instead he said, "Can't we talk here?"

"Mark, I'd really appreciate it if you'd come to my

room. We can relax and have a good talk. Man to man, for a change."

He could imagine what kind of a man to man talk they would have. "What's it all about, dad? I'm really tired."

"So am I. It's been a pretty tough day and I'd like to get out of these things and relax. Come on, please."

Reluctantly he got up and followed David into his room. He sat down uncomfortably as David went into his bathroom-dressing room, turned on the water taps, washed his face and hands, put on a dressing robe and came back. He poured himself a glass of wine from the decanter that was on the table near his favorite chair.

"How about you, Mark. Would you like some?"

"No, I don't drink." You'd think his own father would know that. Words ran through his mind as he recalled the look on his father's face, holding him by the shirt. He squirmed now in the chair.

"Look, Mark," David began, his voice low and easy, "I know what happened the other night was tough on you. I've got a temper—I guess that's no secret to you." David sensed Mark's tenseness, but went on. "I was wrong to come at you all at once that way. I admit it—"

Wow, Mark thought, what a great admission for the big ME to say he was wrong. Well, maybe someday they'd even make it to the moon if the great David Reid could admit that. Mark said nothing.

"Look, I want us to be friends. I'll say again that I'm sorry about *some* of the things I said to you, Mark, but I had my reasons and I still do." . . . Solly, Silverman, this Wallace . . . what did they know? Lawyers and a movie producer . . . their *world* was Jewish, they still lived in a ghetto, never mind if they made more money than their fathers had ever dreamed. A high-class ghetto, but *still* a ghetto. He had moved out, struggled, fought and spent his life to *build* something for himself that belonged now in the wider world outside. Every time one of them came too close, threatened his place in the real world, he could see it all coming apart, see himself tumbling back to the ghetto.

. . . All of them, even his son's friend, were a threat. And he would protect himself no matter who or where or what the cost . . . He looked at Mark, wondering if he could ever understand and knowing as he thought it what the answer was. Still, he needed to try to keep his son.

He sipped his wine, eyeing Mark, who glared back at him. It was moments like this that the boy infuriated him, reminding him of another boy and another father long ago in a ghetto tenement, a long time ago when Isaac got the word of God straight from heaven, and expected his son David to swallow it whole.

Forcing back his memories and the sudden rush of anger, he said in as calm a voice as he could muster, "You know, Mark, parents aren't always right and I've already said I wasn't right to lose my temper with you. But I have learned a few things that can be of use to you, and one of them is that if you want to get ahead in this world and have a good life you've got to be friends with the right people. You were seeing too much of that Wallace boy—"

Mark shook his head. "Look, dad, I don't know about any of this stuff. All I know is the Wallaces are the nicest people I've ever met. As far as I'm concerned, telling me I'm not supposed to see Jeff Wallace is just being crazy—"

David took another sip of wine; he wasn't going to let Mark get to him. "No, it's far from being crazy . . . Mark, do you think the Wallaces were born with that name?"

"How do I know?"

"Well, I do know, and believe me they weren't."

"How do you know?"

"I know because, well, Wallace just isn't a Jewish name—"

So I was right, Mark thought miserably, and said aloud, "Well, so what does that mean? They're still nice people. Maybe that's their real name, but even if it's not, they'd be the same no matter what, whether it was Smith or Jones. What difference does a name make?"

He wished he could really tell him and get it over with—and was dismayed by the temptation. "You're missing the point. What I'm saying is that when people have to go to the trouble of changing their names, that *usually* means they have something to hide . . ." (He should know.) "Now do you begin to understand what I'm saying?"

"I don't know, dad, it's all too complicated for me. Names, the Wallaces being Jewish. . . . I just don't understand any of this . . . By the way—what the heck are we? I mean, what *religion* are we?"

David swallowed hard. This was an impossible situation that he had been maneuvered into, again thanks to Katie. She'd said she'd never have another religion (he'd forgotten he'd also said the same). She should at least have done it for her beloved son, and now what could he say? "Well, Mark, we haven't worried much about things like that. I can tell you this, though. *You have nothing to be ashamed of.*"

"Big deal, I never thought I did . . . Look, dad, maybe we can talk about this some other time. I'm really worn out . . . may I be excused?"

David knew he had not gotten through to him, but there would be other nights and other times—this was only the beginning.

"Okay, I know it's all pretty confusing, you just haven't come up against situations like this before. But you'll be experiencing more of them from now on, and more than anything else, Mark, I want us to be friends and for you to feel that you always can come to me for help or advice. Will you at least remember that?"

Mark went to the door; he did not look at David as he muttered under his breath, "Yeah, I'll remember that." He closed the door quickly behind him, not wanting his father to see the tears that were suddenly making it difficult for him to see even what was right in front of him.

The following months helped more than anything David could say or offer. Mark had developed into a young man of generosity, of very little vindictiveness.

He was flexible and—like Katie before—had an inbred need of family. He also had an unquenchable need for love, and to give love, and the ability eventually to bounce back from hurt and anger. He had compassion, he responded to gentleness, he froze in an atmosphere of hostility and anger. He also had a spine—and when it came to settling for his principles he would not capitulate.

David wanted a son back. But if in the process Katie was more and more separated from Mark, the person she cared most about in her life, well, maybe her loss was well-deserved.

It was an intricate, double-edged game. Shortly after the first of the year it began in earnest.

"Mark," David asked one evening, "what happened to the car?"

"What do you mean?" Mark asked sullenly, not looking at David.

Disregarding the reaction, he said, "I mean you haven't been working on it since Christmas."

Mark looked up now and appraised David. This was the first time his father had shown any interest in the car. Why now? . . . What did his father care if he took the back road with Katie on the way to school in order to avoid Jeff in the morning? What did he care if the car was a painful reminder that he and Jeff had worked on it together, that they used to talk far into the night about how the car would be when they finished it, lying awake in the dark on the nights when he'd been invited to sleep at the Wallaces' or when Jeff slept over? What did he care? And, besides, Mark had promised himself he would not accept another dime even as a loan from his father for the car, he was going to build it all on his own if it took forever.

"That's right, I didn't want to."

"How come?"

"Because I haven't *felt* like it."

"Why?"

God, his father could be dense. "I guess I just haven't been in the mood."

"I know, but you wanted to have it all built by your sixteenth birthday, which is only two months away."

"So what?"

David was teaching himself to have patience. He'd better, he thought. "Mark, I know you've been very angry at me and I'm sure you've thought you'd never be able to forgive me for coming between you and your friend. Believe it or not, I'm not that dense (Mark looked up, startled). I also realize nothing I say at this time in your life is going to convince you that one day you'll thank me . . ."

Mark sighed.

"I'm trying to make up to you for what you think I've done. I'm asking you to start all over again—the way you once asked me to do with your mother—"

God, was he going to bring that up again?

"Mark, I wish you'd also remember this. You'll have a lot of friends in your life. Some of them will stick and most of them won't. I'm your father . . . I'll stick. Besides, and believe this or not . . . (Maggie was momentarily beside him now) . . . I happen to love you—"

Mark had begun to stand up, but was rooted to the ground. He studied his father. He'd never spoken to him like this before. Perhaps it was difficult for a man who had been raised an orphan to say what he felt. That was pretty much what Ralph Hansen had told him once. He was still convinced his father was terribly wrong about the Wallaces, about Jeff, but, even if he didn't come out and say so, maybe his father's dealings with *some* Jewish people had turned him against all Jews, which Mark felt was wrong. He knew that all people were not the same, and he could never blame the Wallaces for whatever his father had thought was wrong with some other Jewish people . . . Anyway, he knew in this area he and his father would always be in total disagreement. Putting that aside, though, whether they agreed or not, wasn't his father entitled to his feelings? Did he have a right to hate his father for trying to do what he honestly seemed to think was best for his son . . .? At least for the first time his father really wanted to be a father. Should he turn him away? Did he want to . . .? "Okay, dad, I'm going to think about what you said."

David held out his hand to Mark, then pulled him close. They were like a father and son together for the first time in a long time.

Later that evening David lay awake wondering if he ought not to keep the house in Tahoe now. He was sure Katie would not come up to the lake with them . . . so as not to antagonize Mark, he'd ask her anyway. If Mark blamed her when she declined, well, that was okay with him. Besides, it would be good for him to revive himself for a few weeks at a time. He would hire a housekeeper on those days when he had to come back on business to the peninsula; he would make sure that Mark invited enough boys to occupy himself through the summer when he was away. This summer would really cement their friendship, Mark would forget about Jeff, Katie would be less important in his life. And he'd begin to have a life again. . . .

Mark had refused additional money to complete his car, even after he and David had come to an understanding that evening, and for a while the vestiges of resentment lingered. He wanted to prove to his father that he could do it on his own.

"Mark, I like the idea that you don't feel because your father's got a little money you can always expect a handout," David said, "but the point is this, you can't work after school and keep up your grades. It's just too difficult. Ask me—I know, and I don't see any point in your going through the same thing when it's not necessary. If I thought it was a character-builder or something, I'd say go ahead and kill yourself. But really, nobody ever got character by pointlessly knocking himself out. Okay? A deal?"

Mark looked down at his shoes. His father was becoming really decent. Even his mother had said love doesn't always last forever. Well, neither does hate . . .

At last on his sixteenth birthday Mark revved up the motor on the Red Chariot. Up the driveway he went with a fanfare from his friends from school who came over for the launching. Behold, there she went, red and shiny with white vinyl upholstery, and two of the most enormous solid chrome headers on either side.

From that day on he was the most important boy at school. He parked the Red Chariot out in front and nobody dared touch it, well, at least not after the time he let them know how strongly he felt.

One day after school he found three boys he hardly knew sitting in his car. Controlling his anger, he said, "Okay, fellas, out!" All three of them began to laugh and mimic Mark. One of the boys sitting on the trunk, his feet on the upholstery, said in a falsetto voice, "Okay, fella, out! or Marky-warky will slap your wrist."

Mark stood glaring at the driver. "Okay, I'm telling you for the last time . . . out, fellas!"

They all laughed uproariously. "Better not talk like that to Marky or he'll tell the principal, and boy, will we be in trouble! Wheee . . ." They screamed with laughter, stamping their feet.

The third boy said, "Better watch out—old man Reid's a big man in town and he'll put us in jail for not being polite to his Marky-warky—" Before he'd finished Mark had reached over, pulled the driver out of the seat and had the boy on the ground. The other two immediately jumped over the side of the car and were on top of Mark, pinning him to the ground.

"Okay, hot stuff, what are you gonna do now?" Mark squirmed and kicked. He ripped his shirt trying to pry himself loose as his knee came up and hit one of them in the stomach. He yelled in pain. Mark stood up, but the other two were taking pot shots at him. By now a crowd had gathered.

"Damn you!" Mark said, blood trickling from his nose and running into his mouth. "Why don't you fight me one at a time and I'll take you on?" But they were all over him, now he was down on the ground again and they were belting him. He finally managed to get loose while the spectators cheered for one side and then the other, their hands cupped around their mouths, everybody with an opinion. "Leave him alone, two against one, that's not fair" . . . "Come on,

Mark, you can take 'em, they're chicken" . . . "Hey, you better break it up, you guys, fighting on school ground" . . . "Oh, God, I can't look," one of the girls said, putting her hands up to her face and looking between her fingers. . . . "Give it to 'em, Mark" . . . "Come on, Mark."

Soon the principal stood before Mark, holding the other two boys by the backs of their shirts, and someone said, "Just when it was getting interesting," but Mr. Whittaker said, "Everyone go on home—"

When the crowd had dispersed he said, "Okay, now tell me, who started this?"

Mark forced himself to his feet. He could hardly stand. He picked up a part of the torn shirt and wiped his face, and felt his nose—he thought it was broken.

"Okay, come on now, who started this?"

Nobody said anything. Mark just stood, gaining his strength back slightly as he balanced himself against the car, pressing his nose—it was still bleeding. He also had a black eye.

"All right, I want you to go to the locker room, Mark, and wash up, and I want to see the three of you in my office immediately." He turned and crossed the school grounds followed by the three of them.

After Mark had washed he examined himself. Now that the nosebleed had finally stopped, the worst damage was that his eye was almost closed. When he got to the principal's office, Mr. Whittaker was seated behind his desk, his face stern.

"All right, now someone start to talk." No one said a word. He pointed to the boy who had been behind the wheel. "Okay, Pete, let's have it."

"It really wasn't anything."

"I see. How about you, Bud, anything to say? And you?" pointing to the third boy. A head shake was his answer. "And you, Mark?" Same. "All right, I've had plenty of trouble before from the three of you so you're suspended for two weeks. You, Mark, are off the basketball team for the rest of the semester."

The three left, kicking up their heels in the hall, free for two weeks. When Mark realized he wouldn't be able to play in the best game of the year, he wished he could have taken these creeps one by one.

When he got home, Katie was so shocked she decided to go up to school the next morning. What kind of ruffians were they, anyway?

David laughed and said, "I think that's great, Mark, there's nothing like a black eye to get a little respect. I hope you kicked the hell out of them." He shook his head, no he hadn't done that, and he begged Katie to drop it. She did, but not without protest.

He was secretly pleased at his father's approval. Now he could hardly wait for June.

CHAPTER THIRTY

June finally arrived after a seemingly endless winter.

"Well, you always wanted us to go to the lake together, and this time we're going," David told Mark.

It was hard to break old habits—"Dad, can you get away?"

"Yes. I have some things going on but they'll just have to wait."

"You sure?"

"You bet. I think it's time we got away together for a while. We'll leave the day after school lets out. You ask as many boys as you want to stay for as long as they want."

Mark wanted to hug his father. "Hey, dad, I've looked forward to this."

"Me too, Mark. It'll be great for all of us—"

That night Mark said to Katie, "Mom, isn't this the greatest? Dad's going up to the lake with us this summer—"

"I'm not going this year, Mark." (Thereby unwittingly fulfilling David's expectation.)

God, it was starting all over again. Now that he had his father the way he wanted him, he was beginning to have problems with his mother. She had to put a damper on everything.

"Why, mom? Give me one good reason why?"

She could have given him many good reasons why. David had not asked her. It would mean going to even greater lengths to keep out of each other's way. At least at home she had her own room, her greenhouse, her piano, her volunteer work. They could at least operate as civilized enemies under one roof. But in

Tahoe there would be no place to retreat, and the danger of an outright eruption would be too great. So she declined, knowing full well that David never wanted her in the first place. For one wicked moment she was tempted to say yes.

"To begin with, I really think this would be a wonderful thing for just you and your father. You've talked to me about it so many times, how your friends go away with their dads, and now you have the chance." She suspected she was not being very clever . . .

"It's not the same," he insisted. "They go away for only a week or two, but this is different."

"Did you ever think that I just don't feel like going?"

"Sure," he said, nodding his head in defiance, "sure. But I know that's not the reason and so do you."

She looked at Mark. My, how he had changed. She wasn't sure she could understand. Was it all part of growing up? He was, after all, sixteen, no longer a little boy. She had never known him to take her to task this way before except that one time about David's coming home.

"Mark, it hurts me that you're acting this way . . . just what is the reason you think I'm not going?"

"You're not going because you want to blame dad for everything and you know it."

"That's unfair."

"But it's true! If it weren't, you'd come."

"I'm sorry, but I have some things to do too—I have to please myself occasionally. Besides, you'll be with your father, and that's something you've looked forward to for a very long time."

"Okay, mom, if that's the way you feel."

He walked out of the room. Wasn't it strange, Katie thought, Mark had always seemed able to excuse David through all the years for *his* absences. The summer that he was involved with Maggie Kent and hadn't come up once to the lake, Mark had thought how sad it was that his poor father remained at home working so terribly hard on the shopping center while they enjoyed all that he had worked to get. Katie wondered how much compassion Mark would have had if he had known the real reason. She was tempted to find out, but knew it would be self-defeating. Mark needed to love his father and to think the best possible of him. If that were to be changed now, it would be David, not she, who would manage it.

That summer was the best in Mark's life. And for David it was a time to escape and relief such as he'd never imagined possible. He swam with Mark, learned the fun of boating and let Mark teach him how to water ski.

In the beginning Mark called Katie twice a week and continued to try to persuade her to reconsider. She could not, so he eventually gave up.

The next two years seemed to slip by with relative ease for Mark. He entered the Red Chariot in the Hillsborough Concourse d'Elegance, won first prize in the custom-built cars division and was on the cover of *Hot Rod* magazine. He went out for track and broke his own record. More than one girl at school said she'd give her eyeteeth to date him. He was neither shy nor aggressive with them. His phone rang incessantly and he was invited to every party. Scholastically he was an A student in everything but math, which he hated. His best subjects were English, history, and literature, which was still his favorite subject, and he was drawn to art and music; and now foreign languages that he'd fought so hard against were coming easily to him. In the senior yearbook he was prominent in the-most-likely-to . . . "We expect great things from our budding tycoon. Like father, like son. Good luck, Reid." When he graduated, it was with honors. From here on his whole life seemed secured and planned for him.

What the yearbook did not say or know was that what he hated most in all the world was his father's business; and now there seemed to be no alternative. David had taken it for granted that when the time came he would go into the organization and become his right arm. He depended upon Mark to carry on, and in recent years had trained him and taken him on business trips. Mark enjoyed the varied places they went, as well as being with his father, but his mother always being home alone and his father saying, "Why don't you get your mother to come? . . . it would be so nice if she were along, there's really no need for her to stay home . . ." took the edge off things. Mark did try with his mother, who always refused (except for once, when she had tried for Mark's sake. That one time had been such a disaster that even Mark had been unable to ignore the truth of the situation). There would be an exchange of angry words, and he would blame her for not co-operating with his father and brusquely leave her room, thinking that she always seemed to want to play the part of the martyr. . . .

CHAPTER THIRTY-ONE

Spring, 1954

"Now, there are two fundamentals with which we must concern ourselves . . ." That was the last of the lecture Mark heard as he sat listening to Professor Wheeler. He wanted it to appear that he hung onto every word, but he was, in fact, thinking about why he had come to UCLA in the first place. The longer he stayed the more he disliked it. A year and a half had come and gone since the day he drove down. He was accustomed to a country atmosphere and had misgivings about being so completely cut off from his friends, and family—whom he'd almost reconstructed, such as it was, single-handed. Menlo School for Boys didn't count because that too was familiar territory, as well as being only twenty minutes from home.

Then there were misgivings about a fraternity. He had selected one out of the three that had rushed him after discussing the final choice with his father. In fact, he now turned to David for most all of his decisions, David making it clear that, of course, in the final analysis he had to make up his own mind. So David suggested—only suggested, mind you—that Mark select the one that was considered to be the most desirable on campus—the boys he would meet there all came from prominent, influential families, and the friendships bound to develop during four years of living together would certainly do him no harm in later life. . . .

"Be selective," David said. "It's better to be alone than to throw in with just anybody—"

Well, he had considered his father's opinion, but not without some beginning self-searching. At Hillsborough he had no real decision of that kind to make—for the most part the kids there came from the same well-to-do background. Also at Menlo. When he went to Burlingame his friends were mostly from upper-income middle-class families, and he didn't much notice or care what their fathers did. He always tried to play down that his father was wealthy so that he would be accepted—being a rich man's son could be a problem.

Now he was on a new threshold. Still feeling uneasy about it, he forced himself to consider his father's advice and finally accepted the so-called best fraternity on the campus, at least the one that seemed to have the most prestige. But after living there for a year and a half he couldn't forget or overlook the initiations and the hazings. He detested the blackballing of two boys, one of whom almost committed suicide, and he was repulsed by the comments on the incident: "If he was that weak-minded, then who needed him?" . . . "He didn't belong if he couldn't take it" . . . "This is when you separate the men from the boys" . . . They were not only snobs, they were bigots. It had only been for his father's sake that he'd worried he might not be accepted, but when he was asked to put down his religion he entered "none." That—so far as he knew, of course—was the truth, and he'd be damned if he'd fudge it. They'd have preferred it if he'd gone to a private boarding school, and they raised a few eyebrows at his "no religious preference" notation, but he was otherwise seemingly out of the approved mold and so was accepted. He hated every minute of living there, but he stayed, feeling that after all the right fraternity was so important to his father and he at least owed him that. . . .

He recalled conversations with both his parents—separately, of course—about his choice of college. They went, he realized, very much as one might have predicted. His mother, wanting him near home but not wanting to influence him unduly, saying that she honestly didn't see any special reason for him to go

East to college when they had such fine places as Stanford right at home, and being obviously delighted when he told her that was sort of what he'd decided as well. And then his father changing all that the summer he graduated from high school, the two of them alone at the lake, spending lazy summer evenings on the moon-lit deck, David casually asking him if he'd made up his mind about Stanford and Mark wondering what his father thought and drawing out of his father precisely what David wanted him to draw out: like his mother, agreeing that going East wasn't necessary; that he really could get a good education in his chosen (by David) field, Business Administration, almost anywhere, but that he really needed to start going out on his own just a bit more, get out from under his mother's influence—of course, he hastened to add, "I don't mean she's purposely done anything wrong, but . . ."—and so that left UCLA, not too far but at least clearly away from home . . . And later, Mark deciding his father was right, that it was time he stood on his own more and made his own decisions and stuck to them and so he decided on UCLA. Of course he couldn't know that his father's motives went beyond helping him strike out on his own, that they included the relief David would feel at not having to pretend so much with Katie as long as Mark was out of the house for extended periods, and he knew as well that Katie would be angered at this change in plans, feeling, as she did, deprived by Mark's absences from her during the summer with his father. As for Katie, she tried not to show her disappointment, doubting that in the process she was entirely successful, or that she once again was not coming across to her son as the martyr of the piece. It appeared that David had, once again, had his way. . . .

Mark was brought up sharply as he saw everyone getting out of their seats. He stood up and walked out of the lecture hall along with the rest. He walked around the campus listlessly for a while, then sat down, took out a letter he had received from Jeff and re-read it.

Jeff was at Harvard, his father's alma mater, and apparently loved it. Mark wondered why he couldn't be more like Jeff, be more sure of himself and what he was doing. He felt part of it at least was the subjects he was taking. Never before had he found school so unrewarding and difficult. He disliked his professors, disliked being in classes so large that he felt like a number rather than a name. The first year he barely passed. At the beginning of the second year he found himself only slightly more resigned.

At home for an Easter vacation, he tried speaking to his father about it.

"Dad, I've never had such a tough time in school before. I just don't know what's wrong with me."

David looked at his son. "Let me give you a little piece of advice. To begin with, you've always had things come fairly easy for you, right?"

Mark nodded.

"You got good grades without any sweat because you excel in the things you like to do . . . but life is one big challenge with lots of self-discipline needed, and if you don't have that, it beats you down. Take my advice, Mark, whether you like it or not, beat the hell out of it. Remember that what you're doing is only a means to an end, the best part of learning is your life, and that still lies ahead. . . ."

"Thanks for the advice, dad. I'll try harder." But Mark's perfunctory answer to his father's fatherly advice left him no less dissatisfied.

He took the Red Chariot out and drove around town, visiting with his friends from home. They talked about the colleges they were attending and for most of them it was all great. One was going to be a doctor, a few had joined the Air Force, and all of them said how lucky he was, he really had it made. . . . One afternoon, not really thinking why, he drifted out to Burlingame High and looked around. There was a whole new set of faces; it seemed as though he'd been away for a hundred years. He actually felt old as he stood there, remembering that this was where he'd spent maybe the best moments of his life. He looked for his old track coach, more fond of him than of any other teacher, even including Ralph Hansen. Neil

Swanson had been his mentor, had encouraged Mark to go out for pole vaulting, worked hard with him—how well Mark recalled the patience Mr. Swanson had had with him and the hours they'd spent together. Unfortunately Mr. Swanson was away for the Easter vacation . . . Suddenly Mark had an enormous desire to go over the bar. He looked around the school for the janitor and saw Mr. Jenkins, who must have been there for fifteen years. Mark was delighted as he called out, "Hi, Mr. Jenkins, remember me?"

He adjusted his wire-framed glasses. "Sure, you're Mark Reid, one of the best pole vaulters we ever had here."

Mark's face lit up. "I didn't think you'd remember."

Taking his handkerchief out of his back pocket and mopping his forehead, Mr. Jenkins said, "I'm not that old, you know, I remember boys from ten years back."

Mark shook his head. "That's great, Mr. Jenkins. I wonder if you could do me a favor?"

"What's that?"

"Could you let me use a pole? I kind of feel like going at it again—"

The old man scratched his head. It was against the rules during vacation to take any of the equipment out of the locker room; but after all, Mark had brought a lot of glory to old Burlingame, it didn't really seem too much to ask. "Well . . ." he said slowly, "I shouldn't do it, but come on and I'll fix you up."

First he jumped eleven feet; he was breathless, then put the crossbar higher; he jumped over, hardly making it, he was so out of practice. He inched it up higher and made it—barely. This time he was determined to see if he could still make thirteen. He backed off, stood poised for the right split second that he always felt before taking off for the vault. A peculiar feeling always came over him when he dug his cleats into the ground, and when he felt the momentum within himself grow to bursting, he vaulted up into the air, missing the crossbar as it came down on him, and landed heavily on his feet, twisting his ankle. He sat in the sawdust looking ahead at the playing field and watching the new kids playing softball. As though to compensate for his present failure, memory evoked the sound of cheering from another day only a few years ago. What wonderful days those were. He had promised himself then the one thing he never would do was go into his father's business, and here he was, preparing for that very career. How had *that* happened? Well, what was he really suited for? When he asked himself what he would rather do, he had to answer in all honesty that he had no idea. His life was ready and waiting for him when he finished next year. Maybe, Mark thought wryly, he ought to lie back and enjoy it . . . like the old bad joke about the lady being raped . . . which ironically put him in mind of the first girl he'd ever had any sexual relationship with, well . . . sort of a relationship.

It had been at one of the sorority dances. He'd danced with this one particular girl, lithe and intense, who danced very close to him. Whenever he looked around, she was always there. Later she took him by the hand and led him to her parked car. "Let's get away from this, it's so boring . . ."

He couldn't remember what he'd said—probably nothing—as he got in. He winced, though, at the memory of his sudden apprehension—apprehension nothing . . . naked fear—which he doubted he'd ever forget. They drove to a small place off-campus, stopped the car, turned off the motor, switched off the lights and before Mark knew it his zipper was down, he was pulled on top of her and she was kissing him with her mouth wide open and going through all kinds of gyrations . . . within seconds it was all over for him. It was awkward, and frightening; and for the girl even further from being satisfying. "Get out of my car, you little pipsqueak, giving me the idea on the dance floor you knew what it was about . . . Get out!" She opened the door, he got out and she drove away, leaving him standing there. He was ashamed, he'd been so clumsy, and angry with himself because this was the first time he'd ever been with a girl in that kind of situation and he didn't really know what to do. For one month he worried that she might be pregnant. He was terrified. The next time he had anything to do with a girl, he promised himself, it at least would be on his terms. Thinking about it now, he was able to laugh. He was barely eighteen when that happened, green as apples from Burlingame High. It had been his first encounter, a sort of rape itself, and it had been perpetrated on *him,* especially his pride. . . .

He got up off the ground, brushed the sawdust from his pants, got into the Red Chariot and drove home, having learned something of more value than his college courses to date. . . .

Time could be cruel, and generous. And it at least could always be depended on . . . never to stand still.

With new determination—if not conviction—Mark returned to school. The first day that classes resumed, he had an eight o'clock in the morning; his next class wasn't until one in the afternoon. Too restless to go back to the fraternity house for the time in between, he walked aimlessly about the campus. Finally he went to the student cafeteria, bought a doughnut and a glass of milk, found a table and sat down to read. Across the table from him sat a young man with sandy-colored hair and blue eyes. They nodded at each other.

"Hi," Mark said, "you're in my psych class, aren't you?"

"Yes, I am. What are you reading?"

"Oh, this crazy thing"—he showed him the title.

"I took that last year—it's rough, I know. Incidentally, my name is Eric Brauch."

"Glad to know you. I'm Mark Reid. You had trouble with it too?"

"At first, but there's sort of a formula. If you can get that, you've got it made. Here, let me show you." Eric turned to a page and began to show Mark the fundamentals and the trick in working out the answers to equations.

"It's simple when you do it, but I'd never find the same answer in a million years."

"Yes you would. Let me show you again." He began with another problem.

"That's great," Mark said. "I think I'm almost beginning to get it—"

"Listen," Eric said, "if you get into any trouble I'd be glad to help—"

"You would?" Mark said in amazement—this guy was a total stranger.

"Sure I would."

"What fraternity do you belong to? I just might take you up on your offer."

"I don't belong to any fraternity; I live at home with my folks. Let me give you my phone number." Eric wrote out the number on a small piece of paper and handed it to Mark.

"Boy, that's great. I sure do appreciate this."

"Forget it, happy to help. Well, I've got to get back to class. Nice meeting you, Reid, see you around."

Mark watched as he disappeared. What a nice guy. He then turned back to try the problems on his own. Finally he gave up. It was all so simple when he'd been shown, but for some reason the technique wasn't working at all now.

He slammed the book shut and thought he'd get back to the fraternity house, maybe call his mother, as promised, instead of waiting for this evening. His last class was over at four. Feeling really down, he went back to his room and started working at his math—by now his most terrifying, and most despised, subject. Skipping dinner, he kept at it until six, by which time he wanted to tear the book to pieces. Finally he picked it up and threw it against the wall, then stretched out on his bed, totally frustrated. There was no doubt about it, he was going to flunk, he knew it. He thought, guiltily, of his father's injunction . . . "Do the things that come hard, it develops character," et cetera, et cetera. Staring up at the ceiling, arms crossed over his chest, he suddenly remembered—what was his name? Getting up, he went through his pants pockets for the number but couldn't find the slip of paper. He looked again, then remembered putting it between the pages of the book, which was on the floor. He picked it up, flipped through until he found the piece of paper, went downstairs to call.

"Hello," the voice at the other end said. It was a thick, guttural, foreign-sounding voice.

"Is this the Brauch residence?"

"*Ja.*"

"I wonder if I could speak to Eric Brauch, please."

"*Ja*, I go call him to the phone."

Mark waited. "Hello?"

"Er, yes," Mark said, feeling embarrassed for a moment. Here he had just met this guy and already he was asking help from him. "This is Mark Reid. Remember? We met in the cafeteria today."

"Sure, Mark. What can I do for you?"

"Listen, you could do me a big favor—"

"Sure."

"Explain once more how you get the answer . . . Wait a minute, I have the book right here—"

Before Mark could turn the page, Eric said, "Look, why don't you come over?"

"You mean it?"

"Sure, if you feel like it. It's a lot easier if we sit down together and go over it—"

"I'm not interrupting anything?"

"No, not at all. Besides, it won't take more than a half-hour. It's pretty simple when you catch on—"

Mark was reluctant, but he was also desperate. "When shall I come over?"

"Let's see, we're having dinner now. Say about seven-thirty, okay?"

"And how, it's okay. I'll be there. Thanks a lot."

Eric gave him the address, and not knowing how long it would take, Mark left at seven o'clock. The Brauchs lived in a white two-story stucco house about five blocks from Wilshire Boulevard, one of many such dwellings along a wide boulevard lined with palm trees. A few of the lawns appeared in need of reseeding, and some of the houses could have used a coat of paint. It was seven forty-five when Mark rang the bell—he hated being late.

A short, solidly built woman in a blue cotton dress, braids wrapped around her graying blondish hair, answered.

"*Ja?*" she said through the screen door.

This must be Eric's mother, Mark thought. "Yes, I'm Mark Reid, I'm here to see Eric."

She appraised him, then nodded. "I call Eric."

Mark stood uneasily before the open screen door as he heard Eric being called: *"Mach schnell, einer deiner Freunden ist hier."* Having come to America with the Brauchs, Hilde spoke only German. Although she understood English perfectly, Eric had long since given up trying to get her to speak it; nevertheless he always responded in English.

"Okay, Hilde, tell him to come up."

"Ja," she said, making her way back to the door and taking it off the hook. Mark felt her eyes on him as he went up the stairs. Eric was waiting outside his room.

"Hi, still having trouble with this?" taking the book from Mark.

"You're not kidding. Incidentally, I hope your mother didn't mind my coming over."

"She's not my mother, but she's like one of the family. Hilde's lived with us for years. Come on in." Eric shut the door behind them. The room was sparsely furnished with a bed, dresser and a long folding table where Eric worked. There was a wooden chair in front, another near Eric's bed and a faded green mohair upholstered chair with a matching ottoman. On the wall was a large poster of a kibbutz, and on the table was strewn an assortment of books: engineering, economics, *Mein Kampf*, *A History of the Jews*, *The Rise and Fall of the Roman Empire*, *War and Peace*, books on contemporary Israel, Karl Marx, the philosophy of Nietzsche, and an assortment of other subjects totally arcane to Mark.

"All right, let's get down to cases," Eric said. "Now here, let's take this example." Turning to the page, he pulled the chair up to the table and they sat down.

Two hours later Mark began to see the clearing in the wilderness. "I thought I'd never get it through my skull. God, Eric, I don't know how to thank you."

"Forget the thanks, and if you have any more trouble, let me know. I'll see you in psych anyway, and you can tell me how it's coming."

"I sure will. Thanks again, Eric."

"Forget it."

That night Mark had his first sleep uninterrupted by worries about flunking out of school. He was always going to hate math, no matter what, but at least he understood it enough now to feel he had a reasonable chance of getting through. And it was less his father's exhortation to conquer the things you liked least than the unexpected aid of a new friend that had done the trick. . . .

In the next few weeks Eric and Mark saw one another in their psych classes, then started having lunch together, and one day Eric said to Mark, "How about coming to my house for dinner?"

"Hey, I'd like to."

"Okay, how about Wednesday?"

"Great, what time?"

"Six?"

"I'll be there. So long." He waved and each went his separate way.

Things, Mark decided, were decidedly looking up.

As Mark parked in front of Eric's house, it occurred to him that this was the first time he'd been invited to a Los Angeles area home modest, to say the least, in comparison with the grand manses of Beverly Hills and the San Fernando Valley he'd been invited to on weekends by his "brothers." Just noting the difference made him wonder for a moment if he were turning into a snob like them. He didn't think so, but he did realize that his own world had been remarkably closed and circumscribed by the ways of the rich or at least the upper middle class. His own home seemed palatial as well compared to the Brauchs' with its small living room, overstuffed couch and matching chairs. A large grand piano seemed to overpower the room. "Meet the right people, the important people . . ." his father had said. Well, he had met them, and few interested him. Still, sitting here, he felt vaguely uneasy, and resented feeling it. He really liked Eric more than anyone he'd met so far at college, but it might still be best to keep it on a casual basis.

He could not even invite Eric home . . . the first thing his father would ask was "What does his father do? Who is he? Where does he come from?"

They were up in Eric's room going over an assignment when there was a knock. Through the door Mark heard, *"Dein Vater ist zu Hause, kommen Sie, es ist Abendessen."*

"We'd better go on down. Hilde just said my father's home," Eric told him.

It all seemed very strange, Mark thought, as he followed Eric down into the living room to meet Mr. and Mrs. Brauch. Mr. Brauch was of medium height, distinguished looking with a shock of white hair. He wore very thick lenses, but somehow this did not detract from his appearance; he still maintained an air of distinction. Eric's mother was a woman almost her husband's height with violet-blue eyes, but in spite of her height she was delicate, near-fragile. Her feet were small for a woman her size and her hands were exquisite, the fingers artistic and tapering. At first the impression she gave was one of studied aloofness, and there was something about her that seemed distinctly old-fashioned; as the evening wore on, though, she became somewhat more friendly. On the whole her personality seemed to contrast with Mr. Brauch's—an outgoing man of warmth and wit. In fact, Mark realized that Eric was like his father, outgoing but with just a trace of inner reserve that commanded respect.

Suddenly the door opened and Adrienne walked in. As she passed the living room where Mark and her family had been waiting for her, she stopped at the entrance and said, "I'm sorry I'm late but it couldn't be avoided," then hurried upstairs to her bedroom, tossed her books on the bed, ran a comb through her hair, returned quickly to the center of the living room, apologizing again for keeping everyone waiting.

"Mark, this is my sister Adrienne."

Mark nodded.

"Adrienne, this is Mark Reid."

"Hi, Mark."

Hilde came in to announce dinner. Everyone walked into the dining room just across the narrow hall opposite the living room. They were seated, Eric next to Adrienne, Mark across the table facing them; Mr. and Mrs. Brauch sat at opposite ends. There were flowers in a Meissen bowl and matching candlesticks, the silver was heavy German, and the china the oldest pattern of delicate Meissen. Hilde, dressed in a white uniform with a starched apron over it, brought in a tureen of soup and placed it before Mrs. Brauch. She never spoke to the family at all throughout dinner, going about her chores as though she were a servant, which confused Mark. The first night he had come to see Eric she had called out in such intimate terms that he even thought she was his mother, but seeing her standing almost at attention in this dingy little dining room, as though she were serving the aristocracy of old Germany, all seemed out of focus.

Mrs. Brauch ladled out the thick lentil soup with large pieces of frankfurter sausage floating on the top. She did it with a kind of elegance, as though it were a well-known ritual. Mark, who had never had lentil soup before, found the taste somehow foreign; he didn't like it, it was too spicy; he ate most of it, though. When he placed his spoon down, Mrs. Brauch asked in a soft accent, "May I offer you more?"

"Oh, no thank you, Mrs. Brauch. I've had plenty. It was delicious."

"*Und* you, Werner?"

He replied with barely a trace of accent that he would have some more. Hilde was at his side immediately. Mrs. Brauch then asked Adrienne. She declined, no, she had had enough, but Eric took another half-portion. The plates were then removed, and Hilde brought in a platter of sauerbraten that had a thick raisin sauce over it and thin, lacy-crisp potato pancakes on the side, with applesauce and a bowl of marinated shredded red cabbage. Mark ate the potato pancakes, which he loved, but when it came to the sauerbraten he could hardly eat it. He remembered fleetingly when he was a small boy he could never eat in anyone's house, because they couldn't cook like his mother. He noticed that both of the elder Brauchs ate holding their knives in their right hand and their forks in their left, and when they put their knife down it was placed to the side of the plate rather than across it. Mark assumed that this was the European style and in the best tradition; but this was the first time that he'd ever met foreign people and their customs seemed so odd, unlike the American. What Mark liked best of all about the dinner was dessert. Hilde had made a strudel with the thinnest, most flaky-delicate dough he had ever tasted, and the apples, raisins and nuts truly melted in his mouth.

During dinner there had been very little conversation, and Mark felt an awkward silence as he looked across the table to Eric and Adrienne. For the first time he took a really good look at her. Her hair was more blonde than Eric's, and her eyes were an intense green. She was, in fact, quite beautiful, far more so than he'd thought when she'd come rushing in and he had not really had time to look at her. She, too, it seemed, had inherited her father's warmth and charm.

When dinner was over they all talked at once, speaking about their day, how had it gone? After her classes, Adrienne taught remedial reading at the YMCA to a group of boys from South America, which was why she had been late . . . "And your day, Eric, things went well?" Werner Brauch asked . . .

Mark just sat back listening to the conversation, taking it all in, noting how interested they were in one another. Soon Else said, "Come, we go inside and let Hilde clear away." They all left the table and moved into the living room. After a very short time Adrienne excused herself, saying she had a lot of studying to do. She turned to Mark, smiled and said, "Nice meeting you, Mark."

"Thanks, same here."

When she was gone, Eric asked to be excused because he and Mark wanted to go over some work they were reviewing for mid-terms. The two of them went up to Eric's room.

No sooner had they begun to study than from downstairs came the sound of someone playing the piano. It was magnificent. Mark stopped in the middle of what they were discussing and listened. Eric was surprised by Mark's shift of attention, having no idea that Mark would enjoy listening to Schumann. Perhaps it was because Mark appeared so athletic, which was rather silly when he thought about it. After all, what does brawn have to do with appreciation? When they met it was always at school, and they spoke only of things related to their studies. All he knew about Mark was that he came from the suburbs outside San Francisco and that his father was in the real estate business—nothing more nothing less—and Mark never asked anything about him; so these two young men were, in reality, unknown quantities to one another.

"Do you like music, Mark?"

"I sure do." Mark listened more intently as he heard the intricate arpeggios being played as if by a concert pianist. "Who's that playing?"

"My mother."

"Really?"

"Yes. She would have been a concert pianist if it hadn't been for—"

"My mother plays the piano too, but not like that," Mark said, unaware that he'd cut Eric off—or rather that Eric had interrupted himself.

"That accounts for it."

"Accounts for what?"

"That you like this kind of music."

"That's right. I sort of cut my eyeteeth on Brahms."

How little you knew about somebody from outward appearances struck Eric, as it often did. "We could go to some concerts together if you'd like."

"I sure would."

"That's great, because I can get in for nothing."

"How come?"

"Adrienne plays in the symphony."

"She does? That's terrific. What instrument?"

"The viola."

"Isn't that great? What's she going to be when she gets out of college, a musician?"

"No, a teacher."

"Oh. How old is she?"

"Two years younger than me, nineteen."

"Where does she go to school?"

"UCLA."

"Oh . . . Say, your mother is really good."

"Well, if you like it all that much you'll have to come over some night when we get together, just the four of us, and really have a jam session." Eric laughed. "Jam session! My mother would faint away dead if she knew I used that expression about the sacred three B's—you know, Beethoven, Bach and Brahms."

"What instrument do you play?"

"The flute, and my father plays the violin."

"Boy, that must be an incredible thing for all of you—"

"Well, music has always been pretty important in our lives."

Mark was fascinated, he'd never met a family like this. It was as though they were from another world.

"You play the flute?" he asked, shaking his head.

"Yeah, that's right. I really love the instrument. My poor mother could faint, I think, when I play along sometimes with Benny Goodman records . . . he gets some terrific sounds. Do you like Stan Getz?"

"Sure."

"I have a whole collection of them. We'll play them sometime." Eric looked at the time. "Listen, we'd better get cracking at the books." He turned to the page he had earmarked, but Mark no longer felt like studying. He'd become so captivated by the Brauchs that he could think of nothing else, and all the awkwardness he had felt earlier in the evening seemed to have dissipated itself. He simply had never encountered anyone like them, and his curiosity was beginning to peak.

"Let's knock off studying tonight, Eric, if you don't mind, and just talk."

"Okay, sure." Eric closed the book and waited.

"Eric, I hope you won't be offended, but your family is so unusual . . . at least to me . . . that I'd really like to know some more about them."

"Such as?"

"Your mother and father were obviously born in Germany."

"Well, my father was, but not my mother; she was born in Switzerland."

"And you and Adrienne were born here?"

"No, we were born in Germany too."

"You were? Believe it or not, I've never met anyone who wasn't born here—no, I shouldn't say that, my mother was born in England. But outside of that—well, isn't it ridiculous?"

"It's not ridiculous at all."

"I think it is."

"No, it's really not. You live in a very small suburban community where there aren't many foreign-born people and where those that are tend to be the Japanese gardener or the Italian grocer or the Irish maid, or whatever."

"Now that you mention it, I guess that's true. I never thought much about it before . . . Why did your family leave Germany?"

"Because of Hitler." There was bitterness in his voice.

"Oh, I see, sure . . ."

Eric looked at Mark, then added, "My father realized we should leave before the real persecution began."

Mark was confused. Why would they be persecuted? They were Germans. "Was your father in the government?"

Eric looked at Mark in amazement, then asked, "Didn't you know we were Jewish?"

Mark stared. How stupid . . . how *ignorant* he was, he thought. Not only hadn't he met foreigners before, but the only Jews he'd ever met were the Wallaces, and they were as different from the Brauchs as Jeff was from Eric. How could he know, how could you *tell*? The name certainly meant nothing to him, any more than Wallace did. (Though no doubt more attention to what's in a name, such as his father would have had, would in turn have alerted him, if he'd cared about such things.) Still, if he had thought about it at all, he'd have merely assumed it was German. It had surely never occurred to him, even during the conversation . . . He grew uncomfortable as he thought of his father, and in spite of himself felt the old guilt about defying his father working at him once again. He tried to change the subject, not wanting to give in to his discomfort and leave abruptly, but all he could manage in answer to Eric's surprise was, "No, I didn't know," and then added casually, he hoped, "Hey, Eric, maybe we had better get back to the books, all your help keeps needing to be repeated to penetrate this poor old brain . . ."

"Sure, Mark," Eric said, then added, "but maybe you'd rather call it a night . . . matter of fact, I think I would. I'm really beat . . . how about you?"

Mark looked at him, then at his watch. "I guess I'm with you. Thanks, Eric . . . for everything."

"Any time." Eric's voice was friendly as before. He led Mark down the stairs, waited while Mark thanked his mother on the way out, and stood at the open front door until Mark had gotten into his car and driven off.

Mark drove about for a long time trying to sort things out. He had no idea what Mr. Brauch did, and he couldn't care less. Why his father felt as he apparently did about Jews he couldn't imagine . . . of course he'd never come right out and said it in so many words, but it *seemed* the only explanation behind his strained reasoning for not wanting him to see Jeff Wallace . . . nothing else made much sense. And yet he hadn't wanted to confront him with it directly . . . he hadn't actually said it, so maybe he was uneasy himself about it and calling him on it could make things worse . . . Still, he'd better take it easy with Eric—not that he accepted his father's feelings any more than he ever did—not get so close to Eric as he had to Jeff and then not be able to invite him to his house, introduce him to his father, and risk embarrassing and hurting him . . . Of course, he could just say the hell with it, and maybe he was coming to that kind of independence and self-confidence—God, he hoped so—but it didn't seem there just yet. He'd finally managed a kind of friendship and even occasional warmth—in most *other* areas—with his father. It had taken a long time and it was very important to him, especially after all the years growing up when he'd sensed his father really didn't much like him. He decided the change had become noticeable when he was about the only person his father saw at the apartment in San Francisco and developed when he agreed—even wanted—to come back home . . . It would be tough to give that up. Well, he'd see Eric at school only, keep it light for both their sakes, not risk a repetition of the uneasy scene tonight . . . or the awful one with Jeff.

Later that night he called home, as though compelled by some need to touch base with his father . . . perhaps to test out his own feelings and decision. Katie answered the phone. Suddenly he decided he wanted her to come down for the weekend, but as they talked he thought better of it and decided he'd better try to work things out on his own.

In the next few weeks Mark was courteous and friendly when he saw Eric, but didn't linger too long to chat. Eric was pretty sure he knew why, but refused to let it bother him. He'd been through too much in his twenty-one years to let a little sideways anti-Semitism at UCLA bother him. It was also hard not to like Mark—though unbelievably naïve about many things, he seemed a nice kid who really hadn't had much to do with the world, or the world with him. An only child raised in a secluded suburban town, Mark probably had never *met* a Jew, or at least a *goyische* one whose family couldn't be mistaken for Wasps. He wasn't about to condemn Mark out of hand . . . not *yet*, certainly. After all, he was late getting into the real world. He'd wait and watch how he made out. . . .

Mark also had been thinking how late he was in making up for all the years he'd been sheltered from the world. His parents may have thought that they were doing the best thing for him, but now he felt a real sense of loss. His life seemed drab and uninteresting. The fellows at the fraternity seemed even more out of the same mold. It was time to begin finding out about life and letting it touch him. It was time to try to put aside the nagging guilt and worries about consequences and to take some chances. He decided to start with a phone call . . .

"Hello." It was Adrienne.

Mark was startled, he'd assumed Hilde would answer.

"This is Mark Reid, how are you?"

"Fine. I'm afraid Eric's not here, he's at the library."

"When will he be back?"

"About nine, I guess."

Damn it, he'd finally gotten up the nerve to call and now . . . "Well, please tell him I called . . ." He was about to hang up, then stopped abruptly and was astonished to hear himself say, "What are you doing tonight?"

Surprised, Adrienne answered, "Studying."

"How about leaving it? Would you like to go for a ride?"

She thought a moment. Why not? "Okay."

"I'll pick you up in a half-hour." He hung up before she could say no, feeling like a kid who'd just gotten away with something wonderfully forbidden.

Mark was there in exactly half an hour. Hilde came to the door when he rang and invited him into the living room, where Mr. Brauch was reading something that looked like a medical journal and Else was working on her tapestry. She said graciously, "Good evening, Mark. Come in, Adrienne will be down in a moment."

He sat down uneasily and said to Werner Brauch, "How are you this evening?"

"Fine." He put the magazine aside. "Eric tells me you're from San Francisco."

"Well, not exactly; near San Francisco."

"Beautiful city, we visited there only once, I'm sorry to say, some five years ago. I believe it the most beautiful city in the United States, don't you agree, Else?"

She answered without looking up. "Yes, very picturesque." Obviously for her it could never quite compare with Zurich or Cologne.

Adrienne had come into the room. How pretty she looked in the blue sweater and skirt, Mark thought, her hair falling softly, just tucked behind her ears.

"Ready?" she asked.

"Yes."

She bent over and kissed first her father. "Good night, papa," then her mother. When they got into his convertible they sat for a moment without speaking, then Mark turned to her and asked, "What would you like to do?"

"Nothing, just drive. Isn't that what you wanted to do?"

"Now that I'm here, I really don't care." God, he felt like a schoolboy.

"Well, then, let's just drive with wild abandon." She laughed, and the sound of it almost put him at his ease, made him feel it was going to be all right.

For a long time they drove without speaking, enjoying the easy feeling, until they got to the beach and parked. Mark turned off the motor and they listened to the sounds of the waves that quietly came up and touched the sand, making marvelous patterns as they receded.

"Do you like walking along the beach in your bare feet?" Adrienne asked.

"I've never done it."

"Really?"

"No, I mean, yes, believe it or not. There seem to be a lot of things I've never done—"

"You should try it sometimes, it can be great fun."

"I believe you."

"Why did you ask me out?"

"Oh, well . . . because I felt like company."

"Don't you have a girlfriend?"

"I have a few."

"Why didn't you call one of them?"

Mark tried to read her face in the moonlight. My God, was it possible she was as uneasy as he'd been? Somehow he doubted it. "Well, as a matter of fact, I was calling Eric. But for some reason I'm happy he wasn't home." He waited for a response; when it clearly wasn't forthcoming he said, "Would you like to be a witness to an American first?"

"Yes, what is it?"

"Let's take off our shoes and you can teach me how to go wild and run along the beach."

She laughed again and said, "Let's."

They raced each other along the beach in the moonlight, laughing and catching each other, and by the time they fell down from happy exhaustion Mark said, "You're going to think I'm some kind of a weirdo square, but do you know this is just about the most fun I've ever had in my life?"

"Really?" She brushed her hair back with her fingers. "You've apparently missed a lot. How old are you?"

"Twenty."

"Well, they say it takes boys longer—" She was quick to smile.

"I don't know about anybody else, but I sure feel like I qualify as a late bloomer."

He could hear the smile in her voice as she challenged him, "Come on, I'll race you back to the car."

She was off, with Mark chasing her. When they reached the car they brushed off the sand, put their shoes back on and got in. Mark started the engine and they drove off, stopping for ice cream sodas at a drive-in where they began to talk about *her* and what she planned to do with her life.

"When Eric and I graduate from college my family is moving to Israel."

Mark became suddenly upset at the notion of not seeing her, and Eric . . . "Why Israel . . . I mean, what will you do there?"

"What we'll do is help build a new and wonderful nation. That's where the challenges are. It's kind of like the settling of America, only better."

"Why better?"

"Because everyone's together, working for the same goal. Do you realize that Israel is the only country in the world that doesn't have any anti-Semitism?"

Mark's heart pounded, thinking of his father. Clearing his throat he said, "Do you find much of it here?"

"It varies, but it doesn't affect us so much. And please don't think I don't love this country—I do. So does my father and Eric. The only one who will never be an American is my mother."

"Why?"

"Oh, I don't know, she says Americans are gauche and uncultured—"

"Do you?"

"No."

"Even after living here all this time she still thinks that?"

"Yes, but it's only because she's so German. We couldn't even get her to speak English for the longest time. She either spoke German, or French when she didn't want Hilde to understand."

"My mother speaks French."

"Is she French?"

"No, she's English."

Adrienne looked at the clock on the dashboard. It was ten-thirty and on Tuesday nights she never dated. "Mark, if you don't mind, I really have to get back."

He flashed on the lights, and a car-hop took the tray from the door.

Later, walking Adrienne to her door, he asked, "Can I see you again?"

"If you'd like."

"I would like. What about Saturday night?"

There was no hesitation. "Great. Thanks for the soda."

"Thanks for the evening—it was the best I ever had."

She waited for him to get into the car and drive off.

That night Mark refused to think about his father, except to reflect that, ironically, in their fashions, Adrienne's mother and his father had more than a little in common. Mostly, though, he thought about how lovely and fresh Adrienne was, and how he was going to be able to wait for Saturday to come.

It wasn't easy, but finally it arrived and he found

himself ringing the Brauch doorbell. When Adrienne answered it, he knew his anticipation had been more than justified. They went to the movies, the picture turning out to be very sad—something about two star-crossed lovers. Adrienne sobbed out loud, to her embarrassment, and as the tears rolled down her cheeks she fumbled about in her purse for a handkerchief. Mark, noticing, reached in his back pocket and handed her his. During the film he kept looking at her out of the corner of his eye. She seemed to live to the fullest every anguished moment the lovers shared. The ending was deliciously sad.

As they left the theater Mark said to her, "You're certainly affected by things, aren't you?"

She looked up at him. "Of course, aren't you?"

"Yes, I guess I am . . ."

"I know it's hardly original or very sophisticated, but I remember the first time I read *Romeo and Juliet*. I thought I'd die . . . I love tragic love stories—in fact, I confess I don't have a good time unless I cry." She smiled. "But that's only at the movies. I'm not so crazy about the idea in real life."

They went to a drive-in and ordered sodas again, the same kind as the first time. Sipping hers, Adrienne asked, "Do you like picnics, Mark?"

"You know, I don't think I've been on one . . . oh yes, once when I was very young, but not since." He thought about his mother and father, who never went on picnics or, in fact, did much of anything else together.

"Mark Reid, where have you been all your life?"

"You know, I've just begun wondering the same thing myself . . . Hey, how would you like to go on a picnic tomorrow? I mean, it's Sunday and all, and seeing as how I've been so deprived—"

She hesitated a moment. "Well, I have a date to go to the beach . . ."

"Couldn't you break it?"

"That wouldn't be very nice, would it?"

"No, it wouldn't." He looked directly at her, and managed to keep a straight face.

She looked away severely, then back at him, and

laughed as he finally broke up too. "All right, but you wouldn't like it if I stood you up, would you?"

"I'd hate it, but then, I wouldn't let you do that to me."

"You sound pretty sure of yourself."

"For some reason I am, and I'm just getting started—"

"Really? It sounds like you've mapped out an itinerary for yourself."

"That's right. You're just liable to open up a whole new world for me."

"Well, I wouldn't want to impede the progress of young Mark Reid's development, now would I? Still, I don't want you to think I'm fickle."

"Are you?"

"No, not at all."

"Okay. What time tomorrow?"

"Say eleven. Oh, and incidentally, Eric and his girlfriend were going to the beach with us. Is it all right if I ask them to come along?"

"Of course, that would be great!" Mark said, wishing he'd been able to say what he really wanted—which was, I'd rather not.

"It will be fun. By the way, Eric's really engaged to this girl."

"I didn't know Eric was going steady."

"Yes, they'd like very much to get married."

"Well, why don't they?"

"Because of money. They've gone together since high school. As a matter of fact, they've never gone with anybody else."

"That's sure a long time to go steady!"

"Not in their case. They're awfully well-suited, she's like our family."

He envied this girl . . . he envied this family. . . .

CHAPTER THIRTY-TWO

On Sunday Mark picked up Adrienne and Eric, and met Dina for the first time. She had freckles and light red hair, rather a large-boned girl, somehow not what he would have imagined for Eric, but like they said, love was in the eye of the beholder. As it turned out, she was as well-read and as educated as Eric, and they loved not only the same things but each other. They acted as though they had been married for years.

Early in the morning Hilde had baked chickens, cut them up and wrapped them in waxed paper, prepared her own potato salad—like from the old country, she said. If it were from the old country, it had to be good. She put the homemade cakes and cookies in a picnic hamper along with fresh fruit, pickles and olives. Just before they got to the picnic grounds, they bought cold cokes from a store nearby. Then they drove until they found a clearing under a huge horse-chestnut tree where Adrienne and Dina spread out the white linen cloth. Hilde could have thought of nothing more barbaric than eating from paper plates, so she'd packed china ones. It was enough that the Brauchs had to endure the indignities of a drive-in culture, so far as she was concerned. And she wasn't satisfied with the china plates, but had sent along a second set of the Brauchs' silver.

While the girls set out the food, Eric and Mark tossed a softball to each other. Soon, clanking two forks together, Adrienne called out, "Okay, come and get it."

The lunch was a rare treat for Mark. The smell of fragrant grass turning summer brown wafted through the air of the countryside. The sound of crickets seemed all around. A giant butterfly flew by, Mark wondered what rendezvous it was going to keep. But above all the rest, the warmth he shared with the others made this a very special occasion.

After lunch Dina and Eric changed shoes for a hike through the woods. As they were leaving Adrienne said, "Don't lose your way or we'll have to call out the Rangers," and Dina, laughing, called back that they'd leave string to mark their trail, like Tom Sawyer and Becky.

After they'd gone, Mark helped Adrienne clean up and put things back in the hamper. The two of them then lay on the ground, looking up at the sky. Mark broke off a piece of grass and put it between his teeth. "You know something, Adrienne, this is just about the most beautiful day I've ever spent, thanks to you—"

"Why, thank you, sir."

"I mean it."

"Well, I'm glad, except you sound almost underprivileged—"

"More like underdeveloped. Anyway, thanks for coming to the rescue."

She smiled. "What kind of a little boy were you, Mark?"

"I don't know, I guess pretty much like the ones I grew up with."

"What was it like for you, growing up, I mean?"

"I really don't know how to answer that."

"Well, where did you go to school?"

"A small country school, by city standards."

"You mean that was grammar school?"

"Yeah, and then I went to a boys' academy for a while."

"Did you like it?"

"Not in the beginning, but then I did."

"And after that?"

"A suburban high school. Also pretty small."

"Did you go out for sports?"

"I played basketball and went out for football in my sophomore year, but I got the biggest kick out of pole vaulting."

"Were you good?"

"Fair."

"What else . . . ?"

"Well, nothing much, I guess."

"What did you and your family do in the summer?"

He wished she hadn't asked him that. How could he tell her that his mother and father had hardly spoken to each other for years, that they only stayed together because he had forced them into an artificial reconciliation and had felt guilty a long time now for having interfered with their lives when he probably had no right . . . matter of fact, he'd almost come to feel that in a way he'd blackmailed them into getting together again . . . if you could call it that. All he said to her was, "We own a place at Tahoe, go there every summer."

"Well, that sounds like good fun."

"Sure . . . what do you do on vacation?"

"Just ordinary things, like what we're doing now."

"They don't seem so ordinary to me."

They were silent for a while, then: "How do you like Southern California?" Adrienne asked.

"I don't."

"Really? Then why did you decide to come here?"

"I thought it was a good idea to get away from home—"

"Did you?"

"Did I what?"

"Get away from home?"

He got up on one elbow, turning over onto his side. "If you're going to get serious, I'll have to give that some serious thought . . . and now enough of the saga of Mark Reid. How about you, and your family? I'm really very curious."

"Well, it's a long story that begins way back, long before Eric and me."

"Tell me."

"You really want to know?"

"Yes, very much. I wanted to ask Eric, but was afraid he'd think I was prying."

"Then you don't know Eric very well—you can ask him anything."

"You're right, I don't, but I'd like to . . . and you too."

"Well, you asked for it . . . My mother was born in Zurich, my father in Cologne. They're second cousins, in fact."

"Isn't that unusual? I mean, I don't know anybody who's married to their cousin—"

"Well, it happens occasionally in Europe. My great-grandfather's sister married a young man by the name of Hoffman and moved to Switzerland. The Brauchs had lived in Cologne since 1790—actually the house that Eric and I were born in was the same house that my great-grandfather built."

"Hey, that's something . . . Then what?"

"Well, my father met and fell in love with my mother while he was on holiday. They got married soon after that and spent their honeymoon in Italy." Her voice fell off as she spoke now and she seemed far away.

Quietly Mark encouraged her to go on, and she came out of her reverie. "My father's a physician, you know."

Mark was shocked. He'd called him "Mr. Brauch" and no one had corrected him. In fact, now that he thought about it, he did remember seeing Mr. Brauch reading what looked like a medical journal and thinking it sort of strange.

"Yes, the Brauchs have been physicians for generations. My father and his father and grandfather all graduated from Heidelberg University."

"That's what I call tradition . . ."

"I guess so. Anyway, getting back to *our* saga, Eric was born in the same year Hitler became Chancellor of Germany, almost on the exact day in April—by the way, Mark, how much do you know about Germany during Hitler?"

"I'm ashamed to say, not so very much. Mostly what's in a history textbook—"

"Well, that's understandable. I only asked because I don't want to bore you with things you already know."

"Please, I'd appreciate hearing it from you, I mean, if it isn't too—"

"No, that's okay. Most of it I've had to be told. Well, when Hitler came to power the German Jews had lived more or less free of persecution for a long time, so it was nearly impossible for them really to believe even Hitler would harm them . . . I'm talking about at first. Sad to say, some of the Jews in business resented the labor unions so much—at the time Germany had some of the strongest unions in the world—that they supported Hitler in exchange for his promise to do away with the labor unions. I don't mean all did or even most, but a few did and they learned to regret it. And there were some other Jews who were more afraid of Communism, which had become a powerful force in Germany just before the Nazis took over. You have to remember that Germany was just coming out of the breakdown of the Weimar Republic and Germans—and remember most German Jews considered themselves Germans first and Jews second—were still feeling disgraced by its defeat in the First World War. The time was perfect for Hitler.

"At first the Jews felt sort of small subtle changes that were very gradual, and hardly anyone—Jews or non-Jews—thought Hitler would use them as a scapegoat for all Germany's troubles and as objects of hate to unify Germany any way he could. Some did see what was coming, and my father was among the first of them. By 1935, the year I was born, there were even signs at the hospital. Patients were beginning to go less frequently to the Brauch doctors. It was a barely noticeable thing, but it was there, and yet my father's father wouldn't for a moment believe that he would be turned on by his fatherland. Remember, he was a *German* born and bred, and proud of it. He'd fought with the Kaiser. He couldn't believe they'd ever attack the respected house of Brauch. Then by

1938, our father told us, he sensed war was coming and that if we didn't get out it was soon going to be too late. He tried to convince his father to leave the country and go to England with us—he had an uncle there who'd been a professor in a teaching hospital for several years—but grandfather was too proud and he refused to go. After that my father did the only thing he thought he could do—he got us together and we left in the middle of the night. My father doesn't like to talk much about this, but I know leaving his father behind—his mother had died five years earlier—was something he still hasn't gotten over. I doubt if he ever will—"

"You can hardly blame him for that," Mark said, fascinated and horrified by her story.

"No, of course not . . . and not for his foresight, either, in gradually sending a few family things out of the country to England in care of his uncle. They were things that had been in the family for centuries —paintings, mementos . . . hardly anything's left now except a set of Meissen china."

Adrienne stopped and stared ahead. The shadows of the chestnut tree had lengthened, and a soft breeze ruffled the grass.

"What happened to them? I mean the paintings and the rest?" Mark said.

"They were destroyed in the blitz. All that beauty that stood for three hundred years of the Brauch family literally went up in smoke . . ."

"God, how awful. What else happened to you when you got to London?"

"Well, to begin with, Jews had to be vouched for with affidavits, you know."

"No, I didn't—"

"Yes, but this was one problem my father didn't have, thanks to my great-uncle already being in London."

"Oh, and then I suppose he went into his uncle's hospital there?"

"No, it was impossible for him to practice medicine."

"Well, what did he do?"

She hesitated then answered, "He became an orderly. My grandfather would have died if he'd known, but that's all they'd let him do."

"That must have been rotten for him . . . and what about your mother?"

"She took a job in a factory—she'd never worked at anything in her life. But actually we were lucky, we were just thankful to be together, and for a year things went along fairly well."

"It must have been tough just the same."

"Yes, I suppose so—especially not knowing the language. My father was the only one who spoke English."

"Then what happened?"

"When England entered the war, we children were evacuated to the country."

"Were you and Eric together?"

"No, that was the worst part—we were sent to different places. I didn't see Eric again until the war was over."

"God, how awful."

"Yes, it was, because as children the two of us were almost inseparable. I think being apart from him was even worse than being separated from my parents."

"What happened to them?" He was almost afraid to ask.

"Well, one night during the blitz my father was right in the thick of the attack and lost the sight of one eye."

"My God—"

"He also can't see too well with the other, which of course made all the difference in the sort of thing he could eventually do."

"And when the war was finally over?"

"We came to America, but my father's sight was so bad he couldn't study enough to take the examination that was required for foreigners."

"So what does he do now?"

"He's a darkroom technician. He develops film in the X-ray department of a hospital."

"Boy, that must be really tough, I mean for someone who'd been a doctor, whose whole *family* had been doctors . . ."

"It really was, but I doubt if anybody where he works even knows he's a physician."

"That's some story—" It was hard to say much of anything that didn't sound fatuous.

"Yes, I suppose it is. In nineteen years I've had a lot happen to me, but we all realize how lucky we are . . ."

She hid her eyes with her hands, and Mark wanted to hold her.

"I wish I knew what to say to you, Adrienne, but all I can say is that it really is the most terrible thing—"

"No, the most terrible thing is that the world let it happen, and go on happening until six million Jews were dead. There's enough blame for everybody, Jews as well as Gentiles. Everybody is entitled to feel guilty, my father says. Except that doesn't bring anybody back."

"It's important to remember, though, isn't it? Otherwise it could happen again."

She nodded and smiled. "You're a pretty quick study, Mark Reid."

"Thanks . . . well, maybe about some things . . . And what about Hilde?"

"She came to work for my mother as a nursemaid when Eric was a year old. She originally lived in a small village on the Rhine . . . By the way, she isn't Jewish, in case you're wondering."

"How does she happen to be with you now?"

"When my family was getting out of Germany, she came to my father and told him she couldn't stay in her own country any longer—not if it could be so barbaric that it would exclude the Brauchs! She was taking her chances even working for us, let alone being friendly."

"That really is something . . . Didn't she have a family?"

"Only a married sister living in Hamburg that she didn't feel close to. Anyway, my father took her along, and she's been with us ever since."

"The first night I came to see Eric, she opened the door and I thought she was your mother."

"Well, in a way . . ."

"And then the night I came to dinner, I thought she was a servant—"

"No, believe me, Mark, she's anything but. We all love her. She's family. Still, because of her inbred training and background, the night you came to dinner she couldn't resist reverting to the past for the sake of my mother and father. And let me tell you something else . . . Do you know that Hilde actually does work as a domestic for other people. She insists on it, and until just recently also insisted on contributing her earnings to our family."

"I think that's beautiful. And so, by the way, are you."

"Thank you, Mark."

It was like a feeling of reverence. He not only wanted to kiss her, but to hold her close and somehow make up to her for his past ignorance, and especially the misguided thoughts of his father about her people. For the moment, all he could manage was to say, "I'd like to kiss you."

"Then why don't you?"

He put his arms around her, gently placed his lips against hers, and for the first time knew what it was to kiss a girl with all the love and desire that was in his heart.

That night he lay awake for a very long time, wondering at the destiny that had led him to Adrienne, grateful for it, and thinking too of his father . . . and of Ralph Hansen telling him, "Remember this, Mark, your father can't be the most important thing in your life . . ." Now, for the first time, he truly understood those words.

As the weeks rushed by, Mark found himself transported into a world of Adrienne's "ordinary" pleasures. He saw her constantly, and his relationship with Eric deepened as he learned from him. Not having had a religion of his own to fall back upon, and never especially regretting it until now, he became fascinated to learn about Eric's . . . and Adrienne's. The idea of a faith that had undergone near-annihilation for centuries and yet retained its strong identity in the world fascinated him. Judaism was a living history of five thousand years. Jews were the first to recognize a living God when all the world worshipped idols; they offered the world enlightenment, guidance and truth by the ten commandments. The whole Christian world lived by that edict, or at least claimed to. All of this gave Mark reason to think about this ancient, mysterious people. Adrienne had said that they encompassed the world, and yet they had one common bond between them. Judaism was like a universal language for them, even though linguistically they often might not understand each other. Eric fed Mark's curiosity with history, not theology, suggesting as well a number of books that Mark read with the excitement of discovery.

His education, thanks to Adrienne, hardly stopped there. Each Wednesday night during the symphony season he sat through rehearsals, and when the concerts began he attended with Eric and Dina.

As Adrienne sat on-stage, Mark found so much of his attention drawn to her that he hardly heard the music. After the concert was over, the four of them would go to the drive-in for something to eat—Adrienne was always too nervous to eat before a performance. He had begun to see more through her eyes when they went to a play or a movie. They would talk about the story and why the characters had reacted as they had, Mark usually having one explanation and Adrienne another. A play, a piece of sculpture, the color of the sky—*nothing* for Mark was quite the same as it had been before. On Sunday mornings they would play tennis or drive out to the beach, where they had found a special cove that both of them had begun to feel was especially their very own. They rented tandem bicycles for rides through the park, Adrienne bringing wonderful poetry to read to him while he lay with his head in her lap.

Life was perfect . . . almost. He still detested the courses he was taking, never feeling that what he was doing would ever be satisfying. One night he spoke to Adrienne about it.

"Mark," Adrienne said, "did you ever sit down with yourself and ask just what it was that you *enjoy* doing?"

"Yes, but I don't have to ask—I enjoy being with you."

"I don't mean that and you know it. What I'm talking about is if you're not happy with any of the courses you're taking, did you ever stop to think that you could change?"

"Change to what?"

"That's what I'm asking."

"Well, let's face it, what am I good enough at to be especially interested in?"

"Don't you know?"

"No, I don't seem to have any leaning for anything in particular."

"If you didn't have to make a living doing something, what would you choose to do?"

He hesitated. "You laugh and I'll—"

"You know I won't."

"Okay. Well, if I could do anything I wanted I think I'd like to try to write—"

"Then why don't you?"

"Aside from the obvious question of talent, I don't think I'm really free to do that—"

"Why not, what's so important holding you back?"

"I have to be practical."

"So be practical."

"Suppose I wanted to become a beachcomber, I could hardly do that."

"Sounds pretty good to me."

"Oh come on, Adrienne, I mean seriously."

"All right, seriously, but tell me about this being practical."

"Well, I have an obligation to make a living, eventually."

"I know that, but why do you have to go into business if you don't like it?"

"Why? Because my father expects it and I owe him—"

"Oh, does he, and do you?"

"Yes, and besides, it's what I *want* to do."

"Really? Well, in that case, why are you so unhappy about your work so far? I think if I were taking something I disliked so much I'd think about a change—"

"Yeah, well for you that's easy to say."

"But not for you?"

"No."

"Why not?"

"Because your father's not expecting certain things from you," he said with some bitterness.

"Well, I don't think your father has the right to expect 'certain' things from you on *his* terms."

"Now wait a minute, Adrienne, you don't understand—"

"What don't I understand?"

"That my father has a large business and he expects me to take over someday and—"

"Really? . . . Well, what would happen if he didn't have a son . . . then what?"

"If . . . if . . . The point is, he does, and besides there's nothing else I especially want to do."

"Nothing, Mark?"

"No, it's not like you and Eric. You know you're going to be a teacher, and Eric's going to be an engineer."

"Yes, but we are because we want to."

"Well, that's where we're different. I told you I never really thought about doing anything in particular."

"Don't you think you should start?"

Mark laughed. "Just like that?"

"Yes, just like that. Listen, Mark"—she was becoming annoyed at his stubborn resistance—"do you know what I think? Never mind, I'll be happy to tell you . . . I think you're too dominated by your father—"

Mark got up and for a moment was angry with Adrienne. After all, this had been his decision, his father had *said* he could do anything he liked, or go anywhere he wanted to . . .

"You're wrong about my father." But before the

words were out of his mouth, Jeff Wallace clouded his memory, as did the realization that someday he would have to confront his father with Adrienne Brauch. "Let's not discuss it anymore," he said abruptly.

"Fine, but remember—it really is your life, Mark, not your father's." He'd heard it before. He knew it was right. Except . . . They remained silent for a time. Finally Adrienne said, "All right, I know you don't want to talk about it, but suppose I make one suggestion?"

Not looking at her, his arms folded across his chest, he said, "Okay, just one."

"Why don't you tell your father you've tried but this isn't what you want to do?"

"I have. Well, not in so many words . . ."

"And?"

"And he advised me that everything is not a bed of roses, not to mention that you have to do some things you don't like—"

"Oh . . . that's so archaic. If your father was a shoemaker, you should be the same? That's some choice he gave you—inherited drudgery."

"Well, the real estate business is hardly that—"

"Yes, I know, but if you don't like it, it is."

"Listen, I don't want to talk about it any more."

"Now don't get peeved, Mark."

"I'm not peeved."

"Well, if you're not peeved, I'm going to say one other thing."

"Obviously I guess I can't stop you. Go ahead."

She smiled. "Thank you for your generosity." And then: "Change your major."

"To what?"

"Well, you say you like writing. Why not try taking a course?"

"Oh sure. My father would really love that—"

"Your father's not going to college, you are and it's you that's got to be satisfied."

Of course, she was right. Besides, hadn't his father said almost the same? Whether he meant it or not? Well, she'd put the cap on a decision he suspected he'd been coming to for quite a while . . . He at least had finally decided he was *not* going into the real estate business. And with the decision came the admission to himself he didn't quite have the courage yet to tell his father . . . not this, or a few other matters sure to blow the roof off. Still, it was a big start. In more ways than one.

CHAPTER THIRTY-THREE

It was Mark's twenty-first birthday, and after taking separate congratulatory calls from his mother and father . . . yes, everything was going fine; no, he wasn't going to be lonely, he'd be with some friends, he'd see them soon . . . he picked up Adrienne and they drove to the beach. He didn't say a word the entire ride out.

After they'd parked, Adrienne turned to him and broke the silence. "Mark, correct me if I'm wrong, but this is supposed to be your birthday, not a funeral. Do you mind telling me what's wrong?"

"Nothing."

"Oh, thank you. Well, if you're going to be sullen and silent you can do it alone. I'd like to go home, if you don't mind."

He reached over and took her hand. "I'm sorry, Adrienne, I know I'm less than great company and I don't know if I can get up the nerve to tell you why." How could he tell her? He didn't want to risk what they had, maybe never see her again. . . . Still, she was going to know eventually. He took a breath and plunged in.

"Adrienne, I'm going to tell you about my family —I mean, what the Reids are *really* like. My mother and father have been incompatible for years. I love my mother, but I think I blame her as much as my father for what happened, even though for a long time I thought it was all my father . . . as a kid I hardly saw him, but I finally learned to accept that and over the last few years we've gotten pretty close, except—"

"You know, Mark, this is the first time you've ever

spoken about them to me. Of course, I've wondered why—"

"I'm about to tell you, and I *hope* you'll understand . . . I said my father and I had gotten much closer over the years, and in many ways I admire him, except for one thing."

"And what's that?"

"Please, Adrienne, this is going to be very difficult for you to understand . . . I'm not sure I can even say it—"

"It's quite simple, you can just say your father doesn't want you to become involved with a Jewish girl. Am I right?"

He looked at her in astonishment.

"Yes," he said softly.

"Well, let me tell you something. My family's not all choked up with joy about the fact that I'm seeing so much of you, either. Quite frankly, my mother has spoken to me about it. You know, Mark, this isn't so simple for me either."

"I know it's not, I realize it even more now."

"Mark, don't be afraid to answer this. You know some parents just don't want their children to marry outside their religion because they think it will cause needless trouble. And then there are people that are pure and simple . . . 'anti-.' Is your father anti-Semitic?"

A long, long pause. "Yes, I think so, or at least something close to it. He's never come right out and said it, but things he's said . . . well, that's what they seem to add up to. I'm damned if I can understand it either. He was an orphan, he had a tough life—"

"Well, you better understand this, Mark. Whether or not he'd accept me, I'll never accept him, knowing that—"

He pulled her to him. "Please, Adrienne, don't say that."

"Yes, I have to."

"Please, I'm betting he'll come around and see how wrong he's been—"

"I wonder."

"Look, Adrienne, he's really a smart man, and he'll

have to come to his senses when he realizes how much you mean to me—"

"I find *that* difficult to believe."

"Please at least try. He's never known anyone like you and your family and when he does he'll love you as much as I do. Just let me work this out my own way, please?"

She looked at him. "I love *you*, Mark. We'll try to work it out."

He kissed her. "For starters, I'm going to call him tonight and tell him I'm resigning from the fraternity."

"How will that solve anything?"

"I don't want to belong anymore—I never did, really. I only stayed because it was so important to him. But it's been getting worse and worse . . . the dumb snobbery, the hazings, and now at least I have my own reason to get out. I guess that's what I was looking for, or rather waiting for. Well, I'm not so passive now. And mostly that's thanks to you, Adrienne."

"*That* I'm very glad to hear."

"I'm going to take a small apartment somewhere. I want us to be together. I want very much to be with you, Adrienne. Will you do it?"

She looked at him without speaking or smiling, then, very gently, took his face in her hands and kissed him. It bore its own special eloquence—and commitment.

That night he called David and told him he'd decided to resign from the fraternity. He listened to the expected attempts to get him to think it over, and ended politely by saying he'd made up his mind. It was very much a first in his life with his father. Well, he thought, as he hung up, like they say, better late than never.

They looked in the Sunday paper for apartments not too far from the university, and found a lovely bachelor apartment about two years old, furnished with a plaid studio couch, large black vinyl chair, round Danish breakfast room table with four chairs and a black-and-white tweed rug. There was even a pool, and the rent wasn't bad at all. Mark took a six months' lease. They were deliriously happy.

It was a time of firsts . . . he felt as never before that he was his own man, that he really was separate from them and on his own, and their first night together was the most special of them all . . . the first time that he and Adrienne made love to each other, giving and sharing as though they had invented the experience just for themselves. Nothing in all the world compared to her, he thought, as she lay next to him that night. For Adrienne Mark had been the very first. Later they spoke in the darkness about how wonderful life was, that with all the hatred and unhappiness that existed in the world there still remained a place for love and lovers. Far beyond the words they spoke went their feelings, and they lay together, holding one another as if trying to keep as long as possible the specialness that had happened for them.

The apartment had come to mean their own private domain, where no one else was welcome or needed. Adrienne, with Mark's agreement, told Dina, whom she knew she could trust to keep her confidence, not to mention provide an excuse to her parents on nights she stayed with Mark. She disliked the deception, but her parents were much too conservative to understand, and she had no wish needlessly to hurt them.

Mark continued to be curious about Judaism, and finally asked Adrienne if he might go to temple with her on a Friday night. She was delighted, and thought her parents would be pleased as well.

They picked the following Friday night, and Mark was invited to dinner with the Brauchs. He still wasn't crazy about the food and, smiling to himself, wondered if he ever would be. Well, *everything* couldn't be perfect in his perfect new world. Hilde brought in the tureen, this time filled with yellow chicken soup and matzo balls, soft and feathery-light to the touch. That dish he was beginning to enjoy more, but when the pieces of gefilte fish with horseradish the color of beets was placed before him, the small bites just fought his attempts to swallow them down. The chicken was tasty and came with a small serving of noodle kugel, and the dessert was truly delicious —Hilde's sponge cake with fresh strawberries.

By eight o'clock he was seated with them in their family pew, and in spite of himself did feel somewhat out of place, even though Adrienne assured him that services were open to anyone, regardless of their religion, or lack of it. During the cermonial portion of the service he had difficulty in concentrating, looking around instead at the magnificent stained glass windows that evoked so much of man's history. He would have Adrienne explain them later. His mind was intrigued by the chanting and singing of psalms, but it was when the rabbi stood before the congregation and began speaking that Mark's attention was captured:

"What," the rabbi said, "would a man do if he knew this were his last day on earth? In what way would he spend it? How important would the moments become? Would the years of his life become so all-encompassing in that short span of moments that the true meaning of living would be revealed and so he would make the most of that one day for all days, knowing it was to be his last . . . ?"

Afterward the idea lived with Mark. Drifting as he had before, he'd not thought in those terms. Now his life had taken on new meaning, and with it every moment began to take on a new significance.

He talked to Adrienne about his new feeling that a person should never take for granted the promises of tomorrow, and that, as the rabbi had said, no man made a pact with God that tomorrow was guaranteed . . . Adrienne smiled. "You're really learning, darling, you really are. For most Jews, though, what you heard tonight wasn't really such a revelation. It's a theme stressed all through Judaism—that we make the most of every day, living each one as though it were our last."

On Monday afternoon Adrienne went directly

from classes to the apartment, laden down with packages, among which was a small bunch of daisies. She put the groceries away, boiled the spaghetti, made the sauce and when it was finished put it into a baking dish and slipped it into the oven. She cut up the French bread and buttered it, all ready to be toasted, then prepared the green salad, set the table, arranged the flowers in a container that she had bought in the dime store along with two candleholders, and waited for Mark to come home. When she heard his footsteps she ran to greet him.

"Happy anniversary, darling." It had been one month since they had taken the apartment. He scooped her up in his arms and twirled around with her.

"Happy anniversary to you . . ." He sniffed. "What's that?"

"Your very favorite, matzo balls and gefilte fish."

He winced.

"Actually it's spaghetti and salad. Can I put garlic on the French bread?"

"If you can stand me."

"It's a deal—if we can stand each other after that, nothing can come between us."

They talked about the day. Mark could even tolerate his classes, fortified as he was by the anticipation of next year, when he would change his program. Adrienne told him about her group of Chinese boys she was teaching English to and how much she adored them. But the best news of all she kept for after dinner.

When they'd curled up next to each other she said, "Mark, I think I did something today you'll be pleased about."

"You're going to have a baby?"

"No, but suppose I were?"

"So I guess I'd have to marry you."

"Who knows, I might even accept. But to get to more, or less, serious matters . . . I enrolled us in a creative writing course at the ICC—"

"The *what* . . . ? What the hell does the Interstate, Commerce Commission know about writing—?"

She laughed delightedly. "No, silly, ICC also, you should forgive the expression, means Israel Community Center."

"Oh, well, apologies from the goyim. Anyway, darling, I think that's just great! Also, I love you. Remind me to tell you about it."

"I intend to, constantly."

A Tuesday night, nine o'clock at the Center . . . "Now for your next assignment I want you all to prepare a short piece, no more than a couple of pages, on the five senses—what it means to hear, see, feel, smell and taste. Now, any questions? No?" Nobody could think of anything, so the instructor dismissed the class.

On the way to the Brauchs, Mark said, "God, that's really tough when you think about it."

"It certainly is. Now go home and think."

"Check, madame slave-driver." They kissed, and Mark went back to the apartment and she to her home.

That night he lay awake for hours. Finally, giving up to the pressure of his thoughts, he got out of bed, found a pencil and paper, sat down and began to write, trying to make sense from the jumble in his mind. The notion of having only one day to live came back to him—and so it was taking off from this that he began to work out the assignment.

> If it were possible for me to know the day before I die, I think I would suddenly be aware of the little things that say I am alive . . . To awaken to the fragrance of morning after a spring rain. To bite into a juicy red apple. To hold in my hand a velvet rose and let my fingers caress the petals. To listen to the sound of music being played by two hands, just ten fingers capable of lifting me beyond the dimension of time, to listen with my eyes closed and not be envious because it is other hands that play instead of mine. To walk through a meadow and listen in silence to the life that surrounds me, while the sun's

warmth filters through the trees and a leaf drifts to the ground. And I'd look at the blue sky, with my feet planted in the moist earth, and shout at the heavens: God, how I love life!

At the apartment the next day Adrienne asked him, "Did you think about the assignment?"

"Yes."

"Okay, let the slave driver hear what you've come up with."

He walked to the table, picked up the paper and brought it back to her.

Amazed, she said, "You mean you've already done it?" and without waiting for an answer began to read . . . When she'd finished and slowly looked up at Mark there were tears in her eyes.

"Is it that bad?" he asked, hoping he was making a joke but not convinced that he was. "I knew I wasn't F. Scott Fitzgerald, but at least I hoped I wouldn't drive you to tears—"

"Oh, Mark, I think it's really lovely, so touching and true and vulnerable. So *you*, in fact. Maybe that protected life you led taught you more than you imagined—at least it left you open to feel and let your feelings come through. Thank God you're not sophisticated and self-conscious when you put yourself on paper. Mark, please, I'm no critic and I realize this is only a beginning, but at least it should prove to you that you won't be wrong to start believing in yourself, to take some chances and not get committed to a life that you *know* you don't want because you don't think you have any alternatives. You do . . ."

"You're making quite a speech for a non-critic. Seriously, do you really mean it? You're not just saying all that because you know I want to hear it?"

"I mean it, darling, and I wouldn't insult you by saying it just to make you feel better. Can I show it to Eric?"

"Yes, but let's not tell the world just yet that a new genius is born." He was trying to contain his pleasure at her reaction, and finding it almost impossible to do so.

"Oh, Mark, I love you. I want to do all the romantic things with you . . . starve in a garret, be your worst critic . . . Darling, please try to take this a little seriously. Please, I think you can do it. It would be awful not at least to try . . ."

He gave her a bear hug. "Thank you, thank you"—he looked up—"whoever You are that gave me this."

She made him feel it was actually possible. And she made him forget, at least for the moment, two people named David and Katie. For him, there was only this woman he held here in his arms.

The months slipped by, eased by anticipation of the coming September when he would begin the classes that would be his first commitment to, as Adrienne had said, at least trying to see if he might make it as a writer. He would say nothing to either of his parents . . . plenty of time for that just before returning to school next September. And suddenly he thought about summer, and what it would mean not seeing Adrienne for three whole months.

He thought of not going home at all, and realized it would mean the kind of break he wasn't ready for —not to mention being the worst move he could make if he had any hope of bringing his father around when he told him about Adrienne . . . But this he was certain of, whatever happened, it would be the last summer, the last any time he intended to be apart from Adrienne. But for now the thought of their being separated brought on near-panic.

It was the weekend before the end of the semester, and they were going to spend it together, thanks to Dina, with whom she was ostensibly staying. They were to go to the Hollywood Bowl, and when he picked her up at Dina's, Mark would try not to show what he felt, knowing it would only spoil their last weekend together. But that night as he lay next to her the mood stayed with him. Her head was on his shoulder, her finger touching his cheek.

"Mark?"

"Yes?"

"What's bothering you?"

"How do you know anything is?"

"You're not very good at pretending."

"Well, I've been thinking about this summer."

"Me too."

"And . . . ?"

"We wait until next September, what else?"

He got out of bed and stubbed his toe in the dark. "Dammit!" he swore under his breath, then switched on the lamp and sat in the black vinyl chair, his face sober. "If I had a father that wasn't so damned blinded—"

"I know, Mark, but you said it would take time."

"I know I did, and now I think I'm the one who can't wait."

"Well, you've never even spoken to him about us —"

"That's true . . . but it won't be much longer. I'm going to have it out with him as soon as I get home. He'll see it my way, or—"

"Mark, come back here and stop worrying, please."

He got into bed and she put her arms around him. "Darling, we knew this wasn't going to be easy."

"No, but it won't be any easier later."

"I know, but what are you going to say, 'Look, dad, I'm in love with this Jewish girl—' "

"Something like that . . ."

"May I ask you a very honest question?"

"Of course."

"Honest, now . . . Do you think he'll accept me or —"

"I don't know."

"Well, if he doesn't, then *I* honestly don't see much future for us." She said it very quietly.

"God, Adrienne, don't say that, don't ever say that again."

"Now wait, darling. You're in love with me now, but try to imagine how you would feel if you could never bring me to your home or if he disowned you? . . . And think how I'd feel."

He started to answer but she cut him off. "Mark, this is our future we're talking about. And how would you feel when we had children and your parents never saw them—how would you feel then?" (She couldn't know that someone named Maggie Kent had said nearly the same words to her mother in explaining why she could not have a life with Mark's father . . .)

"All *right*, let me ask you a question. How much do you love me?"

Adrienne got out of the bed. "I'm not going to answer that. Like they say, if you don't know now, you never will."

"Then how can you say that we don't have a chance if he doesn't accept you?"

"Well, I love you and I don't want to ruin your life over me—"

"Goddamn it, get into bed. I'll work this out in my own way."

She did.

The parting was painful enough. Now, driving back through the valley, Mark thought of nothing else but what was waiting for him . . . how he would begin. The next days might very well decide whether he lost Adrienne, or his father . . . or even both?

By the time he reached Rosehaven Road and turned into the garage he was physically and emotionally exhausted. Katie came rushing out to the car.

"Mark, darling, you're finally home! I'm so excited to see you—"

He kissed her, told her he was happy to be home too.

David was in his room when Mark knocked. "Dad, it's me."

David rushed to the door and put his arm on Mark's shoulder. "Come on in. My God, I'm glad to see you. Was it hot in the valley?"

"It sure was. How are you, dad?"

"Great."

"How's everything going with San Jose?"

"Problems, but then who doesn't have those?" He sat down. "I guess you're ready to go up to the lake?"

"Yeah, I suppose so." Mark sat down wearily and David looked at him.

"What's the problem, Mark?"

He didn't want to talk about it tonight. "Nothing, dad. We'll talk about it tomorrow. I'm really very tired."

David was looking at him closely. Mark was obviously very worried about something. A pregnant girl? Oh well, par for thc course at twenty-one . . .

"You have some girl trouble, Mark?"

He looked quickly at his father, feeling as though his mind had been read. How could he know? It was much sooner than he'd planncd, but maybe this was the time . . .

"Dad, could I talk to you . . . I mean really talk?"

"Of course. What's the problem?" And anticipated with, "Did you by chance get a girl into trouble? Don't worry too much, it won't be the first time—"

Mark bit his lip. How *did* he begin? "Look, dad, I'm not in trouble and I haven't gotten anybody into trouble, but I am in love."

David sat back and laughed. "Well, that's not so tragic, people fall in love. So what's the problem?"

Why couldn't he find the magic word? "Dad, I'm very much in love with the most marvelous girl I've ever met, or will ever meet."

"So fine, I'm glad to hear that, but what's so tragic? What is this, '*Madame Butterfly*' or something? What is she, Japanese or—"

"No . . ." Mark said. "Matter of fact, she's Jewish."

"Well, I'll be damned." And to himself thought, maybe he was. With the thought came the fear, and with it anger, and now there was no more restraint as there had been in the past when he'd talked to his son. Now, looking at him, feeling an unreasoning hatred born out of his fear, he exploded.

"You fool, you damned little fool. How in the world could you let yourself get into something like this? What happened, is she pregnant . . . ?" And saying it, winced at his crudeness but couldn't stop, his anger raging out of control now as he saw his whole life coming apart, all the work and suffering going for nothing . . . "Damn you, *answer me.*"

"No," Mark said, his anger nearly matching his father's.

"No, what? What the hell do you mean?" And saying that, knew the eerie, terrifying feeling that he was somebody else, somebody from nearly twenty years ago showing his rage at a boy who had just renounced *his* father's faith . . .

"No, she isn't pregnant, not that it's your business."

"Don't take that tone with me. Where did you meet her, how long have you been seeing her?"

"I met her through her brother at college, and I've been seeing her about six months."

"Well, that's nothing, then. You can just forget her, do you hear me, Mark?"

Mark stood up. "You have no right to tell me who I can love, you have no right—"

Now David stood up. His hands were clenched. He would try to recover his poise, talk sense to the boy, maybe there was still time . . . "Oh yes, Mark, I really do have a right. I am your father, and you are my son, and as long as you are, and take my money, I have that right. Now, you simply break off with this girl—"

"Her *name* is Adrienne Brauch, and you have no right to say anything about her or to tell me anything about her without even knowing her—"

"Except I don't want to know her. I have no intention of knowing her. That is final."

Mark turned to the window, shaking. He had done this all wrong. He should have waited until tomorrow, as his instinct had begged him, but his father had somehow made him feel it was the time. Obviously it wasn't, maybe it never would be, but he had to calm down, right now. Adrienne had said that if his father didn't accept her, she might not marry him. He'd been so glib about assuring her that wouldn't happen, that he'd work it out. But how was he working it out?

"Look, dad," he said, fighting for control, "I don't want us to argue. I want you to understand. So far you've never come out and said why, but obviously you have something against Jews"—there it was, finally out in the open now. "Even if you were right—and you're not—why would you blame somebody for their religion? Adrienne isn't any more responsible for being Jewish than I am for being what I am . . . whatever *that* is . . . I'm telling you that if you met her, you'd feel very differently—"

"No," David said, defiantly, feeling unaccountably as though somehow their roles were reversed, he the boy and Mark the man. "I suppose she's the reason you decided to move out of the fraternity house too?"

"No, not altogther."

"I see, in other words you've been living together."

"No, not exactly—"

"Well, you were or you weren't. Which is it?" He was shouting now, and saying the words as though condemning something unspeakable . . . as Isaac once made him feel about his decision?

"I still don't think it's any of your business, but to set things straight, we're seeing each other at times in my apartment but we aren't living together." He felt ashamed for Adrienne. His father made it sound so cheap and sordid.

"All right, now let's get down to cases. What do you intend to do about her?"

"I intend to marry her as soon as I get out of college."

"I see. In that case, you are out of college as of now, because if you think you're going to do me the favor of allowing me to support you while you proceed to marry her—"

"Dad, that doesn't really worry me"—which was less than true, if he were honest, despite Adrienne's expansive encouragement about his prospects as a writer—"but your unbelievable attitude does. What *do* you have against Jews to make you so set against a girl you've never even met?"

"I don't have to give you my reasons" (How could he?) "although I did try once when you took up with those Jews across the street. I tried, not putting it in so many words, but you wouldn't hear me. You wouldn't understand that there's a threat to you too, that I'm trying to protect you too against things that you just don't know anything about—"

"*What* things? You're not making any sense to me, I'm sorry, but you just aren't."

"Well, maybe this will make some sense. You marry this girl, you and I are strangers, we don't know each other. You'll see how it feels to be on your own—"

"That's fine with me. I don't need your money. You managed without it, you've told me often enough."

He didn't wait for a response as he turned and walked out of the room. My God, no wonder his mother could never live with him. It was his way and no other. Give in to him and everything went fine. Stand up to him and he wanted to wipe you out . . . What had happened, he wondered, to the warmth and friendship that had developed between them? . . . that he thought had developed.

Later that night Katie came to his room and sat on the edge of the bed. She did not turn on the lamp, knowing he would rather she didn't see his face.

"Mark," she said softly, "I heard everything, but by now you know I can't do anything about you and your father."

"I know."

"You know I've tried never to come between you and him, but tonight I'm telling you . . . if you love this girl, whoever she is, no matter what she is, you marry her."

"Do you mean it, mom? You heard she was Jewish?"

"Yes, dear, *yes*. You marry her."

"Oh God, mom."

"But love her, Mark, be sure you love her, and then marry her."

He put his arms around her. "Mom, I've been so wrong about an awful lot of things—"

Nervously she hurried on. "Now, I want to meet this girl."

Mark looked at his mother. "You mean it? She's so beautiful, and wonderful. You'll love her. I can't understand dad. It's crazy, like an obsession—I just couldn't get through to him."

Katie looked at him, and for the moment saw the little boy, the child that had lain at her breast. What lies and deceptions we've given you, she thought, while we cheated you of your heritage, your birthright. Why did I allow David to do this to our lives? Why? . . . And knew the answers, but no longer did they suffice as they once had. Time had done that.

And what did she say to him? . . . that he was suffering for something that happened in an office in New Jersey long ago? . . . that happened long before that between a father who preached scripture to his son instead of love? . . . that his father, now so filled with fear and hatred, who had once been too proud to accept the humiliations of prejudice, had gone so far he'd become what he'd sacrificed so much to escape? And you, my son, the innocent caught between . . . She kissed him, but all she could manage to say was, "Darling, we'll talk some more about this in the morning—"

"Thanks, mom, but if you don't mind I'd like to get away and think this out by myself. I'm going up to the lake for a few days."

"All right. Do what you think is best, Mark. Will I see you before you leave?"

"I don't know, it may be very early, but I'll wake you before I leave if you want."

She kissed him good night, tasting the salt of tears, not knowing whether they were hers, or his. But in that moment she did know what she'd tried to deny before and now finally welcomed . . . She decided firmly that tomorrow Mark would hear the truth, as best she could tell it, and for the first time in his life. Her silence had lasted nineteen years too long, never mind the reasons that once had seemed so compelling. She might lose him, she realized that, but at least she owed him this chance for his life.

The next morning he arose at five after a sleepless night. He dressed, and when he had finished, he went through the kitchen, opened the door and climbed the back stairs that led to the attic where his gear was stored for the lake. At the top of the stairs he opened another door, then switched on the naked light bulb that hung from a cord. The room had accumulated dust and cobwebs since last summer. He felt sick this morning, still outraged yet wishing that his father could have understood, or at least seen him as a *man* whose choice deserved to be respected.

How would he tell Adrienne? How would he support her if she did accept this situation? Would she even marry him now? She'd said . . . Maybe a day or two at the lake by himself would help him sort out some answers. One thing he knew for certain—with or without his father's or anybody else's blessings—he would not live without Adrienne.

Mark reached up to the shelf that held the bright orange lifebelts. As he pulled them down, the whole shelf came off its brackets and everything on it went flying. He bent down to pick the shelf up. Lying open before him was Katie's battered, worn suitcase that she had brought all the way from Poland. The lid of the red satin heart had come apart, and all the contents lay scattered about, the photographs, pictures of Katie and David on their wedding day with Isaac and Sarah, pictures of Katie's mother and father, their marriage license, and his birth certificate. The cigar box lay near the red heart. Mark picked it up and opened it. Sitting down on the floor, propped up against the wall, he began to read the letter from Chaim. He read it twice, then looked at the pictures, then slowly at his mother and father's marriage license, both civil and Jewish, then at his own birth certificate. He sat without moving, hardly able to breathe.

He got up and ran down the stairs, then up the front stairs to Katie's room. He did not knock. It was six-thirty. She was coming out of the bathroom and stopped as she looked at Mark's face. It was ashen white. Throwing the boxes on the bed, he just stood wordlessly before her. Her heart pounded as she locked her fingers and put them against her chest, staring down at the boxes. Quietly she said, "You know, Mark, I believe that God in His wisdom finds the right time to deal with us. I was terribly frightened just now, but do you know, I'm suddenly glad and relieved. I'm sorry you had to find out this way —I had planned to tell you myself this morning, God knows how—but I'm glad it's all out in the open, however it happened . . ."

Mark stood there, shaking his head in disbelief. "You talk about God? When did you ever allow God into our home?" He paused for a breath, then in cold white anger said, "I want to *know*. I want you to tell me. *Now*."

And so she tried, standing there before her son, hands clasped tightly . . . Beginning with her coming to New York from London and meeting David, their falling in love, his being born soon after, and David startling her so with his feelings about being Jewish, seeming to be in fact bedeviled with the feeling and his obsession about not living out his life as he knew it on Hester Street. She tried to explain to Mark the awful irony of his father's apparent anti-Semitism being his way of justifying to himself what he'd done . . . if being Jewish meant to be hated and despised, then there became for him something hateful in being Jewish . . . And if there were Jews who rose as Jews from poverty and the ghetto, they became a threat, a rebuke to him. And now to have a Jewish daughter-in-law . . . "Don't you see, Mark, for him she would be the cruelest reminder of his failure—worse even than I have been."

"But you went along with him. How can you justify *that*?"

"I know it's hard for you to understand—"

"My God, *that* is an understatement for the books, but I'm trying. Go ahead."

"I don't want to make excuses for myself, except I suppose that's really what I'm doing when I tell you I was a very lonely young girl. I wanted you to have a mother *and* a father—not be an orphan as I was at the time. I felt trapped—"

"That's not good enough. I don't think I could ever

have done that to a child of mine, no matter what the reasons—"

"Mark, there's no way I can really make it acceptable to you, and I don't know if you'll ever be able to forgive either of us. Maybe you shouldn't. But I do know that it's one thing to stand in judgment of someone else and say what you would have done in their place, and another to be in that position. I did what I thought was right at the time—what I was able to do . . ."

"Are you sure?"

"No, I suppose I'm really not. I am sure, though, that at least in the beginning your father loved me and I loved him. It went on for me long afterward. When we lived in Chicago it was the middle of the Depression and he worked so hard and could only find a demeaning little job. I think he was embarrassed as much as anything, but things got worse between us and finally he said I didn't have faith in him and he told me to leave. It wasn't really lack of faith, I think, so much as that I was afraid of what would happen to us . . . to my baby, and I ran back to my friends on Hester Street, the only family I felt I had. You've read the letters. You know now about Chaim and how he saved my life. But all through this time we were still very much in love, and when you were so terribly sick I called for your father and he came right away, and we were together again. And all through the years since, right or wrong, I kept on hoping, and praying, that he would one day realize how wrong he'd been . . ."

"It didn't exactly turn out that way, did it , Mother?"

"No, it didn't . . . and the rest you pretty much know. As you grew older I think you must have seen how he felt about me . . . I don't think we probably fooled you as much as we fooled ourselves in thinking so . . . And now you know why he felt as he did—because I was his past that wouldn't go away, that he couldn't escape from. Mark, no matter how you feel now, I ask you please not to let this come between us for the rest of your life. Please, try . . . ?"

Mark turned away. He stood staring out to the

garden and the large sturdy oak he had climbed as a child and began to try to absorb what he'd learned. It was like being reborn, and getting used to an entirely new life, a new person—himself. But one thing was clear now. His father was sick, sick with a malady of the soul. And right now he despised him with a passion he would never have believed himself capable of. It went far beyond his ability to excuse him for wanting to reject the suffering that Jews had had to bear for centuries. He recalled something that Adrienne had said . . . "My family were annihilated for no other reason than the fact that they had the temerity to be born Jews." . . . Did his father think he owed nothing to *them*? He thought of his mother, and for the first time with a shock thought of *her* as a Jew. She said she'd felt trapped . . . he began to understand what it must have been like . . .

Katie was sitting perfectly still, hardly daring to breathe as she waited for the verdict. After what seemed like an eternity, he turned and faced her. "Mother, I love you. I think you made a terrible mistake because you did stay, even though I think I'm beginning to understand why. But it *was* a mistake . . . not just for me but for you too. It was because you *were* so young that you should have left." He paused. "No, I guess I have no right to judge you. I'm convinced you did feel you were doing what you thought was right . . ." Suddenly he understood why she had sent him away to school, not wanting him to see them, especially his father, as they really were . . . The one too long suffering, the other playing a role that denied his son the right to choose, trying to poison his mind against the very people who were his closest allies—in more ways than he could have imagined at the time. And now too he understood why his mother couldn't bear to come up to the lake. And suddenly something else—

"Mother, all those times, why didn't dad come up to the lake that first summer we had the house?"

She didn't answer. Was she still going to explain him?

"Don't hold back anything if you ever want me to trust or believe you again."

It was such a relief that it seemed an indulgence. But of course he had a right to know everything . . . "All right, Mark. Your father had a mistress for almost two years—"

"Oh my God, how stupid I was. And I thought it was your fault, you seemed so unyielding without any reason. God, mother, I'm sorry—"

"You were young. There was no way you could have known, and I suppose I was too proud, and hurt—"

"You are not, mother, supposed to be perfect, and I think now that you have taken too much on yourself. I was young, but not so young I couldn't have known. You see, I think I am stronger than either of you thought . . ."

Standing there, looking at him, she felt a shiver of excitement. It was like looking at somebody changing before her eyes from a child to a man. For too long she had seen him as the child, not wanting (like so many mothers before her) to see the inevitable growth in her own—and inevitable loss to herself. "I think you are right, Mark. I only hope you are strong enough to survive the anger I am sure you feel. I can tell you it is not an easy thing to live with . . ."

He went to her and embraced her, holding her for a long moment. "I love you, mother, very much . . . And now I think I have to speak to Mr. *Reid.*"

He turned and left with the boxes in his hand, went across the hall to David's room and opened the door without knocking. His face felt like a stone mask. David was sitting at his desk, about to pick up the telephone. When he looked up to see Mark he started to rise and was interrupted by Mark's, "Stay where you are—*father,* I have a few questions to ask you."

Mark put the boxes down on the desk and stood facing his father. David didn't need to go through the contents; he knew what was in them. Now the muscles in his jaw grew taut. A kind of paralyzing numbness took over all his features, and through it the sense of fear too pervasive to be felt acutely, and with it all the absurdly—even to him—superficial reaction that somehow it wasn't *fair* . . .

He fought for control. "Where did you get these?"

"Don't worry about that, just answer my questions. I want *you* to explain."

"Explain what? . . . What do I have to explain to you?"

"Why you never gave me, why you kept from me the thing I was most entitled to, my knowing where I came from, *who* I was—"

"You don't know what you're talking about, Mark, now—"

"For the first time in my whole life I finally know *exactly* what I'm talking about. All the pieces are suddenly beginning to fit." He took a deep breath, then went on. "I think you're a weak, obsessed man. You couldn't stand up and face what Jews have been facing for centuries. You traded what they gave you for what you thought you couldn't have if you stayed a Jew—"

"Now just a minute, Mark, you're angry and there's nothing to say to you right now that will make this right, but don't think you understand everything so fast, let me—"

"*No*, not this time. This time *you're* going to listen. I'm not going to be taken in any longer. It's too late for that, and it's about time, Mr. *Reid*. You're right about one thing, I don't understand—I don't understand how you could have expected to get what you wanted by throwing away, no, destroying the greatest thing in your life." He fortified himself with a deep breath. "Why, did you know, Mr. Reid, that in Los Angeles some of the richest and most successful people are *Jews*, and I hear tell that there are some Jews who aren't starving in other parts of the country. And of course that isn't the point. It doesn't really matter at all—the money or the business success or the fine house. What matters, I've been lucky enough to discover, is how you feel inside, what you think of yourself. I'm pretty young to find this out, I guess, and I'm damn old, thanks to you, to find out who I am."

He rushed on, not wanting David to interrupt him, not so sure that once interrupted he'd still be able to get it out the way he felt it and wanted to say it. "I have something else to thank you for. Your not letting me be friends with Jeff without giving me any good reason and making it clear even though you didn't come right out and say it that it was Jeff's Jewishness that you held against him . . . well, that only made me start thinking and wondering. You know, you should really have started when I was much younger if you wanted me to accept whatever you said without question. Don't you see, it was *you* who began this. You made me *curious*, very dangerous stuff for a kid . . .

"I just want to tell you that I don't ever intend to see you again. I don't want to know you. You are out of my life. There was a time when I was afraid I might lose the most precious thing in my life because I was afraid to lose you. Believe me, I'm not afraid any longer. Maybe you'll want to think about that . . . Mr. *Reid.*"

He walked from the room, shutting the door firmly behind him.

David got up. He paced the floor, then slumped down in the same chair that had known and held one other person in despair. The memory of Jim Fowler would live long in that room. David buried his head in his hands and, finally, he cried, "Isaac, Isaac, the circle has been completed. Did you hear *my* son? . . . You have your revenge, old man . . ."

Mark went to Katie's room and told her he was driving back to Los Angeles. He gave her Adrienne's address and said he would be staying at his apartment. He kissed her good-bye and drove to the office of the San Mateo *Times,* where he placed a notice in the personal section of the Want Ads:

TO WHOM IT MAY CONCERN

This is to state that Mark, son of David Rezinetsky, known as David Reid, from this day on will be known as Mark Rezinetsky, religion Jewish, from his birth.

He paid for the advertisement, then went to a public telephone and called Adrienne.

"Darling, I'm coming back today. I won't explain to you now, but we're going to be married."

She started to say something and he interrupted. "I'll tell you all about it when I see you. Oh, yes, we're going to be married in temple. Another thing, I love you." He hung up, got back into the car and drove off, less sure that he could make good on every one of his brave words in recent hours than that, finally, he was at least free to try.

CHAPTER THIRTY-FOUR

Summer

Katie stood in the hall waiting for the taxi to arrive. She had her suitcase packed, the one that had been with her through all the years, that held the promises and the defeats. David came out of his room, almost gray, stood at the first landing and looked down at her.

"You're leaving too?"

When she looked up at him, she felt neither pity nor hatred. She felt nothing except that he was, remarkably, a stranger with whom she had shared a long, long night.

"Yes . . . I should have done this a long time ago."

They still looked at each other. David asked, "Will you stay?" He would spare them both the "please."

"No, David, not now, there's no reason any longer."

"Where will you go?"

"I'm going to my son's wedding. . .and I pray that one day I may be given the joy of seeing my grandchild come into this world."

How strange, she thought. There was a marker that lay somewhere in a lonely cemetery. The tall reeds must have long since covered it. Born out of that event, their life together had begun with an ending. . . it seemed fitting that it should end now with a beginning.

Names were suddenly in her mind, as they must have been in his. . .Isaac, Birdie, Abe, Solly, Chaim, Jim Fowler. . .He would be alone with his ghosts, and hers. Perhaps they would instruct him. If he listened. If there was still time.

The taxi driver rang the bell. Katie opened the door, picked up the suitcase in her hands, and walked out without looking back.

ABOUT THE AUTHOR

CYNTHIA FREEMAN was born in the section of New York City she writes so vividly about in *A World Full of Strangers*, and moved with her family to California. She has lived most of her life in San Francisco with her husband, a prominent physician. They have a son, a daughter and three grandchildren. A believer in self-education, Cynthia Freeman has been determined, since childhood, to pursue knowledge for its own sake and not for the credentials. Her interest in formal education ceased in the sixth grade, but, at fifteen, feeling scholastically ready, she attended classes at the University of California as an auditor only, not receiving credit. Her literary career began at the age of fifty-five, after twenty-five years as a successful interior designer. Since writing *A World Full of Strangers*, Cynthia Freeman has authored *Fairytales*, *The Days of Winter* and, most recently, *Portraits*, all of them bestsellers.

A Preview of

Cynthia Freeman's

New Novel

FAIRYTALES

This book will be available in Bantam paperback in March 1978. The *San Francisco Sunday Examiner and Chronicle* says, "The novel bridges several generations in the tradition of the great family sagas. With a gift for narration first seen in A WORLD FULL OF STRANGERS, the author tells a sweeping story of the trials, joys and sorrows of the numerous characters, skillfully brought to life."

1

It was one of those glorious mornings in Santa Barbara that sojourners from the damp, dismal fog of San Francisco dream about, in fact, look forward to every year. The men were already waiting in teams of twos and fours to get on to the green lush golf course. It was the promise of a great day for eighteen holes of golf as they stood swinging their clubs limbering up, but Catherine Rossi couldn't have cared less as she lay alone in the middle of the luxurious oversized bed, in the luxurious oversized room reserved at the Biltmore for herself and her famous husband. The famous Dominic Rossi. Famous stud, that's what he was as far as she was concerned. He'd given her seven famous children, hadn't he? Well . . . this morning Catherine had it up to here. Every time she thought about last night she did a slow burn as her anger smoldered . . . How dare he not remember to make arrangements for her to be seated at the speakers' table alongside of him and all the other dignitaries? Good question . . . how come? Wasn't that where the future United States senator's wife belonged? . . . he'd better believe. That's where she and four of his famous children belonged . . . but where were they seated . . . at a round table in the shadows, in the corner like paying guests. She doubted if anybody knew she was present, but more important, did anyone give a damn? Especially Darlin' Dominic standing up on that platform making speeches with such dramatic flair that would have made Marlon Brando look like a piker . . . why he could easily have won an Academy Award and knowing Dominic, he would have accepted it. Well, there was one advantage . . . in case of fire she was so close to the exit she sure as hell would have had no problem getting out fast . . . why the very idea . . .

How dare he treat her likc she was some insignificant Sicilian wife cooking pasta. Well, the odds were eight would get you five in Las Vegas that Dominic Rossi would be the next U.S. senator from California, that he was a winner, invincible. No contest. There was no one that could come up against him and place, much less win. But that's what *they* thought. There was one person who could beat him. Indeed there was. And by God, she would even if it meant her marriage. What marriage. Why she hadn't had a husband in the last six-and-a-half years. He'd gone off this morning to pursue his quest on the campaign trail without her, and Catherine Antoinette Frances Posata Rossi was tired of taking second place and today, more than any other day, she remembered who and what he was when she married him, a starving young attorney from San Francisco. But angry as she was, Catherine wanted to be fair, if even begrudgingly, with herself (and at this moment, it was damned hard to be perfectly fair). He hadn't been exactly poor, since his father and all of the Rossi brothers from Sicily had made it big in fish, or produce, or booze, or whatever they made it in after one generation. But nonetheless, he wasn't her equal when he'd come down to New Orleans that summer to meet her. Bet your little Sicilian ass he wasn't. Why her family had been American born for three generations. Southern born, and they were rich, *really rich.* However they got rich, by now they could afford to forget that Pasquale Posata had jumped ship at New Orleans without papers and melted into a society struggling in a civil war. So with all that going on, who noticed an immigrant from Sicily? His heritage of survival from the old country had trained him well, he found a very lucrative business in rumrunning for the North and gunrunning for the South. He did anything and everything that was illegal or illicit, but the most important thing was his shrewdness to stay out of jail and above all, not to get deported. As far as he was concerned, it didn't make one damn little bit of difference who won, as long as he came out in the end with more than he had started and *Mama mia,* that he did. When the dust had settled, and the fray was over, Pasquale Posata decided to remain in this most divine, magnificent country of opportunity because where else in the world, but in America, could anyone become a millionaire over night from a revolution. When he thought about it, he laughed. In all the twenty years of his life, he'd known nothing but chaos and revolution in the old country, but out of that, one either found himself dead or starving, and here, from revolution, you could become rich.

Now he decided to become respectable and a gentleman. He changed his name to Peter and married an impoverished southern belle of Italian extraction with a crumbling dilapidated mansion and a ruined plantation. But he needed her and she needed him. Not only did he restore the mansion and eventually yield the greatest harvest of tobacco in the state, but he produced four sons and two daughters and Peter Posata was a very happy man. Life had been good to him. *Mama mia,* had life been good to him. He would even have been happier had he been able to foretell that, from the Sicilian earth from which he had come, four generations later, out of his loins would emerge a woman of prominence and distinction.

But this morning, Catherine Rossi wasn't concerned with her lineage nor her great-great-great-grandfather, her mind was filled with the past which didn't go back quite so far. It went back to a lavish garden party given by her parents, who lived in a house one hundred and fifty years old in perfect repair, one of the best in the Latin Quarter, furnished with the most elaborate antiques, and there she met, for the first time, Dominic Rossi, fresh out of Harvard. The meeting was more than casual or coincidental, although it was made to appear so. However, the Rossis of San Francisco and the Posatas of New Orleans had met on many occasions through mutual friends and relatives in their travels and through the years had developed a strong bond of friendship and it was they who had decided it was important the two young people meet. When Catherine's mother, in her most diplomatic, gracious manner, mingled with her southern accent, mentioned that Dominic Rossi was to be their houseguest for a time, Catherine exploded. "You mean, Mama, you're bringin' him here so as I can marry him, and that's the truth . . . isn't that the truth?"

"Now, Catherine, that's no way to talk to your Mama."

Catherine's Sicilian blood, of which there was more than a little residue after all the generations, bubbled. "Maybe not, Mama, but that's why you're havin' him come. Why, you'd think I was an old maid."

And that's what Catherine's Mama really thought. With the few eligible Italian young men in New Orleans from the best families, for some reason Catherine, pretty, petite five-foot-three, brunette, brown-eyed little belle that she was, had more beaus than one could count, but not one proposal. She was going on twenty-five and not one on the horizon and Mama knew why. It was because Catherine lacked her southern, quiet, coquettish style. Instead, Catherine was blunt and outspoken, half scaring, if not discouraging, the young men, and Mama swore it had to come from the Posata side, not hers. Rosa Ann was like *her*. She knew when to say yes at the right time, how to appeal to a man's ego which was the only way to grab a man at the right time, and that was why Rosa Ann, who was only eighteen-months younger than Catherine, was married and expecting her second child. Well . . . God almighty, somethin' had to be done even if it took importing a northerner, or more to the point, a westerner who was two years younger than Catherine, but Mama had read *Gone With The Wind* and decided she would think about that tomorrow (as Scarlett had suggested). But when Catherine saw Dominic Rossi for the first time, entering the garden with the orchestra playing softly, with his father at his side, her blood did bubble, not from anger this time, but from passion. He was virile, handsome, six feet tall with a shock of dark auburn hair, with a clear light complexion. His charm and smile were captivating as was his amazing wit which added to his allure, but he also had made a name for himself as best halfback of the year at Harvard. However he wasn't all brawn, there was a brain so keen and exceptional it had taken him to Harvard at the age of sixteen, from where he graduated first in the top ten, magna cum laude. Yes, sir, the moment she saw him, she could have swooned (if that were the sort of thing Catherine did) as he approached her, standing in that celestial setting with the violins playing in the background, dressed in the most exquisite, most expensive apricot silk organza dress (that Mama or money could buy) with lots and lots of ruffles and on her pretty little feet were four-inch heeled silk shoes to match. Her hair was coiffed to perfection (because Mama always knew a woman's crowning glory was her hair). She pursed her lips in a rather Mona Lisa style, crinkled her eyes as an inner smile tickled her. Yes, sir, by God, Dominic Rossi had met his mate in Catherine Posata and she made up her mind then and there she was going to marry him, make no mistake about that. In spite of his size, she was every inch the woman to handle him. The two fathers embraced one another around the shoulders as Catherine and Dominic looked into each other's eyes for a moment. The spell was broken as Angelo Posata said with enormous pride, taking Catherine's diminutive hand in his, "May I present my daughter, Catherine . . . this is Dominic Rossi."

He answered smiling (beautiful teeth, she thought), "I can assure you this is a pleasure I've looked forward to for a very long time."

"I wouldn't be at all surprised," Catherine answered in her most extravagant southern accent, narrowing her eyes and thrusting back her chin.

For a moment, he inclined his head to one side as though he hadn't heard her, then looked her squarely in the eyes, smiled and laughed as she joined him in the laughter. The two fathers walked away, leaving them alone. "Would you like to dance?" Dominic asked.

And Catherine answered, "Would you rather dance or make love to me?"

This time he stood speechless and for Dominic Rossi, that was a rare situation. He took her by the hand and led her to the furthest part of the garden where he sat her down on a stone bench, half laughing, and said, "You know, beyond a doubt, you're the most curious girl I have ever met. I'm not sure if you're happy or unhappy to have met me."

"Well, I kinda think that's sort of an accomplishment if I can keep a big lawyer guessin' what my motives are."

"Oh . . . well, in that case, I want to make love to you." He took her arm and gently stood her up.

"Now, you just hold on for one minute. What makes *you* think I want to make love to you?"

"Because you asked me."

"That's right . . . I asked you a question, but all questions require answers and my answer is I wouldn't let you make love to me," she responded with that Mona Lisa smile.

"Oh, I'm not so sure of that," he said, holding her close to him, but she pushed herself back.

"Now, you listen to me. You know, as well as I do, that this is nothin' more or less than an arrangement, an arrangement made between our parents, expectin' me to say 'Yes' and 'how sudden all this is,' when the time came for you to pop the question and I should be coy and all nervous-like and excited. Well . . . for your information, Mr. Barrister, I want you to know I don't enjoy playin' these kinda games and I want you to know from the very beginnin' I'm gonna say yes because I do want to marry you. I didn't think I would, but I do. So anytime you want to ask me, don't hesitate."

Dominic started to laugh. Not at her and she knew it, but at her complete candor and lack of inhibition, then quite seriously, looking at her, he said, "You know, when I came down here, I had the same doubts and reservations, but of course I wasn't aware you knew why I was coming. Suppose I tell you something?"

"Yes, please do."

"Beyond a doubt, you're the most staggeringly honest person I've ever met. In fact, you're overwhelming and in these few minutes, I probably know more about *you* than most people do who go together for a long time. And can I tell you something even funnier?"

"Yes, please do."

"I know it's crazy, but I think I'm in love with you. Is that possible, just like that?"

"It's possible, but I wouldn't worry too much about it. If you don't now, you will before you leave."

They both laughed, then quietly and gently he took her in his arms and said, "Catherine, will you marry me?"

She said, with unmistakable languor in her voice, "I thought you'd never ask."

The next few months found Mama Posata as close to heaven as she'd ever come in this world, with all the excitement and frenzy of the impending nuptials. There was trousseau shopping which was not only expensive, extensive and endless, but there was china, silver, crystal and linens to be purchased. After God and church, there was nothing Mama loved quite so much as spending money, clothes, luxury, finery and parties. The whole thing was just about the most exciting thing that had happened to her since Rosa Ann's wedding. But for Catherine, her firstborn, after all, she wanted this to be one of those weddings the likes of which New Orleans had never witnessed. The largest chapel in the Cathedral was filled with an assortment of Rossis who had descended upon the city for days now. Like locusts, they had come all the way from San Francisco. And the Posatas hadn't been Catholics for that many generations not to make their enormous presence felt, with all the uncles, aunts, cousins, nieces, nephews, distant relatives and near, and with a select number of friends, handpicked, there were five-hundred people at the Posata-Rossi wedding and reception. If Garibaldi had the amount of food and champagne that was served at that dinner, he could have united Italy a lot quicker.

Dominic was so dashing and handsome that every girl breathed a little harder when they saw him dance, holding his new bride, all shimmering and soft and satin and lace. When he smiled down at her, tightening his hold around Catherine's thin waist, bringing her closer to him, it was certainly obvious to anyone observing, the promise of what would be theirs later tonight.

2

Catherine sighed deeply and nostalgically in that darkened, lonely room. Yes, sir, what a night it was. The promises of love, devotion, fidelity. Oh, my God, the things people tell each other in moments of passion. How the hell could she ever have predicted at that moment her life could possibly have turned out the way it did? As for love, in or out of bed, well . . . there'd been little of that in the last ten-and-a-half years. She sighed again, ran her tongue over her dry lips . . . she felt lousy this morning. How else could she feel, after last night when she had stolen quietly away, unnoticed, from that overpeopled, overheated, overfed multitude, listening to the great Dominic Rossi expounding all the virtues, panaceas, solutions and promises for saving that most grand sovereign state of California and all its inhabitants from the iniquities of the Republican Party. He stood like the messiah delivering the Sermon on the Mount. Catherine wanted to throw up.

She was in bed with a terrible headache when he returned finally, well after midnight, all charged up, exhilarated, excited and confident that California was his oyster. Switching on the bedside lamp, he sat on his side of the bed, taking off his shoes and socks, then undressed. Going into the bathroom, he showered, then brushed his teeth. By God, he felt good . . . his batteries were so charged up by the time he got into bed, he found it impossible to sleep. Turning off the light, he lay in the dark with his hands behind his head and reviewed the evening. Yes, sir, he'd made the right impression, said the right things, scored the points . . . in fact, he had them all eating out of his hand. Catherine moved closer to the edge of the bed away from the candidate for the senator from California, as far away as she could without falling out.

God, where the hell did he get his stamina? He had enough of that to fortify twenty men and here his family, his wonderful, marvelous, devoted family, who all adored him so, worried about his health, saying that Dominic was taxing himself to the point where they thought if Dom kept up this pace, he'd have a heart attack. Heart attack . . . Hell, what a laugh! He was strong as a horse. His family . . . there sure was no love lost there. Even from the very beginning when she'd come to live in San Francisco as a bride (already two weeks pregnant) with her young struggling husband. And the feeling was perfectly mutual, they couldn't tolerate her any more than she could them, putting on such airs, never letting them forget she was an heiress. She made sure, from the very beginning, that the custom of the Rossi clan getting together constantly was going to stop, if she had anything to say about it and she did. Eventually the invitations dwindled. In no uncertain terms, Catherine made it perfectly clear she had married *him* and not his family and if he wanted to pursue his long familial attachments, it would have to be without her. Naturally, Dominic didn't take that without a few rebuttals, which didn't make her yield one inch, and after all the fights and arguments had run their course, Catherine achieved her point. Dominic saw less and less of the family, which they regretted, but knew why, which only intensified the animosity they already felt for her. However, Catherine's southern Sicilian background had taught her not to dwell upon things of unimportance, so she simply shrugged her shoulders and ignored the fact that Dominic was more than terribly chagrined, embarrassed and unhappy when he attended family affairs, of which there were many . . . especially engagements, weddings, communions, graduations, birthdays, etc, etc., usually alone, always having to give the same excuse that Catherine was not well or had taken a little holiday back to New Orleans to visit her family. His voice startled her, suddenly interrupting her thoughts in the silent dark room. Oh, if he'd only stop talking. My God, she had a headache . . .

"Well, how do you think it went tonight?" he asked. He wasn't really asking she thought, only loving the sound of his own voice.

She could have killed him, but she narrowed her eyes, tightened her lips, caught her breath, swallowed hard and mumbled, "Just the way you planned it . . . right?" He laughed robustly, while to herself she said, you'd better laugh tonight because this will be the last laugh you'll have for a little while in view of the fact I have a little plan of my own all mapped out for tomorrow, your majesty, your royal highness . . . your royal ass.

She was seething inside. Dominic had breakfast early in their room, eating heartily while she, still in bed, observed her husband over the rim of the coffee cup. When he finished, she turned her cheek as he pecked it lightly and quite matter of factly, said his *arrivedercis,* saying he would meet her later in San Diego, then left. Well . . . that was it. Finished, *finito,* and all because he had forgotten last night or didn't even remember she was alive and well and sitting in the back like some morganatic wife not quite good enough to be seated with the king . . . that's right. Okay . . . two can play the game . . . How? . . . Well, I'll tell you, Your Majesty, although I do feel a little ashamed 'cause it's not original on my part . . . I'm just not smart enough to ever have thought of runnin' away from home . . . wish I had, but it sure as hell was the most ingenious idea any political wife had invented up to date so far as I'm concerned, to make a husband realize she was alive and that he owed her a little courtesy . . . so . . . I'm gonna follow the leader . . . gonna do what that brilliant Angelina Alioto did . . . of course she went to the missions . . . so I can't do that, it just wouldn't be cricket to steal her stuff and besides I gotta have a little imagination of my own, so I'm goin' to the Farm . . . well . . . that's not really so unique or original 'cause I've been doin' that for years whenever I needed a rest, but what makes it so excitin' and intriguin' is the runnin' away without lettin' anyone know. . . . That's why I think what Mrs. A did was so smart . . . without lettin' anyone know. . . . Talk about fact bein' stranger than fiction. Well, ain't that the truth. All I can say is . . . God bless you, Mrs. Alioto . . . you sure did emancipate a lotta ladies by showin' us the way. . . . Two can play the game. *Ciao . . .*

Unaware that Catherine has gone to the Farm, Dominic and her children become frenzied at her unexplained disappearance in the middle of her husband's most important campaign. When they don't find her, they go to the police. No one knows that Catherine has "campaign" plans of her own.

Bantam Book Catalog

Here's your up-to-the-minute listing of over 1,400 titles by your favorite authors.

This illustrated, large format catalog gives a description of each title. For your convenience, it is divided into categories in fiction and non-fiction—gothics, science fiction, westerns, mysteries, cookbooks, mysticism and occult, biographies, history, family living, health, psychology, art.

So don't delay—take advantage of this special opportunity to increase your reading pleasure.

Just send us your name and address and 50¢ (to help defray postage and handling costs).

BANTAM BOOKS, INC.
Dept. FC, 414 East Golf Road, Des Plaines, Ill. 60016

Mr./Mrs./Miss ____________________
(please print)

Address ____________________

City __________ **State** __________ **Zip** __________

Do you know someone who enjoys books? Just give us their names and addresses and we'll send them a catalog too!

____

Mr./Mrs./Miss ____________________

Address ____________________

City __________ **State** __________ **Zip** __________

____

Mr./Mrs./Miss ____________________

Address ____________________

City __________ **State** __________ **Zip** __________

FC—9/78